S0-AGH-138

ALEXANDER'S BRIDGE

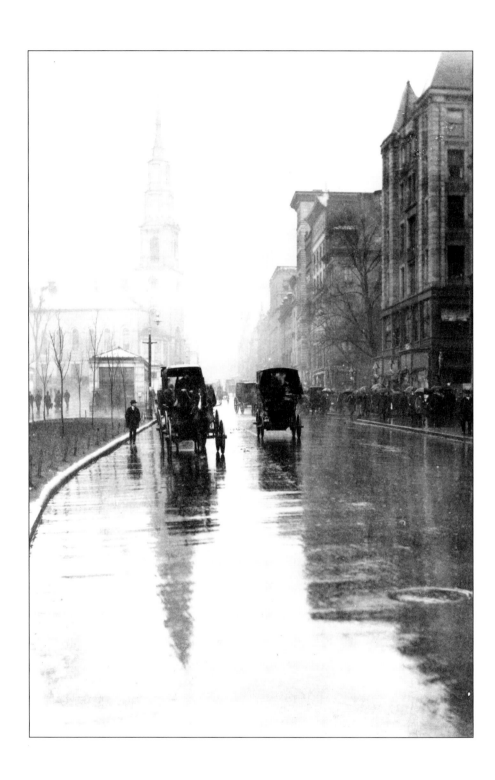

ALEXANDER'S BRIDGE

Willa Sibert Cather

1912

SIMON & SCHUSTER INC.

A CommonPlace Book

I.

Late one brilliant April afternoon Professor Lucius Wilson stood at the head of Chestnut Street, looking about him with the pleased air of a man of taste who does not very often get to Boston. He had lived there as a student, but for twenty years and more, since he had been Professor of Philosophy in a Western university, he had seldom come East except to take a steamer for some foreign port. Wilson was standing quite still, contemplating with a whimsical smile the slanting street, with its worn paving, its irregular, gravely colored houses, and the row of naked trees on which the thin sunlight was still shining. The gleam of the river at the foot of the hill made him blink a little, not so much because it was too bright as because he found it so pleasant. The few passers-by glanced at him unconcernedly, and even the children who hurried along with their school-bags under their arms seemed to find it perfectly natural that a tall brown gentleman should be standing there, looking up through his glasses at the gray housetops.

The sun sank rapidly; the silvery light had faded from the bare boughs and the watery twilight was setting in when Wilson at last walked down the hill, descending into cooler and cooler depths of grayish shadow. His nostril, long unused to it, was quick to detect the smell of wood smoke in the air, blended with the odor of moist spring earth and the saltiness that came up the river with the tide.

He crossed Charles Street between jangling street cars and shelving lumber drays, and after a moment of uncertainty wound into Brimmer Street. The street was quiet, deserted, and hung with a thin bluish haze. He had already fixed his sharp eye upon the house which he reasoned should be his objective point, when he noticed a woman approaching rapidly from the opposite direction. Always an interested observer of women, Wilson would have slackened his pace anywhere to follow this one with his impersonal, appreciative glance. She was a person of distinction he saw at once, and, moreover, very handsome. She was tall, carried her beautiful head proudly, and moved with ease and certainty. One immediately took for granted the costly privileges and fine spaces that must lie in the background from which such a figure could emerge with this rapid and elegant gait. Wilson noted her dress, too,—for, in his way, he had an eye for such things,—particularly her brown furs and her hat. He got a blurred impression of her fine color, the violets she wore, her white gloves, and, curiously enough, of her veil, as she turned up a flight of steps in front of him and disappeared.

Wilson was able to enjoy lovely things that passed him on the wing as completely and deliberately as if they had been dug-up marvels, long anticipated, and definitely fixed at the end of a railway journey. For a few pleasurable seconds he quite forgot where he was going, and only after the door had closed behind her did he realize that the young woman had entered the house to which he had directed his trunk from the South Station that morning. He hesitated a moment before mounting the steps. "Can that," he murmured in amazement,—"can that possibly have been Mrs. Alexander?"

When the servant admitted him, Mrs. Alexander was still standing in the hallway. She heard him give his name, and came forward holding out her hand.

"Is it you, indeed, Professor Wilson? I was afraid that you might get here before I did. I was detained at a concert, and Bartley telephoned that he would be late. Thomas will show you your room. Had you rather have your tea brought to you there, or will you have it down here with me, while we wait for Bartley?"

Wilson was pleased to find that he had been the cause of her rapid walk, and with her he was even more vastly pleased than before. He followed her through the drawing-room into the library, where the wide back windows looked out upon the garden and the sunset and a fine stretch of silver-colored river. A harp-shaped elm stood stripped against the pale-colored evening sky, with ragged last year's birds' nests in its forks, and through the bare branches the evening star quivered in the misty air. The long brown room breathed the peace of a rich and amply guarded quiet. Tea was brought in immediately and placed in front of the wood fire. Mrs. Alexander sat down in a high-backed chair and began to pour it, while Wilson sank into a low seat opposite her and took his cup with a great sense of ease and harmony and comfort.

"You have had a long journey, have n't you?" Mrs. Alexander asked, after showing gracious concern about his tea. "And I am so sorry Bartley is late. He's often tired when he's late. He flatters himself that it is a little on his account that you have come to this Congress of Psychologists."

"It is," Wilson assented, selecting his muffin carefully; "and I hope he won't be tired tonight. But, on my own account, I'm glad to have a few moments alone with you, before Bartley comes. I was somehow afraid that my knowing him so well would not put me in the way of getting to know you."

"That's very nice of you." She nodded at him above her cup and smiled, but there was a little formal tightness in her tone which had not been there when she greeted him in the hall.

Wilson leaned forward. "Have I said something awkward? I live very far out of the world, you know. But I did n't mean that you would exactly fade dim, even if Bartley *were* here."

Mrs. Alexander laughed relentingly. "Oh, I'm not so vain! How terribly discerning you are."

She looked straight at Wilson, and he felt that this quick, frank glance brought about an understanding between them.

He liked everything about her, he told himself, but he particularly liked her eyes; when she looked at one directly for a moment they were like a glimpse of fine windy sky that may bring all sorts of weather.

"Since you noticed something," Mrs. Alexander went on, "it must have been a flash of the distrust I have come to feel whenever I meet any of the people who knew Bartley when he was a boy. It is always as if they were talking of some one I had never met. Really, Professor Wilson, it would seem that he grew up among the strangest people. They usually say that he has turned out very well, or remark that he always was a fine fellow. I never know what reply to make."

Wilson chuckled and leaned back in his chair, shaking his left foot gently. "I expect the fact is that we none of us knew him very well, Mrs. Alexander. Though I will say for myself that I was always confident he'd do something extraordinary."

Mrs. Alexander's shoulders gave a slight movement, suggestive of impatience. "Oh, I should think that might have been a safe prediction. Another cup, please?"

"Yes, thank you. But predicting, in the case of boys, is not so easy as you might imagine, Mrs. Alexander. Some get a bad hurt early and lose their courage; and some never get a fair wind. Bartley"—he dropped his chin on the back of his long hand and looked at her admiringly—"Bartley caught the wind early, and it has sung in his sails ever since."

Mrs. Alexander sat looking into the fire with intent preoccupation, and Wilson studied her half-averted face. He liked the suggestion of stormy possibilities in the proud curve of her lip and nostril. Without that, he reflected, she would be too cold.

"I should like to know what he was really like when he was a boy. I don't believe he remembers," she said suddenly. "Won't you smoke, Mr. Wilson?"

Wilson lit a cigarette. "No, I don't suppose he does. He was never introspective. He was simply the most tremendous response to stimuli I have ever known. We did n't know exactly what to do with him."

A servant came in and noiselessly removed the tea-tray. Mrs. Alexander screened her face from the firelight, which was beginning to throw wavering bright spots on her dress and hair as the dusk deepened.

"Of course," she said, "I now and again hear stories about things that happened when he was in college."

"But that is n't what you want." Wilson wrinkled his brows and looked at her with the smiling familiarity that had come about so quickly. "What you want is a picture of him, standing back there at the other end of twenty years. You want to look down through my memory."

She dropped her hands in her lap. "Yes, yes; that's exactly what I want."

At this moment they heard the front door shut with a jar, and Wilson laughed as Mrs. Alexander rose quickly. "There he is. Away with perspective! No past, no future for Bartley; just the fiery moment. The only moment that ever was or will be in the world!"

The door from the hall opened, a voice called "Winifred?" hurriedly, and a big man came through the drawing-room with a quick, heavy tread, bringing with him a smell of cigar smoke and chill out-of-doors air. When Alexander reached the library door, he switched on the lights and stood six feet and more in the archway, glowing with strength and cordiality and rugged, blond good looks. There were other bridge-builders in the world, certainly, but it was always Alexander's picture that the Sunday Supplement men wanted, because he looked as a tamer of rivers ought to look. Under his tumbled sandy hair his head seemed as hard and powerful as a catapult, and his shoulders looked strong enough in themselves to support a span of any one of his ten great bridges that cut the air above as many rivers.

After dinner Alexander took Wilson up to his study. It was a large room over the library, and looked out upon the black river and the row of white lights along the Cambridge Embankment. The room was not at all what one might expect of an engineer's study. Wilson felt at once the harmony of beautiful things that have lived long together without obtrusions of ugliness or change. It was none of Alexander's doing, of course; those warm consonances of color had been blending and mellowing before he was born. But the wonder was that he was not out of place there,—that it all seemed to glow like the inevitable background for his vigor and vehemence. He sat before the fire, his shoulders deep in the cushions of his chair, his powerful head upright, his hair rumpled above his broad forehead. He sat heavily, a cigar in his large, smooth hand, a flush of after-dinner color in his face, which wind and sun and exposure to all sorts of weather had left fair and clear-skinned.

"You are off for England on Saturday, Bartley, Mrs. Alexander tells me."

"Yes, for a few weeks only. There's a meeting of British engineers, and I'm doing another bridge in Canada, you know."

"Oh, every one knows about that. And it was in Canada that you met your wife, was n't it?"

"Yes, at Allway. She was visiting her great-aunt there. A most remarkable old lady. I was working with MacKeller then, an old Scotch engineer who had picked me up in London and taken me back to Quebec with him. He had the contract for the Allway Bridge, but before he began work on it he found out that he was going to die, and he advised the committee to turn the job over to me. Otherwise I'd never have got anything good so early. Mac-Keller was an old friend of Mrs. Pemberton, Winifred's aunt. He had mentioned me to her, so when I went to Allway she asked me to come to see her. She was a wonderful old lady."

"Like her niece?" Wilson queried.

Bartley laughed. "She had been very handsome, but not in Winifred's way. When I knew her she was little and fragile, very pink and white, with a splendid head and a face like fine old lace, somehow,—but perhaps I always think of that because she wore a lace scarf on her hair. She had such a flavor of life about her. She had known Gordon and Livingstone and Beaconsfield when she was young,—every one. She was the first woman of that sort I'd ever known. You know how it is in the West,—old people are poked out of the way. Aunt Eleanor fascinated me as few young women have ever done. I used to go up from the works to have tea with her, and sit talking to her for hours. It was very stimulating, for she could n't tolerate stupidity."

"It must have been then that your luck began, Bartley," said Wilson, flicking his cigar ash with his long finger. "It's curious, watching boys," he went on reflectively. "I'm sure I did you justice in the matter of ability. Yet I always used to feel that there was a weak spot where some day strain would tell. Even after you began to climb, I stood down in the crowd and watched you with—well, not with confidence. The more dazzling the front you presented, the higher your façade rose, the more I expected to see a big crack zigzagging from top to bottom,"—he indicated its course in the air with his forefinger,—"then a crash and clouds of dust. It was curious. I had such a clear picture of it. And another curious thing, Bartley," Wilson spoke with deliberateness and settled deeper into his chair, "is that I don't feel it any longer. I am sure of you."

Alexander laughed. "Nonsense! It's not I you feel sure of; it's Winifred. People often make that mistake."

"No, I'm serious, Alexander. You've changed. You have decided to leave some birds in the bushes. You used to want them all."

Alexander's chair creaked. "I still want a good many," he said rather gloomily. "After all, life does n't offer a man much. You work like the devil and think you're getting on, and suddenly you discover that you've only been getting yourself tied up. A million details drink you dry. Your life keeps going for things you don't want, and all the while you are being built alive into a social structure you don't care a rap about. I sometimes wonder what sort of chap I'd have been if I had n't been this sort; I want to go and live out his potentialities, too. I have n't forgotten that there are birds in the bushes."

Bartley stopped and sat frowning into the fire, his shoulders thrust forward as if he were about to spring at something. Wilson watched him, wondering. His old pupil always stimulated him at first, and then vastly wearied him. The machinery was always pounding away in this man, and Wilson preferred companions of a more reflective habit of mind. He could not help feeling that there were unreasoning and unreasonable activities going on in Alexander all the while; that even after dinner, when most men achieve a decent impersonality, Bartley had merely closed the door of the engine-room and come up for an airing. The machinery itself was still pounding on.

Bartley's abstraction and Wilson's reflections were cut short by a rustle at the door, and almost before they could rise Mrs. Alexander was standing by the hearth. Alexander brought a chair for her, but she shook her head.

"No, dear, thank you. I only came in to see whether you and Professor Wilson were quite comfortable. I am going down to the music-room."

"Why not practice here? Wilson and I are growing very dull. We are tired of talk."

"Yes, I beg you, Mrs. Alexander," Wilson began, but he got no further.

"Why, certainly, if you won't find me too noisy. I am working on the Schumann 'Carnival,' and, though I don't practice a great many hours, I am very methodical," Mrs. Alexander explained, as she crossed to an upright piano that stood at the back of the room, near the windows.

Wilson followed, and, having seen her seated, dropped into a chair behind her. She played brilliantly and with great musical feeling. Wilson could not imagine her permitting herself to do anything badly, but he was surprised at the cleanness of her execution. He wondered how a woman with so many duties had managed to keep herself up to a standard really professional. It must take a great deal of time, certainly, and Bartley must take a great deal of time. Wilson reflected that he had never before known a woman who had been able, for any considerable while, to support both a personal and an intellectual passion. Sitting behind her, he watched her with perplexed admiration, shading his eyes with his hand. In her dinner dress she looked even younger than in street clothes, and, for all her composure and self-sufficiency, she seemed to him strangely alert and vibrating, as if in her, too, there were something never altogether at rest. He felt that he knew pretty much what she demanded in people and what she demanded from life, and he wondered how she squared Bartley. After ten years she must know him; and however one took him, however much one admired him, one had to admit that he simply would n't square. He was a natural force, certainly, but beyond that, Wilson felt, he was not anything very really or for very long at a time.

Wilson glanced toward the fire, where Bartley's profile was still wreathed in cigar smoke that curled up more and more slowly. His shoulders were sunk deep in the cushions and one hand hung large and passive over the arm of his chair. He had slipped on a purple velvet smoking-coat. His wife, Wilson surmised, had chosen it. She was clearly very proud of his good looks and his fine color. But, with the glow of an immediate interest gone out of it, the engineer's face looked tired, even a little haggard. The three lines in his forehead, directly above the nose, deepened as he sat thinking, and his powerful head drooped forward heavily. Although Alexander was only forty-three, Wilson thought that beneath his vigorous color he detected the dulling weariness of on-coming middle age.

The next afternoon, at the hour when the river was beginning to redden under the declining sun, Wilson again found himself facing Mrs. Alexander at the tea-table in the library.

"Well," he remarked, when he was bidden to give an account of himself, "there was a long morning with the psychologists, luncheon with Bartley at his club, more psychologists, and here I am. I've looked forward to this hour all day."

Mrs. Alexander smiled at him across the vapor from the kettle. "And do you remember where we stopped yesterday?"

"Perfectly. I was going to show you a picture. But I doubt whether I have color enough in me. Bartley makes me feel a faded monochrome. You can't get at the young Bartley except by means of color." Wilson paused and deliberated. Suddenly he broke out: "He was n't a remarkable student, you know, though he was always strong in higher mathematics. His work in my own department was quite ordinary. It was as a powerfully equipped nature that I found him interesting. That is the most interesting thing a teacher can find. It has the fascination of a scientific discovery. We come across other pleasing and endearing qualities so much oftener than we find force."

"And, after all," said Mrs. Alexander, "that is the thing we all live upon. It is the thing that takes us forward."

Wilson thought she spoke a little wistfully. "Exactly," he assented warmly. "It builds the bridges into the future, over which the feet of every one of us will go."

"How interested I am to hear you put it in that way. The bridges into the future—I often say that to myself. Bartley's bridges always seem to me like that. Have you ever seen his first suspension bridge in Canada, the one he was doing when I first knew him? I hope you will see it sometime. We were married as soon as it was finished, and you will laugh when I tell you that it always has a rather bridal look to me. It is over the wildest river, with mists and clouds always battling about it, and it is as delicate as a cobweb hanging in the sky. It really was a bridge into the future. You have only to look at it to feel that it meant the beginning of a great career. But I have a photograph of it here." She drew a portfolio from behind a bookcase. "And there, you see, on the hill, is my aunt's house."

Wilson took up the photograph. "Bartley was telling me something about your aunt last night. She must have been a delightful person."

Winifred laughed. "The bridge, you see, was just at the foot of the hill, and the noise of the engines annoyed her very much at first. But after she met Bartley she pretended to like it, and said it was a good thing to be reminded that there were things going on in the world. She loved life, and Bartley brought a great deal of it in to her when he came to the house. Aunt Eleanor was very worldly in a frank, Early-Victorian manner. She liked men of action, and disliked young men who were careful of themselves and who, as she put it, were always trimming their wick as if they were afraid of their oil's giving out. MacKeller, Bartley's first chief, was an old friend of my aunt, and he told her that Bartley was a wild, ill-governed youth, which really pleased her very much. I remember we were sitting alone in the dusk after Bartley had been there for the first time. I knew that Aunt Eleanor had found him much to her taste, but she had n't said anything. Presently she came out, with a chuckle: 'MacKeller found him sowing wild oats in London, I believe. I hope he did n't stop him too soon. Life coquets with dashing fellows. The coming men are always like that. We must have him to dinner, my dear.' And we did. She grew much fonder of Bartley than she was of me. I had been studying in Vienna, and she thought that absurd. She was interested in the army and in politics, and she had a great contempt for music and art and philosophy. She used to declare that the Prince Consort had brought all that stuff over out of Germany. She always sniffed when Bartley asked me to play for him. She considered that a newfangled way of making a match of it."

When Alexander came in a few moments later, he found Wilson and his wife still confronting the photograph. "Oh, let us get that out of the way," he said, laughing. "Winifred, Thomas can bring my trunk down. I've decided to go over to New York to-morrow night and take a fast boat. I shall save two days."

2.

On the night of his arrival in London, Alexander went immediately to the hotel on the Embankment at which he always stopped, and in the lobby he was accosted by an old acquaintance, Maurice Mainhall, who fell upon him with effusive cordiality and indicated a willingness to dine with him. Bartley never dined alone if he could help it, and Mainhall was a good gossip who always knew what had been going on in town; especially, he knew everything that was not printed in the newspapers. The nephew of one of the standard Victorian novelists, Mainhall bobbed about among the various literary cliques of London and its outlying suburbs, careful to lose touch with none of them. He had written a number of books himself; among them a "History of Dancing," a "History of Costume," a "Key to Shakespeare's Sonnets," a study of "The Poetry of Ernest Dowson," etc. Although Mainhall's enthusiasm was often tiresome, and although he was often unable to distinguish between facts and vivid figments of his imagination, his imperturbable good nature overcame even the people whom he bored most, so that they ended by becoming, in a reluctant manner, his friends. In appearance, Mainhall was astonishingly like the conventional stage-Englishman of American drama: tall and thin, with high, hitching shoulders and a small head glistening with closely brushed yellow hair. He spoke with an extreme Oxford accent, and when he was talking well, his face sometimes wore the rapt expression of a very emotional man listening to music. Mainhall liked Alexander because he was an engineer. He had preconceived ideas about everything, and his idea about Americans was that they should be engineers or mechanics. He hated them when they presumed to be anything else.

While they sat at dinner Mainhall acquainted Bartley with the fortunes of his old friends in London, and as they left the table he proposed that they should go to see Hugh MacConnell's new comedy, "Bog Lights."

"It's really quite the best thing MacConnell's done," he explained as they got into a hansom. "It's tremendously well put on, too. Florence Merrill and Cyril Henderson. But Hilda Burgoyne's the hit of the piece. Hugh's written a delightful part for her, and she's quite inexpressible. It's been on only two weeks, and I've been half a dozen times already. I happen to have MacConnell's box for tonight or there'd be no chance of our getting places. There's everything in seeing Hilda while she's fresh in a part. She's apt to grow a bit stale after a time. The ones who have any imagination do."

"Hilda Burgoyne!" Alexander exclaimed mildly. "Why, I have n't heard of her for—years."

Mainhall laughed. "Then you can't have heard much at all, my dear Alexander. It's only lately, since MacConnell and his set have got hold of her, that she's come up. Myself, I always knew she had it in her. If we had one real critic in London—but what can one expect? Do you know, Alexander,"—Mainhall looked with perplexity up into the top of the hansom and rubbed his pink cheek with his gloved finger,—"do you know, I sometimes think of taking to criticism seriously myself. In a way, it would be a sacrifice; but, dear me, we do need some one."

Just then they drove up to the Duke of York's, so Alexander did not commit himself, but followed Mainhall into the theatre. When they entered the stage-box on the left the first act was well under way, the scene being the interior of a cabin in the south of Ireland. As they sat down, a burst of applause drew Alexander's attention to the stage. Miss Burgoyne and her donkey were thrusting their heads in at the half door. "After all," he reflected, "there's small probability of her recognizing me. She doubtless has n't thought of me for years." He felt the enthusiasm of the house at once, and in a few moments he was caught up by the current of MacConnell's irresistible comedy. The audience had come forewarned, evidently, and whenever the ragged slip of a donkey-girl ran upon the stage there was a deep murmur of approbation, every one smiled and glowed, and Mainhall hitched his heavy chair a little nearer the brass railing.

"You see," he murmured in Alexander's ear, as the curtain fell on the first act, "one almost never sees a part like that done without smartness or mawkishness. Of course, Hilda is Irish,—the Burgoynes have been stage people for generations,—and she has the Irish voice. It's delightful to hear it in a London theatre. That laugh, now, when she doubles over at the hips—who ever heard it out of Galway? She saves her hand, too. She's at her best in the second act. She's really MacConnell's poetic motif, you see; makes the whole thing a fairy tale."

The second act opened before Philly Doyle's underground still, with Peggy and her battered donkey come in to smuggle a load of potheen across the bog, and to bring Philly word of what was doing in the world without, and of what was happening along the roadsides and ditches with the first gleam of fine weather. Alexander, annoyed by Mainhall's sighs and exclamations, watched her with keen, half-skeptical interest. As Mainhall had said, she was the second act; the plot and feeling alike depended upon her lightness of foot, her lightness of touch, upon the shrewdness and deft fancifulness that played alternately, and sometimes together, in her mirthful brown eyes. When she began to dance, by way of showing the gossoons what she had seen in the fairy rings at night, the house broke into a prolonged uproar. After her dance she withdrew from the dialogue and retreated to the ditch wall back of Philly's burrow, where she sat singing "The Rising of the Moon" and making a wreath of primroses for her donkey.

When the act was over Alexander and Mainhall strolled out into the corridor. They met a good many acquaintances; Mainhall, indeed, knew almost every one, and he babbled on incontinently, screwing his small head about over his high collar. Presently he hailed a tall, bearded man, grim-browed and rather battered-looking, who had his opera cloak on his arm and his hat in his hand, and who seemed to be on the point of leaving the theatre.

"MacConnell, let me introduce Mr. Bartley Alexander. I say! It's going famously to-night, Mac. And what an audience! You'll never do anything like this again, mark me. A man writes to the top of his bent only once."

The playwright gave Mainhall a curious look out of his deep-set faded eyes and made a wry face. "And have I done anything so fool as that, now?" he asked.

"That's what I was saying," Mainhall lounged a little nearer and dropped into a tone even more conspicuously confidential. "And you'll never bring Hilda out like this again. Dear me, Mac, the girl could n't possibly be better, you know."

MacConnell grunted. "She'll do well enough if she keeps her pace and does n't go off on us in the middle of the season, as she's more than like to do."

He nodded curtly and made for the door, dodging acquaintances as he went.

"Poor old Hugh," Mainhall murmured. "He's hit terribly hard. He's been wanting to marry Hilda these three years and more. She does n't take up with anybody, you know. Irene Burgoyne, one of her family, told me in confidence that there was a romance somewhere back in the beginning. One of your countrymen, Alexander, by the way; an American student whom she met in Paris, I believe. I dare say it's quite true that there's never been any one else." Mainhall vouched for her constancy with a loftiness that made Alexander smile, even while a kind of rapid excitement was tingling through him. Blinking up at the lights, Mainhall added in his luxurious, worldly way: "She's an elegant little person, and quite capable of an extravagant bit of sentiment like that. Here comes Sir Harry Towne. He's another who's awfully keen about her. Let me introduce you. Sir Harry Towne, Mr. Bartley Alexander, the American engineer."

Sir Harry Towne bowed and said that he had met Mr. Alexander and his wife in Tokyo.

Mainhall cut in impatiently.

"I say, Sir Harry, the little girl's going famously to-night, is n't she?"

Sir Harry wrinkled his brows judiciously. "Do you know, I thought the dance a bit conscious to-night, for the first time. The fact is, she's feeling rather seedy, poor child. Westmere and I were back after the first act, and we thought she seemed quite uncertain of herself. A little attack of nerves, possibly."

He bowed as the warning bell rang, and Mainhall whispered: "You know Lord Westmere, of course,—the stooped man with the long gray mustache, talking to Lady Dowle. Lady Westmere is very fond of Hilda."

When they reached their box the house was darkened and the orchestra was playing "The Cloak of Old Gaul." In a moment Peggy was on the stage again, and Alexander applauded vigorously with the rest. He even leaned forward over the rail a little. For some reason he felt pleased and flattered by the enthusiasm of the audience. In the half-light he looked about at the stalls and boxes and smiled a little consciously, recalling with amusement Sir Harry's judicial frown. He was beginning to feel a keen interest in the slender, barefoot donkey-girl who slipped in and out of the play, singing, like some one winding through a hilly field. He leaned forward and beamed felicitations as warmly as Mainhall himself when, at the end of the play, she came again and again before the curtain, panting a little and flushed, her eyes dancing and her eager, nervous little mouth tremulous with excitement.

When Alexander returned to his hotel—he shook Mainhall at the door of the theatre—he had some supper brought up to his room, and it was late before he went to bed. He had not thought of Hilda Burgoyne for years; indeed, he had almost forgotten her. He had last written to her from Canada, after he first met Winifred, telling her that everything was changed with him—that he had met a woman whom he would marry if he could; if he could not, then all the more was everything changed for him. Hilda had never replied to his letter. He felt guilty and unhappy about her for a time, but after Winifred promised to marry him he really forgot Hilda altogether. When he wrote her that everything was changed for him, he was telling the truth. After he met Winifred Pemberton he seemed to himself like a different man. One night when he and Winifred were sitting together on the bridge, he told her that things had happened while he was studying abroad that he was sorry for,—one thing in particular,—and he asked her whether she thought she ought to know about them. She considered a moment and then said: "No, I think not, though I am glad you ask me. You see, one can't be jealous about things in general; but about particular, definite, personal things,"—here she had thrown her hands up to his shoulders with a quick, impulsive gesture—"oh, about those I should be very jealous. I should torture myself—I could n't help it." After that it was easy to forget, actually to forget. He wondered to-night, as he poured his wine, how many times he had thought of Hilda in the last ten years. He had been in London more or less, but he had never happened to hear of her. "All the same," he lifted his glass, "here's to you, little Hilda. You've made things come your way, and I never thought you'd do it.

"Of course," he reflected, "she always had that combination of something homely and sensible, and something utterly wild and daft. But I never thought she'd do anything. She had n't much ambition then, and she was too fond of trifles. She must care about the theatre a great deal more than she used to. Perhaps she has me to thank for something, after all. Sometimes a little jolt like that does one good. She was a daft, generous little thing. I'm glad she's held her own since. After all, we were awfully young. It was youth and poverty and proximity, and everything was young and kindly. I should n't wonder if she could laugh about it with me now. I should n't wonder—But they've probably spoiled her, so that she'd be tiresome if one met her again."

Bartley smiled and yawned and went to bed.

3.

The next evening Alexander dined alone at a club, and at about nine o'clock he dropped in at the Duke of York's. The house was sold out and he stood through the second act. When he returned to his hotel he examined the new directory, and found Miss Burgoyne's address still given as off Bedford Square, though at a new number. He remembered that, in so far as she had been brought up at all, she had been brought up in Bloomsbury. Her father and mother played in the provinces most of the year, and she was left a great deal in the care of an old aunt who was crippled by rheumatism and who had had to leave the stage altogether. In the days when Alexander knew her, Hilda always managed to have a lodging of some sort about Bedford Square, because she clung tenaciously to such scraps and shreds of memories as were connected with it. The mummy room of the British Museum had been one of the chief delights of her childhood. That forbidding pile was the goal of her truant fancy, and she was sometimes taken there for a treat, as other children are taken to the theatre. It was long since Alexander had thought of any of these things, but now they came back to him quite fresh, and had a significance they did not have when they were first told him in his restless twenties. So she was still in the old neighborhood, near Bedford Square. The new number probably meant increased prosperity. He hoped so. He would like to know that she was snugly settled. He looked at his watch. It was a quarter past ten; she would not be home for a good two hours yet, and he might as well walk over and have a look at the place. He remembered the shortest way.

It was a warm, smoky evening, and there was a grimy moon. He went through Covent Garden to Oxford Street, and as he turned into Museum Street he walked more slowly, smiling at his own nervousness as he approached the sullen gray mass at the end. He had not been inside the Museum, actually, since he and Hilda used to meet there; sometimes to set out for gay adventures at Twickenham or Richmond, sometimes to linger about the place for a while and to ponder by Lord Elgin's marbles upon the lastingness of some things, or, in the mummy room, upon the awful brevity of others. Since then Bartley had always thought of the British Museum as the ultimate repository of mortality, where all the dead things in the world were assembled to make one's hour of youth the more precious. One trembled lest before he got out it might somehow escape him, lest he might drop the glass from overeagerness and see it shivered on the stone floor at his feet. How one hid his youth under his coat and hugged it! And how good it was to turn one's back upon all that vaulted cold, to take Hilda's arm and hurry out of the great door and down the steps into the sunlight among the pigeons—to know that the warm and vital thing within him was still there and had not been snatched away to flush

Caesar's lean cheek or to feed the veins of some bearded Assyrian king. They in their day had carried the flaming liquor, but to-day was his! So the song used to run in his head those summer mornings a dozen years ago. Alexander walked by the place very quietly, as if he were afraid of waking some one.

He crossed Bedford Square and found the number he was looking for. The house, a comfortable, well-kept place enough, was dark except for the four front windows on the second floor, where a low, even light was burning behind the white muslin sash curtains. Outside there were window boxes, painted white and full of flowers. Bartley was making a third round of the Square when he heard the far-flung hoof-beats of a hansom-cab horse, driven rapidly. He looked at his watch, and was astonished to find that it was a few minutes after twelve. He turned and walked back along the iron railing as the cab came up to Hilda's number and stopped. The hansom must have been one that she employed regularly, for she did not stop to pay the driver. She stepped out quickly and lightly. He heard her cheerful "Good-night, cabby," as she ran up the steps and opened the door with a latchkey. In a few moments the lights flared up brightly behind the white curtains, and as he walked away he heard a window raised. But he had gone too far to look up without turning round. He went back to his hotel, feeling that he had had a good evening, and he slept well.

For the next few days Alexander was very busy. He took a desk in the office of a Scotch engineering firm on Henrietta Street, and was at work almost constantly. He avoided the clubs and usually dined alone at his hotel. One afternoon, after he had tea, he started for a walk down the Embankment toward Westminster, intending to end his stroll at Bedford Square and to ask whether Miss Burgoyne would let him take her to the theatre. But he did not go so far. When he reached the Abbey, he turned back and crossed Westminster Bridge and sat down to watch the trails of smoke behind the Houses of Parliament catch fire with the sunset. The slender towers were washed by a rain of golden light and licked by little flickering flames; Somerset House and the bleached gray pinnacles about Whitehall were floated in a luminous haze. The yellow light poured through the trees and the leaves seemed to burn with soft fires. There was a smell of acacias in the air everywhere, and the laburnums were dripping gold over the walls of the gardens. It was a sweet, lonely kind of summer evening. Remembering Hilda as she used to be, was doubtless more satisfactory than seeing her as she must be now—and, after all, Alexander asked himself, what was it but his own young years that he was remembering?

He crossed back to Westminster, went up to the Temple, and sat down to smoke in the Middle Temple gardens, listening to the thin voice of the fountain and smelling the spice of the sycamores that came out heavily in the damp evening air. He thought, as he sat there, about a great many things: about his own youth and Hilda's; above all, he thought of how glorious it had been, and how quickly it had passed; and, when it had passed, how little worth while anything was. None of the things he had gained in the least compensated. In the last six years his reputation had become, as the saying is, popular. Four years ago he had been called to Japan to deliver, at the Emperor's request, a course of lectures at the Imperial University, and had instituted reforms throughout the islands, not only in the practice of bridge-building but in drainage and road-making. On his return he had undertaken the bridge at Moorlock, in Canada, the most important piece of bridge-building going on in the world,—a test, indeed, of how far the latest practice in bridge structure could be carried. It was a spectacular undertaking by reason of its very size, and Bartley realized that, whatever else he might do, he would probably always be known as the engineer who designed the great Moorlock Bridge, the longest cantilever in existence. Yet it was to him the least satisfactory thing he had ever done. He was cramped in every way by a niggardly commission, and was using lighter structural material than he thought proper. He had vexations enough, too, with his work at home. He had several bridges under way in the United States, and they were always being held up by strikes and delays resulting from a general industrial unrest.

Though Alexander often told himself he had never put more into his work than he had done in the last few years, he had to admit that he had never got so little out of it. He was paying for success, too, in the demands made on his time by boards of civic enterprise and committees of public welfare. The obligations imposed by his wife's fortune and position were sometimes distracting to a man who followed his profession, and he was expected to be interested in a great many worthy endeavors on her account as well as on his own. His existence was becoming a network of great and little details. He had expected that success would bring him freedom and power; but it had brought only power that was in itself another kind of restraint. He had always meant to keep his personal liberty at all costs, as old MacKeller, his first chief, had done, and not, like so many American engineers, to become a part of a professional movement, a cautious board member, a Nestor *de pontibus*. He happened to be engaged in work of public utility, but he was not willing to become what is called a public man. He found himself living exactly the kind of life he had determined to escape. What, he asked himself, did he want with these genial honors and substantial comforts? Hardships and difficulties he had carried lightly; overwork had not exhausted him; but this dead calm of middle life which confronted him,—of that he was afraid. He was not ready for it. It was like being buried alive. In his youth he would not have believed such a thing possible. The one thing he had really wanted all his life was to be free; and there was still something unconquered in him, something besides the strong work-horse that his profession had made of him. He felt rich to-night in the possession of that unstultified survival; in the light of his experience, it was more precious than honors or achievement. In all those busy, successful years there had been nothing so good as this hour of wild light-heartedness. This feeling was the only happiness that was real to him, and such hours were the only ones in which he could feel his own continuous identity—feel the boy he had been in the rough days of the old West, feel the youth who had worked his way across the ocean on a cattle-ship and gone to study in Paris without a dollar in his pocket. The man who sat in his offices in Boston was only a powerful machine. Under the activities of that machine the person who, at such moments as this, he felt to be himself, was fading and dying. He remembered how, when he was a little boy and his father called him in the morning, he used to leap from his bed into the full consciousness of himself. That consciousness was Life itself. Whatever took its place, action, reflection, the power of concentrated thought, were only functions of a mechanism useful to society; things that could be bought in the market. There was only one thing that had an absolute value for each individual, and it was just that original impulse, that internal heat, that feeling of one's self in one's own breast.

When Alexander walked back to his hotel, the red and green lights were blinking along the docks on the farther shore, and the soft white stars were shining in the wide sky above the river.

The next night, and the next, Alexander repeated this same foolish performance. It was always Miss Burgoyne whom he started out to find, and he got no farther than the Temple gardens and the Embankment. It was a pleasant kind of loneliness. To a man who was so little given to reflection, whose dreams always took the form of definite ideas, reaching into the future, there was a seductive excitement in renewing old experiences in imagination. He started out upon these walks half guiltily, with a curious longing and expectancy which were wholly gratified by solitude. Solitude, but not solitariness; for he walked shoulder to shoulder with a shadowy companion—not little Hilda Burgoyne, by any means, but some one vastly dearer to him than she had ever been—his own young self, the youth who had waited for him upon the steps of the British Museum that night, and who, though he had tried to pass so quietly, had known him and come down and linked an arm in his.

It was not until long afterward that Alexander learned that for him this youth was the most dangerous of companions.

One Sunday evening, at Lady Walford's, Alexander did at last meet Hilda Burgoyne. Mainhall had told him that she would probably be there. He looked about for her rather nervously, and finally found her at the farther end of the large drawing-room, the centre of a circle of men, young and old. She was apparently telling them a story. They were all laughing and bending toward her. When she saw Alexander, she rose quickly and put out her hand. The other men drew back a little to let him approach.

"Mr. Alexander! I am delighted. Have you been in London long?"

Bartley bowed, somewhat laboriously, over her hand. "Long enough to have seen you more than once. How fine it all is!"

She laughed as if she were pleased. "I'm glad you think so. I like it. Won't you join us here?"

"Miss Burgoyne was just telling us about a donkey-boy she had in Galway last summer," Sir Harry Towne explained as the circle closed up again. Lord Westmere stroked his long white mustache with his bloodless hand and looked at Alexander blankly. Hilda was a good story-teller. She was sitting on the edge of her chair, as if she had alighted there for a moment only. Her primrose satin gown seemed like a soft sheath for her slender, supple figure, and its delicate color suited her white Irish skin and brown hair. Whatever she wore, people felt the charm of her active, girlish body with its slender hips and quick, eager shoulders. Alexander heard little of the story, but he watched Hilda intently. She must certainly, he reflected, be thirty, and he was honestly delighted to see that the years had treated her so indulgently. If her face had changed at all, it was in a slight hardening of the mouth—still eager enough to be very disconcerting at times, he felt—and in an added air of self-possession and self-reliance. She carried her head, too, a little more resolutely.

When the story was finished, Miss Burgoyne turned pointedly to Alexander, and the other men drifted away.

"I thought I saw you in MacConnell's box with Mainhall one evening, but I supposed you had left town before this."

She looked at him frankly and cordially, as if he were indeed merely an old friend whom she was glad to meet again.

"No, I've been mooning about here."

Hilda laughed gayly. "Mooning! I see you mooning! You must be the busiest man in the world. Time and success have done well by you, you know. You're handsomer than ever and you've gained a grand manner."

Alexander blushed and bowed. "Time and success have been good friends to both of us. Are n't you tremendously pleased with yourself?"

She laughed again and shrugged her shoulders. "Oh, so-so. But I want to hear about you. Several years ago I read such a lot in the papers about the wonderful things you did in Japan, and how the Emperor decorated you. What was it, Commander of the Order of the Rising Sun? That sounds like 'The Mikado.' And what about your new bridge—in Canada, is n't it, and it's to be the longest one in the world and has some queer name I can't remember."

Bartley shook his head and smiled drolly. "Since when have you been interested in bridges? Or have you learned to be interested in everything? And is that a part of success?"

"Why, how absurd! As if I were not always interested!" Hilda exclaimed.

"Well, I think we won't talk about bridges here, at any rate." Bartley looked down at the toe of her yellow slipper which was tapping the rug impatiently under the hem of her gown. "But I wonder whether you'd think me impertinent if I asked you to let me come to see you sometime and tell you about them?"

"Why should I? Ever so many people come on Sunday afternoons."

"I know. Mainhall offered to take me. But you must know that I've been in London several times within the last few years, and you might very well think that just now is a rather inopportune time—"

She cut him short. "Nonsense. One of the pleasantest things about success is that it makes people want to look one up, if that's what you mean. I'm like every one else—more agreeable to meet when things are going well with me. Don't you suppose it gives me any pleasure to do something that people like?"

"Does it? Oh, how fine it all is, your coming on like this! But I did n't want you to think it was because of that I wanted to see you." He spoke very seriously and looked down at the floor.

Hilda studied him in wide-eyed astonishment for a moment, and then broke into a low, amused laugh. "My dear Mr. Alexander, you have strange delicacies. If you please, that is exactly why you wish to see me. We understand that, do we not?"

Bartley looked ruffled and turned the seal ring on his little finger about awkwardly.

Hilda leaned back in her chair, watching him indulgently out of her shrewd eyes. "Come, don't be angry, but don't try to pose for me, or to be anything but what you are. If you care to come, it's yourself I'll be glad to see, and you thinking well of yourself. Don't try to wear a cloak of humility; it does n't become you. Stalk in as you are and don't make excuses. I'm not accustomed to inquiring into the motives of my guests. That would hardly be safe, even for Lady Walford, in a great house like this."

"Sunday afternoon, then," said Alexander, as she rose to join her hostess. "How early may I come?"

"I'm at home after four, and I'll be glad to see you, Bartley."

She gave him her hand and flushed and laughed. He bent over it a little stiffly. She went away on Lady Walford's arm, and as he stood watching her yellow train glide down the long floor he looked rather sullen. He felt that he had not come out of it very brilliantly.

4.

On Sunday afternoon Alexander remembered Miss Burgoyne's invitation and called at her apartment. He found it a delightful little place and he met charming people there. Hilda lived alone, attended by a very pretty and competent French servant who answered the door and brought in the tea. Alexander arrived early, and some twenty-odd people dropped in during the course of the afternoon. Hugh MacConnell came with his sister, and stood about, managing his tea-cup awkwardly and watching every one out of his deep-set, faded eyes. He seemed to have made a resolute effort at tidiness of attire, and his sister, a robust, florid woman with a splendid joviality about her, kept eyeing his freshly creased clothes apprehensively. It was not very long, indeed, before his coat hung with a discouraged sag from his gaunt shoulders and his hair and beard were rumpled as if he had been out in a gale. His dry humor went under a cloud of absentminded kindliness which, Mainhall explained, always overtook him here. He was never so witty or so sharp here as elsewhere, and Alexander thought he behaved as if he were an elderly relative come in to a young girl's party.

The editor of a monthly review came with his wife, and Lady Kildare, the Irish philanthropist, brought her young nephew, Robert Owen, who had come up from Oxford, and who was visibly excited and gratified by his first introduction to Miss Burgoyne. Hilda was very nice to him, and he sat on the edge of his chair, flushed with his conversational efforts and moving his chin about nervously over his high collar. Sarah Frost, the novelist, came with her husband, a very genial and placid old scholar who had become slightly deranged upon the subject of the fourth dimension. On other matters he was perfectly rational and he was easy and pleasing in conversation. He looked very much like Agassiz, and his wife, in her old-fashioned black silk dress, overskirted and tight-sleeved, reminded Alexander of the early pictures of Mrs. Browning. Hilda seemed particularly fond of this quaint couple, and Bartley himself was so pleased with their mild and thoughtful converse that he took his leave when they did, and walked with them over to Oxford Street, where they waited for their 'bus. They asked him to come to see them in Chelsea, and they spoke very tenderly of Hilda. "She's a dear, unworldly little thing," said the philosopher absently; "more like the stage people of my young days—folk of simple manners. There are n't many such left. American tours have spoiled them, I'm afraid. They have all grown very smart. Lamb would n't care a great deal about many of them, I fancy."

Alexander went back to Bedford Square a second Sunday afternoon. He had a long talk with MacConnell, but he got no word with Hilda alone, and he left in a discontented state of mind. For the rest of the week he was nervous and unsettled, and kept rushing his work as if he were preparing for immediate departure. On Thursday afternoon he cut short a committee meeting, jumped into a hansom, and drove to Bedford Square. He sent up his card, but it came back to him with a message scribbled across the front.

So sorry I can't see you. Will you come and dine with me Sunday evening at half-past seven?

H.B.

When Bartley arrived at Bedford Square on Sunday evening, Marie, the pretty little French girl, met him at the door and conducted him upstairs. Hilda was writing in her living-room, under the light of a tall desk lamp. Bartley recognized the primrose satin gown she had worn that first evening at Lady Walford's.

"I'm so pleased that you think me worth that yellow dress, you know," he said, taking her hand and looking her over admiringly from the toes of her canary slippers to her smoothly parted brown hair. "Yes, it's very, very pretty. Every one at Lady Walford's was looking at it."

Hilda curtsied. "Is that why you think it pretty? I've no need for fine clothes in Mac's play this time, so I can afford a few duddies for myself. It's owing to that same chance, by the way, that I am able to ask you to dinner. I don't need Marie to dress me this season, so she keeps house for me, and my little Galway girl has gone home for a visit. I should never have asked you if Molly had been here, for I remember you don't like English cookery."

Alexander walked about the room, looking at everything.

"I have n't had a chance yet to tell you what a jolly little place I think this is. Where did you get those etchings? They're quite unusual, are n't they?"

"Lady Westmere sent them to me from Rome last Christmas. She is very much interested in the American artist who did them. They are all sketches made about the Villa d'Este, you see. He painted that group of cypresses for the Salon, and it was bought for the Luxembourg."

Alexander walked over to the bookcases. "It's the air of the whole place here that I like. You have n't got anything that does n't belong. Seems to me it looks particularly well to-night. And you have so many flowers. I like these little yellow irises."

"Rooms always look better by lamplight—in London, at least. Though Marie is clean—really clean, as the French are. Why do you look at the flowers so critically? Marie got them all fresh in Covent Garden market yesterday morning."

"I'm glad," said Alexander simply. "I can't tell you how glad I am to have you so pretty and comfortable here, and to hear every one saying such nice things about you. You've got awfully nice friends," he added humbly, picking up a little jade elephant from her desk. "Those fellows are all very loyal, even Mainhall. They don't talk of any one else as they do of you."

Hilda sat down on the couch and said seriously: "I've a neat little sum in the bank, too, now, and I own a mite of a hut in Galway. It's not worth much, but I love it. I've managed to save something every year, and that with helping my three sisters now and then, and tiding poor Cousin Mike over bad seasons. He's that gifted, you know, but he will drink and loses more good engagements than other fellows ever get. And I've traveled a bit, too."

Marie opened the door and smilingly announced that dinner was served.

"My dining-room," Hilda explained, as she led the way, "is the tiniest place you have ever seen."

It was a tiny room, hung all round with French prints, above which ran a shelf full of china. Hilda saw Alexander look up at it.

"It's not particularly rare," she said, "but some of it was my mother's. Heaven knows how she managed to keep it whole, through all our wanderings, or in what baskets and bundles and theatre trunks it has n't been stowed away. We always had our tea out of those blue cups when I was a little girl, sometimes in the queerest lodgings, and sometimes on a trunk at the theatre—queer theatres, for that matter."

It was a wonderful little dinner. There was watercress soup, and sole, and a delightful omelette stuffed with mushrooms and truffles, and two small rare ducklings, and artichokes, and a dry yellow Rhone wine of which Bartley had always been very fond. He drank it appreciatively and remarked that there was still no other he liked so well.

"I have some champagne for you, too. I don't drink it myself, but I like to see it behave when it's poured. There is nothing else that looks so jolly."

"Thank you. But I don't like it so well as this." Bartley held the yellow wine against the light and squinted into it as he turned the glass slowly about. "You have traveled, you say. Have you been in Paris much these late years?"

Hilda lowered one of the candle-shades carefully. "Oh, yes, I go over to Paris often. There are few changes in the old Quarter. Dear old Madame Anger is dead—but perhaps you don't remember her?"

"Don't I, though! I'm so sorry to hear it. How did her son turn out? I remember how she saved and scraped for him, and how he always lay abed till ten o'clock. He was the laziest fellow at the Beaux Arts; and that's saying a good deal."

"Well, he is still clever and lazy. They say he is a good architect when he will work. He's a big, handsome creature, and he hates Americans as much as ever. But Angel—do you remember Angel?"

"Perfectly. Did she ever get back to Brittany and her *bains de mer*?"

"Ah, no. Poor Angel! She got tired of cooking and scouring the coppers in Madame Anger's little kitchen, so she ran away with a soldier, and then with another soldier. Too bad! She still lives about the Quarter, and, though there is always a *soldat*, she has become a *blanchisseuse de fin*. She did my blouses beautifully the last time I was there, and was so delighted to see me again. I gave her all my old clothes, even my old hats, though she always wears her Breton head-dress. Her hair is still like flax, and her blue eyes are just like a baby's, and she has the same three freckles on her little nose, and talks about going back to her *bains de mer*."

Bartley looked at Hilda across the yellow light of the candles and broke into a low, happy laugh. "How jolly it was being young, Hilda! Do you remember that first walk we took together in Paris? We walked down to the Place Saint-Michel to buy some lilacs. Do you remember how sweet they smelled?"

"Indeed I do. Come, we'll have our coffee in the other room, and you can smoke."

Hilda rose quickly, as if she wished to change the drift of their talk, but Bartley found it pleasant to continue it.

"What a warm, soft spring evening that was," he went on, as they sat down in the study with the coffee on a little table between them; "and the sky, over the bridges, was just the color of the lilacs. We walked on down by the river, did n't we?"

Hilda laughed and looked at him questioningly. He saw a gleam in her eyes that he remembered even better than the episode he was recalling.

"I think we did," she answered demurely. "It was on the Quai we met that woman who was crying so bitterly. I gave her a spray of lilac, I remember, and you gave her a franc. I was frightened at your prodigality."

"I expect it was the last franc I had. What a strong brown face she had, and very tragic. She looked at us with such despair and longing, out from under her black shawl. What she wanted from us was neither our flowers nor our francs, but just our youth. I remember it touched me so. I would have given her some of mine off my back, if I could. I had enough and to spare then," Bartley mused, and looked thoughtfully at his cigar.

They were both remembering what the woman had said when she took the money: "God give you a happy love!" It was not in the ingratiating tone of the habitual beggar: it had come out of the depths of the poor creature's sorrow, vibrating with pity for their youth and despair at the terribleness of human life; it had the anguish of a voice of prophecy. Until she spoke, Bartley had not real-ized that he was in love. The strange woman, and her passionate sentence that rang out so sharply, had frightened them both. They went home sadly with the lilacs, back to the Rue Saint-Jacques, walking very slowly, arm in arm. When they reached the house where Hilda lodged, Bartley went across the court with her, and up the dark old stairs to the third landing; and there he had kissed her for the first time. He had shut his eyes to give him the courage, he remembered, and she had trembled so—

Bartley started when Hilda rang the little bell beside her. "Dear me, why did you do that? I had quite forgotten—I was back there. It was very jolly," he murmured lazily, as Marie came in to take away the coffee.

Hilda laughed and went over to the piano. "Well, we are nei-ther of us twenty now, you know. Have I told you about my new play? Mac is writing one; really for me this time. You see, I'm com-ing on."

"I've seen nothing else. What kind of a part is it? Shall you wear yellow gowns? I hope so."

He was looking at her round, slender figure, as she stood by the piano, turning over a pile of music, and he felt the energy in every line of it.

"No, it is n't a dress-up part. He does n't seem to fancy me in fine feathers. He says I ought to be minding the pigs at home, and I suppose I ought. But he's given me some good Irish songs. Lis-ten."

She sat down at the piano and sang. When she finished, Alexan-der shook himself out of a reverie.

"Sing 'The Harp that Once,' Hilda. You used to sing it so well."

"Nonsense. Of course I can't really sing, except the way my mother and grandmother did before me. Most actresses nowadays learn to sing properly, so I tried a master; but he confused me, just!"

Alexander laughed. "All the same, sing it, Hilda."

Hilda started up from the stool and moved restlessly toward the window. "It's really too warm in this room to sing. Don't you feel it?"

Alexander went over and opened the window for her. "Are n't you afraid to let the wind blow like that on your neck? Can't I get a scarf or something?"

"Ask a theatre lydy if she's afraid of drafts!" Hilda laughed. "But perhaps, as I'm so warm—give me your handkerchief. There, just in front." He slipped the corners carefully under her shoulder-straps. "There, that will do. It looks like a bib." She pushed his hand away quickly and stood looking out into the deserted square. "Is n't London a tomb on Sunday night?"

Alexander caught the agitation in her voice. He stood a little behind her, and tried to steady himself as he said: "It's soft and misty. See how white the stars are."

For a long time neither Hilda nor Bartley spoke. They stood close together, looking out into the wan, watery sky, breathing always more quickly and lightly, and it seemed as if all the clocks in the world had stopped. Suddenly he moved the clenched hand he held behind him and dropped it violently at his side. He felt a tremor run through the slender yellow figure in front of him.

She caught his handkerchief from her throat and thrust it at him without turning round.

"Here, take it. You must go now, Bartley. Good-night."

Bartley leaned over her shoulder, without touching her, and whispered in her ear: "You are giving me a chance?"

"Yes. Take it and go. This is n't fair, you know. Good-night."

Alexander unclenched the two hands at his sides. With one he threw down the window and with the other—still standing behind her—he drew her back against him.

She uttered a little cry, threw her arms over her head, and drew his face down to hers. "Are you going to let me love you a little, Bartley?" she whispered.

5.

It was the afternoon of the day before Christmas. Mrs. Alexander had been driving about all the morning, leaving presents at the houses of her friends. She lunched alone, and as she rose from the table she spoke to the butler: "Thomas, I am going down to the kitchen now to see Norah. In half an hour you are to bring the greens up from the cellar and put them in the library. Mr. Alexander will be home at three to hang them himself. Don't forget the stepladder, and plenty of tacks and string. You may bring the azaleas upstairs. Take the white one to Mr. Alexander's study. Put the two pink ones in this room, and the red one in the drawing-room."

A little before three o'clock Mrs. Alexander went into the library to see that everything was ready. She pulled the window shades high, for the weather was dark and stormy, and there was little light, even in the streets. A foot of snow had fallen during the morning, and the wide space over the river was thick with flying flakes that fell and wreathed the masses of floating ice. Winifred was standing by the window when she heard the front door open. She hurried to the hall as Alexander came stamping in, covered with snow. He kissed her joyfully and brushed away the snow that fell on her hair.

"I wish I had asked you to meet me at the office and walk home with me, Winifred. The Common is beautiful. The boys have swept the snow off the pond and are skating furiously. Did the cyclamens come?"

"An hour ago. What splendid ones! But are n't you frightfully extravagant?"

"Not for Christmas-time. I'll go upstairs and change my coat. I shall be down in a moment. Tell Thomas to get everything ready."

When Alexander reappeared, he took his wife's arm and went with her into the library. "When did the azaleas get here? Thomas has got the white one in my room."

"I told him to put it there."

"But, I say, it's much the finest of the lot!"

"That's why I had it put there. There is too much color in that room for a red one, you know."

Bartley began to sort the greens. "It looks very splendid there, but I feel piggish to have it. However, we really spend more time there than anywhere else in the house. Will you hand me the holly?"

He climbed up the stepladder, which creaked under his weight, and began to twist the tough stems of the holly into the framework of the chandelier.

"I forgot to tell you that I had a letter from Wilson, this morning, explaining his telegram. He is coming on because an old uncle up in Vermont has conveniently died and left Wilson a little money—something like ten thousand. He's coming on to settle up the estate. Won't it be jolly to have him?"

"And how fine that he's come into a little money. I can see him posting down State Street to the steamship offices. He will get a good many trips out of that ten thousand. What can have detained him? I expected him here for luncheon."

"Those trains from Albany are always late. He'll be along sometime this afternoon. And now, don't you want to go upstairs and lie down for an hour? You've had a busy morning and I don't want you to be tired to-night."

After his wife went upstairs Alexander worked energetically at the greens for a few moments. Then, as he was cutting off a length of string, he sighed suddenly and sat down, staring out of the window at the snow. The animation died out of his face, but in his eyes there was a restless light, a look of apprehension and suspense. He kept clasping and unclasping his big hands as if he were trying to realize something. The clock ticked through the minutes of a half-hour and the afternoon outside began to thicken and darken turbidly. Alexander, since he first sat down, had not changed his position. He leaned forward, his hands between his knees, scarcely breathing, as if he were holding himself away from his surroundings, from the room, and from the very chair in which he sat, from everything except the wild eddies of snow above the river on which his eyes were fixed with feverish intentness, as if he were trying to project himself thither. When at last Lucius Wilson was announced, Alexander sprang eagerly to his feet and hurried to meet his old instructor.

"Hello, Wilson. What luck! Come into the library. We are to have a lot of people to dinner to-night, and Winifred's lying down. You will excuse her, won't you? And now what about yourself? Sit down and tell me everything."

"I think I'd rather move about, if you don't mind. I've been sitting in the train for a week, it seems to me." Wilson stood before the fire with his hands behind him and looked about the room. "You *have* been busy. Bartley, if I'd had my choice of all possible places in which to spend Christmas, your house would certainly be the place I'd have chosen. Happy people do a great deal for their friends. A house like this throws its warmth out. I felt it distinctly as I was coming through the Berkshires. I could scarcely believe that I was to see Mrs. Bartley again so soon."

"Thank you, Wilson. She'll be as glad to see you. Shall we have tea now? I'll ring for Thomas to clear away this litter. Winifred says I always wreck the house when I try to do anything. Do you know, I am quite tired. Looks as if I were not used to work, does n't it?" Alexander laughed and dropped into a chair. "You know, I'm sailing the day after New Year's."

"Again? Why, you've been over twice since I was here in the spring, have n't you?"

"Oh, I was in London about ten days in the summer. Went to escape the hot weather more than anything else. I shan't be gone more than a month this time. Winifred and I have been up in Canada for most of the autumn. That Moorlock Bridge is on my

back all the time. I never had so much trouble with a job before."
Alexander moved about restlessly and fell to poking the fire.

"Have n't I seen in the papers that there is some trouble about
a tidewater bridge of yours in New Jersey?"

"Oh, that does n't amount to anything. It's held up by a steel
strike. A bother, of course, but the sort of thing one is always having to put up with. But the Moorlock Bridge is a continual anxiety.
You see, the truth is, we are having to build pretty well to the strain
limit up there. They've crowded me too much on the cost. It's all
very well if everything goes well, but these estimates have never been
used for anything of such length before. However, there's nothing
to be done. They hold me to the scale I've used in shorter bridges.
The last thing a bridge commission cares about is the kind of bridge
you build."

When Bartley had finished dressing for dinner he went into his
study, where he found his wife arranging flowers on his writing-
table.

"These pink roses just came from Mrs. Hastings," she said, smiling, "and I am sure she meant them for you."

Bartley looked about with an air of satisfaction at the greens and
the wreaths in the windows. "Have you a moment, Winifred? I have
just now been thinking that this is our twelfth Christmas. Can you
realize it?" He went up to the table and took her hands away from
the flowers, drying them with his pocket handkerchief. "They've
been awfully happy ones, all of them, have n't they?" He took her
in his arms and bent back, lifting her a little and giving her a long
kiss. "You are happy, are n't you, Winifred? More than anything

else in the world, I want you to be happy. Sometimes, of late, I've thought you looked as if you were troubled."

"No; it's only when you are troubled and harassed that I feel worried, Bartley. I wish you always seemed as you do to-night. But you don't, always." She looked earnestly and inquiringly into his eyes.

Alexander took her two hands from his shoulders and swung them back and forth in his own, laughing his big blond laugh.

"I'm growing older, my dear; that's what you feel. Now, may I show you something? I meant to save them until to-morrow, but I want you to wear them to-night." He took a little leather box out of his pocket and opened it. On the white velvet lay two long pendants of curiously worked gold, set with pearls. Winifred looked from the box to Bartley and exclaimed:—

"Where did you ever find such gold work, Bartley?"

"It's old Flemish. Is n't it fine?"

"They are the most beautiful things, dear. But, you know, I never wear earrings."

"Yes, yes, I know. But I want you to wear them. I have always wanted you to. So few women can. There must be a good ear, to begin with, and a nose"—he waved his hand—"above reproach. Most women look silly in them. They go only with faces like yours— very, very proud, and just a little hard."

Winifred laughed as she went over to the mirror and fitted the delicate springs to the lobes of her ears. "Oh, Bartley, that old foolishness about my being hard. It really hurts my feelings. But I must go down now. People are beginning to come."

Bartley drew her arm about his neck and went to the door with her. "Not hard to me, Winifred," he whispered. "Never, never hard to me."

Left alone, he paced up and down his study. He was at home again, among all the dear familiar things that spoke to him of so many happy years. His house to-night would be full of charming people, who liked and admired him. Yet all the time, underneath his pleasure and hopefulness and satisfaction, he was conscious of the vibration of an unnatural excitement. Amid this light and warmth and friendliness, he sometimes started and shuddered, as if some one had stepped on his grave. Something had broken loose in him of which he knew nothing except that it was sullen and powerful, and that it wrung and tortured him. Sometimes it came upon him softly, in enervating reveries. Sometimes it battered him like the cannon rolling in the hold of the vessel. Always, now, it brought with it a sense of quickened life, of stimulating danger. To-night it came upon him suddenly, as he was walking the floor, after his wife left him. It seemed impossible; he could not believe it. He glanced entreatingly at the door, as if to call her back. He heard voices in the hall below, and knew that he must go down. Going over to the window, he looked out at the lights across the river. How could this happen here, in his own house, among the things he loved? What was it that reached in out of the darkness and thrilled him? As he stood there he had a feeling that he would never escape. He shut his eyes and pressed his forehead against the cold window glass, breathing in the chill that came through it. "That this," he groaned, "that this should have happened to *me!*"

On New Year's day a thaw set in, and during the night torrents of rain fell. In the morning, the morning of Alexander's departure for England, the river was streaked with fog and the rain drove hard against the windows of the breakfast-room. Alexander had finished his coffee and was pacing up and down. His wife sat at the table, watching him. She was pale and unnaturally calm. When Thomas brought the letters, Bartley sank into his chair and ran them over rapidly.

"Here's a note from old Wilson. He's safe back at his grind, and says he had a bully time. 'The memory of Mrs. Bartley will make my whole winter fragrant.' Just like him. He will go on getting measureless satisfaction out of you by his study fire. What a man he is for looking on at life!" Bartley sighed, pushed the letters back impatiently, and went over to the window. "This is a nasty sort of day to sail. I've a notion to call it off. Next week would be time enough."

"That would only mean starting twice. It would n't really help you out at all," Mrs. Alexander spoke soothingly. "And you'd come back late for all your engagements."

Bartley began jingling some loose coins in his pocket. "I wish things would let me rest. I'm tired of work, tired of people, tired of trailing about." He looked out at the storm-beaten river.

Winifred came up behind him and put a hand on his shoulder. "That's what you always say, poor Bartley! At bottom you really like all these things. Can't you remember that?"

He put his arm about her. "All the same, life runs smoothly enough with some people, and with me it's always a messy sort of patchwork. It's like the song; peace is where I am not. How can you face it all with so much fortitude?"

She looked at him with that clear gaze which Wilson had so much admired, which he had felt implied such high confidence and fearless pride. "Oh, I faced that long ago, when you were on your first bridge, up at old Allway. I knew then that your paths were not to be paths of peace, but I decided that I wanted to follow them."

Bartley and his wife stood silent for a long time; the fire crackled in the grate, the rain beat insistently upon the windows, and the sleepy Angora looked up at them curiously.

Presently Thomas made a discreet sound at the door. "Shall Edward bring down your trunks, sir?"

"Yes; they are ready. Tell him not to forget the big portfolio on the study table."

Thomas withdrew, closing the door softly. Bartley turned away from his wife, still holding her hand. "It never gets any easier, Winifred."

They both started at the sound of the carriage on the pavement outside. Alexander sat down and leaned his head on his hand. His wife bent over him. "Courage," she said gayly. Bartley rose and rang the bell. Thomas brought him his hat and stick and ulster. At the sight of these, the supercilious Angora moved restlessly, quitted her red cushion by the fire, and came up, waving her tail in vexation at these ominous indications of change. Alexander stooped to stroke her, and then plunged into his coat and drew on his gloves. His wife held his stick, smiling. Bartley smiled too, and his eyes cleared. "I'll work like the devil, Winifred, and be home again before you realize I've gone." He kissed her quickly several times, hurried out of the front door into the rain, and waved to her from the carriage window as the driver was starting his melancholy, dripping black horses. Alexander sat with his hands clenched on his knees. As the carriage turned up the hill, he lifted one hand and brought it down violently. "This time"—he spoke aloud and through his set teeth— "this time I'm going to end it!"

On the afternoon of the third day out, Alexander was sitting well to the stern, on the windward side where the chairs were few, his rugs over him and the collar of his fur-lined coat turned up about his ears. The weather had so far been dark and raw. For two hours he had been watching the low, dirty sky and the beating of the heavy rain upon the iron-colored sea. There was a long, oily swell that made exercise laborious. The decks smelled of damp woolens, and the air was so humid that drops of moisture kept gathering upon his hair and mustache. He seldom moved except to brush them away. The great open spaces made him passive and the restlessness of the water quieted him. He intended during the voyage to decide upon a course of action, but he held all this away from him for the present and lay in a blessed gray oblivion. Deep down in him somewhere his resolution was weakening and strengthening, ebbing and flowing. The thing that perturbed him went on as steadily as his pulse, but he was almost unconscious of it. He was submerged in the vast impersonal grayness about him, and at intervals the sidelong roll of the boat measured off time like the ticking of a clock. He felt released from everything that troubled and perplexed him. It was as if he had tricked and outwitted torturing memories, had actually managed to get on board without them. He thought of nothing at all. If his mind now and again picked a face out of the grayness, it was Lucius Wilson's, or the face of an old schoolmate, forgotten for years; or it was the slim outline of a favorite greyhound he used to hunt jack-rabbits with when he was a boy.

Toward six o'clock the wind rose and tugged at the tarpaulin and brought the swell higher. After dinner Alexander came back to the wet deck, piled his damp rugs over him again, and sat smoking, losing himself in the obliterating blackness and drowsing in the rush of the gale. Before he went below a few bright stars were pricked off between heavily moving masses of cloud.

The next morning was bright and mild, with a fresh breeze. Alexander felt the need of exercise even before he came out of his cabin. When he went on deck the sky was blue and blinding, with heavy whiffs of white cloud, smoke-colored at the edges, moving rapidly across it. The water was roughish, a cold, clear indigo breaking into whitecaps. Bartley walked for two hours, and then stretched himself in the sun until lunch-time.

In the afternoon he wrote a long letter to Winifred. Later, as he walked the deck through a splendid golden sunset, his spirits rose continually. It was agreeable to come to himself again after several days of numbness and torpor. He stayed out until the last tinge of violet had faded from the water. There was literally a taste of life on his lips as he sat down to dinner and ordered a bottle of champagne. He was late in finishing his dinner, and drank rather more wine than he had meant to. When he went above, the wind had risen and the deck was almost deserted. As he stepped out of the door a gale lifted his heavy fur coat about his shoulders. He fought his way up the deck with keen exhilaration. The moment he stepped, almost out of breath, behind the shelter of the stern, the wind was cut off, and he felt, like a rush of warm air, a sense of close and intimate companionship. He started back and tore his coat open as if something warm were actually clinging to him beneath it. He hurried up the deck and went into the saloon parlor, full of women who had retreated thither from the sharp wind. He threw himself upon them. He talked delightfully to the older ones and played accompaniments for the younger ones until the last sleepy girl had followed her mother below. Then he went into the smoking-room. He played bridge until two o'clock in the morning, and managed to lose a considerable sum of money without really noticing that he was doing so.

After the break of one fine day the weather was pretty consistently dull. When the low sky thinned a trifle, the pale white spot of a sun did no more than throw a bluish lustre on the water, giving it the dark brightness of newly cut lead. Through one after another of those gray days Alexander drowsed and mused, drinking in the grateful moisture. But the complete peace of the first part of the voyage was over. Sometimes he rose suddenly from his chair as if driven out, and paced the deck for hours. People noticed his propensity for walking in rough weather, and watched him curiously as he did his rounds. From his abstraction and the determined set of his jaw, they fancied he must be thinking about his bridge. Every one had heard of the new cantilever bridge in Canada.

But Alexander was not thinking about his work. After the fourth night out, when his will suddenly softened under his hands, he had been continually hammering away at himself. More and more often, when he first wakened in the morning or when he stepped into a warm place after being chilled on the deck, he felt a sudden painful delight at being nearer another shore. Sometimes when he was most despondent, when he thought himself worn out with this struggle, in a flash he was free of it and leaped into an overwhelming consciousness of himself. On the instant he felt that marvelous return of the impetuousness, the intense excitement, the increasing expectancy of youth.

6.

The last two days of the voyage Bartley found almost intolerable. The stop at Queenstown, the tedious passage up the Mersey, were things that he noted dimly through his growing impatience. He had planned to stop in Liverpool; but, instead, he took the boat train for London.

Emerging at Euston at half-past three o'clock in the afternoon, Alexander had his luggage sent to the Savoy and drove at once to Bedford Square. When Marie met him at the door, even her strong sense of the proprieties could not restrain her surprise and delight. She blushed and smiled and fumbled his card in her confusion before she ran upstairs. Alexander paced up and down the hallway, buttoning and unbuttoning his overcoat, until she returned and took him up to Hilda's living-room. The room was empty when he entered. A coal fire was crackling in the grate and the lamps were lit, for it was already beginning to grow dark outside. Alexander did not sit down. He stood his ground over by the windows until Hilda came in. She called his name on the threshold, but in her swift flight across the room she felt a change in him and caught herself up so deftly that he could not tell just when she did it. She merely brushed his cheek with her lips and put a hand lightly and joyously on either shoulder.

"Oh, what a grand thing to happen on a raw day! I felt it in my bones when I woke this morning that something splendid was going to turn up. I thought it might be Sister Kate or Cousin Mike would be happening along. I never dreamed it would be you, Bartley. But why do you let me chatter on like this? Come over to the fire; you're chilled through."

She pushed him toward the big chair by the fire, and sat down on a stool at the opposite side of the hearth, her knees drawn up to her chin, laughing like a happy little girl.

"When did you come, Bartley, and how did it happen? You have n't spoken a word."

"I got in about ten minutes ago. I landed at Liverpool this morning and came down on the boat train."

Alexander leaned forward and warmed his hands before the blaze. Hilda watched him with perplexity.

"There's something troubling you, Bartley. What is it?"

Bartley bent lower over the fire. "It's the whole thing that troubles me, Hilda. You and I."

Hilda took a quick, soft breath. She looked at his heavy shoulders and big, determined head, thrust forward like a catapult in leash.

"What about us, Bartley?" she asked in a thin voice.

He locked and unlocked his hands over the grate and spread his fingers close to the bluish flame, while the coals crackled and the clock ticked and a street vendor began to call under the window. At last Alexander brought out one word:—

"Everything!"

Hilda was pale by this time, and her eyes were wide with fright. She looked about desperately from Bartley to the door, then to the windows, and back again to Bartley. She rose uncertainly, touched his hair with her hand, then sank back upon her stool.

"I'll do anything you wish me to, Bartley," she said tremulously. "I can't stand seeing you miserable."

"I can't live with myself any longer," he answered roughly.

He rose and pushed the chair behind him and began to walk miserably about the room, seeming to find it too small for him. He pulled up a window as if the air were heavy.

Hilda watched him from her corner, trembling and scarcely breathing, dark shadows growing about her eyes.

"It . . . it has n't always made you miserable, has it?" Her eyelids fell and her lips quivered.

"Always. But it's worse now. It's unbearable. It tortures me every minute."

"But why *now*?" she asked piteously, wringing her hands.

He ignored her question. "I am not a man who can live two lives," he went on feverishly. "Each life spoils the other. I get nothing but misery out of either. The world is all there, just as it used to be, but I can't get at it any more. There is this deception between me and everything."

At that word "deception," spoken with such self-contempt, the color flashed back into Hilda's face as suddenly as if she had been struck by a whiplash. She bit her lip and looked down at her hands, which were clasped tightly in front of her.

"Could you—could you sit down and talk about it quietly, Bartley, as if I were a friend, and not some one who had to be defied?"

He dropped back heavily into his chair by the fire. "It was myself I was defying, Hilda. I have thought about it until I am worn out."

He looked at her and his haggard face softened. He put out his hand toward her as he looked away again into the fire.

She crept across to him, drawing her stool after her. "When did you first begin to feel like this, Bartley?"

"After the very first. The first was—sort of in play, was n't it?"

Hilda's face quivered, but she whispered: "Yes, I think it must have been. But why did n't you tell me when you were here in the summer?"

Alexander groaned. "I meant to, but somehow I could n't. We had only a few days, and your new play was just on, and you were so happy."

"Yes, I was happy, was n't I?" She pressed his hand gently in gratitude. "Were n't you happy then, at all?"

She closed her eyes and took a deep breath, as if to draw in again the fragrance of those days. Something of their troubling sweetness came back to Alexander, too. He moved uneasily and his chair creaked.

"Yes, I was then. You know. But afterward . . ."

"Yes, yes," she hurried, pulling her hand gently away from him. Presently it stole back to his coat sleeve. "Please tell me one thing, Bartley. At least, tell me that you believe I thought I was making you happy."

His hand shut down quickly over the questioning fingers on his sleeves. "Yes, Hilda; I know that," he said simply.

She leaned her head against his arm and spoke softly:—

"You see, my mistake was in wanting you to have everything. I wanted you to eat all the cakes and have them, too. I somehow believed that I could take all the bad consequences for you. I wanted you always to be happy and handsome and successful—to have all the things that a great man ought to have, and, once in a way, the careless holidays that great men are not permitted."

Bartley gave a bitter little laugh, and Hilda looked up and read in the deepening lines of his face that youth and Bartley would not much longer struggle together.

"I understand, Bartley. I was wrong. But I did n't know. You've only to tell me now. What must I do that I've not done, or what must I not do?" She listened intently, but she heard nothing but the creaking of his chair. "You want me to say it?" she whispered. "You want to tell me that you can only see me like this, as old friends do, or out in the world among people? I can do that."

"I can't," he said heavily.

Hilda shivered and sat still. Bartley leaned his head in his hands and spoke through his teeth. "It's got to be a clean break, Hilda. I can't see you at all, anywhere. What I mean is that I want you to promise never to see me again, no matter how often I come, no matter how hard I beg."

Hilda sprang up like a flame. She stood over him with her hands clenched at her side, her body rigid.

"No!" she gasped. "It's too late to ask that. Do you hear me, Bartley? It's too late. I won't promise. It's abominable of you to ask me. Keep away if you wish; when have I ever followed you? But, if you come to me, I'll do as I see fit. The shamefulness of your asking me to do that! If you come to me, I'll do as I see fit. Do you understand? Bartley, you're cowardly!"

Alexander rose and shook himself angrily. "Yes, I know I'm cowardly. I'm afraid of myself. I don't trust myself any more. I carried it all lightly enough at first, but now I don't dare trifle with it. It's getting the better of me. It's different now. I'm growing older, and you've got my young self here with you. It's through him that I've come to wish for you all and all the time." He took her roughly in his arms. "Do you know what I mean?"

Hilda held her face back from him and began to cry bitterly. "Oh, Bartley, what am I to do? Why did n't you let me be angry with you? You ask me to stay away from you because you want me! And I've got nobody but you. I will do anything you say—but that! I will ask the least imaginable, but I must have *something!*"

Bartley turned away and sank down in his chair again. Hilda sat on the arm of it and put her hands lightly on his shoulders.

"Just something, Bartley. I must have you to think of through the months and months of loneliness. I must see you. I must know about you. The sight of you, Bartley, to see you living and happy and successful—can I never make you understand what that means to me?" She pressed his shoulders gently. "You see, loving some one as I love you makes the whole world different. If I'd met you later, if I had n't loved you so well—but that's all over, long ago. Then came all those years without you, lonely and hurt and discouraged; those decent young fellows and poor Mac, and me never heeding—hard as a steel spring. And then you came back, not caring very much, but it made no difference."

She slid to the floor beside him, as if she were too tired to sit up any longer. Bartley bent over and took her in his arms, kissing her mouth and her wet, tired eyes.

"Don't cry, don't cry," he whispered. "We've tortured each other enough for to-night. Forget everything except that I am here."

"I think I have forgotten everything but that already," she murmured. "Ah, your dear arms!"

7.

During the fortnight that Alexander was in London he drove himself hard. He got through a great deal of personal business and saw a great many men who were doing interesting things in his own profession. He disliked to think of his visits to London as holidays, and when he was there he worked even harder than he did at home.

The day before his departure for Liverpool was a singularly fine one. The thick air had cleared overnight in a strong wind which brought in a golden dawn and then fell off to a fresh breeze. When Bartley looked out of his windows from the Savoy, the river was flashing silver and the gray stone along the Embankment was bathed in bright, clear sunshine. London had wakened to life after three weeks of cold and sodden rain. Bartley breakfasted hurriedly and went over his mail while the hotel valet packed his trunks. Then he paid his account and walked rapidly down the Strand past Charing Cross Station. His spirits rose with every step, and when he reached Trafalgar Square, blazing in the sun, with its fountains playing and its column reaching up into the bright air, he signaled to a hansom, and, before he knew what he was about, told the driver to go to Bedford Square by way of the British Museum.

When he reached Hilda's apartment she met him, fresh as the morning itself. Her rooms were flooded with sunshine and full of the flowers he had been sending her. She would never let him give her anything else.

"Are you busy this morning, Hilda?" he asked as he sat down, his hat and gloves in his hand.

"Very. I've been up and about three hours, working at my part. We open in February, you know."

"Well, then you've worked enough. And so have I. I've seen all my men, my packing is done, and I go up to Liverpool this evening. But this morning we are going to have a holiday. What do you say to a drive out to Kew and Richmond? You may not get another day like this all winter. It's like a fine April day at home. May I use your telephone? I want to order the carriage."

"Oh, how jolly! There, sit down at the desk. And while you are telephoning I'll change my dress. I shan't be long. All the morning papers are on the table."

Hilda was back in a few moments wearing a long gray squirrel coat and a broad fur hat. Bartley rose and inspected her. "Why don't you wear some of those pink roses?" he asked.

"But they came only this morning, and they have not even begun to open. I was saving them. I am so unconsciously thrifty!" She laughed as she looked about the room. "You've been sending me far too many flowers, Bartley. New ones every day. That's too often; though I do love to open the boxes, and I take good care of them."

"Why won't you let me send you any of those jade or ivory

things you are so fond of? Or pictures? I know a good deal about pictures."

Hilda shook her large hat as she drew the roses out of the tall glass. "No, there are some things you can't do. There's the carriage. Will you button my gloves for me?"

Bartley took her wrist and began to button the long gray suede glove. "How gay your eyes are this morning, Hilda."

"That's because I've been studying. It always stirs me up a lit-tle."

He pushed the top of the glove up slowly.

"When did you learn to take hold of your parts like that?"

"When I had nothing else to think of. Come, the carriage is waiting. What a shocking while you take."

"I'm in no hurry. We've plenty of time."

They found all London abroad. Piccadilly was a stream of rapidly moving carriages, from which flashed furs and flowers and bright winter costumes. The metal trappings of the harnesses shone dazzlingly, and the wheels were revolving disks that threw off rays of light. The parks were full of children and nursemaids and joyful dogs that leaped and yelped and scratched up the brown earth with their paws.

"I'm not going until to-morrow, you know," Bartley announced suddenly. "I'll cut off a day in Liverpool. I have n't felt so jolly this long while."

Hilda looked up with a smile which she tried not to make too glad. "I think people were meant to be happy, a little," she said.

They had lunch at Richmond and then walked to Twickenham, where they had sent the carriage. They drove back, with a glorious sunset behind them, toward the distant gold-washed city. It was one of those rare afternoons when all the thickness and shadow of London are changed to a kind of shining, pulsing, special atmosphere; when the smoky vapors become fluttering golden clouds, nacreous veils of pink and amber; when all that bleakness of gray stone and dullness of dirty brick trembles in aureate light, and all the roofs and spires, and one great dome, are floated in golden haze. On such rare afternoons the ugliest of cities becomes the most beautiful, the most prosaic becomes the most poetic, and months of sodden days are offset by a moment of miracle.

"It's like that with us Londoners, too," Hilda was saying. "Everything is awfully grim and cheerless, our weather and our houses and our ways of amusing ourselves. But we can be happier than anybody. We can go mad with joy, as the people do out in the fields on a fine Whitsunday. We make the most of our moment."

She thrust her little chin out defiantly over her gray fur collar, and Bartley looked down at her and laughed.

"You are a plucky one, you." He patted her glove with his hand. "Yes, you are a plucky one."

Hilda sighed. "No, I'm not. Not about some things, at any rate. It does n't take pluck to fight for one's moment, but it takes pluck to go without—a lot. More than I have. I can't help it," she added fiercely.

After miles of outlying streets and little gloomy houses, they reached London itself, red and roaring and murky, with a thick dampness coming up from the river, that betokened fog again tomorrow. The streets were full of people who had worked indoors all through the priceless day and had now come hungrily out to drink the muddy lees of it. They stood in long black lines, waiting before the pit entrances of the theatres—short-coated boys, and girls in sailor hats, all shivering and chatting gayly. There was a blurred rhythm in all the dull city noises—in the clatter of the cab horses and the rumbling of the busses, in the street calls, and in the un-dulating tramp, tramp of the crowd. It was like the deep vibration of some vast underground machinery, and like the muffled pulsa-tions of millions of human hearts.

"Seems good to get back, does n't it?" Bartley whispered, as they drove from Bayswater Road into Oxford Street. "London always makes me want to live more than any other city in the world. You remember our priestess mummy over in the mummy-room, and how we used to long to go and bring her out on nights like this? Three thousand years! Ugh!"

"All the same, I believe she used to feel it when we stood there and watched her and wished her well. I believe she used to re-member," Hilda said thoughtfully.

"I hope so. Now let's go to some awfully jolly place for dinner before we go home. I could eat all the dinners there are in London tonight. Where shall I tell the driver? The Piccadilly Restaurant? The music's good there."

"There are too many people there whom one knows. Why not that little French place in Soho, where we went so often when you were here in the summer? I love it, and I've never been there with any one but you. Sometimes I go by myself, when I am particularly lonely."

"Very well, the sole's good there. How many street pianos there are about to-night! The fine weather must have thawed them out.

We've had five miles of 'Il Trovatore' now. They always make me feel jaunty. Are you comfy, and not too tired?"

"I'm not tired at all. I was just wondering how people can ever die. Why did you remind me of the mummy? Life seems the strongest and most indestructible thing in the world. Do you really believe that all those people rushing about down there, going to good dinners and clubs and theatres, will be dead some day, and not care about anything? I don't believe it, and I know I shan't die, ever! You see, I feel too—too powerful!"

The carriage stopped. Bartley sprang out and swung her quickly to the pavement. As he lifted her in his two hands he whispered: "You are—powerful!"

8.

The last rehearsal was over, a tedious dress rehearsal which had lasted all day and exhausted the patience of every one who had to do with it. When Hilda had dressed for the street and came out of her dressing-room, she found Hugh MacConnell waiting for her in the corridor.

"The fog's thicker than ever, Hilda. There have been a great many accidents to-day. It's positively unsafe for you to be out alone. Will you let me take you home?"

"How good of you, Mac. If you are going with me, I think I'd rather walk. I've had no exercise to-day, and all this has made me nervous."

"I should n't wonder," said MacConnell dryly. Hilda pulled down her veil and they stepped out into the thick brown wash that submerged St. Martin's Lane. MacConnell took her hand and tucked it snugly under his arm. "I'm sorry I was such a savage. I hope you did n't think I made an ass of myself."

"Not a bit of it. I don't wonder you were peppery. Those things are awfully trying. How do you think it's going?"

"Magnificently. That's why I got so stirred up. We are going to hear from this, both of us. And that reminds me; I've got news for you. They are going to begin repairs on the theatre about the middle of March, and we are to run over to New York for six weeks. Bennett told me yesterday that it was decided."

Hilda looked up delightedly at the tall gray figure beside her. He was the only thing she could see, for they were moving through a dense opaqueness, as if they were walking at the bottom of the ocean.

"Oh, Mac, how glad I am! And they love your things over there, don't they?"

"Shall you be glad for—any other reason, Hilda?"

MacConnell put his hand in front of her to ward off some dark object. It proved to be only a lamp-post, and they beat in farther from the edge of the pavement.

"What do you mean, Mac?" Hilda asked nervously.

"I was just thinking there might be people over there you'd be glad to see," he brought out awkwardly. Hilda said nothing, and as they walked on MacConnell spoke again, apologetically: "I hope you don't mind my knowing about it, Hilda. Don't stiffen up like that. No one else knows, and I did n't try to find out anything. I felt it, even before I knew who he was. I knew there was somebody, and that it was n't I."

They crossed Oxford Street in silence, feeling their way. The busses had stopped running and the cab-drivers were leading their horses. When they reached the other side, MacConnell said suddenly, "I hope you are happy."

"Terribly, dangerously happy, Mac,"—Hilda spoke quietly, pressing the rough sleeve of his greatcoat with her gloved hand.

"You've always thought me too old for you, Hilda,—oh, of course you've never said just that,—and here this fellow is not more than eight years younger than I. I've always felt that if I could get out of my old case I might win you yet. It's a fine, brave youth I carry inside me, only he'll never be seen."

"Nonsense, Mac. That has nothing to do with it. It's because you seem too close to me, too much my own kind. It would be like marrying Cousin Mike, almost. I really tried to care as you wanted me to, away back in the beginning."

"Well, here we are, turning out of the Square. You are not angry with me, Hilda? Thank you for this walk, my dear. Go in and get dry things on at once. You'll be having a great night to-morrow."

She put out her hand. "Thank you, Mac, for everything. Goodnight."

MacConnell trudged off through the fog, and she went slowly upstairs. Her slippers and dressing gown were waiting for her before the fire. "I shall certainly see him in New York. He will see by the papers that we are coming. Perhaps he knows it already," Hilda kept thinking as she undressed. "Perhaps he will be at the dock. No, scarcely that; but I may meet him in the street even before he comes to see me." Marie placed the tea-table by the fire and brought Hilda her letters. She looked them over, and started as she came to one in a handwriting that she did not often see; Alexander had written to her only twice before, and he did not allow her to write to him at all. "Thank you, Marie. You may go now."

Hilda sat down by the table with the letter in her hand, still unopened. She looked at it intently, turned it over, and felt its thickness with her fingers. She believed that she sometimes had a kind of second-sight about letters, and could tell before she read them whether they brought good or evil tidings. She put this one down on the table in front of her while she poured her tea. At last, with a little shiver of expectancy, she tore open the envelope and read:—

BOSTON, FEBRUARY—

MY DEAR HILDA:—

It is after twelve o'clock. Every one else is in bed and I am sitting alone in my study. I have been happier in this room than anywhere else in the world. Happiness like that makes one insolent. I used to think these four walls could stand against anything. And now I scarcely know myself here. Now I know that no one can build his security upon the nobleness of another person. Two people, when they love each other, grow alike in their tastes and habits and pride, but their moral natures (whatever we may mean by that canting expression) are never welded. The base one goes on being base, and the noble one noble, to the end.

The last week has been a bad one; I have been realizing how things used to be with me. Sometimes I get used to being dead inside, but lately it has been as if a window beside me had suddenly opened, and as if all the smells of spring blew in to me. There is a garden out there, with stars overhead, where I used to walk at night when I had a single purpose and a single heart. I can remember how I used to feel there, how beautiful everything about me was, and what life and power and freedom I felt in myself. When the window opens I know exactly how it would feel to be out there. But that garden is closed to me. How is it, I ask myself, that everything can be so different with me when nothing here has changed? I am in my own house, in my own study, in the midst of all these quiet streets where my friends live. They are all safe and at peace with themselves. But I am never at peace. I feel always on the edge of danger and change.

I keep remembering locoed horses I used to see on the range when I was a boy. They changed like that. We used to catch them and put them up in the corral, and they developed great cunning. They would pretend to eat their oats like the other horses, but we knew they were always scheming to get back at the loco.

It seems that a man is meant to live only one life in this world. When he tries to live a second, he develops another nature. I feel as if a second man had been grafted into me. At first he seemed only a pleasure-loving simpleton, of whose company I was rather ashamed, and whom I used to hide under my coat when I walked the Embankment, in London. But now he is strong and sullen, and he is fighting for his life at the cost of mine. That is his one activity: to grow strong. No creature ever wanted so much to live. Eventually, I suppose, he will absorb me altogether. Believe me, you will hate me then.

And what have you to do, Hilda, with this ugly story? Nothing at all. The little boy drank of the prettiest brook in the forest and he became a stag. I write all this because I can never tell it to you, and because it seems as if I could not keep silent any longer. And because I suffer, Hilda. If any one I loved suffered like this, I'd want to know it. Help me, Hilda!

B. A.

9.

On the last Saturday in April, the New York "Times" published an account of the strike complications which were delaying Alexander's New Jersey bridge, and stated that the engineer himself was in town and at his office on West Tenth Street.

On Sunday, the day after this notice appeared, Alexander worked all day at his Tenth Street rooms. His business often called him to New York, and he had kept an apartment there for years, subletting it when he went abroad for any length of time. Besides his sleeping-room and bath, there was a large room, formerly a painter's studio, which he used as a study and office. It was furnished with the cast-off possessions of his bachelor days and with odd things which he sheltered for friends of his who followed itinerant and more or less artistic callings. Over the fireplace there was a large old-fashioned gilt mirror. Alexander's big work-table stood in front of one of the three windows, and above the couch hung the one picture in the room, a big canvas of charming color and spirit, a study of the Luxembourg Gardens in early spring, painted in his youth by a man who had since become a portrait-painter of international renown. He had done it for Alexander when they were students together in Paris.

Sunday was a cold, raw day and a fine rain fell continuously. When Alexander came back from dinner he put more wood on his fire, made himself comfortable, and settled down at his desk, where he began checking over estimate sheets. It was after nine o'clock and he was lighting a second pipe, when he thought he heard a sound at his door. He started and listened, holding the burning match in his hand; again he heard the same sound, like a firm, light tap. He rose and crossed the room quickly. When he threw open the door he recognized the figure that shrank back into the bare, dimly lit hallway. He stood for a moment in awkward constraint, his pipe in his hand.

"Come in," he said to Hilda at last, and closed the door behind her. He pointed to a chair by the fire and went back to his work-table. "Won't you sit down?"

He was standing behind the table, turning over a pile of blue-prints nervously. The yellow light from the student's lamp fell on his hands and the purple sleeves of his velvet smoking-jacket, but his flushed face and big, hard head were in the shadow. There was something about him that made Hilda wish herself at her hotel again, in the street below, anywhere but where she was.

"Of course I know, Bartley," she said at last, "that after this you won't owe me the least consideration. But we sail on Tuesday. I saw that interview in the paper yesterday, telling where you were, and I thought I had to see you. That's all. Good-night; I'm going now." She turned and her hand closed on the door-knob.

Alexander hurried toward her and took her gently by the arm. "Sit down, Hilda; you're wet through. Let me take off your coat— and your boots; they're oozing water." He knelt down and began to unlace her shoes, while Hilda shrank into the chair. "Here, put your feet on this stool. You don't mean to say you walked down— and without overshoes!"

Hilda hid her face in her hands. "I was afraid to take a cab. Can't you see, Bartley, that I'm terribly frightened? I've been through this a hundred times to-day. Don't be any more angry than you can help. I was all right until I knew you were in town. If you'd sent me a note, or telephoned me, or anything! But you won't let me write to you, and I had to see you after that letter, that terrible letter you wrote me when you got home."

Alexander faced her, resting his arm on the mantel behind him, and began to brush the sleeve of his jacket. "Is this the way you mean to answer it, Hilda?" he asked unsteadily.

She was afraid to look up at him. "Did n't—did n't you mean even to say good-by to me, Bartley? Did you mean just to—quit me?" she asked. "I came to tell you that I'm willing to do as you asked me. But it's no use talking about that now. Give me my things, please." She put her hand out toward the fender.

Alexander sat down on the arm of her chair. "Did you think I had forgotten you were in town, Hilda? Do you think I kept away by accident? Did you suppose I did n't know you were sailing on

Tuesday? There is a letter for you there, in my desk drawer. It was to have reached you on the steamer. I was all the morning writing it. I told myself that if I were really thinking of you, and not of myself, a letter would be better than nothing. Marks on paper mean something to you." He paused. "They never did to me."

Hilda smiled up at him beautifully and put her hand on his sleeve. "Oh, Bartley! Did you write to me? Why did n't you telephone me to let me know that you had? Then I would n't have come."

Alexander slipped his arm about her. "I did n't know it before, Hilda, on my honor I did n't, but I believe it was because, deep down in me somewhere, I was hoping I might drive you to do just this. I've watched that door all day. I've jumped up if the fire crackled. I think I have felt that you were coming." He bent his face over her hair.

"And I," she whispered,—"I felt that you were feeling that. But when I came, I thought I had been mistaken."

Alexander started up and began to walk up and down the room.

"No, you were n't mistaken. I've been up in Canada with my bridge, and I arranged not to come to New York until after you had gone. Then, when your manager added two more weeks, I was already committed." He dropped upon the stool in front of her and sat with his hands hanging between his knees. "What am I to do, Hilda?"

"That's what I wanted to see you about, Bartley. I'm going to do what you asked me to do, when you were in London. Only I'll do it more completely. I'm going to marry."

"Who?"

"Oh, it does n't matter much! One of them. Only not Mac. I'm too fond of him."

Alexander moved restlessly. "Are you joking, Hilda?"

"Indeed I'm not."

"Then you don't know what you're talking about."

"Yes, I know very well. I've thought about it a great deal, and I've quite decided. I never used to understand how women did things like that, but I know now. It's because they can't be at the mercy of the man they love any longer."

Alexander flushed angrily. "So it's better to be at the mercy of a man you don't love?"

"Under such circumstances, infinitely!"

There was a flash in her eyes that made Alexander's fall. He got up and went over to the window, threw it open, and leaned out. He heard Hilda moving about behind him. When he looked over his shoulder she was lacing her boots. He went back and stood over her.

"Hilda, you'd better think a while longer before you do that. I don't know what I ought to say, but I don't believe you'd be happy; truly I don't. Are n't you trying to frighten me?"

She tied the knot of the last lacing and put her boot-heel down firmly. "No; I'm telling you what I've made up my mind to do. I suppose I would better do it without telling you. But afterward I shan't have an opportunity to explain, for I shan't be seeing you again."

Alexander started to speak, but caught himself. When Hilda rose he sat down on the arm of her chair and drew her back into it.

"I would n't be so much alarmed if I did n't know how utterly reckless you *can* be. Don't do anything like that rashly." His face grew troubled. "You would n't be happy. You are not that kind of woman. I'd never have another hour's peace if I helped to make you do a thing like that." He took her face between his hands and looked down into it. "You see, you are different, Hilda. Don't you know you are?" His voice grew softer, his touch more and more tender. "Some women can do that sort of thing, but you—you can love as queens did, in the old time."

Hilda had heard that soft, deep tone in his voice only once before. She closed her eyes; her lips and eyelids trembled. "Only one, Bartley. Only one. And he threw it back at me a second time."

She felt the strength leap in the arms that held her so lightly.

"Try him again, Hilda. Try him once again."

She looked up into his eyes, and hid her face in her hands.

IO.

On Tuesday afternoon a Boston lawyer, who had been trying a case in Vermont, was standing on the siding at White River Junction when the Canadian Express pulled by on its northward journey. As the day-coaches at the rear end of the long train swept by him, the lawyer noticed at one of the windows a man's head, with thick rumpled hair. "Curious," he thought; "that looked like Alexander, but what would he be doing back there in the day-coaches?"

It was, indeed, Alexander.

That morning a telegram from Moorlock had reached him, telling him that there was serious trouble with the bridge and that he was needed there at once, so he had caught the first train out of New York. He had taken a seat in a day-coach to avoid the risk of meeting any one he knew, and because he did not wish to be comfortable. When the telegram arrived, Alexander was at his rooms on Tenth Street, packing his bag to go to Boston. On Monday night he had written a long letter to his wife, but when morning came he was afraid to send it, and the letter was still in his pocket. Winifred was not a woman who could bear disappointment. She demanded a great deal of herself and of the people she loved; and she never failed herself. If he told her now, he knew, it would be irretrievable. There would be no going back. He would lose the thing he valued most in the world; he would be destroying himself and his own happiness. There would be nothing for him afterward. He seemed to see himself dragging out a restless existence on the Continent— Cannes, Hyères, Algiers, Cairo—among smartly dressed, disabled men of every nationality; forever going on journeys that led nowhere; hurrying to catch trains that he might just as well miss; getting up in the morning with a great bustle and splashing of water, to begin a day that had no purpose and no meaning; dining late to shorten the night, sleeping late to shorten the day.

And for what? For a mere folly, a masquerade, a little thing that he could not let go. *And he could even let it go,* he told himself. But he had promised to be in London at midsummer, and he knew that he would go. . . It was impossible to live like this any longer.

And this, then, was to be the disaster that his old professor had foreseen for him: the crack in the wall, the crash, the cloud of dust.

And he could not understand how it had come about. He felt that he himself was unchanged, that he was still there, the same man he had been five years ago, and that he was sitting stupidly by and letting some resolute offshoot of himself spoil his life for him. This new force was not he, it was but a part of him. He would not even admit that it was stronger than he; but it was more active. It was by its energy that this new feeling got the better of him. His wife was the woman who had made his life, gratified his pride, given direction to his tastes and habits. The life they led together seemed to him beautiful. Winifred still was, as she had always been, Romance for him, and whenever he was deeply stirred he turned to her. When the grandeur and beauty of the world challenged him—as it challenges even the most self-absorbed people—he always answered with her name. That was his reply to the question put by the mountains and the stars; to all the spiritual aspects of life. In his feeling for his wife there was all the tenderness, all the pride, all the devotion of which he was capable. There was everything but energy; the energy of youth which must register itself and cut its name before it passes. This new feeling was so fresh, so unsatisfied and light of foot. It ran and was not wearied, anticipated him everywhere. It put a girdle round the earth while he was going from New York to Moorlock. At this moment, it was tingling through him, exultant, and live as quicksilver, whispering, "In July you will be in England."

Already he dreaded the long, empty days at sea, the monotonous Irish coast, the sluggish passage up the Mersey, the flash of the boat train through the summer country. He closed his eyes and gave himself up to the feeling of rapid motion and to swift, terrifying thoughts. He was sitting so, his face shaded by his hand, when the Boston lawyer saw him from the siding at White River Junction.

When at last Alexander roused himself, the afternoon had waned to sunset. The train was passing through a gray country and the sky overhead was flushed with a wide flood of clear color. There was a rose-colored light over the gray rocks and hills and meadows. Off to the left, under the approach of a weather-stained wooden bridge, a group of boys were sitting around a little fire. The smell of the wood smoke blew in at the window. Except for an old farmer, jogging along the highroad in his box-wagon, there was not another living creature to be seen. Alexander looked back wistfully at the boys, camped on the edge of a little marsh, crouching under their shelter and looking gravely at their fire. They took his mind back a long way, to a campfire on a sandbar in a Western river, and he wished he could go back and sit down with them. He could re-member exactly how the world had looked then.

It was quite dark and Alexander was still thinking of the boys, when it occurred to him that the train must be nearing Allway. In going to his new bridge at Moorlock he had always to pass through Allway. The train stopped at Allway Mills, then wound two miles up the river, and then the hollow sound under his feet told Bartley that he was on his first bridge again. The bridge seemed longer than it had ever seemed before, and he was glad when he felt the beat of the wheels on the solid roadbed again. He did not like coming and going across that bridge, or remembering the man who built it. And was he, indeed, the same man who used to walk that bridge at night, promising such things to himself and to the stars? And yet, he could remember it all so well: the quiet hills sleeping in the moonlight, the slender skeleton of the bridge reaching out into the river, and up yonder, alone on the hill, the big white house; upstairs, in Winifred's window, the light that told him she was still awake and still thinking of him. And after the light went out he walked alone, taking the heavens into his confidence, unable to tear himself away from the white magic of the night, unwilling to sleep because longing was so sweet to him, and because, for the first time since first the hills were hung with moonlight, there was a lover in the world. And always there was the sound of the rushing water underneath, the sound which, more than anything else, meant death; the wearing away of things under the impact of physical forces which men could direct but never circumvent or diminish. Then, in the exaltation of love, more than ever it seemed to him to mean death, the only other thing as strong as love. Under the moon, under the cold, splendid stars, there were only those two things awake and sleepless; death and love, the rushing river and his burning heart.

Alexander sat up and looked about him. The train was tearing on through the darkness. All his companions in the day-coach were either dozing or sleeping heavily, and the murky lamps were turned low. How came he here among all these dirty people? Why was he going to London? What did it mean—what was the answer? How could this happen to a man who had lived through that magical spring and summer, and who had felt that the stars themselves were but flaming particles in the far-away infinitudes of his love?

What had he done to lose it? How could he endure the baseness of life without it? And with every revolution of the wheels beneath him, the unquiet quicksilver in his breast told him that at midsummer he would be in London. He remembered his last night there: the red foggy darkness, the hungry crowds before the theatres, the hand-organs, the feverish rhythm of the blurred, crowded streets, and the feeling of letting himself go with the crowd. He shuddered and looked about him at the poor unconscious companions of his journey, unkempt and travel-stained, now doubled in unlovely attitudes, who had come to stand to him for the ugliness he had brought into the world.

And those boys back there, beginning it all just as he had begun it; he wished he could promise them better luck. Ah, if one could promise any one better luck, if one could assure a single human being of happiness! He had thought he could do so, once; and it was thinking of that that he at last fell asleep. In his sleep, as if it had nothing fresher to work upon, his mind went back and tortured itself with something years and years away, an old, long-forgotten sorrow of his childhood.

When Alexander awoke in the morning, the sun was just rising through pale golden ripples of cloud, and the fresh yellow light was vibrating through the pine woods. The white birches, with their little unfolding leaves, gleamed in the lowlands, and the marsh meadows were already coming to life with their first green, a thin, bright color which had run over them like fire. As the train rushed along the trestles, thousands of wild birds rose screaming into the light. The sky was already a pale blue and of the clearness of crystal. Bartley caught up his bag and hurried through the Pullman coaches until he found the conductor. There was a stateroom unoccupied, and he took it and set about changing his clothes. Last night he would not have believed that anything could be so pleasant as the cold water he dashed over his head and shoulders and the freshness of clean linen on his body.

After he had dressed, Alexander sat down at the window and drew into his lungs deep breaths of the pine-scented air. He had awakened with all his old sense of power. He could not believe that things were as bad with him as they had seemed last night, that there was no way to set them entirely right. Even if he went to London at midsummer, what would that mean except that he was a fool? And he had been a fool before. That was not the reality of his life. Yet he knew that he would go to London.

Half an hour later the train stopped at Moorlock. Alexander sprang to the platform and hurried up the siding, waving to Philip Horton, one of his assistants, who was anxiously looking up at the windows of the coaches. Bartley took his arm and they went together into the station buffet.

"I'll have my coffee first, Philip. Have you had yours? And now, what seems to be the matter up here?"

The young man, in a hurried, nervous way, began his explanation.

But Alexander cut him short. "When did you stop work?" he asked sharply.

The young engineer looked confused. "I have n't stopped work yet, Mr. Alexander. I did n't feel that I could go so far without definite authorization from you."

"Then why did n't you say in your telegram exactly what you thought, and ask for your authorization? You'd have got it quick enough."

"Well, really, Mr. Alexander, I could n't be absolutely sure, you know, and I did n't like to take the responsibility of making it public."

Alexander pushed back his chair and rose. "Anything I do can be made public, Phil. You say that you believe the lower chords are showing strain, and that even the workmen have been talking about it, and yet you've gone on adding weight."

"I'm sorry, Mr. Alexander, but I had counted on your getting here yesterday. My first telegram missed you somehow. I sent one Sunday evening, to the same address, but it was returned to me."

"Have you a carriage out there? I must stop to send a wire."

Alexander went up to the telegraph-desk and penciled the following message to his wife:—

I may have to be here for some time. Can you come up at once? Urgent.

BARTLEY.

The Moorlock Bridge lay three miles above the town. When they were seated in the carriage, Alexander began to question his assistant further. If it were true that the compression members showed strain, with the bridge only two thirds done, then there was nothing to do but pull the whole structure down and begin over again. Horton kept repeating that he was sure there could be nothing wrong with the estimates.

Alexander grew impatient. "That's all true, Phil, but we never were justified in assuming that a scale that was perfectly safe for an ordinary bridge would work with anything of such length. It's all very well on paper, but it remains to be seen whether it can be done in practice. I should have thrown up the job when they crowded me. It's all nonsense to try to do what other engineers are doing when you know they're not sound."

"But just now, when there is such competition," the younger man demurred. "And certainly that's the new line of development."

Alexander shrugged his shoulders and made no reply.

When they reached the bridge works, Alexander began his examination immediately. An hour later he sent for the superintendent. "I think you had better stop work out there at once, Dan. I should say that the lower chord here might buckle at any moment. I told the Commission that we were using higher unit stresses than any practice has established, and we've put the dead load at a low estimate. Theoretically it worked out well enough, but it had never actually been tried." Alexander put on his overcoat and took the superintendent by the arm. "Don't look so chopfallen, Dan. It's a jolt, but we've got to face it. It is n't the end of the world, you know. Now we'll go out and call the men off quietly. They're already nervous, Horton tells me, and there's no use alarming them. I'll go with you, and we'll send the end riveters in first."

Alexander and the superintendent picked their way out slowly over the long span. They went deliberately, stopping to see what each gang was doing, as if they were on an ordinary round of inspection. When they reached the end of the river span, Alexander nodded to the superintendent, who quietly gave an order to the foreman. The men in the end gang picked up their tools and, glancing curiously at each other, started back across the bridge toward the river-bank. Alexander himself remained standing where they had been working, looking about him. It was hard to believe, as he looked back over it, that the whole great span was incurably disabled, was already as good as condemned, because something was out of line in the lower chord of the cantilever arm.

The end riveters had reached the bank and were dispersing among the tool-houses, and the second gang had picked up their tools and were starting toward the shore. Alexander, still standing at the end of the river span, saw the lower chord of the cantilever arm give a little, like an elbow bending. He shouted and ran after the second gang, but by this time every one knew that the big river span was slowly settling. There was a burst of shouting that was immediately drowned by the scream and cracking of tearing iron, as all the tension work began to pull asunder. Once the chords began to buckle, there were thousands of tons of iron-work, all riveted together and lying in midair without support. It tore itself to pieces with roaring and grinding and noises that were like the shrieks of a steam whistle. There was no shock of any kind; the bridge had no impetus except from its own weight. It lurched neither to right nor left, but sank almost in a vertical line, snapping and breaking and tearing as it went, because no integral part could bear for an instant the enormous strain loosed upon it. Some of the men jumped and some ran, trying to make the shore.

At the first shriek of the tearing iron, Alexander jumped from the downstream side of the bridge. He struck the water without injury and disappeared. He was under the river a long time and had great difficulty in holding his breath. When it seemed impossible, and his chest was about to heave, he thought he heard his wife telling him that he could hold out a little longer. An instant later his face cleared the water. For a moment, in the depths of the river, he had realized what it would mean to die a hypocrite, and to lie dead under the last abandonment of her tenderness. But once in the light and air, he knew he should live to tell her and to recover all he had lost. Now, at last, he felt sure of himself. He was not startled. It seemed to him that he had been through something of this sort before. There was nothing horrible about it. This, too, was life, and life was activity, just as it was in Boston or in London. He was himself, and there was something to be done; everything seemed perfectly natural. Alexander was a strong swimmer, but he had gone scarcely a dozen strokes when the bridge itself, which had been settling faster and faster, crashed into the water behind him. Immediately the river was full of drowning men. A gang of French Canadians fell almost on top of him. He thought he had cleared them, when they began coming up all around him, clutching at him and at each other. Some of them could swim, but they were either hurt or crazed with fright. Alexander tried to beat them off, but there were too many of them. One caught him about the neck, another gripped him about the middle, and they went down together. When he sank, his wife seemed to be there in the water beside him, telling him to keep his head, that if he could hold out the men would drown and release him. There was something he wanted to tell his wife, but he could not think clearly for the roaring in his ears. Suddenly he remembered what it was. He caught his breath, and then she let him go.

The work of recovering the dead went on all day and all the following night. By the next morning forty-eight bodies had been taken out of the river, but there were still twenty missing. Many of the men had fallen with the bridge and were held down under the débris. Early on the morning of the second day a closed carriage was driven slowly along the river-bank and stopped a little below the works, where the river boiled and churned about the great iron carcass which lay in a straight line two thirds across it. The carriage stood there hour after hour, and word soon spread among the crowds on the shore that its occupant was the wife of the Chief Engineer; his body had not yet been found. The widows of the lost workmen, moving up and down the bank with shawls over their heads, some of them carrying babies, looked at the rusty hired hack many times that morning. They drew near it and walked about it, but none of them ventured to peer within. Even half-indifferent sight-seers dropped their voices as they told a newcomer: "You see that carriage over there? That's Mrs. Alexander. They have n't found him yet. She got off the train this morning. Horton met her. She heard it in Boston yesterday—heard the newsboys crying it in the street."

At noon Philip Horton made his way through the crowd with a tray and a tin coffee-pot from the camp kitchen. When he reached the carriage he found Mrs. Alexander just as he had left her in the early morning, leaning forward a little, with her hand on the lowered window, looking at the river. Hour after hour she had been watching the water, the lonely, useless stone towers, and the convulsed mass of iron wreckage over which the angry river continually spat up its yellow foam.

"Those poor women out there, do they blame him very much?" she asked, as she handed the coffee-cup back to Horton.

"Nobody blames him, Mrs. Alexander. If any one is to blame,

I'm afraid it's I. I should have stopped work before he came. He said so as soon as I met him. I tried to get him here a day earlier, but my telegram missed him, somehow. He did n't have time really to explain to me. If he'd got here Monday, he'd have had all the men off at once. But, you see, Mrs. Alexander, such a thing never happened before. According to all human calculations, it simply could n't happen."

Horton leaned wearily against the front wheel of the cab. He had not had his clothes off for thirty hours, and the stimulus of violent excitement was beginning to wear off.

"Don't be afraid to tell me the worst, Mr. Horton. Don't leave me to the dread of finding out things that people may be saying. If he is blamed, if he needs any one to speak for him,"—for the first time her voice broke and a flush of life, tearful, painful, and confused, swept over her rigid pallor,—"if he needs any one, tell me, show me what to do." She began to sob, and Horton hurried away.

When he came back at four o'clock in the afternoon he was carrying his hat in his hand, and Winifred knew as soon as she saw him that they had found Bartley. She opened the carriage door before he reached her and stepped to the ground.

Horton put out his hand as if to hold her back and spoke pleadingly: "Won't you drive up to my house, Mrs. Alexander? They will take him up there."

"Take me to him now, please. I shall not make any trouble."

The group of men down under the river-bank fell back when they saw a woman coming, and one of them threw a tarpaulin over the stretcher. They took off their hats and caps as Winifred approached, and although she had pulled her veil down over her face they did not look up at her. She was taller than Horton, and some of the men thought she was the tallest woman they had ever seen. "As tall as himself," some one whispered. Horton motioned to the men, and six of them lifted the stretcher and began to carry it up the embankment. Winifred followed them the half-mile to Horton's house. She walked quietly, without once breaking or stumbling. When the bearers put the stretcher down in Horton's spare bedroom, she thanked them and gave her hand to each in turn. The men went out of the house and through the yard with their caps in their hands. They were too much confused to say anything as they went down the hill.

Horton himself was almost as deeply perplexed. "Mamie," he said to his wife, when he came out of the spare room half an hour later, "will you take Mrs. Alexander the things she needs? She is going to do everything herself. Just stay about where you can hear her and go in if she wants you."

Everything happened as Alexander had foreseen in that moment of prescience under the river. With her own hands she washed him clean of every mark of disaster. All night he was alone with her in the still house, his great head lying deep in the pillow. In the pocket of his coat Winifred found the letter that he had written her the night before he left New York, water-soaked and illegible, but because of its length, she knew it had been meant for her.

For Alexander death was an easy creditor. Fortune, which had smiled upon him consistently all his life, did not desert him in the end. His harshest critics did not doubt that, had he lived, he would have retrieved himself. Even Lucius Wilson did not see in this accident the disaster he had once foretold.

When a great man dies in his prime there is no surgeon who can say whether he did well; whether or not the future was his, as it seemed to be. The mind that society had come to regard as a powerful and reliable machine, dedicated to its service, may for a long time have been sick within itself and bent upon its own destruction.

EPILOGUE

Professor Wilson had been living in London for six years and he was just back from a visit to America. One afternoon, soon after his return, he put on his frock-coat and drove in a hansom to pay a call upon Hilda Burgoyne, who still lived at her old number, off Bedford Square. He and Miss Burgoyne had been fast friends for a long time. He had first noticed her about the corridors of the British Museum, where he read constantly. Her being there so often had made him feel that he would like to know her, and as she was not an inaccessible person, an introduction was not difficult. The preliminaries once over, they came to depend a great deal upon each other, and Wilson, after his day's reading, often went round to Bedford Square for his tea. They had much more in common than their memories of a common friend. Indeed, they seldom spoke of him. They saved that for the deep moments which do not come often, and then their talk of him was mostly silence. Wilson knew that Hilda had loved him; more than this he had not tried to know.

It was late when Wilson reached Hilda's apartment on this particular December afternoon, and he found her alone. She sent for fresh tea and made him comfortable, as she had such a knack of making people comfortable.

"How good you were to come back before Christmas! I quite dreaded the Holidays without you. You've helped me over a good many Christmases." She smiled at him gayly.

"As if you needed me for that! But, at any rate, I needed *you*. How well you are looking, my dear, and how rested."

He peered up at her from his low chair, balancing the tips of his long fingers together in a judicial manner which had grown on him with years.

Hilda laughed as she carefully poured his cream. "That means that I was looking very seedy at the end of the season, does n't it? Well, we must show wear at last, you know."

Wilson took the cup gratefully. "Ah, no need to remind a man of seventy, who has just been home to find that he has survived all his contemporaries. I was most gently treated—as a sort of precious relic. But, do you know, it made me feel awkward to be hanging about still."

"Seventy? Never mention it to me." Hilda looked appreciatively at the Professor's alert face, with so many kindly lines about the mouth and so many quizzical ones about the eyes. "You've got to hang about for me, you know. I can't even let you go home again. You must stay put, now that I have you back. You're the realest thing I have."

Wilson chuckled. "Dear me, am I? Out of so many conquests and the spoils of conquered cities! You've really missed me? Well, then, I shall hang. Even if you have at last to put *me* in the mummy-room with the others. You'll visit me often, won't you?"

"Every day in the calendar. Here, your cigarettes are in this drawer, where you left them." She struck a match and lit one for him. "But you did, after all, enjoy being at home again?"

"Oh, yes. I found the long railway journeys trying. People live a thousand miles apart. But I did it thoroughly; I was all over the place. It was in Boston I lingered longest."

"Ah, you saw Mrs. Alexander?"

"Often. I dined with her, and had tea there a dozen different times, I should think. Indeed, it was to see her that I lingered on and on. I found that I still loved to go to the house. It always seemed as if Bartley were there, somehow, and that at any moment one might hear his heavy tramp on the stairs. Do you know, I kept feeling that he must be up in his study." The Professor looked reflectively into the grate. "I should really have liked to go up there. That was where I had my last long talk with him. But Mrs. Alexander never suggested it."

"Why?"

Wilson was a little startled by her tone, and he turned his head so quickly that his cufflink caught the string of his nose-glasses and pulled them awry. "Why? Why, dear me, I don't know. She probably never thought of it."

Hilda bit her lip. "I don't know what made me say that. I didn't mean to interrupt. Go on, please, and tell me how it was."

"Well, it was like that. Almost as if he were there. In a way, he really is there. She never lets him go. It's the most beautiful and dignified sorrow I've ever known. It's so beautiful that it has its compensations, I should think. Its very completeness is a compensation. It gives her a fixed star to steer by. She does n't drift. We sat there evening after evening in the quiet of that magically haunted room, and watched the sunset burn on the river, and felt him. Felt him with a difference, of course."

Hilda leaned forward, her elbow on her knee, her chin on her hand. "With a difference? Because of her, you mean?"

Wilson's brow wrinkled. "Something like that, yes. Of course, as time goes on, to her he becomes more and more their simple personal relation."

Hilda studied the droop of the Professor's head intently. "You did n't altogether like that? You felt it was n't wholly fair to him?"

Wilson shook himself and readjusted his glasses. "Oh, fair enough. More than fair. Of course, I always felt that my image of him was just a little different from hers. No relation is so complete that it can hold absolutely all of a person. And I liked him just as he was; his deviations, too; the places where he did n't square."

Hilda considered vaguely. "Has she grown much older?" she asked at last.

"Yes, and no. In a tragic way she is even handsomer. But colder. Cold for everything but him. 'Forget thyself to marble'; I kept thinking of that. Her happiness was a happiness *à deux*, not apart from the world, but actually against it. And now her grief is like that. She saves herself for it and does n't even go through the form of seeing people much. I'm sorry. It would be better for her, and might be so good for them, if she could let other people in."

"Perhaps she's afraid of letting him out a little, of sharing him with somebody."

Wilson put down his cup and looked up with vague alarm. "Dear me, it takes a woman to think of that, now! I don't, you know, think we ought to be hard on her. More, even, than the rest of us she did n't choose her destiny. She underwent it. And it has left her chilled. As to her not wishing to take the world into her confidence—well, it is a pretty brutal and stupid world, after all, you know."

Hilda leaned forward. "Yes, I know, I know. Only I can't help being glad that there was something for him even in stupid and vulgar people. My little Marie worshiped him. When she is dusting I always know when she has come to his picture."

Wilson nodded. "Oh, yes! He left an echo. The ripples go on in all of us. He belonged to the people who make the play, and most of us are only onlookers at the best. We should n't wonder too much at Mrs. Alexander. She must feel how useless it would be to stir about, that she may as well sit still; that nothing can happen to her after Bartley."

"Yes," said Hilda softly, "nothing can happen to one after Bartley."

They both sat looking into the fire.

ABOUT THE PHOTOGRAPHS

Front cover and page 1: Unidentified Bostonian, c. 1910. Culver Pictures, Inc., New York, New York

Pages 2–3: Public Garden, Boston Commons, with State House and Park Street Church visible in skyline, 1906. Society for the Preservation of New England Antiquities (SPNEA), Boston, Massachusetts

Page 4: Study in Beebe House, Beacon Street, Boston, 1911. (Detail) SPNEA, Boston, Massachusetts

Page 5: Residence, Commonwealth Avenue, Boston, late nineteenth century. Boston Public Library, Boston, Massachusetts

Pages 6–7: Architect's office, Boston, 1900. Maine Historic Preservation Commission, Augusta, Maine.

Pages 8–9: Hell Gate Bridge under construction, New York City, 1916. Culver Pictures, Inc., New York, New York

Page 10: Gaiety Theatre, London, England, 1910. (Detail) Hulton Getty Picture Collection Limited, London

Page 11: London Music Hall actress, c. 1900. Hulton Getty Picture Collection Limited, London

Page 12: Boston Commons, 1914. SPNEA, Boston, Massachusetts

Page 13: Boston Commons and State House, c. 1910. SPNEA, Boston, Massachusetts

Pages 14–15: Photograph of a festive dinner from an unidentified Massachusetts family album, 1892–1893. Boston Public Library, Boston, Massachusetts

Page 16: Tremont Street, Boston, 1915. Bostonian Society, Boston, Massachusetts

Back cover: Signature and photograph of Willa Cather, c. 1912. Willa Cather Pioneer Memorial Collection, Nebraska State Historical Society, Lincoln, Nebraska

ABOUT THE AUTHOR

Born in Virginia in 1873, Willa Cather moved with her family nine years later to Red Cloud, Nebraska. Though she only lived there for thirteen years, Cather's memories of Red Cloud inspired her best fiction. In 1896 she left Nebraska to embark on a full-time journalism career that took her first to Pittsburgh and then to New York, in 1906, where she eventually became managing editor of *McClure's*, a magazine that published Mark Twain, Thomas Hardy, Stephen Crane and Jack London. It was while she was on assignment for this magazine, in 1907, that she met Sarah Orne Jewett, who would become an important mentor to the younger writer. At a time when Cather was imitating Henry James, whose influence is felt in her first novel, *Alexander's Bridge* (1912), Jewett offered Cather this advice: "Of course, one day you will write about your own country. In the meantime, get all you can. One must know the world so well before one can know the parish." Indeed, in *Alexander's Bridge*, set in upper-middle-class Boston and London, one can see her infatuation with urban sophistication. The following year Cather turned to the Nebraska prairies, a subject she knew most intimately in her breakthrough novel *O Pioneers!* (1913), which she dedicated to Sarah Orne Jewett. Eventually, Cather left magazine editing and was able to devote herself to creative writing after 1912. Among her novels are *Song of the Lark* (1915), *One of Ours* (1922), which won the Pulitzer Prize in 1923, *A Lost Lady* (1933), *The Professor's House* (1925), *Death Comes to the Archbishop* (1927), and *My Antonia* (1918). Her short story collections include *The Troll Garden* (1906) and *Youth and the Bright Medusa* (1920). She continued to make her home in New York City until her death in 1947, making annual visits to Jaffrey, New Hampshire, where she is buried, and Grand Manan, an island off the coast of New Brunswick.

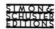

Simon & Schuster Inc.

Rockefeller Center

1230 Avenue of the Americas

New York, New York 10020

This book is a work of fiction. Names, characters, places, and incidents either are products of the author's imagination or are used fictitiously. Any resemblance to actual events or locales or persons, living or dead, is entirely coincidental.

Compilation copyright © 1997 by CommonPlace Publishing, LLC

All rights reserved, including the right of reproduction in whole or in part in any form.

Simon & Schuster Editions and colophon are trademarks of Simon & Schuster Inc.

10 9 8 7 6 5 4 3 2 1

Library of Congress Cataloging-in-Publication Data

Cather, Willa, 1873–1947.

Alexander's bridge / Willa Sibert Cather.

p. cm.

"A CommonPlace book."

ISBN 0-684-81907-4

1. Bridges—Design and construction—Fiction. 2. Married men—Massachusetts—Boston—Fiction. 3. Mistresses—England—London—Fiction. 4. Civil engineers—Fiction.

I. Title.

PS3505.A87A7 1997

813'.52—dc20   96—42550

CIP

Punctuation and spelling in this edition are based upon the original 1912 text.

This edition of *Alexander's Bridge* was produced by CommonPlace Publishing and designed by Samuel N. Antupit. The text of this book was set in the 1924 Monotype version of John Baskerville's 1753 design. When first introduced in England, Baskerville was hailed and derided as an innovative typeface with few classical references; the thick/thin contrast within the letter greatly influenced later modern designers of type. The display face, Cushing Oldstyle, was issued in 1895 by American Type Founders and copied by Monotype in 1904. This sturdy, compact face reflects the bold, slab serif Clarendons of the nineteenth century.

Research by Susan Chitwood has enriched the photographic portfolio of this book. Film for the photographic portfolio was digitally produced at Computertech in Stamford, Connecticut. The book was printed and bound by Oddi Printing, in Iceland.

Raves Fo̶

S0-BRA-287

RIVINGTON STREET

"Gallops along at a satisfying pace...with women characters who think seriously and passionately about work, politics, friendship and sex...Extraordinary"
        The New York Times Book Review

"A stirring novel of both passion and intelligence—the kind you would stay up all night to read."
        Hartford Courant

"Well-researched and skillfully written, sweeping the reader along with rich characterizations and a plot humming with dramatic momentum"
        Publishers Weekly

"Has an appealing, gutsy warmth...Especially satisfying"
        Kirkus Reviews

"Meticulously researched...A story the reader is deeply involved in from first page to last."
        Milwaukee Journal

Other Avon Books by
Meredith Tax

Union Square

Avon Books are available at special quantity discounts for bulk purchases for sales promotions, premiums, fund raising or educational use. Special books, or book excerpts, can also be created to fit specific needs.

For details write or telephone the office of the Director of Special Markets, Avon Books, Dept. FP, 105 Madison Avenue, New York, New York 10016, 212-481-5653.

RIVINGTON STREET

MEREDITH TAX

AVON BOOKS ◆ NEW YORK

AVON BOOKS
A division of
The Hearst Corporation
105 Madison Avenue
New York, New York 10016

Copyright © 1982 by Meredith Tax
Front cover illustration by Ben Wohlberg
Published by arrangement with William Morrow and Company, Inc.
ISBN: 0-380-70907-4

All rights reserved, which includes the right to reproduce this book or portions thereof in any form whatsoever except as provided by the U.S. Copyright Law. For information address Permissions Department, William Morrow and Company, Inc., 105 Madison Avenue, New York, New York 10016.

First Avon Books Printing: February 1990

AVON TRADEMARK REG. U.S. PAT. OFF. AND IN OTHER COUNTRIES, MARCA REGISTRADA, HECHO EN U.S.A.

Printed in the U.S.A.

OPM 10 9 8 7 6 5 4 3 2 1

___ACKNOWLEDGMENTS___

I did the research for this book at the Schlesinger Library at Radcliffe, the Tamiment Library at New York University, the New York Public Library's Jewish room and general reading rooms, the fashion library at the Metropolitan Museum of Art, and the archives of the YIVO Institute for Jewish Research. Many thanks to all of them for their help. Thanks as well to Liz Ewen, who was kind enough to let me see her forthcoming book on Jewish and Italian women on the Lower East Side.

Sections of the following, all out of copyright, are quoted herein:

"When You Know You're Not Forgotten by the Girl You Can't Forget," by Edward Gardener and J. Fred Helf;

"Heaven Will Protect the Working Girl," by Edgar Smith and A. Baldwin Sloane;

"London," by William Blake;

"*Le Voyage*," by Charles Baudelaire;

"Old Black Joe," by Stephen Foster.

My women's group and my women writers' group gave me much encouragement in the early stages of this enterprise. Special praise and thanks go to Beverly Elkan, Myra Murray,

Ann Snitow and Sharon Thompson for help ranging from practical support to close reading to emotional sustenance. Thanks to Billy Friedman for encouragement when this book was no more than an idea; to Kris Glen for being a facilitator; to Harriet Wasserman, my agent, for her help and faith in me; and to Harvey Ginsberg, my editor, for teaching me how to write a novel.

The women of my family trained my ear and helped me with research; special thanks to my mother, Martha Tax, my aunts Rose Lucoff and Esther Mosher, my cousin Hannah Klein and the memory of my grandmother.

The most personal thanks to Marshall and Corey, for being there.

To the women's movement—past, present and future—and especially to my daughter, Corey

CHARACTERS

(* denotes a historical character)

Moyshe Levy, a cigar maker and Bundist of Kishinev
Hannah Levy, his wife
Rosa Levy ⎫
Sarah Levy ⎬ their daughters
Ruby Levy ⎭
Rachel Cohen, Sarah's closest friend

Avigdor Spector, a printer and Bolshevik of Ludlow Street
Joe Klein, a staff member of the ILGWU
Roman Zach, an avant-garde painter
Tricker Louis Florsheim, a pimp and strong-arm man
Denzell Sloate, an aristocratic flier
Laetitia "Tish" Sloate, his sister, a suffragist

Kishinev, Russia:
"Bubbe" Minde Ginsberg, Hannah's mother
Becca Ginsberg, Hannah's aunt
Shmuel Ginsberg, Hannah's cousin
Benya Rogovin ⎫
Zvi Herzog ⎬ members of the local Bund
Rabbi Isaacson, chief rabbi of Kishinev
Avrom Herzog ⎫
Mr. and Mrs. Yakov Feldstein ⎬ pillars of the temple
Pavel Peshkoff, a Russian socialist tobacco worker

The Lower East Side:
Rabbi Ezra Cohen, Rachel's father, of the Gradz *shul* on
    Norfolk Street
Bertha Cohen, his wife
Milke Kretskes, their neighbor
Solly Fein, a meat peddler
Hymie the Suspenders } other peddlers
Menachem the Fish
Yetta Breynes, a midwife of Rivington Street
Yahkne Breynes, her young daughter
Kalman Garfinkle, a kosher butcher of Rivington Street
Shprinzel Garfinkle, his wife, also known as *Fafonfnik*
Rosalie Garfinkle, their daughter
Goldie Golovey, a matchmaker
*Dopey Benny Fein, a leading gangster
*Abraham Cahan, editor of the *Jewish Daily Forward*
*Benjamin Feigenbaum, president of the United Hebrew
    Trades
*John A. Dyche, secretary-treasurer of the ILGWU
*Jacob Panken, a socialist lawyer
*Abe Baroff, president of Local 25 of the ILGWU
*Ida Grabinsky of the Equal Voice movement

The Triangle Waist Factory:
Molly Hurwitz
Becky Zinssher
Fanny Jacobs } strikers
Minnie Fishman, an anarchist
Mrs. Rosenblum
Mr. Rabinowitz
*Harris and Blanck, the big bosses
*Bernstein, the foreman
*Jake Goldfarb, the strong-arm man

Margolis Modes:
Herman Margolis, president
Abe Greenfeld, his foreman
Morrie Katz } workers
Nahum Tabachnik

The Feminist Movement:
*Mary Dreier, president of the New York Women's Trade
    Union League

*Helen Marot, executive secretary of same
Prue Gruening, a suffragist from Buffalo
*Mrs. Alva Belmont, a society matron and suffragist

Berliner's Department Store:
Ira Berliner, its founder and president
Isabelle Berliner, his wife
Benjamin Berliner, their son
Fritzi Edelin, head designer

William Denzell Rensselaer Sloate II, president of the Sloate Consolidated Bank and Trust, father of Tish and Denzell
Caroline Longworth Sloate, his wife
*Samuel Gompers, president of the American Federation of Labor
*Alexandra Kollontai, a traveling Russian revolutionary
*Superintendent Whittaker, of Occoquan workhouse in Virginia

CONTENTS

"If I am not for myself, who will be for me? If I am only for myself, who am I for? And if not now, when?"

RABBI HILLEL

BOOK ONE

Not Like Lambs

to the Slaughter

I

In the later years of the last century, an avalanche began in Russia. First little pebbles moved, then big, until everything fixed seemed to shift and tremble. The power of the Czar, the misery of the peasants, the position of women, the persecution of the Jews—all these were suddenly opened to question. History was speeding up. The bedrock of Russian society began to change shape unpredictably, becoming fluid and slippery, so that a careless or unlucky person could lose her footing.

Hannah Levy peered cautiously around her door one morning in March 1903, and surveyed her courtyard in Wood, a suburb of Kishinev named for the wooden roofs of its huts. Only Jews with jobs could afford such luxury. Peddlers, day laborers, and others who lived off the air dwelled in Grass, in mud dugouts with grass growing on their roofs. Rich Jews— merchants, bankers, saloonkeepers, factory owners—lived in style in New Town, near the marketplace. In all these neighborhoods, Jews and Gentiles were sprinkled together like salt and pepper, mixed but distinct.

Hannah looked up at the sky. The last stars were fading over Kishinev. The air was clear. It would be a fine spring day. "Fine for some," she muttered. To Hannah, there were no fine days in Russia. She was a short woman in her thirties with a round body, a beautifully modeled face, and rough brown curls she pushed impatiently aside as she walked toward the small lean-to that served as a chickenhouse. She paid no attention to the religious law requiring a married woman to crop her head and wear a wig, or at least cover her head with a kerchief. Though she kept kosher and observed the Sabbath like everybody else, she had no interest in tradition. Her attention was on survival.

Glancing quickly around to ensure that no one was stirring, no lantern shining in the windows of the other houses on the courtyard, Hannah ducked through the low door of the chickenhouse. Quickly setting the sleeping birds out of the way, she began to rake the sawdust on one side. Soon she came to a small piece of board, which she clumsily removed. Every morning it was the same at this point: Her hands fumbled and her breath caught in her throat as she rushed to make sure everything was as she had left it, scrabbling with her fingers in the space beneath the board, squinting in the dim light. Then, with a shuddering sigh, she relaxed. No one had found it. The money was still there.

Hannah's family was a living illustration of how fast the world had changed. She and her mother stood on opposite sides of a great crack in the history of the Russian Jews, the year 1881. Before then, the Ginsbergs, like most of their people, lived in a *shtetl* village, Volvelnya, little more than a handful of huts thrown down on a mountainside. There they raised vegetables and chickens for food and scratched out a poor living from trade. Everything the family owned was made by someone living within twenty miles of them and no one had ever been farther from the village than that.

Volvelnya was surrounded by a sea of sometimes hostile but basically indifferent Russian, Polish, and Moldavian peasants who came there to market and get drunk. Occasionally a few rowdies attacked the Jews. Once Hannah's father Yossel was badly beaten, and in his father's time there had been a pogrom, incited by the local landowner. *Shtetl* life had its uncertainties, and its poverty and ignorance were proverbial; still, it was sweetened by the security of long custom in a setting where everyone knew all about everyone else's grandparents. In Hannah's mother's day, those who left for the city were few and remarkable.

For Hannah, such community was only memory. When she was twelve, the May Laws of 1881 decreed that Jews could no longer own land or farm it; they were to be moved into the cities of the Pale, the traditional area of Jewish settlement in eastern Russia and Poland. Why? Who knew? The Czar said they had to move, so they did, even though Minde Ginsberg, Hannah's mother, could hardly bear to leave the place where she was born and the graveyard where her parents were buried. She left looking backward, like Lot's wife.

The Ginsbergs drifted first to a small town where Yossel could find no work, then to a larger town, and finally to Kishinev, capital of the province of Bessarabia and an industrial city of a hundred thousand. There factories sprang up to greet them, places new under the sun where hundreds of people worked together under one roof. In Kishinev there were garment and cigarette factories, vineyards, lumber mills, canneries. It was as if the same forces that had driven the Jews from the land had created these places to receive their bodies, put their hands to work, and crush their souls between pieces of metal. So Minde Ginsberg said. But she had a magical way of thinking, unsuited to industrial life.

In Kishinev, Yossel found work in a sawmill, where his hand got caught in a machine. He died of blood poisoning, a lingering death in delirium, screaming as he lay in his bed to go home to Volvelnya, where he could rest. Minde would not go into a factory after that. She supported her family as well as she could as a midwife and seamstress while young Hannah went out to work in a tailor shop, where she stayed until she married Moyshe Levy in 1888. Then she came with her mother to the two-room house on Nicolaevski Street in Wood, where her three girls were born, and where she ran a little dry-goods store in the front room and raised a few chickens in the courtyard.

Every morning Hannah Levy was the first in the chicken-house; every night she was the last, not even permitting her daughters to help her. No one knew why. She was glad enough for their assistance the rest of the day, in her frantic rush to do the cleaning, marketing, and cooking, saving every kopeck she made, never buying a thing they could do without—not a tablecloth, not a bit of jam for their tea. The Levy hut was one of the worst in Wood, with a mud floor, chinks in the walls, and wooden shingles that were perpetually coming off so the rain got in. More than once Moyshe Levy had asked her, "Should we try to find something better?"

"This is good enough," she would answer. "Are we the Rothschilds, we should live in a palace?"

He would shrug and drop the subject. Whatever his weak-
nesses as a husband, Hannah thought, at least he didn't interfere about money. He turned his pay over like a good man
should, without even asking for a reckoning. She found it
harder to manage the children. Her oldest, Rosa, longed for a
dowry and a proper wedding; Ruby, the baby, wanted a new
doll; and how Sarah complained about her shoes! She had to
wear Rosa's cast-offs. It was true they were too big but what
could Hannah do? She had no money to spare.

Of course the neighbors gossiped and speculated: "Where
does it go?" Moyshe had a good job for a Jew, in Leiberman's Cigarette Factory. Hannah had her chickens and the
little shop. "Where does all the money go? Their children
walk around half-naked and there's not a chair to put your
bottom on," said Fishman next door. Hannah knew. She
heard the rumor that Moyshe was a miser, hiding his gold in
the mattress, a rumor that sent every kid in the neighborhood
over to poke and pry. She knew the nasty tale spread by Mrs.
Zaretsky that Moyshe was a secret drinker who spent all he
made on vodka. She heard the lie that she herself was a good-
for-nothing spendthrift, as careless with her money as her
words and wasting both upon the air.

Hannah stuck out her chin and kept her own counsel despite such provocations. What you can do, do; what you
have, hold; what you know, keep to yourself. So the saying
went and so she did. Nor did she worry about the children's
complaints. "So your shoes are too big," she told Sarah.
"You should be glad you've got shoes. You should have
grown up in Volvelnya, then you'd know how to be poor."
Of course they suffered a little; wasn't that part of life? The
main thing was it should go for something. Their poverty had
a purpose. In a few years her family would understand and
forgive her without question.

Hannah unwrapped the bundle on the chickenhouse floor
and stared at her treasure: six silver spoons from her aunt, a
little gold ring left by her grandmother, and—five hundred
rubles! The savings of years of endless labor, almost enough
to buy the border and the passage for six people. And then—

America! The *goldineh medina*.

Everyone in Wood knew Hannah wanted to go to America.
When the letter carrier hollered in the courtyard that Mrs.
Twirsky had a letter from her son in New York, Hannah

would drop whatever she was doing to rush around the corner to Number 14, where Mrs. Twirsky was busily sharing her correspondence with the neighbors. There had been a letter yesterday:

"Dear Ma, I got a good job now in cloaks not so much money as I hoped but here is some it is all I can spare as prices are high so you should save and come over. Many people here are shaving off their beards and dancing even on *Shabbos* with women I am your beloved son Itzik."

"He never wrote that himself," muttered Hannah.

"What's that you say, Mrs. Levy?" inquired her neighbor sharply. "And have you heard lately from your father's second cousin in Minnesota, the one who was going to send for you, I should live so long? My Itzik's been there two years, still he writes, a good boy."

"I'll give him your good wishes when I see him in New York," retorted Hannah. Mrs. Twirsky just laughed. But Hannah had almost enough money now, as long as it was safe, as long as no one found the hiding place. Her eyes glared into the distance and her jaw worked as she ground her teeth, thinking. She could do whatever scrimping was necessary to secure happiness for her family. Mortgaging the present to buy the future was good business. But what about Moyshe Levy?

"He'll never come," she whispered bitterly. He would tell her that he loved her but the revolution was here. And she would stay forever, still too much of a fool to take the children and go. She shook her head, covered up her treasure, and fed the chickens. An early rain had left puddles in the courtyard and the morning sun gilded them, turning the dirt into a pavement of gold. It looked like the street in the steamship-company poster she had seen, showing the happy American workers coming home on payday with bundles of money on their backs. Hannah pursed her lips. Would she ever see such wonders? Things didn't come that easy. "Does a roasted chicken fly into your mouth?" she asked the sun ironically, and went quickly into the house.

The Jewish labor exchange, or *birzhe,* was where the old Kishinev marketplace had been. A patch of ground with a well, a bagel-woman, and a man selling tea from a samovar on a cart, it was filled with people looking for work. There were factory workers between jobs, porters, itinerant carpenters, roofers and furniture menders, delivery men and chimney sweeps, ragpickers and peddlers, all trying to pick up a day's wage. Some wore the long side curls and untrimmed beards of the Chassidim; others, the assimilated, had shaved or at least trimmed their beards. Some wore felt hats and long medieval coats, others Russian tunics and workers' caps, for every kind of Jew came to the *birzhe*, even members of the Bund.

The Bund, as the General Jewish Workers' Union of Lithuania, Poland, and Russia was known, had three purposes: to build labor unions in the Pale, to overthrow the Czar, and to defend the Jews against their enemies. Its members used the *birzhe* as a forum where they could pass news and literature, relay instructions, and argue with their competitors—scholars and mystics, freethinkers and pious, Labor Zionists and territorialists—all seeking converts at the labor exchange. While the authorities knew this went on, they could not end such discussions without closing the *birzhe* itself, which they were unwilling to do because it was central to the city's economy.

At the moment, the only policeman in the old marketplace was busy flirting with the bagel-woman. It was Friday afternoon and the week's labor had been concluded; still, the *birzhe* was crowded with workers going from the industrial district back to Wood and Grass. One of them, a tall man with bright eyes and a big moustache, had already gathered a crowd.

"Here it is, the Sabbath, and look at us—dirty, raggedy, half starved," he said, drawing people to him as much by his smile as by the confidence in his voice. "How many of us will have chicken on the table tonight? We work twelve or fourteen hours a day and barely have the strength to eat when we get home—if there is anything to eat. We have holes in our roofs—if we have roofs. We can't afford to send our children to school—if they could get in under the quota. Do you call this living?"

"There you go again, Moyshe Levy," said the Rabbi sourly as he passed through the *birzhe* on his way to the old synagogue. He was a portly, serious-looking man with a fur hat and a long black coat with an astrakhan collar. "I should have known that if I saw a crowd of ne'er-do-wells, you'd be in the middle of it."

The men in the marketplace smiled in anticipation, for Moyshe Levy and the Rabbi were old antagonists who delighted in scoring verbal points against each other. Their Friday night encounters were a bit of comic relief at the end of a hard week.

"Why, Reb Isaacson, can it be you?" said Moyshe in mock astonishment. "What are you doing in the *birzhe* with us common people? Surely you're not looking for an honest job? Have you come to see our misery so you can preach to our employers to pay us higher wages?"

The old man with flowing locks who accompanied the Rabbi began to hop up and down with irritation. "Aren't we in *golus?*" he cried. "What can we expect but suffering? Didn't God ordain it this way to punish us for the sins of our ancestors, and who are we to complain about God's will?"

"Shame on you, Avrom Herzog, blaming the crimes of the Czar on God," said Moyshe. "The Czar is responsible for his own sins, just like my boss Jacob Leiberman. I suppose God was the one who told Leiberman he should pay me only six rubles a week because I live in *golus?*"

"Jacob Leiberman is a pillar of the temple," said the Rabbi ponderously. "I will hear nothing against him." Several men in the crowd hooted.

"We all know what side you're on, Rabbi," said Moyshe with a smile. "We remember the way you used the synagogue to recruit scabs during the tannery strike. You certainly turned the tannery workers away from religion, I'll give you that."

"Since when are you concerned about the workers' religion?" cried the Rabbi, stung.

"But Rabbi, even the Torah says that every seventh year the Jews shall free all their slaves," said a new arrival, an innocent-faced, clean-shaven man in a wool cap. "What about us poor wage-slaves? When will the good Jewish employers in your congregation set us free?"

"Benya," said Moyshe happily, going over to clap him on the back. Benya Rogovin was one of his oldest friends and comrades. "Ah, Benya, don't you know we can't expect to get justice until the Messiah comes? That's why it's a sin to form labor unions."

"We can't get into the schools because we're Jews," said Benya. "We can't become doctors or lawyers because we're Jews. We can't own land because we're Jews and we can't even leave the Pale and go where there are more jobs. If we aren't killed in a pogrom, we're drafted and sent to die in some foreign country. But if we protest against any of this, the Rabbi tells us we are offending God. Is God in favor of anti-Semitism?"

"Beware!" thundered the Rabbi, pointing his finger at them. "Beware of these serpents in workers' clothing! They will get us all driven out of the little paradise we have left. Bad as things are, they could still get worse. Who are we, barely tolerated wherever we go, to meddle in the politics of a country kind enough to receive us? Remember 1881 and the pogroms these revolutionaries brought down upon our heads. They assassinated the Czar, but who suffered for it? Turn away from them now and go home to your Sabbath dinners like God-fearing people, lest we bleed again for their foolishness!" With this he threw up his hands dramatically and left the marketplace.

As the little crowd began to disperse, Benya Rogovin pulled a folded newspaper from his pocket and handed it to Moyshe. "He's right about one thing anyway," said Benya softly.

"What?" said Moyshe, staring at the headline.

"Read it out loud."

"People, listen," said Moyshe urgently, stopping their drift away from the *birzhe*. "Here is *Bessarabets*, the government paper. The headline says, 'Jews Murder Christian Child.'" He began to read, translating from Russian into Yiddish as he went. " 'The infamous Jews, not satisfied with the blood of our Saviour, take that of innocent Christian children to use in their Passover rituals. They crucified a little boy this week in the suburb of Dubossary. The police have kept this information secret, fearing to excite all true Christian warriors against this foreign scum. These Jews should have been expelled from Russia long ago. They steal our money, murder our children, and drink our blood. Death is too good for them.'" Moyshe lowered the newspaper, his face ashen. The crowd was frozen. In the silence, his whisper rang out clearly:

"Pogrom."

By the time Moyshe reached home that night, the candles were lit and the Sabbath table was ready. "What happened, Moyshe?" said his wife. "Why are you so late?" In answer, he handed her *Bessarabets*. Hannah, who seldom read Russian, spelled out the letters haltingly by the light of the Sabbath tapers. The three girls gathered around, listening. Any one of them could read better than she but none would have thought to take the paper from her. Halfway through the article Hannah put the paper down, her face white, and Ruby, the youngest, began to cry.

They sat down to a dinner that was one of their few observances of religious custom. Friday was the only day of the week the Levys had meat, usually one of Hannah's chickens. On weekdays they lived on black bread, an occasional egg, and the "Jewish fruits"—potatoes, onions, cucumbers, beets, cabbages. Usually they gobbled the chicken down as soon as it reached the table, but tonight no one had an appetite. Even Ruby, who always cleaned her plate, merely pushed the food around. Soon Hannah laid down her fork.

"Listen to me, Moyshe," she said intensely. "Now is the time. If we go to America now, we can still escape. I can find a way if you will help me."

He looked at her in astonishment. "Why do we always have to go through this? Our fight is here. How could I run away?"

"You're going to stop a pogrom all by yourself? Who are you, the Messiah?" They glared at each other across the little table. Then Sarah, their middle child, sprang up and rushed to stand next to her father.

"He won't be alone!" she cried. "I will be with him! And so will the rest of the Bund!"

Hannah's eyes flashed. All the anger and terror she felt for Moyshe but dared not show welled up in her when she looked at Sarah, her child but so little hers. "Oh, yes, the heroic girl revolutionary," she mocked her. "She will save her people single-handed. Even though she can't keep her shoes on."

"Another dinner spoiled by fighting," whispered Rosa to

the air. At fourteen, she was a dark-haired beauty and her
mother's right hand. But, unlike Hannah, Rosa was an ac-
commodator, looking only for a niche to fit herself into while
the family quarrels raged around her head. She would emerge
from these unscathed, still everybody's good girl. She loved
her family, but she hated the way they lived.

It was not so much their poverty. That was to be expected,
though regretted. When the boy she wanted could not marry
her because there was no dowry, she was unhappy. "Is there
no way we can find a hundred rubles?" she asked Hannah.
But when Hannah said no, Rosa adjusted. There was no point
in wishing. She found another boy, the son of a poor cobbler
from Grass.

"Why marry such a poor one?" asked her mother. "Wait,
you're young yet. What's the rush?"

"I'm fourteen," said Rosa. "Another two years and I'll be
an old maid."

"Wait a year," Hannah begged. Rosa finally agreed. She
was in no special hurry to marry but wanted a quieter life and
a house of her own. She had heard enough of Hannah and
Sarah's fights, these bits of family drama that blew up in one
moment and blew over the next. For them these battles, and
even the pain they caused, seemed to break the rhythm of an
otherwise dull household life. Or so it had been until the last
year, when Sarah had begun to follow her father everywhere
he went instead of staying home with the other girls.

Hannah still grieved over this defection, though she knew
she was being foolish. She wasn't even sure which she was
jealous of: Did she envy Sarah her hours trailing after
Moyshe, or was it Moyshe she resented, for capturing her
daughter's mind? She studied Sarah with irritation. She even
looked like her father, with that dark skin and thin face and
those horrible pigtails that would never hang straight. Sucking
on the insides of her cheeks, kicking her stool legs—she was
so restless, so unlike other girls. Who would ever marry her?

At the other end of the table sat little Ruby, licking a spoon
and staring dreamily into the dying flame of the candles. She
was as placid as Sarah was fidgety, but Hannah worried about
her, too: She seemed to have no sense. Probably she was
pretending she was someone in her Bubbe's stories, a princess or a wood fairy. At least it kept her quiet. "Stop that,
Ruby," she snapped as the child's thumb stole toward her

mouth, a habit that reasserted itself at bedtime, even though she was six years old.

"Let her be, Hannah," said Bubbe. "She's tired."

Bubbe was Ruby's protector and the chief source of comfort in the lives of all her grandchildren. How old she looks tonight, thought Hannah, staring at her mother. Every so often she realized Bubbe would not live forever. Her teeth were nearly gone and she couldn't walk fast anymore. Still, she was spry, like a tough old hen. She looked like one, too, with her sturdy body and skinny neck, her thin hair pulled into a tiny bun, her eyes darting about, missing nothing, while her head twisted on its long neck like a chicken's did, surveying the barnyard. She was almost as strong as ever, but her mind was not what it had been.

As Bubbe grew old, she seemed more and more to feel the loss of the farm, of her village of Volvelnya, and the countryside itself. She told stories of people she had grown up with, dead now or scattered by the winds, unfindable. Several times a month she walked miles out of town into the forest, taking Ruby and Sarah along for company. She said she went to gather herbs, for she was a wise woman and a midwife. But Hannah knew she went to smell the trees, hear the birds, dabble in the river, and get away from the city with its dust, its closed-off houses, its hard streets and its Gentiles. She had never gotten used to living so close to Gentiles; in the village they lived apart from the Jews, but here they were only a street away. "They should have their own place," she whispered, adding a *"kinehora"* to avert the evil eye.

Bubbe was a storehouse of methods for avoiding the ill luck that plagued her people: admonitions, cures, charms, nostrums, and preventive measures against curses of all kinds. "If a baby laughs, slap it until it cries—Lilith steals happy children." "Never praise a child or you'll bring down the evil eye." "Never say a child is good; the good die young." "If you play with fire, you'll wet your bed." "Don't play with your shadow; it makes you stupid." "Burn all your fingernail parings and loose hairs—a corpse that has anything missing will never enter Paradise."

She was the children's reliable guide to the rules of Jewish life in Russia and they loved her without question. And she loved them in return: Rosa for her good nature, Sarah for her temper, and Ruby because she was the baby. Ruby followed her grandmother everywhere and imitated all she did; she dreamed Bubbe's stories, copied her needlework, and accompanied her on her trips to the cemetery, where Bubbe went often to visit her family: her husband Yossel, her brother Max, her sister Basha. Not her parents. They were still in Volvelnya, a hundred miles away, their graves overgrown and untended. They had no one to come and talk to them, no one to tell them the family news, no one to invite them to the bar mitzvahs and celebrations. Against her will she had abandoned them, leaving them in the earth of another town, and not a day went by that she didn't grieve for this double death.

Nor did she feel she was really settled in Kishinev until Yossel died and was buried in the cemetery. Then she had roots, some piece of the ground that was of her family, some stake in the continuation of the place. The afternoons she spent in the graveyard were little reunions, with Ruby tagging after to be introduced and take up her relationships with elders who had died before she was born. There was no hard line, no wall between the dead and the living for Bubbe. In their silent grass-grown way, the dead took an interest, making regular if unnoticed appearances at family occasions, coming in dreams to prophesy or give advice, helping her fill in the words to an old song when her mind dimmed as it so often did these days. Her long-dead mother observed her kitchen habits silently, making sure she kept kosher, and when Bubbe measured out her flour for the Sabbath loaf she rapped the cup against the side of the bowl three times, just as her mother had, and felt her mother's presence in the deed and in her. It was a comfort, and she passed it along to her wide-eyed, absorbent grandchild. In later years Ruby too would rap the cup of flour against the side of the bowl three times, just so, in unspoken invocation.

Ruby also studied her grandmother's needlework, for Bubbe was a master of all the useful arts and there was much to learn. She had the most beautiful shroud in all of Kishinev, white embroidery on fine white linen. So thoroughly had she ornamented it that there was almost no space left.

"You'll be the best-dressed woman in Paradise, Ma," Hannah would tell her. And Bubbe would smile, picturing herself dancing proudly before the Lord as David did before the Ark, her hair thick again and flowing out behind her, and

Yossel coming up to say, "How like a girl you look, Minde, in your white dress."

Bubbe could do anything with a needle. She could copy any garment, tailor a coat to fit, create miracles with a ball of old yarn unraveled from some shawl full of holes and rolled again to make a sweater for a child, or stockings if there was not enough for a sweater. Her current preoccupation was crocheting yards and yards of strip lace "for Rosa's dowry." It rolled from her fingers as if from a machine.

"I don't know what you think all that lace is going to go on," said Hannah frequently. "She's not a millionaire's daughter." But Bubbe paid no attention. She taught Ruby how to make lace too, and the child edged her doll's dresses with it.

Ruby had two dolls—Harriet Eugenie, a wooden peg-doll made by her father, and Jessie, a rag doll made by Bubbe. Sewing for them was her favorite pastime. They wore copies of her mother's or Rosa's dresses, made from scraps with surprising skill and fanciful additions of feathers or bits of embroidery. Ruby had a precise eye for color, line and form, the play of light through leaves. While Sarah leaped over puddles, Ruby stopped transfixed by the rainbows in them. In a culture that did not prohibit graven images, she might have become a painter. As it was, she could do needlework, and so her visual sense became inextricably fused with the household arts, beauty and use together. The loveliest thing she had ever seen, a thing that filled her whole body with delight, was not a painting—she had never seen a painting—but a heavily embroidered peasant shawl at a fair.

As the women cleared the table and cleaned the room that served as kitchen, living room, and bedroom, Ruby retired to a corner with her dolls and Sarah went outside to sit with her father while he smoked the Sabbath cigar he always purloined from Leiberman's Cigarette Factory. She stood on one leg, staring at him.

"Are you going anywhere tonight, Papa?"

He nodded.

"Can I come?"

"Not tonight," he said. He rose, kissed her good-bye, and said, "Tell your mother I'll be home late." Then he was off; she watched him go around the courtyard wall and vanish. It

wasn't fair. If they were going to fight the pogrom, she
wanted to help plan it too.

She shrugged and unwrapped the rags her mother insisted
she wear on her feet to keep Rosa's too-big shoes from falling
off and getting lost. Free, her toes wiggled ecstatically. Pins
and needles! Up she darted all in one motion like a jack-in-
the-box and swept into the center of the courtyard, spinning
around and around wildly with her braids flying, until she
collapsed in the dirt in a heap, her breasts heaving. They were
still tiny, a child's breasts, but starting to bud with secret
aches and itches. She cupped her hands around them and
stared up at the stars.

They were so high up, so far away. Their light was flickering and cold, not friendly like that of the moon. She would
give light too, she thought, but not cold like that. Not hot
oven-light either, like Mama. She would be like the bonfire
the *goyim* had at midsummer festival—huge and red with
licking flames, snapping and crackling wood, light and heat
all moving together. She stretched her arms wide, digging her
bare feet sensually into the dust of the yard until they were
half buried.

To be free like that bonfire! To have your spirit and body
and everything free to burn like flame! To push your toes into
the dust and not have to worry about Mama yelling! To run
barefoot through the streets without having old women whisper "Tsk tsk!" To be able to stand up and say whatever you
want, write whatever you want, yell, shout, and not get into
trouble or get arrested and sent to Siberia like Papa's friends.
She was filled with a sudden rush of feeling for all the poor
prisoners, all those who had ever struggled or gone hungry or
had to wrap rags around their feet. Her eyes filled with tears
and her heart nearly burst with longings her mind had no
words for. She flung her arms wide to the stars again. "Freedom!" she whispered. Nor was this all vainglory. At the age
of eleven, Sarah Levy was a runner for the Bund.

She had fought hard for this status. Though the Bund had
youth affiliates in the north, where it was strong, Sarah was its
youngest member in Kishinev and her father had not wanted
her involved. But Sarah had followed him, sneaking after him
when he'd gone out in the evenings. For months he had made
her go home whenever he caught her but, Sarah recalled grinning, he did not always catch her. She had located the group's

secret printing press, behind the butcher shop of a Hungarian named Sygorny, and one day, consumed by curiosity, she had crept in and sat with her ear glued to the inside door. Suddenly it opened and she fell in. "Who is this kid?" whispered a terrified voice, and Sarah bleated, "Papa!" and ran to her father's lap.

She was not yet a fully accepted member of the Bund. But they let her become an apprentice when Moyshe, by now proud of her determination, said, "I give up. If I say no, she'll follow me anyway." And Sarah had gradually convinced the others that she could be useful as a paper cutter and folder, distribution expert, spy, and lookout. After all, who would suspect a little girl running in alleys? She was in no danger, she assured them, because no one ever noticed her.

Zooming about the city like a small black bat in her gabardine coat, braids flying behind her, Sarah played protector of her people, listening in on the conversations of strangers, swooping down on garbage piles for contraband, skimming fields and skittering through alleys—a messenger of light. No puddle could deter her, no cobblestone could trip her, no pothole could make her fall: Sarah the sure-footed, the mountain goat. Not for her the life of a stirrer-of-pots and mama's girl—leave that to Rosa. Not for her the fancies of princesses and frogs that preoccupied Ruby. Sarah dreamed of deeds of blood like those of the revolutionary martyrs her Papa had known, with their brave deaths on the scaffold. Exalted, she climbed onto the shaky ridgepole of the chickenhouse in her bare feet. Poised there, silhouetted against the sky, she whispered, "I am proud to die for freedom!" and jumped—*splat!*—into the courtyard dust.

"What was that noise?" asked Rosa, sticking her head out the door. "Is that you, Sarah? Come in, it's late. Oh, are you dirty! Mama will kill you—the water's all used up and you can't wash your feet until tomorrow!"

But Hannah was too engrossed in an argument with her mother to give Sarah more than a routine slap.

"Don't America me," said Bubbe, rocking back and forth on her stool. "Don't tell me, Change your place, change your luck. I changed my place once already and that was bad enough. This is where I'm staying until the Messiah comes. If

God had wanted us to move around, He would have made us
with wheels."

"I will not bring my children up in a hut with a mud floor
and death hanging over their heads like a knife on a string!"
shouted Hannah. "We can never find peace here!"

"Even a stone can grow moss if it stays in one place long
enough," said Bubbe placidly.

"We've been in Russia hundreds of years and still they kill
us," said Hannah, wringing her hands in her apron. "Can't
any of you see?" Her face shattered like a pane of glass as
the tears broke from her eyes; then she threw her apron over
her head and ran into the corner, where she huddled, sobbing.
The children watched, aghast. Hannah never cried.

The three Bundists sat in half darkness in the little room
behind Sygorny's shop. They had come by devious routes,
spaced fifteen minutes apart as was their custom to avoid police observation, to try to struggle through to a plan. That
there would be a pogrom was certain. The relentless anti-
Semitic propaganda of the newspaper *Bessarabets,* the government's suppression of its only rival paper, and the frequent
conferences of its editor, Pavolaki Krushevan, with not only
the Governor-General but the Minister of the Interior in St.
Petersburg, all showed which way the state was tending. It
was true there had never been a pogrom in Kishinev. But, as
Benya said, perhaps no one had tried to organize one before.
And Easter, traditional open season on Jews, was fast
approaching.

Clearly the Bund should try to organize self-defense. But
how? Their prestige was relatively high. They had done good
propaganda work. With the help of Pavel Peshkoff, a Russian
workmate of Moyshe's who had access to a horse and cart,
they had built a distribution network for illegal literature that
reached over the border into Rumania. And they had won a
number of supporters in their successful work in the tannery
strike two years before. But two of their members, including
the only woman, had been arrested since and they were now
so small that military leadership seemed out of the question.
Only one of them, Moyshe, had even a gun. Was it possible
that they could organize the Jews of Kishinev to defend themselves? In living memory, this had never been done in Russia.
The enormous weight of tradition—hundreds of years of sur-

vival through meekness and flight—combined with the quietism of the religious authorities, made this almost unthinkable.

"We can at least agitate about self-defense in the *birzhe*," said Benya. "We can urge people to get weapons. Some of the workers might do that."

"We have to reach the middle-class people, too," said Moyshe. "And those who are religious. Or anyway try."

"Forget about them," said Zvi Herzog contemptuously. As a middle-class student himself and the grandson of Rabbi Isaacson's chief disciple, he felt he could speak with authority. "They'll bribe the police to keep the Black Hundreds out of the New Market area and let it go at that."

Benya agreed. There was nothing to be gained by appealing to people like that. The Bund was proudly a working-class organization.

"We can't just dismiss them without giving them a chance," argued Moyshe. "Let's go to the *shul* and make a public appeal. We need their help. Maybe some of them will see reason."

"The *shul* is filled with crazy old men like my grandpa," said Zvi. "Even if you could get them to listen, they could never do any fighting. They're useless."

But Moyshe insisted until they gave in. "I don't think it will come to anything," said Benya. "But I'm willing to go to *shul* as long as you do the talking when we get there. After all, what have we got to lose?"

The Levy children stayed up for hours that same night, too agitated to sleep. In their bed above the big oven they whispered, poked, giggled, kicked, and bounced up and down. Sarah was still engrossed in her dinner-table battle with her mother.

"I will fight for the people," she said defiantly. "Mama can't stop me."

"If you fight, you die," said Rosa. "Do you want to die?"

"If you don't fight, you also die," said Sarah.

"That's true," conceded Rosa, and laughed. She was not interested in politics. "But girls shouldn't fight. If you do, it's common and coarse and nobody will marry you."

"Nobody will marry her anyway," said Ruby. "Mama said so."

They both giggled.

"I don't care," said Sarah, tossing angrily in the bed. "Who wants to get married and sit around the house all day and cook and clean? I want to go out to work and have adventures, like Papa."

"Girls aren't supposed to have adventures," said Rosa.

"Well, I'm going to," said Sarah. "And if I don't get married and I see a man I like, I'll just take him for a lover."

Rosa and Ruby both gasped.

"Jewish girls don't do that," said Ruby. "Stop kicking me with your dirty feet."

"You ought to be ashamed of yourself, Sarah," said Rosa authoritatively. "You know what happens to girls who do it. You would have to leave home. Nobody would ever marry you. Even if it happens in a pogrom, nobody can marry you. That's the law. Even if the Russian boys catch you bathing in the river and do something bad to you, you can't get married. The law doesn't care that it's not your fault. What if you had a baby? You would have to go to America all by yourself, or be like Simme the whore down by the river, and Ruby and I could never talk to you again."

A bulky shape suddenly loomed out of the shadows near the bed. "And why could you never talk to Sarah?" said Bubbe. The three girls were silent. "Secrets?" She poked Ruby fondly.

"We were just talking," mumbled Sarah.

"Tell us a story, Bubbe," said Ruby, throwing her arms around the old woman's neck. "We can't sleep. Please?"

The old woman chuckled. "What kind of story do you want?" She pulled over the bench from the table and settled her weight upon it. It creaked responsively. She took her lace from her apron pocket and began to crochet automatically, as the light of the moon shone in the one small window near the roof and through the chinks in the walls, where the snow drifted in winter.

"A story about men and women and marriage and sin," said Rosa with relish.

"I'll tell you the story of Rivke the Rabbi's wife and the bargain she made with a water demon," said Bubbe. Then she sat straighter and, crocheting all the while, began to speak in what Ruby always thought of as her "story voice," deep and sonorous, as much like singing as like her ordinary way of talking. Bubbe had learned most of her stories from her grandmother, who had learned them from her own bubbe; Ruby could envision an endless chain of grandmothers, like the wooden Babushka dolls the Russians made one inside the other, going back to the beginning of time itself. The first grandmother, the fount of all stories, had lived when stories really happened and was herself conversant with wood fairies and water demons, magical rabbis and even a princess or two.

"Long ago, yesterday, in a certain village, not high, not low, not near, not far, lived a pious and hard-working woman named Rivke," said Bubbe. "She was married to the famous Rabbi Eliezer, a rich man and a learned one. He was so wise that students came from all over Russia to study at his side, but he wouldn't have anything to do with women. He hardly spoke to Rivke or his children, just *davened* all day with his pupils, learning by heart the Talmud, reciting all the commentaries, and working up an appetite. Then at night he and his students came home to Rivke. She would have laid ready a white cloth on the table, fruit in a bowl, food for an army— there were even chairs enough for everyone to sit down at the same time, so rich was this Rabbi Eliezer.

"But who do you think did all the work for this crowd? Who else but Rivke and her seven daughters. From morning to night they broke their backs cooking and cleaning, going to the stream to wash, rubbing the clothes against the stones to get the dirt off. Even on the Sabbath they could hardly rest. And did she get a word of affection as a reward for it all? Never. The Rabbi would say, 'The Talmud says it is better to talk to a woman and think of God than talk to God and think of a woman, but I am a holy man so I can talk to God and think of God and never talk or think of a woman at all.'

"For a long time Rivke bore her burdens in silence. But who knows what goes on in a woman's heart? In her heart, she must have rebelled, for why else would the water demon have chosen her, a woman never beautiful and no longer young, the mother of seven children already?

"One day when Rivke was alone, pounding her white tablecloth against the stones in the stream, the demon rose out of the water. *Oy*, he was horrible to look at, covered all over with hair. He had long claws like a rake. 'I will give you three wishes,' he told Rivke. 'Three times you may call on me at your convenience. But the third time I will take you away with me to *Yenne Velt* to be my bride and pick the lice out of my hair.'

"Rivke did not like this idea at all, because the demon was not only terrifying but also extremely ugly, covered with warts and long black hair. On the other hand, her husband was very similar in appearance and she had to pick the lice out of his hair too. So she went home and held her tongue. What else could she do? If she told the Rabbi, who knows—he might do something shameful, like divorce her. So she went about her business and hoped it would all come to nothing.

"That night one of the students spilled wine on the white tablecloth. Now, you know what it's like to get wine stains off something white."

The girls nodded, hypnotized, though none of them had ever seen a white tablecloth.

" 'Oh,' cried Rivke, 'I wish you hadn't done that!' Immediately the bottle of wine got back up again, the stain leaped off the tablecloth and back into the bottle, and the conversation went on as if no one had noticed anything. But Rivke clapped her hand over her mouth because she knew one of her wishes was gone.

"The next night, a fishbone caught in her oldest daughter's throat. As she stood there watching her child turn purple in the face, she cried, 'I wish there was something I could do!' Suddenly a huge wind blew into the room and threw her to her daughter's side, where she gave her a tremendous *klop* on the back and the bone jumped out of her mouth.

"Now Rivke was worried, as you can imagine. She knew she had only one wish left. And with her tongue, it would soon be gone. 'If I have to be damned for eternity,' she told herself, 'let it at least be for something.' So she called her seven daughters to her. She looked at them, the joy of her life. Who would provide for their happiness? Rabbi Eliezer would probably marry them off to his worthless students and they would live the rest of their lives without appreciation. In a quaking voice she cried, 'I wish my seven daughters were well-married to seven good, hard-working men who would care for them and not scorn them and build good families full of affection!'

"No sooner had she spoken than her daughters were standing under seven 'chuppas, each with the man who had been destined for her: a blacksmith, a baker, a butcher, a tailor, a printer, a carpenter, and a tanner, all skilled at their trades and doing well, and not a rabbi among them! Then, with a huge gust of smoke like from a stopped-up chimney, the demon appeared. 'I claim the woman Rivke as my bride,' he cried in a terrible voice, and she disappeared from living view from that day forward. But I believe she lived as a queen in *Yenne Velt*, with hundreds of servants, for the demon was a king among his own kind."

There was a long pause. The children sighed.

"Let that be a lesson to you girls," said Bubbe pensively. "Don't marry a man who reads a lot of books."

"Everybody up," shouted Moyshe the next morning. "And put your best clothes on—we're going to *shul!*"

"*Shul!*" gasped Sarah, who had been in the synagogue only twice before, both times to say the mourners' prayers for baby brothers who died young. "Why are we going there, Papa? Did you start to believe in God again?"

"*Tchah*, said Moyshe. "Don't be silly."

"Then why?"

"You'll see."

An hour later she elbowed her way to the front of the women's balcony, disregarding Hannah's hissed, "Sarah, get back here." In the balcony, as on the ground floor of the synagogue, the poor were restricted to the back rows, but Sarah wanted to be where she could see what was going on, and the ladies were indulgent and let her through. She stared at them—the same women she saw daily in the marketplace, but how different they looked. Gone were their aprons and stained weekday garments. The poor ones, like Hannah, wore clean clothes and wigs, or scarves too fine for everyday, while the rich sported shawls, bangles, embroidery, and jewels galore.

In the front row sat society. Mrs. Feldstein, the brewer's wife, had on a red wig and big shiny earrings that bobbed when she tossed her head. She called, "Let her in. Come here, child," and Sarah, grinning ingratiatingly, wiggled into the narrow space between Mrs. Feldstein's broad hips and those of the next lady.

"I'm surprised to see a little girl like you at *shul*," said Mrs. Feldstein. It was true; there were a number of boys downstairs, but she and Ruby were the only children in the balcony.

Sarah shrugged. "My papa brought us," she said. "And why not? I suppose girls have brains too and can learn Torah if that's the kind of thing they like to do. I wouldn't care for it myself."

"Oh ho," said Mrs. Feldstein, clapping her jeweled hands. "Listen to her!"

Sarah stared out over the railing. She had an excellent view of the ceiling, beautifully painted with angels inside a circle of Hebrew letters. Animals adorned the walls: an ox, a leopard, a lion, a reindeer, two doves, and Leviathan with his tail in his mouth. The signs of the zodiac were painted between the beasts. On the eastern wall there was a stage with some men on it. Sarah recognized Mr. Feldstein among them. At one side was the elaborately carved cabinet that held the Torah, the hand-written scrolls of the Law. Facing it were the rows of seats: the front pews with velvet cushions for the town's elite, then the pews for those with less prestige but still enough money to buy them and, in the back, the common pews where the workers crowded together. Sarah picked out her father there, sitting with Zvi and Benya. People kept turning around to stare at them.

In the balcony, the *zogerkeh,* who read the service aloud in Hebrew for the women to parrot—since even in wealthy families few girls were taught the sacred language—rapped her knuckles on the bench for silence. The service was beginning. Downstairs, Rabbi Isaacson cleared his throat.

"Today," he said, "the Torah portion will be read by Yakov Feldstein, who has donated fifty rubles to the poor."

Reading the Torah portion was an honor reserved for those who were able to make large contributions to charity. Feldstein came forward. He was a big, jolly-looking man who owned a vineyard, a brewery, and a tavern on Armenia Street—though he held the latter in the name of his Gentile foreman, since the government barred Jews from the saloon trade. As he picked up the Torah, a commotion arose in the back of the *shul.*

"What's going on back there?" said Mrs. Feldstein, craning her neck.

A tall figure detached himself from several men who tried to restrain him and broke for the front of the synagogue. Running up to the pulpit, he banged his hand on the railing and shouted, "I forbid the reading of the Torah!"

Sarah sighed proudly. "That's my papa."

There was pandemonium below as men ran into the aisles or stood up, shouting, until the Rabbi held up his hand for silence.

"What is your grievance, Moyshe Levy?" he said. "And why have you disturbed this service, you who never set foot in this synagogue? Why should God-fearing men listen to such as you?"

As the congregation began to debate the merits of hearing him, their voices rose with increasing intensity to the balcony, and Sarah heard her father bang his hand on the pulpit's railing again and cry, "I have come to save your lives!" In the pause that followed, he went on, "There will be a pogrom next Sunday, on Easter Day. We must act to defend ourselves and our homes."

A woman screamed in the back of the balcony and noise broke out anew.

"What makes you think there'll be a pogrom?" asked Feldstein in astonishment. "I haven't heard anything about one."

"Don't you read *Bessarabets?*" called Benya Rogovin from the back.

"Nobody pays attention to *Bessarabets,*" said a man in the first row. "It's always been anti-Semitic."

"Not like this."

A man in the middle of the room rose and came forward. "I live next door to a Russian policeman," he said. "My neighbor told me not to ask him any questions but said I should leave town for Easter."

"A pogrom is coming," cried Benya, walking down the aisle. "There can be no doubt. And even if it doesn't, can it hurt us to be prepared for once? Enough of lining up like calves at the slaughterhouse. We must arm ourselves and organize groups to defend our communities."

"Why should we do that?" asked Feldstein. "That's what we pay the police for."

"You may pay off the police," said Moyshe bitingly. "But those of us who live in Wood and Grass do not. Who will defend us if we don't defend ourselves?"

"Fighting back will only provoke the police," said a man

with a long beard. "You know how they feel about self-defense. It is always the same. If you resist, you only make it worse. If you are fated to die on Easter, you will die; if not, you won't. Why cause trouble and make it harder for everybody?"

"That's right," said Avrom Herzog, standing up near the front of the room. "We were put in Russia to be punished for the sins of our forefathers. You don't fight God's punishment. When God thinks we have suffered enough, He will send the Messiah to lead us back to Palestine. Until then we must submit."

Zvi Herzog yelled furiously from the back, "God didn't tell you to sit there like a calf and stick your neck out for the butcher, you silly old man."

Avrom Herzog, suddenly shaking, looked around in bewilderment. "Who is that yelling?" he stammered. "I can't see so good. Who's back there?" Painfully, he threaded his way toward the back rows. Suddenly he gave a shout of joy. "It's my grandson!" he cried, throwing his palsied hands in the air. "Such a long time I haven't seen you, Zvi. How come you don't come by the house any more?" Zvi stared at the floor in mortification as the old man prodded him with a bony finger. "Lost your tongue? Answer me why you don't come by my house? Ashamed to see me now that you're a radical?"

"That's not it and you know it," shouted the boy in embarrassment. "You told me I should keep away if I don't believe in God."

The crowd seemed to hold its breath as Zvi stood straight, his cheeks burning, staring at the ceiling, and old Avrom appeared to be debating something internally. Then he shrugged, broke into a grin, and leaped at his grandson, catching him in his skinny arms. "Look at him, my only grandson," he cried to the congregation. "It's true he's a fool, God help him, but I'd rather hear foolishness from him than wisdom from a stranger!" With a sigh, the assembly relaxed and Sarah heard chuckles as the old man caught Zvi in his arms and danced him through the aisle in a clumsy Chassidic twirl. There was a sort of yearning motion visible in the pews, especially those in the back, as if people were leaning toward the men of the Bund, longing to be a community again with an end to these splits that tore one generation from another. "Listen to me," cried Avrom Herzog. "He came back. The boys all came to *shul!* Would they have bothered to warn us if they didn't care? They don't have a lot of respect for the Torah but at least they're trying to help."

"Maybe they're right, we should defend ourselves," said another old man in a back row. "What have the old ways gotten us?"

Again the controversy raged. The Bundists won some allies, especially among those in the back of the room, but the men in front seemed unwavering in their opposition to any action. The majority of the congregation was undecided, as far as Sarah could tell, and wanted to believe there would be no pogrom.

At last the Rabbi spoke: "It is clear that we have not enough information to make a decision today. Therefore, Mr. Feldstein, I, and other members of the synagogue will go to the Governor-General to ask him if there is going to be a pogrom and to plead with him to use his soldiers to prevent one if necessary."

A murmur of approbation swept the *shul.*

Moyshe Levy rose. "Do that if you want to," he cried. "But those who want to defend themselves, come and meet outside."

Sarah leaped from her seat. Undeterred by her mother's call, she catapulted down the stairs and was waiting in the courtyard when her father arrived with a handful of others, still arguing. She counted them. Including the men from the Bund, there were only ten in all.

"What are you doing here, Sarah?" said Zvi sharply. "You should be with your mother. This is no place for little girls."

"It is too," said Sarah hotly. She was still muttering defiantly to herself when her father pushed her through the gate into the arms of her mother and Hannah dragged her home.

II

Three nights later there was a knock on the Levys' door. Rabbi Isaacson stood there, imposing in his long coat and black fur hat. "Good evening, Mrs. Levy," he said. "I've come to talk to your husband. Perhaps you and the rest of the family could go next door for a few minutes?"

"Of course," she said, flustered, and swept them out the door.

Moyshe looked at his old antagonist warily. He motioned to their one chair and seated himself on a wooden barrel. "Have a seat," he said. "Cigarette?"

The Rabbi shook his head. "I thought for a long time before coming here tonight," he said heavily. "To be frank, for you I wouldn't bother, but there is your family. They are innocent. And there is the danger to the rest of the community."

"What are you talking about?"

"I saw the Governor-General today."

"Oh, you came to report to the Bund. How considerate," said Moyshe, who could never resist baiting him.

The Rabbi sighed. "Something came up in the course of our discussion. But first I should say he assured me there would be no pogrom and said he is authorized to use troops to protect us. I also spoke to the bishop at the seminary."

"Him," said Moyshe. "What did he have to say?"

"He said our fears are groundless." The Rabbi paused uncomfortably, then admitted, "He did ask me if it is true that we use the blood of Christian children in our Passover services. Naturally I told him this was a slander, completely without foundation."

"That must have been a comfort to him."

"Moyshe Levy, I did not come here to debate with you but to do you a favor," snapped the Rabbi. "I advise you to listen." The room became very quiet. "After we finished discussing the pogrom, the Governor-General asked me to wait. He said someone wanted to speak to me. He brought in a man I have never seen before, a policeman from St. Petersburg. This man said he was tracking down people who had been troublesome for years and asked me if I knew a Jew named Meyer Levinsky. I said I did not. He told me this person might be living under another name, and he described the fellow, who, he said, was a notorious revolutionary wanted by the Vilna police. The description fitted you."

"And what did you tell him?" said Moyshe softly.

"I could not lie. And I have the rest of the community to think of. I hope I did the right thing. I said that if there were any such person in Kishinev, he was not a member of my congregation and that I associate only with God-fearing Jews."

"That was all?"

"He seemed satisfied to let it go at that."

Moyshe let out his breath. "Well, well. Imagine that. A notorious revolutionary from the north, missing for years, and they're looking for him in Kishinev. Isn't that peculiar?"

"Moyshe Levy," said the Rabbi sonorously, "you must leave town."

"Why?"

"Don't be an idiot! If you don't care about yourself, think of your wife and daughters. Are you determined to be a martyr? This man is serious. It won't be long before he finds someone to lead him to you."

"I'll deal with it after Easter," said Moyshe.

"You're still worried about the pogrom? I told you the Governor-General gave me his word; there won't be one. And even if there is, what can you do with your handful of people? You have delusions of grandeur."

Moyshe scowled. "Since we have had no support from you and the other leaders of the community, we probably will accomplish little," he said bitterly. "Many will die. I appreciate your concern for my safety, but it seems a little misplaced under the circumstances. So many are in danger. Perhaps you have come to salve your conscience."

The Rabbi rose stiffly, dignified. "I can see there's no use talking to you. I should have known better. I thought I could at least save your life but you are determined to throw it away and be a martyr. No doubt the police have good reasons for looking for this Meyer Levinsky, whomever he may be. I hope he is a wiser man than you.''

Meyer Levinsky was born in Kiev into a merchant dynasty so thoroughly assimilated that they spoke Russian rather than Yiddish at home. His father bought him a place in one of the Russian schools that admitted a small quota of Jews, and there he mixed with the most enlightened boys in the city. Like them, he was infected by revolutionary fervor, reading Herzen, Turgenev, and Chernyshevski's *What Is To Be Done?*, throbbing to their indictments of the poverty and ignorance that lay upon Russia like a curse. Filled with youthful ardor, he vowed to be one of the brave spirits who would drag Russia into the modern age. This had nothing to do with Russia's treatment of the Jews. He was barely conscious that he was a Jew. He decided, however, to apply to the rabbinical seminary in Vilna, telling his father it would be a stepping-stone to the university and help him to get one of the few places open to Jews. In fact, he went to Vilna to find the revolution, for that northern city was the center of radical activity in all Eastern Europe.

This was a period of crisis in the Russian movement, and many ideas and tendencies competed for Meyer's allegiance. There were socialists who taught clandestine economics classes to workers. There were others who "went to the people," dressing as peasants and settling in the countryside to agitate against the Czar; they felt the seeds of the future society lay in the traditional peasant commune. And there was Narodnya Volya, the People's Will, the terrorists. Convinced that open political work was impossible in the face of Czarist repression, they made the machinery of despotism itself their target: the local police chiefs, the officers of the secret police, and at last even the Czar, Alexander II. Many of the angriest and most determined students were drawn into the circles surrounding Narodnya Volya, convinced that once the Czar was assassinated the peasants would rise up, kill their landlords, and inaugurate a new age of freedom. Meyer Levinsky was one of them.

On March 1, 1881, Narodnya Volya succeeded in their most cherished ambition, killing the Czar. Meyer waited impatiently for the promised uprising. Instead came a wave of pogroms. "Ninety per cent of all revolutionaries are Jews," stormed the government newspapers. The implication was clear. The results followed in Kirovo, Odessa, Berdichev, Balta, Kherson, Chernigov, Poltava, Ekaterinoslav, and Kiev. And Meyer Levinsky began to remember that he too was a Jew and his family was in Kiev.

Discussion in his circle was at first confused. This was not what they had expected. But, in the end, most of the students decided they must follow the peasants' lead. Spurred by assassination, popular discontent had given birth to a mass movement as they had always hoped it would. True, the movement had temporarily focused on the Jews (due to their position as tavernkeepers, moneylenders, and rent collectors, the intermediary exploiters of the peasantry), but it would inevitably get to its more powerful enemies in time. The circle issued a manifesto hailing the pogroms as the first stage of the revolution.

Meyer could not believe the decision was correct. He decided to return to Kiev to see for himself how revolutionary the progrom was. Filled with foreboding, he went home and found his father's house undamaged, his family well. "I was afraid something had happened to you," he said with relief. "I heard about the pogrom."

"We're all right," said his father complacently. "We were able to bribe the chief of police to keep the mob away from this part of town. They only went into the poor neighborhoods."

All the contradictions in Meyer's mind converged at that moment and he swayed. "He's sick," his mother cried, and they caught him as he fell. He was in bed for a week, and arose ten pounds lighter, his purpose in life shaken. Were most Jews like his father? Was it possible to reconcile being a revolutionary and being a Jew? He had to find out. He became a wanderer in the working-class areas of Kiev. There were whole neighborhoods he had never entered in all the years of his childhood. He talked to the wounded and the families of the dead. He saw which homes and shops had been destroyed. His father was right; only the poor had suffered violence.

How could people say all Jews were usurers, he wondered; how could he have believed such lies? These people were starving, living in miserable hovels, dressed in rags. He looked around his father's house: the rich rugs, the carved furniture. He kissed his mother good-bye with the feeling he might never see her again. "A line is being drawn," he said. "And we are on different sides of it."

He returned to Vilna to find his circle in disarray. Following the assassination of Alexander II, the police had rounded up all the student radicals they could find. Many of his comrades were already in prison and an officer had been to his lodgings looking for him. He would have to leave town at once. He was fortunate to find a comrade who had several forged passports, stamped but with the names left blank. "What do you want to be called?" he asked. "Do you want the same initials? Do you want a Jewish name?" Meyer Levinsky nodded dully. "How about Moyshe Levy?" By evening, he was reborn; he took his passport and walked out into a street that ran for three years and spanned the continent.

Moyshe Levy worked his way slowly south, sleeping in fields or in the homes of poor Jews who gave him charity. At first hand he witnessed the terrors of 1881, the "cold pogrom" that drove Hannah's family from Volvelnya and accomplished by administrative means what violence had not. He saw thousands of homeless people, ejected from their ancient villages and pushed into the cities of the Pale, demoralized, fearful, bewildered. He wandered with them, blown by the same winds through the same years, covering Russia on foot. From them he learned Yiddish, halting at first, then fluent. Working as a day laborer, he became strong and bronzed under the sun, and when his beard and moustache grew long, he let them—what did he care if he looked like a Jew? After a while, he forgot there had been a student called Meyer Levinsky, or a world where the revolutionary uprising was just around the corner. Now he lived day by day. Slowly he inched south, with some vague idea of getting to Palestine through Turkey, until at last he came to Bessarabia—her fertile black soil, her orchards and vineyards, and her bustling little city, Kishinev, expanding and full of jobs. He got a job in a tannery, then another making cigars. Perhaps he should stay awhile.

Then he met Hannah Ginsberg and forgot any plans that did not include her. She was the most beautiful girl he had ever seen, and he realized with a pang that he had seen few girls at close range and this was something to regret. Hannah's hard

life had not yet lined her face or dented her high spirits. Her
eyes laughed up at him and she shone with a pink glow.

"I think you're beautiful," he told her the second time
they went walking in the forest. "I want to marry you.
You're a girl with common sense. You have what I need."

"This may be true," she said. "But I have no dowry."

"What's a dowry to me?" said Moyshe. "I'm not a merchant; I'm not making a business deal. I'm a worker. I need a
wife who can work."

"I can work."

"I need a wife who can love me. Can you love me?"

"Do I know?" laughed Hannah.

He kissed her until she gasped and pushed him away. "Do
you know now?" he asked.

Her eyes were soft. "I can love you, Moyshe Levy," she
said. "If you want me, you can have me." Later she whispered, "Will you teach me how to read?"

And so, at the age of twenty-six, Moyshe Levy entered the
blissful dominion of the senses. Work became something he
did to fill in the spaces between nights. He had never known
such intimacy with another person. "I am a man now," he
told himself, content. "Not a pure-minded student with a
bomb, not a Russian, not a Jew, just a man who can love and
who works with his hands."

Still there was something he missed. He didn't know it
then. Hannah became pregnant and Rosa came, and an ache
began to grow in him like a cavity in a tooth, until sometimes
his whole body echoed with it. Hannah was engrossed in the
baby and didn't notice. Soon she was pregnant again with
Sarah, then with two boys that died one after another; then
Ruby was born. Moyshe was a good family man, but there
was a vacant space in his heart. He tried to fill it by starting a
tobacco workers' *kassy*. Unions were illegal in Russia but
kassys—primitive mutual-aid groups that were organized as
insurance societies—filled some of their functions for the
Jewish workers. In 1901, when Ruby was four, a stranger
came to the tobacco workers' meeting. It was Benya Rogovin.

"I have come to talk to you about the Bund," he told
them. And as he spoke, Moyshe began to feel the empty
place within him fill with bubbles like champagne. Soon the
movement had once more become the center of his world. He
loved his family, but this was his work, the core of his iden-

tity, the thing that shaped his life and gave it continuity. Only in the revolutionary movement could he be both Meyer Levinsky and Moyshe Levy.

It was the night before Easter, the time of pogroms, and Hannah sat up late, staring at the wall, waiting for her husband to come home.

They had been married almost fifteen years. The first ones were pure joy. She had to smile still, recalling the delight they had taken in each other. He was so different from other men she had met, not like those lumps of curd cheese with their limp side curls, wrapped up in their books, or like those crude and grabby ones either. He had the strength of a worker, the education of a scholar, and, what was more, he loved her. Their first years had been sweet, honey in the comb. Now the honey was long gone and the comb hung empty in the hive, rattling drily in the wind.

Love, passion—who had time? There was enough work for an army, fetching water, cutting wood, washing clothes in the stream, not to mention the cooking and cleaning and mending and marketing, and trying to make a penny on the side, first with the chickens, then with the little dry-goods store. It wasn't that you stopped loving, but you stopped paying so much attention. And while you were looking the other way everything changed.

Her eyes filled, remembering. She had looked away for a few years to take care of the children and when she looked back, he was gone. Oh, not in body. His body she could have whenever she wanted it. Which was too often, judging from all those pregnancies, the three girls, those two heart-breaking little boys who died, and then, my God, the miscarriages, she didn't even know how many. How reproachfully he had stared at her during those early years when the girls were small, as if she neglected him from choice. It was so unjust. Her heart ached with relived exasperation. There just wasn't enough of her to go around. Love and laughter in the evening—those were luxuries for the rich, who had maids to do their wash. Hannah went to bed each night aching with fatigue, with a list of tasks left for the morrow weighing on her mind.

Little by little Moyshe had started being away in the evenings. She'd hardly noticed at first. Then she began to ask where he'd been. He was evasive. She wondered if he had another woman. It was months before she'd heard what he was up to, when the neighbors started asking her questions about the Bund. As if she knew anything! It was embarrassing.

Politics! He could never discuss them in a way that made sense to her. All right, things were bad in Russia—did that mean you should risk your life trying to change them? What about your family? At first she tried to get him to explain, but he always thought she was attacking him. You'd think a man with so much education could make things clear. None of his answers met her deepest question: "Why? Why do you leave me at home every night?" Of course this was not a question she asked. She knew better than that, because there was only one reply she would have believed and she didn't want to hear it. In the end, she knew, he would leave her. How could it be otherwise? He would find some younger woman who was educated and who shared his crazy ideas. He'd given up on Hannah; he hadn't asked her to a meeting in years. Sarah he took with him, but not his wife.

He hadn't even told her the secret police were after him. So much was she in his confidence. She had to hear it from the Rebbetzin in the marketplace. And what could he be thinking of, to go on as if nothing had happened? He wouldn't be able to do that much longer; he'd have to face facts once he came home and found she knew. He'd have to run for the border. They all would. It wasn't the way she'd hoped they'd go to America but at least now he would come. He'd have no choice, unless he wanted to be sent to Siberia. So the family would stay together.

It was very late when Moyshe came home. Hannah was dozing at the table and sprang up with a cry. The moon shone in the open door.

"Why did you wait up?" he said. There was a bulge under his jacket. A gun, she thought. He turned his back to her and put something in the cupboard where she could not see. She let it pass in her haste to confront him.

"The Rebbetzin told me the police are hunting you. How could you hide this from me? We'll have to leave the country now."

"I'm not going, Hannah," he said wearily. "I have responsibilities."

She stared at him, unable to find words. He sat down at the table, his head in his hands. "But, Moyshe," she whispered, then broke off. There was nothing to say that could bridge this gulf. Responsibilities, he said—as if he had none to her or the children. "What about us? Don't you know they'll watch the house—they might arrest us all!"

"Then you leave. Go to Peshkoff's hut in the woods. He'll shelter you and help you get out of the country if that's what you want. I'm not going."

Tears ran down her cheeks. So it was over then; the decision was made. They sat in the darkness, the table between them. At last she said, "All right, then, I'll take care of the children. Don't you worry. You do what you want. Fight. Die. There's nothing I can do about it. You don't care."

He looked up pleadingly. "Hannah," he said, his warm hands reaching for her icy ones.

"It's no use talking," she said shakily. "How will I ever be able to forgive you, even if we live?"

She rose and they went to bed. They made love that night with a kind of desperation, as if each thought it was the last time. Even as they did, Hannah felt a dryness blowing in her mind and tears running down her face.

When she woke, he was gone.

It was Easter morning. She stared up at the sun, wondering what the day would bring. It shone mercilessly on her features. She had aged years in a few hours; lines of worry and fear that had hidden themselves under her still-young skin had appeared in the night and etched themselves into her face.

Her mother, still half asleep, went out into the courtyard and shuffled over to the gate to look into the adjacent street where the Gentiles lived.

"Hannah!" she screamed. "Hannah!"

Hannah rushed to her side as the neighbors ran out to see what was happening, Mrs. Fishman still clutching her nursing baby to her breast. Bubbe had flung her apron over her head and was rocking back and forth like a demented bundle of laundry.

"Look at the houses," breathed young Mrs. Fishman. "They put crosses on them. Not the Jewish ones, the others." The Jewish houses, naked without crosses or icons, stood out as if under a spotlight.

"It's for the Angel of Death," said Fishman shakily. "It's like in Torah where God told Moses to make a mark on the Jews' door and the Angel of Death passed over their houses and spared their first born but he smote the first born of the Egyptians."

Bubbe's apron dropped from her face. "Rosa," she whispered. The Easter bells rang out, carrying their message of redemption to the world. Hannah pushed her mother toward the house. "Pack bread and water for you and the children," she said. "Hurry."

She wouldn't be able to take them all to the forest. Bubbe and the children were too slow. They'd be caught.

"We'll hide upstairs in the shed behind Zaretskys'," said Fishman. "You hide there too, Mrs. Levy."

"Maybe," said Hannah. "I'm going to shoo the chickens away first so nobody will get them." She had her own idea of how to hide and where was safest. She evicted the fowl from the chickenhouse and began to dig. In no more than five minutes she had pinned ten rubles in a handkerchief to her waistband inside and buried the rest once more. She ran into the house.

"Bubbe," she said, "give me your ring, I need it. Sarah, Rosa, Ruby, your earrings. You too, Ma." There must be nothing to glint and catch the light, nothing a bandit might see and tear from an ear or cut from a finger. Besides, they were gold. Whatever happened, gold should stay in the family. "Rosa, your ring."

Rosa clutched her hand. "No! What for? It's mine."

"Rosa, this is a pogrom," said her mother.

"You think they're going to kill me for a ring, Ma?" She gave a high-pitched laugh. "If they're going to kill me, it won't be for a ring. I'm keeping it."

Hannah turned away. She would not waste time arguing. "Ma, Ruby, Sarah, come with me." She peeked outside. The neighbors were all hiding, their windows covered; no one could see. She led the two girls and her mother to the chickenhouse and pushed them gently in, one by one. "Go in and don't come out until I return for you," she whispered fiercely. "Do you understand me, Ma? No matter what you hear or what you think is happening, don't come out. Don't worry about me and Rosa; we'll be all right. Don't make noise, don't cry—I mean you, Ruby—or cough or sneeze. Nothing they can hear! The Angel of Death may pass over this whole courtyard but he's got no way to know you are in here. He will pass over a chickenhouse unless you give yourselves away."

She spoke with ferocious emphasis. All three nodded. She
looked at them. Her mother, fumbling her fingers and clutching her lace, seemed suddenly old and more than a little
crazy. Could she be counted on? Ruby, tear-streaked, was
already breathing hard and sucking her thumb. She would fall
asleep in the dark of the chickenhouse like a bird whose cage
had been covered. Sarah stared back at her mother, biting on
the insides of her cheeks, her eyes dark with knowledge.

"Sarah, I am putting you in charge. Don't let either of
them leave the chickenhouse until I get back, even if it gets
dark. Only if another whole day passes and there is no noise
and I have still not returned, only then can you come out—
you alone, Sarah—to see what's happening. Can you keep
them safe?"

Sarah nodded proudly. Her mother had never before shown
such confidence in her.

"No heroic deeds?"

Sarah shook her head.

"All right then, I'm going. Be safe." She blew them a kiss
and went into the house. Rosa sat at the table, sobbing
pitifully.

"Oh, Mama, I'm so scared," she whispered and clung to
her. Hannah held her tight.

"Rosa, listen. I want you to go to cousin Shmuel's in
Grass. There's a very good hiding place there, a cave right
inside the riverbank, remember? We hid there once when we
went swimming and some men came?"

Rosa nodded, her face brightening. "They'll never find us
there," she said. "You can't even see the entrance from
outside."

"You must take Auntie Becca and Shmuel to the cave. Tell
them I said to go with you. I'll come for you as soon as I can,
tonight if possible, otherwise tomorrow. Stay there until I
return."

Rosa dissolved into tears again. "But where are you going?
I want to stay with you, Mama."

"You can't," said Hannah flatly. "It's too dangerous.
You'll be safe in the cave. I'm not even sure how to find
where I'm going."

"But why can't we both stay in the cave?" protested Rosa.
"I need you with me."

"Because we have to get out of Russia. I'm going to find a
horse and cart so we can get away. We're going to America."

"America!" Rosa's face was transfigured. "But where will we get the money?"

"I know where to get the money, but we need a cart to get across the border."

"What about Papa?"

"I don't know," said Hannah helplessly. "I don't even know where he is. What can I do? It's all on my shoulders now. If he wants to find us, he will. Come, let's go."

As they walked through the courtyard gate, she stopped for a moment and looked back at the house as if for the last time. Then she pulled her shawl firmly about her and set out, head high. She and Rosa parted at the crossroad where one street led to Grass, the other into the woods.

"Can't I go with you, Mama?" Rosa made one final appeal.

"No," said Hannah. "Good-bye, my love, my little girl, my right hand. Be safe." She kissed Rosa on the forehead and on the lips, then turned and walked down the road toward the forest. Wrapped in her shawl, she seemed to Rosa like one of the giants in her grandmother's tales, strong enough to carry the world on her shoulders.

The Kishinev pogrom of 1903 began after Easter services on Sunday, April 6, and lasted into the evening of April 7. Its carnage was on a scale considered large until the modern era. Forty-seven Jews were killed, ninety-two were seriously wounded, and five hundred were injured. Seven hundred Jewish houses were destroyed. Six hundred stores and businesses were looted. Two thousand families were ruined economically. The number of women and girls raped is unknown because most were ashamed to report the crime. The victims of the Kishinev pogrom were, almost without exception, poor or working-class Jews; the rich were able to buy protection from the police.

The pogrom was well coordinated. Most of the Black Hundreds were seminarians, government employees, or students. They were organized into bands of fifty which converged on the Jewish quarters of the city on Sunday afternoon. These bands included a number of Albanians and Macedonians who had apparently been sent to town for the pogrom and who disappeared after it. They began by looting and attacking houses and businesses, concentrating mainly on the destruction of property. When the police made no effort to stop this, the rioters progressed to massacre and gang rape, making their way out into the working-class suburbs, where the worst outrages took place on Monday, April 7.

Although Russian newspapers did not record these events, several foreign papers, including the *New York Journal-American*, sent reporters to the scene. Their stories shocked all who read them and led to a number of protest meetings and demonstrations abroad. They told of babies who had their brains dashed out against buildings or were torn apart savagely in the presence of their parents; of men who were tortured, had their eyes gouged out, or had nails hammered into their brains. The *shammus* of the synagogue was beaten to death on the altar as he vainly tried to defend the Torah, which was desecrated and ripped to shreds.

The bishop passed through the rampaging mob on his way home from Easter services and blessed them from his carriage.

On Sunday evening, the first day of the pogrom, a delegation of Jewish leaders waited on the Governor-General. They were told he had no authority to intervene without further orders from St. Petersburg. The *London Times* subsequently revealed that he had been instructed to take no action, and quoted a letter to him from the Minister of the Interior: "It has come to my knowledge that in the region entrusted to you wide disturbances are being prepared against the Jews, who exploit the local population . . . your Excellency will not fail to contribute to the immediate stopping of disorders which may arise by means of admonitions without at all having recourse, however, to the use of arms." When the Governor-General finally called out his soldiers at 6:00 P.M. Monday, one shot sufficed to disperse the rioters and stop the pogrom. But by then most of the damage had been done.

The Jews made only one organized attempt at self-defense, despite the fact that they outnumbered the rioters by at least ten to one. A group of one hundred fifty Jews fought back on the second day of the pogrom, in the New Market. The police then appeared for the first time and arrested a number of them. As a result of the Kishinev pogrom, consciousness of the need for self-defense rose. The next wave of pogroms, which followed the 1905 revolution, was met with armed resistance throughout the Pale, most of which was organized by the Bund. Emigration also increased as a result of the Kishinev pogrom. With help from the B'nai B'rith and the

Jewish Colonization Society, Kishinev Jews left for America at the rate of three hundred a week.

Sarah stopped minding the chickenhouse smell after the first hour, and was glad to be there in the fusty half-light. The straw dust tickled her nose, but it was a familiar tickle, and the cramped lean-to was a shield against the noises outside: breaking glass and splintering wood, running feet that sounded like herds of horses, screaming and wild laughter, and the repeated terrifying cry, *"Byei Zhidoff! Byei Zhidoff! Kill the Jews! Kill the Jews!"*

Ruby slept fitfully. Bubbe muttered to herself, crocheting and reciting charms to keep the family safe. Sarah sat with her arms folded about her knees, trying not to think. The shadows inside the chickenhouse deepened as night fell.

Ruby stirred and woke. "I want to go outside."

"No," said Sarah forcefully.

"But I have to pee."

"Use the corner."

Ruby began to whimper.

"There, there, little one," said Bubbe. "Lie down again, and I'll tell you a story." And she began to recite tale after tale of princesses, forest spirits, wizards, demons, ogres, knights, saintly rabbis, talking animals, and poor woodcutters' sons. Whenever the children grew restive or frightened, she wove magical fables around them like a protective cloak, a wall of imaginary dangers shielding them from the pogrom raging outside.

Hannah had been to Pavel Peshkoff's hut in the woods only once, two years before, on a summer picnic. Then Moyshe had led the way and she had paid little attention. Now she racked her brain, trying to remember landmarks, wondering whether this wasn't all a mistake, a serious error of judgment. It was still not too late to turn back. But if she did, they would never escape to America. Still, the image of those two little white faces staring at her from the dark of the chickenhouse kept returning.

The first time a cart came along the road, she ducked into the forest to hide. The cart was full of drunken peasants from a neighboring village, and as it passed she heard them bragging about how many Jews they were going to kill and how much loot they would take and how many Jewish women they would possess. After that she stayed well off the road.

As a result, she got lost. She became more terrified with each hour. Her legs moved with dogged efficiency, but her mind returned compulsively to all the possible disasters that could befall those she loved. At dusk she came to a hut that looked familiar, but then they all looked the same. What if some stranger were inside and she alone in the woods, with her money, at night? She trembled so that she had to hold onto the wall of the cottage for support. Then she took a breath and knocked loudly on one side of the door, poised for flight if necessary.

"Who's there?" said Pavel Peshkoff, sticking his head out the window. Her knees buckled as she collapsed, sobbing with exhaustion and relief.

Inside she explained: She wanted him to help her get a wagon and bring her mother and the children to his house to hide, then get them across the border, with Moyshe if possible, if not, without. Peshkoff had often taken his brother's wagon into Rumania, sometimes to trade, sometimes with bundles of illegal revolutionary literature hidden under sacks of potatoes or bran. He agreed to tell his brother he wanted to help a friend sell potatoes, and to offer him five rubles for the loan of his cart and horse, five more upon their return. Two hours later, it was done and they set out, Hannah hidden at the bottom of the wagon. It was midnight and all was quiet in Wood; the rioting had stopped at ten o'clock. Seeing at once that Moyshe had not come home, Hannah got her mother and the two tear-stained, smelly children out of the chickenhouse, put them in the cart, and covered them and herself with sacking. Packed together in the wagon, the family set out for the cave in the riverbank.

Suddenly Peshkoff stopped the horse. People were camped all along the river. Even under the straw, Hannah could hear their yelling and singing.

"I can see their bonfires," said Peshkoff. "We can't get through." Without waiting for an answer, he turned the horse and headed for the forest. By midnight they were well on their way to safety.

If Rosa is deep in the cave, she may be all right, Hannah told herself desperately. It was a big cave. It went back a long way and the entrance was hidden. But a mother should be with her children in time of danger. Why had she left her?

Despite her frantic pleading, Rosa had been unable to persuade her great-aunt Becca to leave the shelter of her own courtyard for the uncertainties of a cave in the riverbank.

"I could never make it," Aunt Becca said. "I'm too old and fat and my legs are crippled. If your mother says you should go there, go. You don't have to stay with me." But Rosa did not want to go alone. Staying by herself in a deserted cave, prey to anyone who ventured in, was even more terrifying than staying where she was.

Easter Sunday passed quietly in Grass, though Rosa heard noises of riot from the center of town. She kept wondering where Hannah was. After ten, the night became still, except for the singing near the river. The sky was dark, with stars scattered over it like pinfeathers sticking out of a quilt. Rosa stared out the window a long time, listening for her mother's step in the yard.

Fear crashed down on her with daylight the next morning, and she hid under the coverlet shivering for an hour before she rose. Shmuel and the other men of the courtyard were patrolling nervously with big sticks they did not seem to know how to hold. Great-aunt Becca rocked back and forth in a corner, praying. As the day went by, they began to hear fighting in the distance. The pogrom had reached Grass.

"The men must leave," said Becca. "They will kill the men. They won't kill the women but God help the ones they catch."

A few men wanted to stay and fight. Greenspoon had a crowbar, Mahlkin a length of lead pipe. Two others had butcher knives. The rest of the Jewish men, knowing they were no warriors, took Becca's advice and left.

In a hurried conference, those remaining in the Asia Street courtyard decided that all the children and most of the women should hide in the loft under the roof of Number 13. They would be safer off the ground. Becca refused to climb the shaky ladder, however, insisting she was too fat and it would break. Rosa felt she had to stay with her. They huddled with some other women in a dugout shed behind Shmuel's hut, feeling exposed and insecure, particularly since there were gaps in the walls and a large hole in one side.

In midafternoon, Rosa heard a howling, almost like a pack of wolves coming nearer. It chilled her. Then a voice so close it seemed beside her said, "Where are they, anyway?" She looked through a chink in the wall and saw the courtyard filling with men, thirty or forty of them. They were led by three students from the seminary. The intruders looked silently around. No one stirred. There was a faint, immediately stifled cry from the loft.

"Greenspoon's baby," breathed Aunt Becca.

It was enough. The men ran at the loft like bees swarming. Greenspoon and the other three defenders jumped out of the ground floor of the shed, but were immediately overpowered. Rosa covered her eyes, shuddering, but could not block out their grunts and moans as they were beaten to death.

A voice cried, "Look what I found."

She peered out quickly. A bandit was standing at the loft window holding the baby. As she stared he yelled. "Catch!" and threw it out of the second-story window. One of his fellows ran up under the window holding up his long knife as if playing some sort of game, and as Rosa watched, unbelieving, his arm shot into the air and he skewered the child on the blade as if it were a piece of meat. The infant gave one pitiful bleat, convulsed, and was still, as the bandit ran gaily around the yard, waving his knife with its appalling burden, sprinkling blood behind him.

Rosa could not watch after that. Nor could she stop watching. She would put her eye to the chink in the wall, then pull away, unable to face what she saw, overcome by nausea and horror, stuffing her hands into her mouth so that she would not retch or make a noise. Most of the mob were up in the loft, where their howls mingled with the screams of their victims in a queer cacophony. A repeated high shriek rose above the rest.

"That's little Feya," whispered Becca. Rosa had met Feya Wouller many times. She was a pretty girl, about twelve years old. She kept screaming. The women in the shed rocked miserably back and forth; most, like Rosa, had their hands over their mouths. There was a flurry of sound and fighting outside; someone had broken from the loft. Becca peeked through one of the cracks in the shed. "It's Feya's mother," she breathed.

"Save her, help, please help!" cried a woman. "There are twenty men—they're killing her—she's only a baby!" She ran screaming from the courtyard and they heard her steps disappear into the unknown. Feya's cries continued for some time. Gradually her voice grew fainter. At last it stopped.

"Dead," whispered Rosa. She could imagine such a death.

The men straggled out of the loft one by one. Some were laughing.

"That's enough here," said another. "Let's go to Gostinna Street." They surged out of the yard.

Rosa sank stiffly to the cold mud floor of the shed. She lay curled there for some time, every muscle rigid and aching. She kept hearing Feya's cries in her mind. The other women murmured softly around her, like pigeons cooing, and as Rosa's body slowly began to relax, she fell asleep, overtaken by shock. When she woke a half-hour later, there was only one thought in her mind: Hannah. Where was she? Where were Sarah and Ruby? Were they still alive?

What if Hannah was alone on the road and met men like those? Rosa began to shake at the thought, her teeth chattering. Abruptly she turned to the wall and vomited up the bile that had collected in her stomach all that terrible afternoon. If Hannah had been there, she would have wiped her face with a cold cloth. "Mama," Rosa whispered. "I want my mama." She had never felt so alone in her life.

What if Hannah were back home, waiting for her? If she hadn't found her at the riverbank, and she hadn't come to Asia Street, where else could she be? She would never leave for America without her. Nothing at that moment seemed to matter but holding her mother tight again, hearing Hannah's voice say her name, feeling those strong arms around her. Rosa became more and more fidgety. It was true that Mama had said to stay with Becca, but she meant while the pogrom lasted. The danger was past now. There was no reason to stay any longer. Probably even Papa was home by now; it had been almost two days. She couldn't stand not knowing if they were all right. The anxiety became overwhelming. After another hour she suddenly whispered, "Aunt Becca, I have to go home now," and slipped through the hole in the side of the shed before the old woman could protest.

Free at last to run, Rosa shot through the streets like a panicked deer, hiding in doorways, scampering through the dirty alleys of Grass and the cobbled roads of the city proper, unable to look down because of the horrors in the gutters, unable to look ahead for fear of what might be coming around the corner. The pounding in her temples felt like the beat of her mother's voice calling, "Rosa, Rosa," and she was no

longer sure if Hannah was calling her home or telling her to
go back.

When she reached Nicolaevski Street, she didn't even look
around the courtyard, but burst into the house crying,
"Mama, Mama!" The house was dark. There was no one
there, only broken furniture and ripped-up comforters and pillows, with feathers all over the place. "Mama," Rosa whispered uncertainly. Then she heard the door hinge creak
behind her.

She whirled to run, too late. An arm circled her throat,
cutting off her wind, so she could only mouth the words,
"Oh, no," as she felt the knife at her throat and the dress
torn from her shoulders. What happened after that was painful
beyond imagination, the choking, the hitting, the ripping and
rending between her legs until she felt she was being torn in
half clear up through the top of her mind and she cried out in
agony, "Mama! Mama!"

Moyshe could not remember a time when he had not been
running. It seemed he had run for two days without stopping
for breath, doing reconnaissance, then taking part in the defense of the New Market. His comrades and the hundred-odd
supporters who rallied to them had begun to drive away the
mob when the police came and starting arresting Jews. They
took Benya and Zvi. Moyshe had not stayed to find out who
else was caught. He did not return to his own house until
midafternoon Easter Monday. Trusting Hannah's competence
and assuming his family was safe with Peshkoff, Moyshe had
hardly thought about them until he saw the looted streets of
Wood, filled with broken crockery and blood and feathers,
millions of feathers from the laboriously made pillows and
comforters of the Jews. His house was empty. Panting from
his run, he leaned against the wall, his ears ringing, suddenly
filled with fear. He had no idea where his family was. He did
not even know if they were alive. If they had been hurt—or
killed—they might be in the Jewish Hospital, where the
pogrom victims were being taken.

The wards were filled with the wounded. Moyshe Levy
knew so many of them; his progress was slow, exchanging a
word here, a handclasp there, shedding tears with them. His
own family was nowhere in the wards.

Nor were they laid out in the courtyard with the dead. Yet
how easily they might have been, for so many were stretched

on the ground, eyes staring, mouths gaping. Even Mrs. Fishman from next door was there, sitting with the body of her baby. Weeping, she explained: She had run from three men and one hit her on the head with a club, knocking her unconscious. She fell on her baby. When she came to, she found the infant dead, suffocated under her body. Moyshe spent a few silent minutes with her, then went on down the rows of bodies.

The dead stared up at him like fish. Some had been tortured. One man had nails sticking out of his eyes and temples. A woman had had her tongue cut out. At one end of the yard, raised on a bench as if lying in state, lay old Kopel Kainarsky from Mountezeskaya Road near the slaughterhouse. He had been beaten to death, then his stomach had been cut open and stuffed with feathers, hundreds of feathers. They drifted down his side and stuck in his clotted blood.

The absurdity of it struck him as nothing else had, and he began to tremble at something absolutely beyond his understanding. He knew all the explanations for why people might want to kill Jews and why the government stirred them up to do so, but the logic did not mesh with this. What reason could make anyone want to cut open an old man's belly and stuff it with feathers? It was not the act of a thinking being.

Moyshe shook his head as if trying to get water out of his ears, and fled from the courtyard and a reality that was no longer comprehensible. Like a blind giant, he ran through the streets, Samson looking for a pillar to hold on to until he could gather the strength to pull the city down. It was after dark when he returned to Nicolaevski Street.

He found Rosa sprawled in the doorway, naked, bloody, dead.

Only then did he feel the extent of his folly and his loss. He slumped against the door, looking at Rosa. His throat was dry, his head dizzy and light. Tears he could not shed roared like a waterfall in his ears. He could hear his own breathing and each rasping breath sounded like thunder.

The loss of a child is the most brutal of losses.

She lay across the threshold, her face cut and bruised, her eyes staring emptily, blood smeared like paint over her thighs and belly. One finger, her ring finger, was missing.

He had not been there to protect her. Puffed up by vanity as Hannah had said, as the Rabbi had said, he had gone out to

defend the whole community while his own child was violated and slaughtered. There was no way he could understand
his own life. It all seemed changed in the light of this,
darkened, distorted, and loathsome, as if seen through the
back of a scratched mirror. He was not the man he thought he
was. He was a man who let his children die.

He hardly dared wonder what had become of Hannah and
his other daughters. Whatever it was, they were gone from
him, for even if they lived, what could they do but turn away
when they saw what had happened to Rosa? As he grimaced
at the thought, a gust of wind swept through the house, picking up piles of pink-dyed feathers from the floor and throwing
them in his face like confetti. He choked and was blinded,
struggling to wipe his eyes and nose and mouth free of the
matted fluff, coughing and retching until he could breathe
again.

The effort released something that had been blocked and he
began to sob. Lifting Rosa in his arms, he laid her on the
table, covering her with his jacket. As he took it off, his gun
fell thumping to the floor.

He stared at it. He could make no sense of anything he had
done or anything that had happened, but there was still his
gun. They had taken all he loved. For centuries they had done
whatever they liked, with no resistance, at no cost to themselves. It was enough. He hadn't been able to stop them but
he could make one of them pay. It didn't matter who. They
all had blood on their hands. Dreamily he picked up the gun
and walked into the city in search of someone to kill. He
would not run. He had been running all his life, except for
those first years with Hannah; he had run for years upstream
through water, fighting the current with every step, but no
matter how he struggled the water still flowed in the other
direction. Now he was being swept away by the river, drowning with his family, but he would take one of them along.

He turned the corner of Armenia Street, past Feldstein's
burnt-out tavern, and walked toward the police station. An
officer was standing underneath the portico. "He'll do,"
thought Moyshe. He raised his pistol and shot him twice in
the eye, then threw down the gun and walked away as calmly
as he had come. The policeman sank to the ground behind
him, but Moyshe did not look back. He wandered aimlessly
on through the city, a strange peace on his face. His mind
was blank, his eyes stung, he could hardly see. When he

reached home, he took up his station at the bench beside his daughter's corpse, sitting *shiva,* as his head sank slowly upon his breast. Soon he was asleep with his eyes still half-open, unseeing.

Sarah was the first to find him, tumbling out of Pavel Peshkoff's wagon, crying, "Papa! Papa! You're here!" He started awake, squinting and gasping, and threw his arms around her with a sob.

Then she noticed the table. Eyes wide with horror, Sarah pulled back the cover and saw how Rosa had died.

They made small cuts in their clothing, as was the custom, and sat up all night around Rosa's body despite their over-whelming weariness. Bubbe insisted. She seemed to go crazy when she saw the place where Rosa's ring finger had been, crying in a frenzy, "She needs it to get into Paradise!" She insisted the finger must be found. In the dark of night, with only one candle, Bubbe got down on her hands and knees—after other searchers had failed—and, wheezing with effort, patted every inch of the floor to no avail.

"No one can get into Paradise if they have something miss-ing," she moaned. "You know that, Hannah. I always taught you that. The trumpet will sound and the dead will stand up and the inspector will come and she will be imperfect. How will he know it isn't her fault? Maybe he won't believe her." She sat holding Rosa's left hand, rocking back and forth and weeping.

Hannah grimly sorted through her wrecked household pos-sessions, her face set in stone. There was only one thought in her mind: She asked me to stay with her and I left. For this I was spared.

At midnight one of the men from the burial society knocked and leaned through the opening of the door. He was so tired he could barely speak. "How many?" he said. Moyshe held up one finger. "May your sorrows grow no heavier. Tomorrow at ten in the morning is the funeral. Some of the brothers will come to help carry the body. Have you got a shroud?"

"For such a young girl?" said Hannah harshly. "She hadn't even made her wedding linen yet."

"You're so stupid," shouted Bubbe, jumping up in a frenzy. "She'll wear my shroud. What else would she wear?

She'll be ready, don't you worry. We know how to behave. I'm an old woman, what does it matter what I wear?''

"Ma," said Hannah, "you don't have to do this."

"Don't tell me what I have to do," said Bubbe. "What kind of mother are you, leaving her alone?" Hannah's composure cracked then and she turned to the wall, while Bubbe continued to mutter accusations as she knelt down and began to dig under the floor for her shroud, which she had buried before the pogrom. "Let her have it, my lovely girl, the only dowry I can give her now." She dressed Rosa in the white embroidered linen, crooning as she combed her hair, "See what a beautiful bride she would make."

"I can't stand it," whispered Hannah. She had to get away from that demented voice. She took the lantern. Moyshe rose as if to come with her but she would not even look at him, so he sank back down to the floor, his head on his hands. He had hardly spoken since they returned.

It was some time before Hannah came back into the house, carrying a dirty, heavy sack. "Help me, Sarah." They took it into the center of the room. Then, without comment, Hannah pulled it open and poured a great clinking stream of gold unceremoniously onto the floor. They gasped. It was a fortune: piles and piles of coin gleaming in the light of her lantern.

"Mama!" exclaimed Ruby. "Where did you get so much money?"

"It's ours." Hannah's voice was flat. This was to have been her hour of triumph, the moment that explained each penny pinched, the time when they understood what she'd been doing all these years. Rosa was to have stood beside her, gaping happily at the sight and then, hugging her mother ecstatically, she was to have cried, "Who needs a dowry now!"

"It's our passage money," said Hannah. "For America."

"America!" Sarah began to cry. It was only as escape became a possibility that she understood how terrified she was. She threw her arms around Ruby, almost knocking her down.

Ruby struggled in her embrace. "How are we going to get to America?"

"I will take you over the border to Bucharest," explained Pavel Peshkoff. "You can take a train to Vienna from there. The American Jews in Vienna will help you get the rest of the way." He looked at Moyshe, who stared inscrutably at the money, and whispered to Hannah, "Is Moyshe coming?"

Hannah shrugged helplessly. She did not know. She hadn't said a word to her husband since their eyes had met over Rosa's body.

"Come outside," she told him curtly. Moyshe seemed to have lost his strength; he staggered and she had to support him as they stood in the wrecked courtyard. The moonlight shone iridescent on his ravaged face and the dusting of feathers still in his hair. "Well," she said, "are you coming with us or not?"

He looked at her in astonishment. Was it possible that she still wanted him to come in spite of all that had happened? "What do you want me to do?"

"What do you think?"

His eyes glistened. "I want to come with you, Hannah, if you can forgive me. We are a family, after all."

A flicker of hope she had not felt in years moved inside her. Perhaps they could yet make peace with each other, leaving the anger, the misery, behind in Russia. Even with Rosa dead. If he really loved her still and cared about his children, they could start over. It meant something that he was willing to come. He had never considered it before. He was reaching out to her, saying he had been wrong. That could not be easy for him. There was a sad smile on her lips as her thoughts raced ahead to the journey. "What about the secret police? Are they still after you?"

A helpless supplicant, Moyshe remembered there was one thing he still had to offer. She would not think him entirely useless when she knew. He gave the information to her like a present. "I killed one."

She gasped. "You killed a policeman?"

He nodded proudly. "I shot him. At the police station."

The light in her eyes died and she stared at him grimly. "So you're really on the run now."

He looked at her without understanding, his mind so rusty he could hardly make it work. "Nobody saw me."

But her face was a mask again, her voice empty as she turned from him, telling herself she should have known there was some hidden reason he'd agreed to emigrate. It was the blood on his hands and his fear of the police that would bring him to America, not love of her.

She and Sarah packed what little there was—a few dented cooking pots, a ragtag and bobtail assortment of clothing, one brass candlestick that had survived everything. Bubbe would not let them touch her things, nor would she speak to them. When Hannah whispered, "Ma, let me make a bundle for you," the old woman merely glared at her. At last Hannah gave up. Sarah could run back for her grandmother's things after the funeral.

Fine velvet-draped caskets holding the desecrated Torahs, which had to be buried, led the procession of thousands of Jews that wound through the poor neighborhoods of Kishinev. The rows upon rows of new-made graves awaited them, each with its wooden marker. Standing silently at Rosa's grave, each of the family threw a fistful of ground in after her, then waited to receive condolences. The crowd surrounding them parted like waves as the Feldsteins approached.

"I was a fool," said Feldstein without ceremony, coming up to Moyshe. "I say it before everyone. I was a fool. I thought money could buy safety and I was wrong."

"Who died in your family?" said Sarah.

"We were lucky; we escaped with our lives through the grace of a servant, but we lost everything we had. I'm a poor man now. And I've learned my lesson. This must never happen again."

"What are you going to do to stop it?" said Moyshe.

"Whatever I can. I'm speaking up so you all can hear me and remember. The Bund can call on me. Next time or any time, if I have money, it's for guns. And I'll be holding one of them."

Bubbe was the last to throw dirt on Rosa's grave. That done, she sank heavily onto the ground herself, as if she wished never to rise again. She looked around at the family graves, shaking her head vaguely. "Rosa, Yossel, Basha," she mumbled. *"Oy, oy, oy."*

"Get up, Ma," said Hannah, trying to pull her to her feet. "We have to go soon." She couldn't budge her.

"I'm not going," said Bubbe.

Hannah froze, appalled, realizing for the first time what her mother had been saying all night. "Not going? But you have to go."

"I'm staying with my dead," said Bubbe. "I left my family dead in Volvelnya already. I'm not leaving the other half here with no one to tend their graves." She settled herself more firmly into the ground as if it were a nest. "I promised you when we got married I would never leave you, Yossel," she said. "And I'm staying like I said I would."

"But Bubbe, we need you." Ruby was whimpering, terrified, clinging to her.

"So does Rosa."

"Rosa's dead," said Sarah. "We're alive." Then she covered her mouth in horror at her own words.

"That's why I have to stay. You have each other. She has only me."

"What good can you do her now!" Hannah screamed, shaking her. "It's too late, Ma! Nobody can help her now!"

"Stupid," said Bubbe, shaking her head pityingly. "I have to find her finger."

"Oh, my God," Hannah covered her mouth. "You're doing this to get at me, I know you are. We're not staying, no matter what you do! I won't sacrifice my living children so you can tend these graves!" She fell to her knees, pulling at her mother. "Please get up, Mama, please. We can't leave you!" But Bubbe pursed her lips and sat like a rock.

One of the young men from the burial society stood nearby, eager to assist. "We will find the finger, don't worry," he said. "We're sweeping the streets, getting up all the blood and hair and everything. We will bury it so everyone can rise complete on the last day."

"In a mess like that!" shouted Bubbe. "What good will that do? My Rosa's finger, someone else's hair, another's blood, all mixed up together?" She began to sob, imagining it. "How they will cry out for their lost bodies." Then her face shifted and she put her finger slyly to her lips. "I am an old woman, no reason for me to by shy or ashamed. I can tell the inspector what they did to the girls, so he will let the mutilated ones into Paradise and not hold it against them. Rosa could never say the words herself, but who could tell it better than me? I am her grandmother, after all."

Shmuel pulled Hannah aside. "Go," he said. "You mustn't let her keep you here. You see how she is. She could never stand the journey anyway. We'll take her home with us. Don't worry."

Hannah wept against his shoulder. "I can't bear to leave her."

"Go," Bubbe shrilled. "Go already if you're going. I'm

not getting up from this ground till you're out of my sight."
She covered her head with her shawl like a turtle backing into
its shell.

Moyshe came back from the cart. "Pavel thinks we should
start; we have a long way to travel before dark."

They said their good-byes. Hannah embraced her mother,
who ignored her; then, choking, she ran for the wagon. Ruby
wailed miserably and clung to her grandmother. Sarah walked
stoically to the cart, head high despite the tears in her eyes,
then suddenly broke and ran back. Throwing herself upon the
old woman, she snatched a piece of crocheting from her
pocket. "To remember you," she said defiantly. Clutching
the strip of lace from Rosa's dowry, she kissed her Bubbe
again and ran off without looking back, while the old woman
turned her empty crochet hook round and round in her
fingers.

They would always remember her like that.

Traveling through the next days, Hannah saw her mother at
every turn in the road. When they drove through the forest,
'the spirits of the wood from Bubbe's stories seemed to come
out of the firs and shimmer in the air, whispering, "Go back,
go back. How can you leave her?" When they walked
through a swamp to save the horse, the lady's slippers and
long grasses seemed to clutch at Hannah's ankles, saying,
"Go back, go back," and she remembered the way her
mother gathered them for medicines. In the mountains, the
cold winds knifed her to the heart, wailing, "Go back, go
back," and she could hear Bubbe's voice behind them and
wondered what gave her the power to summon the winds.

But Hannah did not go back. As they went over the mountains in the cart she felt the living fabric of her family, the
web that knit her personality together, slowly stretch and
grow thin until a hole appeared here and there, and the integ-
ument of her life ripped and was rent forever. It would never
be whole again.

"I had to leave, Ma," she whispered in torment. "My
children can't live here. You are my roots, you are everything
that went before. Now I have nothing to hold me down and
will blow in the wind like milkweed for all of time. But my
children will put down new roots in a more friendly soil."

BOOK TWO

*By the Waters
of Babylon*

I

"I can't stand any more," Moyshe shouted, throwing the handful of coins down on the ramshackle table of orange crates. "Here, take it, there it is, everything I've made today. I tell you, Hannah, I will be a peddler no longer!"

Rotten bananas, all that were left of the week's stock, lay about the floor where he had flung them. Their sweet scent filled the air, already heavy with tension. Hannah, tight-faced, stooped wearily to pick up these New World fruits, unknown to any of them just a few years before.

"Hannah," he pleaded, "I wasn't made to be a businessman."

She turned her face away, her mouth tight. The girls leaned stiff as plaster casts against the wall. Sarah's eyes were tense with her mother's fear: This was it then. She would not be able to finish high school. She was thirteen. After her fourteenth birthday, as soon as it was legal, she would get a job. She had to. It didn't matter how bright she was, how good with numbers; it didn't matter that her teacher said she could do great things if she tried. They needed the money. Ruby, next to her, turned her back on the scene, trying to blot it out and think of something else. She stared blankly out the little window onto the airshaft, playing with one of her curls.

"It's my fault, I suppose!" cried Hannah suddenly, whirling on her husband. "It's my fault you can't support your family! At least in Russia you could do that, even if you weren't good for anything else!"

There was a long silence as they glared furiously at each

other. They had fought before, more and more often under the strains of life in this new country, but this quarrel had the ring of finality.

Moyshe's voice was bitter as he said, "It would have been better if I'd died in Russia with Rosa. Then I could no longer hear these reproaches. You want to be rid of me, Hannah? I'll give you your freedom; you can marry again—a shopkeeper, an allrightnik, some kind of success story. That's what you want, isn't it?"

"Listen to how he taunts me. Hear how he pities himself! Do you think I like it, rising at dawn and crawling through the dark streets to get a bundle of work to carry home on my head? Do you think I like slaving over gabardine all day, basting seams for other people to wear at three dollars a week piece rate? Is this why I came to America?" She bit her lip. Didn't he know how it hurt to have her children rush home from school to help her slave in this dark hole, never knowing if she'd make the rent that week or have enough money for bread for supper, since so much depended on how well he'd done on his barrow? If only he showed some initiative, tried harder to sell, went farther from the neighborhood with the pushcart—but all he wanted to do was talk about Russia, not paying attention, letting those little bastards, the Midget Gorillas, steal his fruit and tip over his cart.

Hannah looked at him contemptuously. He stared back, his eyes burning. Then he muttered, "Oh, what's the use of talking to you," and, grabbing his coat, slammed out the door. Sarah's cry, "Papa, come back!" floated after him down the stairs.

Sarah cried herself to sleep that night on her bed made of three orange crates and a blanket, hiding her head in her arms so the others would not hear her. Hannah lay awake. Even her exhaustion could not still the burning thoughts that wound over and over in her mind like thread upon a spool. She was not used to sleeping alone. She missed the sound of Moyshe's breathing next to her, the warmth and weight of his body on the other side of the mattress. Not that they were such lovers anymore. He was too angry with her. What did he hold against her; why did he blame her for his coming to America? Had she forced him? Had he forgotten he'd killed a policeman and had to run for his life? Yet he was so bitter. Even when her mother had died and she needed him most, he'd turned his back on her.

Eight months after they'd come to New York, they got a letter from Shmuel saying Bubbe was dead. "She was never right in her mind after you left," he wrote. "She kept calling for her father. She thought she was a little girl back in Volvelnya and kept crying for him to take her home. We had trouble keeping her with us. One night when we were sleeping, she got out. It was very cold and she had only a nightgown on. The people in the next street found her in the morning, in the snow, but by then she was dead. We buried her next to Rosa and Yossel. We are with you in our thoughts. Love, Shmuel."

How they had mourned. The children were inconsolable; it was like leaving Kishinev all over again. Numb with grief, Hannah had turned to her husband, needing his love and comfort dreadfully. Sunk in his own misery, he could not respond. He lay there, his back turned like a wall, frozen with bitterness at his fate, torment over Rosa's death, hatred of this strange country and longing for home. True, she had not forced him to come here, but he would never have come if not for her. In his mind, it became her fault. She had thought coming to the United States would solve all their problems. Now let her live with it.

Hannah, bewildered, had nowhere to turn in her pain. She had so seldom asked for comfort that it seemed impossible it would not be there the one time she needed it. She sank in upon herself, sitting up late, staring at the kitchen wall, grieving for her mother and Rosa while the others slept. Once Sarah woke up and Hannah told her helplessly, "I knew it would be like this. I knew Bubbe would die and it would be like ashes in my mouth. It is how she punishes me." There was no escape from the burning loss and the guilt. And Moyshe, who should have held her and comforted her, blamed her too, she thought angrily, lying sleepless now on her mattress. If he really loved his family, he would adjust to America; other men did. He wouldn't have to push a cart full of bananas all his life. She had gotten them out of Kishinev and she would lift them out of this Bowery hole. They had progressed already; they had blankets and pillows, even one mattress, they who had come with nothing, who had lost every stick and stitch they had in the pogrom. Who could forget those nights they spent on the bare floor with only their coats for blankets, that first winter in New York?

Fortunately, she was strong. She carried those heavy bundles of gabardine, forty or fifty pounds, up five flights of stairs each day, until the room became a miniature factory covered with piles of fabric. She and the girls sewed late into the night, their hands black with lint and their heads sinking down upon their work until they slept, so exhausted they were unable to creep into their corners. It was a wonder the girls could get up for school. Sarah got good marks, too. Ruby didn't do so well; the teacher said she didn't listen. It was hard to know whether this was fatigue or just her usual dreaminess. Anyway, they all still had their health, thank God, no sign yet of that consumptive cough she heard so often, echoing through the tenement walls. Let them just keep their strength for a few more years, until they could afford a decent supper and didn't have to go to bed hungry. Let them just live until they too could reach for the milk and honey that flowed in the sweet streets of New York for those who could buy.

Oh, the foods of the New World. The meat that ran yellow with fat and the bread white as snow, all the marvels she had seen and could not keep her mind from dwelling on when she was hungry. What foods they would eat when they became rich: that American sugar, soft to the touch, not having to be hewn with a knife out of the rocklike brown ore they called sugar at home. Russian sugar was tough; you could hold a lump between your teeth for a whole glass of tea and still have some left for tomorrow. American sugar melted in your mouth at the first sip—but so what? It was cheap enough; she would have some in her lifetime. And soft rolls, bread, sweet cakes of the twenty different kinds they made in New York. What plenty, she mused, holding her stomach to still the gnawing pains.

"One more year," she murmured. "Give me one more year and we'll be all right." If Moyshe returned. She wondered where he was now, walking or talking or sleeping, and with whom. Plenty of husbands ran away in America; the papers were full of ads looking for them. Deserted wives were commonplace. She sat up in bed, clutching her breasts, breathing hard. Was Moyshe capable of such a thing? She could go on and be strong as long as the family was together—but if Moyshe had really left, what would become of them all?

It was nine o'clock that night before Moyshe slowed down, exhausted by his own frenetic pace. He had been walking the streets of the East Side for hours, not heeding where he was going, and his steps had brought him unawares to the Brooklyn Bridge. Suicide Bridge. He walked a little way out onto it, looking over the dark, rippling waters. The waters of Babylon.

There we sat down, yea, we wept when we remembered Zion. Spring would be coming soon in Bessarabia. The snows would begin to melt and green shoots push up through the earth. The river there was close enough to touch, dark like this one but warm, with the smells of home. In the evening, the birds would call out in fright at the sound of his boots when he came to the riverside to meet his comrades. Tears rose in his throat. I do what I can to help from here but my work is an ocean away; how can I sing the Lord's song in a strange land?

How he detested this country. It outraged his senses. Everything was off scale. The buildings were too high for such narrow streets. Where was the sun? How could it get in? And where were the trees? It had been over a year before he understood that not all New York was as dark and packed as the East Side. One day his pushcart wanderings took him above Fourteenth Street and he saw wide avenues and grassy parks. He'd hated America all the more since then. In Russia everything but the light of the sun had been taken from the Jews. Here they took even that.

All was corrupted, even Yiddish, the language of his own youthful diaspora. The words pretended to be those he knew but their souls had changed. In America, all words meant one thing: money. Familiar words like "freedom" and "democracy" turned out to have dollar signs beside them. Even votes were for sale—votes, for which they were fighting a revolution in Russia. To see his own countrymen sell their votes like *goyim*, taking the two Tammany dollars offered by the local gangsters outside the polls, seemed the final assault.

Two years after he left Russia, in the spring of 1905, a revolution began. While he longed for home and peddled bananas, the workers armed and threw up barricades and, in the cities of the Pale, the Bund led the struggle. How it galled him! It was true what Hannah said, being useful to his family would never be enough for him. It was history he hungered for. Autumn brought a wave of pogroms so well orchestrated that it was clear the Kishinev pogrom had been a government rehearsal for just such an eventuality. As if he had needed a second tragedy to make him see that the first was not his fault, Moyshe had opened his eyes and plunged into a whirl-wind of activity, raising money and organizing help for the victims. He had once more been given a task of heroic scale. The entire Jewish community, even the Germans uptown, had risen in sympathy, holding a vast support demonstration for those in Russia. All the way from Rutgers Square to Union Square, the streets, tenement windows, and fire escapes were black with weeping, cheering people. Moyshe had looked at the crowd with dawning wonder: This was America, true, and he hated it, but these were still his people. There was still work to be done. Perhaps he could make a life here. If only he could get rid of that pushcart!

He shivered. It was cold on the Brooklyn Bridge, with the wind blowing off the river. He shoved his hands into his pockets and his fingertips touched a scrap of paper. He pulled it out to see what it was. As he lit a match, he was filled with elation: It was an address he had written down that afternoon, before the Midget Gorillas and Hannah drove it from his mind. He had looked across the marketplace and there, before his eyes after God knows how many years, was an old friend from his student days in Vilna, just off the boat. Naturally he rushed to greet him, completely forgetting his cart as Hannah had suspected. He chuckled, remembering the providential encounter. His friend had been in New York only two months but had already found a good job in a cigar factory, where they were still hiring. The address was of his boarding house. Moyshe would go there at once, sleep on the floor, and go to work with him in the morning. The time had come to get a real job.

It was eight o'clock the next night when he bounded up the stairs to his home, fortified by a glass of schnapps in the beer garden across from the factory. He made a grand entrance. Ruby and Sarah ran to him and Hannah stared thunderstruck as he announced: "I have a job in a cigar factory! Ten dollars a week! I get paid on Friday!"

Slowly her face relaxed. "Ten dollars a week," she said. "We'll be able to move!"

II

It was spring, 1909, four years later. Hannah leaned out the window of her Rivington Street apartment, taking deep breaths of air and reveling in her new-found freedom. She had taken home her last bundle, sewn the last sleeve on a contractor's coat. From now on she would work only for her family. What luxury! Three years of the combined salaries of Moyshe and Sarah, together with her piecework, had brought them her dream: a flat on a good block, Rivington and Essex, in a corner building, a new-law tenement with running water in every kitchen and a toilet on each landing. Light poured into the parlor and when she stuck her head out, she had a view fit for a queen.

Sighing pleasurably, she surveyed her kingdom, the teeming street. A melting pot they called it, but it was more like a boiling soup kettle, swirling round and round in ceaseless motion. You could never tell what might come to the surface, and her eyes strained perpetually for fear of missing something. All the reserves of energy that had been blocked in Russia, starved for want of sugar and fat, had exploded on the East Side as if some chemical reaction had taken place between the Jews and the New World. Everything here was on a larger scale: colors glowed more garishly, dirt was greasier, people grew bigger, and all the latent exaggerations in their characters flowered. Hannah heard her own voice come out louder than before, her stream of invective in street-corner combats fuller. The unrelenting pressure of the Russian state had been removed and people's lives expanded to fill the new space.

And there were new rules. The children brought them home and Hannah struggled to understand them, trying to separate imperatives from garbage. "You're supposed to have a toothbrush and brush your teeth after you eat." "My teacher wears a hat, not a *babushka*." "If you drink a malted every day, you won't get TB." There were so many pitfalls, from tuberculosis to looking like a greenhorn—even Hannah, an expert on danger, was sometimes at a loss over what to worry about first. But the children were wise, she told herself: little Americans, their accents and gait were already different from hers. They would inherit her kingdom.

Taking her shopping bag and plunging into the life of the marketplace, Hannah threaded her way along the choked sidewalks—six hundred people on every acre of the East Side, more packed even than China. Stalls and awnings burst from the tiny shops onto the sidewalks, pullers-in hollered and grabbed her arm as she went by, pushcarts encroached upon the sidewalk from the other side, leaving almost no passageway.

And here was the world of her delight, after six years still as thrilling to her as an Arabian Nights bazaar. The filth, the crush, the stink, the cacophony of a thousand bickering voices, the yelling of children underfoot, the countless peddlers shouting their wares: pickle vendors with their vats of sours, gherkins, green tomatoes; candymen and their lollipops, licorice sticks, squares of butterscotch ten for a penny; the halvah man and the woman with slabs of broken chocolate. There were carts heaped with dried fruits and nuts—baseball nuts, polly seeds, St. John's bread from Palestine; men who sold knishes or hot sweet potatoes from little metal ovens on wheels; and a fellow who cried "Hot chickpeas! Roasted chickpeas!" Chicken and geese hung by their necks from poultry carts and fish were piled one upon the other, staring upward with glassy eyes. A man peddled hot ears of corn from a vat perched on a baby carriage. Another sold political pamphlets; a missionary dispensed tracts; a vendor of Yiddish sheet music sang free samples; and three little boys practiced a vaudeville routine. There was even an "Irish tenor from Lithuania," singing in English the song of the hour, "I Wonder Who's Kissing Her Now," with a cap in front of him.

She pushed through the crowded street. Look up and you

could see the sweatshop workers hard at it, faces gray as the cloth that drained their lives little by little. Occasionally a worker came out onto one of the fire escapes to gasp for air and she gave him a rueful smile, remembering the lint that had filled her own lungs. The fire escapes were covered with bedding and mattresses, like low-hanging white clouds; clothes hung out to dry between the buildings were getting dirty all over again from the air.

She passed the horseradish vendors, grinding their machines, and the portable soda fountains that sold plain seltzer and malteds and seltzer with a spritz of syrup. Taking a brief detour down Allen Street, she nodded at the building where they had had their second apartment in the shadow of the El. The whores sat on their stoops in the sunlight, faces painted, legs spread, hissing like teakettles at men who passed by. The Levys had moved out of Allen Street fast enough once Hannah understood just how bad a place it was, but not before the girls caught a few sights through uncurtained windows they would have been better off without.

Slowly, gritting her teeth and starving her family as she knew well how to do, Hannah had saved enough to pull them up the ladder one rung at a time: from their first room in the Bowery stews, to dreadful Allen Street, and then to Hester— a place with running water on the landing of each floor, so she no longer had to go downstairs to the pump. Then Sarah quit school and got a job, so there were two salaries coming in and Hannah could stop taking home so much work. And now, at last, there was 123 Rivington Street, a good building, with red- and white-striped bricks and decorations on the windows and a convenient fire escape and a fancy double door to the outside. There they would stay. The neighborhood was full of Rumanians but you couldn't really complain; Hannah liked most of her neighbors except for those stuck-up Garfinkles, the butcher's family across the street. It was a good move; they would be happy here, knock on wood.

There was Malka the Schnorrer, off to do her begging on the Bowery, pregnant as usual and trailing three little kids. She carried her belly high, and Hannah had to laugh remembering the day an Irisher tripped her. When she fell, her belly had tumbled out from under her skirt and revealed itself as a hard cushion.

Such people! How could you know what to make of them?

Just a few blocks away on Mott Street were Chinese men (you never saw a woman there), odd buildings painted red and gold, strange vegetables on the carts, and a sweet smell Moyshe swore was opium. How could you even guess what went on there? On the other side of the ghetto near the river were the Irish, whose gangs and politicians controlled the city, whose little boys tormented Jews. And over on Mulberry Street was Little Italy, its streets as crowded as Rivington Street itself, its women in black with shawls like her own, its noodle stands and operatic street singers and sweatshops just like those of the Jews—run, in fact, by Jews.

And what a collection of Jews there was in New York. There were the uptowners, the *yekkes,* rich fellows from Germany who owned the big factories and stores. They gave you charity with one hand and worked you to death with the other, all with their noses in the air. On the East Side there were *Galitzianers,* low-class types; Hungarians, who thought they were better than anybody else; Rumanians, who cooked their meat with sugar; Poles, a superstitious bunch; and every kind of Russian you could imagine from Muscovites to Ukranians to Litvak intellectuals. There was even a colony around Delancey and Forsyth of Jews from Turkey, who didn't speak Yiddish but talked some kind of Spanish with Hebrew words mixed in. There were the allrightniks, the bosses and shopowners who were making it; and the nebbishes, who were never going to make anything. There was every kind of loser: one-time university scholars working in sweatshops; rabbis who had no congregation since men lost their religion in America; craftsmen who couldn't work at their trade because the American unions wouldn't let them in, like Menachem the Fish, a peddler who'd been a carpenter in Russia.

She stopped at his stall. "You call that thing a herring?" she said, poking it. "My daughter looks more like a herring than that. How much?"

"Your daughter should only have such bright eyes! And look at all that roe—your daughter should only be so fertile. Five cents only and it's killing me, these prices, but I'm a generous man no matter how my family suffers for it."

"Three cents," said Hannah.

"You want to starve my children? You want we should be thrown out into the street? Your husband is working, your

daughter is working, why are you doing this to a poor man?"
he screeched, shaking his fist. "Lilith!"

"You don't want to sell, I don't have to buy." Hannah
calmly wrapped her shawl around her as if to leave.

"Four cents."

"Two for six cents, the one with the roe and that little
piece of nothing over there."

"All right," he said, conceding defeat cheerfully enough
now that the sport was over. "For you I'll make a sacrifice,
two for six cents, only don't tell anybody—and if you're not
satisfied, be sure to come back and complain about it, you
gorgeous doll, you."

Going home, she went slightly out of her way to pass the
stall of Solly Fein the meat peddler. "Hannah Levy," he
sang out in his rich voice, making smacking sounds and
rounding the air appreciatively with his hands. "The best-
looking woman I've seen all day. Come here and *shmooz*,
buy a little something, anything you want as long as I can get
close to you! Come and see, I got some nice sausages, a soup
bone. I'll make you a bargain; for you, I'll even deliver."

"Let him deliver," guffawed Hymie the suspender man,
festooned front to back with black braces cascading down his
person till he looked like a lopsided feather duster. "Appetizing Solly! He'll put a sausage in your oven! He'll give you a
piece *kishke!*"

Hannah stuck her chin out like a queen and passed without
a word, but she did snap him a glance like a rubber band back
over her shoulder and, surprised to catch his appraising eye,
flushed. A low-class man, that Solly Fein, a vulgar man, but
nice-looking, you couldn't deny it. And at least he noticed
her.

Nor was she altogether surprised when, a week later,
Moyshe said, "You know Solly Fein, the meat peddler? He's
looking for a place and wants to know do we have room."

"We have one boarder already," said Sarah.

"So what?" said Ruby. "Do it, Ma. With another one we
can get forks to go with our spoons."

"I don't know," said Hannah. But Ruby kept at her, and
Moyshe said he didn't care, so who was she hurting? She
wasn't going to do anything bad. She didn't even like the
man. But a new face would be a change.

Head bent under the rain, Sarah splashed angrily through the puddles in Washington Square, not hearing the voice behind her calling her name. At last the girl caught up with a gasp and spun her around.

"Rachel," exclaimed Sarah, a smile breaking over her face.

"Didn't you hear me calling you all through the square?" panted Rachel. "I yelled and yelled—Vatsamatter, you don't spik Henglish?"

Both smiled. They had met at their first day at public school, when neither did. Now although they still spoke Yiddish at home, they used English with each other. Rachel was a slight, lovely girl with the curly, orange-red hair occasionally found in Russian Jews and at one time thought bad luck. Although she was too skinny to have been considered a beauty in the old country, Americans stopped and looked after her in the street. "What are you doing around here?" she asked Sarah, linking arms.

"Just walking," said her friend glumly. "I don't want to go home until my pa gets out of work."

"You fighting with your ma again?"

"Not yet, but I will be as soon as I get home. That's why I'm stalling," she said. "What are you doing around here yourself? Since when does your father let you go west of the Bowery?"

"I'm working over here now. By Triangle." Rachel gestured at the line of factories that hedged the east side of Washington Square.

"Triangle Waist?" said Sarah. "Is it as bad as they say?"

"Worse," groaned Rachel. "Don't let's talk about it."

As they trudged companionably east in the rain, Rachel cast a sidelong glance at her friend and suppressed a smile. Sarah was not known for her neatness, and was the despair of her sister Ruby, who was forever trying to smarten her up. It was probably she who had fixed the bright bunch of artificial cherries to the brim of Sarah's old felt hat in a valiant attempt at high style. Alas, the rest of Sarah's costume—particularly her coat, which was almost worn through at the elbows and pulling at the seams—betrayed this effort, while the rain had made her entirely bedraggled. Still, Sarah had charm, thought Rachel loyally. It came from her grace of movement, her dark intensity, and the expressive mobility of her features. She refused to pay attention to her wardrobe, rejecting criticisms and offers of help with equal vehemence. "Nothing I do will make any difference," she told Rachel. "I'll always be a stringbean with a big nose." She also maintained she was too high-minded to care about such things, and if a man was going to love her, it would have to be for her soul, not her clothes. Rachel admired this devil-may-care approach. She was very conscious of her own good looks, since she felt they were all she had to offer, lacking money, connections, education, or familial support.

Sarah, scowling hideously and kicking the puddles, was lost in her own worries. "Do you want to come back with me for supper?" she asked suddenly. "You could help me with my ma."

"I'm supposed to go right home from work," said Rachel slowly. "But if I'm just with you and your father walks me home after, I don't see how my father could make too much of a fuss."

"Poor Rachel," said Sarah sympathetically. Rachel had the worst father of anyone she knew. Reb Ezra Cohen, an orthodox rabbi of the strictest kind, had never worked for wages, devoting his time to prayer and the Talmud, and his wife was little more than his servant. Rachel's oldest brother had run away years before, and her middle brother no longer lived at home, so she was the main wage-earner in the family. She and her father were at each other's throats; he saw any sign of independence on her part as a violation of his patriarchal rights, and she often told Sarah she would leave home were it not for her mother.

"He didn't even want me to work at Triangle because it's not in the neighborhood," she said. "If he could send me there on a leash, he would."

The two girls walked on in silence.

"Are they doing any hiring at Triangle?" Sarah asked finally, with forced casualness.

"The usual. You must have heard how people go in and out of that place. Why? Who's looking?"

Sarah did not answer. The bleak look on her face told Rachel all she needed to know. "Oh, Sarah," she said, "did you get fired again?"

Sarah was always being fired, usually for talking back to the foreman. She was a good worker and had no trouble getting jobs, but keeping them seemed impossible. It made Hannah wild with anxiety.

"My mother will kill me," said Sarah in despair. "She told me the next time I get fired I shouldn't bother to come home."

"You know how she talks. She doesn't mean half of it."

"Half is enough," said Sarah.

The dinner table scene was as bad as Sarah had feared. Hannah's denunciations were pitiless. Even Ruby put her oar in. "Now you'll have to let me quit school and get a job," she told Hannah. "You know we can't get by on one pay envelope and Sarah's never going to work regular. Oh, why couldn't I have had a normal sister!"

Sarah listened, poker-stiff, cheeks blazing. "I didn't get fired on purpose, you know."

"So tell me, brilliant one," said Hannah, "what happened this time? Whose life did you have to save from the capitalist system? I know you would never lose a job on your own account, God forbid. You'd have to be agitating about some terrible injustice."

This was indeed the pattern. Despite her father's instructions to plan carefully and use "tactics," Sarah jumped into every battle, looking to neither side and usually ending up isolated. She claimed she couldn't help herself but Hannah was convinced she didn't try.

What did they expect, Sarah wondered. Did they think she would keep meekly quiet and bow down when she saw the foreman turn the clock back an hour so the girls would work extra time and not know it? Why should they have to buy their own needles and thread and even pay for the electricity they used, covering the boss's overhead for him? Why should they work so long and hard, sixteen hours a day in the busy season, and then go for long months without any work when things were slack? And all for no more than six or seven dollars a week? How could anybody with a sense of right and wrong stand for the arbitrary firings, the sexual insults, the lack of plumbing, the harassment, the way religious Jews were forced to work on the Sabbath, and the lint and scraps lying around, guaranteeing you would die from fire or TB? "We're not animals," she said. "We have our rights."

"Of course you do. Who doesn't?" said Moyshe. "But is this something you tell the boss all by yourself?"

"I'm not afraid of any boss," she flashed back. "This is a free country, it's not Russia. What are they going to do, send me to Siberia?"

"No, they'll just fire you," said Ruby.

"I can always find another job."

"How many shirtwaist shops are there on the East Side?" asked Hannah rhetorically.

Moyshe sighed. Memories of his own youthful impetuosity stirred when he listened to his daughter: that daredevil spirit, that feeling you could change things just by wanting to hard enough. "So tell us what happened this time," he said gently. "We should get at least that much enjoyment out of it."

Eyes flashing, hands waving dramatically, Sarah launched into her story, talking at machine speed. A couple of new girls, learners, had been hired, one a pretty little fourteen-year-old called Leah. Sarah had known the moment she saw her that Leah would have trouble with the foreman, who was notorious for his wandering hands. She made it her business to eat lunch with the girl and, sure enough, her second day there Leah began to cry, telling Sarah how the foreman had pinned her after work the day before and how she could hardly get away. She wanted to quit but couldn't afford to because her father was sick and they needed the money. Because Leah was crying, both she and Sarah were late coming back from lunch and the foreman docked a nickel from each of their salaries.

"Well, I told him a thing or two," said Sarah. "I said, You mean five minutes is worth a nickel around this joint? If I'm worth a nickel for five minutes when I'm *not* here, I ought to be worth at least that much when I *am* here. And that means I should be getting sixty cents an hour, which is the same as $7.20 a day, which means I should be taking home about $43.20 a week. So how come I'm only getting seven? Who's robbing me of my other thirty-six bucks? By this time I'm hollering and everybody stops work to listen."

"Forty-three dollars a week," said Moyshe, impressed. "That's a fortune. Are you sure you did the figuring right?"

Sarah nodded.

"She always was the best in our class in math," said Rachel proudly. "She could do sums in her head just like that."

Even though the foreman was irritated, Sarah probably would not have lost her job had not Mr. Steinfels, the owner of the factory, been there. Noticing that nobody was working because they were all listening to Sarah, he fired her on the spot.

"I can see why you got excited, Rachel," said Moyshe reflectively, "but you can't defend the whole working class single-handed. You need a union."

"Tell me about it," spat Sarah, her cheeks red with anger. "Don't you know I've tried to organize every place I worked since I was fourteen? Don't you remember I'm one of the only three girls in the shirtwaist union, and there aren't too many men either? What am I supposed to do, work miracles?"

Moyshe was taken aback. Sarah seldom got angry with him; to him, she was still the little girl who had followed him whenever he went to the Bund office and who imitated him in all she did. She had often told him that the shirtwaist industry was different from the more stable and well-organized cigar factory where he worked. In shirtwaist, the work force was mostly female. Only the male cutters and pressers had unions, and they didn't seem to care about helping the rest, maintaining that girls were unorganizable because all they wanted to do was get married.

"Things sure are tough," said Rachel into the stunned silence, trying to make peace. "The place I'm working now is so bad I think we could do something if we only had an organizer. I can't do much—I don't know how and my father won't let me go to union meetings. There were some people there once who tried to start a union, but they got thrown out before I came and now there's a Triangle company union instead. The bosses and foremen are in it right along with the workers, and all the members have to pay dues or they get fired."

"Sarah should get a job there," said Moyshe.

"That's what I was thinking," said Rachel. "Then maybe we could bring in a real union."

Sarah could hardly believe her ears. One minute they were yelling at her for being a lousy organizer and the next they were asking her to organize Triangle Waist. But she had to get a job somewhere, and it couldn't hurt to give it a try.

"All right," she shrugged. "I'll go there tomorrow."

* * *

While Rachel's mother, Bertha, shyly thanked Moyshe for walking her daughter home, her husband glared at the socialist, the infidel. "I suppose you think having him walk you makes it all right for you not to come straight home," he said after Moyshe left. He sniffed twice, as was his habit, and the supercilious expression on his face became more intense as he stared at his rebellious daughter. He was a pale man, his shoulders hunched and his belly paunchy from years of inactivity. His beard, still black, was streaked with gray and his bald head was imperfectly covered by an embroidered skullcap.

"Ezra," said Bertha, "Rachel only had dinner by her girlfriend, nothing so terrible." Such pleas for moderation had little effect on him since he never listened to a word his wife said.

"One night it's dinner at the house of a freethinker, the next thing you know, she'll be sneaking out to a dance."

"And why shouldn't I go to a dance like other girls?" said Rachel. "How am I supposed to meet somebody?"

"You see? You see how wild they get in this country?" The Rabbi addressed the heavens. "No daughter of mine will dance with men in public. You'll meet your husband on the day you get married, like your mother and grandmother before you." He went to the corner, sat down in the velvet chair he'd brought from Russia, and began to rock agitatedly, looking at his wife.

"Two sons only you bore me, two sons to say Kaddish for me after I am gone. One has run off, God knows where, and the other has turned out a worthless *Americaner,* caring for nothing but money, with a slut of a wife so loose in her kitchen I'm afraid to eat from the *trefe* food. And look at this reprobate girl of yours." He pointed at Rachel. "I spend all my days studying the Law for you women so I can get you into Paradise, and what do I get for it? She goes her own way, gives me back talk, wants money of her own to squander on herself, reads Christian books, and writes papers in English so I can't read them!" He pulled a book and a few sheets of paper from his desk and waved them about. "What are these?"

"They're mine!" said Rachel, springing up. "Give them back to me."

"Mine?" he mocked her. "There is no *mine* in this house.

English writing. To whom are you writing in English yet and without my permission? I am your father; I am responsible for you. Look at this book—I can't even read it to see if it is suitable. For all I know, it is a Christian missionary book.''

"It's a story from the library, *Les Misérables*. If you hadn't made me quit school when I was twelve, I'd be reading it there.''

He addressed the heavens once more. "You hear how she talks? You see how she throws my poverty at me?'' He spat the words at her. "And is it not only right and proper that you should support the father who brought you into the world, so your mother should not have to bear this burden alone? And would two more years of school help you to get married? No, the opposite; a man wants a housekeeper, not a scholar. And to whom are you writing letters in English behind my back?''

"I'm not writing anybody,'' said Rachel. "That's not a letter. It's an exercise to improve my English.''

"It is not necessary for women to write things,'' he replied loftily, tearing it up. "The Lord is not interested in the thoughts of women.'' He turned his chair around so he faced the corner, and began to mutter prayers to himself, still rocking back and forth. Rachel stared at him with hatred. Though his words could enrage her, they seldom made her feel remorse. They had a deeper effect on her mother, a pious woman who believed as he did. Rushing to her husband, Bertha whispered, "Calm yourself, beloved, calm yourself. You are right. The soul of woman is nothing but a little raisin, a little dried-out raisin.''

Ezra Cohen had been born into the rabbinical dynasty of Gradz, a small town in Poland where for centuries the spiritual leaders of the community had also acted as the Czar's local administrators, even to receiving a portion of the taxes. When the rabbi of Gradz learned that Ezra was to be drafted, he was incredulous at this violation of his hereditary privilege, and quickly smuggled his son across the border. The Cohens traveled rich, with silver candlesticks, feather comforters, the desk and the velvet armchair, and even a fur-lined coat for Reb Ezra. But most of these things had been sold for food while he was waiting for his children to grow old enough to support him. He was even reduced to selling some of his Hebrew books.

Although many of his acquaintances suggested that he get a

pushcart if not a job, the Rabbi refused to entertain this idea, endeavoring as much as possible in his reduced circumstances to continue the scholarly life that was his birthright. As leader of an impoverished tenement-room *shul* composed of fellow exiles from Gradz, he received a stipend so small that it was no wonder he pulled Rachel out of school as soon as she was big enough to pass for fourteen.

Rachel had loved school. She mourned her education as if it had been a bridegroom, and continued to drown herself in books. They were her only escape from a meager and confined existence in which she was expected to do without money, clothes, romance, even friendly visits. She had hoped to continue at night school until she got her diploma, but her father would not allow it. He thought it improper for a girl to go out alone after dark. She felt he had condemned her to be a factory worker all her days, or to marry merely to escape the factory.

Neither was the fate she had chosen, for Rachel longed to become a writer. At night, when the snores of her family and the boarders informed her they would not interfere, she would pull a sheet of paper from her father's desk and sit up late, writing by the dim light of the streetlamp outside. She spent weeks laboring over primitive folk novels like the Cinderella stories her mother read in Yiddish, or perfecting epic tales of nobles and the French Revolution, modeled on her own library reading. Though her English was still imperfect, she had developed a surprisingly forceful Yiddish prose style.

On this night, her thoughts returned to the newspaper she had been reading at Sarah's. Unlike her own family, which read only the orthodox *Tageblatt*, the Levys took the East Side's popular Yiddish socialist paper, the *Jewish Daily Forward*. Whenever Rachel got the chance, she read its correspondence column, "A Bundle of Letters," in which readers poured out their woes, their ideas, and their life stories. Each got his own tailor-made answer from Abraham Cahan, the editor. Rachel had long contemplated writing a letter to the *Forward*. She would wait no longer.

Dear Mr. Editor,

Will you tell me please what a Jewish girl is supposed to do in this country? Is it like the old days in Russia when the father was the slave of the Czar and the girls

were the slaves of the father? Here in America we have
no more slavery, so how about the family?

Because I want to keep one dollar for myself out of
my wages to buy clothes, books, and paper; because I
want to know and learn and go to night school; because I
want to read English books from the library, my father
says I am an ungrateful child who wants to be a Christian. He prides himself on his holiness. He thinks he is
the most important rabbi in New York and that he alone
is keeping the light of Torah burning on these shores.
But he is working my mother into her grave. He nagged
my oldest brother till he ran away and he set such an
example of what a saint is like that my other brother
decided to be a devil instead, so he became a sweatshop
boss.

Jewish men are supposed to start each day by thanking
God they were not born women. My father says this is
because women have no souls and must depend on men
to get them into heaven. But I think it is because women
have to suffer so much. At home we have our fathers
and brothers, and when we go to work the men try to
touch us or sit too close on the benches and tell us dirty
stories to watch if we blush. If we do, they say, "Aha,
she understands what we're saying, just see her blush,"
but if we pretend not to hear, they say, "Look at this
one, she doesn't even have the modesty to blush." Because we work so hard and earn so little, we want only
to escape from the factory into marriage, but when we
do we get a baby every year and a husband who treats us
like a servant girl. So tell me please, Mr. Editor, what is
your advice for a Jewish girl in America on how to handle these problems?

                                        Sincerely, R.C.

The letter appeared in the *Forward* a week later, with a
pithy response from the editor.

Dear R.C.,
    We cannot offer any solution to your immediate prob-
lems, which are part of our people's historic battle between religious obscurantism on the one hand and progress on the other. We have printed your letter because it

so eloquently portrays the sad lot of young girls in our community, caught between the pressures of the old world and the new. We advise you to go on with your writing; you have a natural gift for it. Come and visit our office; submit more letters and articles to the *Forward*. We also hope that when the time comes for you to marry, you will choose a socialist and a freethinker, and not either a tyrannical patriarch like your father or an American money-grubber like your brother.

Rachel got another response to her letter. Several helpful neighbors, members of the Gradz *shul* who were also readers of the *Forward*, had no trouble figuring out her identity and rushed to show the paper to her father. By the time she got home that night, he had worked himself into a frenzy, and he beat her severely with a strap. "If you ever dare slander your family to the freethinkers again," he swore, "you will be cast out and be dead to me and your mother from that day on."

But Rachel was not deterred. The next evening after work, she hurried to the *Forward* office, introducing herself as the writer of the letter, and asked to see the editor. She was sent into the back room where Cahan sat, poring over European newspapers. He was a small, fine-boned man with a bristling moustache and searching, impatient eyes behind rimless glasses. He peered over them at her.

"So?" he said. "What can I do for you?"

"I'm R.C., the girl who wrote the letter you printed," she said shyly. "You said I should come here."

"Yes," he said, studying her. "You write well, popular Yiddish style, eloquent. We can use more of this kind of thing. Write us some stories about life in the neighborhood, conditions in the shop, problems that concern women. Next time we'll pay."

Rachel's eyes widened. "You'll pay me?"

"It won't be a fortune," he said drily. "And we pay only for things we print, so I wouldn't give up my job yet if I were you. But we'll pay something—a little at first, a little more if you write regular. Where do you work?"

"Triangle Waist."

"So write me a story about that and bring it in when you get it done."

Rachel floated home. It was too good to be true, to think

she could actually earn money by writing. Let her father rant; other men, wiser far than he, saw her true worth. Still, she'd have to think up an assumed name so she didn't get into trouble. She rolled several around on her tongue experimentally: Rosalind, Alicia. She finally settled for plain old Sadie. Sadie Waistmaker.

Looks weren't everything to Ruby. But they were a lot. She also liked good clothes and an air of wild romance. By the age of twelve she had found the paragon of all these qualities in Boris Thomashevsky, star of the Yiddish stage. She pasted his picture on the wall above her bed, where she could look at it every night. She dreamed of his coming through the door of 123 Rivington Street, dressed in cloth of gold as he had been in *Alexander, Crown Prince of Jerusalem,* sinking down on his *zaftig* knee, throwing out his arms and declaiming, "As on wings I come, beloved, here to thee."

Ruby saw all of his plays at the People's Theater, saving every penny she could get her hands on for matinee tickets, or begging benefit tickets from her father (for Thomashevsky, once a cigar worker himself, was sympathetic to Moyshe's union and often let them stage benefits). Ruby loved the heady atmosphere of the theater: the shirtwaist girls and milliners come to see their idol, the mothers with their crying babies, the peddlers of candy and soda. She always got an egg cream herself when she had a few cents to spare—not often, since even the cheapest seats cost a whole quarter. Ruby enjoyed a crowd, but best of all, she loved the plays. She loved them all indiscriminately. She loved the ones about ghetto girls who were kidnapped by Chinamen in pigtails and forced into white slavery. She loved the ones about poor students who were falsely accused of committing some terrible murder or of being revolutionaries, sentenced to death or Siberia, and only saved at the last minute by the love of a good woman. She loved the jolly songs and dances that interspersed these sad tales, lightening them up a little; and her heart expanded till it seemed to fill the whole room when the high voice and rolling r's of the great Thomashevsky throbbed to the tune of one of his wonderful songs about his *Yiddisheh mama.* Even Hamlet took time off to sing such a tune, broken-hearted at his mother's grave.

Hamlet was one of her favorite plays, partly because Thomashevsky—portly, with a noble profile and long black curls—looked so nice in tights. Rachel, always a big reader, told her scornfully that this play was not the real *Hamlet* at all, but what did Ruby care? It was real enough for her. Poor Hamlet! His father died of grief in his home town in Russia when Hamlet's uncle—a wicked rabbi from a crazy sect—courted his wife away from him. Hamlet, meanwhile, off studying at the seminary, had to rush home for his father's funeral, only to find out it was his mother's wedding besides. What a scene! Aided by his faithful girlfriend Ophelia, Hamlet gave the sinners a real piece of his mind, reciting beautifully right in the middle of the stage so you could get a good look at him in his costume. And what thanks did he get? His uncle accused him of being a revolutionary and tried to get him sent to Siberia!

Moving as this scene was to Ruby, it could not equal the pathos of the one in the graveyard with the windmill, the arms of which actually moved. When Ophelia was brought in on her bier, Hamlet almost tore his clothes off in the frenzy of his mourning; then he got married to her even as she lay there dead. Ruby's tears flowed unconfined when he followed by dying of a broken heart himself.

After matinees, she often waited outside the theater with a score of other girls, hoping to see Thomashevsky come out in his top hat, silk cape, and gold-headed cane and get into his chauffeured limousine. He ennobled the whole neighborhood. If only she could meet a man like the great Thomashevsky.

Sarah had been waiting outside the shop since six-thirty; you'd better not be late at Triangle or they'd send you home and you'd lose a whole day's pay. When the bell rang, she filed up the four flights of stairs with the rest and went to her place in one of the dark back rows of machines. Only the front rows got any daylight and the manager had not yet turned on the gas. He never did until work was actually beginning, one of the small economies that made the firm so profitable, though it meant the girls had to stumble to their machines and set up in near darkness.

"What are we working on today?" she asked Becky Zinssher, a robust, talkative girl who worked next to her. It

was Sarah's second week at Triangle Waist and she was still
learning the ropes.

"Probably those cotton batiste waists we did yesterday,"
said Becky, "the ones with the ruffled jabots."

Sarah groaned. "I hate that batiste. It's so light it always
gets pulled threads."

"Everything this year has such high necks," commented
Mrs. Rosenblum on her other side, "with these fancy ties on
them." She nursed her year-old baby as she spoke. Every
morning she carried him to the factory to nurse. When work
began, his eight-year-old sister carried him home tied to her
back. At noon the girl brought him back, wailing with hunger, for his next feeding. The baby was not thriving on this
schedule.

"He looks peaked and blue, like my baby brother before he
got diphtheria," whispered Becky, but Mrs. Rosenblum had
little choice. Her husband had come down with the dreaded
"sweater's disease," tuberculosis, and was coughing his life
away in a charity sanitarium out West, leaving her with three
mouths to feed, including her own, which she seldom had
either the time or energy to fill. Sometimes her daughter fed
her while she was nursing.

The forelady passed down the row, depositing bundles at
each girl's place. "You're on buttonholes again," she told
Sarah. She gave Becky the job of pleating, tying, and attach-
ing the lacy jabots that would spill from this shirtwaist's collar down its front.

Shirtwaists, or high-fashion fitted blouses, had come into
existence at almost the same time as the throngs of women
workers who bought them, shortly before Sarah came to the
United States. They were popularized on every magazine
cover by the famous illustrator Charles Dana Gibson and his
"Gibson girls." Perfect for office work under a dark suit,
acceptable for factory use with the sleeves rolled up, the shirtwaist was an item designed specifically for the needs of the
working girl, enabling her to vary the least expensive part of
her costume several times a week instead of having to wear
the same dress to work every day. As the press frequently
noted, the ready-made shirtwaist was a truly democratic article, available in a wide range of fabrics, styles, and prices,
adaptable, modern, and quintessentially American. The
cheaper shirtwaists were poorly made in extreme styles that

changed radically from year to year; their seams were small, without "give," and their stitching, done by learners, was seldom perfect. It didn't matter. Priced to sell at a dollar or two, these blouses were meant to last a season, not a lifetime; they could be discarded when the style changed. Hannah was scandalized by these poorly sewn, disposable garments and had not yet stopped talking about the shoddy workmanship and poor design of the first cheap waist Sarah had bought three years before. But if her mother preferred durable clothes with a handmade aesthetic, Sarah followed most of her generation in choosing cheapness and frequent change.

The shirtwaist industry, centered in New York, was dominated by two or three major firms like Triangle Waist and Leiserson's, but it was also served by hundreds of tiny "cockroach shops," which sprang up one week and vanished the next, victims of poor managerial judgment, cutthroat competition, or insufficient capital. These tiny shops were able to stay in business only because of the way they exploited their workers, some of whom slaved twenty hours a day in the busy season, at rates that were forever declining. These workers were mostly female, largely underage, and entirely unorganized. Although there was a shirtwaist union, Local 25 of the International Ladies' Garment Workers' Union, it was remarkable mainly for its smallness and lack of success.

During the busy season, Local 25 would pick up members because people were earning enough money to pay dues. But when the slack season came, their money would vanish and they would drop out, leaving only a few diehards like Sarah. "How can you organize in an industry like this?" Abe Baroff, president of the local, would cry. "How do you even find the thousand little cockroach shops? And who do you send to talk to them when you have only twenty members to begin with and they're all working full-time themselves?"

He knew the answer. So did Sarah. Every good Russian radical knew it—the shirtwaist industry could be organized only by a general strike that could reach all the workers. Nothing else would keep the little shops from doing work on the sly for the big ones and undermining any strike. But what did that mean Sarah should do at Triangle Waist?

"It's easy for you to say, Use tactics," she told her father.

"But the forelady watches us all like a hawk and if I make any trouble, they'll fire me just like that."

"Look for the issues, the ones that bother everybody, not just you young girls. What are the men upset about? The older women? The religious people?"

"I don't know. I mainly talk to girls my own age."

"Then find out," he said. "There are three floors in the shop, aren't there? You probably haven't even met anybody on the other two yet. You have to wait; it takes more than a couple of weeks to get something going."

So Sarah waited and looked around, sewing mechanically while she tried to understand.

"Slow down, Sarah," hissed Becky. "You're stacking up on me." There was a big pile at Sarah's right hand and a much smaller one at Becky's.

"Oh, I'm sorry," she said. Sarah was a fast worker—too fast sometimes. Though she was paid by the piece, it was pointless to pile up a greater number of shirtwaists than Becky could handle. The piece rate for buttonholing would be lowered if the owners thought the work could be done so quickly. Then the other girls who did buttonholes would get mad at Sarah because they would all have to work harder to make the same money. Nobody with any sense would want to be a pacemaker, even to get in the bosses' good books. Sarah put her work down and gazed furtively about her. Rows on rows of girls working, heads bent in concentration. Looking up, she saw the pipes festooned with great swags of lint and dust and filth, hanging like wisteria blossoms from vines. The place was foul.

"Tra la la," caroled Becky suddenly, and Sarah awoke from her daydreams to find Bernstein, the manager, bearing down on her with murder in his eye. Resting was strictly against company rules. She pretended she was rubbing out a spot in the material, while Becky created a diversion, singing loudly in atrociously accented music-hall English:

When you know you're not forgotten,
By the girl you can't forget,
When you find the girl you left behind
Is thinking of you yet . . .

Distracted, Bernstein passed Sarah and snapped, "That's

enough, Becky, this isn't the Palace," while Becky retorted with a grin. "But, boss, I have to practice my act. My big chance is just around the corner." Even Bernstein had to laugh at Becky. "Not during working hours," he said, and walked on.

Sarah breathed a sigh of relief. "Thanks, Becky," she said, and the other girl winked at her.

"Appetizing" Solly Fein, known to his intimates as "the landladies' delight," was a veteran of boarding-house sieges and kitchen-table campaigns. He changed lodgings frequently, seeking out likely prospects in the street as he peddled his wares. This way of life had many advantages: An amorous landlady was known to be more generous in the items of food and laundry, and the sexual benefits prevented him from throwing himself away on the wrong girl. Anyway, he preferred mature women.

Hannah gave him no more than a speculative thought or two before he moved in, but then she found that she couldn't get away from the man. He was around the house more and more, and it was upsetting, the way he would put his hand on her sometimes when no one was looking or press his knee against hers at the table. She always frowned and pulled away, but he smiled meltingly and paid no attention. She was becoming flustered. She didn't want to make a thing of it by asking him to leave or by starting an argument. Besides, that could be embarrassing—what if he denied everything and laughed at her? So she decided to ignore him. After all, she didn't even like the man. Still, he was a handsome one, rosy-cheeked, fleshy, strong you could tell, and hairy on the arms and back. She could see the hair on the shoulders through his shirt when he was sweaty. It gave her a funny twinge.

They were often alone together. Moyshe was never home at night and Sarah would work late, then go to the union or out with her friends. Ruby went to the settlement house three nights a week for lessons in modern housekeeping, fine sewing, and dancing, and the other boarder, who had been a chaperone at first, had suddenly decided to move to Cleveland. So Solly and Hannah would sit in the little dark kitchen of an evening—she refused to go into the front room with a man like him—and he would tell her dirty stories. Terrible, they were. She was ashamed to listen with her bare face hanging out, and she would slap at him and tell him what she thought; but she had to admit some of them were funny, and sometimes she could not help letting out a big belly laugh. Then he would smile into her eyes and tell her how beautiful she was.

It didn't mean a thing to her.

But she was lonely. For the first time in years she had some breathing room during the day, and all she could do with it was mourn her dead. The pain hadn't lessened by being postponed. She couldn't stop asking herself who was tending her mother's grave, and Rosa's. She didn't even know if Shmuel and Becca were still alive; she hadn't heard from them since the second pogrom, the one in 1905. Longing for family left behind, for the town she had lived in so long, she felt like cursing God for making her choose between home and survival.

"Curse God and die," the devil said to Job. What about God—did He hear her thoughts all the way across the ocean? Was He in America too? Never observant herself, Hannah had been content to leave matters of ritual to her mother and religious speculations to her husband. Moyshe, for his part, seemed to think she'd taken on his atheism with his name. In fact, she had simply put off considering such questions for lack of time. Now they swooped down on her with eagles' claws. If there was a God, what was He doing? Where had He gone? Had He fled earth in disgust? Had He abandoned the Jews? One or two of her mother's stories hinted at this possibility; others blamed the Jews for their own misfortunes or spoke of the glory to be when the Messiah came. He was a long time coming. In the meantime, she searched for some meaning in the tragedies of her life and could find none.

If only she could talk to someone about it. But Ruby was just a kid, Sarah was too preoccupied, and Moyshe, if he had listened at all, would only have made speeches about superstition. Anyway, it was years since she and he had discussed such things. And how could she believe he would take her seriously, he, who had been to the *yeshiva* and had read so many books. If he had any questions of his own, he certainly didn't tell her about them. All he did was go to union meetings, radical forums, Workman's Circle educationals, socialist rallies, who knows what, as though he didn't even know what country he was in.

To be a revolutionary in Russia was one thing. It was dangerous and unwise, but at least you could understand it. But to be a revolutionary in America was crazy. There was no czar here. There were no pogroms. Jews could work at any kind of job they wanted. Anyone could better himself. Only a born malcontent would be an agitator in a country like this. Yet Moyshe still complained about everything the government did. Obstinate and ungrateful, Hannah thought; he had gotten the habit of being discontented and now he couldn't stop. A dog without teeth still gnaws at a bone, and what can you expect from an ox but beef?

If he loved her, it would be different, but he never gave her a look. You'd think she was an old hag. She was only forty, not a gray hair in her head, her breasts still firm. Maybe there was a little too much padding around the hips but some men liked that. Some men appreciated her. Was it wrong to enjoy the compliment? Was it wrong to have thoughts? If people were damned for having bad thoughts, everybody would be damned. And who was she to worry, when she wasn't even sure there was a God?

It wasn't that Moyshe neglected her completely. He still did the expected on Friday nights and occasionally at other times, but you could tell his heart wasn't in it anymore. A minute or two and it was over and done with, not like the old days. She couldn't help wondering if it would be the same way with another man. Solly Fein wasn't the man her husband was. He was a little vulgar, a little gross, but what good was Moyshe's sensitivity to her? She didn't get any of the benefits. Better a steady dime than a dollar that never comes. Solly Fein might not be perfect but he was around.

One summer night, something happened. Solly was sitting at the table reading the *Tageblatt*, moving his lips with the effort, she noticed. She was sitting there, peeling potatoes into a bowl in her lap. He wasn't paying attention to her; his arm lay relaxed on the table: big, rosy, well-muscled. It was covered with a sprinkling of reddish brown hairs lying flat against the skin, gleaming in the light from the lamp. Each little hair shone tiny and distinct; she could have counted them. She couldn't look away. Her breathing became hoarse and irregular and a melting sensation turned her legs to jelly and rooted her to the chair. She could not have moved for a dollar. Suddenly he looked up and met her eyes. Blushing like a girl, she jumped to her feet muttering, "I'm going to catch some air," and fled from the room. She heard him chuckle behind her, and wondered with dreadful excitement if he would come down the stairs after her. But he did not. He knew when to wait.

The next week was his birthday. She baked him a small sponge cake and he brought home a bottle of schnapps to celebrate. They had three glasses each. Hannah got giddy and as she struggled to her feet, she let him put his arm around her. Suddenly he was pulling her up next to him, his hand going all the way under her arm and onto her breast. As his left hand cupped her breast, her nipple lifted by itself and hardened responsively—she could no nothing to stop it. She felt as though she had no bones at all and she could only lean heavily against him. He laughed a little, and still saying nothing, turned her to him. Then his big hands went up under her skirt, closing tightly around her buttocks, stroking her slowly, softly, and pushing her insistently against him. In front he was as hard as a rock and big, pressing himself into her, grinding until she moaned. It had been so long since someone had really wanted her. Then they were in the back room and he was on top of her and the rest was more or less as she had known it would be from the time she began to think about it: the little curly hairs on the back of his shoulders, his broad haunches moving under her hands, the salty smell of him all over her. She tried to remain detached, as if this terrible thing were being done by some other woman but she had no control over herself at all. She writhed and cried out like an animal. He was well satisfied. He laughed in her ear, the whiskey heavy on his breath, his big lips all over her face as he kissed her and rubbed himself against her luxuriantly, again and again until she cried out with pleasure.

The next morning she could not meet anyone's eyes, but Ruby told her she looked pretty, like she'd had a good night's sleep, and Solly smacked his red lips as he ate.

All that summer she coupled with him fiercely, as if she were frantic to make up for her many years of loss and knew she had only a short time in which to do so. The moment they were alone he would smile at her or run his hand carelessly over her and she would become weak, wet, barely able to stand. He would take her without a word, smiling all the while, caressing her, rubbing up against her until she cried out for him and he felt a gush like a fountain spurting forth from inside her, watering the desert. It was that gush that made him stay so long, that and the knowledge that he brought it out of her against her will. For she still did not like the man. He was a poor thing next to her husband. He thought of nothing but his wallet and his *putz* and his gut. But he was there and Moyshe was not, and he wanted her, and with him for a moment she could forget everything but the need of her body. That he cared for her no more than she did for him was evident; what would happen when one of them tired she did not know. She also worried about someone finding out. What would the girls think? But Ruby was too dreamy to notice, and while Sarah disliked Solly, she was totally involved in her own life. As for Moyshe—when did he even look?

At least these worries kept her from thinking about God all the time. Still, when she was alone, guilt descended upon her like a leaden cloud, and she knew with dread that God indeed existed and was in America. How could she excuse her conduct? A light woman, unfaithful to her husband with a man she didn't even love—what could be said in her defense? At such moments she would move restlessly around the apartment as if driven by some wind. If not for fear, sinning would be sweet, so the saying went, but she was not ready to stop yet and if she was going to do it, she should at least enjoy it. Hadn't she suffered enough? If God had been attending to business and had left her Bubbe and Rosa, she would never have done such a thing. She wouldn't have been able to with Bubbe in the house. God is the one that should feel bad, not me, she thought; still, she knocked the wooden table superstitiously as she passed, just in case it would do her some good.

III

The hot August sun still beat down upon the park bench in Washington Square even though the long workday had ended. The five girls in shirtwaists and dark skirts sat there wilted, in exhaustion, listlessly examining their pay envelopes.

"Every year I make less instead of more," said Rachel. "Shouldn't it be the other way around?"

"I think they took out half my pay this time," complained Becky Zinssher. She counted up. "I lost two of those numbers they pin on the sleeves and got docked a dollar each even though I finished the work. Then I was late once, another dime. Needles, thread, electricity, rent for those lousy crates they give us to sit on—at these prices you'd think they could at least give you a chair. There's nothing left in here hardly. I wanted to get a ticket to a show but I'll be lucky if I can buy a soda."

"I don't know what I'd do if I didn't live home," said Fanny Jacobs, a tired-looking fifteen-year-old who had been working at Triangle for four years. "These girls who have to board out and save money to bring their families over from Russia—how do they do it?"

"Why? How much money do you get to keep?" said Rachel. "I have to give my mother my whole pay envelope."

"I keep fifty cents for clothes," said Fanny.

"Seven dollars is all I got," said Molly Hurwitz, shaking her head. She was a pretty girl with long brown hair elaborately done in a big pompadour. "At the rate it's going, I'll be working for nothing by the time I'm twenty. My God, what a life. Last night when I was coming home along the Bowery, this guy says to me, 'Hey, what's a pretty girl like you doing wasting it in a factory? I could tell you how to have an easy life and make good money, too.' What do you think, girls? Are we just being stupid?"

"Oh, come on," said Fanny uncomfortably.

Becky stood and put her hand upon her breast, raising her eyes dramatically to the heavens. "Oh, Father in Heaven," she intoned, "look down upon this frail creature and increase her wages that she may not sin. When she walks down the Bowery tonight and the foul villain plies her with wine and deceiving compliments, will this poor factory girl yield? Will she be defiled?"

"Never!" Rachel rose and took Becky's hands. "She will look the villain in the eye and sing," and they chorused together:

> Stand back, villain! Go your way,
> Here I will no longer stay,
> Although you were a Marquis or an Earl.
> You may tempt the upper classes
> With your villainous demitasses,
> But Heaven will protect a working girl!

Fanny and Molly applauded politely but Sarah ignored them, staring absently into space.

"What's the matter with you?" said Becky, gently kicking her ankle.

"I'm thinking."

"Don't tell me, I know, about the union. Kiddo, if you can bring a union into Triangle Waist, you can work miracles. I'll let you be my manager and get me into the Ziegfeld Follies like Fanny Brice."

The five girls were all in Local 25 and had signed up some sixty others. But it wasn't enough. There were four hundred workers in the Triangle Waist Company, and too many of them were still in the company union, the Triangle Waist Benefit Society, formed to keep a real union out. Its president was the company manager, Bernstein, and the rest of its officers were all relatives of the two big bosses, Isaac Harris and Max Blanck. Yet people stayed in it, particularly the older workers who had been at Triangle for a long time, seeming to believe that they were part of a "happy family," as Bernstein put it. The younger, more fiery workers who were discontented had been terrorized by his goon, Jake Goldfarb, or by the bosses' forelady relatives, who crept around in the new rubber-soled shoes that Sarah was sure had been invented just for them.

Like most of the big garment factories, Triangle was run on the team system. Bernstein hired contractors, men who were usually tailors, and promised them so many dollars to make so many shirtwaists. He gave each one a team to work under him: two basters, three operators, one finisher (usually a very young girl, paid next to nothing), and a presser. All of these were women except the presser, and the contractor had to pay all of them out of his assigned sum. Since Bernstein was always lowering the piece rates and the amount he paid the contractors, the girls' wages declined until the average pay was six or seven dollars a week, and each girl had two bosses over her, the contractor and Bernstein himself. It was a system designed for minimum efficiency and maximum stress.

Of all the factories in which Sarah had worked, Triangle was the most repressive. There were rules for everything. No talking. No singing. No leaving your own department. No eating. No dawdling in the bathroom—Bernstein had a special spy outside the toilet door. No soliciting money for any purpose. No belonging to outside organizations—that meant unions. The girls were searched at the end of each day and all the doors, even the doors to the fire escapes, were kept locked to prevent petty theft.

"Ouch, my head," said Molly, poking around in her pompadour. "They searched my hair again and pushed the rat out of place."

Sarah was taken aback. "What do they think you're going to hide in your hair?"

"Bernstein told me once they found a girl who had four shirtwaists bundled up inside her pompadour instead of a rat."

"That I would like to see," said Becky.

"Did you get any union cards today?" Rachel asked Sarah.

Looking furtively around, Sarah undid one button of her shirtwaist and reached inside her corset. "Look," she said, pulling out two bits of red cardboard. "Belle Grossman and Lily Pestalozzi."

"How did you get Lily? She doesn't speak any English."

The company had recently been hiring Italian girls and seating them next to Russians. Since few of either nationality spoke English, it made them harder to organize.

"She knew the word for union," said Sarah. "That was the only one she needed."

"So we have more than sixty cards now. Not bad," said Rachel.

"Yes, but we only have girls. We have to figure out a way to get some men and some of the older women with families. Otherwise they'll scab on us if we go out."

"It's harder for them," said Becky. "They've got kids so they're scared. Molly, you were there when they had that strike a couple of years ago. Were the older women in that?"

"Sure," said Molly. "We all were."

"What happened?"

Molly told the story. There had been two subcontractors, Jake and Morrie, who wanted more money to pay their workers. Bernstein had told them to get out of the shop if they weren't satisfied, and sent Goldfarb to throw them out. Jake had yelled to his fellow workers for help, and when Goldfarb threw him down the stairs, everyone got up and walked down right after him. They stayed out for three days, but none of them knew what to do and there was no money for benefits in the union treasury, so they ended up going back to work. After that, Bernstein brought in the benefit society. Molly and Fanny, who had been at Triangle the longest, were members.

"But they never hold any meetings," said Fanny. "They take dues out of my pay envelope but I never get anything for them."

Sarah snorted in disgust. She was continually amazed at what other people were willing to put up with. "How can you belong to a union that has your boss for the head of it? Don't you know your friends from your enemies?"

"Sarah," said Rachel warningly, "not everybody has a father like yours."

"I don't have a father at all," said Fanny in a small voice.

"I'm sorry, Fan," mumbled Sarah. "I didn't mean it." She was doing her best to control her tongue, but though she had managed to stay out of trouble at work, she still blurted out things when she was with her friends and got them mad at her half the time. She sighed. It was hard. The pressures of the factory got on her nerves, the petty persecutions made her furious, and there was no one to yell at. "What do they think we are!" she would rage on the way home, and Rachel would answer, "I know. But watch it. And watch your face, too— it's almost as bad as your mouth. Anybody can tell what you're thinking just by looking at you."

Now Sarah made her face still and listened.

"They told us it would be a benefit society when it was set up," said Molly, "but they never pay out any benefits when people get sick. I bet they wouldn't even pay burial money. Probably Bernstein just keeps it all."

"They should give benefits for the high holidays," said Fanny. "Poor old Rabinowitz told me he owes money yet from Passover because he stayed out and he had to buy special food for his whole family. Now that Rosh Hashanah's coming he's scared of the expense. That's not right. They should give these men and older women with families something."

Rachel stared at her. "I bet a lot of the older workers would like that idea," she said slowly, "the ones in the benefit society."

"Who wouldn't like some more money?" said Becky.

Sarah and Rachel looked at each other. "Money for the high holidays," Sarah whispered, "a benefit. I would never have thought of it in a thousand years. Fanny, Molly, why don't you bring it up to the benefit society? You're both in it, you've been paying out all this time—how about somebody getting something back?"

"I don't want to get into any trouble," said Fanny.

"You won't get in trouble if there are enough of you," said Sarah. "Ask around. I bet everyone will think it's a great idea. Who could possibly object? Except the bosses' relatives, of course."

A week later forty workers told Bernstein they wanted to see some of the benefit society money to give a ten-dollar holiday bonus to the men and women with families. One of the big bosses, Max Blanck, was in the office. He said it would be all right, though Fanny told Sarah that Bernstein looked like he'd have a heart attack. The workers in the benefit society were jubilant. But when they went in for their checks at the end of the day, Bernstein stormed at them. He said it was a plot to destroy the benefit society by emptying its treasury, and he wouldn't sign the checks. He said he would lend them money if they were so hard up and take it out of their pay a little at a time.

The workers were infuriated—to be raised so high and cast so low. They had already spent the money in their minds. What kind of a benefit society never paid anything out? What had happened to their money? Had Bernstein pocketed it? How could they even find out? If only they had a real union! Acting on information from Sarah and Rachel, Local 25 called a meeting for Triangle workers on September 22, held in secret to prevent spying. "Come alone," Sarah warned. "Don't tell anybody where you're going. You never know who's a fink around here."

Clinton Hall was dark as the workers approached it. The shades were drawn and it was impossible to see from the outside that anything was happening. That night one hundred fifty Triangle workers joined Local 25—including every member of the benefit society except for Bernstein, Goldfarb, and the bosses' relatives.

The next night Rachel and Sarah went to the union hall to report. When Rachel saw that Joe Klein, a handsome young man on the union executive board, was there, she poked Sarah in the ribs. Everyone knew Joe had a thing for Sarah.

"Hello, girls," he said, smiling a welcome. "Going to the dance?"

"Going?" said Sarah. "Our local's giving it."

Local 25, wasting no time in following up on the Triangle meeting, had scheduled a grand ball to be given jointly with the *Forward*, on Saturday, September 25. There were going to be two bands, one Jewish, one Italian, and speakers in three languages. The union had reason to celebrate; the Triangle events were just one sign that the shirtwaist industry was finally starting to organize. As far back as July, workers in Rosen Brothers, a small shop, struck when the management refused to meet the contractors' prices. They stayed out for five weeks and won all their demands. Their victory encouraged another strike, at the large Leiserson factory at 26 West Seventeenth Street, where a hundred union members walked out on September 3. When Leiserson hired strong-arm men or *shtarkers* to intimidate the pickets in front of his factory, a number of the strikers were severely beaten. One member of the union's executive board, Clara Lemlich, even had to be hospitalized. True to its socialist mission, the *Forward* spread the news through the Yiddish-speaking community—but the Italian girls whom Leiserson hired as scabs could not read Yiddish. They could look out of their shop window, however, and see other workers being beaten. After a week or so, four or five Italian girls walked out in solidarity, and joined the union, to be soon followed by others. The officers of Local 25 were elated; hence, the ball.

"Are you going to dance with me, Sarah?" asked Joe Klein. She backed away with a grin.

"I'll dance with anyone who's a union man," she said, then ran down the stairs with Rachel right behind her.

"He really likes you, Sarah," said Rachel, as they walked down the street arm in arm.

Sarah shrugged. She liked Joe Klein well enough, but thought him a little light-minded. While she enjoyed his attentions, they also made her uneasy. In some ways she still felt as she had when she was eleven and swore she'd never marry. Men were not that important. "I can't be bothered worrying about Joe Klein," she told Rachel airily. "Once you start thinking about boys, you stop being able to think about anything else. I've seen it happen lots of times."

"You mean you're never going to get interested in boys?" It was a state of mind Rachel could hardly imagine.

"I don't say never," Sarah assured her. "But I want to make my mark first. I want to do something that will make people sit up and take notice, like Joan of Arc or Sidney Carton in *A Tale of Two Cities*." They had read Dickens in school.

"But this is America. How can you be guillotined here?"

Sarah had to concede the point. "I don't know what I'll do exactly, but I'm certainly not going to fall in love, at least not until after the strike. This isn't the old country, where you have to get married by seventeen or be an old maid. I've got time and we both have plenty of other things to worry about right now."

The next day at work, her words were confirmed. Bernstein called an open meeting of the benefit society, to which all were invited.

"Somebody ratted," whispered Rachel. This was indeed the case. Bernstein was irate.

"I have been informed that some of you girls are talking about a union," he said mournfully. "This fills me with sadness. I've been like a father to you and now you stab me in the back. I've done my best to make you happy. We all have. We kept the factory open when we really didn't have enough work just so you girls would get paid. We took lofts in the most modern building on the East Side just so you could be in a clean, safe place, with steel scaffolding and fire escapes."

"Only the doors to them are locked," whispered Sarah. Rachel kicked her.

"You can't belong to two rival organizations at the same time," he continued. "That's against company rules. You're going to have to choose between our benefit society and this outsiders' union. Why should strangers with axes to grind come in here and disrupt the peaceful atmosphere we've always maintained? Do you want to pay dues to some fancy walking delegate with a diamond stickpin instead of paying them into your own benefit fund? Our benefit society operates for the mutual good of everyone here. Anyone who is a traitor to it is not the kind of person we want to employ at the Triangle Waist Company. So you have two days to choose which you want to belong to. I know some of you have been hot-headed and acted in a way you now regret, going to strangers with family problems. It's not too late to come back into the family. It's up to you."

Over the next two days, the tension in the factory became palpable. No one was completely sure that the older workers would remain firm. On Saturday afternoon at closing time, Bernstein called them together once more.

"I've come for your decision," he said. "You can all join the benefit society now. I have your cards here."

A pool of silence settled in the room, growing longer and wider until it became unbearable. Then old Rabinowitz stepped forward. "It might as well be me," he said. "Boss, we tried out the benefit society already and it didn't work so good. We got no benefits. Now we're going to try out the union for a while."

Bernstein stared at him in cold disbelief. Goldfarb, the strong-arm man, stepped toward him, clenching his fists. Rabinowitz looked around in helpless appeal. There was an awful pause.

Then Sarah stepped forward and took the old man's right

arm. Rachel took his left, and the other workers crowded
around him until he was ringed by a solid mass of people.
Goldfarb looked uncertain. He had never been required to hit
women workers. He turned to Bernstein for instructions. With
an impatient gesture, Bernstein rose and went back into the
office, followed by Goldfarb and the bosses' relatives. The
workers stood there, staring at each other, slowly beginning
to smile. Rachel bit trembling lips; tears welled up in Sarah's
eyes.

"Oh boy," said Becky Zinssher loudly. "Oh boy, am I
proud of us! If Florenz Ziegfeld himself came in here right
now to offer me a job, I'd tell him to go jump in the river."

Their mood of elation held through the dance that night.
Every Triangle worker who had not yet joined Local 25 did
so, while the music played and Sarah danced on and on with
Joe Klein, laughter bubbling up inside her.

That Monday work began as usual. At ten in the morning,
Bernstein blew the whistle. "I have an announcement," he
said, and read from a piece of paper. "The Triangle Waist
Company regrets to inform you that we are closing for a
month because of lack of work." He walked out. The workers stood dumbfounded.

"It's true business is off," said Fanny doubtfully. "Some
other places are closing down."

"Even if there's not as much work as last month, there's
enough to keep open," said Rachel.

Sarah ran to Clinton Hall. "Something is fishy," she said.
The next day proved her correct. The *Tageblatt* carried a big
box ad: "Three hundred workers wanted Triangle Waist
Company. No experience necessary. Union members need
not apply."

"LOCKOUT AT TRIANGLE WAIST!" screamed the
Forward in response. "UNION DECLARES STRIKE!"
Sarah was one of the first to volunteer for picket duty.

"I thought unions were legal in America," said Moyshe
sardonically after the first week of the shirtwaist strike.

Labor organization in 1909 was in a no-man's land between respectability and criminality. While the trade-union
movement was growing, especially among skilled craftsmen,
many people still regarded it as un-American. In 1903, a
presidential commission was set up to arbitrate a coal strike.

It laid out the government's approach to labor relations, a philosophical defense of scabbing: "The right to remain at work where others have ceased to work, or to engage anew in work which others have abandoned, is part of the personal liberty of a citizen, that can never be surrendered, and every infringement thereof merits and should receive the stern denouncement of the law."

Even the use of the word "scab" was sometimes considered such an infringement by the courts, which made no pretense at neutrality in battles between capital and labor. In 1908, a year before the shirtwaist strike, the Supreme Court ruled that the Sherman Anti-Trust Act applied to unions just as much as to monopoly corporations, judging that the hat makers of Danbury, Connecticut, were members of "a vast combination" trying to force employers to unionize "against their will" in order to "control the employment of labor." In one decision after another, the courts ruled out boycotts, protective legislation, the closed shop, and even peaceful picketing.

So thoroughly was the majesty of the law on the side of the manufacturers that the owners of Triangle Waist could probably have obtained an injunction against picketing that would have crippled the strike. But either because they were ignorant of these American refinements or because they judged the union so pitiful that such expense was unnecessary, they did not do so for some time.

They hired gangsters instead.

Tricker Louis Florsheim was a handsome man by anybody's standards, young, well built, healthy-looking, with that special glow found in men who make their living partly from their looks: actors, singers, politicians, pimps. Like Ruby Levy, Tricker was a follower of the stage, indiscriminately patronizing both the Yiddish theater and the English melodramas on the Bowery. He often said he might have become an actor himself had his start in life been more propitious, but, alas, he was an orphan, denied the benefits of a mother's love. She died before he left Russia with his father, who followed her to heaven in short order, after contracting tuberculosis his first year in New York. At the age of ten, Tricker was left to the tender mercies of his aunt,

Shprinzel Garfinkle, wife of Kalman Garfinkle, the kosher butcher of Rivington Street.

Tricker disliked being a poor relation and spent as little time at the Garfinkles as possible; he received his education on the street instead. Running with the Midget Gorillas, he played hooky, stole candy and fruit, wrecked pushcarts, fought the neighboring gangs for turf and reputation, and harassed the women on Allen Street. Many of his childhood friends in the Midget Gorillas—Joe Klein, for one—grew up to become respectable citizens, but Tricker was unusually bold and tough and caught the attention of an older boy named Crazy Butch, leader of a gang of "kid dips" or pickpockets. An orphan like Tricker Louis, Crazy Butch had slept on the streets of the Lower East Side from the time he was eight, progressing from paperboy to pickpocket. On turning thirteen, he celebrated his bar mitzvah by stealing a dog, naming it Rabbi, and teaching it to snatch purses whenever he whistled "Dixie." Tricker became part of his bicycle gang. Crazy Butch would ride down Second Avenue on his bike until he found an opportunity to crash into a pedestrian, preferably an old woman. As a crowd of bystanders gathered, he would scream at her, push her around, perhaps even kick her, and while the indignant crowd's attention was thus engaged, his kid dips would go through their pockets.

By the time he was fifteen, Tricker Louis was making twelve dollars a week and spending most of it in the fifty-cent brothels on Elizabeth Street. He had gotten his first taste of sex from the tough babies who ran with the Midget Gorillas, and had gone on to experiment in the Jewish houses on Allen Street, but the women there were too old and too homey. They reminded him uncomfortably of his aunt. The Elizabeth Street girls were young—very young, usually no more than fourteen and sometimes only ten, sold to American entrepreneurs by their *padrones* in Italy. Men came from all over the city on Saturday nights, lining up outside the houses in a carny atmosphere created by the pullers-in, who yelled, "Come on, fellows, come and get it. Little heifers fresh off the boat from Palermo and Napoli, a whole ship full of virgins just come in!" But Tricker soon learned that if he went to Elizabeth Street at off hours, things were quieter and more relaxed. The little white-faced bewildered girls who spoke no English were pathetically grateful for a kind word or a handful of sweets, while the older ones—whom he preferred because they were less terrified—would soon do anything he asked for no charge if he spoke to them politely and told them he loved them.

Though the Garfinkles disapproved of Tricker's activities, they could do little to control him. After his third arrest, his uncle Kalman kicked him out of the house, saying he was bad for business. From that time on, Tricker lived off women. He had two regulars, Ida Odessa and Sally the Goose, and a rapid turnover of young girls. His name was a byword on Rivington Street, where all the children had been warned to stay away from him, since he preserved an interest in his old neighborhood, keeping an eye open for any promising young beauties coming into bloom. Ruby Levy had possibilities, he thought, and he always smiled nicely and raised his derby when he saw her, unless her parents were around. Tricker had a healthy respect for Moyshe Levy's size, though nothing but scorn for his political opinions. He was a Tammany man himself, proud of the fact that Big Tim Sullivan, boss of the Lower East Side, had spoken kindly to him and promised to use him in the next election. If he got into politics, people would have to show a little manners and stop spitting on the sidewalk when he passed. Tricker hungered for reputation and was bitterly hurt by the attitude of people on his old block. Just because he wasn't dumb enough to slave away in a factory getting consumption, they looked down on him.

People had such stupid prejudices; they'd make a hero out of a bank robber, but a man who used his brains instead of his muscle and helped women make a living, they called scum. Not that Tricker planned to stay in the business all his life. Someday he would become famous, with his name in the paper for some first-class crime or other (the fantasy got vague at this point). Then people would hold him in the same awe as they did his friend Steel Kishkes, so named because he had proven that no amount of bloodshed could turn his stomach. They would even cross the street when he passed, as they did for King Indian, another friend, who dressed in black from head to toe, starting with a ten-gallon hat, and was mysterious about his ancestry, admitting only to close friends that the blood of Spanish noblemen and Indian princesses flowed in his veins. An unkind rumor had it that King Indian's father was actually Irving Mandelbaum, owner of a dry-goods store in Brownsville, but Tricker Louis considered such allegations tasteless and would not have considered repeating them.

If one of his dreams was of infamy, Tricker the Outlaw, another was that he would make the transition from a life of crime to respectability, perhaps through politics, and acquire a home, wife, family, rosy babies nestled round a fireplace—the works. Tricker was sentimental about home and hearth, never having experienced either. Someday he would marry a proper girl from a good family, and hang a picture of his mother over the mantel. He carried such a picture with him at all times, considering it his good-luck charm, and showed it tearfully to the eager little shopgirls and factory workers he took to the theater. Moved by this display of filial devotion, they thought he possessed real depth of feeling. Tricker was not above exploiting his own emotions.

"I cannot ask you to marry me now," he would say lugubriously. "I haven't enough money to provide you with the home you deserve. Just a few months of some soft work would put us both on Easy Street, but—" He would break off and shake his head. "I could never ask a woman I loved to do that for me."

Tricker specialized as a maiden-taker. He broke girls in. His looks and technique had seldom failed him: professions of love and matrimonial intentions, hot eyes looking long into theirs, whispers in their ears, lost-boy helpless looks, gentle fingers on arm and thigh. Girls were so dumb. He'd never met one he couldn't handle. After they worked for him for six months or a year, he sold them to a house. He had standing arrangements with two madams, Sadie the Chink and Jennie the Factory. It was all very businesslike.

In fact, it was becoming a bore. This kind of thing was all right for a kid, but he was twenty now, looking for more serious work. Like most of his buddies he doubled as a *bolagula* or strong-arm man, a higher-status occupation than pimping. Consequently he was pleased when he received word in September 1909 that Jake Goldfarb wanted to see him. Quickly putting on his gray derby with the concealed pistol inside, Tricker hurried over to Essex Street and the Silver Dollar Saloon, hoping that Goldfarb, who had a steady job as a gorilla in a shirtwaist factory, had something promising to offer.

The Silver Dollar Saloon, a Tammany joint whose floor

glistened with silver dollars set into the wood, was filled with
the usual grifters, gunmen, variety artists, hookers, *shtarkers*
and fixers, dope peddlers and floating politicians, holdup men
conferring in corners and racetrack touts in from New Jersey.
Goldfarb waved him over to his table and, a busy man, lost
no time in getting to the point.

"Tricker, I got some business for you," he said. "The
Triangle Shirtwaist Company is on strike. The boss wants
some gorillas to keep the pickets busy so they won't get in the
way of the scabs going in."

"How many?"

"Three or four men, seven or eight hookers. Ten dollars a
day for the *shtarkers*, seven-fifty for the girls, and fifty dollars extra for you."

"What does he want girls for?" said Tricker. The use of
sluggers was not uncommon in labor disputes, but in the past
they had always been men.

Goldfarb shrugged. "The pickets are girls, so it'll look better in court if we have girls charge them with assault. Anyway, they got his goat. The boss says he wants to put them
trouble-making broads in their place, walking up and down
the street in front of the shop like that."

"Okay."

"You won't have any trouble getting girls to do this?"

"Oh, no," said Tricker Louis. "They'll think it's a nice
change."

The third morning Sarah went picketing she found them
lined up in front of the shop: four goons, ten prostitutes, and
Bernstein. She knew one of the men, a shirttail relative of
Garfinkle the butcher. She'd seen him hanging around the
block making eyes at the girls, and the fact that she recognized Tricker Louis made her feel more secure. She noticed
he avoided meeting her eyes. He probably recognized her too
and was scared she'd tell the Garfinkles on him. If the other
shtarkers were no more than cheap neighborhood punks like
him, Sarah wasn't going to be intimidated, even when they
all started yelling insults and dirty names. She refused to admit that there was anything nerve-racking about walking up
and down the street trying to talk scabs out of going inside the
shop, never knowing when you'd be jumped by some tough
or slugged by some hooker.

Or by the cops. She and Molly were picketing together the day after the scabs came, when a prostitute stationed in front of the factory pointed to Molly's pompadour and cried, "Look at that haystack! Let's see if there's any rats in it!" She grabbed Molly's hair and began to pull viciously. Molly yelled, "You stop that!" and punched her in the eye, and the cop who'd been watching arrested Molly for assault.

Sarah was chasing a scab at the time, a little girl who raced to get in the door. "Don't you go in there," Sarah cried, heading her off. "Can't you see how they treat us? Don't work for them!" The girl, who couldn't have been more than twelve, burst into tears and bolted for Washington Square like a frightened pony. Bernstein darted out the door to catch her, but he wasn't fast enough. Turning on Sarah in frustration, he began to slap her around, calling to the police, "Arrest this bitch. She's a troublemaker. Did you see how she chased that little girl away from her job?" By the time the cop threw Sarah in the wagon, her face was black and blue. Judge Corrigan gave her and Molly suspended sentences, since it was their first offense, but warned them against further picketing. It took them just that long to learn whose side the law was on.

"I wouldn't have believed it," muttered Hannah, bathing Sarah's face that night. "Not in America."

But Sarah was lucky next to Rachel. At least her parents backed her up. When Rachel was arrested, her father almost threw her out of the house for dishonoring his name. He nagged her half to death about getting another job; the family was short of cash. "Walking the streets like a bad girl! Bringing no money in!" And Rachel's brother kept saying that if she didn't like working at Triangle, she should work for him. "Keep it in the family." They drove Rachel to distraction with their fussing; the strike itself was tense enough. Fortunately some of the workers in the Gradz *shul*, hearing of the situation, kicked in a little extra money for their rabbi, "for strike benefits."

Neither the Yiddish press, the union, nor Bernstein could imagine a strike without a male leader, so Joe Zeinfeld, a tailor, had been publicly identified as the organizer of the strike. He was often on picket duty and Bernstein singled him out for retribution. On the morning of October 4, he was picketing with Sarah when three gorillas bore down on him, pulled him into the alley behind the shop, and proceeded to beat him senseless. Running to help him from the other end of the block, screaming at the top of her voice, Sarah darted into the alley and attached herself to the back of the nearest thug, trying to pull him off. He turned, swatting at her as if she were a fly. It was Tricker Louis.

"Mind your own business, girlie," he growled, pushing her away, but when she returned to punch him, he threw her against the factory wall and broke two of her ribs. "Say anything about this to my aunt and I'll kill you next time," he whispered as he hit her methodically over and over again.

Holding her sides in agony, each breath a needle through her lungs, Sarah staggered out of the alley to the nearest cop. "Help," she breathed. "They're killing a man in there."

The cop arrested her for interfering with an officer in the conduct of his duty. She had to wait three hours in the Jefferson Market Court, nearly fainting, before she was sentenced and fined. It was late afternoon before Sarah managed to get to a doctor who could strap her ribs. She spent the next week in bed. Zeinfeld spent it in the hospital.

Rachel had been helping in the *Forward* office in her spare time, working on stories and getting experience. She was there when she heard the news. "Please let me write this one up, Mr. Cahan," she begged and he decided to feature the story, sending a photographer to get a picture of Sarah in her bed, looking unusually frail and angelic. Rachel's story, written under the pseudonym "Sadie Waistmaker," had many colorful details of the kind Cahan loved:

TRIANGLE HEROINE BEATEN BY VICIOUS GANGSTER

Interviewed by the *Forward* upon her bed of pain in her family's small but tidy Rivington Street flat, Miss Levy was asked if she recognized any of her assailants.

"You bet your life I did," she answered swiftly. "The leader was a cheap crook named Tricker Louis, whose family lives across the street from me: Garfinkle the butcher. I must have seen the rat a hundred times."

As a result of Rachel's story and the *Forward*'s many follow-up bulletins on her health, Sarah became an East Side heroine. Strangers stopped Ruby in the street to press a few pennies into her hand "to help with the doctor bills" and to ask how the strike was going.

Tricker Louis's name also became a neighborhood byword, but not in the way he had wished. Beating up a local union girl to break a strike was not looked upon kindly, and the neighbors muttered darkly about what they would do to him if he dared show his face on Rivington Street again. Everyone who went into Garfinkle's shop commented loudly on the case, glad to have a chance to score a point against Shprinzel, with her sour face and her pretensions. The butcher's family was not popular. For one thing, they priced their meat too high; people bought from them only because they gave credit, or when they were in too much of a rush to go all the way to the market, where the prices were better. Besides, the Garfinkles were clearly future allrightniks; they thought they were too good for the neighborhood—didn't their daughters buy clothes uptown?

Hannah had a particular dislike of Shprinzel Garfinkle (whom she always called *"Fafonfnik"* because of the way she talked through her nose), and she took delight in standing outside the butcher-shop door, loudly detailing her daughter's injuries to anyone who'd listen. Then she would drop her voice significantly and point to the butcher's wife within. "The apple doesn't fall far from the tree," she'd say with a wise nod.

All this upset Shprinzel Garfinkle so much that she told Tricker Louis to stay away from the shop. "It makes me sick what you did, and there's a lot of feeling in the neighborhood. The Levys have friends. It's bad for business."

Tricker couldn't understand what all the excitement was about. He had never thought the Levys of any importance, except for their two daughters. While the oldest always kept her nose in the air, the youngest, Ruby, used to look at him with interest the way good girls sometimes did, and he'd entertained friendly thoughts of her. Now the family became a symbol of all his way of life denied him. If he could win them over, if they could learn to respect him, anyone could.

This feeling was confirmed when Joe Klein tracked him down at McGuirk's Suicide Bar, so called because of the number of prostitutes who'd killed themselves there. Although he and Joe had been pals in the days of the Midget

Gorillas, their paths had diverged when Joe got a job in a cloak makers' shop and now they seldom met. He pushed into the bar looking mad and waving the newspaper.

"Is this true?" he said fiercely. "Did you do this, Tricker?"

"Business, Joe, business," said Tricker placatingly.

"Touch her again and I'll kill you," said Joe. "She's my girl."

"I didn't know," said Tricker. "No offense meant. I was only doing my job."

"Some job, beating up girls," said Joe. "Breaking strikes."

Tricker was stung. "You've got no right to say that to me. If you union guys had the brains you were born with, you wouldn't send girls like that out on a picket line without any muscle to protect them. If you weren't such cheapskates, you'd hire me instead of letting the bosses buy up all the gorillas for their side."

Joe stared at him in surprise. "You mean you would work for the unions?"

"Sure, if you paid us. You think I like having people spit on me when I go by? You think I like being told to keep off my own block? I'd like to be on the side of the good guys for a change, too."

"But we can't pay you. There's no money in the treasury."

Tricker shrugged. "Then we can't do business. Get in touch with me if things look up."

"Keep your hands off my girl in the meantime," said Joe, still angry.

Tricker nodded sympathetically. He understood how Joe felt; he didn't like it when his girls got roughed up either.

Ruby ran up the stairs calling, "Mama, mama," with three packages in her arms. Hurriedly she moved the furniture away from the parlor window. Tearing the paper off one of her parcels, she removed a piece of bright flowered chintz and some tacks. Taking off her shoe, she nailed the fabric over the window, using her heel for a hammer, then looped it back on each side with a length of ribbon and more tacks. The light shone through the fabric, making it look like a field of flowers.

"Look, Ma," she cried, "a curtain. Like the Americans have."

Hannah stared at it, wiping her hands unnecessarily on her apron. A smile trembled at the corners of her mouth as she touched the chintz with one finger.

"So fine," she whispered. "It lights up my whole front room. Look at it—it reminds me of the flowers back home."

Ruby laughed, nearly dancing with excitement as Hannah stepped back into the doorway and re-entered to get the full effect. She pronounced judgment: "Like a millionaire's parlor!" Then she frowned. "But Ruby, where did you get it?"

"I bought it!" crowed Ruby. "With money I earned!" She had planned this moment for weeks, keeping her secret, staying late at the settlement house. "A lady was watching my sewing class. She said how fine my work was and did I want to sew for her. So I helped her make a fancy ball dress and she paid me three dollars!"

"Don't tell me this cost three dollars?" said Hannah, appalled at such extravagance.

"No, no, Mama, I got other things too," said Ruby, unwrapping a second parcel. "But first look what the settlement lady gave me. She had some cloth left over from the dress and she gave it to me—look, a great big piece of silk for a princess!" She held out the fabric, about three-quarters of a yard of pinkish beige satin. Hannah stroked it gingerly.

"So heavy," she whispered. "So precious." In all her life she had never touched such fine cloth.

"It's not enough for a whole shirtwaist so I'll use it for the waist section and piece the bodice and sleeves," babbled Ruby, pulling things out of the third parcel. "I spent the other two dollars on these." Finery seemed to explode out of the package: yards and yards of mauve silk ribbon in several widths, rose velvet ribbon, buckram for stiffening, beige muslin for the lining, whalebone for collar, cuffs, and the brassiere section of the waist, a yard of fine beige net, thirty-six tiny uncovered buttons, and eight skeins of silk embroidery floss in different shades of pink, rose, and green.

"What is all this?" asked Hannah in bewilderment.

"I'm going to make me a shirtwaist like Rivington Street has never seen," said Ruby thrillingly. "Like nobody on the East Side could even imagine, like for a princess to wear to a ball!'' She held the satin next to her face. "Look, Ma, the color." It brought out the pink in her complexion and the lights in her brown hair. She went over to her second bag and pulled out a magazine with a pink cover. "The lady let me have her pattern book when she was finished with it— *Harper's Bazaar*. I'll show you the pictures of what I'm going to make." She flipped eagerly through the pages, past drawings of fancy hats with huge flowers and plumes, long elaborate gowns, and delicate slippers. "Here it is," she said. "Inexpensive waists, it's called. It says they cost only five dollars to make, but I know how to buy, I can do it for two with the free material."

"Five dollars!" said Hannah. "By you this is inexpensive?"

"Look at these two pictures," said Ruby, unheeding. One was a shirtwaist with an elaborate lace yoke, buttons down each side, a high boned collar with a lace medallion in the center, and a double sleeve. A tight lace undersleeve ending in a ruffle was topped by a silk oversleeve that stopped just below the elbow and was edged with ribbon.

"It's a Paris model," said Ruby, and read aloud: " 'Meteore silk blouse; self-covered buttons; Irish lace on yoke and lower sleeves.' I'm going to take the yoke from this one and the embroidery and cut from this other one." She indicated a sketch on the next page. " 'Sage-green satin and net waist; flowers embroidered in blue and mauve.' You embroider on top of the net so the flowers go like squares in the little holes; it's called darned net. It looks like crocheted lace, doesn't it? I think I'll use the sleeve from this one," she went on, turning another page to show Hannah a shirtwaist with an ornate full sleeve made of alternating stripes of fabric and velvet ribbon, with velvet bows parading down the middle.

Hannah looked at her thirteen-year-old daughter in dismay, struggling to find words. "Ruby, where are you going to wear this? The ladies in this book are rich ladies from uptown. They go around in carriages."

"Oh, there'll be someplace I can wear it when I'm a little older," said Ruby.

Hannah shook her head in bewilderment. "You can't wear such a thing on the East Side—people will laugh at you. They'll say, 'Look at that *schlemiel* of a girl, a piece of nothing making like she's a lady.' You just spent enough money for our whole family to eat for a week on these pieces of ribbon—what's wrong with your head? We've got no kings in our family. Sarah's on strike and we can hardly make it through the week on just your father's pay. We don't have a clock. We don't have enough blankets. It would be nice to get you a cot so you wouldn't have to sleep on three chairs for the rest of your life. You need a winter coat and so does your father. And you go out and spend the first money you make on this? What are you, crazy?"

With all the passion of adolescence, Ruby burst into tears. "I knew you'd say that. I knew it would be like this. You never like what I do, none of you. Nobody ever wants good things but me. Nobody cares about being American. There's nothing nice in this whole house except this curtain. There's no money for anything, ever. Why did we come to America if it's going to be like this? Why didn't we just stay in Russia and die?"

Hannah shook her head. She loved Ruby dearly and indulged her in small ways, feeling she sometimes got overlooked in the family storms that centered on Sarah. But this was ridiculous.

"All my life I never had one nice thing," wept Ruby. "I never said anything about it because I know there's no money. I wouldn't ask. I never had a bought doll to play with. I never had a piece of clothes that wasn't worn by two or three people first. I never had a single thing that was just for me. Well, I earned this money myself and I want this, I want one thing that isn't made over and cheap and stingy and a bargain—one thing good enough for an American!"

"But Ruby," said Hannah weakly, "this is a princess shirtwaist, not something you can use. You've got nowhere to go in it."

"That doesn't matter," cried Ruby. "It's something fine to *have* that I want even if I never wear it for ten years!"

Hannah had been young once herself with no money for finery. She nodded slowly, remembering.

"Oh, Mama," said Ruby, hurriedly wiping away her tears. "Does that mean it's all right—I can do it?"

"I think you're crazy," said Hannah. "And to me it's wrong to spend so much money on something like this. But the money's gone already and crying won't bring it back. And you did earn it yourself. So go ahead."

Ruby smiled ecstatically. "You'll see," she vowed. "When you see me trying it on, you'll understand." Her face clouded over. "One thing more I have to ask you." She darted into the little back room where Hannah had a special box in which she kept her treasures: their vaccination papers, Moyshe's first immigration papers, her wedding ring. Ruby took from it a roll of fine handmade lace as delicate as an ivory cobweb. She came slowly back to her mother and held it out in her palm. "I want to use this."

"Bubbe's lace!"

Ruby nodded defiantly. Hannah was shocked. To think of using the lace Bubbe was making for Rosa's dowry, the lace Sarah had ripped from her hands in that last wrenching farewell, seemed like blasphemy.

"It's all we have from her," she said fiercely. "And you want to use it on this *mishegas?*"

"Bubbe would have let me," said Ruby, tearful again. "She loved me."

Hannah tried to think it through. It was true that Bubbe had been the most practical of women, making nothing except for use. And she had loved Ruby. Ruby had been her shadow. She probably would have given her the lace rather than let it sit hidden dully away in a back room

"Sarah won't like it," she sighed finally, consent in her voice. She unrolled the lace on the table. The strip was very long. "There's more here than I thought," she said decisively. "You can use only half, Ruby. The rest I will keep for Sarah."

Ruby frowned. It was a real waste to give lace to Sarah. She didn't care about clothes. But it would be futile to argue with her mother on this point. "All right," she said, and smiled joyfully as Hannah cut the strip of lace in two. Smoothing each ribbon, each scrap of finery lovingly, Ruby began to fold her treasures.

Hannah watched her, troubled in her mind. "Ruby," she said, "one thing I'm sure you know—a princess shirtwaist doesn't make a princess. Like your Bubbe used to say, if the castle falls, its name is still castle; if the dunghill is raised up, its name is still dunghill."

"Not in America," said Ruby radiantly. "Here we don't have to worry about ancestors. People go from rags to riches.

I can do anything that's in me to do. That's what my teacher says. That's what America is all about."

"*Oy vay*," whispered Hannah, for the first time appreciating the extent of her problem. There could be nothing but trouble ahead in this degree of illusion.

The strike brought Sarah long days of adventure and companionship she had not known since childhood. She woke each morning full of excitement. It was partly the danger: the fights outside the shop, the intimidations of the goons and their women, the abuse of the police, the threat of jail. When she saw herself and her friends take these assaults in stride, she began to rethink her idea of heroism: maybe it wasn't being guillotined or burned at the stake, but an everyday affair.

As September turned to October and November, the days grew cold, with freezing rains that soaked through the thin coats and shoes of the girls on the picket line. Between the weather and their starvation diets, some of the strikers became sick. Sarah was ashamed to eat much herself, now that she wasn't bringing in any money, for Hannah was hard put to feed them all on Moyshe's wage alone. But Sarah was well off next to many. Fanny was the sole support of her mother and baby brother, except for a little piecework her mother did at home. She was getting two dollars a week strike benefits, but how could they live on that when they'd barely made it before on seven? If Fanny didn't complain, Sarah certainly wouldn't.

Still, it was hard to be so cold and hungry and afraid every morning and watch other people going off to their jobs without ever thinking about the strike. The Jewish press printed strike news when there was any, but these stories were discouraging: The enemy seemed so strong, the union so weak. The police got more outrageous every day. They called out to girls who were passing the factory, "Looking for work? Plenty of jobs at Triangle." Detectives were stationed outside the union office at Clinton Hall to keep notes on who went in and out, in order to give evidence of conspiracy in court. On October 19, detectives broke into a strike meeting, bringing Goldfarb, the Triangle Company goon, and two other thugs in with them. The cops stationed themselves around the room, arms folded menacingly and nightsticks on the ready, while

Goldfarb jotted down names and pointed out ringleaders to the gorillas. It was impossible to continue the meeting under such conditions. Next day, every picket who had been there was arrested. It was Sarah's third arrest; she was fined three dollars and Judge Corrigan said the next time he saw her he would send her to the workhouse as an incorrigible trouble-maker.

The fines were becoming a problem for Local 25. Its treasury was empty. Its officers turned to their International, the Ladies' Garment Workers' Union, for help. But the secretary-treasurer of the International, John A. Dyche, was a conservative who did not approve of the strike. The next time Sarah went to Clinton Hall, she found the president of Local 25, Abe Baroff, with his head in his hands.

"What are we going to do?" he said. "We've got no more money and I don't know how we're going to get any. The American unions won't help; they don't even seem to know we're on strike. Maybe we'll have to give in."

"No!" said Sarah, but she couldn't come up with any solution. How could one tiny local union defeat not only a big firm like Triangle Waist, but the police and courts as well?

"You know, Sarah," said Ruby that night, "one time at the settlement house a lady gave a talk. She had on the most beautiful dress, Mama, lilac silk crepe with plum inserts . . ."

"Who cares what she was wearing, get to the point," snapped Sarah. Anxiety was making her bad-tempered.

"She was from the Women's Trade Union League. They're uptown ladies who want to help women on the East Side get unions. I think they're for woman suffrage, too," said Ruby. Her voice trailed off. She didn't like to admit she'd paid more attention to the lady's costume than to her speech. "Why don't you see if they can help?"

"Help what? Does this have something to do with the strike?"

"I told you," said Ruby. "There are some ladies who want to help. They gave me a paper. I think I still have it." She went off to rummage among her things, reappearing shortly with a handout. It read:

THE WOMEN'S TRADE UNION LEAGUE
OF AMERICA
WHY IT IS:

There are six million working women in the United States. The average wage of these women is under $6.00 a week. The purchasing power of $6.00 is inferior food, inferior clothing, inferior shelter.

Six dollars allows no margin for (1) illness, (2) recreation, or (3) education.

Unorganized, badly paid women workers lower men's wages.

Organization is education. Women in the past met their problems as personal—which they were. They now through organization are learning to meet their economic problems as social—which they are.

THE WOMEN'S TRADE UNION LEAGUE
OF AMERICA
WHAT IT IS:

1. Organization of all workers into trade unions.
2. Equal pay for equal work.
3. An eight-hour day.
4. A minimum-wage scale.
5. Full-citizenship for women.

Sarah read the leaflet over and over, feeling as if rockets were going off in her head. American ladies! She didn't even know any; still less had she imagined they could be a possible source of help. It was almost more than she could grasp; she wanted to rush and find them immediately. She looked at the address: East Twenty-third Street. Uptown. She couldn't go there now; it was already dark. She would do so first thing in the morning. She clasped her hands prayerfully under the table. Maybe help would come. Then she looked irritably at her younger sister. "I can't believe you've been sitting on this the whole time and never said a word, Ruby," she said. "Do you know what a difference these women could make?"

"I'm sorry," said Ruby humbly, "I forgot." She was in awe of Sarah and seldom initiated conversations with her. She surmised—correctly—that Sarah thought her a poor, flighty creature with no social conscience. From time to time she would try to listen to the discussions Sarah and Moyshe had about politics, but her head would immediately fill with cotton wool, making her feel so stupid she stopped listening. Privately, without fully admitting it even to herself—for the Levys were a fiercely loyal clan—she thought Sarah a bit crazy and blamed her father for it. He had turned Sarah's head in childhood, while they were still in Russia. It was too bad. She'd never have a normal life now, much less become rich as Ruby intended to do—an intention she kept to herself, though she suspected her mother would not be unsympathetic.

Sarah was lost in her own dreams. "I'll go see these women tomorrow," she said. "How do you get to Twenty-third Street, anyway?"

"Go west on Houston to Broadway and walk north," said Ruby. "It's a long walk. Where Broadway crosses Fifth Avenue, that's Twenty-third."

Hannah stared at her in astonishment. "How do you know?"

"I go uptown sometimes," said Ruby airily. "After school."

Moyshe put down his newspaper. "Uptown? What for?"

"To go to the fancy stores."

"The fancy stores," said Sarah. "Why? You don't have any money."

"I like to look at the clothes," said Ruby. "I like to see how they're made."

The next morning Sarah collected Rachel and Becky Zinssher, and they began the long trek uptown to the Women's Trade Union League, walking arm in arm, chattering, shivering, huddled together for warmth. Although the November morning was gray and the winds gusty, the skies were clear and the air smelled sharp and clean. As they walked, the East Side's dirt and congestion, beards and caftans, pushcarts and fire escapes and tenements, began to fade. After its raucous but beloved voice dwindled to a whisper, Rachel began to hear a new voice, soft at first, then insistent, a melodious hum that seemed to come from Broadway itself as it widened out, from its increasingly grand buildings, its black motorcars, its well-dressed pedestrians. The voice spoke in English and it said, "You're a long way from home, aren't you, little girl?"

Above Fourteenth Street only a sprinkling of people were
out so early, mainly men. They walked slowly and confidently in their warm clothes, sometimes smoking cigars;
they talked in low voices without yelling or gesticulating the
way everyone did downtown. A few of them stared as Sarah
and Becky chattered excitedly in Yiddish, oblivious. Rachel
became embarrassed.

"Hey," she said. "Talk English—we're not on the East
Side anymore."

They looked blankly at her for a moment, then switched.
But Rachel, who had spent hours practicing her pronunciation
so she could talk the way her teachers did, knew they still
sounded funny. Foreign. The elegant stone office buildings,
the fine shops, the Palladian villas they passed stared down,
their windows so many lorgnettes through which to peer at
these intruders.

Rachel stared back, lagging behind. On the East Side, she
seldom looked up from her feet, the sidewalk, her thoughts,
shutting out the squalor and the bustle. Here she rubber-
necked until her eyes bulged and her neck muscles hurt. The
marble of the mansions, carved in spirals and cascades; the
stateliness of the granite houses with their pilasters and ornaments; the exquisite tracery of the wrought-iron balconies; the
poignancy of the curve of one particular window; the sudden
and unutterable coziness of a little mansard roof, all pierced
Rachel's eyes with ecstatic pain. Her senses reeled with her
first experience of aesthetic order.

At the corner of Twentieth Street she stopped, wide-eyed.
"Wait, look a minute. It's Lord and Taylor."

Sarah and Becky obediently halted.

"That's where Rosalie Garfinkle, the butcher's daughter,
buys her clothes," said Sarah with a sniff. "Or so she claims.
Ha. I bet they wouldn't even let her in."

"Get a look at that hat!" said Becky respectfully. "Can
you believe the size of those plumes?"

But Rachel said nothing, reduced to silence not by the
clothes but by the building itself, reaching up into the clouds,
seven stories high and built of a cast iron so pure in form,
painted such a brilliant white, that she thought at first it was
marble. On the top was a funny little cubicle of a roof with a
wrought iron grille around it and a round window. Under it
were more windows, each row larger than the one above,

stately and dignified, with arches. A pain stabbed Rachel's heart and she clutched Sarah's arm for support. "It's like a bird," she whispered, "or an angel. It could fly right off the ground."

Sarah snorted. She hated it when Rachel became poetic. "'Build thee more stately mansions, O my soul,' like the poem we learned in school. Come on, let's go." They walked in silence for a few blocks until Sarah said, pointing uptown, "Look at that funny building. It's like a big piece of cake." The Flatiron Building rose, pristine in its newness, wedge-shaped against the sky.

"I wonder how it stays up?" said Becky nervously. "It's awful high, isn't it? It must be ten or twenty stories." They counted. Twenty. "I wouldn't like to be under that in a strong wind."

"Anyway, we're here," announced Sarah. "This is Twenty-third Street. That must be where we want to go." And she pointed to a small brownstone house sandwiched in between two larger, newer edifices.

Helen Marot, executive secretary of the New York Women's Trade Union League, arrived at her office early that morning. Several times a week she came in at seven-thirty to take advantage of the early-morning quiet and clear her desk. When the doorbell rang at eight o'clock, she looked up in surprise and walked quickly over to peer through the glass. An enormous smile lit her plain face, transfiguring it, when she saw who was outside.

Although the League had opened shop in 1904, it had met with little success in recruiting masses of women workers. There were some, of course—a few from the East Side garment shops, some American-born white-collar workers, even a handful from New Jersey—but these remained isolated cases rather than pathfinders for a working-class army that would follow in their steps. Most of the active members of the League were middle-class women who were sympathetic to labor—"allies," they called themselves.

Helen Marot was one of the most steadfast of these. Thin-faced, in her forties, wearing a mannishly tailored business suit, a plain white shirtwaist, and a tie, with wire-rimmed glasses and hair pulled back severely, she looked the picture of a New England spinster. But if her exterior was stereotypi-

cal, her mind was unconventional, alert, wide ranging, and
systematic. Years of service as an industrial investigator and
statistician had made her a partisan of trade-unionism as well
as a confirmed feminist.

She scanned the three girls who entered her office with a
delighted eye: garmènt workers from the East Side, undoubt-
edly, but what could they want at this hour? Something must
have happened. They introduced themselves as she bustled
about making tea. The thin dark one, Sarah, was the leader.
She could tell that by the determination in her face and the
way the other two turned to her. She wasn't pretty in any
conventional sense but what intensity, what passion, spoke in
those dark eyes! The redhead, Rachel, was the prettiest and
the best-dressed: pink-white skin and Grecian features but an
abstracted look, as if she were more attentive to her own
thoughts than to any problem before her. She kept staring at
the furniture and the pictures on the wall. The big buxom
one, Becky, was cracking jokes. How she towered above the
other two. Most of these East Side girls were runtish, poorly
nourished as children, no doubt, but she was as tall as any
American, and what a hat! The child must have made it herself and modeled it after that of some vaudeville star. A little
vulgar, unquestionably, but what an innocent grin on that
round face, what puppyish friendliness in those brown eyes—
you couldn't help liking her at once.

Helen poured tea, then listened with growing excitement as
they told her everything: the conditions at Triangle, the sister
strikes, the attacks by the police and the hired thugs, the
courts, the fines, the fear. The strike was clearly important:
three shops and it had gone on for weeks already though the
union was, as usual, mismanaging it. These Jewish unions
with their narrow range of East Side contacts, probably completely restricted to Russian socialists, were in her opinion
completely unable to summon up the resources in money,
publicity, legal assistance, and organizational skills that were
necessary for any major organizing drive. Well, that was
what the Women's Trade Union League was there for. This
strike might well provide the League with the opportunity it
had sought to prove itself to the labor movement and make its
name known among the women workers.

"The police seem to be outdoing themselves," she said.
"The first thing we must do is get independent observers

down there to back up your story. The idea of arresting four-teen-year-old girls for picketing!"

"Is it really against the law to picket?" asked Rachel.

"Certainly not," said Helen. "It's part of your First Amendment right to freedom of speech; that's in the Constitution. Unfortunately, laws are enforced by policemen and interpreted by judges, and most men in these groups are unsympathetic to labor. So their interpretation of the law may differ from mine. And until more people know about what's going on down there, the police will keep getting away with murder."

Sarah was not sure she understood. "You mean the police will stop arresting us if there are stories in the American papers?"

"It won't be quite that easy," said Helen wryly. "They're used to having a free hand on the East Side. But I think we can do something if we can alert the progressives and reach out to other women. It's about time these Cossacks learned there is a women's movement and we will not tolerate having girls arrested and jailed merely for trying to earn more than six dollars a week!" She tapped her pencil on the desk for emphasis as she spoke, and with her last words, the pencil snapped in half.

Rachel stared. She had thought Helen Marot unmoved by their story; her New England face had so little expression. Now she noted her shiny eyes and compressed lips. The woman had not only been moved, she was enraged and entirely on their side. Rachel smiled hopefully. For the first time she believed that help might come.

As soon as the three girls left, Helen Marot telephoned Mary Dreier, president of the New York League, who came over to the office at once for a conference. They agreed they must move immediately.

"Someone should go down there tomorrow morning," said Mary Dreier. She was a delicate woman in her late thirties, with flyaway blonde hair and china-blue eyes. Only the set of her jaw and the frown lines on her forehead belied the sweetness of her smile and indicated that she was anything more than a lady of leisure. The women's movement had given meaning to her life, which would otherwise have been bounded by tea parties and drives in the park, afternoons at the museum and evenings at the opera.

"Why don't you go yourself, Mary," said Helen. "It will be easier to get the press interested if you've been personally involved."

"I'd like to. Those girls are probably exaggerating. I can hardly believe people get arrested for no cause at all, but I'll go and see for myself."

How odd she looked, thought Rachel at six the next morning, standing there in her fur coat and hat, watching the picketing, her chauffeured car waiting in the next street. She was very friendly. She introduced herself to the strikers the minute she came, explaining that she had come as an impartial observer so she could testify as to what was happening. The policemen and Bernstein didn't like having her there. They kept staring at her and muttering to one another. Finally the sergeant confronted her.

"Who are you and what are you doing here?"

Mary Dreier looked surprised, then smiled pleasantly. "I am a citizen and a taxpayer and I'm here on behalf of the Women's Trade Union League, of which I am president, to see whether the constitutional rights of these strikers to peaceful picketing and freedom of speech is being upheld by the law." She nodded in dismissal.

Bernstein couldn't bear being left out; he ran over in a rage. "What did she say, Ladies' Union League?" he said. "No lady would belong to a union; that's for scum. She's some kind of uptown scum come down here to cause trouble!"

Mary Dreier raised her eyebrows. "You must be the manager. I've been told you've hired gangsters and fallen women to terrorize these strikers. Is this true?"

"Of course it's not true. I've been hiring workers, honest workers," he sputtered. "You're nothing but a dirty liar."

Mary Dreier gasped. A wealthy woman, the daughter of a cultured German-born manufacturer, she had led a sheltered life and such abusive language was never used in her presence. She turned to the law for protection. "Officer, this man called me a dirty liar. Aren't you going to do something?"

"I never saw you before," said the cop. "How do I know you're not a dirty liar?" He walked away. Bernstein laughed. Mary Dreier stood for a moment, almost in shock, then threw back her head and walked over to Rachel, grabbing her picket sign. "I'll hold that," she said furiously. "I'm beginning to see what you're up against."

The strikebreakers were coming to work. Rachel and the others began to follow them along the sidewalk, calling, "Don't go in there. They treat us terrible. They'll do the same to you."

"Don't go to work in Triangle Waist!" sang Mary Dreier in imperious tones. Two or three little scabs stopped to stare. What was this rich lady in a fur coat doing on the East Side? Was she the boss's wife?

"Unions are necessary," she told them. "We must all support them. Only through unions will women be able to obtain decent wages and working conditions. These girls are on strike for you, for all working women. You must support their struggle and not scab."

"All right, ma'am," said one of the little girls with a curtsy. She took her friend's arm. "We're going home now, see?"

"You come back here," screamed Bernstein.

But they ran off. Mary Dreier grinned in elation and took Rachel's arm. As the two of them chased after the scabs, they did not notice Bernstein conferring with Tricker Louis and the woman called Ida Odessa, who suddenly confronted them with a police sergeant in tow.

"Officer," said Tricker, pointing at Mary Dreier, "I want you to arrest this woman. She threatened my companion. We were just walking along, minding our own business, when she called out, 'Don't go in there or I'll kill you.'"

"Yeah," said Ida Odessa with relish. "She told me she'd kill me if I went in there to work. I want her locked up."

"You're under arrest, miss," said the obliging sergeant and led Mary Dreier away without further ado.

The police captain at the Jefferson Market Station was appalled. Didn't these cops on the beat understand anything? He apologized profusely. "They were never supposed to arrest a lady like you, ma'am," he said. "That was not at all within the scope of their duties, and I hope you will accept my sincere apologies and we can let this unfortunate mistake die right here. I will speak severely to the officer in charge."

But Mary Dreier had no intention of letting the matter die. She held a press conference that night at her Sutton Place

home, and the American city editors, who had previously ignored the strike or treated it as a bit of East Side local color,
suddenly found their angle:

SOCIETY WOMAN ARRESTED ON FALSE CHARGES;

SAYS POLICE COLLUDING WITH SWEATSHOP

OWNERS AND PERSECUTING GIRL VICTIMS!

SUTTON PLACE RESIDENT, MISTAKEN FOR

STRIKER, SAYS WOMEN MUST STICK TOGETHER!

IS THIS RUSSIA OR AMERICA, ASKS YOUNG GIRL STRIKER?

Soon the papers were full of pitiful young immigrant girls;
vivid Russian revolutionaries; Broadway hookers and their
pimps; street-corner toughs like those favorites of the city
desks, Steel Kishkes and King Indian; and, of course, benev-
olent society ladies. Checks and offers of assistance followed
the reporters to the union hall, and the wise men of the Jewish
labor movement began to take note.

With the arrest of Mary Dreier and the publicity it brought
the strike, the movement of shirtwaist workers into the union
became pronounced. More joined each week, and sympathy
strikes began at two firms that were doing secret scab work
for the Triangle bosses. The activists of Local 25, including
Rachel and Sarah, were convinced the time had come to call a
general strike of the whole shirtwaist industry. But John A.
Dyche was still adamantly opposed. "The International
doesn't even have the money to pay strike benefits to the
people already out, and now these Russian hotheads want to
call a general strike," he snorted to Joe Klein.

"They say a general strike is the only way they'll ever be
able to reach the rest of the industry," said Joe. "Look,
how's it going to hurt to call a meeting at least? You know
the local is going to do it sooner or later; you might as well
give in gracefully."

"Never," swore Dyche. But eventually he bowed to pressure, and a mass meeting was scheduled for November 22 at

Cooper Union. Samuel Gompers himself, president of the AFL, agreed to speak; the call went out in the *Forward;* and the flow of new union members into the office at Clinton Hall became a flood.

On the night of November 22, Sarah, shifting restlessly in her chair, looked around at the enormous crowd of shirtwaist workers. The place was a sea of ''Merry Widow'' hats and so many girls were there that even Cooper Union, with its two thousand seats, couldn't hold them all. The union staff had to go around hiring one overflow hall after another. Soon meetings were going on at Astoria Hall, Beethoven Hall, and the Manhattan Lyceum as well, with runners ready to dash from one place to another when something was decided. Even so, it didn't look as though anything would be settled very soon. The session at Cooper Union had already lasted for what seemed an eternity. What a bunch of windbags, Sarah thought impatiently. Some of the girls had fallen asleep on their friends' shoulders; others were whispering. It was no wonder, they were tired after a hard day's work. Sarah bit her lip, looking at the platform. What could those men have been thinking of to plan a meeting this way?

Becky poked her in the ribs and she jumped. ''Is this going on all night?'' she whispered loudly, and the girls in front of them turned and nodded in agreement. ''What do they think this is, one of their socialist meetings? These women still have things to do when they go home. Some of them are going to start leaving unless something happens pretty quick.''

The line of speakers covered the platform. Benjamin Feigenbaum of the *Forward* and the United Hebrew Trades was chairing; he sat near the podium. Behind him were arrayed: Samuel Gompers; Mary Dreier (the only woman speaker); the East Side's beloved socialist lawyer, Meyer London; Jacob Panken, another socialist lawyer; Joe Goldstein from the baker's union; Bill Coakley from the lithographers; Max Pine and Bernie Weinstein from the United Hebrew Trades; and Ab Cahan of the *Forward.* The leaders of Local 25 weren't even on the stage, having been happy to relinquish the honors to more experienced speakers. Only half of these had spoken so far, several in English, which few in the audience could understand. Gompers, as predicted, had said they shouldn't strike unless it was absolutely necessary, but if it was, they should stick together. Others too had advised moderation and prudence. No one had put forward any plans or given any concrete direction. What was the matter with them?

"Sarah," hissed Rachel from down the aisle, "do something!"

"What?"

Fanny reached over Becky's statuesque form and clutched Sarah's hand. "Just get up," she whispered. "It'll be all right. Say we want a strike."

Feigenbaum had just finished introducing Jacob Panken. If he starts, he'll go on forever, thought Sarah, and she was suddenly on her feet and in the aisle, pushing her way forward and shouting, "Mr. Chairman! Mr. Chairman!"

Heads craned to find out who it was. The whispering stopped. A few girls in the back stood up in order to see better. Feigenbaum came to the edge of the stage calling, "Who's that? What's the matter?"

Sarah stepped into the circle of light at the front. Her knees could barely hold her up. "I have to say something," she said weakly.

Jacob Panken opined that this was quite irregular; he had just begun his speech. Goldstein mentioned that if she had wanted to speak she should have told the committee. Besides, they had too many speakers already. Cahan said, "She is a striker, after all." A certain amount of platform bickering became visible. But Feigenbaum held out his hand and helped her onto the stage, saying loudly, "She's the striker from Triangle who got beat up and she's been active in the union from the beginning, so who has a better right? Step back for a minute, Jacob."

Sarah stood at the center of the stage and swayed. For a moment her mind went blank with terror and her lips would not move. "Go ahead, Sarah," whispered Feigenbaum. "Do you want to wait until Jacob's done?" Sarah shook her head and took a deep breath; her fear receded as her anger returned. The hand she was stretching forward in unconscious appeal turned to a fist.

"I am sick of listening to speeches that go on and on," she said in her high, passionate voice. "I am sick of people telling me to be careful. All my life people have said, 'Wait, don't make trouble'—we've done that for enough years and where has it gotten us? You all know me; I work at Triangle Waist. I've been working in the trade since I was fourteen. I've been harassed like you, underpaid like you, and I've been on strike for four weeks. I've been beaten up, I've been arrested three times, I've gone hungry. I don't mind if it will build the union.

"We need a union in shirtwaist. It's the only way we can get decent pay, clean places to work, standards in the industry. These bosses don't realize they depend on us; they think we need them more than they need us. Without us they can't make a dime. Let them learn respect. Let them see the spring season coming on and them with no stock. Let them worry about making ends meet. We can hold out longer than they can because we know how to go hungry already; we've got experience at starving.

"They think they can scare us back to work with gorillas and police. They don't understand where we come from. Police and persecution are nothing new to us—didn't half of us run to America to get away from the Black Hundreds? And here we are in the land of freedom, facing the police once more, but this time there's nowhere left to run. We have to fight. But since this is America we can fight in the open.

"All of us have to strike together. Triangle can't do it alone; your shop can't do it alone. If we go out one by one, the bosses will use one shop to scab on another. They'll subcontract the work and we'll end up cutting our own throats. If we want to build a union, we must all go out together. We must hit them with one fist!" She held her arms wide in appeal. "I call for a general strike!"

Pandemonium broke out in Cooper Union. Thousands of girls, previously quiet, began to shout, "Hooray!" and "Strike! Strike!" waving their arms and stamping their feet. Feigenbaum hugged Sarah ecstatically. Tears were streaming down his face. He waved his hands for quiet, to no effect. "Help me quiet them down so we can vote," he asked Sarah. She put her finger to her lips, saying, "Shh," and slowly the crowd stopped talking and waited in excited silence.

"Do you mean faith?" cried Feigenbaum. "Will you take the old Jewish oath?" The women's heads nodded as one. He held out his right hand. "Hold out your hands and repeat after me," and as he said the words two thousand hands stretched forward and two thousand voices repeated, "If I turn traitor to the vow I now pledge, may my hand wither from the arm I now raise."

Then pandemonium broke out once more and Sarah was swept from the stage into the arms of her friends, who were cheering, crying, and jumping up and down.

"We did it!" yelled Becky.

The speakers sat astonished on the stage, forgotten.

"What was that thing they swore in Yiddish?" Joe Coakley asked Cahan.

"It's from the Bible," he said. "If I forget thee, O Jerusalem, may my right hand lose its cunning."

Gompers stared at the cheering, weeping girls, shaking his head in disbelief. "Never in all my years in the labor movement have I seen a strike meeting like this," he told Mary Dreier.

"Why, no, you've never seen one that was mostly women before," she said, with her sweet, determined smile. "Have you, Mr. Gompers?"

BOOK THREE

*The Joy of
the Struggle*

I

Ten thousand shirtwaist workers marched slowly down to City Hall on December 4, 1909, faces set, arms linked, hands clenched. The Bowery had never seen a more dignified parade. In the weeks since the strike had begun, more than two hundred women had been arrested. Many others had been beaten. Sarah, in the forefront of the march, still favored the side where Tricker Louis had broken her ribs, but her spirits were ebullient and, head high, black eyes dancing, she was photographed innumerable times by the press, who had adopted her as the personification of the militant young womanhood emerging on the East Side.

Sarah's features also impressed themselves upon another observer, Avigdor Spector, a young man who had arrived from Russia only the week before. He trailed along at the side of the march, wondering what it was all about since most of the signs were in English and he could not read them. He ended up following the demonstration all the way to City Hall. It was the first thing he'd seen in America that seemed familiar, yet its differences from Russian demonstrations fascinated him: the American parade was much more orderly; the marchers bore neatly painted signs clearly made by professional sign painters; and all of them looked comparatively prosperous. Certainly they were less ragged than his comrades at home, and there were fewer mothers carrying babies among them. The most striking contrast was the sprinkling of richly dressed women, some even wearing furs, among the strikers. Avi could not understand who they were or why they were there, but, from that day forward, he became interested in the strike, following its progress in the newspapers, going to its public meetings—where he frequently noticed Sarah Levy, who reminded him of the movement girls back home— and trying to understand the American labor movement.

The well-dressed women who had perplexed Avi Spector were suffragists and members of the Women's Trade Union League, now playing a major organizing role in the strike. The first few days after the Cooper Union meeting had been completely chaotic; Clinton Hall was jammed floor to ceiling with bewildered young girls who had walked off their jobs as directed but had no idea what they were supposed to do next. The streets were more crowded than on the High Holidays, packed with bodies in a confusion of pushing and yelling and waving and cheering and asking directions, with no one in charge and nobody giving clear instructions. The League had brought order to this bedlam, with the help of strikers like Sarah, who was captain of the Triangle workers. Each shop had its own captain and held daily meetings where picketing was arranged and strike benefits distributed.

Near the head of the march on City Hall, four strikers carried a large banner reading, "150 Employers Agree to Union Demands." Some of the little cockroach bosses panicked as soon as the general strike began. Knowing a few days of idleness would bankrupt them, forty settled within twenty-four hours. The bosses in the big factories were not so easily cowed. Harris and Blanck of Triangle Waist Company even organized an employers' association—Sarah called it a "bosses' union"—in which everybody swore not to recognize Local 25. "No workers will tell us how to run our business," they said.

Recognition of the union was the chief demand of the general strike. There were others: wage increases, a shorter work week, four paid holidays a year, no discrimination against union members after the strike, an equal division of work in the slack season, and no more paying for needles, thread, electricity, machine rental, and stools. From now on each worker would be a wage earner in her own name, as an individual, not as a part of some contractor's team forced to take whatever he wanted to give when the envelope was divided up.

Still, all these demands were trivial next to union recognition. In economic terms, recognition meant Local 25 would be able to bargain for the whole industry and set uniform wage scales and hours. Employers called this "the closed shop" because it meant that all shirtwaist workers would have to join the union and companies couldn't hire some girls on the union pay scale and others on a scab scale, giving the latter group most of the work. The smallest shops, the ones that could not pay their workers a living wage and still make a profit, would be driven out of business, and, in the long run, this would be good for the industry and those who worked in it.

Yet all of these reasons for stressing union recognition could not account for the passion with which the strikers held to this demand. As Molly Hurwitz put it, groping for words, "Recognition means they have to admit we're people, not just hands. They have to see we're human beings like them." Listening to her, Rachel thought that this was the one thing they were least likely to do.

Molly stopped marching for a moment, bent over with a cough. Her eyes were bright, her cheeks flushed. Rachel was worried about her. Molly had gotten sick picketing in the cold rain; she had no proper winter coat or boots and of course she wasn't getting enough to eat. None of them were. There wasn't enough money in the union treasury to go around, and Molly spoke for all of them when she said, "I can't take the money. There are too many that need it more. Look at Mrs. Rosenblum, look at the men with families."

Neither hunger nor cold had deterred the strikers from turning out in vast numbers to march to City Hall that December day. Rachel had never been part of so large a crowd before. She felt as if her heart would jump out of her body when she looked back and saw the black mass snaking out of sight behind her. She didn't know whether she wanted to cry or cheer, so she winked at Becky and said, "My, don't we look swell and I do mean you." They had all worn their best, but Becky was particularly resplendent in a new black picture hat trimmed with tulle and three enormous red roses. Rachel knew without asking that she'd trimmed it herself. Becky's tastes always aspired to the theatrical.

At City Hall, a line of mounted police was waiting for them. Since the city had refused them permission to use the park, they had to continue to march around it while their delegation went in to see the mayor. The orderly character of the march disintegrated at this point. Ranks broke and reformed, and Sarah ran back along the procession looking for her friends. Sighting Becky's enormous hat, she dived into the line, giggling, "Quick, hide me, girls, before anybody else takes my picture—I'm sick of being famous. What a reason to get your face in the paper—being beat up by Tricker Louis."

"That's not why," said Fanny. "It's because you've done so much for the strike."

"The reporters don't care about that," said Sarah. "All they're interested in are gory details. And the League women are just as bad, telling everyone how poor and hungry we are. It's embarrassing."

"They've been a big help, Sarah," said Rachel.

"I know. But sometimes they make me mad. They talk like we're just a lot of charity cases." While Sarah knew the help of the League was indispensable, spending time with women so different from herself made her uncomfortable. What did they want, anyway? Even Moyshe had been unable to illuminate that question. Rachel, on the other hand, was sure she knew.

"They want us to join the women's movement, of course. What's wrong with that?"

This was but one of several issues on which Rachel and Sarah were beginning to develop distressing differences of opinion.

Even though Rachel and Sarah had known each other since their first day in public school, the strike had deepened their friendship. They spent hours together each day, on the picket line, in meetings, at the union hall, soliciting money, or, often enough, just kidding around.

Sarah found herself worried, however, by Rachel's lack of seriousness. Rachel had always been romantic, influenced by silly novels, but now that she had so much free time, her imagination was getting out of hand. Sarah supposed it was because she was so pretty, with her long waist and elegant profile, her slim figure, her skin as white and clear as any rich girl's, and that hair like flame. Men were always asking to meet her and crowding around her in the union meetings. Of course, Rachel wasn't allowed to go out with men. Her father said that he would pick her husband when it was time for her to stop working and until then she could spend her time with girls or at home. Rachel said she didn't care. She wasn't interested in any of the men she knew anyway. Behind her back, the union boys called her "the Duchess."

"She thinks she's too good for us," Joe Klein told Sarah.

"She just hasn't fallen in love," Sarah defended her. But privately, she had to admit he had a point. Rachel said she wasn't attracted to East Side men because they reminded her of her father. They all talked too much. The political ones were too bossy and the allrightniks had no soul.

"What do you want, the moon from the sky?" said Sarah, sounding like her mother. She could have taken Rachel more seriously if she didn't talk about love all the time; so much theoretical fervor and so little practical interest seemed an odd combination. Rachel continually pressed Sarah for details of what happened when Joe Klein walked her home from meetings and dances, as he did increasingly.

"Does he hold your hand?"

"I already told you," Sarah would sigh.

"Does he ever kiss you?"

"Certainly not." When pressed, Sarah admitted that he had tried once or twice, but she ran upstairs. Rachel was outraged.

"I don't think you're very modern in your sex attitudes, Sarah," she said with a sniff. "Maybe Minnie Fishman is right about you. She thinks you're a prude."

Minnie Fishman worked on another floor at Triangle Waist, so neither Sarah nor Rachel had gotten to know her until the strike. They found she was full of surprises. "What a mouth!" Rachel exclaimed after their first encounter. "And she looks so sweet!" It was true; Minnie, a red-cheeked apple dumpling of a girl, had iron in her soul and vitriol in her mouth.

"Gunpowder!" she'd cry. "Give the boss a dose of kerosene!" Then they would all shush her quickly before anyone could hear.

Minnie was an anarchist. She had read Bakunin and heard Emma Goldman speak and thoroughly approved of assassination, though she had never tried it herself. She even spoke with approbation about free love. Sarah thought she was a bad influence on Rachel. She had loaned her several issues of Emma Goldman's magazine, *Mother Earth,* and since Rachel couldn't possibly take them home, she'd prevailed upon Sarah to keep them for her. This meant Rachel had to come to

Rivington Street to study them, and the conversations that followed were torment to Sarah.

"Emma Goldman says women naturally want sex fulfillment the same as men do," Rachel reported one afternoon. "How about that? Listen: 'A large proportion of the unhappiness, misery, distress, and physical suffering of matrimony is due to the criminal ignorance in sex matters that is being extolled as a great virtue.' That's us, Sarah. We are ignorant and kept so for the purposes of the master class. Nobody tells us anything, even our mothers. We owe it to ourselves to learn about sex so we don't ruin our lives by marrying the wrong man and having too many babies."

"I'm not sure I want to get married at all," said Sarah.

"Of course you do, just not an old-fashioned bourgeois marriage where the woman is the servant, chattel, and sex possession of the man, like our mothers are, but a full union of equals."

"My mother isn't anybody's chattel," objected Sarah. "If anything, she's the boss."

"You just think that because she bosses you. I actually feel kind of sorry for your mother. Your father never pays any attention to her or takes her anywhere or even kisses her."

"They're a little old for that sort of thing," said Sarah, shocked.

"I wonder how it feels to fall in love." Rachel stared dreamily at the wall. "To have your whole body sway with feeling, to melt with passion at one glance from his eyes." She sighed. "Do you feel like that with Joe Klein?"

"No, and I'm sick of hearing about it," said Sarah. "Love, love, love—can't we talk about anything else?"

Rachel contemplated her through narrowed lids. "What are you afraid of?"

"I'm not afraid of anything!" cried Sarah. "I'm bored."

Rachel merely nodded superciliously and went back to reading *Mother Earth*. The conversation made Sarah furious, especially because she really was afraid to think about sex and hated to admit it. How could she explain, even to Rachel, what came over her? Sometimes she would get as far as imagining herself alone somewhere with Joe, in the country perhaps, by a brook, with willows, and he would take her in his arms and bend her head back in a swooning kiss. But as soon as Sarah would begin to give herself up to the fantasy, there'd be a crash like a door slamming and a scream would echo through her head, her own scream. She would clench her eyes shut to keep the picture out but not in time to stop her from seeing that white young body and all the blood. She would sit numb, shaking with the effort of trying not to remember what had happened to Rosa.

Joe Klein was a union man and a dedicated one, but he didn't want to be poor all his life. Was that so terrible? He wasn't asking to be a millionaire, just comfortable. He'd saved up a little money and was thinking of putting it into a building in Brownsville. Nobody in his family had ever owned land. But to hear Sarah, you'd think he was J.P. Morgan.

"Some union man," she sniffed. "A climber. Eugene V. Debs said he wanted to rise with his class, not from it. If you put half as much time into figuring out how we can win this strike as you do into thinking about real estate, we'd all be better off." She drove him crazy.

"You know all the answers, don't you?" he asked hotly. "A slogan for everything."

You'd think he was some kind of criminal, the way she went after him. Wasn't he working for the union at a fraction of what he could have made if he went into jobbing or man-ufacturing the way his mother wanted him to? His mother was another one, nagging at him all the time, only in the opposite direction from Sarah: He should make something of himself, get somewhere. Look at so-and-so's boy, going to medical school, and this other one's boy, only thirty and already he owns a factory; oh, that the Lord should send me such happi-ness before I die.

His mother hated Sarah, the wrong kind of girl. He shouldn't throw himself away as she had when she'd married his father, that good-for-nothing. His father and Sarah, two of a kind, all mouth and no money. "Look at her," his mother said disparagingly. "Skinny, no flesh on her bones, running around all the time. She looks like something left out in the rain. What do you see in this girl, Yossel? What have I done to deserve you should disappoint me this way?"

When she wasn't going on about Sarah, she was yelling at him for not coming into the store. He wasn't going to throw his life away behind the counter of a little hole-in-corner candy shop; wasn't it enough she had his two sisters? He felt a certain resentment, even though he knew she was a deserted

wife with three kids. She wanted them to have it easier than
she had. But there was something a little grasping about his
mother, narrow-minded. He could see why the old man had
skedaddled, and he wanted a woman of larger views for himself, a woman whose whole life wasn't just her family and a
little store. A modern woman.

Like Sarah. She knew how to act in the world. She had
views on every subject. She read books and newspapers and
had mixed with all different kinds of people, even Gentile
rich ladies. She insisted men treat her as an equal. It even
made him a little uneasy, the way she harped on politics,
arguing that women were as good as men and that they should
have the vote. Sometimes he wondered whether he wanted his
girl to be so militant, always going to meetings, even getting
beat up in a strike, though of course that was not her fault, it
was that bum Tricker Louis. Still, it was a contradiction: the
very things that drew him to Sarah also threw him off. If they
got married, she'd have to settle down. In marriage, you
wanted someone stable. His mother kept saying she had
found just the wife for him.

"Why don't you call Gussie Rabinowitz? She's dying to
hear from you."

She probably was, though he didn't want to be conceited.
The one time they'd met, Gussie certainly had seemed to like
him. She was a dish, too, *zaftig* with blond curls and a rich
father who was a Tammany Hall lawyer and fixer. Word had
even reached Joe that Rabinowitz himself had been very impressed by him. With his looks, his good accent, his nice
manners, his warm personality, and his union connections,
Joe was a natural for a political career, according to Rabinowitz.

"So call her," urged his mother. "What are you waiting
around for? I know—it's that Sarah Levy who's holding you
back."

So he called Gussie; yet even before he saw her again, he
knew how he'd feel. She was a nice enough girl, but limited.
She didn't have Sarah's spark, though half the time Sarah
wouldn't let him even kiss her. What was it that kept bringing
him back to her? Maybe she did remind him of his pop, that
long-lost ne'er-do-well idealist who'd skipped town when he
was a little kid.

And she didn't defer to him the way other girls did. Most
girls fell all over him, agreeing with every word he said. Not

Sarah. She wasn't impressed. He liked that. It showed quality. She had a poor opinion of him; all right, that gave him something to work against. She was a challenge.

Hunched beside the lamp, Ruby labored over her princess shirtwaist. Her work was so fine that Hannah had to squint to see where one stitch ended and the next began.

"How come you never go out anymore, Ruby?" asked Solly Fein irritably.

"I've got too much to do."

First she made the embroidered yoke. She cut the beige net to fit the pattern, which curved intricately in Gothic convolutions, dipping to a pointed lozenge in the center where she was to embroider a large peony. She duplicated the pattern on stiff paper, and basted the net on i., making delicate tucks at the throat line. Next, she carefully cut out the satin bodice, holding her breath. She couldn't afford to make mistakes with the satin; it could not be replaced. She basted the underside of the satin to the net, then turned it to the right side and bound the edges in buttonhole stitch, using old-rose silk embroidery floss and stitching over a cotton cord to add height to the binding.

When she had finished, the yoke was securely backed in satin and outlined in dark pink. She then cut away the paper backing between the net and the fabric, and began her embroidery, in a pattern of peonies, chrysanthemums, and curling tendrils and leaves. She stuffed the larger flowers and leaves with cotton as she went, to give a three-dimensional illusion. She worked the one large and two small peonies in a rose and lilac satin stitch, filling their centers with mauve French knots, and did the leaves in short-and-long stitch, pale green. She used both pale green and olive for the stems, which she outlined in buttonhole stitch. The curling vines were a medium green. There were eight chrysanthemums of varying sizes embroidered in pink, beige, and old rose, with ivory highlights.

This embroidery took Ruby four weeks. When it was done she carefully cut the satin from behind the net yoke, and bound the edges underneath with more buttonhole stitch. The front of the shirtwaist was now finished: a pinky-beige satin bodice and a net yoke, transparent except for strategically placed embroidered leaves and blossoms. Her round pink shoulders would peek out from behind the pale chrysan-

themums, while the shadow between her young breasts would
be discreetly, erotically hinted by the curve of the darker
peony, lilac and rose, and the trembling of the pale green
leaves that twined around it like a lover's fingers.

On Wednesday, December 15, 1909, the Women's Trade
Union League arranged a special fund-raising meeting at the
exclusive Colony Club, and Sarah was asked to be the main
speaker.

"Say whatever's on your mind about the strike," Helen
Marot told her. "But throw in some details about your own
life that will personalize the story. You must remember these
women know nothing whatsoever about you shirtwaist girls,
the way you live, or conditions in the East Side shops.
They're society women; they've never worked a day in their
lives." Her voice betrayed a certain contempt. "They are as
ignorant of economic life as babies, for all their wealth and
influence, but they are well intentioned, and, heaven knows,
you need their help. Reach them, move them, get them emotionally involved. If they become interested they can be a
powerful force for good—and give a lot of money to the
strike fund."

Rachel and the other strikers whom Helen chose to come to
the Colony Club said only a few words each. Helen Marot
herself gave the main outline of the events of the strike, along
with a plea for help. Unfortunately, her manner was rather
dry and the audience responded apathetically. It would be up
to Sarah to inspire them. But Rachel feared that Sarah would
not be at her best in this setting. She hated rich people. She
had begun to scowl even before they reached the elegant
building with its facade of intricately checkerboarded bricks,
and she became as stiff as a poker once they were inside the
enormous drawing room.

It was a brilliant room, with gleaming ivory-painted woodwork, ivory walls, gilt chairs and velvet settees, carved
wooden tables, and a few fantasies in wicker. Its wide, light
windows were fronted by feathery potted palms. Some of the
shirtwaist girls, used to dark, cluttered, dingy quarters,
gasped as they entered, and Rachel murmured, "Everything's
so white—it's like being out in the snow."

"Yes, isn't it extraordinary," said Mary Dreier enthusiastically. "Elsie de Wolfe did it a few years ago. She has
such a genius for doing rooms that now she's decided to give

up acting and make a business out of it. Interior decoration, she calls it. Her own apartment on Irving Place is quite stunning, all ivory, like this.''

It had never occurred to Rachel that the process of pulling a room together implied a choice among various possibilities of style, color, and ornament. Selection of this kind was not a part of life on the East Side. Mere acquisition—just having anything, a chair, a table, a piece of spare cloth to pin over the window at night—was enough to worry about. Rachel could hardly imagine a state of mind, an ease of livelihood, a graciousness of schedule that would permit pondering over household furnishings: bric-a-brac, fresh flowers, carved wooden tables, velvet and silk brocade. She thought about the possibility for some time. Elegance. She found it a pleasurable if quite unaccustomed field for thought.

Not Sarah. She barely looked around, just sat staring grimly into space. Rachel knew she was terrified. As soon as they had entered the room and she had seen the hundreds of elaborately gowned, jeweled, and coiffed society women sitting on gilt chairs staring at her, Sarah had clutched Rachel's sleeve in an iron grasp. Rachel squeezed her hand now. "You'll be fine," she whispered. "Go on, Sarah, give 'em what-for.''

Sarah took a deep breath, thinking, There's no way, there's no way I can make these rich women understand anything. She scanned the room until her eyes met those of Becky, down the row, who gave her a big wink and the high sign. Sarah closed her eyes, opened her mouth, and began to speak.

Afterward she couldn't understand what all the fuss was about. She couldn't even remember what she'd said. She knew she'd told them about Russia, Papa in the early days, and the pogrom. Rosa. Bubbe. Coming over in steerage. Mama taking home bundles and their working after school. Her wanting to study but having to get a job. Then the jobs, one after another, and always getting fired when she spoke up against intolerable conditions, and still not being able to keep herself from speaking up. Then Triangle Waist and the strike. The gorillas, the beatings, her broken ribs. The League's help, the general strike. The continual harassment, the fear of the police, of arrest, of losing all. She did not remember crying out, "We came here to get away from the Cossacks and

we find them here before us, in blue uniforms with the courts
backing them up.''

When she finished, there was silence, then thundering applause that seemed to go on too long. She felt so weak she
had to lean on a table. Rachel hugged her and whispered,
''Oh, Sarah, you really did it. You even had me crying,'' and
Sarah looked up and saw that a number of the beautifully
dressed ladies were wiping their eyes or discreetly blowing
their noses and that the collection plate Helen Marot was
passing was piled high, not with coins but with dollar bills.

Then came tea: silver teapots and coffeepots, creamers and
sugarbowls, with the sugar in little cubes you took with silver
tongs shaped like birds' claws. There were plates of tea sand-
wiches: watercress, cucumber, some kind of meat paste,
some kind of creamy cheese; trays of fancy pastries and tea
cookies; edifices of whipped cream and fruit piled high inside
ladyfingers; silver bowls of fruit—even grapes, in December—and nuts and chocolate. And pieces of fine damask you
were supposed to wipe your dirty mouth on, and silver
spoons. But, Sarah noted, no toothpicks.

She found herself sitting next to Helen Marot, which was a
good thing since she helped her deal with all the society
women. Sarah was still drained from her speech, tense and a
little sharp, like a string tuned too high. She remained seated
as the ladies came up and bent over her in their beautiful
gowns so their décolletages showed and told her how much
they liked her speech and how wonderful and brave she was
and how they did think her work was simply splendid and
how it all sounded very dreadful down there on the East Side
and if they could help in any way—at which point Helen
would break in with a smile and ask them to sign up as volunteer pickets or fund raisers. Finally the crowd around Sarah
thinned enough so she could drink her tea. She was churning
inside. She hated being fussed over. Everything in her
heritage warned her that so much favorable attention could
only bring bad luck.

''You really reached them, Sarah,'' murmured Helen.
''You even had Mrs. Belmont blowing her nose.''

''Who's she?''

Helen smiled wryly. ''Of course, you don't read the society pages. She's the one with the pug nose over there in a
blue dress. She's married to the subway system—Oliver Haz-
ard Perry Belmont, you know? She made her daughter Con-

suelo marry the Duke of Marlborough for his title. It was a great scandal at the time, the bride driving to the wedding in tears and so forth.''

Sarah was shocked. ''What's a woman like that doing here?''

Helen shrugged. ''She's on our board. She's terribly keen on women's rights, a militant suffragist. Of course she's always threatening to set up new organizations if the old ones don't do as she likes, but she's very supportive and free with her money.''

''I can understand how someone like that might be a suffragist, but I can't see why she'd support unions. Her husband breaks strikes.''

''Well, perhaps this is a way of demonstrating her independence from him,'' murmured Helen with a rather cynical smile. ''In any case, their money doesn't come from the garment industry. I've also heard that the original Belmont was a Jew who changed his name when he came over.''

Sarah shifted uncomfortably in her chair and Helen looked at her quizzically. ''You know, Sarah, if you had a little more experience, I'd say you should try to become a full-time organizer after the strike. You're a natural speaker.''

Sarah looked blank. ''What do you mean, be on the union staff?''

''Are there any women on the staff?'' Helen paused. ''Don't bother to answer. No, that's not what I mean; there are other ways. We should think about it.'' Her eyes surveyed the room, seeming to click off possibilities as Sarah lapsed into thoughts of her own.

It was strange how the union officers were all men. Most of the workers were women, but there weren't even any women in on the negotiations. She'd never really thought about it before. It was disturbing, and she wondered about the reason. Maybe there weren't any girls who wanted to be negotiators or have union jobs. Or perhaps you were supposed to ask somebody for these jobs and the girls didn't know or didn't think of it, so only the men asked. Probably custom had something to do with it, too, and the shyness of most of the women who always assumed men could do better. But it didn't have to be that way.

If they won the strike, the union would have more dues money and could hire more walking delegates. That would be the time to ask. As Sarah imagined what it would be like to work full time for the union, a delighted smile spread over her face. Just think of being able to spend all your time organizing other girls! A woman could understand what they were thinking and how to reach them. She'd be able to visit them at home, too, and in their boardinghouses, without people talking. How wonderful it would be to have such a job! First she would organize all the shirtwaist girls into groups, according to where they worked, and visit the shops regularly to check on conditions and keep up morale. Then she'd go after the really young ones, the little kids who slaved away in the white-goods industry making underwear. And when all of them had been organized, she'd start in on the laundries.

Surely Helen was mistaken if she thought women were deliberately kept out of union staff jobs. No women had asked, that's all; and the men had problems of their own; they couldn't think of everything.

Rachel was sitting next to an extremely thin and extravagantly dressed young woman with a lace collar so high her neck looked a foot long. A dark green chiffon scarf wound round her chestnut curls like a Greek fillet, and her tiny face, dwarfed by this coiffure, was as pointed as the head of the fox fur draped over her shoulders, biting its front paws. She wore a bottle-green redingote bordered with embroidery made of braid sewn down in serpentine curlicues, and her skirt was the tightest Rachel had ever seen. How could she walk in it? Her steps were, indeed, small and mincing, Rachel noted, as the girl went to fetch a second helping of cake, then sat languidly down again.

"My name's Tish Sloate," she murmured. "I adore cream cakes, don't you?"

Rachel smiled shyly. She could not take her eyes off the girl, who had now positioned herself in her little gilt chair at the most acute angle Rachel had ever seen assumed by the female body. Her back must have been forty-five degrees from the chair. Rachel tried to figure out why that seemed so unusual and nearly gasped as she understood—this woman must not be wearing a corset! Rachel herself wore only a light one, but she could not bend at all between her ribcage and her waist, and even sitting down demanded all her concentration. But it couldn't be. No one went out without a corset. It would be like going naked.

Rachel suddenly realized she was staring and the girl was

staring right back at her, eating meditatively and licking her spoon like a cat. Her eyes were a startling green shot with yellow. Embarrassed, Rachel looked away.

"Hmm," said the girl. *"Dites, qu'avez-vous vu?"*

"What?"

"Nous voulons voyager sans vapeur et sans voile!
Faites, pour égayer l'ennui de nos prisons,
Passer sur nos esprits, tendus comme une toile,
Vos souvenirs avec leur cadres d'horizons.
Dites, qu'avez-vous vu?"

After a moment, Rachel realized she was reciting something in a foreign language. But surely she must understand English? She was an American. Nonplussed, Rachel smiled politely and said nothing.

"Baudelaire," said Tish Sloate.

"What does that mean?"

"Oh, you don't speak French?" said Tish. "Sorry. It means: 'I'm bored, give me a vision, tell me what you've seen.' Well? What have you seen?"

"Me?" said Rachel. "Nothing much." She thought for a moment, then said daringly, "The depths but not the heights."

"Really?" said the girl with interest. "Just the reverse of me. I've only seen the heights. What do you think of that?" She smiled brightly, and her long elegant hands moved in constant exclamation as she spoke.

"I don't know," said Rachel. She had no idea what to say to this person and decided that honesty was her only possibility.

The girl looked at her narrowly. "You disapprove of me, don't you?"

"Why should I?" said Rachel. "I don't even know you."

"Hmm, a good point," said Tish. "I suppose I'm making an ass of myself for a change. You see, I'm feeling a bit desperately out of my element at ye olde Colony Club. It's my mother's club, and full of her friends, like Mrs. Belmont over there, gaping at me like a dying guppy. Mother begged me not to come today. She was afraid I'd disgrace her; I often do. But I did so want to hear about the East Side and the strike and meet you girls. And when I heard your friend speak I thought, 'I must change my life.' But then I thought, 'Oh, what's the use, they'll all hate me anyway, because they're so terribly strong and brave and principled and hard-working and I'm such a useless creature.' Do you see?''

Rachel didn't, but was eager to find some point of contact. She sensed a rancor similar to her own behind all this green-eyed brilliance and exclamation.

"My parents are mad at me, too," she confided. "Especially Papa. He thinks I'm an ungrateful daughter. He's against the strike and is sure it will lead me into prostitution if not atheism, and that I'll never get married now."

"Isn't that extraordinary?" said Tish. "That's almost word for word what my father said when I got kicked out of Vassar."

"Why were you kicked out?" Rachel wasn't quite sure what Vassar was, but clearly one could ask this creature anything.

"For a number of reasons. There was a rather too intense friendship with a teacher, for one," and Tish darted a glance at Rachel to see if she understood. Rachel looked as blank as ever. "Then there was a little scandal involving a suffrage meeting for Mrs. Pankhurst, the English militant, you know? She was touring and I wanted her to speak at college but they wouldn't let me have the auditorium or the gymnasium. So we had to hold the meeting in the local cemetery. The papers got hold of it, of course, and it was all rather dramatic, I confess, particularly since the spirit moved me to come in a nun's habit. I can't quite remember why, but I suppose it had something to do with my general feeling about women's colleges. And I was irritated with the college president. Anyway, the meeting was bad enough and then I was observed not long after driving through the countryside in a Lagonda, with a most unspeakable young man at a most indecorous hour and worst of all, I shudder to say, holding a lighted cigarette in my hand. So I was expelled."

"Smoking!" exclaimed Rachel in delight.

"Yes. Ladies don't. Have you ever?"

"No. Is it nice?"

"Not really," said Tish. "In fact, it's revolting, but it produces the most entertaining looks on the faces of one's elders, not to mention on those of all the suitable young men, otherwise known as stuffed shirts, whom one's parents wish one to marry. Do you plan to marry?"

"Eventually," said Rachel. "But not anyone I've met."

Tish laughed. "My sentiments exactly. If only one could marry someone without having to meet him, what a world of tedium could be avoided. We really are rather similar despite our differences in what my mother insists upon calling 'breeding,' aren't we? How about food? I adore it; it's my one sincere passion."

"I never feel I've had quite enough of it," grinned Rachel. "You might call it unrequited love in my case."

"Then let me get us both some more dessert so we can go on exchanging girlish confidences," said Tish, rising gracefully and going to the tea table. "Oh, look—raspberry fool!" She seized an ornate arrangement of berries, whipped cream, and ladyfingers, and dance it over to Rachel with little mincing steps, caroling, "I'm just a fool over raspberry fool!"

"Will you look at Laetitia Sloate," said Mrs. Belmont across the room. "I really must speak to that child's mother."

Rachel and Sarah went home on the Third Avenue El. It was late and they were tired. Sarah was, in addition, annoyed with Rachel, who had hardly come near her all afternoon. It was bad enough to have to listen to her gush about love all the time, but if she was going to have her head turned by the Colony Club—well, two people could only be best friends if they had the same kind of values.

"Who was that girl you spent the whole time with?" she asked jealously.

"Her name's Tish Sloate. As in Sloate Consolidated Bank and Trust."

"Hmph," said Sarah. "Of course you can't trust people like that." It would only bring Rachel pain to get her head turned by some rich girl who would then drop her.

"How do you know?"

"Why would a rich girl want to be friends with you?"

"Oh, for heaven's sake," said Rachel impatiently. She was increasingly tired of what she thought of as "Sarah's preaching." Just because Sarah knew more than she did about unions didn't mean she was right about everything. The strike had opened new worlds of experience to Rachel; away from her grinding daily labor and the repressive influence of her parents, she felt herself growing, stretching mentally. She would not be held back by anyone. Sarah got mad whenever she did anything on her own; even Rachel's working at the

Forward, which she could hardly criticize, made Sarah glower. Ab Cahan had been very nice to Rachel, almost like a good father. He let her work on the paper as often as she liked and even said he might give her a real job someday. For Rachel, the *Forward* office was a university; she loved to hear the men argue about poetry and theater and international politics. Sarah's response was to sneer at intellectuals, just the way she sneered at love.

She was even more nasty about Rachel's interest in the women's movement. Rachel was fascinated by the world of feminism—the uptown ladies, the Village intellectuals, the reformers, the suffragists, the militants, even the millionaire women. Their understanding touched her own experience at many points and she was drawn to them, wanting to copy their manners and be at home with their ideas. She could learn things from these women that she never could from the socialist men on the East Side, even Cahan. The men all lectured too much, and she privately dismissed them as rabbis like her father, looking for radical congregations. She had not the same resistance to listening to women, so she understood more. She wanted to be friends with Tish Sloate. She would not let Sarah run her mind and her life and keep her chained to her side.

"So what if they're rich and we're poor," she said. "We're all women. To them, that's the main thing; it makes them want to help us. And as far as I'm concerned, we need all the help we can get."

"That's just what they want, to convince us we're all sisters together! The trouble with you, Rachel, is you have no more class consciousness than a two-year-old child."

Rachel's cheeks burned with anger. "And the trouble with you is that your head is so full of cut-and-dried slogans from your father that you've no idea what it's like to be a woman!"

"What's that supposed to mean?"

"Your father has always let you do whatever you want. You stay out late at night; you do hardly any housework. Nobody tries to make you get married. What do you know about how most girls feel? I have more in common with some of those rich girls than I do with you."

Sarah was stricken; did Rachel really think that? "It's not true," she cried. "If we lose our strike, that rich girl won't care. She won't go hungry. We can't depend on people like her; we have to count on ourselves and on the working class!"

"What kind of help have we gotten from the working class?" snapped Rachel. "Except for the East Side unions, the men don't give us money. As far as that goes, how much have your precious Joe Klein and the International done for us?"

"They're doing all the negotiating!"

"Has it ever occurred to you to wonder why we're not doing our own negotiating?"

Sarah jumped as if she'd touched a nerve; it was the same question she'd been circling gingerly in her own mind. "We're too busy picketing, of course," she said in a tone that brooked no argument.

Rachel exploded. "Boy, you're dumb sometimes! I don't know what's going to become of you. I really don't. Either you'll marry the first union man who asks you or else you'll never marry and spend your life fronting for big-mouths like Joe Klein, doing all their work for them and never asking why they get a salary and you don't!"

Sarah felt as if she'd been hit; there were tears in her voice as she spoke. "I don't need to hear you tell me that, Rachel. I know what you're really saying, it's just what my mother says, that I'm some kind of freak and nobody will ever marry me."

Rachel knew she'd gone too far; she tried to apologize but Sarah wouldn't listen.

"Now that I know what you think of me, you don't have to come around me anymore," said Sarah very proudly. "I don't need friends like you. Just stay away from me and my house. And don't come and get me for picket duty tomorrow, either."

"All right, I won't! I'll go to the *Forward* office instead and work on my story. At least there people listen to what I'm trying to say instead of jumping down my throat!"

They parted without even saying good-bye.

That night Rachel cried herself to sleep. She knew she had hurt Sarah far more than she had meant to and that Sarah had misunderstood what she'd been saying. They had been best friends for six years and a life stretching on without Sarah was unimaginable. Sarah was her refuge from her family, the one to whom she told her dreams, the only person in the world she loved without ambiguity. "But it can't be that I have to agree with her about everything," she wept into her pillow. "That's not friendship."

Sarah tossed on her cot half the night, preparing denunciations. Rachel was her only close friend her own age. Drawn into adulthood young, she could be silly only with Rachel, joking around and for a moment or two sloughing off her sense of world-historical responsibilities. Sarah often retreated into a prickly shyness that cut her off, and many thought her arrogant. Rachel was her bridge to other girls, and she had assumed they thought the same way about basics. "But she really thinks she's something all of a sudden," muttered Sarah in confusion. How like Hannah she had sounded on the El—so superior. "Well, if that's what she thinks of me, it's better I should know it now. She'll see." But what she would see, Sarah did not know.

Friday morning Sarah went to picket duty alone. She was soon joined by Fanny Jacobs. There were few strikers there and the policeman in charge saw his opportunity to make an arrest without any trouble. After a brief conference with Bernstein, who was standing at the Triangle door welcoming scabs, the cop arrested them. By the time the League women found out and came to the Jefferson Market courthouse, Bernstein had already testified that Sarah and Fanny were notorious anarchists and prostitutes, and they had been sentenced to five days in the workhouse.

That same Friday morning, Hannah was busy scrubbing the walls and floors, going over the cracks with carbolic acid to keep out roaches.

"If you don't care about religion, how come you go through this every Friday?" asked Ruby.

Hannah sniffed defensively, aware that she had become much more observant of late. Her continuing sin with Solly Fein weighed upon her mind and though she knew it was silly to think God could be bought off so easily, she clung to a childish calculation that he might let her off easy on sex if she straightened up on kosher housekeeping. Thursday night and Friday had become a frantic bustle, a hysteria of purification after which Hannah collapsed, exhausted. But she was not about to explain this to Ruby.

"Don't be such a dummy," she told her impatiently. "Doesn't every Jewish lady in the building stand on top of her chairs and tables to paint the cracks so the roaches shouldn't come out on *Shabbos?* Am I supposed to have the only place with no carbolic? I might as well send the roaches a dinner invitation. Now get out of here with your questions. Go to school."

Ruby clattered down the stairs, abashed, and Hannah smiled triumphantly; once more she had used sarcasm to shield faith.

After finishing the walls she began to scour the stove and the shelves. She was hard at work, her sleeves rolled up, her hair disheveled, when she heard heavy footsteps clumping up the stairs and stopping in front of her door. There was a commanding knock.

"Who is it?" yelled Hannah, wiping her hands and pushing at her hair ineffectively. It had to be a stranger. The neighbors didn't knock.

A lady's voice said, "Goldie Golovey the *shadchen,*" and Hannah opened the door. An amazing figure entered. Monumental beyond fatness, swathed richly in brown bombazine and draped additionally in the classical manner by a blue silk shawl with black beadwork, she was as startlingly outsized as a caryatid holding up a temple. Her own pediment was triangular, of garnet-colored velvet with a brown veil and a blue feather. Her genial red face bore a wide smile and a brown mole with a tuft of hair; she had a gold tooth and a beady brown eye, and she carried a carpetbag. She graciously extended her large hand. On it sparkled a rose-cut diamond; another bloomed upon her vast bosom, plunked in the middle of a big gold brooch shaped like a lozenge. Hannah gasped and crossed her fingers behind her back to avert the evil eye, just in case.

She knew who the woman was, of course. The *shadchen* or matchmaker was a familiar figure on the East Side. Her carpetbag was full of Kodak pictures of would-be brides and grooms, with copious notes on the appearance, character, and financial standing of each. The pious rich and prudent all-rightniks of the East Side did not believe in newfangled ideas like love; marriage was a business arrangement conducted between families, and the Goldie Goloveys of this world were created specifically to facilitate matrimony between shy nubile girls and old goats who'd made a bundle, between hard-working but plain daughters and widowers who needed a housekeeper and stepmothers for their brats, having killed one wife already through overwork and breeding. A terror to the young girls who hid at the sight of her, Goldie Golovey was a godsend to unworldly uprooted parents who wanted gentle scholarly boys with no infidel taint for their daughters.

"Is it okay I sit down and rest my feet?" she inquired. "I'm glad to find you at home and I want you should know right away, I haven't just come, I've been sent."

"Sent?" Hannah exclaimed in alarm. "Mrs. Golovey, I must tell you that in this house we're freethinkers. Also my daughters are still young and when they get older they'll want to pick out their own husbands."

"*Feh*," said the guest delicately. "So let them. Though by me thirteen and seventeen ain't so young already to be looking, and who says young ones have got the sense to pick good? A marriage is a bargain that should last a lifetime, and it takes a wise mature head. You know the saying, God sits above and makes matches below, but relax, relax, I haven't come here to talk about your daughters."

How did she know the girls' ages, Hannah wondered, then realized she probably knew the age and condition of every girl on the East Side. Why had she come? Hannah sat uncomfortably, avoiding the visitor's eyes and focusing on her diamond brooch.

"You like my jewel?" said Mrs. Golovey. "The gift of a satisfied customer." She inclined her head graciously and continued, "You have a boarder, Solomon Fein."

Hannah sat up with a jerk. Had he been going around trying to marry off the girls? She'd kill him! "Yes," she said cautiously. "So?"

"It's about him I've come to talk to you. He's been a customer of mine for more than a year already but I can't satisfy him—money he wants, good looks, youth, family, all together, and what has he got to offer in return? He ain't going to make a fortune peddling from a wagon. So how can I find for him such a match? Everybody knows that money follows money. Still I keep trying, because there's something about the man I like; he's well set up, strong in the arms, a sweet tongue in his mouth, so I keep on looking and hope somebody will come along, an older daughter maybe with a rich father and younger sisters dying to get married who can't budge until she's out of the way. And I think I finally found the girl."

Hannah listened, frozen, her mind in turmoil. Why was this awful woman telling her all this?

"Everything is coming along—Solly agrees, the father agrees, the girl is overjoyed. And then the mother starts making with the questions. 'Mrs. Golovey,' she tells me, 'what about his character? I hear he's a chaser, no woman is safe around him, he goes after his landladies, his customers, any woman who walks by. I don't want my Rosalie married to this.'"

"Rosalie!" Hannah shot the name out like a bullet.

The *shadchen* laughed richly in her throat, a noodle-pudding laugh, oozing with cream. "Well, Mrs. Levy, they told me you were nobody's fool. I can see what you're thinking: How many Rosalies can there be on the East Side?"

"The one I'm thinking of was born Rivke, put on display for years in the window of her father's butcher shop, like an old brisket, but still no takers."

"Well," sighed the *shadchen*, "it's true she's getting a little long in the tooth but we can't all be beauties and she's an even-tempered girl with many good points, such as her father's store, a nice butcher shop for a meat peddler to marry into."

"A robbery shop, charging two pennies more on the pound than the shop on the next block but giving credit so they can draw in the poor and suck their blood—this is the family you mean?"

Hannah was seething. Of all the people to get mixed up with he had to pick the Garfinkles? Bad enough their connection to that gangster who beat up Sarah, even worse that Mrs. *Fafonfnik* herself, full of hot air and so proud you'd think she never peed, strutting around the neighborhood in her fancy dresses ripped under the arms because she was getting so big and was too much of a slut to sew them, fancy dresses stained with sweat, lording it over the block and boasting with her *fonfe, fonfe, fonfe*, talking through her nose like she always had a cold: "I hab to tell you, Brs. Leby, such a bargain by Rosalie got by Lord ab Taylor's ubtown." Rosalie was a homely, freckle-faced redhead, getting into her late twenties, and spiteful from hanging on the vine waiting to be picked.

"Rosalie," said Hannah venomously. "A bust like a balcony sticking out in front and a nose like a drainpipe, still dripping."

The *shadchen* was watching her closely. "So what's it to you, Mrs. Levy? You seem so upset."

Hannah's hands twisted in her apron but she tossed her

head. "Upset? I'm not upset, why should I be upset? I'm
only—surprised—that somebody I know would want to tie
himself up with a family that's the hate of the neighborhood,
but it's none of my business. It's his life."

"That's what I hoped you'd say, because I tell you straight
out, there's been talk and Mrs. Garfinkle sent me to find out
what's what."

"Talk? What kind of talk?" So it was as she had feared,
the big-mouthed lout had bragged. Her hands turned cold. Lie
with a dog, you get up with fleas. She had known the man's
character; why hadn't she listened to her own warnings?

"Oh, it's not just about you they talk, it's him and all his
landladies. Don't you know what the men on the pushcarts
call him—appetizing Solly, the landladies' delight?"

Hannah took a deep breath as she felt the blood rush to her
face, telltale. Frightened, appalled, she tried to assess her
position. They couldn't really know anything. They were
only guessing. She could put a bold face on it, and who
would trust the bragging word of a man like Solly Fein unless
the woman admitted it or acted guilty herself? She might have
sinned and maybe she would pay for it, but that was between
her and God. It was no concern of Fafonfnik's or of this
terrible matchmaker. Nobody was going to shame her in the
neighborhood if she could help it. Better pain in your heart
than shame on your face. She drummed her fingers dangerously on the table, staring at the *shadchen* with narrowed
eyes.

"Are you trying to tell me that woman across the street
thinks I'm one of Solly Fein's *tchotchkies?*" she said fiercely.
"Is that what she thinks?"

"Oh, no, she doesn't *think*," said the matchmaker hastily,
"not *think*, only *wonder*, so she sent me to find out."

"I'd like to see her have the nerve to say it to my face!"
yelled Hannah, rising and beginning to stride about the room,
banging on furniture. "Who does she think she is, dirtying
my name in the neighborhood, talking about me to strangers!
You see how you make the blood rush to my face with such
an idea? You know what we call that in Russia? We call that
spilling blood, when you make somebody ashamed like that.
Doesn't that stupid cow have the brains to know that when
you spill someone's blood you make them your enemy? Who
does she think she's calling a whore, just let her come over
and say it here!" Hannah kicked the table for emphasis.

Mrs. Golovey was taken aback.

"Mrs. Levy, Mrs. Levy, calm yourself down. I didn't mean to upset you. I'm sure Mrs. Garfinkle has no such idea. She never said anything about you in particular. She was only worried about the man's reputation in general. You know how people talk. And as the saying goes, even if people don't believe a whole slander they believe half of it, so I said, Why not ask his landlady, that's all, no offense meant and none taken as they say in America, I certainly hope."

"So it was your idea, not hers," said Hannah, tight-lipped. "Well? What are you going to tell her?"

"Why, I'll tell her the truth," said the *shadchen* innocently. "That as far as you're concerned, there's nothing to these stories. That is what you said, isn't it? He never did anything bad with you?"

"Of course not!" The two women looked at each other for a long, measured minute until the matchmaker hoisted herself from her chair.

"Then I'm satisfied," she said. "The wedding can go ahead."

Hannah sighed. "Tell the Garfinkles I wish them all the happiness they deserve," she said in a sugary voice. "I'll dance at their wedding."

The woman left and Hannah sat shaking, hugging herself at the narrowness of her escape. She had never deceived herself about Solly's character. But she had not known she would endanger her reputation merely by sharing a roof with him. She had assumed their affair was secret and safe and had not thought about him very much during the day, keeping her regular life and her evening pleasures separate in her mind. But he had brought her, without her consent, into his own daytime world; he had fouled and humiliated her. Her cheeks burned, imagining him joking about her with the other peddlers on Essex Street. She saw him nodding when her name came up, as if he could tell a thing or two if he wished, and his friends laughing and taking her name lightly. And now she was to be seen by the world as his creature, soiled by his use.

She felt like scouring her whole body as she had the floor. All her *Shabbos* cleaning was worthless if she was dirt in the eyes of the neighborhood. Could they really believe such things of Hannah Levy, who carried herself so proud? She was not that kind of woman, She might have made a mistake but it was not the kind of mistake that was in her nature; she did not hold herself cheap. She would show them. She would dance at his wedding indeed. She would not let herself be tainted by a rumor that could never be proved, that was merely slander from a loose-living man.

Hannah was in this agitated state when she found out about Sarah's arrest. There was nothing she could do since no visitors were allowed on Blackwell's Island. She paced the floor like a caged animal, almost glad of a plausible reason for her red eyes, her pent-up hysteria. Because of the arrest, Moyshe stayed home to sit with her that night and the next, which was not only a comfort but also delayed the hour of confrontation with Solly Fein.

When it came, she congratulated him coolly on his engagement and got her shawl. He put his hand on her arm and said in his insinuating way, "I'll be right across the street, you know. I'm sure we'll still see a lot of each other."

"You don't think I'm going to start buying meat at those robbery prices just because you're there!" She opened the door.

"Where are you going?"

"To visit the woman whose daughter's in jail with my Sarah. You think I'm going to stay here with a man of your reputation?" And down the stairs she went.

He could never catch her alone after that. Soon he stopped trying. He had enough to do getting ready for his wedding and fixing up the little flat above the store. He was always philosophical about the end of an affair. "Easy come, easy go," he would say to himself and start looking for the next.

Hannah was less well-prepared and much less experienced. She resigned herself to the stasis that was to be her life from now on. She would live for her children, a thankless business though common enough. She could not understand how, loathing Solly as she did, she could lie sleepless next to an unknowing Moyshe and burn for him still. Consumed by resentment and longing, she imagined him with Rosalie, laughing at her. If he talked about her to that silly bitch, she would kill him, then kill herself, and she lay in cold torment, imagining that ending.

But she showed none of these feelings. She was composed and distant with Solly, though she could not resist letting fall some remarks about his intended. Correctly diagnosing this as jealousy, Solly smiled to himself and spent more time away from the house.

"If you ever get lonely," he said, "you can drop across the street."

"I don't get lonely," said Hannah Levy.

Little Fanny Jacobs cried when the cop who arrested her pinched her bottom. She flinched when the men at the station-house leered and beckoned. She clung to Sarah, who stared gravely, taking it all in, wondering why the men were acting like this. Was this what Rachel meant when she said Sarah didn't know how it felt to be a woman? It couldn't be that the cops really thought the girls were whores because they walked the street carrying picket signs. They just said that to make them feel bad. Or was the point to scare them, to make them feel they had to give up the strike and stay home, behind some door guarded by a father or husband, so they had a man's protection? Joe would like me to do that too, she suddenly thought. That's why he wishes I weren't so involved in the strike. It makes me too hard to protect. He doesn't like it that I want to take care of myself.

After an inedible dinner, the prisoners were loaded into a cart with barred windows and taken by boat across the river. As soon as they arrived on Blackwell's Island they had to change into prison uniforms, one-piece striped dresses of heavy coarse wool. Fanny completely disappeared within hers; even after it was pinned up at the hem and sleeves, she could hardly move because of the weight of the cloth.

They were put to work the next day sewing uniforms. The material was hard and stiff, and after a few hours their finger-tips were covered with bloody little punctures from the wrong end of the needle when it wouldn't go through the goods. Sarah was faint with hunger and fatigue; Fanny was in an even worse state. Neither had been able to eat the rotten food given them the night before; neither could eat again that night, though Fanny forced down some moldy bread and Sarah chewed on a nearly raw potato.

The women with whom they shared their cell and most of the women they saw at dinner were clearly prostitutes. Sarah had always wondered what that was like. Did they hate it? Did they get used to it? How did it feel when they did it? Did it hurt every time? A lot of her questions about prostitution were really questions about sex. Some of them talked as if they liked it. A few asked her and Fanny who they were, then made fun of them for being strikers. "You got to be crazy to work in a factory for six dollars a week when it's so easy to make money," said one. "Think of having to strike and get beat up for nothing."

Fanny kept peering around nervously. "I keep wondering if I'm going to run into this girl who used to live in our building. Would I be embarrassed!"

"Who was she?"

"She used to do it with the big boys after school, behind the stairs in the back. They paid her a quarter. Somebody told her pa and he kicked her out. Then I heard she went into a bad house."

You couldn't grow up on the East Side without knowing something about sex, no matter how innocent you were supposed to be. There were the whores sunning themselves on Allen Street, where Sarah used to live, the rough talk from the fellows in the shops, the heckling from some of the push-cart peddlers and street types. The intimacies of tenement life were themselves educational; the couples entwined on the fire escape or humping on the roof in the hot pale August nights as if they didn't know they were surrounded by a whole ghettoful of neighbors also sleeping outside to escape the heat; the noises that came up the airshaft, especially on Friday nights when it was a man's Sabbath duty to pleasure his wife—Mr. Breynes downstairs made so much noise every night of the week that Hannah called him "the saint." Why? "To him every day is the Sabbath."

But no matter how Sarah strained her ears to hear if any wild thumpings were coming from the tiny back room her parents shared, she never heard a sound. She wondered why, to the extent that she could bring herself to think about it. Impossible to ask, even to hint. Sexual matters were no less unmentionable in the Levy household than they were in the homes of pious families like Rachel's.

Why did women become whores? The explanations she had heard involved forced abductions and white slavers, innocent young country girls seduced by big-city men, and working women who could not survive on their wages and turned to sin to escape starvation. Many of the tales Sarah heard in prison did not fit these patterns. The worst was one she heard her first night, lying in the dark pretending to be asleep and eavesdropping while the whores in the cell exchanged life stories. There was one who said she was twenty-five though

Sarah thought she looked forty. Her mother had sold her when she was five; she had borne a child of her own at eleven. Now she whispered in the dark, fear in her throat, "I'm almost down to the bottom. I was a kid trick. I was in an uptown house in the Tenderloin, then I slipped down to Fourteenth Street, then to the Bowery, and now I'm working the Chinatown dance halls and all that's left are the back rooms on the waterfront. Then it's the Potter's Field."

Sarah lay there stiffly, trying not to make a sound. *Why?* Sold as a baby by her own mother, seeing her future so plain and so hopeless—how could she know it for what it was and do nothing to stop it? She should make a bomb and throw it; she should kill somebody. Sarah wanted to leap up and shake her until her bones rattled and she fought back. But whom would she fight? Lying there tormented, Sarah suddenly saw as if projected on the cell wall that cold white Kodak imprinted forever on her brain. The dead girl lay on a table with blood all over her stomach and between her legs, her left hand dangling off the side, one finger missing.

Then the steel door that was always poised ready in her mind slammed shut and Sarah was alone in the dark, closed and clenched and terrified, with one thought blazing clear, It could happen to anyone. To any girl. To me.

A reception committee waited at the dock to greet the returning strikers. Rachel hung apart from the rest, fearing that the things she'd said on the El were unforgivable. She dreaded the ugly scene that might take place when Sarah saw her; perhaps she would denounce her as an opportunist; perhaps she would just pretend she didn't exist and cut her dead. The boat docked. The imprisoned strikers stepped from it and were immediately engulfed in the welcoming crowd. Rachel saw Sarah poke her head up and peer anxiously about. Their eyes met.

"Rachel!" Sarah shouted joyfully, and ran to her, throwing her arms around her so hard she almost knocked her down. Rachel began to cry.

"Oh, Sarah," she said, "I was so worried about you. Are you all right?"

"Sure."

"You're not mad at me?"

Sarah laughed. "Even *I* am not that crazy. At least, not when I'm in jail." Rachel sniffed, and began to laugh, too.

Then Mary Dreier came rushing up, bubbling with excitement. The League had made big plans for the next day: They
had decided to adopt a tactic of the suffrage movement—the
automobile procession. Instead of using Fifth Avenue as the
suffragists did, this motorcade would honk its way through
the narrow streets of the Lower East Side. Its banner-draped
cars would carry strikers and their society allies, providing a
feast of ironic contrasts for the gentlemen of the press, who
showed every sign of loving the pageantry.

"What do you think, Sarah?" said Mary Dreier. "Isn't it a
fine idea?"

Sarah was dazed. After the silence and introspection of jail,
this was more bustle than she could comprehend all at once.
"I don't know," she said. "I've never been in a motorcar."

"You get in front, Rachel," ordered Tish Sloate, opening
the door of the huge gray Hispano-Suiza. "Then everyone
can see you. If you put your union button on your hat it will
show from the window. You get in back with me, Molly, and
we'll hold both ends of the banner so it will go around the
back of the car."

"What does it say?" asked Molly. She was tremendously
excited.

"It says, 'The Workhouse Is No Answer to a Demand for
Justice.'"

"Tish," said the young man in the driver's seat, "aren't
you going to introduce me?" Rachel looked at him. He was
extraordinarily handsome, blond with fervent moustaches,
wearing a tall fur hat, plaid gaiters, and a tattersall-check
motoring ulster. He also seemed to have remarkably good
teeth.

"I have to remind Tish of her manners now and then," he
said in a stage whisper, leaning closer. "As her brother I'm
responsible for her conduct, and I'm sure you've noticed that
it's frequently dreadful."

Rachel dimpled.

"My chauffeur is called William Denzell Schuyler Sloate
III, commonly known as Den so as not to be confused with
William Denzell Schuyler Sloate I, also called Grandpa, now
deceased," rattled Tish in flutelike tones. "Or with William
Denzell Rensselaer Sloate II, our revered parent, known as
William or Sir. And these lovely ladies, Den, are Rachel Co-
hen and Molly Hurwitz."

To the extent that it is possible to bow from behind the wheel of an automobile, he did so.

As the enormous motorcars threaded their elephantine way through the congested streets of the East Side, tying up traffic and forcing the pushcarts to make way, Rachel found herself unable to tear her eyes away from the golden profile of Denzell Sloate. He seemed to return her interest, glancing at her from time to time and finally turning to stare with a look that combined admiration and the liveliest curiosity. Rachel felt herself blush.

"Eyes on the road, Den," commanded his sister. "You almost ran down a peddler just now. You can stare at Rachel some other time."

"When?" he asked eagerly. Molly giggled.

"I told you she was pretty," said Tish, "but I thought you were so besotted with your Frenchwoman that you'd never notice. Denzell's quite a case," she continued despite his protesting murmurs. "He only falls in love with unsuitable objects. First it was Uncle Schuyler's mistress, a singer. Then when Daddy shipped him off to Europe, he took up with a showgirl in the Folies Bergère."

"At least I'm warm-hearted," said her brother. "You never fall in love with anyone at all. It's positively abnormal."

"Simple prudence," said Tish. "A girl can't afford to throw her heart around like a tennis ball. Rachel and Molly and I are preserving ourselves for Mr. Right, aren't we, girls?"

"Sure," said Molly, still giggling.

"Yes indeed," said Rachel demurely, smiling at him out of the corner of her eyes.

"How will you know when you meet him, Rachel?" said Denzell.

"By the melting sensation in the region of my heart."

He chuckled. "Did you get that out of a book?"

"Many books," said Rachel.

"You know, my brother was quite taken with you," said Tish a few days later. "He said you were the most beautiful girl he'd ever seen and raved on at some length about your titian hair. Then he asked me to invite you to tea. I said you wouldn't want to take time off from the strike but promised him I'd mention it."

Rachel shrugged indifferently. "I don't mind one way or the other, but it sounds like your brother falls in love with every woman he meets—or at least every 'unsuitable' woman."

"Not really," said Tish. "Usually he just admires them from afar. He doesn't chase them; he's too lazy. In fact, they chase him. At least Uncle Schuyler's mistress did, worse luck. Mostly Denzell falls for women who'll treat him cruelly, like La Belle Dame Sans Merci, or women who are married. That's what I meant by unsuitable."

"Oh," said Rachel. "I thought perhaps you meant Jewish. Or poor."

"Well, those are points in your favor, there's no getting round it. Dark, flaming exotic—you know, right out of *Ivanhoe*. Den and I both seek forbidden fruit rather a lot. Our family's so stuffy, one has a positive need to kick over the traces. At least *we* do. Our older brother Sonny works in the bank with Father."

"So all I am is a gesture of rebellion?" said Rachel lightly.

"More than that, love," protested Tish, "but if you could hear Mother going on and on about blood and breeding—I mean, it does get sickening. She and Den had a row about it only this morning. He said our class was too inbred and that's why he and I are so peculiar; the line needs new blood. Healthy peasant stock. Mother nearly fainted. Hmm, do you suppose he meant you, Rachel?"

Rachel just smiled coolly and shrugged. But her heart turned over.

Hannah's period was a month late before she realized it. She never gave it a thought until one day, putting a clean rag in the box she kept for the purpose, she realized there were too many there. Had she missed a month? The blood drained from her face and she sat down suddenly as she remembered her nausea the last few mornings. When had she had her last period? Before Sarah was arrested? Before the *shadchen* came? She counted back on her fingers, frowning in concentration.

It had been seven weeks. And she was never late.

She gave a little groan and covered her mouth. Caught! So this was to be her punishment, to bear the child of a man she hated while he and his loathsome bride smirked at her from across the street; to have her husband turn from her in sorrow, perhaps even cast her out, and her daughters hold her in contempt. Before long the whole world would see what had happened and know of her shame—for inevitably the infant would resemble his father, the grossness of his features proclaiming his parentage.

Or perhaps she would die in childbirth, leaving her husband and children without a home. Or be crippled. At best, she would be worn down by the rigors of carrying at her age, by the nightmare of her guilt, by the poverty they would again plunge into with another mouth to feed. How cruel it was that it should happen now, when she had come so far and suffered so much and just gained this little plateau where she could begin to breathe easy for the first time.

She never doubted for a moment that the child was Solly's. If Moyshe had been going to make her pregnant he could have done so at any point in the last thirteen years; he didn't have to pick now. No, this child was one of sin, visited upon her in retribution. She would pay—oh, how she would pay—for her one slip, with a life made bitter, a life of condemnation and self-disgust, of revulsion from her own flesh and from the child who was her guilt made visible.

Shivering violently, holding the wall for support, Hannah made her way to her bed and lay down, limp with terror. Thirteen years since she was last pregnant! To think of going through all that again, even under better circumstances, would be hard enough—the carrying, the pain of labor, the danger. How many women bled to death? How many died of infection? At least in the old country she'd had her mother for a midwife. Bubbe could be trusted; she knew the magic charms and ceremonies to ward off evil, and how to clean you out afterward with her little wooden paddle so no infection could take root. But it was still a risk. She remembered the five or six miscarriages she had suffered, bleeding all day and not knowing why, and then she had been a young woman!

You went through all that and half the time the baby died anyway. A feeble mewing cry and it was gone. You did what you could to keep a child alive. You cleaned it with oil. You swaddled it quickly with clean bands of linen. You kept the windows closed tight so no fresh air or sunlight could get in. You buried the cord and the afterbirth deep in the earth, with the proper ceremony, so no malign influence could reach them. You hung curtains over the windows; you pinned psalms above the doorway; you let no one look at the child directly without spitting three times to keep off the Evil Eye. But none of it was sure. She had done all this for Rosa, for Sarah, for Ruby, but also for her two little boys who had died just the same, without even time enough on earth to be circumcised. No one knew how to keep them alive. She held her womb and sobbed.

She could not go through all this again. She had suffered enough. She would not raise a child of spite, acid in her womb, a changeling from across the street.

But it was God's punishment. You can't go against God's will.

She screwed her eyes tight with the effort of thinking it through.

They said it was God's will she should stay in Russia, too. They said this was the punishment given the Jews for their sins in the early days. She had not accepted that. She had rebelled against such stupid fatalism. She had not stood still for the Black Hundreds and she would not give in to this.

There was a thing Bubbe did with her little wooden paddle early in a pregnancy if the mother wanted it. It was not safe. It was not painless. If it went wrong, you could die. But you could die from any of it. No one can choose her death. But she can choose her life. It was only seven weeks; only a little seed. It hadn't quickened yet. There was no sin.

She rose and went to the back of the drawer where she kept her savings in a black coinpurse. The sum was pitifully small. But Yetta Breynes was her friend and a good, clean midwife. She would let her pay by installments and she would keep her mouth shut, too. If, God forbid, Hannah began to bleed, Yetta would do what she could to help her. And if she could not help her, and the worst came, Yetta would protect her memory and never tell Moyshe or the children what she'd done. She was a good woman.

Hannah bit her lip until it bled, fighting the fear and the sorrow. Then she took her coinpurse in her hand, wrapped her shawl around her head, and started slowly down the stairs to the midwife, the abortionist.

Hannah bled for three days after the abortion. After another week of spotting, she went downstairs for a second scraping. She told no one the cause of her pain, letting them assume she was suffering from an unusually severe period. It was too bad Moyshe was not pious, she reflected ironically; perhaps then he'd have left her alone for a week after her uncleanliness. As it was, she had to rebuff him twice. This was not her usual practice. The first time he assumed she was just tired; the second, he asked questions.

"Are you sick?"

She shook her head, lips pursed.

"Are you mad at me?"

She began to shake her head again, then stopped suddenly, realizing she was furious with him. You couldn't exactly say this was all his fault, but if he'd been a better husband she would never have looked at Solly Fein. If he hadn't taken her for granted, ignored her year after year, hurt her so she could hardly stand it, how could she have turned from him to a pig like that? She sniffed.

"What have I done?" Moyshe was bewildered.

What could she tell him? Certainly nothing about Solly. She merely sniffed again, dolefully, and got under the covers. Turning her back to him she lay in the dark, grinding her teeth. Let him see what it felt like to have questions but no answers.

Long after she fell asleep Moyshe lay puzzling about his marriage. Was something really wrong? He did not approach Hannah again for two weeks, by which time her body had healed and she accepted his caresses in her usual matter-of-fact way. But a seed of uneasiness had been sown in his mind. He watched her through the following weeks more attentively than usual. She let him look, nursing her anger, glad he was finally worried. It was about time.

The strike went on and on, the big shirtwaist shops in the Waistmakers' Association still refusing to budge on the issue of union recognition—or, in their terms, a "closed shop." Finally the ILGWU negotiators agreed to a settlement without recognition and presented it to the body of strikers for ratification. They called a mass meeting for this purpose on December 27—but the strikers who came were so outraged at the idea of the proposed settlement that they shouted down Joe Klein and refused even to vote.

After this, the employers' association refused to attend further negotiating sessions and the strike began to lose public support. Among those who washed their hands of it was Samuel Gompers. The League women were furious at such lack of solidarity, but by the end of January, with no settlement in sight, Helen Marot began to agree with the union staff that the only thing to do was settle with the remaining shops on the best terms the union could get. Nothing was to be gained by prolonging the strike further. The workers in more than three hundred shops had already gone back to work with substantial gains. Most had union contracts. The union itself had come of age with the strike; it had gained thousands of new members and would be in a good position to fight the battles to come.

The employers were also tired of the strike. Shop by shop, the union began to settle on whatever basis it could without further votes. On February 8, the Triangle Waist Company signed an agreement with Local 25 of the ILGWU. Wages were raised but the union got few concessions on working conditions or safety. The scabs who had worked during the four-month strike were kept on, and there was no guarantee that all the union members would get their jobs back.

A week after the Triangle settlement, the entire general strike was officially ended. Despite the fact that some workers returned with little protection, it had been a great victory and a milestone in the history of the American garment industry. The workers had stayed out during the bitter winter months and had built a union strong enough to last.

"And that's not all," Helen Marot told Sarah. "You've won recognition for women. Before the strike, everyone said women would never make good trade unionists—they were too flighty and too easily scared. Nobody can say that anymore because of you Russian girls. You really showed them. It will be easier to organize all the others because of you."

II

Rachel hugged her secret, walking home. It was the night of Sunday, February 9, 1910; the next day work would begin again at Triangle Waist. But she would not be there. She had found another job, one where she could think and read and study, where she could talk to people and learn, where she would follow her own bent and become the self she was meant to be—she was now a full-time writer for the *Jewish Daily Forward*. She smiled to herself, remembering how funny Mr. Cahan had looked, brushing his moustache with his fingers and peering up at her from under his shaggy eyebrows.

"A column for girls?" he had asked. "Why girls?"

"Listen to me, Mr. Cahan, just listen." She had rattled out the words in her eagerness to explain her idea. "You got a lot of new readers in the strike, women who bought the *Forward* because it had the best strike stories. I ought to know, I wrote a lot of them. But do you think these girls are going to keep reading the paper now that they're back at work? Not unless we do something special. Readers they're not in the normal way of things; they don't have the money or the time. So the question is, How do we keep them reading the *Forward?*"

Her voice rose as she talked and several members of the staff, attracted by this enthusiasm, came over to see what was going on.

"We have to write about what they care about, from their point of view," said Rachel. "A column of advice, that's the ticket—a column by me!"

"Advice about what?" said Ben Schlesinger, the managing editor.

"Everything," said Rachel. "Boys, parents, friendship, marriage, votes for women, unions, love, clothes, entertainment, working girls' budgets, recipes, stories that reflect their own tastes in their own language."

"And educate too, I hope," said Cahan.

"It could be good publicity," said Schlesinger. "We could run a box on the front page saying something like, 'As a public service, in tribute to the historic strike of the waist-makers, the *Forward* is proud to present a new feature, Advice to Young Girls, by Miss Rachel Cohen, late of Triangle Waist Company. Letters solicited.' How does that sound?"

"Wonderful!" said Rachel, who had hardly dared hope her idea would meet with such a warm welcome.

"You'll have to use your own name, you know." Cahan chewed on his moustache. "No more Sadie Waistmaker."

"Oh," said Rachel slowly. She hadn't thought that part through.

"So all right." Cahan nodded decisively. "We'll give it a try. You can start right now. A column a day at ten dollars a week, how's that?"

Now, hours later, her first column drafted and accepted, Rachel almost skipped along the icy sidewalk. A new life! No longer to be just a pair of hands, working for somebody else, but a mind working for herself as well as for others! Even the knowledge that she must tell her parents could not dim her joy. She would hoard her achievement to herself this one proud night, then face her father in the morning.

She had never seen him in such a rage, shrieking and hitting her like a man gone mad. "A writer!" he shouted his red face looming over her, his graying beard writhing with demonic energy. "A writer for the freethinkers!"

He moaned as if possessed: "Can I earn money for my thoughts, my writings? Do they send me money for writing about Torah, the commentaries, things of holiness they should value? *Drek!* Profanation! That's all they care about in *golus!* Me they ignore; let him starve—a tiny congregation, a handful of the worthy. The others, they don't even see me; it's like I'm not in this country at all. But you they pick, a girl, a useless brainless gadabout who goes on strikes and writes in a *goyisheh* language some rubbishy thing or other, who knows what, nothing of value, nothing holy. What do you know that they should pay you to write it down?"

He hid his head in his hands, sobbing broken-heartedly, and knelt upon the floor in lamentation. "My God, my God, why hast thou forsaken me? Why art thou so far from the words of my groaning? So King David cried, 'I am a worm, and no man; scorned by men and despised by the people. All who see me mock at me!'" He threw himself against the wall, beating upon it with his fists in an ecstasy of sorrow.

"Why did we come to this Godforsaken country where everything is backward, where the fathers are ground into dust and the children exalted as kings, where all I was has fallen from me? I curse this country in the name of Abraham, Isaac, and Jacob. I curse the Jews, who have broken Thy Holy Covenant. And so it is written that our sons and daughters shall be given to another people while our eyes look on and fail with longing for them all the day and it shall not be in the power of our hand to prevent it, so that we shall be driven mad by the sight which our eyes shall see."

He wailed and dashed the pots and pans from their shelf with one sweep of his hand, then looked wildly about the room for something to throw. Rachel's mother was hiding behind the stove; Rachel cowered against the wall. Distracted by some thought, he stumbled to his shelf of books and started pulling the volumes down, flinging them roughly on the floor and stamping on them, sobbing, "There, get there, get ground to dirt, that's all you're worth in this country!" His wife cried, "Ezra, no!" but was afraid to come out, and Rachel could see the neighbors crowded in the hall outside the door, listening in horror but unwilling to interfere.

The rabbi sat down upon the floor, suddenly pensive, stroking his beard sadly. "I should be right now sitting in the back room of the Gradz *shul*, studying my Rashi with the other holy men, going home to my family house, rich, well-kept, a good dinner on the table, with my two sons who have been studying with me all day, and following behind us a fine, big congregation. And where is my congregation? A handful of poor tailors, hardly a *minyan* even on *Shabbos*. Where are my sons who should be rabbis like their fathers before them; where are my *kaddishes*? One runs off God knows where to get killed by Indians or convert to be a Christian; he doesn't even write his mother. The other one's forgotten all the Hebrew he ever knew and thinks only of money, doesn't even cover his head. And my daughter," he cried, agitated again, "what about her? A writer for the atheists, whoring around at all hours of the night!'' He grabbed Rachel's arm and pulled her to her feet. "You wish to leave your people, well, go then! Get out of my house!'' But Rachel could not break away; he was holding her too tightly while at the same time hitting her madly with his other hand. His ring cut her above one eye and the blood ran down her face so she could barely see.

"Stop it, Ezra!'' her mother cried abruptly. Running from behind the stove, she clung to his arm with all her might so Rachel could wrench herself loose. She ran to the door.

"I'm going,'' she cried, trying to wipe the blood from her eye. "Be it on your head! Good-bye, Mama.''

Then she escaped down the stairs as he broke from her mother and came after her, cursing and throwing pots and pans and holy books like hailstones to plague her in her flight.

She came up to the door of 123 Rivington Street hesitantly; she had never been there without Sarah before, let alone to ask such a favor.

"Can I come in, Mrs. Levy?'' she called, then breathed, "Oh,'' as she realized it was washday.

Every Monday Hannah was up long before the sun. By five-thirty she had her kitchen clean, her washtubs filled with water—one with hot and soapy water with the laundry soaking in it, the other with cold clear water for rinsing—and the boiler on the stove heating more. Kneeling on the floor, she rubbed the clothes against her washboard, then dropped each piece into the steaming wash boiler and swished it around with a stick. Next she dumped it into the tub of clean water, swirling it until the soap was out and it was cool enough to touch. Then she wrung it out vigorously and put it on a piece of newspaper on the table, where it sat until she had accumulated enough clean clothes to make it worthwhile to stop, take them out to the fire escape to hang, and change the water. That was the worst part. She bent over and picked up the heavy tub, groaning *"oy"* as she felt the strain in her back. After she had repeated this whole sequence several times, the ironing began.

"You're working hard today,'' said Rachel faintly, leaning against the doorjamb. The cut above her eye was still raw, her face was puffy from crying, and the bruises were beginning to come out. Hannah didn't look up, however; she was attending to her work.

"It's Monday," she grunted. "At least I got water in my kitchen these days, not like Allen Street where I had to fetch and carry from the yard." She glanced at Rachel, then screamed and ran to her. "My God, sit down, you look like you might faint. Who beat you up? Don't tell me it's that Triangle Waist again. I thought the strike was settled! Where's Sarah, in jail?"

"No, no," said Rachel, laughing weakly. "I didn't go to Triangle. My father did this."

"Your father!" Hannah dipped a clean rag in cold water and began to sponge Rachel's face, wiping away the tear stains and dried blood. "I never heard of such a thing."

"He was mad because I got a job on the *Forward*."

"The *Forward?*" Hannah stopped, confused. "But that's a desk job! What's his problem?"

"It's against his religion," whispered Rachel. She seemed to be losing her voice. "He threw me out."

Hannah pursed her lips grimly. Any man who'd do something like this to his own daughter was worse than a criminal, religion or no religion.

"You'll move in here with us, Rachel. We've got plenty of room since Solly Fein's gone and you're like one of the family already. You can sleep with Sarah on the mattress."

Rachel leaned her head thankfully on Hannah's strong shoulder. "I was hoping you'd say that." Her voice broke. "I don't have anywhere else to go."

It took two days for Rachel to gather the courage to go back to her parents' apartment on Norfolk Street for her things. She took Ruby and Sarah along for reinforcement. As they entered the ramshackle tenement building where the Cohens had a third-floor flat, a door suddenly opened and Milke Kretskes, the first-floor neighbor, poked her head out. Seeing Rachel, she gasped.

"You can't go upstairs," she cried. "Stay down here by me. Come, have a glass of tea."

"Thank you but I have to get my things," said Rachel politely.

Ruby held up her hand for silence. "Listen. Something's happening up there."

A chorus of male voices, chanting sonorously, reverberated through the old building. *"Yis gaddal v'yiskaddash shmey rabboh, b'olmoh dee v'roh chir-usey, v'yamlich malchusey,*

b'cha-yeychon uvyo-meychon, uvcha-yey d'chol beys yisro-
eyl, ba-agoloh uvizman koreev, v'imru omeyn."

"That's Kaddish," said Rachel. "What's happened?
What's the matter?" She trembled. "Has something happened to my father?"

Milke gave her a pitying look and spat three times, *"puh*
puh puh," to avert the evil eye. Rachel trembled, then gave a
little cry.

"It's for me, isn't it? They're saying Kaddish over me.
That's why you won't let me go up; they're sitting *shiva* on
me up there!" She threw her hands over her ears. "Oh, my
God, it's my death they're wishing on me." She faltered, the
prayer for the dead pursuing her around the tiny hall. "I can't
go up there, Sarah. I can't go to my own Kaddish. You and
Ruby will have to get my things."

She darted into Milke's apartment and the sisters went
slowly up the stairs, terrified. Their shadows loomed huge on
the steps before them. Sarah pushed open the apartment door.
Inside it was dark, tenebrous, already haunted. The windows
were shrouded; the mirror next to the door was covered with a
black cloth. A single candle burned in the middle of the floor.
Around it sat shapeless figures, a *minyan*. As Sarah's eyes
became used to the darkness, she recognized Rachel's father
and brother among them. Rachel's mother sat in the back,
behind the circle. One of the men had begun to chant a
psalm, "Who shall ascend the mountains of the Lord and
who shall stand in His holy place?"

Sarah cleared her throat. "Mrs. Cohen," she said loudly,
"we've come for your daughter's things."

The rabbi stiffened; his wavering shadow was distorted
against the wall. "I have no daughter," he rasped. "My
daughter is dead."

"He that hath clean hands and a pure heart, who hath not
taken My name in vain and hath not sworn deceitfully," the
singer continued.

Rachel's mother stared at the girls beseechingly, nodding
her head in the direction of the corner near the door. There
were two bundles there. Ruby went over to them inquiringly,
and Rachel's mother nodded. Without another word, each girl
took a bundle and bolted down the stairs. The psalm floated
after them.

Sarah's life, too, had changed radically on the day work

began again at Triangle Waist. With the others she had lined up in front of the shop before it got light. "Lots of people on picket duty today," Becky had yelled. Everyone laughed. They had come to work, not picket, eagerly waiting for that first pay envelope with which they could begin to make good on the debts accumulated during the strike to landlords and butchers and *landsmanschaft*. The factory whistle blew: six o'clock. The door opened. Standing in it, framed against the light of the stairwell, barring the way, were Bernstein and Goldfarb. Bernstein had a list in his hand and, as he checked off each name, Goldfarb let the worker through.

"Etta Rosenblum."

She went in.

"Molly Hurwitz."

She went in.

"Fanny Jacobs. Rebecca Zinssher."

Each of them passed through the gate.

"Sarah Levy."

She pushed her way up to the door. Goldfarb barred it with his huge arm. "Well?" she said. "Aren't you going to let me in?"

A silence fell on the crowd as Bernstein looked her up and down.

"You think I'm crazy, I should let you into my shop?"

"What do you mean? You signed a contract; you have to take me back."

"I didn't sign anything said I have to take back agitators." The veins stood out in his forehead. "I'm management here. I got the right to pick and choose my help; nobody's going to dictate to me. Get out of here, you anarchist bitch—get off my property!"

"I'll go to the union," said Sarah.

"Go ahead." He laughed scornfully. "You think they're going to call another strike just for you? You're finished in this industry—not just by me, by the whole association. You're going to pay for the trouble you caused. You won't work in Triangle, you won't work in Bijou, you won't work in any shirtwaist shop in New York." He smiled. "Triangle is going to look good to you before you're done hunting for a job."

Sarah was stunned. Despite all her experience, she had never imagined getting blacklisted. She looked at the line of workers in appeal. They stared back terrified, begging her silently: Don't ask us. She tried to smile. Then, with a leaden gait, she walked what seemed an endless winter block to Washington Square and collapsed on a park bench.

Two hours later she stumbled up the stairs to the union office and leaned against the door frame. Her face was streaked with tears. John A. Dyche, Abe Baroff, and Joe Klein stared at her in consternation.

"I've been blacklisted," she said.

Joe was surprised by the frisson he felt at the news. Maybe now she would turn to him for protection. Though he dismissed the thought as unworthy, he could not keep a foolish smile from troubling the corners of his mouth.

It took a while for all of them to hear and digest her story, and decide what the union should do.

"The company's trying to provoke us," said Dyche. "They know we could never get the workers out again after they've just gone back; they want us to call another strike and fall on our faces, so we'll look bad."

"But we'll look like schmucks if we let them blacklist Sarah and don't do anything," said Baroff. "We have to respond."

"They'll never take me back no matter what we do," said Sarah in despair. "Bernstein said I'd never work in shirtwaists again. It's the only work I know." She began to cry helplessly, and Joe put a comforting arm around her. Baroff made a sorrowful face.

"It's a shame, when I think about how hard you fought and all you went through. At least it didn't go for nothing. We have a real union now, and that's what we fought for, isn't it?"

Sarah looked up, remembering a conversation with Helen Marot that seemed years ago. Now was the time. "Is it true we have enough dues money now to hire a real staff, with walking delegates like the cloak makers have?" she asked through her tears.

"You bet." Baroff was glad to change the subject. "We were just talking about whom to hire."

"How about me?"

They all gaped at her. A sick silence fell. She looked from one to the other, suddenly unsure of herself. "What's the matter, somebody walk over all your graves?" She tried to laugh. It didn't work.

Baroff cleared his throat. "Sarah, you're a girl."

"So what? Most of the industry is girls."

"It's ridiculous," said Dyche impatiently. "Let's not waste time discussing it. I'm surprised at you, Sarah. All right, you need a job, but you should think about the union. Do you want us to be a laughingstock in front of the whole AFL?"

Sarah took a deep breath. So she'd been wrong. All this time she'd thought of them as comrades, as equals fighting together. She had been so sure they felt the same way. She flushed with pain and anger. "I'm not worried about the AFL and it's not just a job I'm after. Hiring me would help the union; I'm a good organizer."

"Now, Sarah," said Baroff, "try to look at it objectively. A walking delegate has to be able to negotiate with the boss on a daily basis. He has to be able to win the boss's respect and fight it out with him man to man. Seriously, do you think you could do that? The bosses aren't like us, you know; they don't listen to women."

"I'm a good fighter," said Sarah.

Dyche snorted. "Too good. You fight with everybody. A walking delegate has to be a stabilizing influence on the industry. We don't want a wildcat strike popping off every time he walks into a shop to settle a grievance. We don't need any irresponsible little girls in that job. The strike is over. It's peacetime, time to settle down. Even if you were a man I'd still think you were too hotheaded to be a walking delegate."

"It's not true!" She turned to Joe in appeal. He hadn't said anything. Surely he at least would come to her defense. "Ask the women in the League," she faltered. "They said I was a natural organizer."

That got Joe. He threw back his head and glared at her. So that's why she was coming here stirring up all this trouble; those rich women had put her up to it. She didn't care how it made him feel to be on the spot like this, caught between her and the staff. She did whatever that bunch of old maids told her. It was useless waiting for her to realize she was a woman and she needed a man. She'd starve before she turned to him. There was no hope for their relationship.

"Is that where you got this crazy idea, from that bunch of rich ladies you hang around with?" he said coldly. "If you want to be a union organizer, you should have enough sense to stick to your own class."

She turned white at the betrayal. It hurt more then she would have believed. Her lip trembled. "So you don't think I'm good enough to work for a union? You think maybe you're a better organizer than I am? You've held down a staff job for two years, so tell me, what makes you so qualified?"

"Why pick on me?" he said irritably. "Am I the only one here? It's not a question of good enough or not good enough. The job isn't suitable for a woman. It wouldn't look right. What would people say if we let a girl do this kind of work— that we weren't men enough to do it ourselves?"

"Funny how nobody worried about that when I went on picket duty," she said. "I don't remember any of you getting beaten up, but of course I didn't get paid for that. It's only when it comes to a salary that people get concerned."

The other two men looked at Joe Klein in appeal. He sighed and took Sarah's elbow. "Listen, you've had a hard day, and we're all edgy. Why don't you come for a cup of coffee with me so we can talk in a more relaxed way?" Before she knew what was happening, he'd guided her out the door and shut it behind him.

She leaned against it. "I thought you were my friend," she whispered.

"Don't be this way. You know I care about you too much to let you do a job like this. I'm trying to protect you."

"Protect me!" she breathed incredulously. "Protect me!" She could find no more words. Instead she stepped back and hit him across the face with all her strength. He staggered back against the door. "I hope I never see you again!" she said, and ran downstairs.

Joe pulled himself up and patted his smarting face. No doubt it was red all down one side. He went back into the office, nearly ill with tension. Dyche and Baroff looked at him expectantly. He would have to save face.

"I thought I heard a slap," said Dyche. "Fresh?"

Joe shook his head ruefully. "No, I didn't touch her. But you know Sarah. It's like you said, she's a little hotheaded to be a walking delegate."

Sarah walked the snowy streets for hours before she finally stalked into the office of the Women's Trade Union League. Helen Marot was there alone.

"Sarah, what's the matter?" she exclaimed. "Why aren't you at work?"

Sarah sank into the nearest chair, shivering with cold. She told the story as quickly as she could. "I've been walking all afternoon. I don't know where to go. I don't know what to do."

Helen had listened with growing outrage, but her voice was sad. "It will take time to change the union."

Somehow that was the last straw. Sarah leaned back in her chair. She was almost too tired to speak, but she had to let it out.

"There's no place in the world for women like me," she said hopelessly. "I have nothing left. They took my job. They took my hope for the future. I've always stuck up for everybody, but when I needed them, no one was there, even the man I thought was my real friend." Tears had begun to roll down her cheeks again. She hadn't cried so much in one day since she left Russia.

Helen paced the room, biting her lip; for the moment Sarah's pain was her own and she would have done anything to soothe it. Surely it could do no harm to tell the child her news a few days early?

"Sarah, listen," she said urgently. "I wasn't supposed to tell you yet. We were going to announce it at a meeting. But I will anyway. Some rich women are going to donate money to the League so we can hire an organizer. Our board met yesterday and decided our highest priority is to build on the gains we made during the strike and spread the gospel to other girls on the East Side. We want to offer you the job."

Sarah looked up, dazed. Helen had to repeat the offer twice before she could take it in. Even then she could think of nothing but how contemptuous the union men would be when they heard. Joe would say she couldn't get a labor job so she went and got one from a bunch of rich suffragists. He didn't even think the League was part of the labor movement. He'd say she had gone over to the other side. But what was she supposed to do; who had betrayed whom? She needed a job. She wanted to be an organizer. The union wouldn't hire her and the League would. The choice wasn't a choice at all.

Unfortunately, she half agreed with Joe's sentiments about the League. They weren't labor people. And how could she organize women into the union if she was working for them?

"I wouldn't want to go against the union," she said cautiously.

Helen looked at her in surprise. "Why should you? That's

not what we want. Your job would be to work with the new
girls in the union, to educate them about their rights and duties as members and enable them to play a larger role in the
movement. We also want your help with a few other things,
our campaign for the eight-hour day and our suffrage work,
but surely this would be no problem?''

"I don't think so. I just don't quite understand what the job
is.''

"Well, to be honest, we're not quite sure ourselves. It's an
experiment; we'll have to work out the rules as we go. We've
never had a working-girl organizer before. Some of the board
thought we ought to send you to college first, but Mary and I
felt practical experience was more important, and you already
had that. What do you say, Sarah? The salary would be ten
dollars a week.''

Sarah's eyes widened. It was more than she had ever
earned in her life.

As Solly Fein's wedding approached, Hannah became increasingly nervous. The wedding would be a test of her composure; her poise must give the lie to any notion that she
cared a fig if the man got married. The event would also
indicate where her reputation stood; she must be alert for significant leers or whispers. Most of all, her family must appear
together, united as if by a steel strap, exemplary in every
way.

If only she had something nice to wear. It had been so long
since she'd spent any money on herself that all her dresses
were twenty years out of fashion. She spread her few good
things on the table. They made a pathetic display. When
Ruby came home from school, Hannah was still sitting there,
head in hand, staring at a dark blue taffeta gown.

"What are you doing, Ma?''

Hannah sighed. "Trying to decide what to wear to Solly's
wedding.''

"Not that thing, I hope. It must be a hundred years old.''

"It's not," Hannah protested. "It's from when I got
married.''

"You can't wear a Kishinev dress to a New York wedding.'' Ruby's scorn was withering. "You'll look like you
just got off the boat.''

Hannah spread her hands helplessly. "It's as good as new.
Bubbe made it to last, not like this factory-made stuff you get

now. Look at the beading. She even cast over the seams. And it's good taffeta. So maybe the style isn't so up-to-date, but it's got years of wear in it.''

"It's got a stain on the bosom."

"There's a tear in it, too," Hannah admitted, "here on the skirt where I caught it on a nail in the photographer's wagon, that time we had our picture taken. I sewed it up but it still shows."

"You should have a new dress," said Ruby. "You haven't had one since I can remember. At least a new shirtwaist to wear with a skirt."

"My skirt's worse than this is," cried Hannah in despair. "The material is all rusty-looking. And we don't have the money for clothes for me. The little bit we've got is for spring clothes for you girls. I'm an old woman, what do I need a new dress for?"

"You're not old, Mama. If you only dressed American you'd look better than half the women on this block. But in this *shmatteh*, I don't know . . ."

She examined it closely. Twenty years ago in Kishinev it must have been high style: taffeta with a fitted bodice and leg-of-mutton sleeves, a shawl collar with jet beadwork, and a skirt so full it cried out for a crinoline. The bodice was intricately draped and gathered, a style still acceptable when executed in silk mousseline or chiffon, but hopeless in a stiff material like taffeta: each fold stuck out like an iron bar.

"Let me see it on," said Ruby. "Maybe we can figure something out."

Hannah looked at her dubiously. It was true she was good with a needle, taking after her Bubbe, much more skilled than Hannah herself. But she was only a fourteen-year-old kid. What did she know? And with her fancy ideas, who knew what she'd come up with? Still, Hannah had a hunger to look good at Solly's wedding. Slowly, she began to remove her apron, then her housedress.

"You've still got a good shape, Ma," said Ruby, "a natural S-curve. You hardly need a corset."

Hannah nodded. She knew she had kept her figure. Her breasts were a trifle lower than they had been, but a matronly, rounded bosom was the style, especially if you had plenty behind to balance it off. She put on the dress.

"Turn," said Ruby. She turned. Ruby pulled at the skirt critically.

"There's two, three yards of extra material in here, and maybe another yard in the sleeves. Let me see how the collar's made." She examined it. "We could take off the collar and fill in the bosom with net. That would be more modern and the net wouldn't cost more than a dime, fifteen cents. I could embroider it."

She walked around Hannah, frowning.

"Wait, I know," she said suddenly. "I'll take the whole skirt off! It's only gathered at the waist; that's nothing. I'll remake it so it's fitted down to the knees, gored so it hugs your body, then flaring out, maybe with a little train. I think there's enough goods; it's a big skirt. Then I'll take off the sleeves and piece a new bodice with the material from them—cut low, none of these pleats—and fill it in with chiffon or net. I'll use the same chiffon to make new sleeves, with trim from what's left of the old ones. Then to top it all off, a choker made from the jet beads—they're good ones, handmade. I'm telling you, Ma, you'll be a knockout!"

"Choker?" said Hannah weakly. "I don't even know what you're talking about."

"It's the latest thing. It's a real high collar, so tight it looks like you could choke from it. They also call them dog collars."

"I don't want to look like a dog," protested Hannah.

"Oh, Ma," said Ruby with an indulgent smile. "It's the fashion. Fafonfnik will have one, wait and see. Isn't it worth a little discomfort to show those Garfinkles up?"

Hannah had to admit it probably was. "But if you go taking my only good dress apart, Ruby, you be sure you put it back together again," she warned. "I don't know from this fancy sewing."

"Don't worry, I'll go tomorrow to where I get my remnants. I'll pick up a little piece of chiffon, maybe some ribbon damaged in a corner where nobody will see—give me fifty cents and I'll have you looking like a million bucks!"

In the end, she was able to get enough bronze net and navy chiffon for both the sleeves and the bodice, and still have change left over for some thin gold braid for a belt.

"Ma," she swore as she took the taffeta dress apart, "if you aren't dressed to kill, my name isn't Ruby Levy."

I spent so long on Mama I forgot about myself, thought Ruby bitterly a few weeks later, looking at her own meager wardrobe. There was nothing in it she considered appropriate for a major social event like Solly's wedding. She had only two dresses and both were children's styles; her mother still insisted on dressing her like a kid.

The main point of contention was length. Schoolgirls wore short dresses, said Hannah, and until Ruby was out of school she would do the same. She could nag night, nag morning—it would make no difference. Hannah even insisted that Ruby wear aprons to school—as if she would ever get a dress dirty! And when Ruby pointed out in exasperation that thousands of girls of fourteen were already working and walking around in long skirts and shirtwaists, Hannah simply said, "Let them."

She had yielded on only one point, the length of the suit Ruby made for spring—and that was merely because it was expensive and supposed to last for years. Ruby had not been allowed to make a full-length skirt, but Hannah did let her get enough material to make a big hem, so the skirt could be let down when the time came.

Hannah underestimated her daughter's ingenuity. Instead of making an enormous hem as instructed, Ruby cut off the skirt below the knee and finished it with a buttonhole placket. She used the hem material for a button-on extension, her own idea, which brought the skirt to adult length when attached. She had not yet shown her mother the finished product. Now, poring over her choices the night before Solly's wedding, she resolved that she would wear her new skirt long or not go at all. She was tired of being treated like a little girl.

She modeled her suit after supper, changing downstairs at the Breynes in order to make a grand entrance, with Yakhne Breynes following her, a giggling entourage of one. "Ladies and gentlemen,"· crowed Yakhne, who was only eight and a great admirer of Ruby's, "may I present the new original Ruby Levy in her own invention— the convertible skirt."

Ruby twirled. Everyone stared in astonishment. The little bolero jacket and princess cut of the waistline showed off her burgeoning figure to advantage, while the gray flannel of the suit brought out the blue of her eyes.

"That's your new suit," said Hannah. "What did you do to it?"

Ruby unbuttoned the skirt extension with a flourish. "One minute a child, the next a woman!" she announced grandly. "Convertible!"

Hannah got down on her hands and knees to inspect Ruby's

work. "You little devil," she muttered. "Going behind my back."

"Can I wear it to the wedding?" Ruby begged.

Hannah grunted noncommittally, turning the skirt extension in her hands. Then her shoulders began to shake. She laughed until tears ran down her face and she had to sit helplessly, shaking. "I was hoping I could keep you in short skirts until you got a little more sense," she wept. "But I guess you're too smart for me. There's no way I can keep you from growing up, no matter how hard I try."

Ruby had been playing lookout on the fire escape for over an hour before she called, "They're opening the door, Ma, hurry up!" Hannah rushed outside. The fire escape—indeed, every fire escape on Rivington Street, and all the windows and stoops as well—was lined with people settled like heavy, overdressed pigeons on the metal stairs, their eyes fixed on the door that read "Garfinkle's Meat Strictly Kosher." The wedding coach, a rented horse and buggy, awaited. The bridal party was about to embark on its journey to the New Essex Street American Hall ("All Electrified; Wedding Parties Catered"). Although this was a journey of a mere five blocks, the neighborhood would scarcely have considered the wedding legal had the family gone on foot.

"Here they are," said Ruby. "Look at Solly. *Oy*, I'm dying."

Solly was resplendent in rented tails. His balding head gleamed as if waxed. Looking at the fire escapes, bowing to the neighbors, he put on his silk top hat and waved his hand like a king receiving homage.

"By me he looks like an undertaker," said Hannah sourly. "You can't make a silk purse out of a sow's ear and you can't make a prince out of a meat peddler."

"Here comes the bride, big, fat, and wide," rang out a child's soprano from the next fire escape. "See how she waddles from side to side."

"Look at that dress," said Ruby, shaking her head. "Would you believe a gown like that on a shape like hers?"

Rosalie Garfinkle emerged, heavily veiled in lace with an elaborate edifice of artificial orange blossoms as a crown. Her dress, rented for the occasion as were all the bridal clothes, was white satin, cut in the latest hobble-skirt style which, while it made walking difficult, was very becoming to the slender figure. Rosalie didn't have one.

"She looks like a stuffed cabbage," said Ruby.

Fafonfnik came out next, in olive-green satin with a choker. Her hat was so enormous she could hardly get through the carriage door.

Hannah sniffed contemptuously. "Such a klutz! If she fell on her back, she'd break her jaw."

They went inside to collect the family for the wedding. Moyshe was still struggling to button his only suit. He looked at Hannah bemused, as if he'd never seen her before.

"That's a new dress," he said. "You look beautiful."

All the way down Rivington Street, Hannah kept smoothing her dress self-consciously, hoping he was right. How she longed to put their eyes out with her splendor. Ruby had indeed performed a miracle of tailoring, more even than Hannah realized. The gentle contours of the gown's bodice and the svelte lines of its fitted skirt showed her figure to its best advantage. The high beaded neck accentuated the graceful sweep of her throat and bosom, and the dark blue fabric pointed up the pinks and whites of her skin and the blue of her eyes. The dress was in the very latest fashion. Even Ruby had gasped when Hannah tried it on, crowing, "Mama, you look like a magazine cover!"

By the time they arrived, the New Essex Street American Hall was a blaze of light. Hannah, unused to electricity, had to shield her eyes from its brilliance. As the guests entered, the wedding bard or *badchen,* doubling as master of ceremonies, yelled out their names and the bride's parents came forward to welcome them. Fafonfnik's face froze when she saw Hannah's gown.

"My God, it's the latest style," she whispered, grimacing. Then, with an unconvincing smile, she declaimed, "Mrs. Levy, how nice you could come. I just love your dress. I saw the same one in Saks. You look so fancy I hardly recognized you."

"This old thing?" said Hannah, a thrill of triumph running through her frame. "Why, this is just a *shmatteh* my girl fixed up for me. I wasn't sure it was good enough to wear to a society wedding."

The whole East Side was there. Hannah noticed there was even an underworld contingent and hoped with a sinking heart

that Tricker Louis Florsheim hadn't been invited. He was,
after all, a family connection. But she didn't see him. There
was an outpost of Central Park West near the front of the hall:
wholesalers, she thought sagely, nodding to herself. Hannah,
an expert on social stratification, knew they were the guests
who'd kick in the heavy gifts: the carpets, furniture, silver.
The Levys themselves were giving the bride a small but tasteful ashtray, and plenty of their neighbors couldn't manage
that much.

The band played a processional and, as Hannah settled into
her seat, Solly marched in seconded by his best man, Hymie
the Suspenders. Hannah had never seen him without his
cascade of merchandise before; he was skinnier than she'd
thought. The two men stationed themselves under the
chuppah, the purple velvet canopy heavily embroidered in
gold that stood at the front of the hall. With a fanfare, the
bride entered, preceded by her "leaders," namely her sisters
Leah and Shayndel, who guided her in a circle around Solly,
seven times. Hannah shook her head disapprovingly; didn't
these dumb *Galitzianers* do anything right? "In our family,
we circle three times."

The rabbi held up a glass of wine and recited a *brocha,*
then gave it to the pair to drink. Hymie the Suspenders
handed Solly the ring. The rabbi lifted the bride's veil for a
moment, as if showing Solly the goods, and Solly nodded,
saying rapidly, "Behold thou art betrothed to me with this
ring in accordance with the law of Moses and of Israel." He
put the ring on Rosalie's finger. Now came the moment everyone had been waiting for, the reading of the marriage contract, which would reveal both the bride's dowry and the
amount she would get back if the marriage didn't last. Without this legal document, no wedding was valid. The rabbi
read through it rapidly.

"On the fifth day of the week, the twelfth day of the month
of Heshvan in the year 5672 since the creation of the world
according to the reckoning we use in the city of New York in
the United States of America, Solomon Fein, son of Yikhor
Fein of Lemberg, said to this maiden Rivke Garfinkle, daughter of Kalman Garfinkle of New York, 'Be thou my wife
according to the law of Moses and Israel and I will work for
thee, honor, provide for and support thee, in accordance with
the practice of Jewish husbands, and agreed at that time to set
aside for thee two hundred American dollars due thee for thy

maidenhood, which belong to thee according to the law of the
Torah, and thy food, clothing, and other benefits which a husband is obligated to provide, and I will live with thee in accordance with the requirements prescribed for each husband.'

"The dowry that she brought from her house in silver,
gold, valuables, clothing, and household furnishings, together
with one year's rent on the second-floor flat above the
butcher's shop and one-third interest in the business of Garfinkle Kosher Butchers, all this the groom accepted," concluded the rabbi.

"One-third of the business," said Ruby. "Not bad."

After the bride and groom signed the contract, the rabbi
read the Seven Blessings and handed the pair another glass of
wine. Rosalie sipped from it; Solly finished it; and the rabbi
wrapped the glass tenderly in a napkin and placed it under
Solly's foot. Solly stepped down with gusto and the small
crack of breaking glass rang through the hall, symbolizing the
fall of the Temple—though Ruby remembered her grandmother's whispering that a glass wasn't the only thing that got
broken on a wedding night. The crunching noise released all
the pent-up celebratory energies of the waiting crowd.
"Mazeltov" and "Good luck" rang through the hall as the
band swung into the traditional dance, *"Chassen, kalleh,
mazeltov,"* and the guests parted in the middle like the Red
Sea as Solly danced Rosalie down the aisle and out into the
hall for the moment of privacy that completed the marriage
ceremony.

"The kosher dance!" called the *badchen*, asserting his role
as master of ceremonies. "Time for the kosher dance." In the
old country, it was forbidden for Jewish couples to dance
together. Men danced only with men, women only with
women—except at a wedding, where this ban could be sub-
verted by the use of a handkerchief. The man held one corner, the woman the other, and so they danced together; and
thus it was on this occasion. Fafonfnik danced with her husband while the *badchen* did the honors with Goldie Golovey
the *shadchen*, who looked like a gigantic dancing prune in a
costume of dark brown velvet. As the kosher dance wound
down, Hannah heard her say to Fafonfnik, "Shprinzel, are
you going to do the mother-in-law dance?"

Various wags in the company took up the cry: "The
mother-in-law dance! The mother-in-law dance!"

"How am I supposed to do that?" asked Fafonfnik crossly. "You all know Solly's mother is dead."

Goldie Golovey whispered something in her ear, and a wicked smile spread over her face. She nodded her head decisively. Then, much to everyone's surprise, she marched across the floor toward Hannah Levy, who waited nervously, wondering what was happening.

"Mrs. Levy," Fafonfnik said loudly, "since Solly's mother ain't here maybe you should stand in for her, being as how he boarded with you so you're giving him away, if you know what I mean?"

Hannah turned pale, but lifted her head regally. "Certainly, Mrs. Garfinkle," she said courteously. "I'd hate for you to miss a dance you waited so long to do."

"Listen to the needling!" cried the *badchen*. "You'd think they were really relatives!" And the laughter became general as the band swung into the traditional tune to the "quarrel dance."

Hannah fought to keep her composure. Was the woman trying to humiliate her in front of everyone? Was she announcing to the world that Hannah had some kind of special relationship to Solly Fein? Or was she merely calling her old enough to be his mother? She stepped proudly into the mother-in-law dance, sweeping through the "quarrel" steps, flying at Fafonfnik with her arms raised high as if she longed to deliver real blows, then falling back just in time, never missing a beat. Back and forth she danced, as the onlookers laughed and clapped their appreciation. By the time the music ended and the two women gave each other the customary formal embrace which ended their rivalry, Hannah was flushed with exertion. She stepped back quickly, removing her hands from her enemy's back and wiping them on her skirt.

"*Oy*, a *shvitzer!*" she cried merrily. As Fafonfnik hissed and the crowd laughed at the Yiddish pun, which meant not only a sweaty person but also a big-mouthed braggart, Hannah curtsied politely and returned to her family in triumph. Then the band struck up a *freylaks* and couple after couple swept onto the floor and bounced through one Russian jig after another. The American-raised children stared as their parents, including Moyshe and Hannah, stamped their heels on the floor like whips cracking, one two, dancing in lines and circles, back and forth, up and down, side to side, until there was a roll of the drums and the *badchen* called, "Ladies

and gentlemen! Dinner is ready downstairs, so if you'll line
up with the gentlemen escorting the ladies and the wedding
party first, we can have the procession—''

His words were lost. The younger members of the crowd,
who had sat through a dreary ceremony, then watched their
elders do incomprehensible old-country dances for what
seemed an interminable length of time, moved purposefully
and swiftly, while the children simply ran at the sound of the
word "dinner," cutting off the wedding party at the stairs and
creating a bottleneck as the bride's relatives battled them un-
successfully for precedence. When the *badchen* finally beat
his way downstairs and got to the head table, he found the
seats had been usurped by a motley company of scrawny
kids, some beginning to bang on their plates with their
spoons. It took him fifteen minutes of appeals to the Almighty
and their parents to get the seats cleared for the wedding
party.

Not even then were the children allowed to eat, though the
waiters did put drinks on the table: bottles of wine and pitchers of grape juice, seltzer, slivovitz, and celery tonic. Hannah, fanning herself from her exertions, took some of the
latter to help get her through the announcements of the wedding presents and the reading of telegrams. But first came the
groom's sermon, a solemn part of any wedding. Solly rose,
looking less confident than usual.

"The Torah portion I have chosen today," he mumbled,
"is from Judges 14." He stammered through the Hebrew,
reading badly; each time he made a mistake, he was corrected
by any number of ancient men. Then he went through it again
in Yiddish, for the women: "Out of the strong came something sweet, out of the eater came something to eat."

Hannah snorted. "Trust him to make up a sermon about his
gut."

"This comes from the story of Samson," he said. "You
remember how he wanted to marry the Philistine woman and
he saw a lion and killed it, and then a whole bunch of bees
started swarming in the body of the lion so he took the honey
and served it at his wedding. And he asked a riddle of the
Philistine woman's relatives, how something sweet came
from something strong and so on like I said before."

"Tchah!" Goldie Golovey was scandalized. "A Philistine
wedding he gives us."

"So here is the meaning I get out of my Torah portion. Like Samson, I have taken a wife."

"Only not a Philistine," said Fafonfnik loudly.

"Though as my *machetuneste* points out, she is not a Philistine," Solly agreed. "However, she does come from meat, just like the honey did, seeing as how her father is a butcher. And also I am strong, like the Torah says, 'Out of the strong came something sweet.' So my sermon is about Rosalie and me and it means that when I am working by my father-in-law, his meat will be twice as sweet even as before, so you should all buy at Garfinkle's and this is the end of my Torah portion."

"He's made the groom's sermon into an ad." Moyshe was astonished. But he noticed that while the rabbi was disapproving, Garfinkle the butcher didn't mind a bit.

Then, at last, the waiters began to serve the food, bringing platters of chopped liver, herring, deviled eggs, and little meatballs, along with crackers and rye bread, as the *badchen* read out the list of gifts, from the most insignificant toothpick to the lordly money gifts of the relatives ("from the bride's parents, Kalman and Shprinzel Garfinkle, one thousand dollars with much love") and the elegant items sent by well-wishers in the business community ("from Jacob Stampfels, wholesale butcher, one Brussels carpet"). The list was a reflection of the Garfinkles' status and connections, and some of the guests, too poor themselves to have a cloth on their table or a rug on their floor, ground their teeth as they listened. But their envy added spice to the meat—at least they could fill their bellies off the rich, this once, and dance with someone else's wife.

After the gifts came the telegrams, most of which began with the words "charges prepaid," indicating that the sender was rich enough not to have to pay on the installment plan.

"Charges prepaid. Lots of *naches*, your Aunt Dora." There was clapping at a table near the front.

"Charges prepaid. Roses are red, violets are blue, all the luck in the world I wish to you. Mr. and Mrs. Oscar Rubino, wholesale meat."

And so it went, as more and more food arrived on the tables: roast chicken and brisket, roast potatoes, sweet potatoes and potato *kugel, kishkes,* carrot *tzimmes,* and seven different varieties of pickle—the food kept coming on, as if Garfinkle had decided to feed the whole East Side for a week from his own shop: meat, meat, and more meat. The men drank too much, the women talked too much, and the children ate too much and then began to chase each other. The uproar intensified until the music in the background could hardly be heard. As the younger people began to do "American dancing," their parents migrated from table to table, looking for gossip. There was considerable speculation about how long Solly Fein would remain faithful.

"Look, he's already dancing with one of her sisters, a waltz yet," Yetta Breynes whispered to Hannah.

And indeed, as the evening wore on, the groom cast amorous glances haphazardly in all directions, dancing with his new relatives and his old mistresses and all the women whom he hoped would someday attain that station. He asked Hannah Levy to dance, but she refused, clinging to Moyshe's arm.

"I'm old-fashioned," she said for all to hear. "I dance only with my husband," and sailed away looking like a dark rose. Later, secure in her triumph, she stood against the wall and watched the company, a sardonic angel floating above the gathering.

Sarah, she noted, was being pursued by that old goat Menachem the Fish, who left his wife and six children guzzling food in a corner so he could dance with all the maidens. Sarah danced with him once, head pulled stiffly back to avoid his slivovitz reek and the dribble on his beard, then fled from spot to spot, finally taking refuge in a crowd of old *yentas* in the back of the hall, where she peeped out from time to time to see if Menachem was hovering near. He always was.

Lovely Rachel was dancing like a graceful stick with everyone who asked her, smiling a little wooden smile, looking pensive in the intervals. Why so sad, Hannah wondered. Was it her lost home she grieved for? Did she miss her mother? Was she thinking of her own wedding, sure to be a poor thing without a paternal dowry or parental send-off? Did she have her eye on some young man who'd disappointed her, and was that why she showed so little interest in any of her partners?

Little Ruby was nowhere to be seen. When Hannah finally searched, she found her sequestered in a back room in animated conversation with Tricker Louis Florsheim, who was looking even more handsome than usual in honor of his cousin's wedding. With a gasp of horror, Hannah pulled her child up, slapped her on both cheeks, and dragged her from the room in tears. Taking her out into the alley, she turned upon her.

"What's the matter with you, talking like that to a pimp!"

"He's not a pimp," sniffed Ruby.

"What are you talking about? Everybody knows he's a maiden-taker. And you dumb enough to let him soft-soap you! My God, Ruby, think how he beat up your sister!"

"He says that was all a terrible mistake," wept Ruby. She had thrilled to Tricker's story, which was of a complexity and improbability usually found only on the stage. "He was forced into a false position by a jealous rival. He didn't know she was my sister or he would never have done it."

Ruby wiped her round blue eyes, hoping her mother would not forbid her to see Tricker Louis anymore. He looked more like Boris Thomashevsky than any other boy she'd met, and anyway, how could it hurt to talk to him?

Hannah looked at her with sour disfavor. "Dumb like a cow," she said oracularly. "Not fit to be let out alone. Ruby, if I ever catch you anywhere near that fellow again, I swear I'll lock you up! I won't even let you go to school. Letting a man like that get close to you. Just think what would have happened if Sarah had found you—there would have been a riot." Shuddering, she dragged Ruby back into the main hall with stern instructions not to leave her sight. Ruby spent the rest of the evening dancing with a fat old man with a gray moustache. When questioned later, she was not even sure of his name, though she thought it might be Moscowitz or Margolis.

"So what were you talking to him about all night?" asked Hannah.

"Nothing much," said Ruby airily. "Clothes. I told him about my convertible skirt."

As the evening wore on, Hannah noticed her husband staring fixedly at her from across the room in a way he hadn't done in years. She couldn't imagine what had got into him; maybe it was the dress. Embarrassed, she smoothed her skirt and looked up again. He was coming toward her. She caught her breath. The look on his face took her back years with such a rush of feeling she could hardly bear it, so painful had the loss of it been. He held his arms out to her and they danced.

"You are beautiful tonight, Hannah. More beautiful even than you were as a girl."

She looked at him blankly. She hardly knew what to think. Of course he had been drinking. But imagine, after all he'd put her through, him coming up to her and flirting like a kid. Did he think that would make everything all right?

He held her closer. "It's been a long time since we were alone together," he murmured. "Maybe we should save up and take a little trip. We could go to Coney Island for a weekend."

"And leave the girls alone? Are you crazy?" After what had happened with Ruby that night, she could hardly leave her alone for even an hour. She had already decided to keep that story to herself, at least for the duration of the wedding. Moyshe and Sarah were unpredictable and she didn't want any scenes.

He sighed. The influence of the wine, the dancing, the wedding, had brought all his sentiment to the surface. He thought how lovely she was, regretted how far apart they had grown, and for the moment could not even remember why they had. As if years of resentment and coldness had never taken place, he spoke his heart simply, "I love you, Hannah," and kissed her cheek.

She jerked her head back as if stung, her heart pounding like a sledgehammer. Then she leaned on his shoulder, cursing herself for showing so much emotion in public. But of all the times to pick, he had to choose now, when there was no way she could discuss her feelings? Today of all days she must seem to be on top of the world; she must not falter in her self-possession, even though a wild hope swept through her as the blood rushed in her ears. Was it possible that grown men and women could fall back into a love they'd left behind.

But Moyshe would never return to his pre-Bund self; he wouldn't give up politics. So what common ground could they have? The hope pounded on, impervious to reason, but she would not heed it. She pushed him away and left the floor as soon as the dance ended. Still he pursued her, not wanting to understand.

"Hannah? What's wrong?"

She looked him full in the face, smiling amiably for all to see. "When I needed you, where were you?" she whispered. "Do you remember? Now you're here, but do I need you? Think it over."

He shook his head, suddenly depressed. He would never

understand her. But he knew enough not to push her further tonight; he had gotten all the answer he would get from Hannah, always full of words on the unimportant things and silent on the big questions. He would have to do as she said. He would have to think it over.

At the end of the evening Hannah stood once more against the wall, taking stock. Achievement played like an organ inside her head. She had done what she'd planned and been rewarded beyond expectation. After so many deaths and so much pain she was all she had been and more. She had learned to stand alone. Now, divested with honor of her lover, able to take or leave her husband, with her two girls almost grown, she could bask in the warm sun of afternoon triumph, like a full-blown rose.

She had won. She had brought them here out of death and fire and danger, against impossible odds and with great sacrifice, and now everyone must admit she had been right. She gazed at her friends and her enemies, at the dancers hopping up and down, at the heaped tables with children playing under them, at the couples giggling in corners, at the rowdy boys chasing one another, at her husband staring at her from across the room, and as the scene spun before her eyes in a wild spiral of color and light, a saturnalia, she was overcome by a wave of sweeping love for what she saw, the muck and glory all together, and she had to shut her eyes to keep the tears from showing.

BOOK FOUR

Tempered

in the Fire

I

At four o'clock on March 25, 1911, Sarah began to walk downtown from the League toward Washington Square. The day was pleasant; and, ambling along Fifth Avenue, she did not at first notice the sirens. The sound was common enough. But as more and more fire trucks raced past her, shrilling their panicky cries, she saw people running ahead of her and a pillar of smoke rising above Washington Square. Then she too began to run, as if her life were at stake, hoping desperately that it was not what she feared.

Triangle Waist was ripe for disaster. The piles of oily rags and lint under the tables could burst into flames spontaneously; it had happened before. The whole place could go up in seconds; even the air itself, filled with cotton dust, could catch fire. Everyone who worked there knew she was risking her life, but what could you do? You had to eat. And bad as Triangle was, most other garment shops were no better. "We tried, during the strike," thought Sarah. "We brought it up. But they said the building was fireproof."

It had better be fireproof because God only knew how anybody would get out. The stairway was so narrow only one person could pass at a time. The elevator was tiny. There were no sprinklers. The fire escapes were rickety things that would hold only a few people—and at that, they didn't reach the ground. Triangle was on the eighth, ninth, and tenth floors of the building and the fire escapes ended thirty feet in the air, above a glass roof edged with iron spikes. But the girls would be lucky to find the fire escapes, with the fire doors always locked to prevent thieving and the fire escapes themselves hidden behind huge iron shutters, barred and locked. No one even knew who had the keys. She gasped as she ran, her eyes half-shut with terror.

Washington Square was filled with people, many of them relatives of Triangle workers who had run up from the East Side when they heard the sirens. A police cordon held the crowd back as women in shawls, screaming their children's names, tried to break through and get closer. Firemen were hosing down the building, but their water didn't reach the top stories and the ladders on the trucks were useless; the tallest extended only as far as the sixth floor. The fire nets were lying tattered on the ground, ripped to shreds by the impact of the bodies that lay on top of them, girls who had jumped two and three together, holding each other, into the flimsy nets. Their corpses littered the pavement. A few policemen were tagging them with numbered labels, then covering them with tarpaulins and loading them into wagons to be taken to the morgue. And still the girls kept jumping.

The windows were an inferno. A frieze of black silhouettes poised against the light on the ninth-floor ledge kept moving, changing, as the workers jumped hopelessly one by one and their number was replenished from the hell inside. Some were already in flames and they fell like burning matches, going out in the air. Others, like weighted rag dolls, plummeted from certain death to certain death and landed with an unforgettable little thud like no sound Sarah had ever heard before. Fanny, she thought at the sight of each childish form; Molly, at each slim, tall one; Becky, she whispered when a big round girl fell. A thousand pair of eyes stared up as helplessly as her own, and the water in the gutters ran pink with blood.

A plump shape with an enormous picture hat joined the others in the ninth-floor frieze. The deliberation of her movements, her seeming calm, caught the eye of the crowd. Sarah shoved her fist into her mouth—surely only one girl at Triangle would put on her hat to die, surely only one carried herself with quite that air.

"Becky!" she screamed.

Slowly, almost dreamily, the silhouetted figure on the fiery ledge reached up and unpinned her hat. As if throwing a bridal bouquet she tossed it into the wind, and it floated down lazily, much more slowly than the falling bodies. It was no more than forty feet above the crowd when it suddenly burst into flame, like a burning leaf in the air. The girl on the ledge spread her arms wide as if calling the watchers to attention; one side of her skirt looked as though it had caught fire. Quickly she opened her pocketbook and pulled out her pay— a few bills, a handful of coins—and with a typically Becky gesture, combining generosity and bravura, threw the largesse wide as if saying, "This at least they won't get." Her skirt was definitely on fire now. Still she did not jump. Rather she stepped gracefully out into the air as if onto a dance floor, lifting her arms in one last embrace of the life she loved. Sarah covered her eyes but could not block out the sound of Becky's body hitting the ground. The crowd screamed, but the screaming inside Sarah's own skull drowned them out as she opened her eyes and saw her friend's body, broken, spread-eagled on a pile of other dead girls.

By eight o'clock the fire was extinguished but the streets were still full of people: East Side women with shawls on their heads, men with hats and long beards, like wraiths haunting the spot where their children had died. They moved in an endless stream from the factory to the police station to the morgue and back again, calling the names of the lost, asking if anyone had seen them.

A small figure stood motionless on Greene Street, across from the gutted factory. It was Sarah. She had not moved in some time. Her shirtwaist was filthy and full of holes left by flying sparks; her face was ravaged, streaked with soot and tears which rolled continuously down her cheeks. Passersby eyed her curiously but she did not see them. She was listening to the voices in her head.

"Make them pay," the voices said. "Remember us. You have to talk for us now." There was Becky's voice and Molly's, little Fanny's, Mrs. Rosenblum's. Even her sister Rosa was there.

Sarah shook her head pitifully. "Please," she begged. "I'm not strong enough. I don't know how." But they wouldn't listen to her. They never had. They made her go up on the platform every time. She bowed her head miserably and whispered, "All right, you win. I'll represent you."

Avi Spector knew Sarah by sight. He had seen her many times since that parade down the Bowery, and had often sought opportunities to take his mother and sister to hear her speak, for she remained for him a touchstone, a combination

of the old Russian fire with something new and American that
thrilled him. He had never spoken to her. Now he stared at
her for some time before he shook her arm gingerly. "Miss
Levy?" It was no use. She seemed to hear nothing.

It was night. The streets were still crowded, but it was
getting late and he couldn't leave her there. Rough people,
sensation seekers from other parts of town, were flocking
around, and who knows what kind of carrion crow comes out
after a tragedy, looking for easy pickings. He wanted to escort her home, but had no idea where she lived.

"Miss Levy?" he said again, but she gave no sign that she
heard him. Decisively, he took her arm. If he held it firmly,
he could support her weight and take her to his mother and
sister. They would know what to do.

Gittel heard him on the stairs and came out onto the landing. "Avi," she said, "there's been the most terrible fire at
Triangle Waist—"

"I know," he said, "I was there."

Then she saw that he was not alone. "Why, that's Sarah
Levy, the girl from the strike," she breathed. "Was she in
the fire?"

"I don't know," he said. "I can't get her to talk. She was
standing on the street and I couldn't leave her there. She's all
wet from the hoses."

Their mother bustled out. "Get blankets," she ordered.
"Gittel, boil water for tea. I saw people like this in the
pogrom; you have to keep them warm."

They put Sarah on the divan in the front room and wrapped
her up. She was as cold as ice. Mrs. Spector made tea with
sugar and fed it to her with a spoon, but still Sarah did not
talk or even look around. She took a few sips, then her eyes
closed and her head fell backward. She was fast asleep. They
went into the hallway. Gittel thought to look in Sarah's
pocketbook for her address, and Avi ran to tell her parents
where she was. Once he had gone, the two women took off
Sarah's wet clothing and Gittel slipped her own best chemise
over the girl's head. Sarah slept on, oblivious.

Hannah was so worried she refused to light the lamps.
"We'll only have to go out again anyway," she kept saying.
She sent Moyshe over to Triangle as soon as he got home, but
he returned two hours later, grief-stricken and bemused, without having seen Sarah.

"There were so many people looking," he said. "She might have been there; I couldn't get close."

No one spoke the thought that was in all their minds: what if she got there early when the alarm was just sounding? If Sarah saw her friends in danger, she wouldn't be sensible. What if she'd gone into the building?

At seven-thirty Fanny Jacob's mother came to the door. Her face fell when she saw them. "I thought maybe," she said helplessly. She put her shawl over her head. "I'll try the police station again," she whispered, and went slowly down the stairs.

At eight Moyshe insisted they light the lamps. No one had eaten. Hannah did not even try to make dinner. Every few minutes she would say, "Moyshe, maybe you should go back again," and he would say, "No. If she's all right, she'll come home. It's better to wait."

At nine a strange young man burst into the room. His coat was slightly singed. "Are you Sarah Levy's parents?" he asked. "She's at my house."

"Is she all right?" demanded Moyshe, tears of relief rushing into his eyes.

"She's not hurt," said Avi Spector, "but I don't think she's all right, either."

A few minutes later they all trooped into the Spectors' two rooms on Ludlow Street. Sarah lay under a pile of blankets and coats, still asleep. Hannah knelt beside her.

"Sarah," she whispered, "it's Mama."

Slowly, Sarah opened her black eyes. They were clouded with sleep and pain.

"Where's Rosa?" she said.

"Oh, my God." Hannah buried her face in the blankets.

"Rosa is dead," said Moyshe. "She died a long time ago."

"Papa," said Sarah. She shook her head as if to clear it and memory flooded in. "I saw Becky die," she whispered. "I saw her jump."

They quickly agreed not to move her that night. Hannah would stay with her, and the rest would return the next day with breakfast. "Thank you for helping my daughter," said Moyshe, shaking hands with Avi as he left.

"I would do it for anyone," said the younger man shyly, "but especially for your daughter. She is a real Russian. You should be proud."

Moyshe looked at him curiously. "I am," he said.

Sarah never really got over the Triangle Fire. It ran through
the rest of her life as an obbligato of despair, for what good
was all her organizing if it could come to so much death
within a year? She rose from her long sleep the next morning,
surprised to find herself on Ludlow Street, glad to see her
mother, polite to the Spectors. She was more subdued than
usual. She was not among the thousands who went to the
morgue to identify the dead, though she did go to many of the
funerals, one after the other, including the mass funeral demonstration for the unidentified corpses. And she went to all
the protest meetings, but somber, dulled, except when she
made a speech. Then she was like a burning brand, fire in her
mouth, but breaking down afterward, holding Rachel's hand
and weeping as if her tears could find no end. Her family
came with her to most of these events and along with them
came Avi Spector.

She did not yet feel she knew this strange young man, but
she was grateful for his presence. He was someone new. He
had no past associations with the shop or the union. This
made him a distraction she welcomed, for she wanted only to
forget as much as she could. That would, she knew, be little
enough.

She could not stop asking why it had happened, as if under
compulsion to extract some meaning from the horror. She
asked Rachel.

"Because of Bernstein," said Rachel, her voice hard,
"and Goldfarb and Harris and Blanck and all the rest of
them. They just won't let us live."

She asked her father.

"You know why, Sarah," said Moyshe. "These tragedies
are constant under capitalism. Workers die at their machines
in a fire, they die in the mines when the mine shaft collapses,
they die in wars that are made for profit the same way the
factories are run for profit. What do the capitalists care if we
go hungry? What do they care if one hundred and forty-six
workers die in a fire because they're too cheap to put in decent fire escapes? With so much unemployment, they can replace those workers more easily than their machines."

She asked the women at the Women's Trade Union
League.

"Because women can't vote," said Mary Dreier. "If

women had the vote, we'd have passed fire laws so strict they'd never dare break them, and we'd get women fire inspectors to make sure. As it is, we have no power even when our lives are at stake."

She asked her mother.

"Why?" said Hannah sharply. "Don't you know that Jews are born to sorrow? In Russia, it's a pogrom; here, it's a fire. But the same people do the dying. So it is, so it has been, as long as Exile." Hannah's fingers trembled over the sock she was darning. Then she said in a curious voice, "It reminds me of the story Bubbe used to tell about God's mother."

"God's mother?" said Sarah in surprise. "Does God have a mother?"

Hannah put down her work, her eyes turning inward. For a moment she looked almost like Bubbe, and she spoke in a faraway voice.

"God's mother always told Him He should bring up His children strict. 'Don't tell them how handsome or smart they are,' she said. 'Don't compliment them or they'll get stuck up. And don't hover over them like a hen. You have to let them fight their own battles. That's how they get strong.'

"She also told Him not to play favorites. He had to be just as hard on the ones that were closest to His heart as He was on all the rest, maybe harder.

"'But they have so many enemies,' God said.

"'That's what life is like,' she told Him. 'It's not all a bed of roses.'

"At first it was hard for God to obey His mother. His children had so much *tsuris* it worried Him. His favorites had an especially hard time; it was centuries before they even settled down in one place. And because they knew they were special to Him, they held themselves apart and other people picked on them. Sometimes He would interfere—you know, part the waves or something like that. But He tried not to do it too often because He knew His children wouldn't become tough if He did too much."

Sarah watched her mother with wondering eyes. This was a side of her she'd never seen. And the story didn't sound like one of Bubbe's.

"After a while God relaxed. His children had lived through the Egyptians. They had survived the Assyrians. Even the Romans couldn't destroy them. So He decided He could leave them alone for a while. He had other things to worry about.

He even took a nap. When He woke up, His mother was shaking Him and yelling in His ear.

"'Wake up, wake up,' she cried. 'Look what's going on down there!'

"He looked down at the earth. There were his children, in Russia. Pogroms were going on all over the place. His mother glared at Him.

"'So?' she said.

"'You told me to leave them alone,' He said. 'You said they'd grow strong if I let them take care of themselves.'

"She gave Him a withering look. 'How strong are they supposed to get?'"

Hannah stopped abruptly. Her hands were shaking. There was a long pause. Sarah felt confused.

"Is that the end of the story, Mama?" she said. "Why does it end like that?"

Hannah raised her eyes. They were full of sadness.

"That's all I know," she said. "I don't know the end."

As the weather grew warmer and the evenings longer, Avi Spector dropped around the corner to the Levys' more and more frequently; soon he and Sarah were seeing each other several times a week. Sarah was still depressed; so many things brought back the image of the dead. Whenever she tried to look ahead, she could feel the past dragging on her skirts; sometimes she got so tired she could hardly hold up her head.

"You never laugh," said Avi gently. "You hardly smile. Is it still the fire?"

"I try to forget," she said. "But what can I do? I'm like that; I don't know how to let go."

"After 1905, I was the same way. I fought in the revolution. I saw my friends shot down. One minute they were running, then they fell. I couldn't even stop to see if they were dead. It took me a long time to get the pictures out of my head."

"Why do such things happen?" cried Sarah. They had gone for a walk on the Williamsburg Bridge and she paused, clutching the railing so hard her knuckles turned white, almost weeping with frustration. "It's bad enough to die, but to die so young!"

He shrugged. "You know what the world is like, Sarah. The question is how to change it. Don't ask why, ask how."

"All right, how?"

He began to laugh helplessly. "I don't know, in this country. In Russia, maybe. But I do know that's the question—how." His English was still halting. "That's my life: To try to make things better, to build a world where injustice will be impossible. More than this I don't know."

Sarah watched him leaning on the bridge. He was so ready to admit there were things he didn't know. Most men on the East Side weren't that humble; Joe Klein certainly hadn't been. Avi smiled quizzically at her. To other girls, she knew, he would not seem a glamorous figure: young, skinny, with a big moustache, curly hair, dark eloquent eyes. He wasn't handsome like Joe. But to Sarah he was gilded with romance. She knew his life story. He was not just an ordinary worker or a future allrightnik like Joe. He was a real revolutionary, a knight armored only in his courage and his reason. She looked down at his hands on the railing, stained with printer's ink. Fighter's hands, she thought.

Impulsively, surprised at herself, she lifted one to her lips. Then she gazed at him with her eyes full of tears. Trembling, he pulled her to him and held her in his arms on the Williamsburg Bridge. Then, very tentatively, he bent his head down and kissed her on the lips. It didn't feel like Joe Klein's kisses at all.

It's not like he's trying to get something from me, thought Sarah. It's like he's trying to give me something. A tremulous, uncertain joy lit her face as he took her arm and they left the bridge to walk home.

Avigdor Spector was born in 1890 in Kovno. His father died before he was ten and the rest of the family went to work, his brother as a carpenter, his sister Gittel and his mother as seamstresses. Avi got a job in a tailor shop. He was a quick and curious child, good with his hands, and his brother, an active Bundist, soon had him carrying messages to Vilna, Grodno, and other nearby cities. Within a year he was also doing technical work: forging passports, smuggling literature across the border, skilled at playing dumb and avoiding arrest. Why did Avi become a revolutionary? He was poor and a Jew, therefore he hated the Czar; his brother was one and he loved his brother; and, besides, it was so much fun. If you had asked him which revolutionary organi-

zation he worked with, he could not have told you; he didn't
know one from the other.

Although Avi was the youngest in his tailor shop, he was
active in organizing a union. Like most unions in the Pale,
this one had a clandestine study group attached and Avi
joined. He already knew how to read and write well enough
to forge documents; now he became sufficiently literate to
study the rudiments of political economy.

The secret study groups were all linked in some way, Avi
was not sure how, and as they grew stronger, they began to
call mass meetings which were held in the forests outside of
Kovno to avoid detection. Avi went to one on May Day
1902. The workers filtered slowly into the woods, one by one
so as not to arouse suspicion, gave the password to the sentry,
and got directions. This was Avi's first big meeting; he heard
two speeches, sang a number of songs, and marched defiantly
with the rest back to Kovno in a group, waving a red flag.
They scattered only when the police began to block the road.
It felt wonderful.

A comrade got him a job with a Vilna printing press the
next year, when he was thirteen, so Avi left his home town to
become an underground printer. The movement was very
bold in Vilna, especially the Bund; and the active people met
informally each day after work in the city's labor exchange,
where they chatted, made plans, and argued. They staged
many strikes the first year Avi came to Vilna, even more the
second year. The 1905 revolution was building. Although the
police watched the exchange closely, the movement was so
strong arrests could not derail it. Avi found this out one day
in 1904 in his first real battle with the law.

The police caught three of his comrades carrying leaflets
and arrested them. The crowd in the exchange protested, crying, "Let them go!" and followed the police, Avi along with
the rest. None of the workers was armed and there had been
no prior planning, yet they gathered in front of the police
station in spontaneous demonstration, shouting and demand-
ing the release of their friends. When the officers taunted
them, one of Avi's friends cut the telephone wires to prevent
any calls for reinforcements and the crowd broke into the police station.

The officers had taken their prisoners upstairs to the second-floor waiting room; now, armed with swords, they
grouped on the landing and slashed at anyone who tried to

ascend the stairs. Avi and others near the back of the crowd got the idea of getting into the station via the roof. They slid down through the attic trapdoor and began to throw stones; this barrage from the rear forced the police down the stairs into the arms of the furious mob. While they were thus occupied, Avi and the others got the prisoners away. Avi was wounded slightly, but escaped arrest—they all did—and the prisoners were taken across the border to freedom that same night. Avi always dated his manhood from this battle.

He was not arrested until the next year, in the failure of the 1905 revolution; he was then sixteen. The Russian prison system segregated political prisoners from ordinary criminals, and he was put into a separate wing of the great prison at Kovno. Avi had never seen so many books in one place. The jail held representatives of every imaginable political tendency, though most were Bundists or *Iskraites*—*Iskra* was the newspaper of the left-wing socialists, or Bolsheviks, as they had begun to call themselves. They and the Bund had deep disagreements about revolutionary strategy, but Avi had never paid much attention to their arguments before. Now, with nothing else to do, he began to listen.

The Bund believed Jews should organize separately and have complete autonomy; *Iskra* said everyone should be in one highly disciplined party. The events of 1905 made Avi favor the *Iskraites*. While the Bund had been the best organized of any group in the area, its very effectiveness and superior size had made it easier for the government to isolate it, claiming that the whole revolution was a Jewish plot and not in the interests of Gentile workers. Hence the wave of horrible pogroms that ended the revolution; his brother had been killed in one. The Bolsheviks argued that the differences between Jewish and Gentile workers could be overcome only by a party in which all were united; this made sense to Avi. He was young, after all; he spoke Russian as well as Yiddish; and he had no particular commitment to any separate Jewish identity. He went to one of the older Bolsheviks and asked to study with him. Soon prison became his university, and by 1908, when he went over the prison wall with twelve of his comrades, he was a theoretical adept. While he fled across the border into Austria, the party got in touch with his mother and Gittel, who sold everything they had to raise passage money for America.

Sarah was enchanted by Avi's story. She had never met a

boy whom she could admire so wholeheartedly. His bravery, his single-mindedness, his lack of egotism were qualities she had found in only one other man, her father. She always said she'd never marry, but marriage to someone like Avi might be different from the usual bad bargain in which the woman was expected to stay home and cook and clean while the man had all the adventures. But was this love? She didn't know.

Rachel was a little uncomfortable in the Metropolitan Museum of Art. She was sure she'd say the wrong thing about the paintings, and she hated being with Tish and Denzell together; they always quarreled and she got stuck in the middle. But if she didn't see Den with Tish, she wouldn't see him at all. He never asked her to go anywhere alone. She, who was always so sure of herself with men of her own background, had no idea how to handle someone like him—rich, Gentile, blond. Their few encounters left her with a flying, ecstatic feeling that troubled her sleep and was like nothing she had ever known.

Today Tish was in one of her moods: tapping her feet and sticking out her chin and elbows so she looked very angular next to the round ladies in the paintings. She was wearing an odd, narrowly draped costume, one of her new French things that were straight up and down with the waist right under her bust, Empire style. It was a weird bright purple, and on her head, instead of the usual matching picture hat, she wore a black silk turban with a white aigrette in front. She looked so peculiar everyone in the Museum stared at her, but she said they were just showing their ignorance and gazed truculently back. She kept asking Rachel and Den what they thought of this or that painting, and making faces at their answers. Rachel sighed and decided to be as quiet as possible. After all, she'd never been in a museum before.

Museum—you'd think it was a church, with the madonnas and crucifixions and saints they had all over the place. Rachel had been brought up to think looking at a church was bad luck; she turned her eyes away whenever she walked down Grand Street past St. Mary's. Now she felt disloyal for looking at the pictures. The nativities were pretty, but the crucifixions scared her. One of them was so gruesome it made her queasy. Jesus looked all gray and dead and they were lowering him into his coffin. The blood oozing out of his cuts was clotted and nasty and seemed to stick up out of the painting;

and the thorns on his head were so very sharp that Rachel glanced around nervously, wondering if people could tell she was Jewish. They better not blame me, she thought; it was the Romans, not the Jews, that killed him.

She had often wondered how Denzell and Tish felt about her being Jewish. Was it just something exotic to them or did they connect it with their religion, like the Irish kids at school who talked about Christ killers and called the Jewish kids mockies because Jews had mocked Jesus. There was another picture by Petrus Christus with nice bright shiny colors showing Christ dead on a white sheet with some funny-looking people pointing at him. Rachel figured they must be mockers. They didn't look Jewish.

She liked the pictures best that weren't about Jesus. There was a lovely round one by Thomas Lawrence of two beautiful children. Their hair was all combed and curled in ringlets; and they were so red-cheeked and healthy-looking that Rachel knew without asking they were rich. No East Side kids ever looked like that. Rachel could tell the picture was special because of the big crowd around it.

"This one is nice," she said shyly and Denzell said it was his mother's favorite. "Cute little kids," he said. Tish snorted furiously, and began to jab the point of her parasol into the floor as she walked.

"Ignore her," whispered Denzell.

Some of the pictures were a little embarrassing. There was one called "The Storm" of a shepherd and his girlfriend running and holding a piece of cloth over their heads like an umbrella. The girl was very pretty with long curls and blue eyes, but she had almost nothing on—just a net gown. You could see everything right through it, even her nipples. Rachel was shocked. Denzell laughed in a funny way. There was another naked one, by Veronese, called "Mars and Venus United by Love." Mars was dressed in armor but Venus had nothing on except pearls. There was a piece of blue cloth draped between her legs but it looked like Mars was going to snatch it off any minute and then those little fat kids with wings wouldn't be much help.

"This is Father's favorite," said Tish nastily. "He likes blondes." Their father was a great patron of the museum and had given it money and several pictures of his ancestors.

They wandered on. Rachel found a beautiful quiet painting of a girl in a funny hat pouring water; the painter was called

Vermeer and the picture was all light and shade, very peaceful. Even Tish liked that one and stood in front of it a long
time. There was also a portrait of Christopher Columbus
looking rather sad; it reminded Rachel of her mother and the
way she used to curse Columbus for discovering America
whenever things went wrong. She did miss her mother
sometimes.

Tish was behaving more and more eccentrically, stomping
her feet and muttering insults under her breath.

"What are you going on about?" asked Denzell.

"You wouldn't understand," she hissed. "I feel as though
I'm being smothered with miles of gauze! Or as if I've been
painted with varnish; it's like a corset over my senses and I
want to peel it off, just peel it off and walk naked to the
world!" Her voice had become quite loud and people were
staring. "I want to see something new, plain, bright. I want
to peel the skin off life and look at its insides! Where are the
modern paintings?"

"Take it easy, old girl," said Denzell. "You're making a
scene."

"Oh bother!" shouted Tish, banging her parasol on the
marble floor. "I don't care! I hate brown varnish! I hate sim-
pering portraits of children! I hate all this old rubbish! I want
to see something new!" People were gathering from all over
the hall to see what was happening. "I've got to get out of
here," she muttered, kissing Rachel swiftly on the cheek.
"Don't worry about me, Den, I'll get home by myself." She
fairly ran from the room. They followed along behind her but
by the time they reached the great marble staircase, she was
nearly down it; they could hear her parasol tap-tap-tapping on
the steps as she ran. Rachel and Denzell looked at each other
wide-eyed. Then Rachel began to giggle. Denzell smiled
happily.

"Let's go somewhere nice and have tea," he said.

I'll go to Two Ninety-One, thought Tish. That will show
them. There were tears of rage in her eyes. "Them" was
mainly her father, who had been ranting to her only the night
before about "291," a new gallery downtown owned by a
photographer named Stieglitz. It even showed photos sometimes, right along with the newest paintings from France. She
had read about it in the paper and asked her father to take her
there, but he refused.

"Two Ninety-One stands for everything I detest," he said. "Anarchy, paganism, and formlessness—all the self-indulgence that is the curse of this modern age!" Very good, thought Tish, she would go there at once and, what's more, she would walk all the way even though her mother said no lady should walk in the streets alone.

She stomped down Fifth Avenue scowling and knocking the tip of her parasol on the pavement with each step, *click click click.* When passersby stared, she blotted them out by closing her eyes halfway, a trick she had mastered in childhood. The tapping of her parasol and the clomping of her heels on the pavement set up a meter in her mind, so that she began to mutter verse pugnaciously at the elegant fronts of the upper Fifth Avenue mansions where her parents' friends lived.

I wander thro' each charter'd street, (stomp, click)
Near where the charter'd Thames does flow, (stomp, click)
And mark in every face I meet, (stomp, click)
Marks of weakness, marks of woe. (stomp, click)

There were plenty of marks of weakness to be seen in Denzell's face if Rachel had the eyes to look, but no, she was blinded by his golden sparkle, the glamour cast by sex. The way he mooned over her was no surprise; Denzell was always mooning about some woman; he needed women to give meaning to his life. And they called that love!

Rachel seemed to be falling for it. Of course, she didn't know any better. She hadn't seen much of the world, and didn't understand where you ended up when you bought the lies that covered up sex, lies that landed women like her mother in big houses with dark old pieces of furniture like gravestones for their death-in-life. There they sat, waiting for the men to come home from their world of business and city lights, having teas and charity balls and arranging marriages and circulating scandals. Blake knew about that too:

But most thro' midnight streets I hear
How the youthful Harlot's curse
Blasts the new-born Infant's tear
And blights with plagues the marriage-hearse.

Any woman who married was a fool. And Rachel was an-

other to be so easily taken in by Denzell; Tish had thought
better of her. Imagine her falling for that poor cardboard cut-
out of a person, that empty *boulevardier*. Of course he'd
swear to love her forever and how would she know that only
meant until she got in the way of his stupid aeroplanes. If she
could only see things straight, if only her mind-forged mana-
cles were not so firmly in place that she could not even see
the other love that reached out to her hidden under a thousand
social forms, the hopeless, undemanding, sisterly love.

There was no point thinking about it. It was not going to
happen. Things did not all work out in the end. You had to
keep your distance, not get so wrought up, keep the light
ironic tone, stop these nonsensical romantic fantasies. A corner of Tish's mouth twitched scornfully and she stuck out her
elegant chin. No one would know, at any rate; that was a
comfort. There was only one woman she'd ever met who
thought about it that way; she was probably still at Vassar.
There were plenty of other things in life. If you were going to
suffer, at least you could have the dignity to do so in silence.

She was approaching downtown now, and the shops were
ending, all the lovely boring shops filled with luxurious
clothes for young matrons done in tasteful pastels and dark
greens and browns and blues. Ladylike clothes, nothing striking. Tish's mouth curled with considerable hauteur as she
looked at her own purple costume imported directly from
Paris, where they knew how to live, where women had stolen
the barest styles and the gaudiest colors right out of the Russian ballet. How people did stare as she walked by; let them.
Her clothes could scream if she could not: "You dowdy
pigeons, see a peacock!"

Was that the Flatiron Building in the distance? Had she
come that far already? Tish caught sight of a sign discreetly
placed in the upstairs window of a small brownstone. It said
"291." Next to it was a picture of some sort. She couldn't
see it clearly from the street but she could tell that it was the
reddest thing she had ever encountered, redder than a rose, a
radish, or even a tomato.

Upstairs were three small, unpretentious rooms and an ex-
plosion of color on their walls: reds, purples, queer acrid yel-
lows, and greens of a bright bitterness. Tish had never seen
such colors used in painting. There was a man there, too, but
she did no more than note his presence, as she gazed trans-

fixed at one of the larger canvases. It seemed to be entirely red.

Gradually her eyes overcame their shock at its extraordinary insistence upon that color and she realized it was a representation of a room, perhaps the artist's studio. An easel and a few odd pieces of furniture were drawn onto the red with yellow lines. The only other accents were in the blotches of color that were canvases leaning against the wall—he had painted in pictures of his other paintings. One was a pink and purple nude, the figure oddly foreshortened—not at all a female beauty of the sort her father liked, hardly even identifiable as a nude woman. There was a sinuous green plant in a vase; its color throbbed against the implacable red of the canvas, the tomato red that kept drawing attention to itself and insisting you follow its flatness around the entire surface of the painting, with no help from any attempt at highlights or shadows or other conventional means of fixing your eye or giving the illusion of depth. It was as if the artist were saying, "What's the difference what it's a painting of—give yourself up to the color." She heard a step behind her.

"Who did this painting?" she asked.

The man answered, "Henri Matisse. Do you like it?"

She turned to look at him. He was a small man with a beard, oddly dressed in a gray wool shirt without a tie or jacket, with a bright blue scarf tied around his neck peasant-style. His eyes were a dark velvety brown.

"I can't tell you," said Tish, raising her long hands expressively. "I've just been to the Metropolitan. I had to leave; it felt like a cemetery. And then to find this—" She shrugged. "I'm usually better at saying what I mean, or even what I don't mean, but this—I've never seen anything like it and it was what I really wanted. That makes me very excited and also frightened because I didn't know there was anything to want that really existed and wasn't just my own oddness. I know I'm babbling, but you can't imagine—" She trailed off.

He regarded her with the warmest interest. "Sometimes it hits people like that," he said.

Her eye caught another painting across the room and she went toward it as though drawn by a magnet: green grass, blue sky, just laid down flat in blocks of color and five enormous naked women, you could hardly call them nudes, ca-

vorting in a circle. They were very, very pink. The whole
thing made the most beautiful free design; it was like a flower
opening to see those huge, loping, ungainly figures. They
were different sizes with their limbs all wrong, grotesque, but
none of that mattered, there was something so joyful about
them. They didn't even have to be women, they might just as
well be flowers because the joy was in the color, the freedom
of the lines, the paint itself, not the identity of the subject.

"I do love this one," she said softly, then turned abruptly.
"Are these paintings for sale?"

"More or less," said the bearded man. "But Steiglitz just
shows them. If people want to buy them, he puts them in
touch with the artist. He doesn't take a commission. That's
not what it's about. Money would spoil it."

"Why does he do it then?"

"It's to help people open their eyes. A lot of people come
here all the time and most of them see things differently when
they leave than they did when they walked in. As you will."

"Yes," said Tish. She liked the paintings and the man.
She liked it not being about money. She would come again.

"I think of Two Ninety-One as a laboratory," he went on.
"For experiments in seeing, I suppose, or chemical reactions
between paintings and people. It's part of the revolution. People won't put up with the old things anymore; they won't be
told what to do and how to act. They want to think for themselves and see things new. Two Ninety-One is about that and
that's why some people hate it."

"Like my father," interrupted Tish.

"Oh, yes?" he said. "Well, they say we're a sign of the
times, part of the general social unrest. So we say, That's
right, yes, we are, we're the art arm of the revolution!"

Tish's eyes were shining with excitement. "That's so
fine!" she said. "Are you a painter too? What's your name?"

"Roman Zach," he said. "I'm a Cubist."

After their afternoon at the Metropolitan Museum, Rachel
didn't hear from Denzell Sloate for two months. She assumed
he had been forbidden to see her, and she knew he couldn't
stand up to his family.

His father, William Sloate, a coarse but energetic banker of
Scotch-Irish descent, had plans for each of his children and
had let them know what was expected of them. His oldest
boy, Sonny, was to marry well and come into the bank. He

did. As befitted her feminine sensibility, Tish was to cultivate the arts, which she did in her fashion; she was also to marry brilliantly. This she had refused to do. Denzell's assignment was more vague; he was to be a credit to the family. He dutifully played football at Princeton and maintained a gentleman's C average, though with some difficulty. He gave up a succession of housemaids, barmaids, divorcées, and "townies" whenever his father told him to.

Denzell had low tastes, perhaps in response to his mother's excessive refinement. Emily Longworth Sloate traced her descent to the Jamestown Colony and seldom stopped alluding to it. Denzell and his father both escaped into the arms of women who were their social inferiors. "Such relationships, while enjoyable, should be brief and purely physical," William warned his son. "Otherwise they can become expensive." When he discovered that Denzell had become attached to a Frenchwoman of dubious reputation, he ordered him home from Paris at once, in the fall of 1909. He did not know that Denzell had fallen in love, not with a *soubrette* but with far more exciting activities taking place at certain airfields outside Paris.

In the United States, aeroplanes were still in their infancy and were used primarily for stunt flying at state fairs. William Sloate had no patience with this fad of his younger son's and ordered him to drop it at once and find something serious to do. Disobeying his father for the first time in his life, Denzell spent much of 1910 at Belmont Park watching the new Curtiss hydroplanes race back and forth to the Statue of Liberty, clocking their time on his stopwatch. When Glenn Curtiss made his historic flight from Albany to New York in only two hours and fifty-six minutes, little longer than the journey took by train, Denzell tried to convince his father that this hobby was of potential use. Someday aeroplanes would be used for transportation, mail, hunting, racing; they might even be adapted by the military in the unlikely event of another war. But his father was adamant.

"It's too dangerous," he said. "As long as your money is in my control, you'll have to stay out of those damned things."

Denzell brooded on this injustice. People had scoffed at railroads and automobiles, and look at them now. Every new invention seemed impractical at first. Aeroplanes were becoming safer every year. People were already perfecting wheels so they could come down on land as well as water, and once they solved the problem of stabilizing a plane so it wouldn't pitch about in the wind, there'd be little danger left. Just because a few reckless daredevils did stunt flying at fairgrounds didn't mean the whole enterprise was crazy. In France they understood such things. Hadn't the builder of the Eiffel Tower himself invested his entire fortune in aeronautical research? Flying was the next great thing, and if his father had any imagination, the Sloate Bank and Trust would be in on it.

In June 1911 Denzell turned twenty-five and came into an inheritance left by his grandmother. He at once placed an order for a new Curtiss hydroplane. It had two seats, double wings, stabilizing floats, and could fly up to sixty miles an hour. Shortly after his tea with Rachel, he left for upstate New York and lessons at the famous Curtiss school.

Although his chief passion was aviation, Denzell was not indifferent to women, especially beautiful ones, and found himself drawn to Rachel Cohen in a less purely sensual way than usual. True, she was a girl of the lower classes; but she was also a brilliant girl, an intellectual, a friend of his sister's. As if his first successful defiance of his father had given him courage to do other untoward things, upon his return to the city he invited Rachel to lunch at a famous midtown hotel.

She had grieved over his neglect and was delighted to accept, astonished to hear he had been away and overcome by the reason for his absence. She had never known anyone who'd been near a plane before and questioned him closely. Denzell was at a loss for words; he was never able to describe his feelings about flight.

"There's nothing like it," he said. "You'll have to come up with me and see for yourself. It's dazzling, that's all."

"Me, fly? I'd be terrified."

"It's perfectly safe," he assured her. "I'm an excellent pilot. And you are strapped in."

"But what if you bump into clouds?"

"They're just fog," he said. "There's no harm in them, really. They do prevent you from seeing where you're going, but I can always tell where I am by the feel of the wind. Come on, say you'll do it."

But she continued to demur, saying finally, with a charming smile, that she would wait until they knew each other better.

"I'm perfectly reliable," he laughed, looking into her eyes. He reached deliberately across the table and took her hand.

She stared at him gravely. The sunlight shone through the window on his golden hair, turning the top of it to pure light. He looked back at her with a little smile. His skin was so pink, his profile as perfect as that of a king on a coin. How could she help loving him? It was as if a prince on a white charger had ridden down Rivington Street to find and claim her.

"I hope we get to know each other much better," he said.

Of course he'd never marry her. He would probably be glad enough to get her outside of marriage, like a showgirl, but Rachel didn't hold herself that cheap. Free love was one thing, between equals or for the sake of an ideal. But free love with a rich man was the same as being kept. So it would have to be marriage or nothing. Yet, sitting there in the restaurant with her hand in his, Rachel was overcome by such a torrent of longing she could hardly keep from snatching his hand to her breast. She looked at him and the air seemed to buzz with all that might happen between them, and her hand felt very heavy. After a while she took it away.

Ruby was content with her job. By the spring of 1911 she was bringing home eleven dollars a week as an assistant designer at Margolis Modes. This was, as she pointed out, four dollars more than Sarah had made at her age.

"I wasn't a boss," Sarah retorted, "or even a boss's flunky."

"I'm not a boss's flunky, either," said Ruby complacently. "I'm a designer—an artist. That's why they pay me high; my work is worth a fortune to them."

Ruby's work was indeed of a high quality, but that was not the only reason she made more than was usual for her age. The boss had a soft spot for her. Herman Margolis was an unhappy man. He disliked his wife and was uncomfortable in their Central Park West establishment. His children had been educated beyond him and considered him low-class. His business was giving him stomach ulcers, so stiff was the competition, so difficult were relations with the workers. In this gloomy picture, Ruby was a spot of pink. She was good with designs and pretty to look at but, most of all, he could talk to her. She took an interest. He poured out his problems by the hour and Ruby listened and asked intelligent questions. Sometimes she even made helpful suggestions.

Ruby liked to hear about the business. She had thoughts of opening her own factory someday. After all, this was America; even a poor boy like Henry Ford could become a millionaire.

"You're not a poor boy, you're a poor girl," said Sarah. "Girls don't make fortunes, they marry them."

"Wait and see," said Ruby airily. She had no idea that most of the men in the shop believed she was Margolis's mistress. She felt like his daughter and assumed he was similarly paternalistic; after all, the man was in his fifties.

She had obtained the job several weeks after Solly Fein's wedding and as a direct result of it. One night Moyshe said, "Ruby, I thought you invented that convertible skirt. Here's an ad for one in the *Forward*."

"What?" said Ruby. "Let me see."

The picture seemed identical in every detail, and the copy read: "New! Remarkable! Margolis Modes Convertible Skirts turns a Little Girl into a Young Lady in no more than the time it takes to button ten buttons! Patent pending."

"I don't understand," said Ruby, her face puckered in bewilderment. "I made it up. I know I made it up."

The next day she wore the skirt to school, with the extension in her bag, and, buttoning it on after the bell rang, made her way to the Division Street premises of "Margolis Modes: Fine Garments for Ladies and Girls for Fifteen Years."

"I want to see the boss," she told the foreman.

She was ushered through the messy, busy loft to a dark cluttered office in the back. A little man with a brush moustache sat behind an oak desk littered with drawings. He looked up.

"You!" exclaimed Ruby. "I danced with you at the wedding! You stole my convertible skirt!"

"You can't prove a thing." He jumped up and waved his foreman out of the room. "I deny everything. It'll never stand up in court."

Ruby just looked at him, her innocent blue eyes full of tears. Then she sat down.

"You've got grounds for nothing, not even a settlement.

The patent's in my name. You should have gotten it patented yourself if you didn't want it stolen. These things happen all the time in the garment industry. You've got to be smart—it's dog eat dog on Division Street.''

Ruby still did not respond.

"Say something," he wailed. "What are you going to do? Are you going to make trouble or aren't you?"

"I saw your ad in the *Forward*," Ruby said conversationally. "My friend Rachel works there. She'd do anything to help me get my rights." She didn't say more. She didn't have to. No business that valued good will could afford to make an enemy of the *Forward*. Margolis Modes was a small operation. Most of its retail outlets were on the East Side. A bad press could make the difference between getting through another season and collapsing.

"No need to talk about the *Forward*," said the little man hastily. "Don't give it another thought. Tell you what, I'll make you an offer. I'll buy the design from you retroactive. I'm not a bad guy, I don't like to cheat people, only I'm desperate for new designs. I've got a *shlub* of a designer who can't see straight, and in this business the look is everything. I could tell you stories you wouldn't believe, such crooks, and anyway I never thought you'd find out. But I'll pay. How much do you want for the design?"

Ruby thought a moment longer. "You need a good designer," she said. "I'm a good designer. I want a job."

"I can't give you a designer's job," said Mr. Margolis, horrified. "You're a little kid. I got fifty-year-old men here working for less than what a designer makes. In this industry, girls are learners on the trim machines or maybe finishers; men are designers."

"Well, I don't ask to be made head designer right away," said Ruby reasonably. "I can't even start work until school lets out. How about assistant designer at fifteen dollars a week?"

"Are you crazy? Fifteen dollars is what a cutter makes!" Margolis was scandalized.

"What does a designer make?"

"Mine makes twenty-five, but he's a forty-year-old man with five children. Also he helps the foreman and he can lift the heavy bundles of cloth. You could never do that."

"Give me ten dollars now, try me out for a year and then make me assistant designer at fifteen," said Ruby. "He can do the lifting and I'll do the designing. Or you can get rid of him after I get some experience."

"You can't be more than fourteen years old. I'll give you seven dollars."

"Nine," said Ruby, "and I promise you won't be sorry."

"This is blackmail," groaned Margolis, but Ruby just smiled.

She planned to begin work in June 1910, but there was a general strike in the cloak and skirt industry, and Moyshe refused to let her start until it was settled. "That's all right," said Margolis philosophically. "I would have had to lay you off anyway; we're not getting any work out."

She began her new job in the first week of September 1910, although Sarah was fiercely opposed to her taking it. "How can I hold up my head if my sister is a boss!" she cried. Moyshe too was against it, but Hannah prevailed.

"You have always done what you thought best," she told Sarah. "You never asked for my approval or for Ruby's. So you're embarrassed. Maybe Ruby was embarrassed when you kept getting arrested. Did you ask her? Now you'll have to let her do what she's determined to do."

"Well, I hope we don't end up staring at each other from opposite sides of a picket line some day."

Ruby became part of a mushrooming ladies' cloak and suit trade. Ready-made garments were in greater demand every season and were being shipped all over the country. By 1910, over fifty thousand people worked in the industry. Although the earliest cloak factories had depended upon women cutters and machine operators, as the work increased and became more lucrative, they were replaced by men—for it was heavy work, and only men were strong enough to slash through the piles of wool twenty layers thick with a special knife, cutting out the pieces. Even when electricity was introduced for both sewing and cutting machines, men kept the jobs, for they all had some lifting involved. Women worked only as finishers and at other light tasks, like sewing on buttons and making trim. Only twenty of the hundred employees at Margolis Modes were female.

Although it was booming, the industry was in a haphazard state. Few of the manufacturers had either the business experience or the acumen to organize their factories in the efficient way then being worked out by Henry Ford and Frederick Taylor, inventor of scientific management. Taylorism eliminated the old craft basis of industry. No longer could workers pursue their tasks by their own methods; jobs were standardized and descriptions of them written by managers in a separate office, who divided and subdivided the work in the interest of greater production. But these modern mass-production methods were not yet common in the garment center, where the hundreds of dirty, overcrowded shops had no sanitation, no fire prevention, no decent light or air, and not much in the way of management, either. Like most Division Street employers, Margolis got his cloth on credit and his designs wherever he could. His work was poorly organized and done in a slipshod manner.

It was Ruby Levy who introduced scientific management to Margolis Modes, making it her business to learn every aspect of the production process and poke into every detail of how the shop was run. She followed the boss around. She followed the foreman, Abe Greenfeld, around. She stayed late, studying the patterns, and though she was not strong enough to wield a cutter's knife herself, she thought of new ways to place the patterns on the piles of fabric so that less material would be wasted. Her own designs were at first simple, but she made sure that the work on them was careful, and several of them sold well. She watched the workers, suggesting various small innovations to Margolis: a new way of doing buttonhole plackets that took less time; a way of ruffling heavy wool that made it lie flat; and constant subdivisions in the labor process.

When Ruby started at Margolis Modes, work was still done on the old section system: a tailor would not only seam a coat sleeve, but also turn under the edges, bind them, and sew in the lining before he passed it on to the next worker. Ruby divided up the work so that one tailor did seaming, another binding, and a third put in the lining. Because each worker did only one operation over and over, he became very fast and the company saved money in labor costs. Of course the workers disliked the innovations—they called them "the speed-up system"—because they made the day more monotonous and put all the control over speed in the hands of the foreman; but the new system was good for the company and that was what counted with Ruby. It wasn't just the praise she got from the boss or the bonuses he gave her when she saved him money; she glowed with pride at how well Margolis Modes was doing.

In 1912, Margolis got rid of his old designer, who was having trouble keeping up, and promoted Ruby, raising her salary to twelve dollars a week. He refused to give her the title or the pay her male predecessor had gotten, saying it would cause too much trouble in the shop and she had to wait until she was twenty-one. But everyone knew what had happened.

To the workers, she was a pariah; her rapid rise and her contributions to speed-up made them despise her. The women called her "that spy" and never spoke in her presence. The men called her "Margolis's *tchotchke*" and held her in contempt. Even the foreman hated her for enjoying more of the boss's confidence than he did himself. If Ruby had been older and more attentive to these matters, she might have found ways to defuse this antagonism. But she barely knew it existed and since she thought of the class struggle as a fairy tale spread by her father, she would have dismissed the hatred of the other workers as mere jealousy if she had noticed it. She was involved in her work, her dreams, and all she was learning about the business.

Ruby usually walked home on Essex Street so she could look over the pushcart merchandise. One day a friendly voice hailed her, "Hello, Ruby."

It was Tricker Louis Florsheim. He walked her part of the way, holding her elbow whenever they crossed a street and inquiring after the health of her family. After that, she frequently ran into him. She didn't mind as long as her mother didn't find out.

Ruby had become the complete young lady, dressing demurely in lacy white shirtwaists with colorful ties or artificial flowers at the neckline, respectable dark skirts, and fetching little bonnets. She wore her brown curls piled high on her head like a grown-up, but her round blue eyes were as guileless as ever. Ruby was an innocent with men. Though many thought her boss was making a fool of himself over a girl young enough to be his daughter, Ruby didn't notice. Though boys whistled when she walked down the street, she barely heard them. And though Tricker Louis was obviously making a point of waiting for her on Essex Street, she hardly gave him a moment's thought.

glish. Patsye Keegan the dope fiend sat with Chaim the Mummy and Birdie Pomerantz the gun moll. Tricker's two favorite madams, Sadie the Chink and Jennie the Factory, were together at one table and at the next were the Boston Brothers, Meyer and Sam, whose real name was Solomon. Then Tricker's eyes met a pair of sleepy-lidded brown ones and his face lit up.

"Benny," he hollered, making his way to the corner table where Dopey Benny sat with two of the boys. Tricker and Dopey Benny (who derived his name not from any bad habits but from a sinus condition that gave him a perpetually sleepy look, like an addict nodding out) had been pals since grade school, when they were the two bad boys who had to sit in the back of the room. Benny was the teacher's special bane, leading the pack in practical jokes, scratching dirty words into the desk tops, and lifting the little girls' skirts. Together the two had stolen fruit and knocked over pushcarts; together they had graduated to the status of full-fledged gangsters with their first indictment. But unlike Tricker, Dopey Benny had done time, lots of it, first in Elmira Reformatory, then upstate at Sing Sing, from which he had recently emerged to become a lieutenant of Big Jack Zelig's in the labor-management relations field. The two men who sat with him, Joe the Greaser and Yoski Nigger, named for his swarthy complexion, were also associates of Zelig's. Yoski, a Sephardic Jew, was the leader of his own little gang, the Jewish Black Hand Association.

Tricker sat down. "I've been filling the boys in on the long-range picture," said Benny. Tricker nodded. Benny had the kind of vision that was needed on the East Side. He had educated himself in prison, struggling through Frederick Taylor's *Principles of Scientific Management* in the Sing Sing library, and he was a great admirer of Henry Ford. Like Ford, Dopey Benny wished to reorganize his industry for greater productivity: he would divide up tasks and territory among various gangs; he would separate planning from execution in order to work on a large scale; and he would draw up long-range programs to avoid the seasonal panics that made life so uncertain.

"Big Jack Zelig was a good man," said Benny, "but he's gone, and let's face it, those mick bastards have given us a chance to reorganize. The employers are still backward in a number of industries, especially garment."

"I don't know about that," said Joe the Greaser. "They hire us."

"Sometimes they hire us," corrected Benny, "but sometimes they hire the Five Pointers. Imagine bringing in Irish gorillas to beat up on Jewish workers! Now how is a crummy little Columbus tailor with his skinny legs and spindly arms supposed to stand off the Five Pointers? Jewish labor needs help, and who is better equipped than us?"

"Are you kidding?" said Yoski.

"The labor relations business has two sides, capital and labor, offense and defense. So far the only ones with any dough have been the bosses. But now the workers have gotten organized. There've been strikes in shirtwaist, cloaks, furs. They can afford to buy their own muscle."

There was a long pause while the men considered the idea. "What makes you think the unions will hire us?" asked Yoski. "I mean the Jewish unions. Aren't they too socialist?"

"I know a guy named Joe Klein," said Tricker quickly. "Grew up on the block with me, used to run with the Midget Gorillas. Now he works for the ILGWU. I've got an appointment to see him."

They looked at him with new respect. His heart glowed. The tide was finally turning; he could feel it. With Benny's help, he would pull himself out of the gutter and win respectability. A steady job working for a union. He could get married. Any girl would be proud to latch onto a fellow like that. How could Ruby's family object to a union man? He would give the situation a few months to get regularized, then hunt her down and pop the question.

II

Rachel was hopelessly in love with Denzell Sloate and Sarah was sick about it. "He doesn't do anything. He doesn't think anything. He doesn't contribute anything. What do you see in him?" she said. "And he's part of the ruling class."

Rachel didn't know what to answer. How could she explain that she did not love him because of qualities?

"He's a person," she said. "You can't turn everything into a category." His blond hair, his blue eyes, his tall straight body, his white teeth, his courage, the way he smiled at her—what did those have to do with money? He was all she had never had; and he loved her. Maybe.

Tish thought not. She was rather sarcastic about it.

"He probably tells you he loves you," she said. "He usually does."

Rachel flushed and looked down at her hands, which had acquired a life of their own and kept picking at the pattern in her skirt.

"Has Denzell had many love affairs?" she asked miserably.

"Many, what's many?" said Tish. "I can think of twenty of my friends he's tried, but I know only one woman he's been serious about, that Frenchwoman. And Father squashed that." She pinched her forefinger and thumb together to illustrate her meaning. "He cut off Denzell's allowance so he had to come home."

Rachel was bewildered. "Did't he want to stay? Surely he could have found some sort of job?"

Tish hooted. "A job? What a giggle! The boy's never worked a day in his life."

"But surely his—woman friend—could have found him something."

"My sweet Rachel," drawled Tish, "the lady was from the Folies Bergère. She'd have slung him out on his ear if he came to her with no money."

It was all very hard to understand. The world these rich Gentiles moved in, their morals, and their emotional laws were inscrutable to her. Nor was she sure she could believe everything Tish said about her brother. There was a hint of jealousy in her descriptions that rendered her verdicts suspect. It was hard to tell if she was warning Rachel out of concern for her welfare or because she liked to keep her friends to herself. Especially since Denzell, in his turn, had warned her off Tish.

"She gets these odd crushes on other women," he said. "There was a teacher at college—the family hushed it up. But I don't think she'll ever marry, unless it's a Boston marriage."

Rachel looked at him blankly. "What's that?"

He raised his eyebrows. "Don't you know? Two women living together? It's not all that uncommon."

"It's not uncommon at all," she said stoutly. "Women live together all the time," and she didn't understand why he laughed. She did hate it when he acted supercilious. And so many things about his world were strange to her that it was hard to know when to ask questions and when to keep still. It was like all the letters about mixed marriages she got at the *Forward*:

"Dear Young Girl's Friend, I work in a shop with a Gentile boy and as things happen we fell in love. It was nobody's plan, still it happened. Now we went to get married but my mother says if I do she will go back to Russia. I don't want her to go back and get killed in a pogrom but if I don't marry this man I will be miserable all my life. What is your advice?"

Cahan had worked out a stock answer to this question, straddling the fence: Maybe you should do this, maybe that, in the long run only you can decide, but it is our observation that marriages between people of different backgrounds often don't work out.

Rachel followed the formula with less and less conviction. She longed to write a very different answer, one full of questions: "Dear Reader, What is it that draws us to these Gentile men? Is it a desire to escape our Jewishness, or our oppression? Is it because we hate ourselves and our people, or because we love the man? Is it something chemical, a physical attraction mainly, or the lure of what is different? Why did I never feel this way for any of the boys in the neighborhood? What am I to do, dear reader? I have already lost one family; can I afford to give up all the rest of my roots for this? I think not, but then I see him and I lose my bearings once again. And I don't even know if he loves me."

Perhaps there was some way to test his feelings for her; she could set him some kind of ordeal, like knights and ladies in romances. Tish was sure he'd never come to the big suffrage demonstration in March; he said he wouldn't make that kind of fool of himself. The next time Rachel had dinner with him, she said demurely, "Is it true you're afraid to come to the suffrage march?"

"Of course I'm not afraid, I just don't fancy it. Think how it would look, me marching with all those women."

"There's a men's contingent," she said. "You could go with the Men's League for Woman Suffrage."

He groaned. "Do I have to?"

"Of course you don't have to." She laid down her fork. "I just thought, from things you said, that you cared about equal rights for women."

He took her hand across the table. "Does it mean so much to you?" he asked softly.

She considered. "It says something about your character. Either you've been misrepresenting your opinions in order to win my approval, in which case you're dishonest; or else you're a friend to women's rights in words but not in action."

"Help!" he cried, laughing and putting his hands in the air. "I surrender! I'll go to the demonstration!"

"That's nice," she said. But she was far from being convinced he'd really do it.

The suffrage demonstration was to be held on March 4, 1912. Tish had been working on it indefatigably, and since the headquarters of the Woman Suffrage Party were in the same building as the office of the Women's Trade Union League, she and Rachel and Sarah often met for lunch. Sarah had stopped being so hard on Tish, once she saw how she worked; and she laughed at her gory tales of suffrage wars among the rich ladies.

"This year Mrs. Belmont says she'll march," Tish burbled. "It's hilarious. She maintains she was absolutely right not to do it in 1910 because the idea was too new, and even last year was too soon for her because it was still mainly radicals marching. But this year the march is going to be really big, proving that the idea has become respectable and is supported by the majority of women. This means that not only is it permissible for a lady of breeding to be in the parade, but in the case of a person of Mrs. Belmont's stature, it is required that she participate in order to raise the tone of the event. On the other hand, Mrs. MacKay, another friend of my mother's, has her own group, the Equal Franchise Society. She told my mother that this year is no different from any other year and that Alva Belmont's change of heart merely confirms what she always suspected—Alva Belmont is no lady. After all, she was divorced."

Sarah was fascinated. "You mean suffragists don't approve of demonstrations? Does the national group have them?"

"Heavens no, they're a really stodgy bunch," said Tish. "If we had to rely on them, we'd never get the vote. It took years to convince the state organization that a demonstration wouldn't set the cause back, and even then they insisted on riding in cars. Our group is the only one that's determined to get the vote even if we have to be unladylike to do so."

"What's unladylike about marching?" asked Sarah. "We marched during the shirtwaist strike. The labor movement marches every May Day."

"My dear girl," drawled Tish, raising an imaginary lorgnette, "that is the point. We wouldn't want to have people mix the suffrage movement up with your lot."

"How many people do you expect?" said Rachel.

"Maybe five or even ten thousand. There were three thousand last year."

"And we're supposed to wear white?"

"If possible. No one should stay away just because she can't afford to get a white skirt—but it does give a graphic image of our unity if we are all dressed the same."

"Hmph," said Sarah dryly. "Nobody I know even has a white skirt. It's a good thing the suffrage movement doesn't have to do its own laundry."

Tish's estimate of ten thousand proved to be low. The *Tribune* counted twenty thousand marching, and everyone agreed there were at least five hundred thousand people watching on the pavement. They filled the sidewalks of Fifth Avenue all the way from Union Square to Columbus Circle to watch what they soon realized was not only a spectacular show but also a historic occasion.

"It was a parade of contrasts," said the *New York Times:* every age and condition of woman was represented. There was Antoinette Brown Blackwell, the suffrage pioneer, in her nineties and so feeble she had to be drawn in a flower-decked carriage; and there were babies in strollers. There were businesswomen, motherly-looking women with their daughters, schoolgirls in uniform and factory workers, socialites and socialists. "There were women who work with their hands and women who work with their heads and women who never work at all. And they all marched for suffrage."

Leading the parade were fifty women on horseback, among them Tish on the big bay mare she had brought in from her family's Long Island estate. They all wore white, with the suffrage ribbon saying "Votes for Women" stretched across their breasts, and straw hats with cockades in the suffrage colors: purple, green, and white. They looked like the cavalry of some Amazon army. Riding in front were society beauty Inez Milholland (a friend of Tish's from Vassar) and Sarah McPeake, carrying a banner between them which read:

> Forward out of error,
> Leave behind the night;
> Forward through the darkness,
> Forward into light.

Next came contingents demonstrating the changing social position of woman. First were a corps of Scottish bagpipers, followed by a woman in a sedan chair: these symbolized the conditions of the past. After them came floats depicting woman's contribution to various industries: spinning and weaving on looms. Then came the women themselves, organized by occupation and demonstrating more effectively than any float the message that they had entered public life in great force and variety. There were professional women: doctors, writers, lawyers, musicians, artists, librarians, social workers. The teachers were there in caps and gowns, the nurses in uniform. After them came at least two thousand industrial workers: milliners, custom dressmakers, shirtwaist makers from the East Side, domestic workers, laundresses. The float of the Women's Trade Union League was there and near it, set a bit apart from the rest, dramatic in its mourning amid all the white, was a solitary black banner. It read, "Triangle Fire—We Will Never Forget. We Want the Vote for Protection," and it was carried by Sarah and Rachel.

A number of marching bands were there, notably the brass band provided by Mrs. Belmont, which played various patriotic airs such as "Marching Through Georgia" and "The Stars and Stripes Forever." Anna Howard Shaw marched magnificently past in her university cap and gown. Mrs. Marie Stewart rode past on a milk-white steed, dressed as Joan of Arc in a full suit of medieval armor. A group of Scandinavian women in national costume brought support from the only countries in the world where women could vote. Children carried banners pleading, "Give mom the vote." Women carried others reading, "Taxation without representation is tyranny" and "All this is the natural consequence of teaching girls to read."

The men's contingent aroused particular derision. Tricker Louis, who was uptown on business, stood on the sidelines with his cronies, yelling "Sissy sissy sissy," while others cried, "Who's minding the baby?" Upon seeing Denzell, a tall Adonis dressed all in white, the crowd sang "Here Comes the Bride."

A company of street speakers from the Woman Suffrage Party carried their own green soapboxes. After the march, they would fan out all along Fifth Avenue and explain the meaning of the day to all who would listen. Most of the marchers, however, when they reached the end point at Columbus Circle, simply joined the crowd of bystanders to see the rest of the parade.

It had begun at five o'clock in Union Square, and it was dark long before the last demonstrators reached Fifty-ninth Street, singing the *Marseillaise*. The military strains floated thrillingly ahead of them, and then their torches came into view and the onlookers gasped. It was the socialist women; their sashes were flaming red; and as they marched up the dark, packed avenue they looked like the revolution come to call.

Throughout the march, Rachel had been looking anxiously for Denzell but had not caught sight of him anywhere. She kept telling herself it must be because the men's contingent was so far ahead. Still, the sinking feeling in her stomach made her aware that her faith in him was less than infinite. As the socialist contingent marched by, there was a whoop behind her.

"Found you!" cried Denzell, and threw his white derby exuberantly into the air. Rachel was weak with relief.

"How did you enjoy your afternoon with the Men's League for Woman Suffrage?" she inquired.

"Whew," he said, "I'd rather join the army than do that again. I wish you'd have a tournament next time so I could ride out and defend you in single combat rather than have to stay in line. I was dying to break ranks and beat some of those hooligans on the sidewalk to a pulp, but of course that would have been bad for the march."

"We don't need any knights in shining armor, Den," said Tish sharply. "Just supporters and allies, thank you. Stay in your place."

"Why did you march, anyway?" asked Sarah. It did not fit her picture of him.

"I'll tell you," he said, pulling out a folded sheet of paper. "Allow me. Richard LeGalliene passed these out," and, clearing his throat, he read:

> *I had my marching orders, that's*
> *Why I marched today,*
> *For all the women that I loved*
> *Were going the same way.*

He looked at Rachel meaningfully and she gazed back at him, her eyes shining. Sarah's heart sank.

Nothing was going quite right for Sarah. She was already tired of her job at the Women's Trade Union League. The Triangle fire had given her a discouraging, if more realistic, sense of what could and could not be accomplished by one woman organizer. Immediately after the fire, the city indicted Isaac Harris and Max Blanck, owners of the firm, on charges of violating the fire laws. The Women's Trade Union League, while awaiting the outcome of the trial, initiated a campaign of fire-prevention education. Sarah spoke on the street corners of the East Side all that year, telling people to call the League if they found dangerous conditions in their shops. Hundreds of calls came in, providing lots of ammunition for Mary Dreier's campaign to get stronger fire laws, but the machinery for punishing violators was cumbersome and ineffective, and the city seemed reluctant to move against them.

"Wait until the verdict in the Triangle case," said Mary Dreier. "Once Harris and Blanck are convicted, all this will become easier."

Harris and Blanck did not seem apprehensive. They hired new premises and reopened for business. They rented a loft on the corner of University Place; it soon transpired that this building was not even fireproof and, as if this were not enough, they placed their sewing machines so that they once more blocked the fire escapes.

"So much for their fear of the law," said Sarah.

Their contempt proved justified. On December 29, 1911, after deliberating only two hours, the jury brought in a verdict of not guilty. The judge had instructed them to vote that way unless they were convinced beyond the shadow of a doubt that the owners of the Triangle Waist had knowingly locked the fire doors at the relevant time and that this, rather than anything else, had caused the death of the workers.

"Not guilty!" cried Sarah that night, reading the paper with horror. "How do they have the nerve to say the words?"

"Look who was on the jury," said Moyshe, reading over her shoulder. "Do you expect businessmen to find Harris and Blanck guilty? Especially with so many loopholes in the law?"

"What do we do now?" Sarah asked Mary Dreier the next morning. "Am I supposed to keep standing on street corners telling people to report violations in the fire laws so we can bring their bosses to trial? They'll laugh in my face."

Mary sighed; she too was discouraged by the Triangle verdict. "It does seem to be a hard world for women sometimes. We'll just have to work harder than ever to get rid of the loopholes, I suppose. But wait until we get the vote and can elect our own judges. Then you'll see some action!"

The League's fire-prevention campaign did have results. Within a few years a Factory Investigating Commission was appointed and completely overhauled industrial legislation in New York State. Sprinkler systems were required by law. Women and children were given the eight-hour day. Sanitation measures were introduced to protect both workers and the public. Other laws were passed regulating ventilation, lighting, lead poisoning, and other industrial hazards. Evidence that Sarah hunted up helped many of these laws pass.

It proved easier to change the fire laws than to win the vote for women, however. There was to be a state referendum in 1912; if women won the vote in New York State, the whole national movement would be affected. The League worked night and day trying to reach union men and get them to vote right. Although she couldn't go along with Mary Dreier, who seemed to think women could clean up the slums, end child labor, and bring universal peace inside of a year once they had the vote, Sarah thought suffrage would help working women quite a bit. As she told Hannah, "We'll have much more influence if we can vote, and we'll be able to get our laws passed more easily. Right now nobody listens to us. And of course, woman suffrage will double the number of working-class votes—socialist votes." She found it fascinating to go around to the men's unions and tell all those pipe fitters and carpenters and teamsters the score. And while some of them said their wives didn't need the vote, others were sympathetic and entered into the argument on her side.

She made a rip-roaring speech at a big suffrage meeting the League held at Cooper Union in 1912:

"The politicians tell us we're too delicate to vote. They say dropping a piece of paper into a ballot box once a year will wreck our feminine charms! Tell that to the laundry workers, standing knee-deep in cold water for fourteen hours a day, doing the washing of the rich! Tell that to the sweatshop workers on the East Side, slaving all through the night for a few cents an hour, stopping in between bundles to nurse babies who will probably die from malnutrition before the year is out! Tell it to us shirtwaist workers—they weren't worried about out delicacy when they sent us to the workhouse! The fact of the matter is that we working women have never had any of those feminine charms they want to protect—we can't afford them! We work as hard as any man; we think as well as any man; and we want every right and privilege the men have, including the privilege of making fools of ourselves every four years as they do by voting for capitalist parties that keep the chains fastened around their necks!"

People crowded around to congratulate her after the speech, though Mary thought she shouldn't have said anything about socialism since it wasn't the League's position. Among those in the crowd was Joe Klein. She hadn't talked to him since she'd been blacklisted, though they'd run into each other from time to time. Now he came up to her.

"You're turning into a real suffragist," he said. "I can hardly tell you from the rich ladies, you look so fine." It was true; since Sarah got her job at the League she'd had to pay more attention to her clothes.

"How's everything down at the union?"

"Never better," said Joe. "Our membership's growing all the time. We even have a lot of new women members since we organized the white-goods workers."

"I've no doubt you can sign them up," said Sarah drily, "but if you want to hold on to them, you'd better do a little more in the way of benefits and women organizers."

"Come on, Sarah," he pleaded, with his most winning smile, "don't hold a grudge. Maybe I was wrong. But how am I going to change my mind if you stay mad at me all the time? Who knows, we might even hire a woman organizer sooner or later if you spent a little time converting me." She had to smile at his nerve.

"People tell me you have a boyfriend," he said. "A printer. Is it true?"

She shrugged. "We go for walks together."

"Serious?"

"We're not about to get married."

"Well, that's a relief. I've thought about you a lot. In fact, to tell you the truth, I've kind of missed having you around to tell me off. How about you and me going out every now and then?"

She shrugged again, but smiled. It was nice to see Joe; he always kept her on her toes. And maybe if Avi had a little competition, he'd show more enthusiasm. He seemed to assume they would just keep going on walks for a few years and then drift into marriage. Maybe because he never put the kind of pressure on her that Joe did, she felt there was something missing in their relationship.

"How about Saturday night?" said Joe.

"I have a standing engagement on Saturday nights," said Sarah primly, "but some other night would be okay. Why don't you drop around Friday after supper?"

By the next spring, Sarah had been going out with Avi Spector for two years, and was also dating Joe Klein steadily. For most girls, she knew, Joe would be the clear winner in this competition. He was handsome, smooth, Americanized, at ease in most situations. A man on his way up, he was already making decent money working for the union and would probably leave it eventually to go into real estate or become a lawyer, possibilities he talked about. They didn't particularly thrill Sarah; in fact, Joe's desire for upward mobility lowered his rating.

So did his attitude toward women. There was always a trace of condescension in his smile. He couldn't be trusted; every time they went out he tried to get away with something and she had to watch his hands like a foreman. And she already knew he was undependable in a crisis—hadn't he betrayed her that day she got blacklisted? Besides, he wouldn't marry her even if she were interested. He was looking for a rich girl or one with political connections, like the daughter of that Tammany lawyer.

Avi would marry her tomorrow if she gave him enough encouragement, but he was so shy she'd probably have to ask him. That was the trouble; her feelings for him were intense but he seemed interested only in friendship. He hardly even touched her. The sensual element so strong in her relationship with Joe was missing from Avi's courtship; she was honest enough with herself to know she needed it. When he talked about his life in the Russian movement, she would have knelt at his feet, so inspiring was his faith, so admirable his devotion. But all that passion seemed reserved for the revolution, not for her.

He was always trying to get her to study—some theoretical tome or some diatribe of the Bolsheviks. She couldn't read such stuff. She was no dummy, but her mind turned to cotton wool when faced with polemics. Why did she have to be an intellectual?

"I work hard all day," she said. "I don't want to come home at night and slave over some book."

She tried once or twice, to please him, but whenever she got to a difficult section she put down the book. Things that came hard made her feel stupid, a feeling she disliked.

"I know all about revolution already," she told Avi carelessly. "I don't need to study; I know from my own experience."

"You don't know enough to convince anybody else," he said. "How are you going to win over people who haven't had your experience?"

She glared at him. Why did he want to make her over? "If

he doesn't like me the way I am, let him find somebody else," she told Rachel.

"You're just looking for a fight," said Rachel perceptively. "He doesn't really think you're dumb; he couldn't possibly."

It was true that Sarah picked fights with him. Partly this was from family habit, but it was also a way to inject some excitement into their relationship and interrupt his lectures. Why did he have to preach at her all the time? It never occurred to Sarah that his stiffness was due to inexperience in romance.

He was so Russian; all he wanted on Saturday night was to sit around in a café and talk politics, or study, or at best go to a very serious play. He never took her dancing; he never paid her compliments. In fact, half the time he criticized her. "You're too hotheaded," he would say. "Your instincts are good but you lack judgment."

But at least he loved her, she did know that—to the degree he knew how to love. His style wasn't romantic and his feeling for her didn't have much to do with her being a girl. He loved her as a socialist.

Moyshe liked Avi very much, seeing him as a younger reflection of himself, and when his union at the cigar factory organized a Fourth of July outing to Prospect Park in Brooklyn, a popular country spot for day trips, he invited Avi to accompany the family.

Prospect Park was the first unbroken expanse of ground Hannah had seen in America. The memory of the Russian countryside hit her like a blow in the chest, and she sat down sadly, looking into space. She could almost see her mother roving underneath the trees, gathering herbs, dabbling in the water. After a time Ruby came to sit with her. Grateful for the company, Hannah took her hand.

"It makes me think of Bubbe, Mama," said Ruby.

"Me, too," said Hannah. They sat in silence.

"She would have hated America," said Ruby finally. "Even Kishinev was too built up for her. She liked the country."

Hannah nodded. "I know it's better that she didn't come. And yet—" She couldn't go on. Ruby squeezed her hand. "You are my rock to lean on, Ruby, now that Rosa's gone," whispered Hannah.

Ruby gazed across the clearing at the others. Avi, Moyshe, and Sarah were having an animated discussion; Moyshe was grimacing and holding something in his cupped hands. Ruby went over to see what he had. It was a ladybug, creeping over each joint of his knit fingers, unable to find an exit.

"This ladybug is like me in America," said Moyshe. He let it go. It flew clumsily over to the trunk of a tree a few feet away, where it began to creep up the bark in an aimless fashion.

"It's not America that traps you," said Avi, lying down to look up at the sky. "It's history. It's time."

"But history isn't set," said Sarah. "We make it as we go. We change it." He smiled at her.

Moyshe leaned back on the grass and stared up through the branches of the trees. "Even the clouds are wipsy here," he murmured. "In Russia the clouds were as solid as marble. They looked like you could carve steps in them and climb to Paradise."

Sarah lay beside her father and put her face close to his. "I thought you were happy in America now, Papa," she whispered. "Do you still miss Russia all the time?"

"Not all the time," he said. "But I miss myself. It's hard to explain. I grew up in the Russian movement. It molded me into a certain kind of person: a fighter, a doer. The times needed heroes. They still do over there. But I am here and there is nothing I can do. I go to my job, to my union, to speeches and meetings, but who am I? I feel myself dwindle into an old man. The things I loved in myself are not needed here."

"We need you, Papa," said Sarah, hugging his arm.

Moyshe smiled over her head at Avi. "You need a father, not a hero," he said. She wouldn't understand; she was too American. But perhaps Avi would know how he felt.

As he rode back on the ferry that night, the lights of the city seemed a hundred miles away. The waves lapped mournfully against the side of the boat. On the deck above them, some Americans were singing, "Gone are the days when my heart was young and gay, gone are my friends from the cotton fields away," and even though Moyshe could not understand the words, he felt the yearning of the music. He looked at Avi, and for a moment Avi shared his longing.

"Oh, Death in Life, the days that are no more," he whispered in English.

"What?" said Sarah.

"The English poet, Lord Tennyson," he whispered back. "I studied him in my English class."

Sarah told Rachel wistfully the next day, "He sat next to me all the way home on the boat and he didn't even try to kiss me. Sometimes I think he likes my father better than me."

Like many of his comrades in Russia, Avi had consecrated his life to politics at such an early age that he had bypassed the sexual agonies of adolescence. Or postponed them. His contact with girls had been all in the context of work and meetings; he had never had to manage a purely social relationship before and did not know what he was expected to do. He was not even sure what he wanted, overcome as he was by feelings of embarrassment or inadequacy when he thought of wooing Sarah, and intimidated by the amount of talk about sex in America. Even the Jews, known in Russia for their puritanism, wore tight-fitting clothes here and went to dancing academies, where they held strange women in their arms. The men at the print shop where he worked talked of nothing but chasing women. Of course, they weren't revolutionaries; but even some of his political friends seemed like hedonists to him.

The Russian movement was more idealistic, he thought. Couples there were purer in their feelings, sometimes even denying themselves sex for the pleasures of a perfect comradeship. Women in the movement were regarded as men's equals; they received the same jail sentences and had the same responsibilities. Avi always made it a point to behave that way to Sarah; his criticisms of her were a sign of respect, and he could not understand why she took them so badly. He treated her as he would a sister, never flirting, always avoiding the passionate impulse that had led him to kiss her on the Williamsburg Bridge. He would do nothing to show that he had thoughts which women might find insulting or impure. Sometimes when Sarah was walking close to him and he took her arm and felt the pressure of her body against his, he could hardly restrain himself. But he was a disciplined man and a revolutionary, so he pulled away.

"I'm not going to be in love with someone who treats me like his maiden aunt," Sarah told Rachel, nearly weeping with frustration. "I don't think he cares about me at all."

"Why don't you see if you can get him to take you dancing?"

Local 25 was giving a dance at a nearby hall that weekend. The three-piece band ground out one waltz after another as the couples on the floor circled more or less in time, some with grace, others with their hands pumping up and down as though they were drawing water from a well. Avi's back was among the stiffest on the floor and he gazed stonily over Sarah's head, eyes fixed, swallowing convulsively. She looked at him in disgust. He was not a bad-looking man at all: well-built, tall enough, with regular features and lovely gray eyes—but without a smile, what have you got?

"You don't know how to dance very well," she observed the third time he stepped on her feet. She was a good dancer herself; she often practiced with Rachel or Ruby. Now she smiled in anticipation as the band swung into a song in the new beat—ragtime—that was sweeping the city.

"Hey, it's the turkey trot," she said excitedly. "Come on, Avi, I'll show you how. 'Everybody's doin' it, doin' it, doin' it,'" she hummed, holding out her arms impatiently, raring to go. He was in an agony of embarrassment as he watched the other couples, holding each other tightly, begin to zip through their paces; he could not imagine holding her like that and bouncing around like a rubber ball.

"I can't do this," he mumbled miserably.

"All right," she said sharply. All her awe of him was for the moment gone; her irritation and resentment were overpowering. She wanted to dance. Why was she saddled with this socialist *yeshiva bucher*? She waved gaily at Joe Klein whom she saw across the floor, and as he walked toward her she ran to meet him and they began to dance.

Avi backed off the dance floor, watching her, white-faced and shaken. She danced again and again with Joe Klein, as if they had some special understanding; she seemed to be happy to have his arm around her. She laughed up at him. She put her hand on his shoulder, his back. Finally Avi could stand it no longer. He marched out onto the floor, seized her arm, and walked her toward the door.

"I'm taking you home," he said.

"Why? It's still early."

But she did not struggle as he got her coat and led her into the street. He was clearly upset. They walked in silence for a block.

"Even if you didn't have the manners to stay with the man who brought you, you might have done so out of regard for my feelings," he said in a tight voice.

She realized she had really hurt him. Her irritation ebbed like water down the drain when she saw the misery on his face.

"I'm sorry," she said in a small voice.

"You should be," he said. His fingers were like iron bands around her arm. All the time he was thinking miserably that she hadn't wanted to be with him. She cared more about dancing with that smooth-faced American than she did about him. He had known about Joe Klein, but not taken him seriously as a rival—the man clearly had no soul. Now he saw that it was Joe Klein she wanted.

"I thought you were a serious person," he said, his voice raw, "not someone who would dance with that fellow like any shopgirl."

"Does being serious mean I'm never supposed to have fun?" She was angry again. "And when did I claim to be better than a shopgirl? And what about revolutionaries, Avi, what do they do? Do they only study and work, nothing else? What about marriage? What about making babies? Do they do that? Tell me, how is the race going to propagate itself after the revolution?"

He blushed, thankful she couldn't see him in the dark. Humiliated, furious, at a loss for an answer, he had never felt more bereft.

"You'd better not say any more," he snapped. "Everything you say just lowers my opinion of you."

She stopped walking, nearly ready to tell him she'd go home alone. The agony on his face stopped her. But who was he to tell her off like this? She had feelings too. All Sarah's scrappiness rose up in her. She loved drama; she loved testing and pushing people to their limit, making sweeping denunciations and having the last word. Did he think he could get away with this, taking her from the dance as though she were some kind of criminal? Working herself into a defensive rage, she mentally listed her grievances: he wanted to make her over; he never wanted to go out and have fun but acted like a rabbi all the time; he argued about everything; he couldn't dance and didn't know how to behave socially; he never said anything nice to her; he never tried to kiss her; he acted as if he were afraid to touch her. Did she have some contagious disease? She refused to think about the things she loved in him, not now, not at this moment.

If he had only been able to reach out and hold her, he might have broken through her anger, but this was the thing he was least able to do. His passion was bricked inside a wall of shyness, hidden behind a screen of words. They got to the corner of Rivington Street and Essex.

"Don't bother to see me to my door," she said coolly.

"All right," he said with equal hauteur.

"Perhaps we shouldn't see so much of each other," she continued. "You obviously think I'm not good enough for you."

He was white, ill-looking. "I would certainly never ask a girl to marry me who cared as little for me as you do." His voice was shaking.

She spared him nothing. "Marry you," she hooted. "Marry you—that's a laugh. And what would we do after we were married—study all night and shake hands at the bedroom door?" Feeling she had gotten off a winning shot, she whirled and ran up the stairs, not leaving him time to reply.

He could not have replied if she had given him half an hour. There was no way in the world he could have responded to that. He was shriveled up in misery. So that was what she thought, that he was no man at all. He walked home cold as a pool of tears, resolving he would never see her again. It hurt too much.

His absence was soon noted in the Levy household. Sarah, miserable and guilt-stricken, cursed her sharp tongue, but merely told her parents they had decided not to see each other anymore and refused to say why. After two weeks, at Hannah's insistence, Moyshe sought Avi out.

"At least tell me what happened?" he said.

But Avi too would not say. "Sarah has no feeling for me," was all he would concede. "She made that plain."

Mystified and grieved for himself as well as for Sarah, Moyshe said, "It doesn't seem fair. Even if you and Sarah have had a fight, why should I have to lose you too? I never had a son."

Avi was touched. He felt the need of a father, and Moyshe had become precious to him. "We could have tea sometimes," he offered, thinking also that through her father, over the years, he would from time to time hear news of Sarah. He would hear when she married. He would hear when she had children. But he would never see her again.

III

In the summer of 1913, Margolis's wife made him take a two-week vacation to settle his family in their summer home in New Jersey. "Abe Greenfeld will be the boss while I'm gone," he told Ruby.

"Who will be foreman?" said Ruby.

"What do you mean, foreman? He will."

"No, he'll be the boss. He'll need somebody to be his assistant. While he's busy doing the things you do, somebody will have to do the things he does."

Margolis had not thought of this. "I suppose you mean you," he said.

"You know I'd be the best."

"Do you have any idea what you're getting yourself into? The men would never stand for it. They hate your guts as is."

"Pooh," said Ruby. "They won't care. And what if they do? It's none of their business. Let them work as hard as I do and they'll get promoted too. Why should I have to stand back just because I'm a girl—this is the twentieth century, after all."

When Margolis told Abe Greenfeld that Ruby was to be temporary assistant foreman, he said, "I don't know, Mr. Margolis, the men aren't going to like it."

"Then they'll have to lump it," said Margolis. "That kid knows the business better than anybody but you and me, and I'm not sure about you. So that's all there is to it."

"I'm worried about Ruby," said Moyshe to his wife as they lay in bed that night. He folded his arms pensively behind his head. "She doesn't understand anything about the world. She can't take a foreman's job in a cloak factory where all the workers are men. She's only seventeen. They'll kill her. I can't understand why she should want to do such a thing.''

"Ruby is ambitious," said Hannah.

"Ambitious for what?"

"She's never exactly told me," said Hannah, "but I think she wants to own her own factory."

Moyshe, for once, was speechless.

Nobody spoke to Ruby as she walked through the shop the next morning. When she got to Margolis's office, she found him pacing the floor.

"I can't do it," he announced immediately. "The men won't work for you. I must have been crazy to think you could be assistant foreman. It was the last straw. They said I have to put you on a regular woman's job or they'll walk out."

Ruby stared at him uncomprehending. "But you're the boss," she said. "You don't have to listen to them."

"Ruby, it's the height of the winter season and I'm already in debt for the cloth. They have me over a barrel. If there's a strike, I'll lose weeks of work; I could even lose the factory. I won't be able to fill my orders. The models won't get into the shop before Christmas. No matter how I feel about you, I'm not going to wreck my whole life to give you a promotion."

"But how can I learn new things if you won't give me any responsibility? If I can't learn here I'll have to look for another job. Is that what you want me to do?"

His self-control cracked. "Oh, Ruby," he whispered, "don't even say it."

"Then stand up to the men. I don't believe they'd walk out. The union wouldn't back them up if they struck over something like this."

He stared at her mournfully. "If you only knew how I feel about you, Ruby, you would take pity on me. You're young, you have time yet. Don't push so hard."

"What are you talking about?"

"The whole shop knows, everybody except you," he cried in a passion. "They all say I'm a fool, an old goat in love with a young girl! Have you no feeling for my position? If you knew how I think of you day and night—"

Ruby stared at him in disbelief, surveying his shapeless

form, his gray brush moustache, his pleading watery eyes. It
was disgusting! He was old enough to be her father! To think
that all the time he'd been leading up to this. The sneerers in
the shop had been right; she was the one who was a fool,
thinking she'd risen through talent alone. They'd told her,
"Nothing special about your work—he just wants to get into
your pants." But she had been so sure of herself and her
gifts. She began to sob, great childish gulps of disappointment. Misunderstanding, hoping, he took her in his arms.

She pushed him violently away. "Leave me alone! I'm
going home. I'll send my mother for my pay."

"But Ruby," he stammered, "you can't just go like this. I
need you."   •

"You don't care about me," she cried. "You're only interested in one thing, just like they said!"

"All right, all right," he cried wildly, "you want the foreman's job, I'll let you have it. Anything—so long as you'll
stay at least until I get back from vacation so we can talk
things over. Ruby?" He touched her chin gently. "Will you
do that?"

"You'll make me temporary foreman?" Her sweet young
face was hard.

He sighed. Maybe they wouldn't really strike. They might
have been testing him. He nodded his head.

She gave him a grudging, tearful smile. "All right, then,
I'll stay until you get back, but don't talk to me about love.
You're too old for me. I just want to learn the business, that's
all."

She did her work the rest of the day with a set face, looking neither to the right nor the left, thinking what a fool she'd
been. Next time she would know better. You couldn't trust a
man. You had to put your faith in yourself and your own
talent and concentrate on getting ahead that way. Men would
only trip you up; they'd wreck your chances at success if they
could. She walked home in a state of furious concentration.
So absorbed in thought was she, in fact, that she nearly
walked into the suave figure that crossed her path to bow at
her, some well-dressed uptown type. He straightened up and
raised his hat. It was Tricker Louis Florsheim.

"Hello, beautiful," he said. "I've gone straight."

What a transformation! Gone were the checked pants and
plaid jacket, the hard derby and diamond pinky ring. Con-
servatively dressed in a dark double-breasted suit, with a dis-

creetly tailored vest buttoned up to his snowy collar and
foulard tie, topped by a Homburg hat, Tricker was barely
recognizable. With a broad smile, he took an elegant leather
card case from his inner coat pocket and extracted a piece of
pasteboard. It read: "Louis Florsheim, Esq. Labor-Management Relations."

"My goodness," said Ruby, taken aback. They talked for
some time. He was handsomer than ever, and treated her so
politely, it soothed her feelings after the bruises of the day.
When he asked her to have dinner with him at the Hotel
Napoleon in midtown that Saturday, she thought, Why not? It
was true that men couldn't be trusted. But she hadn't the
slightest intention of trusting Louis; he was so suspect already
that she could never make the mistake with him she had with
Mr. Margolis. She would go and get dressed up and eat a
good dinner and that was all; if men were going to chase after
her, she might as well get something out of it.

Tricker fairly danced into Joe Klein's office that evening.
"I'm getting married," he crowed. "Congratulate me."

"I didn't even know you were engaged."

"I'm not," said Tricker, "yet. But I will be after Saturday
night. I'm going to take Ruby out to dinner at the Hotel
Napoleon and pop the question."

"Ruby who?" said Joe.

"Levy," said Tricker. "The sister of that friend of yours."

Joe's mouth fell open. "I didn't even know you were acquainted," he said lamely. "Does her family know?"

"Not yet," said Tricker. "First I propose, then we tell the
folks."

"Do you think she'll have you?" said Joe.

Looking in the little mirror on the back of the door, Louis
smiled at his profile and straightened his elegant tie. "No girl
has refused me yet."

Less than five minutes after he left, Joe picked up the
phone and asked for the number of the Women's Trade Union
League. "Sarah," he said, "I've got to talk to you. It's about
your sister, Ruby."

It wasn't every day a girl got invited to the Hotel Napoleon
for dinner. Perhaps it was Ruby's sense of the grandeur of the
occasion that led her to take out her treasured princess shirtwaist; perhaps she just wanted to make herself feel better, for
she was still smarting from her disappointment at work. She

had never worn the waist, packing it away long ago for just such an opportunity. Now she examined it furtively; Sarah was in the room and she didn't want to call attention to what she was doing.

How was she going to get it on? Her mother had been right about the buttons after all. Thirty-six of them marching up the back of the blouse, fastened with tiny crocheted silk loops. "How are you ever going to button all those?" Hannah had exclaimed. "That kind of thing is for ladies with maids." But Ruby had obstinately followed the pattern in *Harper's Bazaar*. I'll go downstairs and find Yakhne Breynes, she thought, slipping the shirtwaist under her wrapper. For a penny that kid would button anything.

Putting her book down, Sarah stared after her. The idiot! Bad enough she wanted to be a boss; bad enough she was a speed-up expert—but to go out on a date with Tricker Louis Florsheim! It was too much. Whatever respect she'd had for her sister was gone. And then on top of it to wear that ridiculous fancy shirtwaist! Sarah had always hated the thing. How shocked she had been when she realized Ruby had used their Bubbe's lace, the lace that was all they had left of her.

"Bubbe made it to be used," Hannah said quietly.

"Well, I'll never use my half," Sarah had vowed. "I'll keep it forever, to pass down. I don't need to dance on my Bubbe's grave to make myself pretty."

And that smug brat Ruby had snapped back, "Nothing could make you pretty." Sarah grimaced. She had half a mind to call off the whole rescue operation and let Ruby take what was coming to her. But blood was thicker than water.

Ruby and Tricker finished dinner and a bottle of wine and began on dessert before he popped the question. He then sat dumbfounded as Ruby, already tipsy, explained at length her reasons for refusing him.

"I don't plan to get married for years, if I ever do," she said in her sweet voice. "You can't trust men anyway, I've found that out, and I want a career. That's more important to me. I love my work and I'm very, very good at it. I've already worked my way up to assistant foreman. That's not bad for a kid my age, you know. And it's just the beginning. By the time I'm twenty-five I'll have my own factory. I'll do all the designs and be the boss and have lots of men working under me. What do you think of the name Rubymodes?'' She went on and on, oblivious.

Tricker sat with narrowed eyes, breathing hard, as his dreams shattered around him. It had never occurred to him that she would refuse—and for such reasons! Was this the girl he had yearned for? For this he had changed his life? Who did she think she was? He had asked her to marry him! And here she was, babbling as if that was nothing. Why, she ought to be down on her hands and knees to him! She ought to be weeping with gratitude!

For this he had stopped pimping? For a stuck-up school girl who thought she could run the world?

He would show her what a mistake she'd made. Taking him so lightly. How he hated her! She was like all of them. The only thing she had to offer was between her legs. His mistake had been to think that she was different. He knew how to deal with girls who thought they were better than he was; he'd done it before.

"Why, that's a wonderful plan," he said. His manner was still soothing and considerate, his voice only a little thickened by rage. He would show her what she was. He would put her in her place. He signaled the waiter. "That deserves a toast," he said. "Two sloe gin fizzes, please. Make them doubles." Girls liked those sweet drinks.

Ruby gulped hers down in no time and he ordered her another. "It's like raspberry soda," she giggled. She didn't feel drunk at all, though she did notice the air was getting funny and Louis's face seemed closer. How magnetic his dark eyes are, she thought, how he resembles Thomashevsky in *Alexander, Crown Prince of Jerusalem*. She hardly noticed it when he disappeared for a few moments to talk to the waiter. She had by then had three sloe gin fizzes. Tricker returned with her coat.

"Are we going home?" she said dreamily.

"In a little while," he said. "First I want you to see how nice it is upstairs."

Deft and speedy as his fingers were, they were not used to such niceties as thirty-six covered buttons. Pressed on top of her in an upstairs bedroom, his tongue exploring her gasping, drunken mouth, his left hand moving caressingly over her

thighs, he found his right hand completely unable to undo the
little crocheted button loops.

Dare he use both hands? He did not want to take any
chances. Would she come to her senses if he suddenly
stopped caressing her? He peered under her half-closed eyelids. She was out. He began to use all ten fingers on the
buttons, with little more success than he had had with five.

Ruby opened her eyes. "What?"

Quickly he unbuttoned his trousers, confident that the eager
pressure of his firm moist member upon Ruby's knickers
would so enchant her that she wouldn't care about anything
else.

Ruby had dressed with great care that morning, donning
not only her princess shirtwaist but also her best drawers,
which were the new closed variety. Her other two pair were
the old-fashioned kind, still widely used, consisting merely of
two separate legs tied around the waist with a drawstring, and
an opening in between. The new knickers were a more substantial barrier than the old would have been. Still, her skirt
was soon above her waist, her corset unlaced, the drawstring
on her knickers untied and his hand exploring within them as
she trembled with the unaccustomed thrills that ran through
her young body. Then she felt him, warm and big and moving on top of her but stopped by her drawers, which were
only halfway down her hips. In a sensual dream, she moaned
a little and moved her pelvis.

"Goddamn it," he swore under his breath, still struggling
with the buttons, frustrated beyond endurance. Maybe he
should leave the blouse alone and just stick it in her, but he
hated to do that while he still couldn't get at her breasts. He
gave a sharp impatient tug at the tenth button, a particularly
recalcitrant one. There was a small ripping sound and a tiny
ping as the button hit the floor.

Ruby opened her eyes. What was that?

She was suddenly aware in a hazy way that things were not
as they should be. Her sense of sartorial morality, more developed than her sense of self-preservation, was awakened.
He had torn a button off her princess shirtwaist! Couldn't he
see how good the silk was?

That was not all he had done. Biting her lips, she realized
what was going on. Those hands—hands which were now
busily engaged with her buttons, crawling all over the silk of
her blouse. She began to squirm violently. "Hey!" she said,

her words muffled against his chest. "Cut that out!" She tried
to push him away. In answer, he shoved his face down onto
hers and kissed her energetically, once more beginning his
explorations of her mouth. This time he met no warm welcome; she struggled, in increasing panic, making emphatic if
muffled sounds of protest.

"Shut up," he said, grinning luxuriantly. He was certainly
not going to stop now.

Finally awakened to her danger, Ruby began to fight in
earnest while he, realizing he had no more time to waste on
buttons, concentrated on holding her with one hand while
pulling down her knickers with his other. If he could just get
them down far enough to part her legs, he would be home
free. The material was heavy cotton, made to last; he couldn't
seem to rip it. Then he had to use one hand to cover her
mouth because she began to shrill, "Help, help!" The stupid
little bitch. Who did she think was going to help her?

The hell with it. She could yell her head off; nothing would
come of it anyway and he could use both hands on her knickers. He grunted, inching the drawstring waist down over her
hips, then her thighs.

Sarah, Rachel, and Moyshe had trouble finding Ruby even
after they got to the Hotel Napoleon. She wasn't in the restaurant and the clerk at the hotel desk was uncooperative. It
wasn't until a motherly-looking lady described a couple she'd
seen going upstairs and Rachel began to talk about the Sloate
family and all their powerful connections that the clerk suddenly remembered the room number of the "young lady
who'd been taken ill."

"You didn't tell me she was a minor," he said self-righ-
teously. "You should have said that when you came in." He
sent a man with a passkey along to guide them.

Barely had the key turned in the lock when they were upon
the struggling pair. Tricker Louis took one horrified look at
the enraged Moyshe and turned to flee, but his pants, down
around his ankles, tripped him. Moyshe lifted him to his feet
by his hair and punched him so hard that Tricker hardly felt
the blows that followed. By the time Moyshe threw him down
in an exclamation of disgust, Rachel and Sarah had dressed
Ruby and wrapped her in Rachel's cloak, still in a drunken
stupor. They made their escape through the hotel lobby, dragging her behind them.

They did not get through Rivington Street unnoticed. A hundred prying eyes saw that Ruby was muffled in a cloak; a thousand whispering voices seemed to fill the street as they passed, saying, "Look, she can't even walk herself." The fire escapes, the streets, and all the windows were filled with faces; those who had curtains moved them aside for a full view, while most just stood and stared, bare-faced. "Look at her hair, how mussed." "They have to hold her up, she must be drunk." "Who knows how many men . . . ?"

Worst of all, Hannah was still awake when they arrived.

"What were you thinking of, to go to a hotel with a man like that, a gorilla, a maiden-taker, a pimp!"

It was four o'clock on Sunday afternoon. Ruby had been too drunk and shocked for interrogation the night before, but from the moment they all arose that morning, Hannah subjected her to the third degree. Moyshe made his escape early, but the girls stayed on. By now they were all exhausted. Still Hannah continued, going over and over the events of the previous night.

"He told me he had changed," sobbed Ruby.

Hannah sat down next to her, took her hands and stared at her teary, blotched face in dour assessment. "Ruby," she whispered, "I'm asking you for the last time. Look me in the eye." Ruby raised her red eyes fearfully. "Did he stick it in you?"

She shook her head passionately back and forth. "No, no, no, I told you already, no, I wouldn't, I didn't let him!"

"But how can I trust her?" Hannah asked the ceiling.

"I told you, they were fighting when we came in," said Sarah wearily.

"Her knickers were still on," said Rachel.

"Thank God for small favors, not that anybody will ever believe it." Hannah shook her head, overcome with the unexpectedness of this misfortune, and slapped her hands down on the table so hard the dishes jumped. "How could she be such a dummy! I still can't understand it! Maybe I should get the doctor to come and examine her," she mused. "He could give us a paper saying she is pure. If she really is."

"Come on, Ma," said Sarah, "don't be crazy. What are we going to do with a paper, put it on the door? Maybe nobody in the neighborhood even knows about this!"

"Fat chance," said Hannah. "In this neighborhood they

know everything." She stared at Sarah meditatively. "And to think you were the one I always worried about. You were the one I was so sure would never get married. And here you are with two boyfriends, and I know you wouldn't be dumb enough to let either one get you without a ring."

Rachel stood up. "I think Ruby should lie down," she said firmly. Fed up with Hannah's hysterics, she took Ruby into the bedroom.

Hannah sat for a moment, then pulled herself to her feet. "I'm going out," she said. "I have some marketing to do." This was not entirely true; she was going to reconnoiter. She stood on the stoop and looked around. Across the street, Fafonfnik and her daughter Rosalie Fein were gossiping in front of the butcher shop with Mrs. Breynes. "Hello, Mrs. Levy," called Fafonfnik, and gestured her over. "How's your daughter?" she said.

"My daughter?"

"The little one who was caught in the whorehouse?"

Hannah gasped. "That's not what happened!"

"They ought to lock men like that up," said Mrs. Breynes viciously. "They ought to geld them like horses so they would leave poor girls alone."

"Yah, yah, you hear such stories," said Rosalie pleasurably, fanning herself. "I heard about this one girl over on Delancey fell for a pimp, got decoyed up to a room he had rented just for that—first he took her, then he let his whole gang in, fifteen men. She had to go to the hospital."

"New York is hard for a mother," said Fafonfnik with odious sympathy. "You got to keep your eye on them every minute, so many dangers. That's why I never let my Rosalie work in a factory."

Rosalie simpered. "I never would have gone anywhere with a bad man," she assured her mother virtuously, "not even when I was a kid like Ruby. You brought me up too good."

Hannah almost cried, "But it was your cousin she went with," but stopped herself just in time. If they didn't know that much about what had happened, all the better. They wouldn't hear it from her. Blushing with rage and shame, she heard Solly Fein murmur, just inside the door, "Like mother, like daughter." It was the final outrage. Without another word she turned and fled down Rivington Street. They are spilling my blood, thought Hannah in agony. They are spilling my blood. She ground her teeth miserably, running through the crowd, wondering how far the rumors had gone and how exaggerated they had become.

By the time she returned home, she was shaking with blind rage. She put her bundles on the table and stared at her daughters. Ruby was sitting silently, gazing at the wall, her face still red and swollen from all her tears. Sarah was reading and Rachel was mending stockings.

"Well, Ruby, you're famous," said Hannah in a thick voice. "The whole East Side knows everything that happened and a lot that didn't." Horrible and bizarre as the rumors had become, there was no cut that hurt more than Solly Fein's. She always said the apple doesn't fall far from the tree. Her shame was reflected in Ruby's. The taunt festered in her mind, like the symbol of everything she had done wrong, now having terrible results in the next generation. How she longed to push it away! She stared at her youngest girl, her eyes bulging, till her anguish overcame her, making her deaf and blind to everything but its commands.

"You did this to me!" she screamed. "You gave them a knife to spill my blood!" Shaking with rage, she swept the bundles she had just bought off the table and lunged at Ruby, slapping her face so hard she fell to the floor.

"Mama!" cried Sarah, starting from her chair, but Hannah was hitting Ruby again and again with her open hand until the room rang with the sound of the blows. Ruby huddled sobbing on the floor, shielding her head with her arms. Hannah looked around wildly for a weapon and her eyes fell upon the broom, but Sarah got to it before she did. As they struggled for possession of it, pulling back and forth, Moyshe came home.

Hannah sat down, shaking, still holding the broom while Sarah and Rachel told him the story. Ruby said nothing, but got slowly up from the floor.

Moyshe shook his head, perplexed. "I don't understand what all this fuss is about," he said. He had been thinking about Ruby all day, going over the past, wondering whether he had been partly responsible for the near-disaster. He had neglected Ruby. All his attention had gone to Sarah, so like him, and he had found his youngest child's ambitions distasteful, her mind uninteresting. Lacking a father's guidance, she had not known how to judge men; it was his fault. Now he smiled at her warmly. "Ruby's going to be all right," he said. "We got there in time; nothing happened to her. So what is the problem, Hannah? Why are you so upset?"

Hannah glared at him defensively. "She's going to be all right," she jeered. "A lot you know about it! What about her reputation? Who's going to save that? Too bad you didn't worry about her a little sooner; none of this would have happened. Too bad you didn't introduce her to some decent young men the way a father should!" She bit her lip, mortified that he had seen her so out of control.

"I admit I haven't been such a good father, but what's gotten into you, hitting Ruby like that?" said Moyshe. "Is it the neighbors you're so worried about, what the neighbors think?"

"I gave the family a bad name," said Ruby abruptly. It was the first time she had spoken in several hours.

"We don't have a bad name," said Moyshe.

They all looked at him uncomprehendingly.

"How could something like this give us a bad name?" he said. "How could one little mistake outweigh all the things we've done? Will people forget my Bund work, the way I raised money and got support for the pogrom victims in 1905? Will they forget Sarah's union work? Will they forget how your mother helps anybody who needs it, feeds everyone, is a friend to all who have trouble? And surely they will think of what a good girl you have always been, Ruby, your gentleness and fine sewing."

Tears came to Ruby's eyes. This praise from such an unexpected source was almost as painful as her mother's blame.

"But they're talking about her all over the neighborhood," cried Hannah, unable to contain her grievance. "They're saying terrible things! Everywhere I went there was nothing else on their lips! How will she ever get married? How will we hold up our heads!"

"I won't have any trouble holding up my head. But I don't understand you, Hannah. What people are saying seems to matter more to you than how Ruby feels. Why is this? You never used to care what the neighbors said. In Russia, they said plenty. Remember how they talked when you married a wild man from out of nowhere? Remember how the old women yelled at you for not shaving off your hair and wearing a wig after you were married?"

Hannah's face grew still, remembering.

"So what has happened? How come you care so much now

about a little gossip, it makes you go crazy?" he asked, really wanting to know. "What made you change?"

She tried hard to think. Her head was numb, like a recent wound. She couldn't make any sense of it. "I don't know," she muttered.

"That's too bad," he said. "I wish you could tell me. As for the neighbors, it's a problem, but we have to handle it politically. There's no reason you should be the only ones to face the gossips. I'm her father, after all." He was silent for a moment. Then he rose and took the big cast-iron cooking pot from the stove.

"Can I have the wooden spoon, Hannah?" he asked.

Mystified, she found it for him.

"Go out on the fire escape," he said, and went down the stairs. They went out. The other fire escapes were deserted; it was dinner time and people were busy inside.

Hannah watched her husband come out into the street below. He was still an imposing figure, bigger than anyone else around. She could not see him well because it was getting dark, but as he went toward one of the streetlamps and positioned himself under it, the yellow light from above picked out his strong features and made them more dramatic than ever. She could not imagine what he was up to. Standing under the lamp he took the wooden spoon and began to beat on the bottom of the iron pan with it; the loud noise resonated through the quiet street like an alarm. Windows were flung open. Heads popped out. Dark shadows filled the fire escapes.

"People," he called in his deep voice. "People, listen to me. This is Moyshe Levy, your neighbor and fellow worker. I have an announcement to make." He continued to beat on the kettle loudly, giving the fire escapes a chance to fill with people. Hannah covered her mouth with her hand. Such a man! You never knew where you were with him. He would be quiet for years, then just when you thought you had him figured, he would break out.

"First of all, I want to thank you for your concern about my daughter Ruby. I want to tell you what happened, since we all know people will talk and they might as well tell the truth. My youngest girl was innocent enough to believe in the honest intentions of a notorious man who pretended he had reformed. However, despite this mistake, she was not harmed.

"Now, if you want to do my family a favor—and I'm sure you'll want to stick by us as we have always done for you—you can ask any questions you might have right now instead of bothering my wife or my daughters later on. That way everything will get cleared up in front of everybody and you can set anybody from off the block straight if they've heard exaggerated rumors. I'm going to stand here in the middle of the street for an hour and anybody who has any questions can come down here and ask me. I am happy to answer anything asked in the spirit of community."

He paused. The block was as silent as if it were the middle of a snowstorm.

"But if I don't get any questions I'm going to assume everybody knows all they need to and will stop any stories from spreading that could injure my family any further. So if I hear about anybody telling lies about my girl, I'm going to think it's done on purpose to hurt us and that might get me mad. Remember, the Bund has a long arm."

He put his hands in his pockets and stood there, huge as a bull, silhouetted magnificently by the streetlight. There was a certain amount of buzzing on the fire escapes but no one came down. Five minutes passed. Then Hannah heard the door of her own building open and shut beneath her and slowly Mrs. Breynes, holding her little daughter Yakhne by the hand, shuffled out in her carpet slippers into the circle of light cast by the lamp. Hannah trembled but her neighbor's voice floated up, clear and strong.

"I brought you a cup of tea, Moyshe."

He thanked her and, with dignity, she turned and padded back into the house. Then voices began to ring out from the windows and fire escapes all around:

"Tell Ruby that Bessie Moscowitz is glad nothing bad happened."

"Ruby's a good girl."

"Give your family regards from the Finklesteins."

Ruby was smiling ecstatically through tears. She and Hannah stayed out on the fire escape, holding each other and watching Moyshe for as long as he stood below. All the love Hannah had denied so long came flooding through her, and she remembered the day she first saw her husband, standing in the Kishinev marketplace, arguing. When he saw her, he turned and stared at her all the way down the street until people in the crowd started to laugh and nudge one another.

Her eyes shone, remembering, and when Moyshe finally
came back up the stairs after his vigil, she said nothing but
went to him and put her arms around his waist and her head
down on his breast as she had when they were young, and
held him as if she could not imagine why he had stayed away
so long.

They lay in bed in the dark, each knowing they had to say
everything they had not said in their many years of loneliness.
Neither knew where to begin. Finally Hannah spoke, almost
in a whisper.

"When you asked me why I was so upset about the neighbors here, when I wasn't in Russia, I said I didn't know. I
know now." She spoke with great difficulty. "It's because,
what else have I got?"

"What do you mean, Hannah?" He spoke gently.

"I have to care about how we look because that's all there
is. It's not like it was."

"What did you have in Russia that you don't here?"

"I had you," she said simply.

He sighed and scratched his head; she could barely see him
in the blackness of the tiny room. She gathered her courage.
"When we were together at first it seemed like we made
something so strong the rest of the world didn't matter. I
didn't care about talk. When the inside is strong, you can
stand blows. But when the inside goes, and all that's left is
the outside—" She stopped.

"When did it go?" he asked. "When I joined the Bund?"

"I don't know," she replied. "Maybe. No, not really. The
girls were little then and I had my hands full; that changed
things too. There were problems, but it wasn't as bad. When
it really hit me was when my mother died. I was so alone
here. I had none of my family. I wanted to die myself. And
you were hard. You turned your back on me."

"Ach," he said in self-disgust. "I couldn't think of anything but myself then. I was so miserable in this country, I
felt so sorry for myself for being here and longed for Russia
so much, all the time, it was like a knife in me. I hated
having a pushcart. I felt like I'd sold my soul."

"You wouldn't even hold me," she accused him, still cold
with the memory of that grief.

"How could I? I was too angry with you for bringing me
here, cutting me off from my comrades and my work. I felt

like I was dying for lack of Russian air. The revolution happened and I wasn't part of it, wandering here like a ghost instead of being part of the struggle. How could I comfort you? I was sick with blaming you."

"But why blame me?" she asked in astonishment. "Is it my fault you killed a man?"

"What are you talking about?"

"What do you mean, what? In Kishinev, in the pogrom."

"Of course, I haven't forgotten," said Moyshe impatiently, "but what's that got to do with anything?"

She couldn't believe he was so dumb; it didn't seem like him. "Why else would you come except to escape the police?"

He stared at her in the dark. Was that what she'd been thinking all these years? "Are you serious?"

"Of course I'm serious." But for the first time, uncertainty was creeping into her voice.

He took her by the shoulders and shook her. "Hannah, think what you're saying. Think! If all I cared about was not being arrested, I would have gone underground. I'd done it before. I could have disappeared into Russia like a fish in the sea; the Bund would have helped me, and I could have continued my work. Think! You'll know this is true if you think about it."

She could hardly take it in. Clinging to the familiarity of misery, she protested, "No. It wasn't for me you came. It couldn't have been. You wouldn't even talk about it."

"I never took it seriously," he said. "I never thought for a minute you could save so much money. I still don't know how you did it. I never thought it was possible for us to come here and, since I didn't want to anyway, I didn't think about it much. But when I finally understood that you really meant it and that you would leave me behind if you had to—it broke my heart. And I had made such a mess of things, how could I hold out against you? I was afraid you wouldn't even want me to come. Everything I'd tried to do had failed, and then to come home and find Rosa like that and know I was responsible for her death—"

"You were not responsible," she snapped. "Foolish talk!"

"I wasn't there to protect her. I was her father and I wasn't there."

"And what about me?" said Hannah. "Was I there? Do you think I haven't thought about it over and over a thousand times, blaming myself till I nearly went crazy from it? I could have taken her with me to the forest. I almost did, but I was afraid she'd be in more danger there—how could I know? I thought she'd be better off with Becca in the cave. But Becca wouldn't go to the cave and she didn't stay with them; she got scared and she wanted to come home—" Hannah's voice faltered. "I blamed myself, but it makes no sense. It's not your fault, it's not my fault. It happened, that's all. We should hate the ones who did it, not ourselves. You did what you thought best. If you had done something else, you would have been a different person and I could not have loved you as I did."

"As you did?" he asked, his words dropping like pebbles into a pond.

There was a long silence.

"As I do," she said.

He stroked her hair reflectively. "Remember Solly Fein's wedding?" he said. "You looked so beautiful to me that day, and I wanted you back. But you turned away."

"I was still too hurt from when my mother died," she said simply.

They looked at each other. It was so dark they could see only the shape of each other's head, the faint gleam that was their eyes.

"Hannah," said Moyshe, "I want you to be my wife again. I want us to be close the way we used to be."

"Moyshe," she whispered. There was a sob in her voice, for always in her there was a tension between holding onto the unhappiness she knew or giving herself up to the possibility of joy. But her hands sought him in the darkness and she kissed him lovingly on his nose, which was the first thing her lips found. And slowly, carefully, with the banked passion of years in each small touch of a finger, knowing that what flowed between them was healing, knowing that they had recovered from the tremendous wounds life had inflicted upon them as much as they could alone, they made slow, thrusting, luxuriant love in the little back room on Rivington Street until they fell asleep in one another's arms.

Ruby paced the shop floor in irritation. It was a good thing Margolis was due back soon because the work was not getting done properly in his absence. They were falling way behind on the winter orders and nobody seemed to care but her. People really take advantage when you give them half a chance, she thought grimly, remembering Tricker Louis. The work just wasn't moving—and Abe Greenfeld, who was supposed to be out there on the floor making it move, was nowhere to be found, as usual.

"Look at that!" she exclaimed angrily, stopping in front of a vast pile of bundles of finished sleeves, tied together in groups of forty each. They had to be taken across the floor to the men who sewed them into the coats and here they were, stacked up, while the men on the other side of the room were almost out of work.

"Tchah," she said impatiently. "Morrie, would you come here, please, and move these sleeves to where they're supposed to go."

It wasn't a question, it was an order. But there was no answer. She looked up. Morrie Katz was standing there with his arms folded lazily across his chest, looking at her through half-closed eyes. There was considerable antagonism between him and Ruby, not without its sexual overtones since he was the youngest and handsomest man in the shop. He hated her all the more for being so cute; it made him sick to think of her fondling that dirty old man Margolis. Now he smiled triumphantly and said nothing.

"What's the matter with you?" said Ruby. "I asked you to move the sleeves. Are you deaf?"

"You're not the boss," he said, and spat.

Some of the other men who worked on sleeves came over to see what was happening.

"Will you fellows please move these sleeves," Ruby said in exasperation. "They're running out of work over there on the other side."

There was a long silence. None of them moved. They didn't say anything, just stood there. Ruby suddenly felt a little nervous.

"What's the matter with you guys today?" she said.

"We don't take orders from girls," said Nahum Tabachnik, a heavy-set older man. "I didn't hear Abe say to move any sleeves."

"Abe always moves them himself if they get stacked up," said Morrie. "Of course, he's a man. He's strong. He can do it."

"Yeah," said his friend Yentel. "That's why foreman is a man's job. They don't give it to girls even if they spread their legs for the boss. Or pimps.'' The men all laughed. So the story had spread this far.

Ruby's cheeks burned red with rage. She looked around helplessly. With a sigh of relief, she saw Abe Greenfeld coming toward her.

"Abe, these sleeves have got to be moved and the men won't move them,'' she blurted.

"Oh, yeah?'' he said. He looked at the men. "What's the story?''

"Why, that's a foreman's job, to help move those sleeves, isn't it, Abe?'' said Nahum. "We told her you always do it. So if she's the temporary foreman, she should do it herself.''

"Oh,'' said Abe Greenfeld. "I see what you mean. They're right, Ruby. I always move some of the stuff when it gets stacked. But I'll tell you what, since you're my assistant you can take half and I'll take half.'' Without further ado he picked up a bundle and ran across the room with it.

Each bundle of sleeves was three by four feet and weighed at least sixty pounds. Ruby was sure she wouldn't be able to carry them. But she was not going to be shamed in front of these horrible men. She would do her best. Her cheeks flaming, she bent down and, sucking in her breath, unsteadily hoisted the heavy bundle up as high as she could, rising slowly from her bent position until she had balanced it against her hips so that most of the weight was on her pelvis. It stuck out above her head so she couldn't see where she was going. She sniffed and started trundling slowly across the room, doing all in her power to keep the load from slipping through her grasp. She was dizzy and her hands felt so weak she could hardly keep hold. She was worried about not being able to see; there was a stairwell on one side of the loft and she didn't want to go that way by mistake. They would just let her fall down it. Terrified, she felt the bundle begin to slip. Somehow she would have to look around the side of it without putting it down too far.

At the moment she twisted her head to one side, putting herself slightly off balance, one of the men cried out in a high falsetto, "Ruby, look out!'' She jerked back involuntarily. The next moment she had dropped the bundle and was down on the floor, screaming in pain, bent double like a hairpin, holding her back. It felt as though someone were driving a red-hot railroad spike into it.

She couldn't even get up; they had to lift her to a standing position. Abe Greenfeld took her home and told her to stay there as long as she had to; he would explain to Mr. Margolis when he returned. Hannah went for the doctor, who bandaged Ruby's back tight and said he would return to look at it the next day and see if it was less tender. He told her to stay in bed and gave her some codeine syrup for the pain.

"Doctor—is it permanent?" whispered Hannah fearfully at the door.

"It's too early to say," he responded. "She'll always have some trouble with it. But she should be able to work again, some kind of work. In a few months, or a year."

Hannah looked after him, appalled. Poor Ruby. And not just poor Ruby. As she began to foresee what this would mean to the family—the medical expenses, the salary lost, the debts they would have to accumulate—she knew that Ruby's disaster was all of theirs. She had thought them free and clear at last, but no East Side family with an invalid could be financially secure.

Hannah covered her face with her apron for a moment, leaning against the doorjamb. Then she went inside to take care of her child.

A few days later Rachel finally consented to go up in Denzell's aeroplane. The atmosphere at the Levys' was so gloomy she had to get out. He was elated. What a wonderful girl, he thought! They had been seeing each other frequently, despite his father's opposition; the thrill of adulthood it gave him to be able to defy his father deepened his attraction to her.

As the world spread out beneath them like a picnic upon a tablecloth, Rachel sat frozen and terrified in the open cockpit, hunched down in her seat behind Denzell's, muffled beyond recognition in helmet and goggles and flying suit and scarves. She was glad he couldn't see her face. She shut her eyes most of the time, unable to bear the sense of exposure to the wind and sky or to stop thinking about what would happen if the fragile construction of wood and metal and canvas that held them up suddenly pulled apart or plummeted to earth.

Finally, cold and miserable, she leaned forward to ask him if they could land, and was surprised by the look of blind rapture on his face, an expression she'd never seen in all the times he'd gazed at her. Disturbed, she sat back. Her sudden motion broke his concentration and he turned to look at her

over his shoulder, smiling brilliantly. His eyes were unbelievably blue. Then he pulled down on the throttle and they
shot into the matching hues of the sky. He yelled something,
but his words were lost in the wind that rushed in her ears.

Even after they came down, Rachel had trouble hearing
him because of the roar left behind by the wind.

"What were you trying to tell me up there?" she said.

He grinned. "I said, Marry me and I'll lay the world at
your feet."

The air was suddenly very hot and still. She stared. Had
she really heard that? "That was a joke," she stated tentatively.

He looked at her, suddenly very serious and a little
frightened.

"No," he said. "It wasn't." He stepped toward her.
Trembling, she broke and ran for her life, away from everything she most desired, afraid to believe in it. He raced after
her and reached her as she came out onto the little dirt air-
strip, caught her by the shoulder, spinning her around, and
held her arms so she couldn't get away.

"Why are you running?" he said passionately. "I thought
you cared about me."

"You don't love me. You can't possibly. You don't want
to marry somebody like me. Think of what your parents will
say, think how your friends will laugh—they'll say you got
me into trouble; they'll think you've gone mad."

He stood there panting from his run. "I know all that. I've
thought about it all, believe me, and the money too. I don't
even know what we'll live on if my father cuts me off for
marrying without his permission, but I don't care. When I'm
with you, I feel like I'm alive. Except for flying, there's nothing I care about but you. Oh, Rachel." He seized her face
between his hands and pressed his mouth down on hers so
fiercely that it was as if he wanted to be lost in her. She met
him with a spurt of flame that left them both shaken, clinging
to each other. He shook his head in wonder and touched her
burnished hair with the tips of his fingers.

They eloped the next month, taking only Tish into their
confidence. Rachel asked for three weeks off from work and
told everyone she was going to stay with Tish at her family's
Long Island house, Nirvana. She didn't tell even Sarah the
truth. She didn't want any scenes to mar her happiness or

shake her determination, and she knew what Sarah would say.

"Where are you going to live after you're married?" asked Tish.

"We haven't worked out the details yet," said Denzell blithely. "We'll decide when we get back from Florida. I suppose we'll stay out at Nirvana for the rest of the summer, unless Rachel wants to keep working, or else we'll get someplace in the city—I don't know. It depends a lot on Father. We won't be able to afford anything fancy on my dividends, though we may have enough to scratch by. Time enough to worry about all that when the honeymoon is over."

Besides Denzell's allowance and the remains of his grandmother's legacy, he had some stock given him as a child. At the rate he went through money, however, Tish did not think he could cover his expenses and a house of his own. His aeroplane alone cost thousands of dollars a year. She was not surprised he was taking this problem lightly; he had never looked farther than a month ahead in all his life. He'd never needed to. She did wonder how Rachel could be so relaxed, but guessed that she had no idea how much money Denzell could spend.

"When are you going to tell Mother and Father?" she said.

"We'll send them a telegram from Palm Beach."

"I know what that means," said Tish with grim resignation. "It means I'll have to calm them down before you get back."

It took her a week to talk her father out of disowning Denzell and another to convince both her parents that an annulment or even a financial settlement was absolutely out of the question. They assumed Rachel was a fortune hunter.

"Maybe at least I'll get a grandson out of this," grumbled her father. "Even if he is half Yid. I just hope the woman isn't totally unpresentable, fat and greasy with hair on her upper lip. Well, I suppose he'll get tired of her sooner or later and then we can pension her off."

Tish had deliberately not told them much about Rachel, leaving it to their imagination. She thought it would help when they found the reality more acceptable than their fears. Perhaps they would be so relieved it would make them generous.

The Florida sun shone in the bedroom window, hotter and brighter than any sun Rachel had ever seen. Outside the window were green spiky leaves and enormous lush bougainvillaea and palm trees silhouetted against a blue sky. Their cabin was near the sea, and she could hear the breakers crashing in the early morning.

She looked at Denzell. He was shaving. Each day he became more beautiful to her, still a stranger, still becoming known. Each night was more surprising. The first had been almost frightening, so much passion mixed with the terrors of initiation, for she had after all only a theoretical knowledge of sex. She feared he would find her lacking, pallid, boring. He had been with so many women.

When she awoke she looked into his blue eyes almost fearfully and found in them such joy, such love, that she relaxed and sank back as into a current of warm water that would take her wherever it went. It took her places she had never imagined, to heights so intolerable that she wept, not knowing whether she wanted to go on or stop, to low warm shallows, where she lay with Denzell for hours, their legs and bodies entwined. Each time was different, yet she could not separate one time from another in her mind and she wondered, How do people have an everyday life if there's this?

When they sat in the garden restaurant like anybody else, she felt a little click of incongruity, as if a camera were going off in her brain, and she wondered how this pleasant, amiable, quite good-looking but really basically unremarkable young man could be the same one who came to her in the dark like some god covered with vines, who made her legs long to curl around him and her tongue to seek him out, who knew where each nerve under her skin lived and how to make it dance, whom she was as folded around and folded within as a snake that eats itself, and from whom she could no more separate than she could put out her own eye. And she thought how astonishing it was that one person could curl inside another in so many different ways. And she marveled that they could sit there in the garden eating melon and reading newspapers like any other married couple.

BOOK FIVE

If Not Now, When?

I

Ruby was out of work for months. For a long time, she just lay on her back, screaming with pain whenever she moved. One doctor came, then another. The first gave her pain killers. The second said that she should lie still and eat well and build up her strength. Their visits cost money. The medicines cost money. The chickens for special rich broth cost money. Soon Hannah's savings were eaten away. But Ruby didn't get better.

"It's like something in her broke, not in her back, but inside," whispered Rachel. She had quit her job but came in from Long Island once a week. "Too many bad things happened to her and she wasn't prepared."

It was true. Everything Ruby had thought secure had been swept away in a series of sharp blows: her job, her reputation, her faith in her own judgment. Even her bodily integrity had been violated, first by the deceptive fingers of Tricker Louis, then by the injury to her back. She knew she should try to stand or at least sit up for a while, but she hadn't the heart. She lapsed deeper into depression each day.

It drove Hannah crazy. She was tormented by the thought that this was another fruit of her sin with Solly Fein, that her punishment, like her shame, was being visited upon her daughter. And she was paying for it herself, too—not only in her worry about Ruby, but in the daily humiliations she suffered in Garfinkle's butcher shop.

Hard-pressed to make ends meet, Hannah was doing what she'd sworn she never would: buying her meat on credit across the street. Each shopping trip was wormwood in her mouth, the more so because everyone on Rivington Street knew of her family's declining fortunes. They had been well off until Ruby hurt her back. Moyshe brought in an average of ten dollars a week; Sarah had earned seven dollars at Triangle but jumped up to ten dollars when she went to work at the League; and Ruby's salary had risen to twelve dollars shortly before her injury. This put their collective income very high on the neighborhood scale.

Of course, they'd had nothing when they came over, not even a stick of furniture. Everything was bought on time from the peddlers on Essex Street. Hannah restrained herself until Ruby began to work, but then she let go. She bought a bedstead for her and Moyshe, feather comforters for everyone, pillows and sheets. She got a sleeping couch for Ruby and a new mattress for Sarah. She purchased a beautiful cut-velvet "living-room suite" in red and blue flowers. She gave away their orange crates and replaced them with proper chairs for the kitchen table, so the family could sit in comfort while they ate. At Ruby's request she bought a large mirror, and a clock for Sarah. She even got a Belgian carpet for the parlor. And, of course, a sewing machine was an investment, not an extravagance, even at five dollars down and fifty cents a week. They would own it outright in fifteen years. Hannah paid off the other items at weekly rates ranging from fifty cents to a dollar-fifty.

Her grandest dream came true when the lady in the corner apartment downstairs left and the Levys moved to the second floor, a vast climb in status. The corner apartments had windows on two sides with light streaming in—and on the second floor, Hannah could fly in and out like a bird, with few stairs to climb. The rent on the new apartment was higher, six dollars instead of four. But they were making good money, so she didn't worry, even with all her payments (including that secret one, her abortion, not yet redeemed). She was still able to save, accumulating dollar after dollar in the little flat tin box under the mattress.

It was all gone now. Not only had Ruby's injury cut twelve dollars a week off their income, but in the winter of 1913 Moyshe was put on half-time. The cigar industry was in a slump. There was too much competition from cigarettes, growing more popular by the year; the boss said a national depression was on the way and he didn't want to stockpile since people would never buy cigars if they had no money for food. By the end of the year the promised depression was upon them, and Moyshe was laid off completely. The Levys' income had gone from the princely sum of thirty-two dollars a week to a pitiful ten dollars, and Sarah was the only wage earner left in the family.

All New York was in the grip of economic crisis. Unemployed men stood on every street corner; mobs congregated in Tompkins Square to listen to agitators. Bread lines grew. Evicted families huddled on the streets with their sticks of furniture, trying to take up collections from neighbors only slightly less impoverished than they. It was a nightmare.

The medical bills continued and the food costs were fantastic. An invalid in the house meant more coal, for Ruby must be kept warm. It meant beef for beef tea to strengthen her blood, and eggs for custards to fatten her up, and of course chickens for chicken soup, the best cure for any ailment, as every housewife knew. Hannah's money didn't begin to reach. She fell behind in her furniture payments. The bill collector repossessed the clock and the mirror, then the sewing machine. The living-room suite would be next.

So Hannah had to get her meat and eggs on credit at Garfinkle's, though the *goslin* charged two cents more on the pound than anybody else, and, what was worse, he weighed in the fat and bones instead of trimming the cuts as any decent butcher would. How it galled her to have to wait while that Solly Fein leered at her, bare-faced, and to catch the grim look on Rosalie's kisser, the spiteful one on Fafonfnik's. As she sank deeper into debt, she could hardly stand to think of the future—the Garfinkles weren't the kind of people you let get a hold on you.

At least she had one consolation. Now that Moyshe wasn't working, he was finally taking an interest in Ruby. He borrowed an old cribbage board and taught her how to play. Soon she could beat him.

"Hey, you're no dummy," he said in surprise.

Her ironic look resembled Sarah's. "You noticed."

Moyshe also began reading aloud to improve his English. Hannah loved this; it helped her with the language too, and it was entertainment for the family. She could sew or darn and listen at the same time. But Ruby didn't like her father's selections, which were largely from the socialist press.

"I want to hear a real story, Papa," she complained. "This is boring. Go to the library and ask the lady for something made-up."

So Moyshe dutifully went and asked for something peppy without too much romance. He came home with an edition of Sherlock Holmes. Soon even Sarah was rushing home from work to hear what happened next, while Hannah repeated each installment in her own words for the benefit of Mrs. Breynes and other neighbors who had no one to read to them in English.

"And, Mrs. Breynes, they were the footprints of a gigantic hound!"

Sarah was so concerned about Ruby that she consulted Tish Sloate at her suffrage office upstairs from the League.

"If we could only get her to do something," she said. "She just sits there all day."

"What is she interested in?"

"Nothing except clothes as far as I can see," said Sarah with some contempt. "She's always been very good at sewing."

"Maybe I could bring her some of my fashion papers from Paris," said Tish. "They're wonderful this year. There's a completely new look. In fact, I've been wanting to get someone to make some copies for me. Do you think Ruby could do that? I'd pay her, of course."

Sarah thought it was possible and began working on her mother to invite Tish to dinner. This was no simple matter; Hannah had never had a Gentile to dinner before. What if she didn't like Jewish food? In the end, she enlisted her neighbors' help and advice, spent days scouring and fixing the place up, and used almost the whole week's budget on one meal, making gefilte fish, potato kugel, roasted chicken, cooked carrots, and even a sponge cake. Tish and Rachel motored in for the occasion.

"I was so happy when you invited me," said Tish rather shyly, thanking her stars she had been blessed with a good appetite. "I always wanted to come here. The food was wonderful and besides I've heard that you, Ruby, are good at sewing. I've been looking all over for somebody who could

copy some of the new Paris styles for me. The woman who
usually makes my clothes won't do it; she says these are too
extreme and that she can't get such bright colors over here."

Ruby hadn't said much during dinner; she had merely sat at
the table and stared at Tish in fascination. Now her eyes glit-
tered. "Bright colors?"

"There's a Frenchman who's doing amazing things with
color and line, very simple, very vivid color combinations
I've never seen before: red with purple, blue with green,
yellow with a very bright cyclamen pink. I've got some pictures here if you'd like to see."

The women all crowded around as she pulled out assorted
magazines and one little pamphlet called *Les Choses de Paul
Poiret*. She opened it.

"Look at these pantaloon dresses," she said. "What do
you think of them?"

"My God," said Sarah. "Pants. Like a man!"

"You can't wear something like that in New York," said
Rachel. "You'd get arrested."

The picture, an elegant line drawing filled in with color,
showed four costumes with loose-fitting pants ending in a
wide cuff; two appeared to be one-piece and the third was a
Chinese-looking suit. The last pant-dress was apparently for
evening wear since it had a very low-cut green bodice ending
in a fluttery lilac tunic, over pants of the same green.

"Let me see," said Hannah, taking the magazine. She
looked at it, shaking her head for some time, then said in
what was clearly an attempt to be tactful, "I think Ruby
should make something else. We don't want to cause any
more talk."

Tish retrieved the magazine gracefully. "There are several
others I like," she said. "Take a look at this one, Ruby."

It was a picture of a slim girl in a long, very simply cut
lemon-colored gown, which was tied under the bust with a
Chinese red cord and tassel. It had a perfectly plain boat
neck, and black fur on the cuffs and around the hem. It was
as different from the ornate and heavily pieced fashions then
current in New York as a lily is from a wedding cake. Instead
of calling attention to each of its parts, it made one bold statement as a whole; the point was line, not fuss. The girl in the
drawing wore a tight-fitting turban, black embroidered with
red lozenges, that completely covered her hair. She appeared

to be vaguely Oriental and was holding a blue parrot in one
hand and selecting a sweet from a plate offered by an apparently Moorish slave with the other, but these were clearly
details of the illustrator's whim and not essential to the
concept.

"It looks like you," said Ruby suddenly.

Rachel and Sarah looked at Tish. It was true; both she and
the model had long, straight, slim bodies which had not been
particularly well-suited to the elaborate and busty fashions of
the past decade but which were perfect for this new style.

"Would you want it in yellow like this?" asked Ruby.

"I don't know," said Tish. "Something bright. We'll have
to see what's in the shops."

The next morning Ruby bravely dressed herself. Her back
still throbbed with pain but she thought she would at least try
to go out. Her legs were weak and tended to buckle.

"I said I'd meet Tish to buy material," she said to
Hannah. Her voice broke. "Could you maybe walk me a
block or two, Mama?" Hannah, overjoyed, rushed to get her
shawl.

Ruby worked longer each day, pushing herself to the limit.
Her torn ligament had in fact healed substantially during her
months of bed rest, though there would always be a weakness
in her lower back. Her main problem at this point was that
her muscles had begun to atrophy from disuse, but under the
inspiration of Paul Poiret's designs, she rapidly grew stronger.

Two weeks after her visit to Rivington Street, Tish had her
first fitting. Ruby's mouth dropped open as Tish slipped out
of her clothes.

"You're not wearing a corset!" she exclaimed.

Tish giggled. "Don't tell," she said. "I never wear one.
I'm so skinny, I don't need one to hold me in and I hate the
way they feel. So I just wear drawers and a petticoat below,
and this thing I made on the top."

Instead of the usual smocklike chemise with a corset laced
over it, Tish had on an extraordinary garment like a loose
bodice with straps that went over her shoulders. It was made
of white cotton and ribbon.

"What on earth is that?" asked Ruby, so fascinated she
forgot her back entirely.

"I had it copied from something in a French magazine," said Tish. "It's called a brassiere, because you put your arms through the straps—arms are *bras* in French. I made it out of two handkerchiefs and some ribbons, or, rather, my maid did. I folded the handkerchiefs into triangles, then fastened them with ribbon in back and over the arms."

"How do you get it on?"

"Over my head," said Tish. "It takes some wiggling."

"You could probably work out a way to fasten it in back or at the shoulders," said Ruby. "Then you could adjust it. Maybe you could use elastic." She examined Tish critically. This was just the kind of problem she could get excited about. "Pull the straps a little higher," she suggested. Tish complied. "It makes you stick out that way."

"Well, we can't have that," said Tish, releasing the straps. "For this dress I have to be as flat as the prairies."

"Pull the part under your arms tighter," said Ruby. "Yeah, that flattens you out. You could make a tuck in it and it would stay like that." She was silent for a moment, lost in speculation.

"Does your back hurt?" asked Tish sympathetically.

"I was just thinking," said Ruby. "Do any of your friends have these?"

"No, I only had enough made up for myself. But I bet they'd jump at the chance to get one."

"It seems to me," said Ruby carefully, "that if this new up-and-down style of yours catches on, we're going to need a new kind of underwear. Corsets were fine for the old S-curve dresses, where you were supposed to stick out in front and behind. They make you look real bosomy even if you're low and kind of wobbly. But now we'll need to be flat."

Tish sat down. "Hmm," she speculated. "I wonder."

A week later, Ruby produced three model brassieres of varying construction, which she had slaved over, staying up late and going twice to Essex Street for supplies. Hannah was so joyful at Ruby's new interest in life that she even consented to model for one of the contraptions.

"This one is for women who are big and low," Ruby told Tish, displaying her first model. "I used my mother as a basis. It holds the woman up and flattens her out at the same time."

As she examined the brassieres, Tish became more and more excited.

"Ruby, this has tremendous implications! It's not just a question of fashion. Corsets are dreadful. They're Victorian. They hurt. You can hardly move in some of them. It was one thing to wear them in the old days, before there was a woman's movement. But now we're agitating for the vote, we're marching in parades, we're going on strikes—we certainly won't wear corsets forever. A lot of my friends have already switched to those light sport corsets that start below your waist so you can breathe. But that's because they don't know there's an alternative. Wait until they find out about these new brassieres!"

She was all for their starting a factory immediately, but Ruby soon realized that she had no idea how complicated it was. Where was their capital to come from? "We'd have to rent a loft, buy machines, hire people, get material. Then we'd have to pay at least one salesman to take them to the stores. Do you have that much money?"

Tish was dashed. She wouldn't come into her own money for years and she knew her father would never finance this sort of enterprise.

"The trouble is, being in business isn't ladylike," she explained. "Ladies are not supposed to be concerned with money at all, let alone start factories."

The more they discussed it, the clearer it became that they could do nothing with their idea for the time being. But they agreed to take out a patent, at any rate, so nobody could steal it as Margolis had stolen Ruby's convertible skirt. They would call the design the New Era Brassiere.

Rachel sat miserably in her secret place behind the clump of oaks at the top of the hill. It was steep, and climbing it left even a healthy person breathless. She was disobeying doctors' orders to come out at all. They had pronounced her constitution delicate, her health uncertain, her condition unpredictable, and her temper so unstable as to necessitate constant supervision. And who knew what strain those years of child labor might have put on her reproductive system? The burden she carried was too precious to risk; she must stay in the house and preferably in bed. For in her womb was the first Sloate grandchild; she had become an incubator, a conveyer belt for the production of little Sloates, and this gave her both higher status and less freedom of movement than she had ever had at Nirvana before.

Looking back, Rachel could hardly remember that her married life had once seemed promising. She had known that the Sloates were rich, of course; that was a given. She had flattered herself she knew what rich people were like. After all, hadn't she visited their haunts before with Tish and Den: the Colony Club, the Metropolitan Museum, various restaurants and tearooms. But she had never been to any of their homes. She had no way of predicting the depth and intensity of her reaction to Nirvana.

Who could imagine she would feel so violated by a mere place? How could she predict the strength of the outrage that made her earlier radicalism seem tepid and abstract? The contrast between Nirvana and the East Side was always with her and each new luxury she saw became a blister on her senses. That tapestry chair in the drawing room was worth a hundred times as much as all the pitiful little scraps of furniture in the Levy flat put together—all those sticks that represented such months of saving and longing, such years of self-denial and labor. It was monstrous that things should be so unequal, intolerable that the labor of thousands of Sarahs and Rachels and Moyshes and Hannahs and Rubys—not to mention the legions of gardeners and maids on the Sloate estate—should go to create splendor and ease for such a few!

No wonder the house felt like death.

Even Tish and Denzell, a colorful pair in the city, seemed to fade at Nirvana, as if smothered by the heat and the velvet hangings, the thick carpets and innumerable tapestries, the omnipresent potted palms and ferns, the huge oil paintings in their gilded frames, the ormolu clocks and lamps with crystal bobbles and Chinese vases and whatnots full of bric-a-brac, the oak furniture carved so heavily that you were afraid to put your hands down on the arms of chairs lest you obscure some craftsman's fantasy. Only their father, robust and red-faced, was immune to the paralyzing gentility of Mrs. Sloate, but of course he seldom came home even on weekends. The pressures of banking were apparently so intense that he had to spend most nights at his club or so the fiction had it; Tish claimed he really stayed with a popsy he kept in a flat in Murray Hill, thus escaping his wife's toils. For Caroline

Longworth Sloate was the spider sitting in the midst of all this
splendor, stinging anything alive and wrapping it up in gauze.

Cold, elegant, haughty, preoccupied with manners and social position, her mother-in-law made Rachel feel a child
again—or, rather, a "street urchin" or a "little Jew gut-
tersnipe." Nothing she said or did was right; nothing ever
would be, from the moment she went for her first walk
around the estate.

"Surely you're not going out like that?"

Rachel had been wearing a simple suit with a white shirtwaist, such as she often wore to work. "Why not?" she
asked, bewildered. "No one will see me but the gardeners."

"I should hate to have even the gardeners see that my
daughter-in-law did not know the difference between city and
country dress," said Mrs. Sloate icily. And Denzell, embarrassed, had to intervene and say that in their rush to get married they had perhaps scanted their attention to Rachel's
trousseau.

That was in the first few days, when Denzell was still bothering to defend her. Before he abdicated. Now he was seldom
at home and Rachel was left to the mercies of her mother-in-
law, pinned like a fly under her unceasing scrutiny. She had
not yet been introduced to any of the Sloates' friends; Mrs.
Sloate opined that Rachel was not quite ready for that. She
would have to whip her into shape first. She spent a good deal
of energy upon this pursuit, endlessly reprimanding Rachel
for her mispronunciations and working-class usages.

"*Been* rhymes with *seen* not with *then*," she would say.
"For heaven's sake, don't say *dresser;* the article in question
is called a *chest of drawers.*" Rachel tried to please at first
but her enthusiasm lagged when she realized that the object of
the exercise was to list the things she did wrong, not to correct them. Every aspect of Rachel's diction, each turn of
phrase, her costumes, the way she did her hair, the way she
moved, the position of her feet when she sat down, all were
subjected to the most piercing and continual examination, all
were found wanting. Under this never-ending inspection,
Rachel's edges became dulled and she lost all spontaneity.
This was to Mrs. Sloate's satisfaction; ladies were not spontaneous. Rachel's highly colored gaiety, her joy in life, the
wit that had drawn Denzell to her dimmed as she wandered
cringing through the forty rooms of Nirvana, hoping to avoid

both her tormentor and the servants who acted as her spies and emissaries.

It was as bad as being at home with her father again. No, it was worse. Her hatred of her father was based on intimate knowledge of his standards, his culture, his means of attack. Here the assaults came from a culture that was strange to her and she was defenseless against them. And Denzell, who should have been her shield, was no help at all.

He was unwilling to admit there was a problem. He didn't like to talk about it. When Rachel tried to explain how she hated Nirvana, he told her not to fuss. "Mother is difficult," he admitted. "She always has been. You just have to not pay attention. Perhaps you could give in on one or two of the smaller things."

Rachel tried, but she didn't know which the smaller things were. They all seemed small, but their total was enormous. Her efforts to please merely brought that contemptuous smile to her mother-in-law's face, the smile Rachel dreaded even more than her barbed words.

Finally Rachel put her back up; if she couldn't please her new family, then she couldn't. She had done all she could. "I won't be made over," she told Denzell defiantly. "You fell in love with me because I was different from the girls you knew—that's what she can't stand. So I might as well stay different. I can't help it anyway."

He shrugged. But when he wouldn't take her away even then, she began to cultivate her hatred like a plant; it was her only means of defense. The bitch, the snob, even her own children hate her, she thought, shooting looks of icy rage at Mrs. Sloate, who didn't seem to mind. Perhaps making Rachel miserable was all the satisfaction she needed.

More and more the house was an assault, an affront to everything she cared about. That Chinese vase—it must have cost enough to keep her father and mother for the rest of their lives! Those cloisonné ornaments—how many years' pay were they worth to a stitcher at Triangle Waist? What a fool she had been to think she could just sail into Long Island like a sweet little boat into a new harbor; what an idiot to forget all she knew about the class system. The house was full of stolen goods; its riches were bled from the bones and lives and children of people she loved.

Though Rachel had always thought of herself as a socialist,

partly because of Sarah's influence, her real anger had been
directed not against any master class but at her father. Now all
that had changed. She was living on the most intimate terms
with America's ruling circle, with the president of the Sloate
Consolidated Bank and Trust, who embodied its holdings in
mines and textile mills, railroads and factories, its influence on
the government and the press, its adventures in Asia and Latin
America. Living with William Rensselaer Sloate II made
Rachel understand class hatred. What a loathsome man, she
thought, with his veneer of culture over the instincts of a beast
of prey; with his general contempt for the rest of the world
combined with his particular scorn for her class and her people;
with his ferocious opposition to unions and any other measure
of progress that might slightly alleviate the suffering caused by
a game in which he held all the cards. And seeing his opposition to reform, she began to understand that she too was no
gradualist; her hatred was too fierce for that. She didn't want
the Sloates to share their crystal chandeliers and potted palms
with the poor; she didn't want them to be more "understanding"; she wanted to line them up against their greenhouse wall
and kill them! Kill them! How dare they heat a greenhouse all
through the winter when the Levys went cold to bed, unable to
afford coal for their stoves.

Her animosity was sharpened by her observations of Mrs.
Sloate. Despite the insufferable way she treated Rachel, despite her arrogance and the blitheness of her assumption that
she knew best on any issue, what a useless creature she was!
She couldn't even dress herself, let alone cook a meal or sew
on a button, and if she were ever sent out to earn a living,
she'd starve to death inside a week. This was what the mas-
ters made out of their women—lapdogs, playthings—no, not
even that, for certainly Mr. Sloate had no desire to play with
his wife. He kept other women for that purpose, in the city.
She was a breeder, nothing more, held in contempt by her
husband and her children alike, and the ferocity with which
she treated Rachel was no more than a reflection of her own
weakness in the world outside Nirvana.

Rachel could see why Tish vowed she'd never marry. The
marriages of her class were horrific. Rachel didn't know how
she'd have stood Nirvana without Tish, who was so clearly
ranged on her side. Oh, she spent her father's money carelessly
enough and she had no idea what it was like to have to work for

a living. But her sympathies were quick and lively, she was a radical democrat in her emotions—and she made no personal distinctions. She never sneered at people for being poor and she hated the starchy, suffocating qualities of the bourgeoisie with a hatred that was almost sharper than Rachel's, bound up as it was with her own desire to live and breathe and her knowledge that women of her class were barely supposed to do so.

Because Tish couldn't stand being at Nirvana, she spent a lot of time in the city, staying at her aunt's. She tried to get Rachel to come with her. "Say you have to do some shopping," she instructed.

But Rachel didn't like to trail along after Tish to her shops and her suffrage meetings, without any place of her own or any money. She didn't like always to be paid for and Denzell, who never had any money, kept her short. That was why they couldn't get their own place to live, he said—and anyway, Nirvana was convenient to the airfield and he had to be there every day, now that he was test flying that new French plane, the Blériot. When Rachel tried to get him to explain how much money there was and where it all went, he smiled and evaded her questions.

She was sure that if he would sit down with her and go over their income and expenses, she could find ways to economize. But he just laughed at the idea. She could not gain entrée into that part of his life on any terms; the money was his, absolutely and only his, and he would give her some when she requested it, though never very much, and that was that.

At first she thought he was simply being tiresome about prerogative: even though he was hardly a breadwinner, never having held a job in his life, he would still control their finances because his masculine pride was invested in the role. But as the first year of their marriage passed, she began to understand that he was terrified to talk about money because his relationship to it was magical. He thought of gold as if it were some god he could appease if he paid proper tribute. Money came from some mysterious source, flowing in a golden stream; you got it because of who you were or because you were lucky or maybe for your smile; and it would go on forever, though its ebb and flow at any particular juncture in the stream were somewhat chancy. You might run out of it for a bit, but you could always borrow against future income, at least if you were a Sloate.

But not if you were married to one.

Longing for escape, missing her friends and the East Side with an intensity like mourning, Rachel even considered returning to work. She could get back her old job on the *Forward,* though the amount she earned there was less than Denzell spent on cigars. But doing this would mean leaving Denzell; it would be burning her bridges with a vengeance, for he would never move to the East Side. He was no settlement worker. She might be able to work part-time on the paper; spend four days a week in the city and return to Long Island for long weekends. Tish frequently did that. She thought it could be just feasible, but when she raised the idea experimentally one evening, Mrs. Sloate said coldly, "I can imagine what the press would make of that. Cinderella returns to the slums. I don't think we need any more of that sort of publicity." And Denzell whispered, "Do you really want to spend three or four nights a week away from me?"

Of course, she didn't; she wanted more of him, not less. And nights were the only time they saw each other. Most of the time, he was at the airfield. He was obsessed with the war that had just begun in Europe, and with America's lack of air preparation.

Rachel had thought him uninterested in politics; but world events had brought to life something in him that she would rather have left unborn. When he talked about the war, he sounded like the yellow press. How ridiculous it was, how naive, to think it was being waged by anyone for purely humanitarian reasons, or to protect what he kept calling "Western Civilization." After all, the Czar was on the same side as England and France, and he was certainly less civilized than the German Kaiser.

"Politics make strange bedfellows," replied Denzell.

Politics wasn't the only thing that did, she thought. And yet their love could still be wondrous; he had that hold over her. He had captured her senses for the first time; she laughed at herself bitterly for being so weak, but what else did she have? Still, as time passed, she grew angrier, boiling at the way he had abandoned her, at his political stupidity, at the complacent way he assumed she had been captured for life by his wandering fingers. The anger grew, like a land mine un-

der her love for him. Would it one day explode? Or would it
rot inside her, a hidden infection; would her life be poisoned
by a festering rage that could find no object but herself?

In October of 1914, she learned she was pregnant. This put
an end to the sexual relationship that was all that remained of
their love; she was delicate, the doctors said; she must avoid
any physical intimacies that might endanger the child. Such
abstinence was customary, they told her, and most women
found it a relief, since everyone knew women did not feel the
need as men did. Rachel was to stay in bed much of the time
and be careful to avoid any stress and exertion.

After she was confined to the house, Rachel's longing for
the East Side became a sickness; she could think of nothing
else. Most of all she wanted Sarah and Hannah. Her own
mother was gone forever, completely out of reach. Sarah she
could telephone at the League; but these conversations were
brief and unsatisfactory and you could never be sure who was
listening in at either end. Besides, she was ashamed to admit
how miserable she was; what if Sarah said, "I told you so"?
Sarah would never allow herself to be locked up in her room;
she would simply pack her bag and walk out. But she had a
mother to go home to.

Perhaps a year and a half at Nirvana had sapped Rachel's
strength; perhaps she had never been good for much to begin
with. She threw up every morning and the rest of the time she
was so tired she could hardly drag herself around. She didn't
know whether it was normal to feel this way when you were
pregnant, and there was no one she could ask. Tish was as ill-
informed on these matters as she was and Rachel certainly
was not going to complain to Mrs. Sloate or the doctors. She
was terrified of giving birth; her ignorance and fear weighed
on her like a stone; but the doctors were worse than no help—
terrifying, remote, male, Gentile, friends of the family. She
couldn't even talk to the servants, who kept their distance,
knowing well which side their bread was buttered on.

Pregnant, fearful, lonely, she reached with memory to the
East Side tenement where she had cowered so many nights
after bedtime, trying to read under the covers by the uncertain
light of the streetlamp outside. Sometimes she had an odd,
mystical vision of herself as child looking across the years to
herself as grown-up, miserable still but in a different room.
What a bond, she thought bitterly, and stretched the hand of

her mind out over the miles to give that child's red curls a caress they had never gotten from anybody else.

"Don't cry, Rachel," she whispered. "It could be worse."

There was a war in Europe and Denzell wasn't in it. Nothing else mattered. He had never wanted anything in his life the way he wanted to be in France, fighting in the air with the Boche. More than ever he spent his time flying, imagining the great duels taking place on the other side of the ocean, practicing dive bombing, circling, and quick drops in altitude, his only audience the squawking gulls from Long Island Sound.

The ground had less and less to offer. It wearied him. So much talk, so much fussing over markets, bonds, furniture, women, Rachel's baby. His and hers both, of course, but he felt little connection with it. As her belly swelled, it only pushed him farther away. Only in the sorrows of the clouds, the pillars of thunder, the arches of electricity, and the damp black fogs that swept in from the Atlantic did Denzell find affirmation. His own cyclones had been pushed so far down they were lost to him; he could not read his own climate except in the passions that filled the tempestuous sky.

There one need not talk, or even hear. In the open cockpit of his Jenny, the wind in his ears and the roar of the engine were so deafening he could often hear nothing for hours after he landed. It was no loss; he didn't miss the tinkling glissandos, the false notes of conversations with which he was never quite in tune. He was able to mimic the formal signals of this world beneath the skies without understanding what they really meant. He could smile and murmur appropriate nothings, but he could not speak his mind because his mind did not live in words.

What could Rachel know of this? She had loved him for his otherness from her, yet he was more different than she could ever guess. How could she imagine to what extent he had already abandoned the human for that no-man's-land in the clouds and a glancing, fleeting, pleasurable vision of his own death, evanescent, his body falling through space while the transcendent part of him remained in the oceans of air.

"This war will change everything," said Moyshe.

From the moment of its declaration in July 1914, he had seen it as a turning point in world history. In a rare but brilliant attack of sympathetic imagination, Ruby went to Rand McNally one day and bought him a large, expensive wall map with money she had earned sewing for Tish. He was overcome with delight and nailed it up immediately with Hannah's approval. "It dresses up the wall," she said.

The map was highly colored, with all the empires clearly marked: red for Britain, blue for France, yellow for Germany. Ruby even bought map tacks so Moyshe could mark the progress of the armies as they advanced: black tacks for Germany, white for the Allies.

"Rubeleh," he said, wagging a reproving finger. "This is not a question of black and white. Both sides are imperialist and don't you forget it." He used his map to considerable effect in making this point to everyone who came to the house.

"Don't call it 'the European war,'" he would tell them. "It's a world war, a war to divide up the world between the great powers. Look here, look at the tacks in Africa, in China, in Turkey—they're even fighting in Palestine!"

His thirst for war news became insatiable. No longer was the *Forward* enough for him; he demanded the English-language papers, the *Times*, the *World*, the socialist *Call*. His knowledge of English improved dramatically. His grasp of military developments became the pride of the whole block and he developed a following of young boys, all of whom were war-crazy. Children dropped in on their way home at night to see if anything new had happened on the map and their grades in geography soared.

In the summer of 1915, the German army thrust into the Russian Pale to open up an eastern front. Suspecting all Jews were a potential fifth column, the Russian army had begun to rid the border areas of them. Hundreds of thousands of unarmed, poverty-stricken Jews were driven from their homes in Lodz, Kielce, Petrokov, Ivangorod, Skiernievice, Suvalki, Grodno, Bialystock, and large areas of Russian Poland. General Yanushkevitch, a hysterical anti-Semite who was in charge of the eastern area, organized pogroms that killed off most of the rest. When the Germans invaded Lithuania, the Jews there were similarly affected. Eight hundred thousand were driven from the frontier areas so rapidly they could take nothing with them, forced across the snowy fields by Russian Cossacks with whips.

Once more the East Side feared for its relatives back home. The neighbors, Moyshe's friends from work, and various café cronies began to drop in on Rivington Street to follow the war news on the map with such regularity that Hannah grumbled. "I'm going to put in a turnstile and give out tickets like the Garden Cafeteria, they should at least pay for their tea." How embarrassed she was, and how proud, when they all chipped in and bought her a samovar for Rosh Hashanah in 1915—a samovar, the Russian symbol of prosperity! She glowed as she polished it.

Only one of Moyshe's companions refused to visit him at home: Avi Spector. Moyshe continued to meet him in cafés: he would not have given up his company for the world now that they were for the first time in agreement about politics. The international socialist movement was in a shambles. Despite their prewar vows of eternal solidarity, the socialist parties of Britain, France, Belgium, and Germany immediately sided with their respective governments when war was declared. The German socialists in the *Reichstag* voted for war appropriations; the French deputies did likewise; and two parties which had been joined in brotherhood the year before were now mortal enemies.

"It's a *shandeh*," groaned Moyshe, "a scandal."

His own party, the Bund, like Avi's Bolsheviks, had not followed the general trend. Both condemned the war, as did the American socialists, for the United States was still at peace. It was possible to be either pro-Ally or pro-German, or even to oppose the whole conflict, and still be a good American, for both the Republicans and the Democrats were resolute that their country should remain neutral. President Wilson had even started to campaign for re-election on the slogan, "He kept us out of war."

II

As a natural consequence of her breakup with Avi Spector, Sarah began to see more of Joe Klein, but the two of them didn't get along any better than they ever had. Still, their quarreling added a kind of bite to their relationship, and at least it gave Sarah something else to think about besides her worries over Ruby and her job, which she was finding increasingly wearisome. She spent most of her time talking to legislators or trying to educate kindly lady sympathizers about life in the working class. The women were terribly well-meaning but they had been so sheltered and were so privileged that they hardly understood a thing she told them. It was as if they spoke a different language. She longed for the tickle of Yiddish in her mouth and the company of her own people.

She had managed to keep in touch with some of the girls from the strike and from Triangle Waist, but with the possible exception of Minnie Fishman, who was so temperamentally different from Sarah that they could never be really close, she didn't know any of them well. Her real friends were dead, except for Rachel, who had sold herself to a rich man and was being held in Babylonian captivity far from home, unreachable. That hurt. Even when Rachel came to the East Side to visit, things weren't the same. There was a distance between them now, a distance put there by money.

When Sarah looked back upon the strike, with all its dangers and privations, she felt a pang of longing for Becky and Molly and Fanny, for Rachel fighting beside her, for a com-

radeship between men and women that now seemed vanished
forever, and for the struggle itself, then so sharp and clear,
now so vitiated and pale. She chided herself for sentimen-
tality, knowing the battle had to take different forms in different periods. Nobody could question the need for stable
unions and they had those now; still, what they had lost
seemed so much more than what they'd gained. It was partly
her nostalgia for the strike and the company of her own people that drew her to Joe Klein.

He for his part was fascinated by the changes time had
made in Sarah, the patina of middle-class culture and feminist
politics she had acquired. She was so full of ideas, so assert-
ive in her quicksilver way, so much more interesting than the
other women he dated—including Gussie, the lawyer's
daughter, who was obliging in every respect but who put him
to sleep. Sarah made him want to eat her up and smash her at
the same time.

Their spooning became more and more passionate, though
she always stopped him short of taking off her clothes. She
liked to tease him, herself too, acting cold then catching fire,
pulling away and pretending the heavy breathing was all his
doing. He could not believe she was really afraid, not her.

"You're a case," he told her scornfully. "You, the big
radical—you're as much of a prude as any rabbi's daughter.
What are you holding out for, a ring? I thought you didn't
want to get married. Maybe you're just scared."

He sensed this taunt would get to her, but had no idea how
it would eat at her mind. If there was one thing Sarah feared,
it was being a coward. The alarm bells went off and the vision of her sister's death still rose before her eyes when she
went too far with Joe; but she couldn't go on like this forever.
She would have to close her eyes and jump into the water.
That was the only way to learn to swim, and it might as well
be with Joe as with anybody else. She even liked him
sometimes.

By 1914 the ILGWU was a force to be reckoned with, and
Joe Klein was proud to think he was one of the men who'd
made it so. The 1909 shirtwaist strike had sparked a wave of
general strikes that had brought unionization to the East Side
garment industry: the cloak makers in 1910, the furriers in
1912, the white-goods workers and wrapper makers in 1913.

The cloak makers' strike was especially long and bitter; many families had nearly starved and there were pitched battles between strikers and gangsters. The workers held out for two months, after which the manufacturers agreed to a compromise set of demands including higher wages, an end to subcontracting, and a method of resolving future disputes by peaceful arbitration rather than strikes. The pact, called "The Protocol of Peace," was immediately proclaimed a model of civilized transactions between capital and labor. Protocols were soon adopted in the rest of the garment trades.

Joe Klein thought protocolism a healthy development: it stabilized the industry and it helped the union grow. Through settlements that made union membership obligatory, the ILGWU enlisted over 90,000 members and became strong enough to hire a number of new organizers and start expanding from New York to the rest of the country. As a result, standards of safety were raised; sanitary arrangements improved; electricity was brought into almost every shop and paid for by the boss. The rule of law, with definite procedures for resolving disputes, began to replace the rule of goons like Jake Goldfarb. Union representatives came and went freely from shop to shop, arguing the workers' grievances.

There were plenty of these, for the protocol was not free of problems and wages were still low. Since most garment workers were paid piece rate rather than by the hour, epic struggles took place at the beginning of each season, when the union and each employer had to agree on the prices for different kinds of work. To escape union pressure and cut costs, a group of employers began to have their pieces made out of town or at nonunion "sub shops." To Joe, such runaway work was the main problem confronting the industry; it could only be solved by strengthening the protocol. To others, like Sarah and Minnie Fishman, the protocol itself and the way the union was run were bigger problems. They thought more militance and more strikes were needed—a nonsensical and childish view, in Joe's opinion.

He heard a lot about Minnie's ideas from Sarah. Joe had never been able to stand Minnie; in the old days Sarah too had found her tiresome and impractical, but now she seemed to agree with Minnie more than she did with him.

"Minnie says the protocol is nothing but a piece of toilet

paper and the bosses' only purpose in going along with it is to make a fool out of the union.''

"What do I need to hear this stuff for?" he shouted. "If I want to hear from Minnie, I'll go out with her, not you!"

"You aren't very responsive to the views of your members.''

He couldn't believe the way Sarah always had to start an argument. What a troublemaker! People like Sarah and Minnie thought the union could get anything it wanted; all it had to do was strike. As if the power of the workers was infinite. Idiots! They didn't realize that strikes ate up the treasury and once that was gone and there were no more strike benefits, the workers would cave in. The more strikes you had, the more you'd lose. Far better to avoid such episodes, which were not only harmful to the treasury but dangerous to the workers, since the bosses always hired goons to break strikes.

And what was a union supposed to do when it came up against the combined muscle of the cops and the courts, the bosses and the *bolagulas?* The ILGWU hardly had the muscle to fight them all off, one on one. Its members weren't teamsters, they weren't construction workers—they were a bunch of girls! Try to send them out against an army of gangsters with pipes and guns! Joe had had no choice but to throw a little business in the way of his old friend Tricker. Tricker had handled it pretty well, and Joe thought it might solve a lot of the union's problems to put a few of the boys on salary, as long as it could be kept quiet. It would never do to let a hothead like Minnie Fishman get hold of that news.

What did she know, anyway? What did Sarah know? Look at her own sister, one of the worst in the industry, redefining job descriptions, bringing in efficiency experts with stopwatches. Joe must have been called down to Margolis Modes twenty times to hear them complain about Ruby. Well, that was over now. She had been taught a lesson. Funny how different two sisters could be.

It wasn't easy working for the union. No matter what happened, he'd end up stuck in the middle. The militants wanted strikes; the men on the floor wanted job control against people like Ruby; and a lot of the women wanted the union to be a glorified benefit society, with all kinds of fringes like health insurance, death payments, unemployment benefits, educational programs, pensions. Somebody had even told him the union should invest in real estate and build a special housing project for its members.

Nobody seemed to understand you could go only one step at a time, and not in every direction, either. You could use the dues money for pensions, maybe even for housing, but not if people were going to go on strike and need it for food. You had to choose; you had to be part of the modern business system. You had to be responsible to your members and to the industry as a whole. He would do what he thought best, no matter what Sarah said, and if she didn't like it she could lump it.

In December of 1914, Sarah had to go to Philadelphia for a daytime meeting with the branch of the League there. She planned to stay overnight at a hotel, and return the next day. Never having been in an American train before, she sat nervously in her compartment as the engine coughed and puffed on the tracks, getting up a head of steam. Then the door opened and a familiar voice said, "Here you are. I've been all up and down the train looking for you."

It was Joe Klein.

"What are you doing here?" she asked in astonishment.

He laughed. "I had to go to Philly on union business, so when I heard you were going I thought we could travel together. Pleased?"

She nodded happily. "Sure."

"Let's have dinner and take in a show if you have time," he said.

That night they went to see *Hedda Gabler*. Sarah found the play shocking and exciting. They drank a whole bottle of wine with dinner; then he said quietly, "Why don't you come back to my hotel?"

She looked at him slowly and steadily and felt her blood rise. It might as well be now. But once she got there she felt like a bucket of cold water had been emptied on her head. She became stiff, terrified, artificially vivacious. She oohed and aahed over the bathroom with its elegant clawfoot tub; she'd never seen one like that before. At home they had an old tub in the kitchen. She thought the flocked velvet wallpaper in the bedroom was nice, too.

He knew she was chattering because she was nervous. That was all right. That was as it should be. It was hard on a woman the first time. Or so he'd been told; he himself had never been with a virgin. His sexual experience had been confined to two sorts of women, whores and willing married women, usually the wives of union buddies who were out on the road or who neglected them. Often the women were older than he, drawn by his good looks and smooth line of talk; you might say he was doing them a favor. Not Sarah. She was a new-minted coin. And now he finally had her. He couldn't wait to get her clothes off.

She lay there huddled under the blanket, naked, glaring at him like a young, trapped animal. Why was she so hostile? He didn't know what to do. Gingerly he put his arm around her. He had to force her head up to get his arm behind her neck; she was as stiff as a board.

The other women hadn't acted like this. They would snuggle up and play with him and make him feel powerful. They would sigh appreciatively when he touched them.

He supposed it was because she was a virgin, but he couldn't get Sarah warmed up. He tentatively put his hand on her breast once more. It was small and cold. She gritted her teeth, her nipple hardened under his fingers and she gave a small involuntary shiver. Her lack of enthusiasm was affecting him. He wasn't even sure he would be able to do anything. It was mortifying.

"Sarah?" he said. His voice came out in an unexpected boom, making both of them start. "You don't have to go through with it if you don't want to."

She crossed her arms over her breasts and stared miserably up at the ceiling. Rosa's image was there, black tender curls of pubic hair and the blood all around. It must hurt unbelievably. She squeezed her eyes shut tight; she had come this far and there was no point in turning back. When you were afraid of something you had to go ahead. That was the time you had to be bravest. This wasn't what had killed Rosa; Rachel said she'd never heard of it killing anybody or at least not very often.

"Go ahead," she said harshly through her teeth. "Do it already if you're going to."

The contemptuous way she lay there, scowling with her eyes squeezed shut, not even willing to look at him, finally got his goat. That was no way to treat a guy. How did she think he felt? He was trying to be considerate of her but she didn't seem to care about him at all. He tweaked her nipple; when she winced, he experienced a little thrill of pleasure. He could tell she didn't want to show any feeling one way or the other. She wouldn't give him the satisfaction.

"What kind of girl are you?" he said. "You don't care about me or anybody. You don't even care about yourself."

She didn't say anything. He couldn't even make her fight with him; she was just going to lie there like a stone and let him do the whole thing and not give anything back. All right, then. She'd asked for it; let her take her medicine. A cruel streak awoke in him. He felt himself begin to harden at last and stand erect, and thought of all the other women who'd told him how big he was and sung the praises of his youth and energy. She was too green to know what she was getting, to appreciate. She'd learn. He chuckled; she was probably terrified. He voicelessly dared her to look at him, to tremble at his girth and muscle, but she just stared fixedly at the ceiling.

He'd give her one more chance. Maybe he could still make her respond to him. He drew his hands slowly over her slender body, watching for the shuddering signs of awakening pleasure, but there was nothing. He stroked her over and over, everywhere, but got nothing. Her smooth skin and little ribs, her young pointed breasts, the feeling of her under his hands and his mouth roused him past forbearance as he pressed kisses on her lips and body, no longer even caring that she shrank back a little under each caress.

Then he could wait no longer and did not even care that he had to force her legs apart like two pieces of jammed machinery and ram his way in, ram and pound himself into her again and again until finally he broke through the barrier and felt himself supreme, thrilling as he exploded inside her, glorying in the feel of her still small bones beneath his weight, the spreading wetness on her loins and his, until finally he slipped out of her and rolled over with a grateful grunt.

Sarah got up immediately. She could not wait to get away. Without a word she walked to the bathroom in tiny wooden steps, afraid to bend her knees because the blood might gush out and ruin the carpet. She walked still-legged as a crow and locked the door and climbed into the cold fancy white tub, sobbing silently with the pain. She sat there with her knees bent and her head resting on them, a burning between her legs and in her belly as though he'd stabbed her. She slowly opened her eyes, and, looking down through her knees, watched a little red puddle form on the bottom of the empty porcelain tub.

There was a knock on the door. "Sarah? Are you all right?"

She didn't answer.

"What are you doing in there?" He rattled the doorknob.

"Go away," she whispered.

"Let me in, Sarah."

In answer she turned on the water so that the noise drowned out his voice. She watched the doorknob as the water began to fill the tub. After a minute the knob stopped jiggling up and down and she knew he'd gone back to bed. She didn't put the plug in the tub but sat there with her head on her knees, watching the red dye which kept splotching out to stain the water and then swoosh down the drain. After a while the color of the water paled to a pink wash, darkest near her body. It got paler and paler.

Like a sunset, she thought. It was then that she understood she was really not going to die. She wouldn't be so angry if she were going to die.

When the water finally ran clear she put the plug in the tub and washed, scouring away the smell and feel of him from everywhere except between her legs. She was afraid to touch herself there. It hurt too much.

Her clothes lay where she had left them a half hour before. She put them on and opened the door. Her hands were clenched but he didn't notice, marveling at the composure of her face.

She really is a tough one, he thought, then asked, "Are you all right?" his voice ringing uncertain even to himself.

She nodded coldly. Then her lip began to tremble and despite her intentions she burst out, "You hurt me! How could you hurt me like that!"

He was taken aback. "It only hurts the first time. You're just not used to it. You'll like it better next time we do it."

She looked at him with a world of scorn and put on her coat. "I'm going back to my hotel."

"Not already," he protested. He'd thought she would stay all night. But she was adamant. He sighed, and patted her cheek tentatively. "All right, then, I'll take you there."

She stepped away. "I'll go myself. I don't want anybody to see us." Silenced by her prudence, he let her depart.

Although she had enough money for a cab, she had never taken one and it did not occur to her to do so now. Pain was a novelty to Sarah but she was inured to discomfort; she walked the mile and a half to her own cheap hotel, where she collapsed upon the bed in her clothes, taking time only to remove her coat and drop it on the floor. She pulled the covers up, hoping she wouldn't start to bleed again because the blood might wreck her dress, and she fell asleep in mid-thought. The next morning she returned to New York.

She avoided seeing Joe for a week or two after she returned. Finally he became uneasy and went to her house. They sat on different steps of the fire escape. She wouldn't let him touch her.

"You hurt me," she whispered accusingly.

"Oh, come on, Sarah," he pleaded. "It won't be like that next time."

But it was a month before she consented to try again, and then it was as much to stop his nagging as because she wanted to. It wasn't as bad the second time; he was so nervous and afraid of hurting her, he could barely do anything. They didn't sleep together for two more months after that, though they continued to go out every weekend. Their sexual misery made the antagonism between them overwhelming. They could no longer escape from argument into sex, since their spooning in itself now had an inevitable conclusion that frightened both of them. As a result, their political debates became even more bitter. Still, they went out religiously, if without enjoyment, as if it was their duty to continue their relationship. They might have gone on that way for years if it weren't for Dopey Benny Fein.

Dopey Benny Fein was a punctilious man who tried to keep out of trouble, but his business competition with the Five Pointers became so sharp that in 1913 he had his boys open fire on them at a party in the Arlington Street Dance Hall. Unfortunately, an innocent bystander was caught in the crossfire, and the new reform district attorney decided to make an example of Dopey Benny, who was harassed and jailed so many times over the next two years that he came to

Joe Klein to appeal for support. He needed more money to defray his legal expenses.

"There's nothing I can do," said Joe. "You have to remember our arrangement is off the books; I pay you out of petty cash. I can't go to my union board for money for you when most of them don't even know you exist."

Dopey Benny took the refusal hard, and thought about it for some time. One thing that distinguished him from lesser gangsters was the care he took to keep accurate business records. He noted all his transactions in a small diary, together with the prices he charged for various services: $150 for wrecking a shop; $100 up for a murder, depending on the victim; $50 for a bomb. The diary also detailed the way he had divided up the city:

Joe the Greaser	furriers, bakers
Yoski Nigger & the J. Black	
Hand Society	
Yoski	livery stables
Charley the Cripple	seltzer deliveries
Johnny Levine	ice-cream trucks
Dopey Benny with	garment—all
Tricker Louis	shirtwaist
King Indian	cloaks
Hudson Dusters	Greenwich Village
	& the West Side
Car Barn Gang	uptown
Gas House Gang	uptown

This diary was Benny's insurance against a doublecross. When he was arrested again, and a further appeal to Joe Klein elicited no more support than the first had, he decided to use it. "KING OF THE RACKETS TELLS ALL," cried the newspapers in February 1915, quoting Dopey Benny profusely: "Different bosses have tried to get me to leave the union and work for them but I always turned them down because I loved those union boys. I thought they were upgrading the whole race. I would have worked for them for nothing if they had treated me right but I can't stand ingratitude."

Among the names he named were those of Tricker Louis Florsheim and Joseph Klein. Both were immediately indicted by a grand jury, along with the leading lights of the United

Hebrew Trades, half the executive board of the ILGWU, and officials of both the cloak makers' and the shirtwaist workers' locals.

The union mobilized to defend itself. Most of the men indicted, as well as their supporters, were bewildered by the turn of events and assumed the whole thing was a frame-up. So did Sarah. But when she went to offer Joe Klein her support, she found him in a semihysterical state, hands shaking, brow sweating, and refusing to talk about it even to her.

"I have nothing to say. The whole thing's a put-up job and that's my final word."

"It's an incredible story," said Sarah. "Imagine them thinking that somebody like you would hire gorillas."

"And what if I did?" he said belligerently. "Not that it's true, of course, but what if the union did hire some muscle— is that so terrible? Didn't it work? Aren't we stronger now than we were in 1910?"

Sarah stared at him, her dark eyes suddenly wary. That time he had called to warn her about Ruby and Tricker, she'd been so panicked she never asked how he found out. And he never told her. She hadn't given it a thought until now.

"Are you friends with Tricker Louis?" she blurted out.

"What do you mean am I friends with him? You think I'm buddies with gangsters?" He began to pace up and down, rubbing his fingers together in an agitated manner. "What a question to ask at a time like this! What are you trying to do, get me to incriminate myself so you can tell your fancy uptown friends and they can run to the D.A.?"

Sarah was frozen by what she saw. How sleazy he looked. Was it possible he had really hired this Dopey Benny? She backed toward the door.

"I can see you're going to stick by me when I'm in trouble," he said sarcastically.

The garment unions held an enormous rally in Madison Square Garden in June 1915, protesting the grand jury indictments of their leaders. Everyone in the movement was there: the Triangle survivors, Ab Cahan, the women from the League, even Samuel Gompers, who made a militant speech about how the government was trying to destroy the labor movement. Morris Hillquit, a well-known socialist lawyer, had agreed to be defense counsel for the indicted union men, and the ILGWU was raising a huge bail fund.

Sarah and Minnie Fishman, to whom she had confided her fears, went to the rally together. They cheered in all the right places and pledged their solidarity; after all, they still had to defend the union, no matter what Joe Klein had done. They walked home past the site of the old Triangle Waist factory; the wrecked building still stood there, a *memento mori.*

"People like Joe, the bosses put the heat on, and they buckle like bad metal," said Minnie. "Like those fire escapes."

Sarah stared at the building, seeing it again as she had on the night of the fire. "He must have had reasons," she said, "but no reasons are good enough. Too many people have died." Her voice broke. "I'm through with him, Minnie."

Rachel leaned, shivering, against one of the big oaks on top of the hill. It was a cold day and she had no business being out, but be damned to them, she thought. Let the doctors threaten her with death and miscarriage; let Mrs. Sloate rave about having her committed. Her father was dead. She had a right to mourn after the fashion of her people. She had a right to tear her hair, to scream and cry and beat her breast, alone, outside, where no one could point at her, where no one could call her crazy. She had a right.

Her family hadn't even told her when the funeral was. They had waited to call her until after he was buried; then her brother got on the phone and stammered out the story from the corner grocery store. Her mother did not even talk to her. The message was clear: Don't come home. Don't make the mistake of thinking you have a home. Despite her father's death, Rachel was an outcast still.

She had done the unforgiveable; she had married a *goy.* Let her live with her choice. The irony was so sharp she caught her breath; she had fled the East Side men with their grabby assertiveness, their prying questions, for a man who would let her be herself, who would leave her alone. Well, she was alone now.

A wave of homesickness swept her like nausea. She could hear her father's voice in her ear, chanting his favorite psalm: "By the waters of Babylon there we sat down and wept, when we remembered Zion. . . . How shall we sing the Lord's song in a strange land?" For the first time she understood his longing for all he had lost, and all the commonplaces about passing things down from generation to generation had a poignancy that twisted in her like a knife. What had she to pass down? Who would be the grandparents of this baby? The Sloates? She wanted none of their tradition.

She clasped her belly as if only the life in it could save her. It was wrong to think of death while she was pregnant, yet she felt herself wavering, fading in and out like a creature in a mist. How often had she told herself, "He wishes I was dead." When he sat *shiva* on her it was like reliving a dream she had had a hundred times. But even as she had wondered if a girl whose parents wished her dead had a right to live, she had clung to life.

There would be no forgiveness from her father now, no reconciliation in the mellowness of advanced age. Never would he tell her he was sorry; never would she kiss his cheek and feel the bristles scratch her lips and smell that sour odor he always had. She could not even weep as black bitterness overwhelmed her. It was all because she was a girl. All the things he would have taken pride in had she been a boy— her joy in learning, her strong will—became a curse because of her sex. You might as well be dead as a girl. She bowed her head painfully, hating the thought even while it swept through her mind, Let it be a boy, dear God, let the baby be a boy.

The day was overcast and cold. She was in her third month. As she ran, stumbling, the long way back to the house, she felt a sharp pain and a wetness. She almost screamed. By the time she finally got upstairs and undressed, there was blood all down her legs and on her petticoat. She didn't tell anyone. Maybe I'll bleed to death, she thought, and fell asleep, exhausted.

That night, in bed, she miscarried. She had lost so much blood she hardly had the strength to pull the bell for the servant.

Mrs. Sloate said vindictively, "I've no pity for her. It's her own fault. She should have stayed in bed the whole time as I did."

Mr. Sloate remarked that he had always thought the lower classes were good breeders.

Denzell brought flowers, like a visitor. Rachel took them with tears running down her face; she didn't know if she was crying for the baby or her father or herself.

"I can't do anything right," she whispered. "I can't even carry a baby."

"There, there," said Denzell, and patted her head. But he did not contradict her.

Roman Zach had no telephone, so on the nights Tish stayed with him she always told people to call her at the home of Emily Doncaster, her friend from the Woman Suffrage Party. She had as usual risen first and washed very thoroughly in the kitchen tub. When he came into the kitchen, wearing only his union suit, she was making up her face in a sliver of mirror that hung over the counter.

He sat down and lit a cigarette, looking at her in his dark, sardonic way. He was a handsome thing, you had to give him that, thought Tish. And at least you could say what you liked in front of him, you didn't have to be careful all the time because nothing could really puncture that ego and make him turn nasty. There was no need to pretend more passion than she felt; he was so self-assured they might even be able to remain friends after she gave him his walking papers.

He smiled at her engagingly. "Why do you come here anyway?" he asked.

She gave him a quick, startled look, then turned to study her own face in the mirror again. "What do you mean?" she asked composedly, ruffling her side hair. She frequently wondered if it had been a good idea to get her hair cut in a Castle bob. She was the first of her set to have short hair. It had been worth it just to see her mother's horror, but perhaps it was too extreme for her thin face. The bang in front did soften it a bit.

"Why pretend?" he said amiably. "I'm not inexperienced and I have some idea how women usually feel about me under these circumstances. And you don't. That's all right; it's your privilege—but it does make me wonder why you bother. What's in it for you?"

She looked at him wide-eyed and expressionless, then took one of his cigarettes and sat down. "Have I done something to injure your pride?" she inquired. Really, the nerve of the creatures. It wasn't enough that you let them do whatever they wanted with you, you were supposed to like it! It seemed she had overestimated him; he was no different from the others. "Do I seem unappreciative?"

For a moment he lost his composure. "You don't understand what I'm trying to say." He sighed. "I don't know how to put it. Look, we're friends, right? I like to go to galleries with you. I like to hear your opinions about my work. I like to talk to you. That's enough. This isn't necessary if you don't want it."

"Well, I must say," said Tish. "You were the one who asked me to pose. You were the one who suggested we go further."

"You can't blame me for trying," he said. "But I wouldn't have pushed it if you refused."

"Of course not," she said mockingly, "not at all. Only I would have found that those pleasant little gallery visits somehow tapered off, that those interesting little dinners and drinking parties with your artist friends suddenly stopped happening, and that all I was learning from you about painting I would have to learn elsewhere. I'm a girl, you know, Roman, it's not so easy for me to do these things without a man along."

He sat back in his chair, looking at her, astonished.

"Do you really think I'd have dropped you if you turned me down?"

"Of course I do," she said. "That's how it is. Men like you don't go around with girls who are just pals. You'd look for someone else to be with and I could hardly expect you to take both of us. Don't act so shocked; you didn't take advantage of me. I knew exactly what I was doing. I mean, I'm delighted to get an education for free when I can but I always know that sooner or later I'll have to pay the price, and between men and women, this is the price. It's cheaper than marriage, anyway."

He thought it over. "I can't say I'm flattered," he said slowly, "but I see your point. You should get your own place in the city—then you could come and go as you pleased."

"My father would never let me," said Tish. He was silent, looking at her through narrowed lids.

"Have you ever been in love?" he asked suddenly.

She smiled a little sadly. "Once."

"Was it different?"

"Yes," she whispered, "quite different."

"What happened?"

She looked at the floor for guidance. "The attachment was

unsuitable," she said primly, "and was broken off. I only fall in love with unsuitable people, just like my brother."

"Well, my goodness," he said, "I'd have thought I was unsuitable enough for anyone, a starving artist in an East Side garret."

"My dear Roman," she drawled, "when I say unsuitable, you've no idea."

"What was wrong with him?" She didn't answer. "Was he married? Jewish? Catholic? Poor? Was it a relative? Your brother?" She smiled and said nothing. "Was it a woman?"

Startled, she dropped her eyes. "How you do carry on. I don't feel like discussing this any more."

He lit another cigarette. "You don't have to be so coy about it. Don't forget I've been in Paris. Women live with women all the time over there. Look at Gertrude Stein. She and her friend go everywhere together; Gertrude sits and smokes and talks art with the men while Alice chats with their wives. Nobody thinks anything about it."

Tish smiled her long, elegant smile. "Hard to imagine," she said sweetly. "Let's change the subject, shall we?"

"Are you in love now?"

She shrugged enigmatically.

"With another woman?"

She began to laugh. "Really, you're too absurd. What difference does it make! The way you're cross-examining me, one would almost think you were jealous."

"Not at all," he said. "Interested. As your friend. Does this woman know you love her?"

She shook her head.

"Why haven't you told her?"

"There'd be no point. It would only ruin our friendship."

Soon after that Emily Doncaster rolled up in her limousine and began to pound on the door downstairs. It seemed Tish had gotten an emergency call from her brother; her sister-in-law had miscarried and was deathly ill. Observing the way Tish turned pale at the news and the speed with which she departed, Roman Zach wondered, not for the first time, at the intensity of her family attachments. He thought that he would like to meet her sister-in-law, Rachel.

Tish burst into the large sunlit room and stopped, appalled. Could only one week have wrought such a change?

Rachel looked like her own ghost. All her color was gone. She lay back upon the pillows, a wan smile barely visible on her face. When she tried to lift a hand in greeting, it fell to the bed. Her features were pinched and sharpened by grief and loss of blood, and her face, its youthful softness gone, was unmistakably Semitic. She looked like a refugee from some European disaster. And Tish realized with horror that the change had not been sudden, but that she had failed to see it; preoccupied with her own feelings, she had let Rachel waste away in the witch's cave and done nothing to help her. Nirvana was killing her; she'd even lost her looks.

"You've got to get away from here," she said loudly, not even thinking of the inappropriateness of such a greeting. "You belong in the city."

Rachel's eyes were full. "Oh, Tish," she whispered. She shut her eyes, as if the weariness of the world lay upon her lids.

Kneeling by the bedside, grasping her hands, Tish held her breath in fear. How wasted and yellow Rachel's hands were. How could she not have noticed, all these months! "You look terrible," she said. "You must have lost quite a bit of blood. You'll need some iron tonic. I'm sure you're depressed too, and no wonder, poor dear. But you'll cheer up once we move into the city. I have it all planned. The three of us will get a flat together in the Village; I've been meaning to talk to you and Denzell about it for weeks."

Rachel tried to smile but couldn't quite manage it. "No money," she whispered. Two tears began to roll down her cheeks, quite evenly matched, Tish noted with one part of her furiously working mind. When Rachel's voice came, it was so faint she could hardly hear it.

"I'll die here," she breathed, not wanting to hear the words herself.

Tish stood up. "Oh, no, you won't," she said with the furious determination she had always had, ever since childhood, when she fought against tears. Then, hitting one post of the oaken bed with a punch that obviously hurt her hand, she went swiftly from the room, leaving Rachel with a thin spark in her mind that hovered between curiosity and hope.

"I want to talk to you," Tish said, bearding her father in his study after dinner. She had carefully considered her approach. "I think it's time I got a pied-à-terre in town. There's really no point in keeping this whole house open over the winter. You and Mother will be in Europe for God knows how long and Denzell is never around anyway. I spend as much time as I can in town and hate to come out here and I find it very tiresome not to have my own place. It's all very well to camp at Aunt Dorothy's, but I can't entertain there, I can't repay my social obligations, I have no room for my clothes. And there's no point in keeping Nirvana open just for Rachel."

"I would never permit you to get an apartment alone," said her father dismissively. "Won't even discuss it." He was intent on the preparation of his after-dinner cigar.

"But I wouldn't be alone," said Tish. "Denzell and Rachel and I can get one together. Rachel would be the perfect chaperone."

"I suspect Denzell won't think much of the idea," said Mr. Sloate drily. "He may prefer to keep her out here." He took an experimental puff.

"Denzell," said his daughter firmly, "could use a chaperone of his own. I'd hate to see him follow in your footsteps, Father."

"What can you possibly mean?"

"I mean merely the pleasures of society in town as contrasted with the difficulties of life with Mother—difficulties of which I know you are well aware, since you too maintain a pied-à-terre, in Murray Hill, I believe?"

He laughed. "Are you trying to blackmail me, young woman?"

"Perish the thought," she protested. "But why should the three of us be condemned to live with a woman that even you cannot abide?"

He laughed again. Disparagement of his wife was one of the ways to his heart, as Tish knew from experience. "I suppose you're old enough," he conceded, "as long as you've got family with you. Where would you want to live?"

"Greenwich Village," said Tish promptly. "I'll start looking tomorrow. I'll need enough money to engage a flat and a housekeeper. Will you see to it?"

Within a month Tish had found a lovely six-room flat with a terrace overlooking Washington Square. Denzell grumbled at the move, pointing out that Nirvana was much more convenient to the airfield and that he would still have to spend some nights on Long Island for the sake of his flying. But Rachel began to display more animation than she had shown in months. The Village, as the new Bohemia was beginning to be called, was not the Lower East Side. It was not home. But it was only a short walk from home, and the sights and people she had longed for.

"I'll feel better in the city, I know," Rachel promised herself wanly. "I'll get my energy back. Perhaps I'll even be able to have a baby."

III

Berliner's Department Store stood at the corner of Fifty-third Street, the center of the golden promenade that was Fifth Avenue. Surrounded by the elegant town houses of the rich and the grand hotels of international café society, it was set in this fashionable residential district like a jewel in an idol's forehead, a focus for the aspirations of the neighborhood.

Only a few years before, the store had leapfrogged up from its first location on Sixteenth Street, vaulting over the backs of its major rivals to a location farther north than that of any other major retailer except Bloomingdale's, much farther to the east. Like treads on a vast staircase, the other great department stores ascended Fifth Avenue to the pinnacle of Berliner's: at the bottom of the stairs was Henry Siegel's, still down at Union Square though about to make the jump to Bryant Park. Then came Bergdorf's at Thirty-second Street and the cluster of fine establishments at Thirty-fourth: Macy's, Saks, and Altman's. A few more steps and there was Bonwit's at Thirty-eighth and then, at last, posed at the top landing like a debutante, came Berliner's. A fantasy in white marble, it offered all the latest conveniences in retailing: both elevators and escalators, full electric lighting on every floor, and a pneumatic-tube system for expediting cash and sales slips. Sumptuous carpets lay underfoot; crystal chandeliers were reflected in gilt-framed mirrors throughout; and the palatial ground floor was a forest of Florentine columns, carved in serpentine and adorned at the summit by plump green cupidons, who appeared to be showering graces upon the beautiful ladies who walked beneath them.

One of these ladies was Tish Sloate, on her way to an appointment with Ira Berliner himself. Tish did much of her extensive purchasing at Berliner's and was a valued customer, frequently waited upon by the head designer, Fritzi Edelin, who presided over the store's famous reproductions of Paris fashions and its vast selection of imported fabrics. While ready-to-wear clothing had become the norm for working girls, society still had its clothes custom-made, either by personal dressmakers or in the workrooms of large emporiums like Berliner's. Consequently Berliner's yard-goods departments employed two hundred fifty people and stretched for three floors (woolens on three, cotton wash fabrics on four, and silks on five), while its ready-to-wear departments were relatively small, selling mainly children's clothing.

Although Berliner's workrooms were a source of prestige as well as custom, the store's main profits were made selling French fabrics and designs to dressmakers, who came from all over the Northeast for the annual spring and fall showings of the latest Paris styles. In New York, the fashionable and the Parisian were synonymous. Each year Fritzi Edelin, a distinguished Austrian-born woman in her forties, made yearly trips to Paris along with Mr. and Mrs. Berliner to buy designs from Poiret, Lanvin, Chéruit, Redfern, Coiullet, Mme. Jenny, Lucille, Callot Soeurs, and the latest nine days' wonder, Chanel. Fritzi selected their more conservative models, on the theory that New York was two years behind Paris in taste; few of her customers made choices as extreme as those of Tish Sloate. "Too Parisian, my dear," she would sometimes reprove Tish.

Through her spies Fritzi kept an eye on the models sold by Bergdorf's, Bonwit's, and the rest, for though no reputable French couturier would sell the same design to two New York stores, it was just as well to be sure. Each season she returned from Paris with hundreds of bolts of designer fabric and the patterns that went with them, so that a model shown in Paris in August could be duplicated in New York by September. And what society wore in September would be worn by the East Side girls a few months later, in cheap, poorly made, ready-to-wear imitations, slightly varied to avoid offending Fritzi, who had a strict proprietary interest in preserving the exclusivity of her models and watched for piracy like a hawk. She consented, however, to let her models be drawn by the artists of *Vogue*, *Harper's Bazaar*, and *Vanity Fair*, since few dressmakers could hope to produce anything resembling the original by studying these sketches. Seamstresses needed patterns at least, and preferably made-up models as well, if they were to duplicate the subtlety of the French effects.

There was consequently a peculiar sharpness to Tish's smile as she tripped through the aisles of the great store, eager to see Fritzi's face when she entered. For Tish was dressed for the occasion in a two-piece Lanvin street costume that had been one of Berliner's most remarkable designs that winter. It had a Russian overblouse with an accordion pleated skirt, ankle length, banded once at midthigh and again below the knee, so the pleats bounced. Berliner's did it in a dull blue crepe de chine, with a contrasting tie collar in a lighter blue, as Lanvin had specified. They never altered fabrics from the designer's original, true to Fritzi's goal of absolute duplication of all things French.

Tish's costume, however, was not blue, a color she considered ingenue. It was bright russet with rose-pink trim; her skirt, moreover, had only one band confining its accordion pleats, which fanned out below the knee to allow for Tish's long stride. These variations were possible because she had not purchased her Lanvin from Berliner's but had it made up in an altered form by Ruby, working from a sketch in *Vogue*.

Fritzi audibly sucked in her breath when Tish entered the office, though she was far too tactful to say anything, merely complimenting her on how well she looked while Ira Berliner came from behind his desk to shake hands. After a considerable exchange of social pleasantries, Tish came to the reason for which she had made this appointment.

"I've got something to show you," she said. "I'd like to take advantage of your expertise, if you would be so kind. A friend and I designed these and made them up. They're a new kind of brassiere."

She pulled out Ruby's three model brassieres and handed them over. The two examined them with interest.

"Well, we carry brassieres, of course," said Fritzi dubiously. "We have for two years now. The younger girls ask for them. But I've never seen any that looked like this. Two of them don't even have any bones."

"Exactly," said Tish. "The point is to suit the model to the needs of the individual wearer. Why should every woman wear the same kind of underclothes? This big model is for an older woman with a large bosom; my partner fitted it on her mother. So naturally it uses bone. A woman who has worn corsets all her life would feel naked without whalebone. These two models are for young girls, and are designed to firm and flatten the bust in a way suitable to the new fashions. They afford the maximum in movement both above and below the waist."

"Fritzi, explain these mysteries to me," ordered Ira Berliner. "How are these different from the models we already carry? Can't women move in those?"

"Our brassieres go from shoulder to waist," said Fritzi. "These stop just under the breast. I'll show you." She left the room and returned with a vestlike shell of bone and lace, still enough to stand up by itself when she put it on his desk. It had a thick center bone running down both front and back, with smaller bones running horizontally back to front on each side, as if a second rib cage were needed on top of the wearer's own.

"This model has been quite popular," said Fritzi, "though some people say it's a bit stiff."

"Stiff," said Tish. "It's armor! A bullet couldn't pass through it!"

"Remember, women like to be held in," said Fritzi. "Last year we had brassieres that were cut down low for evening wear and anyone with a full figure popped right out the top. Very embarrassing; we had a number of complaints."

"But look at this," said Tish, gesturing with the largest of her models. "We achieve the same compression with only two light bones. We use a system of intricate seaming and gusseting that makes all the difference in the world to how you feel. My partner's mother wore this all day and said she had never found it easier to move. And there were no red marks on her flesh when she took it off, either."

Ira Berliner listened in silence with raised eyebrows. He had not realized these things were so uncomfortable.

Fritzi was becoming interested. "What about this one?" She was holding up the smallest of Tish's brassieres. "How does it look on?"

"Well, I'm wearing one." They stared at her. There were no noticeable bulges, no untoward movements under the crepe de chine.

"Look," she said, suddenly bending over to touch her toes three times. They looked. She reached an arm out and swung, imitating a tennis serve. "Perfect for sports," she said. "You see, no wobble."

Ira Berliner began to laugh. He brushed his gray moustache with his fingers. "Charming," he murmured. "Fritzi, we must have some."

"I suppose we could stock a few and try them out," said Fritzi. "We could say you recommend them, Tish. You wouldn't mind that, would you? Where do we order them?"

"You don't understand," said Tish. "These are only models. We hold the patent but we haven't found a way to get them manufactured yet."

Ira Berliner raised his eyebrows. "You are going into business, Tish?"

She laughed flirtatiously. "You know very well I can't do that. A lady in manufacturing? My father would put me in a convent! And my partner can't set up a factory; she's only eighteen. She'd never get financing. Anyway, she's an artist; she wants to design. She's been making these up in a small way for friends but she's tired of it; she says it doesn't pay and we should sell the patent."

"Try Helen of Troy in Bridgeport," said Berliner. "We order a lot of stock from them. They're a good firm. I'll give you a letter to the president and tell him to make you a fair offer."

He carefully penned a letter as she waited. "Be sure to give him a demonstration like you gave us," he said, smiling, as he handed her the paper.

Tish rose to leave. "By the way," she said, "mum's the word outside this room, I trust? I wouldn't like word of this to reach my family."

He shook her hand gravely. "As silent as the tomb," he promised.

As the two women walked down the paneled hall, Fritzi Edelin invited Tish to have a cup of tea before she left.

"You must have known I wouldn't be able to resist asking," she purred. "Who made your dress? One of my girls from the workroom? If I find out who, she'll be sorry she was born. I must say, my dear, you are a cheeky monkey to wear my own design, pirated no doubt by one of my own girls, to an interview here." She smiled to take the sting from her words, but her voice was hurt.

"Why, Fritzi, I'd never do that," protested Tish. "It's true

I wore it to tease you but I'd never go behind your back and bribe one of your people. My partner made me the dress from the drawing in *Vogue*."

"That's impossible. It would never drape like that."

"Fritzi, this girl is a genius. She can do things nobody else can do; don't ask me how. She just looks at the fabric and it drapes itself. And I like to use her because she lets me change things around, like opening up the pleats in this skirt so I don't have to hobble."

Fritzi examined the stitching on her cuffs, her tie, the pleats in her skirt. "I would never have believed it," she said. "Tell me about this girl. What is her name? For whom does she work?"

"Her name is Ruby Levy and she lives on the East Side. She's worked as a designer since she was fourteen, believe it or not, at a place called Margolis Modes. I think they make children's wear. She's taken a short leave from them because she had a little problem with her back, but she's better now and is planning to return any minute. Of course they're offering her the moon."

"And how did you meet her?"

"Through my sister-in-law." Fritzi nodded; no further explanation was necessary. The whole world knew about the celebrated misalliance of Denzell Sloate.

"I keep telling Ruby she should leave the East Side and go where her work will be more appreciated," said Tish chattily. "I don't think she's developing the way she could uptown. But her family is dependent upon her salary and she does have a steady job."

"Still, she has her future to consider," argued Fritzi Edelin. "A young girl must think of that. And what kind of future can she have in ready-to-wear? A flash in the pan, good enough only for the immigrants. Once they have been here a while and have a little money, they will get their clothes custom-made like the rest of us and there will go the whole business, poof! Down the drain!"

This was a pet theory of Fritzi's. Tish had heard it before and let it pass without argument. Instead she said gravely, "What should I tell her to do?"

"Why, you must bring her to me, of course," said Fritzi expansively. "Where else? We're always looking for new talent here and where could she find a more suitable place to learn? She clearly has flair. I can say no more than that until I meet her, but if she seems suitable, I am sure we could match and better any salary offered by one of those horrible East Side firms.''

Fritzi Edelin and the Berliners were German Jews. Like most of their compatriots, they had the liveliest contempt for anything smacking of the East Side and Russian-Jewish barbarism. Berliner's hired very few Russians, and only those who were native-born and had no accent. Fritzi would not, she reflected, be able to use this girl if she were too foreign; she would have to be presentable, not dark or with a thick accent, a greasy face or a moustache, a loud and screeching voice, or any of the other national characteristics Mr. Berliner deplored. He felt even more strongly about the East Side than she did and was involved in a number of projects to reform its morals, manners, language, and religion. He was on the board of the Educational Alliance, set up by the uptown Jews to teach the new immigrants English, and was part of the Kehillah, which was working with the police to stamp out the vice and gambling and prostitution that were giving all Jews a bad name.

So Fritzi could make no commitment to help this girl, who might prove to be quite impossible. But she could at least meet her and see.

While the dresses Ruby made for Tish brought some money into the Levy household, Moyshe was still substantially unemployed. Hannah went so far into debt to Garfinkle that the butcher cut off her credit.

"This isn't the United Hebrew Charities you know," he said. "I'm running a business here."

"And don't you come sucking up to my Solly and asking him for soup bones either," said Rosalie. "I know about women like you. Stay away from my husband."

"Tell him to stay away from me!" retorted Hannah. As if it were her fault Solly leered at her over the counter or tried to reach around to pinch her with his nasty blood-stained hands. She hadn't asked him for anything, but that didn't stop him giving her those bedroom looks, offering in his most seductive voice to bring over a bone if she'd put it in her stewpot. The filthy fellow. "I wouldn't take the time of day from that husband of yours, let alone a soup bone," said Hannah and snapped out the door.

Relations between the Levys and Garfinkles had steadily

deteriorated. Rosalie's marriage was a rocky one—it was in Solly's nature to stray—but she persisted in blaming all the women he ran after, shutting her eyes to his character. Her parents were less deluded and viewed Solly's conquests with even more disfavor. They disliked Hannah for her sharp tongue as well as her past association with Solly, the nature of which they could guess if not prove. While they had to let her buy on credit since she was popular on the block, they made her as unwelcome as they could in the butcher shop—Fafonfnik with her reflections upon Ruby's character and prospects, Garfinkle with his suggestions that Moyshe look for another job in Chicago. Buying meat had become an ordeal for Hannah—one she would now have to endure no more, since her credit had run out. The family would live on bread, cheese, and vegetables.

They did so for three weeks. "I never want to look another cabbage in the face," groaned Moyshe. Then Tish appeared in the doorway, waving a contract.

"Helen of Troy wants our patent!" she sang out triumphantly. "They're offering eight hundred dollars!"

Hannah clutched her heart; Ruby gasped and sat down hard. "You mean I would get half of that?" she quavered.

Tish wasn't at all sure they should take the first offer; they might be able to get more if they held out. "They really want the patent," she insisted.

"Come on, it's a fortune," Ruby said euphorically.

"Four hundred dollars," muttered Hannah, beginning to figure frantically on her fingers as the girls watched bemused. Finally she cried with tears in her eyes, "We can pay the doctors! We can get back the clock and mirror! We can even settle our bill at the butcher's!"

She went into Garfinkle's the next week, cash in hand, choosing the busiest time of day so that everyone would see her.

Kalman Garfinkle was suddenly jovial at the sight of all that cash. "What's going on here? Somebody in your family rob a bank?"

"No," said Hannah grandly, "only my daughter has been paid four hundred dollars for designing a new kind of corset for ladies. It's not so much money for a genius like my Ruby, but we like to pay our bills on time, so from now on I can take my business where they have better quality." Nose in

the air, she swept out of the shop; let them eat their hearts
out.

It took two hundred dollars to pay their debts. With another
hundred, they opened a savings account, since Ruby insisted
this method was safer than keeping such a lot of money under
the mattress. The remaining hundred Ruby kept, at Tish's
orders, as "an investment in herself."

"What kind of an investment?" asked Hannah. When she
found out she clutched her heart again, but it was too late.
Ruby had already spent the money on yards and yards and
yards of wool and silk, trim and binding and ribbon and lace,
a new hat, boots, and even a hair styling at the place Tish
went to, uptown.

"Don't worry about it, Ma," she said irritably, having
doubts on the subject herself. "She promised if I fix myself
up like a lady she'll get me a fancy job uptown at twenty-five
dollars a week. On twenty-five dollars a week we can save up
money like a bunch of Rothschilds."

By the time Ruby went to meet Fritzi Edelin she had been
transformed. Her clothes were elegant, understated, subdued
and tasteful, but in the latest style and the finest material. She
wore expensive Russian leather lace-up boots and glacé kid
gloves. Her brown curls were exquisitely dressed and her
hands as well manicured as any society girl's.

Why, she's a beauty, thought Fritzi, hoping she could
speak English. She waited with bated breath for Ruby's first
words, and heaved a sigh of relief when she heard them: there
was an accent, but it wasn't bad. It was soft, slurred, almost
aristocratic; perhaps they could tell customers she was a Russian princess. In any case, she seemed the quiet type; she
wouldn't talk too much or too loud.

Fritzi's estimate was correct. Besides her dressmaking
gifts, Ruby brought three great assets to her new life. One
was her looks. The second was her quickness at learning
those few things in which she was interested. The third was
her soft, sweet manner. Growing up in a household with
Moyshe, Hannah, and Sarah, she had never had the opportunity to become long-winded; she seldom talked at all, letting their arguments rage over her head and thinking her own
thoughts. She did the same at Berliner's, listening when she
was interested and smiling when she was not. Such calm was

unusual in a young girl. She's a deep one, thought Fritzi
Edelin.

And Ruby came into Berliner's like a queen into her kingdom. Each moment in the great store was like sugar in her
mouth. So this was what she had been waiting for all these
years; this was what destiny had in mind. She had always
known that somewhere in her future lay a mansion of surpass-
ing elegance; now she knew it was a palace of commerce.

There were wonderful new opportunities for women in retailing, or so the other girls who worked at Berliner's assured
her. And Ruby was in a particularly advantageous position;
working directly under Fritzi Edelin, she could really learn
the ropes. Someday she might become a buyer—head buyers
could make fifty, even a hundred dollars a week. And as for
head designers like Fritzi—well, no one knew exactly what
she made, but everyone was sure it was a fortune. Ruby
would start out fitting and cutting patterns designed in Paris,
but after she had been there a year or two, she could perhaps
work her way up to designing for the store's own label for
children, "Little Miss B." This line was jobbed out to various manufacturers on the East Side, and with Ruby's experience in manufacturing, she would be a natural for the work.

"What about women's ready-to-wear?" asked Ruby.
"What's our label for that?"

Her informant sniffed. "Better not let Fritzi hear you ask
that. We don't carry women's ready-to-wear. Our class of
customers wouldn't touch it."

As she had done at Margolis Modes, Ruby studied every
aspect of the store's operation, spending her lunch hours examining the stock, the prices, the customers, department by
department, getting an idea of what there was to sell and who
bought it. Who knew what high position she might rise to;
how could she guess what she might need to know in a year's
time? So she learned it all, every gilded item on the department list next to the elevators.

She learned Artists' Materials, Art Embroidery, Automatic
Pianos, and Books. She examined Bathroom Fittings, Baskets, Boys' Apparel, Blankets and Bedding, Bric-a-Brac,
Blouses, Bathing Suits, Bronzes, and Bicycles. She spent an
hour in Commercial Stationery, watching the customers make
their selections of type face and paper stock. She watched the
little kiosk on the ground floor that sold Cigars and Ciga-

rettes, and was surprised to note that even ladies bought there. She learned Clocks and Cut Flowers and Celluloid Articles and Corsets; she studied China, Cut Glass, Couch Covers, and Curtains; and she spent many hours in Carpets and Rugs, dreaming over the resplendent piles of Orientals laid out upon the floor.

Berliner's had everything for sewing: Dress Trimmings, Dress Goods, Embroideries, Fashion Books, Laces, Notions, Patterns, Ribbons, Sewing Machines, Silks, Veilings, Woolens, and Wash Goods in all weights. In addition ladies could purchase Gold Jewelry, Diamond Jewelry, Furs, Handkerchiefs and Hairgoods, Gloves and Ivory Goods, Hosiery, Kimonos, Leather Goods, Millinery, Perfumes, Plated Jewelry, Petticoats, Rubber Goods (including trusses and special reducing corsets), Shawls, Shoes, Tea Gowns, Toilet Articles, Waists, Watches, Women's Neckwear, and Underwear.

And every sort of professional assistance was available to Berliner's lady shoppers. They could open Charge Accounts, have their clothing Cleaned and Dyed, and put their furs into Cold Storage. The store had its own Chiropodist, Dental Parlor, Electrolysist, Hairdresser, Manicurist, Notary Public, Optician, and Physician—and he was backed by his own Prescription Service. These benefits were for the use of the staff as well as the customers—truly, Ruby would never want for any care again!

You could buy Gymnasium Equipment at Berliner's. You could get a Harness for your horse, or a Hercules Fireproof Safe for your money, or a Lace Portière for your doorway. You could buy a Player Piano complete with Music Scrolls, rent more from the Music Scroll Exchange Library, get a Piano Scarf to drape over its top and a Piano Tuner to fix it up if it got wonky, all without leaving the premises of this one magnificent emporium. Everything was available in Berliner's Department Store in 1915 and Ruby Levy saw it all.

Her one regret was that she could never get her mother to meet her there. "Come on, Ma," she would urge, "come and pick something out for yourself."

"I don't like uptown," said Hannah firmly. She had been to Berliner's only once, with Moyshe, and that was enough. The place was too fancy, too American; she couldn't understand why Ruby would want to work there. It made her feel dirty and dowdy, fat and foreign. The bright lights and the way the crystal chandeliers sparkled in the mirrors hurt her eyes. And it frightened her to see herself everywhere she looked. She didn't even understand what was happening at first. Because the mirrors were so good that there was no distortion in the reflection, she had given a frightened little cry and grabbed Moyshe's arm.

"A *doppelgänger*," she had whispered, pointing at the reflection which obligingly pointed back. How angry she was when he laughed at her.

"I don't like your store," she told Ruby. "I buy where I can bargain so I can bring the price down. I don't like these set prices."

"But, Ma, I get a *discount*," said Ruby.

"Discount, pooh. I can get twice as much off with my mouth. And tell me, what fun is it to go shopping if they won't even give you an argument?"

As the sun poured in the front and side windows on Rivington Street, Sarah and Ruby sat around in their wrappers, even though it was already Sunday noon. Hannah was making a cheesecake, cottage cheese with raisins and a lattice crust, and they were waiting for it to cool when Rachel burst in the door.

"I'm going to have a baby!" she cried joyfully. "I'm pregnant again!"

"Hooray!" yelled Sarah, who knew how Rachel had longed for this news. They crowded around, congratulating her, and Hannah began to cut the cake with a celebratory air. "Well, you're certainly not going to those terrible Long Island doctors this time," she said. "Do you want me to talk to Mrs. Breynes for you?"

"Oh, I'm not going to use a midwife," said Rachel. "I'm going to have my baby in a hospital."

Hannah put down the knife with a horrified thump. "A hospital! God forbid! What do you want to go someplace like that for?"

"I'm not having my baby at home like in the old country," said Rachel. "I want the best and most modern service I can get."

"Now you listen to me," said Hannah firmly. "I've had enough babies, so I should know. You can't do better than Mrs. Breynes. She's clean, experienced, a first-class midwife. And also a friend of the family. You're not sick, you're pregnant—why go someplace where everybody else is dying?"

But Rachel was adamant. She had suffered enough when she miscarried; she wanted her labor to be painless. She was having her baby the modern way, with Twilight Sleep.

"What's that?" said Ruby.

"It's a chemical, scopolamine. They use it with morphine. You get a shot, you go to sleep, and you wake up the next morning with a new baby. You don't remember a thing; they say it's like a night just dropped out of your life."

"I don't believe it," said Hannah. "There's no way to avoid labor pains. Even in the Torah it says, In pain shall thou bring forth children. You think just because you're in America you don't have to go through it like everybody else?"

Sarah was annoyed. "You're such a peasant, Mama. You don't know anything about modern life."

Hannah sniffed. "Modern life, she tells me. Next thing I know you'll be saying women don't have to have babies except when they plan to!"

Sarah began to laugh. She laughed until Hannah became irritated. "Are you going to let us in on the joke?" Then Sarah rose and rummaged among her things, coming back with a dog-eared pamphlet.

"I wasn't going to show you this, Ma, but when I hear such medieval superstition coming out of your mouth, I can't help myself."

"What are you talking about?" Hannah took the pamphlet. It was called *Family Limitation.* "What is this?"

"*Family Limitation!*" Rachel grabbed it. "That's Margaret Sanger's pamphlet! It's the one she had to leave the country for so they wouldn't put her in jail. Where did you get this, Sarah?"

"Minnie Fishman."

"Listen to this." Ruby had taken the pamphlet and, opening at random, was translating into Yiddish. "'It is believed that conception cannot take place if the woman lies on her left side at the time of the act. But it makes no difference which side she lies upon; she can become pregnant if the semen is not prevented from entering the womb.' But why did Minnie give this to you, Sarah? You're not married."

Sarah blushed. Minnie had given it to her during her affair

with Joe Klein, but she had never intended to show it to her family. "No special reason, she just wanted to share."

"Sarah?" Hannah's voice was suspicious.

"Come on, Ma, you know I wouldn't do anything bad." She crossed her fingers, hoping Hannah would not pursue the subject.

Rachel repossessed the pamphlet and began to translate from the introduction. Hannah listened with a troubled face. All this was very hard for her to take in.

"'I feel there is sufficient information given here,'" read Rachel, "'which, if followed, will prevent a woman from becoming pregnant unless she desires to do so. Of course, it is troublesome to get up to douche, it is also a nuisance to have to trouble about the date of the menstrual period. It seems inartistic and sordid to insert a pessary or a suppository in anticipation of the sexual act. But it is far more sordid to find yourself several years later burdened down with half-a-dozen unwanted children, helpless, starved, shoddily clothed, dragging at your skirt, yourself a dragged-out shadow of the woman you once were.'"

Sarah was watching her mother. "Come on, Ma. Don't look so worried—I'm okay."

Hannah shook her head. "That's not what I was thinking." She was silent for a moment, then, "If you knew how it was with us!" she burst out. "The babies would come and then they'd die. We didn't know any of these modern things. We used vinegar, we used herbs, but nothing could stop them from coming and there was nothing you could do to keep them alive."

"But there is something to do if you get pregnant and don't want to be," said Ruby wisely. They all stared at her.

"Who says so?"

"A girl was talking about it at work," muttered Ruby. "The only thing to do is to go to the midwife for a scraping, unless you want to have the baby."

"What is a scraping?" asked Sarah.

Hannah squirmed, remembering her secret. But she was glad there was something she knew more about than these young girls. "They scrape out your insides so you don't have a baby."

"Does it hurt?" asked Sarah.

"Of course it hurts."

Ruby was staring at her mother in fascination. "Have you even had a scraping, Mama?" she whispered.

Hannah's face was a mask. "I've been lucky," she said. "They're dangerous."

Ruby was frozen. "You mean you and Papa—" she stammered. "I didn't know women your age—I mean, I didn't know you still—got pregnant."

Hannah glared at her, standing up to end the conversation. "I'm forty-six years old," she said icily. "I'm not dead yet. And there sure is a lot you don't know."

Living with Rachel and Denzell *en famille* turned out to be more than Tish had bargained for. She had always found her brother irritating; at closer quarters, he became intolerable. His tiresome militarism, so boyish. His stupid singing around the house, war songs, of course, about packing up your troubles in your old kit bag. His avoidance of thought, and the way he made excuses when he didn't come home at night, even though no one asked him where he'd been. It wouldn't have mattered except for Rachel. Tish couldn't stand to see her hurt, especially now that she was pregnant again.

She was due in November. It looked as if she'd be all right this time.

It was hard that he, who obviously didn't care a pin about her, should have the right to run a careless finger over her cheek or touch her hair in the most proprietary way imaginable—and even get a look of gratitude in response—while she, Tish, had to weigh every sign of affection she permitted herself as if on a goldsmith's scale.

The only thing to do was lose herself in work. Another New York suffrage referendum was coming up in November and they needed speakers and organizers upstate. They'd asked her several times and she'd refused. Now she would go. She would pack up her troubles in her own kit bag for there was more than one war on. And she would write poor Rachel lots of letters.

April 5, 1915—Albany

Dear Rachel,

All the legislators are rather short and quite stout and they drink a good deal. I tower about them, terribly *soignée* in my Ruby *modes*, and they are so impressed by my "social position" that they hardly know where to

look, poor things. And I very sweetly ask them to teach
me all their wisdom about the legislative process because
we poor little women have had so few chances to drink
from this fount (which I don't mind saying is a muddy
one indeed, but what would you expect from a lot of
men pigging it up unsupervised all these years?).

On my last day in Albany one very important senator
from upstate took my hand and soulfully mentioned that
he would like to instruct me further, perhaps over dinner
when he next comes to the city, and did I know a charming spot, etc.? I threw up my hands in horror. "Oh, no,
kind sir, I have taken a holy vow not to tête-à-tête with
the opposite sex until women have the vote, so I do hope
you'll use your influence, Senator." And he said,
"Hmm, like Lysistrata," and I said, "Very like." I
hope you are keeping well; do be careful. Love, Tish.

As the war continued, Denzell often went flying at night,
then stayed out at Nirvana alone, falling into bed as the sun
rose. From one or two comments Rachel let drop, he fancied
she thought he was seeing another woman. But no woman
could compare to flying with the whole sky one dark cloud.
He would imagine himself over France, the darkness lit suddenly by flashes of fire. Was that von Richthofen coming at
him from behind that cloud? The Baron lurked like a hawk,
ready to swoop down, but Denzell darted through the air like
a hummingbird, stinging and dancing through the ack-ack
bullets.

He was joined in such fancies by several of his friends at
the club, fliers and Francophiles to a man. How impatient
they were with Wilson, dragging his feet when the greatest
war in history was going on overseas. They would not wait
forever; there were things a man of spirit could do if he
wanted to fight. If worst came to worst, there was the Foreign
Legion.

Rachel wasn't very sympathetic when he talked about
going to France. He couldn't seem to make her understand
how much it meant to him. But when the time came, he
would do what he had to do.

It was just after six o'clock in the evening on May 7, 1915,
when the door burst open and Tish came in, white-faced,
clutching the evening papers. She held them out to Rachel,

who sat up drowsily, surprised. Tish was supposed to be upstate. She smiled at her but as she did so, something went
wrong in Tish's throat and she started to cough helplessly,
drily, covering her mouth, wracked with the spasm.

"What's the matter?" said Rachel, alarmed. "What are
you doing here?"

In answer, Tish shoved the newspapers at her and ran to
the lavatory, where she could be heard gagging and coughing.
When she emerged, her green eyes wide and distended, she
pointed at the newspapers, then collapsed on the sofa, hiding
her face in her arms and curling into its overstuffed cushions
as if she were trying to burrow into them, like some small
animal in a nest of leaves. Bewildered, Rachel picked up the
papers and saw the banner headlines that took up the whole
front page of each:

LUSITANIA SUNK BY HUNS!

GERMANS TORPEDO LUXURY LINER!

OVER A THOUSAND DEAD!

128 AMERICANS ON BOARD!

"Oh, no," breathed Rachel. She read on, " 'At 2:10 this
afternoon a German submarine torpedoed the Cunard liner,
the S.S. *Lusitania,* off the coast of Ireland, enforcing its
blockade of the British Isles. The luxury vessel carried many
prominent New Yorkers, including railroad magnate Alfred
Gwynne Vanderbilt, producer Charles Frohmann, and banker
William Sloate II with his wife, Caroline. The 31,000-ton
vessel, the largest and most elegant liner ever built, sank in
only eighteen minutes . . .' "

Rachel fell silent, imagining such a death: the crash, the
suddenness of the blow, the panic and the screams, the frantic
pushing as you tried to get to a lifeboat, then feeling the deck
break apart under your feet, the icy gray water paralyzing
you, pulling you down, closing over your head. It was a horrible way to die. She went and put her arm around Tish, who
sat up, sniffing.

"I was never right," she said. "I could never please them,
even when I was little. They only cared how things looked,
never how I felt. They were so bad when I got into trouble at
college. They wanted me to get married right away so there

wouldn't be any scandal—they didn't even care who I married, just so they could get me safely swept under the rug before anything else happened.''

She began to cry and threw herself back into the cushions. Rachel kept patting her back and stroking her hair, saying, "There, there," as if she were talking to a child. After a while, her thoughts began to wander to what Denzell would do. He would come into a lot of money now that his father was dead. Would it make him more responsible? Or would he do what he was always dreaming of, and go to France?

The funeral passed, and the mourning period, and still Denzell said nothing of his intentions. Neither woman would have broached the subject for all the world, for fear of encouraging him. So things went on as before, with him spending most of his time at the airfield and Rachel lying around the house, more and more visibly pregnant. And Tish once more grew restless. She was so lonely! All the constraints on her had been removed by her parents' death; she could live as she wished now with no patriarchal voice to forbid her, no hand to cut off funds if she transgressed. She could go anywhere she liked with anyone she liked, but there was only one person she wanted to be with and being with her was worse than being alone. So she went off to Buffalo again to work on the suffrage campaign.

August 8, 1915—Buffalo

Dear Rachel,

I hope my abominable brother is treating you properly; you must be enormous now, poor dear, and it's so hot out. I shall come home the week before Baby is due, which is also, of course, the week after the referendum, God help us. We're making progress but it's just not fast enough, and between you and me and the gatepost, sweets, we're going to lose this round, thanks to Tammany.

I always park my soapbox across from a saloon, since that is where most voters can be found. Then I ring my little silver dinner bell (stolen for this purpose from Nirvana years ago) and my companion, a stalwart local maiden named Prue Gruening, blows on her trumpet and goes into the saloon to fetch the men to hear the noted speaker from out of town. Then I hold forth. Most of the

questions are about temperance, which they fear like
hellfire, or about who will mind the children if the
women get the vote. I enclose a clipping from the local
paper; you will note it spends more time on my parentage and clothes than on anything I said. Par for the
course. Love, Tish

ROCHESTER NOV 2 DEAR RACHEL STOP WELL WE LOST IT
STOP WENT OUT IMMEDIATELY AND HELD A RALLY STOP
NEVER SAY DIE STOP GOING ON A WEEK OF SPEECHES
THEN HOME STOP DO NOT HAVE BABY TILL I ARRIVE
LOVE TISH

Rachel had her baby on November 17, 1915, by Twilight
Sleep. It all went as she had planned and she didn't remember
a thing afterward. The baby was a girl, tiny and sweet. They
named her Caro Rebecca, after Denzell's mother, Caroline,
and Becky Zinssher. Rachel had never felt so proud of anything in her life as she was of that baby. She glowed when
she looked at her. To her sorrow, Denzell's thoughts were
elsewhere. He had known what he had to do from the moment his parents were torpedoed by the Boche, but he was
considerate enough to keep it to himself until the baby was
born. After Rachel had been home from the hospital a month
and his plans were perfected, he announced them one morning in the breakfast nook.
"One of the fellows at the club had the most wonderful
idea, that we should form a special squadron of American
fliers to aid the French—bring our own planes, raise our own
money, and go over there. I said I'd help."
"You're not serious," said Tish.
"Absolutely."
Rachel stared at him, stunned. She had gone through the
argument so many times. America wasn't even in the war. He
couldn't just go and serve in the army of another country. It
was against the law. "You'll lose your citizenship," she said.
"Too true, I'm afraid, at the moment, or so our talks with
the Secretary of State indicate. But that will change. When
America gets into the war, we'll be forgiven. The French
consul says if worse comes to worst we can always enlist in
the Foreign Legion and they'll put us together into our own
squadron as soon as they can."
"What do you mean, the French consul and the Secretary

of State?" Tish was outraged. "How far have you gone with this nonsense without even telling us?"

"I'm not the only one involved. Other fellows have been doing the negotiating. We only got the go-ahead a couple of days ago and even so it will take a month or two to get everything organized. I didn't want to worry you prematurely. The whole thing might have come to nothing."

"Worry us?" said Rachel. "Worry us!"

"I am appalled," said Tish. "Do you know what Father would have said about this? You have responsibilities; you have a wife and child."

"Rachel will be all right," he said, "and I know you'll help take care of Baby. And Father would want me to avenge him. You'll both be proud of me someday for this. You just can't see it straight yet because you're emotionally involved. Think of the butchery going on! We're going to call ourselves the Lafayette Escadrille—repaying the help Lafayette gave our revolution, you know. It's a wonderful propaganda stroke for the Allies: Even as their government teeters at the brink, the young men of America prepare to aid Europe in her hour of darkest need."

Rachel's face was white. "Denzell, you can't go off like this. We've just had a baby."

He looked at her pleadingly. "I'm a flier," he said. "This is the first air war. I can't miss out on a chance like this. You shouldn't ask me."

His eyes begged them not to hold it against him. Then with his sweetest, most engaging smile, he flashed them a salute. "Must be off, girls," he said. "Have to see a general," and he was gone.

The two women stared across the table at each other. Rachel was still stunned.

"He thinks it's all a game," said Tish, "and he doesn't want to be left out. Boys will be boys," and with a nasty smile, she began to clear the table.

Joe Klein tried to make up several times, but Sarah refused to have anything to do with him: the differences between them had become too great. He told himself he was just as glad to stop going out with that self-righteous, cold little prig, and went back to Gussie, the Tammany lawyer's daughter. Since he was still under indictment, he needed all the help he could get. He walked on eggs until the November election of

1915, when the reform district attorney was swept out of office. The first thing Tammany did was drop the indictments of Dopey Benny and the other gangsters. The union also benefited, for the threat hanging over the ILGWU officers vanished at the same time.

This was fortunate, since negotiations were under way in both the cloak and shirtwaist industries. The union announced the terms of the new protocol in February 1916. There were slight gains for the women who worked hourly rates; girls under sixteen would now make twelve cents an hour, while older girls would make fourteen cents their first year and seventeen cents thereafter. An experienced eighteen-year-old could thus earn all of $8.33 for a forty-nine hour week. The male cutters, who got paid by the week rather than the hour, did much better; their wages went from $22 to $27.50. "They have families to support," said Joe Klein.

Radicals like Minnie Fishman thought the union had given away too much. Surely they could win better terms by fighting than by bargaining. Talk of another general strike swept the industry. Faced with this rebellious temper in the rank and file, Joe Klein decided not to submit the new protocol to a general vote. People could vote in their shop meetings, where mutiny could be isolated and contained. Realizing, however, that some outlet for the militance of their workers was necessary, the union and the manufacturers' association agreed on a brief and purely symbolic general strike. As the Association told the press, "The union has asked us to permit the workers in our shops to have a demonstration holiday at their own expense, during which they may be properly registered if they have allowed their union membership to lapse. This holiday will not last more than a day or two. The girls will come back to work just as soon as they can get their new union cards."

Minnie Fishman stormed into Clinton Hall that night and buttonholed Joe Klein.

"What the hell is going on here?" she yelled. "You think we're cattle, we should be herded out of the shop one day and herded back the next without us having a meeting? Who gives you the power to sign a contract without taking a vote?"

"You girls are living in the past," said Joe. "You want everything to be like it was in 1909 for the rest of your lives. We have a structure now; we can delegate. Everything's already been settled."

That night Minnie came to Rivington Street. "You have to

help us, Sarah," she said. "We need a list of all the stewards in the shirtwaist shops. Joe Klein is running a steamroller over us and there's no way we can stand up to him unless we get a group together."

"You mean organize behind the union's back?" said Sarah. "But, Minnie, it's contract time. It's not right. You'll split the union."

But by the end of the evening, she had agreed at least to speak to the women at the League and see what they thought. It was true that they would have to move fast if they were to have any effect on negotiations.

Long after Minnie had gone home and the family was asleep, Sarah lay awake brooding. It made her sick to look back on the past year. Feeling cut off from her roots and marooned in an uptown world, she had slept with Joe Klein to find herself. But when she discovered his betrayal, she had lost her bearings completely and sunk into depression. Now she was filled with rage. After so many years of fighting, the girls had little more than they had won in the first strike. It was his fault. It had to stop. She had to stop him.

But to her dismay she found next morning that the officers of the League were absolutely opposed to her agitating against the new protocol.

"Organize a women's opposition group against the union leaders?" cried Mary Dreier. "Have you lost your mind? It's taken the League years to live down the idea that we were trying to split the labor movement along sex lines—and that's just what you're proposing! One whisper of this would finish us with the AFL. Sarah, I forbid you even to consider this!"

Sarah took it quietly. If there was one thing she had learned at the League, it was when to save her breath. But when she left work that night, she took her address book and her lists of shop stewards with her.

Sarah stayed out of work the next few days, contacting all the girls she'd known, swearing them to secrecy, then telling them the time had come to rebel. "We need the vote in New York State and an equal voice in the union," she said, and the informal network she and Minnie built up began to call itself the Equal Voice Movement. They met each night at Rivington Street.

"You're going to get yourself in trouble calling in sick and

organizing behind the League's back," warned Moyshe.
"And what will the union think?"

Sarah didn't care. She was in a mean and reckless mood.
To hell with the League; she was sick of being ladylike, surrounded by middle-class women all the time. If she wasn't
careful she'd end up living with a roommate or her parents
the rest of her days, getting all her satisfaction from good
works.

How she had wasted her life! For years she had gone to
work doggedly, like a squirrel in a cage, plodding around her
treadmill, telling herself the next time it went around she
would have accomplished something. She felt ill when she
thought of Avi Spector and the way she'd thrown him over
for Joe. The finest, most dedicated man she'd ever known and
she had chosen a crook instead. Now she was doomed to
loneliness. She couldn't even imagine meeting anyone; she
was too hard to please and she seemed to intimidate people.
She had never known how to make small talk or flirt. She
only knew how to be herself and that didn't work with men
no matter what Ruby's magazines said.

She couldn't stand herself or the constraints of her life anymore. It was time to break out and be the old Sarah again,
light in her eyes and fire in her mouth, back with her own
kind of people. And if she lost her job at the League, too bad.

Moyshe too wanted change. He said all the socialist parties
would have to split and form a new International because of
the way so many of them had voted for the war. He talked
Sarah and Minnie into going to Stuyvesant High School to
hear Alexandra Kollontai speak. She was a leader in the Russian women's movement and a Bolshevik like Avi Spector.
Sarah went, faintly hoping that Avi would be there.

The auditorium was so jammed that they could find seats
only near the back. Members of every language group in the
Socialist Party, especially Germans and Russians, swirled up
and down the aisles, elbowing Italian anarchists and American liberals who had come to find out what was happening
abroad. Avi Spector was sitting in front, with two friends
from the Latvian Socialist Federation. Sarah peered around
but couldn't see him.

The speakers filed onto the stage and a man announced that
Madame Kollontai would speak in Russian, with translators
in English and German. Then a slim, elegant figure stepped

up to the rostrum. Masses of curly hair were piled high on her head above a sweet heart-shaped face as beautiful as Rachel's. Sarah thought at first she looked too fancy to be a good revolutionary, but as her high, clear voice rang through the hall, Sarah was completely swept away by what the woman was saying.

She began by attacking the war and the way the socialist parties of Europe had turned against one another, breaking solidarity and following after their own ruling classes. What horrible suffering the war had brought Russia—the starvation, the demoralization—which was, however, meeting its answer in the increasing strength of the revolutionary movement. A new spirit was arising in Russia, and a new generation. In fact, revolution was around the corner! American socialists too must fling aside the worn-out methods of the past and grasp the new! She made a passionate appeal to the young in the audience: "You represent the future, a new age and a new kind of struggle. The war proves that the capitalist system has reached its zenith; it is no longer able to grow by rational means. The forces are already shaping for the last, decisive battle—it is the dawn of a new era, the end of capitalist oppression, the final liberation of all mankind!"

She flung out her arms rapturously as she ended and Sarah, along with most of the other young people in the room, was swept cheering to her feet by a wave of emotion, of desire for union with this ardent hope for the future. She had almost forgotten what it felt like to be this young and new, to know that you could change the world as long as your comrades were beside you and you remained steadfast. Filled with revulsion for all she had been and done these past few years, she thought: Kollontai is right; I feel as she does. Enough of compromise. She had the strength now; she had awakened; she would leave behind everything that made her feel dirty. She would fight the Joe Kleins and their gorillas in a clean, honest, out-in-the-open way no matter what anybody said. And if she lost the first battles her forces would grow stronger till in the end they would win. The union would be theirs again. And then she would be free, free at last to run like a child, to break out and fight, to make everything new, as she had dreamed long ago dancing in the moonlight in a courtyard in Kishinev.

The meeting over, eyes shining, Sarah kissed her father and ran off to find Minnie. They were due at a caucus.

Moyshe's heart swelled as he looked after her, his dearest child, heart of his heart. He, too, had been moved by the speech, but differently, for he was no longer among the young. This year he would be fifty-four. Would he and his children be permitted to enter the promised land together—or would he, like Moses, die still looking at it from afar? How much could one person change in a lifetime; how much was he doomed, as Kollontai said, to remain the child of his age? He had made one staggering leap already in politics, from Narodnya Volya to the Bund, and another in geography, across an ocean. Would he be young enough, resilient enough, to make a third and keep going forward with Sarah, or would he stay, as most of his friends would, fixed in the politics of his youth?

And what of his Sarah, what would become of her? Where would she find her destiny, her happiness? Sighing, Moyshe turned to put on his coat and caught sight of Avi Spector, halfway across the room, staring at the door Sarah had gone out of as if he had seen a ghost. Moyshe shook his head and stood limply, suddenly feeling inadequate to manage even the buttons on his overcoat. Despite the fact that he and Avi met each other frequently, they never spoke of Sarah. When Sarah stopped seeing Joe Klein, Hannah tried to get Moyshe to bring Avi home some night, or, if that was impossible, to bring somebody else home. But he didn't know anybody good enough.

"So get somebody who's not good enough," said Hannah. "She doesn't have to marry him if she doesn't want to. Let her decide."

But he couldn't do that either; he could not introduce her to anyone he knew to be unworthy. It would only make Sarah feel worse than ever if she thought her father wanted her to settle for any man she could get. She didn't have to get married—there were other ways to be useful and productive, maybe even happy.

He and Avi greeted each other, then the younger man suddenly flushed and blurted out, "Was that Sarah I saw leaving?"

"Yes," said Moyshe.

"How is she?" he said lamely.

A taut wire inside Moyshe snapped. "How the hell do you think she is, haven't you got eyes in your head?"

People around them turned and stared. Avi was struck dumb with embarrassment. He motioned toward the door and they walked up Essex Street in the cold. Finally Avi said cautiously, "About your daughter, Moyshe, I only wondered—"

Moyshe interrupted him. "I know, I'm sorry I flew off the handle. I'm just worried about her. She's been so unhappy. I don't blame you for it; her job has been a great disappointment, and this whole business with the union hit her very hard. She has nothing else in her life to balance these things and put them in perspective." His voice trailed off. He didn't want to say too much; maybe he had already.

Avi took the point. There was nothing to balance the work. So she had no one else. Thinking this, he had to know for sure.

"She doesn't have a boyfriend?" he asked timidly.

"Oh, she was going out with that Joe Klein for a while," said Moyshe, "but she never really liked him, if you ask me."

"I always thought she'd find somebody right away. After we broke it off, I mean. How could a girl like that stay alone, so lively, so full of spirit, so beautiful? Such a strong personality. So dedicated, so admirable a person. How could it be?"

Moyshe could no longer contain himself. "What went wrong between you two? She never said."

"She told me to leave," he said simply. "She told me she never wanted to see me again."

"And you listened?" said Moyshe. "You thought this was what she really wanted? Avi. You know what a hothead she is, she says things she doesn't mean fifty times a day."

Avi tried to remember. He had been humiliated. They had quarreled and she had lashed out at him, made him feel clumsy, childish, judged, made him feel unacceptable as a man.

"You can't be too sensitive with Sarah," said her father. "Both of you are too proud for your own good. You have a fight so you don't talk to each other for three years; does this make sense?"

She had made fun of him, let him see that she thought him a greenhorn, convicted him of a lack of sophistication from the height of her American pinnacle. But he had met many women since without ever finding the kinship, the instant flooding of identification he had felt the first time he saw Sarah Levy marching down the Bowery in that shirtwaist demonstration. The Americanization he had deplored in her seemed slight compared to that of girls who thought only of clothes and furniture and catching a man. He felt sorry for them: they were light and silly, they had been denied a political education until it was too late. They humored him when he talked politics, uninterested in his words, paying attention only to his response to them.

Even the movement girls did not please him. And finally, though he had grown more poised, more sure of himself as a man, he gave up, accepting loneliness as the pattern of his life and drowning himself in his political work. He assumed that someday this would change, that when he was in his thirties or forties he would meet someone new and fall in love and get married. Until then he would wait, and the waiting, the deferment, became one of the structures on which he built his life.

Now, all at once, this scaffold of privation was crumbling under the impact of Moyshe's words. Perhaps he could still have Sarah. The ground seemed to shake under his feet as he walked home, ill with anxiety. He could not know without risking himself again. Yet underneath the coldness of February he sensed the possibility of spring. An American spring.

He had been wrong to give up so easily! Was it some atavistic Russian way of thinking, this feeling that he must deny himself life to make a new life for others? It was not right to live like this. Sarah might still want to see him. He would have to find out.

The ten or fifteen girls who had been all Sarah could locate at such short notice poured up the steps of the Rivington Street flat after work, asking, "What's up? What's happened?"

Minnie Fishman, glowering, answered them. "There's going to be a shop stewards' meeting tomorrow night at the *Forward* building. I found out by accident."

"They left me out too." Ida Grabinski, another steward, spoke. "I know why. They're going to tell everybody their phony strike is over and they should go back to work."

"It shows you how brave they are." Sarah's voice was dripping with contempt. "They're afraid to let you into the meeting."

"We should go there anyway," said Ida. She was a recent immigrant from Poland, a real firebrand. "Let them learn they have to reckon with the rank and file. Demand a vote. Demand a voice."

"An equal voice," said several.

If the "Equal Voice" movement lacked a definite program, it had strong desires: more power for women, more democracy in the union, an end to the protocol, and a return to the spirit of 1909. As Ida Grabinski put it: "The union bosses us worse than the bosses. First they tell us to stay home. Then they tell us to go back. We women are the majority of the workers in the trade. We should have a say in what concerns us most."

"You'll come tomorrow night, won't you?" Minnie asked Sarah as the meeting broke up. Although Sarah had been actively organizing, she felt funny about doing so publicly because of her position in the League.

"I don't know," she answered. "I haven't been to the office in days. I keep calling in sick. They'll have a fit if they find out what I've really been doing."

Minnie shrugged. "You might as well be hanged for a sheep as a lamb, but you decide for yourself. I won't beg you." She turned away, then turned back, her face alight with mischief. "You could no more stay away than you could stay home from your own wedding!"

It was true, thought Sarah as she walked the East Side the next day, spreading the word. She couldn't stay away. She had returned to the downtown labor movement and found her youth still there waiting. She had to go where it led her.

The East Side unions routinely held meetings in the *Forward*'s beautiful new building at Rutgers Square. By eight o'clock on February 16, 1916, more than a hundred women were already standing outside the tall building, yelling and hammering on the door, which appeared to be locked. Men were hanging out of the upstairs windows, trying to figure out what was going on. Habitués of the Garden Cafeteria next door kept venturing out into the cold air to see what was happening and running back inside to report.

"It's a shame," said one old man. "They should let the girls in."

"Let us in! Let us in!" chanted the crowd.

"Dictators!" screamed Minnie Fishman. "Black Hundreds!"

"Come out and fight in the street!" yelled Ida Grabinski.

"Go home and wash your pants!" retorted a muffled voice inside.

Minnie looked around furiously and saw Sarah. "Come on," she said, taking her arm. "We'll break down the door!" She grabbed another girl on the left, while others formed a mass behind her. "Watch out, you dirty bastards, here we come!" she sang out exultantly. "A flying wedge! This is how we broke through the police lines in Riga in 1905!"

With a rush the mass of bodies slammed into the door. "Oh," groaned Sarah, as her shoulder crashed against the wood. The group fell back.

"Again!" commanded Minnie and they bashed into it once more, with the force of fifty other bodies behind their own. The impact knocked the breath out of Sarah's body and she would have fallen had she not been held up by the door in front of her and the crowd behind her. For a moment she was dazed and terrified. Then she heard the yelling and cheering and, looking up, saw that one of the hinges had come loose and was curling off the door.

"One more time and we're through!" someone yelled and then they were running at the door again, arms linked, eyes shut. There was a huge, numbing, excruciating crash and the noise of wood splintering, then the door fell slowly inward and they were clambering over the top of it as if it were a barricade. A hundred bodies behind her forced Sarah upward; Minnie was beside her, but as they reached the top Sarah was in front, climbing pell-mell, rushing, not even noticing her torn sleeve and scratched face.

A dark shape guarded the top of the stairs; he stepped forward and the light from the yellow bulb lit the handsome features of Tricker Louis Florsheim, her mortal enemy.

"You!"

His triumphant yell rode over his voice. "Now you're going to get it, you little bitch!" He hit her across the face with all his strength. She fell backward but the mass of bodies behind her held her up, still within his reach. Pulling his heavy boot back he kicked her viciously in the stomach. Sarah crumpled with a little choking cry, and the women behind her passed her carefully down the steps, still doubled over, to the arms of others outside. Tricker Louis had no time to gloat. They were upon him immediately. Furies tore at his clothes, his face, his hair; their fingernails lacerated his carefully tended flesh and shredded his clothes. He could not even

yell for help, only grunt in surprise at the suddenness and fury
of their attack. His jacket was gone, his pants ripped off his
body, his shirt torn from him, then he was down. Countless
pairs of cold, callused little hands picked him up again, mercilessly pushing, hoisting, heaving him at the upstairs door,
using him as a battering ram until the wood at the hinges
splintered and they threw themselves into the meeting,
greeted by consternation in the person of Joe Klein, who
vainly tried to bar the door with his outstretched arms.

Other women threw Tricker Louis down the stairs. He
landed in a huddled, broken lump on the icy pavement, nearly
naked under the February sky. The old men of the Garden
Cafeteria watched silently as the shirtwaist workers still outside kicked him and spat on him and called him names. Finally he pushed himself up on his knees, hunching over in
Neanderthal style to protect his genitals. Looking fearfully up
at the circle of furious eyes, he broke away with a terrified
cry and escaped into the darkness of Essex Street.

The next evening Sarah, ribs bandaged once again, face cut
and bruised, searched through the pages of the *Forward* and
the *Call* for some news of the riot. There were headlines and
stories aplenty about the strike, explaining that it was over
and that forty thousand shirtwaist workers were going back to
work; giving interviews with the union leaders and the Association spokesmen; laying out the terms of the new protocol.
But there was nothing about any disturbance.

"How come there's nothing in the paper?" she finally
asked Moyshe in bewilderment.

"I don't know," said Moyshe. "But I think I'll go find
out."

It was two hours before he came back, looking old and
tired.

"It's the same old *sha, sha, sha*," he said. "You think we
should put stuff like that in the paper, tell the whole city we
can't manage our own union, advertise our problems to the
world, be a *shandeh* to the *goyim*, give joy to the capitalists,
bring those uptown Germans down on our backs again?
What's the big deal, it should go in the paper? A flash in the
pan, a few silly little girls, a handful of anarchist trouble-
makers; they don't represent anybody; they don't know how
to do things in a civilized way; they don't understand how
unions work in America. They want to turn back the clock;
they want it to be 1909 again; don't they know about prog-

ress?'" He threw himself in his chair, glowering. "I won't even repeat some of the things they said you girls needed." His nostrils flared as he took off his boots. Then he looked up with a little grin. "Oh, and by the way, you owe the *Forward* for two doors."

The next day Sarah was fired. Mary Dreier came to the house, twisting her rings on her fingers, nervous, exasperated, uncomfortable.

"You understand we can't keep you on after this," she said. "It would be suicide for the League. We're giving you two months' severance pay. You can come to clear out your desk any time you like, or we'll send your things around with a messenger if you prefer." Mary looked at Sarah with deep reproach. "Oh, Sarah," she said. "How could you?"

Sarah looked back, trying not to show the joy bubbling up inside her. Freedom! At last.

"Really, it is a pity," Mary told Helen Marot later that day. "I don't know what the girl will do to make a living now. But I had no choice. She simply hasn't the temperament for this kind of job."

Minnie Fishman came to see Sarah that night. "Let's face it, we lost this round," she said. "After we finally got in last night, the men adjourned and all went home. How can you have an equal voice if there isn't any meeting? I couldn't even get any of the girls to talk to me, they were so depressed."

"At least we all know each other now," said Sarah. "We can keep in touch, for next time."

"What are you going to do? Are you going to get a job in a shop?"

"Do you think I could get hired? Don't forget I was blacklisted."

"It's been six years. For all you know, they've forgotten all about you. And you could always use a different name."

"If we get into the war, the men's jobs will open up," said Sarah thoughtfully, "and they won't worry about a blacklist then. They'll take any hands they can get."

BOOK SIX

The Bright Future

Rachel received her third letter from Denzell in February 1916. He sounded more elated than she'd ever heard him.

Dear Rachel,

Well, I flew combat for the first time and came back alive. In fact, I have a scalp pinned to my belt! The planes we had for practice were only decrepit old Blériots, not nearly as maneuverable as my Jenny, but once we got out of training they gave us fighting planes, silver Nieuport Scouts, and they handle like a dream. I have to laugh at the way I flew today—we'd practiced diving and darting about in training, but when I got up in the air I was so fascinated watching the battle going on below that I clean forgot to look behind me. Suddenly I heard a ping, and, lo and behold, the Boche had shot a hole right through my wing!

I can tell you I moved fast. The Boche was in a Fokker with a machine gun so I panicked and dropped a hundred feet into a cloud. Then I remembered what I'd been taught, and came up for a peek. The other fellow must have figured he'd gotten me because he was heading back to their side. I came up behind and below him until I had him in range, and then I fired. He went down in flames. It was so easy, I was surprised. Beginner's luck, I guess. Anyway, I'll watch the air instead of the ground next time.

Give the baby a kiss for me and take one yourself.
Love,
                                                    Denzell

Rachel put down the letter bleakly. He hadn't even asked
how they were. His love was just something tacked on at the
end. But at least he was still alive; thank God for small
favors. She folded the letter carefully and went upstairs to put
it with her other mementoes of her husband.

Caro was stirring in her crib. Rachel stuck her head in and
was greeted by an enthusiastic coo. At least somebody cares,
she thought ironically, and leaned over the crib, staring at her
child: three months old, fat legged, blue eyed, and bald as an
egg. Violently excited at the prospect of getting up, the baby
began to babble "ah ah ah" and pedal her arms and legs. One
of her feet caught Rachel in the mouth; she laughed adoringly
and kissed the foot, murmuring, "Silly." If Caro was the prize
she had won by getting married, it was all worth it.

No relationship Rachel had ever known was as perfect and
self-contained as this with the baby. Let Denzell go off halfway around the world; they didn't need him. She and Caro
had a perfect union. They didn't even have to worry about
money since William Sloate had had the foresight to put part
of Denzell's inheritance in trust for his issue. The trustees
were Rachel and Tish, not Denzell, and he had no say in the
disposal of Caro's income, which was enough to keep up the
household.

If only Rachel's mother could see the baby—surely her
heart would melt. Rachel stared wistfully at her child. Sarah
had told Mrs. Cohen of her new granddaughter, but the old
woman refused to visit her. "She says she'll never come as
long as you're married to a Gentile," Sarah reported.

Rachel's mouth drooped bitterly. No matter what she did,
she could not give her daughter the thing that mattered most:
a family. Sarah and the Levys were a rock to lean on but
nothing could make them relatives.

Rachel put her head next to the baby's. "Don't you worry,
pooh," she whispered. "I'm going to love you so much you
won't even know anything is missing. You won't grow up the
way I did, I promise. You'll never be lonely. We're going to
break the chain."

After Denzell left for France, Tish thought quite a bit about her relationship with Rachel. It was Rachel's vibrancy and independence that had first drawn them together; Tish was fascinated by the courage of this gorgeous, rebellious shop-girl, setting her face against her father's will. They were both New Women, sharing a desire for freedom. Tish had hoped that, in time, this affinity could become something deeper. She could use her wealth and position to open a wider sphere to Rachel, nurture her talents, provide a home where she could come to rest, a secure base against the attacks of a hostile world, in which they could love and help each other.

Tish had thought for some years about her love for women. After she was expelled from Vassar she read up on "sexual inversion," as it was called, consulting the works of sex authorities like Havelock Ellis and Krafft-Ebing. She could not recognize herself in their portraits of diseased, tormented women preying on young girls weaker than they. She wasn't like that at all. She found most men boorish and presumptuous; she resented the fact that they had power in the world and she did not; and she preferred the company of women—they were better-looking and more interesting to talk to because they said how they felt about things. She didn't love Rachel because she was wicked or crazed; she loved her because she wanted to be with her and make a life that could please and support both of them.

She had assumed that anyone who resented male authority as much as Rachel did could never fall in love with a man, placing herself in the inevitable position of subordination this entailed. Even if you rejected the status of wife, with all it implied about hearth and slippers, being with a man still made you his creature in the eyes of the world. Thingified! It was in the structure of society and no individual could help participating, even a decent fellow like Roman Zach, who quite liked intelligent women. The only way to avoid being thingified was to stay out of personal relations with men. Tish had thought Rachel understood that. Then she met Denzell, and Tish's hopes crashed with a sickening thud.

True, Denzell was not masterful in any of the usual ways. He was not brutal or overbearing. He did not expect to be waited on. He was simply not there at all; he was so different from her and Rachel that he might as well have been of another species. Rachel may have thought that such a gentle fellow would surely give her room to breathe; but just as he wasn't there to order her around, he wasn't there to help her either. Even against his mother. And now he had gone off to France, leaving Rachel stuck with a baby.

Surely any woman of dignity would have rebelled against such treatment and resolved to make a life for herself! But Rachel just drooped around the house. The metamorphosis of the girl she loved into this weary, baby-obsessed housewife was too painful for Tish to bear. Her Rachel had ceased to exist. This woman was a sister-in-law, not a comrade-at-arms. Hardest to understand was the way she, who had once been on fire for the cause of women, could be content to stay home and mind the house. Was there nothing to do in life but cook meals and diaper babies? They could certainly afford a housekeeper—but Rachel stubbornly insisted on doing the work herself. She had finally consented at least to hire an Italian nursemaid, Marguerita, but she still did all the night feedings and ran the house. Sometimes Tish thought she'd go mad if she had to stay and watch her waste herself any longer.

"I don't see how you can just sit here when the whole world is on fire," she said.

Rachel raised her head from the baby. "You forget, Tish, you had years of rest while you were young," she answered sharply. "I was working in a factory when you were at school and going to parties. Now I'm tired. I have a six-month-old baby I'm going to take care of, and the rest of the time I'm going to loaf if I want to."

She was right, of course, but it only made Tish feel worse, to get so much anger and rejection back when she was trying to help. She couldn't put off the decision any longer; it was time for her to move on. There was work to be done. The leader of the Woman's Party, Alice Paul, wrote continually from Washington, telling her how she was needed there. They were organizing a big push against President Wilson, aimed at the next election—and here she sat, mooning about. If she stayed in New York, she would be miserable; if she left, perhaps Rachel would at least miss her.

"I'm thinking of going to Washington to help with the work there," she remarked. "We're organizing a special railway train for woman suffrage, to tour the country and campaign against that hypocrite Wilson, who says he's for us and then does nothing to help. If we could make a dent in his support, it might teach them all a lesson. What do you think?"

"It sounds like fun."

Not one word of appeal to stay. "I wouldn't want to leave you all alone with Baby Caro."

"Oh, don't worry about us," said Rachel. "We've got Marguerita, and Hannah and Sarah are practically right around the corner. We'll be all right. I wouldn't keep you from this opportunity—it's just your sort of thing, on a grand scale, and you've been so restless all spring, it will do you a world of good to be up and about. I hate the idea that you would let Caro and me keep you from doing what you think is right."

Tish could hardly argue with that. And so it was settled. She left for Washington at the beginning of July.

Brave words notwithstanding, Rachel was lonely with Tish gone. Sarah was not really at her disposal. They visited often, but even though she was still unemployed, Sarah was always rushing around to meetings. "The new left wing," she explained. Like Tish, Sarah tried to draw Rachel into her activities, but she knew better than to push when she said no.

"Have you thought about what you'll do when the baby's older?" she asked on one occasion. "Do you ever still think about being a writer, Rachel?"

Rachel sighed, looking out of the window onto the summer green of the Square; the heat was entirely in tune with her own sluggish maternity.

"I'm so tired all the time," she said. "I have a little notebook where I try to scribble things, but none of them ever amount to anything. I never finish—the baby starts to cry and I go to her, or I remember an errand I have to do before dinner. Each day is full of tasks, yet when it's over, I've accomplished nothing."

"Has Caro started to sleep through the night yet?"

"She has a two o'clock feeding. Sometimes I even wait up for it, since I hate going to bed early anyway; but then I'm really tired the next day because her first feeding is at six. So my sleep comes in bits and pieces like everything else. Listen to me, I heard myself talking and I think, what have I got to *kvetch* about? Look at all the girls who have a baby and no help, or have two or three other kids to look after, or who even have to get up and go to work right after. All I do is sit here feeling sorry for myself." She could admit her unhappiness to Sarah as she never could to Tish. She shook her head. "Isn't it stupid? When I had to fight for every crumb, one little bit of rest seemed like paradise. Now I have all I want and I feel bad."

August 8, 1916—Omaha

Dear Rachel,

You think it's hot in New York, you ought to try Omaha. Thank God corsets are a thing of the past; I'm perishing in lawn. And what a circus this suffrage train is. Everywhere we stop we get out and speechify on the train steps, then fan out to meetings all over town. Exhausting. I have the sweet assignment of appealing to the local high muckamucks. Such comedy, my dear. They still think we're like little puppy dogs, to be satisfied with a pat on the head. You should hear them reassure me:

"Give the President time, he's working up to a more active stand on suffrage."

"He's got the war to deal with. Do you expect him to do everything at once?"

"I don't see what you girls have against the President. Why, he kept us out of war, didn't he? And what could be more important to a mother than to keep her sons out of war?"

I don't know how many of their minds we've changed. But I do know that by making it a campaign issue, we've done more to bring suffrage into the public eye than anyone has in twenty years. The Democrats never wanted to deal with it; they wanted to run their campaign on the war alone. We made that impossible. This in itself is a victory—we've reached so many new people, we've had a hearing in so many little places where we were only a joke before. If nothing else, that'll show them.

Have you heard from Denzell lately?

Love, Tish

The wind's moan had been ominous all day, whipping the branches of the trees in the Square and sending a chill through the room. Rachel lay upon the sofa, shivering, and the telegram dropped from her fingers. So he was dead. He had been

away only a few months and now he was dead. In a way, it
was what he'd wanted. He had flown away from all of them
like a bird let out of its cage; he'd loved the air and the air
had claimed him.

How different life was from the way you planned it. She
remembered the day in the Metropolitan Museum when
they'd walked, the three of them, through room after room of
paintings; she remembered the excitement that had built inside her until she thought she'd explode; she remembered sitting opposite him in the restaurant, looking at his blue eyes,
his golden hair, like one struck dumb. The goose girl and the
prince. She remembered when he told her he loved her, blurt-
ing it out on that little airfield after her first flight, and how
she'd run and he'd chased her across the landing strip and
caught her in his arms.

It was like watching a movie of someone else's life: the
handsome blond flier, the foreign-looking girl, poorly dressed
but pretty—such stereotypes, she thought. She couldn't feel a
thing except the pounding of her heart and the dryness in her
throat. She could sense the grief building inside her, and the
anger, the torment, the rage of her loss, the fear of the future,
the acknowledgment of loneliness, but none of it meant anything yet.

Denzell was fixed now, pinned down. He couldn't change
anymore. She could go back in her mind to the early days and
remember him as he had been when he loved her, without
having to fear what he'd do next. She could forget their battles about the war, forget his childish irresponsibility and her
fear that he would use all the money up in some grotesque
way, leaving her and Caro penniless in a tenement on Norfolk
Street.

She would have to let Tish know. The Woman's Party in
Washington would be able to find her. She would call them
long distance. Tish would come back for the funeral, after
they got the body, but she probably wouldn't stay in New
York long. She was so edgy these days, so restless. It wasn't
like the way it used to be between them.

Imagine him dying like that, in a war not even his own. He
just couldn't wait. Now she had no one.

Except the baby.

And sooner or later, she suddenly knew with distant clarity, she would have her mother again. With Denzell gone, she

would come to visit. She watched that movie too; the shabby old woman creeping up the stairs, knocking timidly on the door, waiting furtively. The pretty girl opening the door. The old woman huddling away from the light, clutching her purse, looking up at the girl. The light on her face. The girl's eyes dilating. Her mouth opening joyfully. Subtitle: "Mother!" They run to each other's arms. Fade. The end.

She would never have a real family, even if her mother did consent to see her. But she did have Caro. She would go up to her room and lie near her, as she often did when she was lonely. Caro would pull her through.

Christmas Day, 1916

Dear Rachel,

I did feel like a pig leaving you and Caro so soon after the funeral, especially with Christmas around the corner. I hope the holidays weren't too grim—if you knew how often my thoughts were with you! But duty called. We sent three hundred women to visit the President today. Some of the more devout among us thought the holiday might soften his heart—that would have been a miracle indeed; you should see the man, stiff and starched as a Congregationalist minister greeting the ladies of the parish. Would you believe he said he had done all he could for suffrage? If it were up to him, of course, etc., but the Democrats wouldn't let him, so we should go and convert them and leave him alone. Here's a man who's shown himself capable of pushing his party any way he likes on the war and a hundred other questions, but is absolutely powerless to shift the legislators one tiny inch on woman suffrage! What rubbish!

We came back to headquarters so angry we didn't know which way to look. We've organized parade after parade; we've had bigger and more influential delegations to see him each time; and none of it has made any difference. We have to find some new tactic, we said, something that will bring our cause before the press and the public, not to mention Mr. Wilson, every minute of the day. Then Harriot Stanton Blatch had the most wonderful idea. She said we should stand in front of the White House gates like sentinels with banners, all day, every day, and the banners will say, "What will you do,

Mr. President, for one-half the people of this nation?''
We will be silent sentinels, sentinels of liberty, sentinels
of self-government—I love it! We were all so excited we
raised a thousand dollars to begin right then and there,
and everyone signed up to volunteer on a rota.

I daresay all hell will break loose now.

Love, Tish

One day about a month after Denzell's funeral, the doorbell
rang and Rachel went to answer it. A handsome, gypsyish
man stood outside.

"Hello," he said. "Is Tish in?"

"Tish isn't here anymore. Who are you?"

"My name is Roman Zach."

"The artist," said Rachel, relieved. "She's told me all
about you. I'm her sister-in-law, Rachel. Would you care for
a cup of tea?"

They sat at the little table overlooking Washington Square
while Rachel rattled on about Tish's suffrage work, her own
regrets that she couldn't do more because of the baby, her
feelings about the war and her widowhood, and her hopes that
the United States would stay neutral. After a spate of talk, she
stopped abruptly.

"How I am chattering," she said with a little laugh. "I
don't think I've talked this much in a week. You're too good
a listener."

"But I'm interested," he protested. "Tish and I used to be
very close but I haven't seen her in a long time and was
wanting to be caught up on all this news."

Rachel thought him very attractive. Tish was always so
absorbed in her suffrage work that Rachel hadn't known she
had time for men. He stayed a long time for a first call, and
when he asked if he might come again, she eagerly consented.

The next time he visited, he brought a little drawing book
and some charcoal pencils with him, and asked if he might
sketch her and the baby. Rachel thought his drawings were
wonderfully lifelike and was pleased when he gave her one.
They walked in the Square with Caro, and he invited her to
his studio for tea the next week.

"To be perfectly frank," he said, "I have an ulterior mo-
tive. I'm hoping you will pose for me. I would like to try a

really large canvas of you silhouetted against my window. Do you have a dark dress you could wear?"

His studio was in a horrible run-down warehouse on Lafayette Street, very unprepossessing from the outside, but inside it was spacious, if not terribly tidy, and there were paintings all around. She stood like a statue in the window, looking out on the street below, thinking her own thoughts. He spent weeks doing one painting after another, and Rachel came to love these quiet afternoons in Roman Zach's studio, where she returned to pose again and again, with the baby off safe with Marguerita. Standing in the winter sunlight that poured through the window, she could stop worrying about Denzell and the future, stop thinking of the baby and chores, and simply sink into herself like a pool. He marveled at how long she could hold a pose.

"You're remarkable," he said. "I've never had a model who could stay still so long. Most people start to shift about or want to talk."

She smiled at him slowly, without speaking. He did not guess at the restlessness at the core of her. Men saw what they wanted to.

Roman complimented her all the time, with unusual skill. Men often exclaimed over her looks and she played along without much interest. But Roman had an artist's eye. He would describe her to herself in the most precise detail: the curve of her nostril, the color of her hair, the angle of her leg under her silk dress. Through him she began to see herself as she never had before, appreciating her own beauty. This was a great gift he gave her.

But when she looked at his paintings she saw nothing of herself, only blotches of color and odd geometric shapes. She didn't see why he needed a model at all.

"Why do you paint like that?" she said. "That's not how I look."

"I'm painting how you are to me, not just how you look," he said. "The window, the light outside, the forms in the room, the way I feel about all them and you."

Rachel looked hard at the painting he was working on. She could recognize the window in the square of moving dashes near the center of the canvas. The shape near it had some relation to her own, but she had no idea what to make of the odd squiggles and geometric patches surrounding it.

"I don't understand painting," she said, discouraged. "I like to look but I never know what to think. When Tish used to take me to the Metropolitan Museum, I'd be tongue-tied. I was always afraid I'd say the wrong thing." He smiled encouragingly. "I guess I only understand words and sounds," she went on, afraid he'd think her an awful fool. "My eye isn't educated, only my ear, because I'm Jewish. No graven images, you know. But I can remember whole passages of Shakespeare just by the way they sound."

"Recite," he suggested. There was an ironic twist to his mouth and he had begun to work on his canvas again.

She resumed her pose by the window, almost whispering the lines:

> How sweet the moonlight sleeps upon this bank!
> Here will we sit and let the sounds of music
> Creep in our ears; soft stillness and the night
> Become the touches of sweet harmony.
> Sit, Jessica. Look how the floor of heaven
> Is thick inlaid with patines of bright gold;
> There's not the smallest orb which thou behold'st
> But in his motion like an angel sings,
> Still quiring to the young-ey'd cherubins;
> Such harmony is in immortal souls,
> But whilst this muddy vesture of decay
> Doth grossly close it in, we cannot hear it.

"What's that?" said Roman.

"Shakespeare," she said. *The Merchant of Venice.* I always feel like the girl in it, Jessica. She's a Jewish girl who runs away with a Gentile and breaks her father's heart." She peeked at him to see if he would follow up this opening, but he said nothing, painting intently and not even looking at her. Rachel sighed. He was clearly more interested in his work than in her life. "I'd give my right arm to write like that," she blurted, annoyed with herself for caring so much about what he thought.

"Why don't you?" said Roman.

"I'm afraid of how angry I get," she said. "If I wrote what I wanted to, people wouldn't like me anymore. When I think of writing about families—that's what I'd have to—the bitterness rises up in me with such force I'm afraid it could destroy the world. And me too," she ended lamely.

He put down his brush and looked at her. "It couldn't," he said firmly. "Believe me. I know. But why are you so angry? If I were, it would be one thing, but you're young, beautiful, you have all the money you need. You could do whatever you want."

Her voice trembled. "For years I had to worry about how I would get through every day. Now I have the time to look back over my life and it breaks my heart, but I'm afraid to write. I can't write about what I feel but I can't write about anything else either, the way I used to for the *Forward*. I can't be flip anymore. So I just don't do anything." She looked at him appealingly, fearful of what he would say. "You're a real artist," she said. "You couldn't understand someone like me."

He shrugged. "If you need to write, you will, sooner or later. If not, it doesn't matter. You didn't really need to."

The Latvian Socialist Federation had called a meeting to discuss the war, a subject on everyone's mind by the middle of 1916. Would the United States be drawn into the conflict? Sarah was late but finally spied an empty seat near the front of the crowded hall. Threading her way down the narrow aisle, she glanced up at the stage and froze. A young man she didn't know was speaking. Behind him were ranged the usual notables: Morris Hillquit; Ab Cahan; and, beside them, Avi Spector. As his dark eyes met hers, a sick excitement began to churn in her stomach. She sat down numbly, still staring at him, until it was his turn to speak and he came forward to the podium.

He seemed nervous and kept looking at her, but grew more confident as he went on, explaining why the United States should stay out of the war.

"They say this is a war to save democracy. In fact, it is an imperialist war for raw materials and control of markets. American banks in foreign countries are forerunners of U.S. troops in the same way that the Spanish missionaries of old paved the way for the conquistadores. Look at our invasion of Haiti, of the Dominican Republic, of Puerto Rico. Look at the army Wilson has sent to crush the Mexican Revolution.

"Imperialism also has a domestic face: strikes crushed by force, brutal police, reactionary judges, the vast unemployment, and the decreasing power of our wages. Our rulers want to squeeze as much profit from our labor power as they could in a colonial situation. For our own sake we must join with the workers in all countries to try to stop the development of imperialism in the U.S."

Watching Avi as he spoke, Sarah was struck by the way he had matured. He was a man now, not a boy. What must he think of her? Did he hate her, or merely remember her with amused condescension as a silly girl from his past? He was clearly an important figure in the left-wing movement. No doubt there were plenty of women crowding around him, eager to offer themselves in one way or another. The thought made her sick. She was glad she was sitting near the aisle so she could get out quickly and not run any risk of bumping into him.

The meeting ended in a disorganized way with people drifting toward the door. By the time Sarah got up, the passageway was clogged. She fought her way to the cold dark air outside, paused a moment on the steps for breath, then plunged into the night in her haste to get away. She was halfway down the block when she heard his voice.

"Sarah! Sarah Levy!"

She turned, confused. Avi raced up, nearly slipping on the ice. He stopped, panting for breath, looking totally unlike the assured speaker of an hour before.

"Your speech was wonderful," Sarah said quickly. Her eyes shone up at him.

"You liked it? Did you agree with it?"

She nodded slowly. "I think so."

"You're not sure?" he pressed, pell-mell. "We could discuss it. I could show you articles from Europe. I have lots of articles."

She didn't say anything.

"I would value your opinion highly," he continued.

"You would?" She was astonished. "Why?"

"You know so much about America," he said simply.

She shook her head. "Every time I think I know something, it changes."

She sounded so sad that his heart went out to her and he forgot his nervousness. "How are you, Sarah?" he asked softly. "Tell me, are you all right?"

She tried to smile and say she was fine, but to her horror, no words came out. She stared up at him bleakly.

"I lost my job," she whispered. "The union has gone to hell. I don't know what I should do next."

"Sarah." His voice faltered. With unsteady hands he reached out and gripped her shoulders, then let them drop, frightened at his own temerity. "Sarah. I would like to hear about all this, as a friend who is concerned for you."

She stared into his eyes until she swayed; it was impossible to look away. The full desolation of the last year suddenly descended upon her. "Oh, Avi," she cried, "I've missed you so!"

His smile split his face like a crack of lightning. Then he took her arm and they walked home together, not even feeling the cold.

A month after Avi and Sarah met again, his mother invited her to dinner. His sister Gittel was out for the evening and at nine o'clock, Mrs. Spector vanished into her bedroom. The two were alone. They sat rather stiffly on the sofa, examining an enormous lot of books, pamphlets, and newspaper clippings piled on the floor next to Avi's left foot. He had been accumulating them for the last three years.

Sarah looked at them all dutifully, though her attention waxed and waned. She was quite interested in the ones about imperialism and the labor movement, and, in other company, might have pored over them with animation. At the moment, she would have been just as interested in a collection of ears of corn or ornamental buttons, as long as they were his; she looked at the pamphlets to please him, she looked because she needed him, she looked because he was one of the three people in the world to whom she might be able to open her heart—and Rachel was lost already, and her father was not enough, so that left only him. As she read, she examined him furtively out of the corners of her eyes, wondering what he thought of her. How did he feel about their sudden reunion? Was there some future for them together, or was his interest of a purely comradely and friendly nature?

Avi was delighted with himself and with the world. Now he knew he had changed in the last three years; how confidently he was able to talk to her, to fill her in on things, to show her his treasures. It was as he had hoped; he was no longer a greenhorn, staring diffidently around, groping for words. He was becoming a personage in left-wing circles,

admired for the way his mind could cut through to the heart
of a complex question. Tonight was a vindication of his hope
that success in that area could spread into others. For wasn't
he sitting here next to Sarah Levy, without even trembling
most of the time, able to focus his thoughts and marshal his
arguments without stammering? And wasn't she listening
with interest, carrying on a civilized conversation, not
glowering at him or bursting out, not angry with him for reasons he could not understand? Apparently they both had
changed.

She was looking down at a clipping now, her face obscured
by her hair. Peering under the waves, he was astonished to
see a tear on her cheek. A feeling of dread seized him like a
toothache. Perhaps she was not as happy as he was that they
were back together again. As he watched, the tear fell to her
knee and she rubbed it into the cloth of her skirt with one
finger. His heart sinking, he put a hand on her shoulder.

"Sarah?" he said. His voice was gentle, concerned. "Is
something wrong?"

She looked up. Her eyes were swimming. "I'm so embarrassed," she said. "I keep thinking of how terrible I was to
you. I'm surprised you don't hate me."

"Don't be silly," he said, with a sigh of relief. "Of course
I don't hate you." She gave a little sob. Her misery made
him forget his self-consciousness; he put his arm around her
and wiped a tear from her cheek. "It's so good to be with you
again," he mumbled, "such good friends."

It only made her cry more. He didn't know what to do to
make her stop. Her body shook with sobs. He stroked her fine
hair but it didn't seem to help. She whispered something he
couldn't hear, something about "friends." What was this all
about?

"I don't understand what's the matter," he said plain-
tively. "I was so happy. I hoped maybe you were too. I was
thinking how nice it was to sit here with you and wondering
whether we should get married and now you won't stop crying and I don't even know what's wrong."

She stopped crying. "What?"

"I was so happy to be with you," he repeated. "I was
thinking we should get married."

She raised her head slowly and looked at him. Her face

was red and wet. She took out a handkerchief and blew her nose. She wiped her eyes. She smiled brilliantly. "Really?"

"Of course," he said. "You know that's what I always wanted."

Her eyes were round and wondering, still pink, as she studied his face, looking for signs. "You really haven't changed?" she whispered, not daring to believe it. "You still feel the same way after all these years?"

"Of course," he said with a little laugh, not understanding the problem. "Why would I change?"

Her smile grew broader and at the same time she began to sniff again, then burrowed into his arms. Her obvious vulnerability, his own new feelings of strength, and the reversal of their positions made the sexual barriers he had always felt simply vanish, at least for the moment. He thought how much simpler things became when you were older, then bent his head and began to kiss her.

She trembled beneath his kisses, responding joyfully, smiling and laughing a little, turning her head breathlessly, whispering to him as he kissed her face and neck with increasing passion. She felt none of the reserve she had with Joe Klein. Her smell, her whispers, intoxicated him. He felt capable of anything as he kissed her lips, her eyes, her hair, her neck, feeling under the high collar of her shirtwaist, even unbuttoning the top button and then the second button so he could kiss the tiny hollow at the base of her throat. She responded with a thirsty, grateful warmth, though not wanting him to think her too experienced, not wanting to have to tell him about Joe Klein. He knew nothing of these fears. Bending over her on the sofa, wanting more and more to feel her under his body, he kissed her with increasing desire, and when his left foot kicked over the pile of pamphlets and books, he did not even notice.

A few weeks later, Avi and Sarah sat in his living room trying to make a budget, his savings book in front of them.

"There's no way I can save more than three dollars a month," he said. "Often I can't save that. I have to support my mother, and Gittel's in school. I can't do it."

"Then we'll never be able to get our own apartment," said Sarah. "We might as well forget about getting engaged.

What's the use of being engaged if you can't afford to get married?"

"We could live here?" he suggested doubtfully.

"And kick your mother out of the bedroom? No thanks, I want my own place. But even if we only got two rooms, it would be six or eight dollars a month. Not to mention furniture. We can't do it."

"Sarah," he said, "why don't you get a job? I don't think the man should be the only one earning money, at least until the children come. There's too much inequality in a marriage if only one has money."

Sarah looked miserably at the floor. "I've been out of the shop almost seven years. I think I've gotten soft."

"Are you afraid?" he asked. "Is it the hours, the filth, the money, the lack of time for yourself? Tell me."

"Let's face it. The last few years have been easy," she said. "As far as work goes anyhow. But the real problem isn't the work. It's that I'm not clear anymore."

"Clear about what?"

"Before, when I was working in shirtwaist, it wasn't just making a living. I was building the union. It was all I cared about. I thought when we got a union we'd have heaven on earth."

"And now?"

She shook her head hopelessly. "I still wish we could make it better. If we could run it—but we aren't strong enough. I'm not like Minnie; I don't say we should smash it and start over. We need a union, even if it's not perfect. But I wish it was different. I wish that somewhere in our lives there could be something we really controlled, that didn't just represent us, but *was* us." Her voice was wistful. "Why can't the union be better than the rest of life?"

"Sometimes I worry about that with revolution."

She looked at him in surprise. "You?" she said.

He shrugged. "I look at our ideals. So fine. Then I look at us, and I think: Somebody can bring these ideals to life but are we the ones? And I wonder, what if by some miracle we actually made a revolution—maybe not here, but in Russia. What then? We would still be us, the same people, formed under Czarism, with all our habits of backbiting and factionalism and *mishegas* as well as our high ideals. Would we be changed overnight into some other kind of person?''

"We were during the strike," said Sarah. "People really were."

"Yes, during the strike. But after—?"

"Ah," said Sarah. "After. I see. What would happen then?"

"I don't know for sure. I have no crystal ball. But I think it might be what you said, that things would go back to everyday life and it might take more than a few years to make it beautiful. We might not be able to do it at all."

"We might not." She gave him a little smile. "But Avi— our children!"

He laughed. "What children? We don't even have the money to get married."

She sighed, shaking her head at him. "Okay, you win. For you, I'll get a job."

He touched her lips with his finger. "Let's go sit on the sofa," he said softly.

She eyed him mockingly. "You men," she said. "You only think of one thing."

He laughed. "That's me," he said, "a hopeless sensualist."

For both of them their physical contact, which had become increasingly passionate though never overstepping the bounds of propriety, was magical. It was like a clear zone which their other disappointments and worries could not reach. Sometimes that worried Sarah.

"Can we really have this?" she whispered. "It's so nice."

He grinned, holding her. "I think so," he said. "We won't have all we want from life but I think we can have this. A little taste of the future society, to keep us going, Sarah."

II

Ruby didn't have to work Saturdays and liked to sleep late, then lie around the house for the rest of the morning noshing, gossiping with her mother, and reading the women's magazines.

"Will you look at this," she said, leafing through the January 1917 *Vogue*. "Brassiere ads all over the place. Helen of Troy knew what they were doing when they bought that patent. I bet they're laughing all the way to the bank now. We shouldn't have sold it."

Hannah shrugged. "We needed the money," she said. "Beggars can't be choosers." She was counting her change, laying it out on the table in neat little stacks of pennies, nickels, dimes, quarters.

"Yeah, but think if we could've held on to it," dreamed Ruby. "Listen to this, Ma. 'You will look so much better when you have discarded the old-fashioned corset cover and selected in its place a brassiere suited to your particular kind of figure.' That's just what we said in 1914."

She glanced at her mother for sympathy. But Hannah wasn't listening. She was figuring in her head, staring at the little piles of coins and whispering numbers to herself. Ruby turned back to her *Vogue*.

"I wonder if the new Paris models are going to make it through the U-boats," she said idly. "There's a war on, you know. That's what everybody says uptown, 'There's a war on, you know.' They're all so worried about the French models. Huh. I wish all those boats would sink to the bottom of

the Atlantic Ocean, then maybe an American designer would
have a chance." She got up and began to rummage in the
cupboard at the thought. "Where did you put the bread,
Ma?"

"There isn't any."

Ruby gave a disbelieving chuckle. "What do you mean,
there isn't any?" she said. "There's always bread."

"My money won't reach," said Hannah in a thin voice. "I
squeeze every penny until it screams but it won't reach."

"I don't understand," said Ruby, sitting down across from
her mother. "What's the matter?"

"What's the matter!" Hannah exploded. "You just said it.
There's a war on, you know. In your uptown world have
prices stayed the same?"

Ruby thought it over. "No," she said. "Lunch has gone
up a dime. Makeup is higher. Lots of things are going up.
Even *Vogue* is going to cost more. I just wasn't thinking."

"You just weren't thinking," mimicked Hannah savagely.
"Well, I think! Every day I go to the market and I think, my
God, how am I going to feed my family? Everything's gone
crazy, up and up, not just a penny a time any more but huge
jumps! Last month potatoes were two cents a pound, now
they're seven. And bread. In one month bread has gone from
seven to twelve cents a pound! The peddlers can't get enough
stock because the farmers are sending it all overseas. People
are speculating, driving up the prices. Menachem the Fish
says even his prices have doubled and half the time he can't
get."

"We haven't had any meat lately either," said Ruby,
"come to think of it."

"Forget meat," cried Hannah. "With you and your father
both working, you'd think we could have meat a couple of
times a week, but I'm lucky to get soup bones. Even chicken
livers I have to pay for these days. A couple of months ago
they gave them away. And the price of chicken! Last month it
was twenty-two cents, then twenty-five, and now that *goniff*
across the street is charging twenty-eight, and what he asks
today the rest will ask tomorrow.

"It used to be I could get meat cheaper than his on the next
block," she went on, nearly weeping with frustration. "Then
I started having to look around, but still, if I walked all over
the place till I found a peddler I could bargain down, I could

find cheaper. But no more! All over it's the same story. What he charges, they all charge."

Ruby was shaken by her mother's distress. "Ma, if worse comes to worse, I've still got my patent money in the bank," she said. "Take it if you need it."

Hannah raised her face, horrified. "I'll cut off my right arm first. That money is for emergencies, for medical, God forbid. Starving is not an emergency," she said with a bitter laugh. "Isn't everybody else on the block starving too?"

All over the neighborhood things were the same; nobody could make ends meet because of the rate of inflation. The price of potatoes and onions was clearly due to the war: profiteers were shipping them to Europe, where people were starving and would pay anything. But what was driving up the price of meat? Traffic at the docks was so tied up that Hannah had heard there was a whole trainload of meat sitting in Chicago rotting, waiting to be shipped out.

Nobody could understand it, except for little Yakhne Breynes, only fifteen years old but such a genius at adding and subtracting that Garfinkle the butcher had hired her to do his books, after school. One Saturday in February she and her mother burst into the Levy apartment.

"Listen to Yakhne," said Yetta Breynes. "She's found something out."

Her story was a strange one. The day before, a delegation of meat peddlers came to the butcher shop. Garfinkle and Solly Fein took them into the back room but forgot to shut the adjoining door. As little Yakhne crept closer, overcome by curiosity, she heard one of the peddlers beg Garfinkle to get the wholesalers to lower their prices—as if he had the power to control meat prices on the East Side.

"We know you're in good with the wholesalers," said the peddler. "We know you tell them how high they can make their prices. But you told them wrong on chicken. People can't pay so much. We have chicken left at the end of the day like we never had."

"The wholesalers charge what the traffic will bear," said Garfinkle. But the peddlers did not seem to believe him. They continued to protest until he finally kicked them out of the store.

Yakhne's curiosity was stimulated by what she had heard. She took the next opportunity to go through the books, where she found a number of peculiar entries, seeming to indicate that the wholesalers were paying Garfinkle instead of the other way around. "Jacob Stampfels, wholesale butcher, $100. Oscar Rubino, $60."

"But I don't understand what they're paying him for," said Yakhne with a mystified air.

"It must be his cut on some deal," said Ruby, whose years in the garment industry had made her wise in the ways of business. "Like for fixing the prices and keeping the peddlers in line. Or maybe he controls distribution, so they can't get their meat into the warehouse without his say-so."

"I know, I know!" jabbered Yakhne excitedly. "I just figured it out! It's Tricker Louis, their nephew, the one who beat Sarah up. He's back! He's been staying upstairs from the shop, not going outside except at night! Rosalie told me he's got connections with the teamsters who carry the meat. He must have fixed it so the wholesalers can't get their meat unless they do what he says!"

Ruby twitched as she always did when she heard Tricker's name. "That figures. He takes a cut, the Garfinkles take a cut, the teamsters take a cut—no wonder prices have gone up! They couldn't get away with it except for the war. Prices on everything else are so high it looks natural."

Hannah's mouth was working as it did when she was in a passion. "The bastards! Here I've been worrying myself half to death about how to feed my family so Garfinkle could get rich! I'll kill him, I'll kill that Solly Fein and his miserable relatives."

Yetta Breynes slammed her hands down on the table and stood up. "Come on, Hannah," she said. "We have things to do. Let's go talk to the neighbors."

There was a crash in the street below. Hannah stuck her head out of the window, then, in one fluid motion, stripped off her apron and ran for the door. So did all the other women in the building, clattering down the stairs like bricks falling in their eagerness to reach the street.

A riot had begun outside.

Hannah never found out for sure who pushed over the first cart on Rivington Street that twentieth day of February 1917. Some said it was the anarchist girl, Minnie Fishman, trying to make trouble. Others attributed it to a stranger, a child, an

agitator, a gypsy; but all agreed the price of meat was the
cause. The peddlers had raised their prices again, and this
time people would not stand for it. Food riots had started the
day before in Brownsville and Williamsburg, where the police had fought crowds of mothers and children for hours
without being able to subdue them. Moreover, Hannah and
Yetta Breynes had talked to most of the block about Garfinkle's price-fixing. Word had spread. By the time Hannah
got downstairs, all the pushcarts in Rivington Street were top-
pling and a general free-for-all had broken out, with women
pouring into the street from all sides to attack the peddlers
with brooms and rolled-up shopping bags.

"What are you telling me, twenty-five cents a pound for
chicken!" screamed Yetta Breynes.

"*Goniff! Goslin!* You've been cheating me for twenty
years!"

Soon the onion and potato peddlers, the bread and pickle
vendors, were caught up in the melee. Minnie Fishman tied
her black shawl to a stick and stood on one of the overturned
pushcarts yelling, "Hooray for anarchy, the black flag
forever!"

"We should go to the Mayor!" cried Mrs. Ashkenazi from
across the street. "We should go down on our hands and
knees and beg him to make the prices lower! That's how they
do things in America; they go to City Hall!"

"No, no, we should go to the *Forward,*" cried Yetta
Breynes, a loyal reader. "We should ask Ab Cahan what to
do."

After an hour of argument and rampaging around, several
hundred women surged out of Rivington Street down Essex,
to be joined along the way by others as angry and frightened
as they until there were at least a thousand of them. Every
housewife on the East Side was out in the street that cold
Wednesday morning, looking desperately for a way to feed
her family. But when they reached the *Forward* building, the
women found little help. Ab Cahan advised them not to be
violent and offered them the use of the *Forward* hall for a
protest meeting that night. Dispirited, they drifted into
Rutgers Square, waiting for something to happen.

Minnie Fishman, never one to pass up an opportunity, got
up on a park bench. "People, hear my story," she cried. "I
was on my way to work this morning when I saw what was

going on and how could I resist helping, since I earn only ten
dollars a week sewing? My family is starving. My brother is
an invalid and can't work. On my ten dollars a week I support
him and my mother besides myself. We live in a two-room
apartment on Delancey Street. I haven't looked an egg in the
face for months. Potatoes are too rich for our blood. We tried
to save money by concentrating on cabbage, but so did everybody else, and now even cabbage is twenty cents a pound.
How will we live?"

There were cries from the crowd: "Bread! We need bread
for our children! What are we going to do?"

"Two things we need: relief and kerosene! The Mayor has
to buy food and distribute it for relief! And we have to go
after these peddlers and teach them a lesson—not only turn
over their carts but pour kerosene on them! That'll show them
who they're dealing with."

"You stop that kind of talk, Minnie Fishman," yelled Mrs.
Ashkenazi, getting up on another park bench. "We're Americans. We don't have to listen to your crazy ideas. What we
need is a petition; we all sign a paper saying we are starving
and send two or three ladies in to give it to the Mayor."

Hannah listened to these suggestions with interest, eager to
do anything that would help. Most of the crowd were of a like
mind, and without waiting for a consensus to be reached,
began to pour out of Rutgers Square down Division Street,
toward City Hall.

When they got there, they found the great iron gates barred
against them. The Mayor wasn't in, a policeman told them
nervously. They should go home. No delegation would be
admitted. The women went wild at the sight of those massive,
almost European gates. They threw themselves against the
bars. They stretched their hands through them imploringly,
crying, "Feed our children!" They shook the bars, screaming, "We want food!" in Yiddish. Many had tears streaming
down their cheeks. Others held babies or clutched toddlers'
hands. Politically inexperienced, not understanding how it
was possible to go hungry in the land of plenty, they had
assumed the Mayor would help them. They had dreamed he
would pass out bread on the spot. They were cruelly disappointed.

"What can we do?" they cried. "Bread! We need bread!"

The policeman told them that if they chose a delegation of

five to come back tomorrow, he would make sure they got in
to see the Mayor. Bella Ashkenazi was nominated, so was
Minnie Fishman; Mrs. Jacob Panken, wife of the well-known
socialist lawyer, was added, along with a rabbi's wife, Mrs.
Teitlebaum. Then, much to her surprise, Hannah heard her
own name being called out. "Mrs. Levy! Hannah Levy!"

"Me?" she said in astonishment.

"Why not?" said Yetta Breynes. "Aren't you Sarah
Levy's mother? You should know all about organizing."

A lady Hannah recognized from the market added, "From
such a family you must have ideas."

To her own amazement, Hannah heard herself open her
mouth and say firmly, "Yes, I do have ideas."

"What are they?" yelled Minnie.

"Well," said Hannah nervously, trying to remember to
speak up, "I think we should go around and tell all the ladies
not to buy onions or potatoes. Or chicken on *Shabbos*.
Today's Wednesday. By *Shabbos* we should have all the
streets fixed so nobody buys these things. That will show
them what we do when they charge such robbery prices."

"Boycott!" yelled someone. "Nobody buys!"

There was such enthusiasm for the proposal that Hannah
did not even go home to make dinner; she was too busy going
from building to building, explaining the riot, the boycott,
and the meeting at the *Forward*. Sarah, Ruby, and Moyshe
sat for an hour in the cold kitchen, bewildered and alarmed,
until Yakhne Breynes ran upstairs with the news. Then they
put on their coats and followed her down to Rutgers Square.

So vast was the mob of women and children assembled in
front of the *Forward* building that it was all they could do to
get into the hall. Bodies were jammed against bodies like rush
hour on the Elevated. Children pushed and screamed underfoot. And a fight for control of the platform was in full swing.
The men from the *Forward* and other leaders of the Jewish
socialist movement plainly assumed that since the meeting
was in their hall, they would run it. They held the stage,
surveying the crowd of women below who had other ideas.
Every time Ab Cahan or Benjamin Feigenbaum or Jacob Panken began to speak, there were boos and shrieks from the
audience. "Let us speak! This is our meeting! We called this
meeting, not you." Mrs. Ashkenazi kept trying to climb up

on the platform, only to be politely pushed off by various
young men.

Finally, accompanied on one side by Hannah Levy and on
the other by Minnie Fishman, Mrs. Ashkenazi mounted the
platform. Bowing to the inevitable, Cahan and the others fell
back. She lost no time in taking advantage of her position.

"You dirty socialists, don't you try to shut my mouth,"
she began irrepressibly. "We don't want to hear from you,
we only want your hall."

Hannah thought this lacked something of the spirit of unity
demanded by the occasion. Others agreed and yelling broke
out all over again. The hall became more and more riotous,
with Jacob Panken and Mrs. Ashkenazi screaming at each
other, until Hannah herself had to step forward and separate
them as if they were her children.

"Behave yourselves, were you born in a barn? Mrs. Ashkenazi, be polite, you're a guest here. Mr. Panken, you'll get
your chance to talk later. Wait your turn and don't be so
pushy."

"Was that Mama?" quavered Ruby, not completely sure
who it had been since they were so far back they could hardly
see.

Sarah blinked. "I think so," she said in amazement.

Mrs. Ashkenazi resumed her oration. "Ladies and people,
we don't want any trouble here. We aren't a bunch of green-
horns who don't know how to act. All we want is food. We
are starving. But we don't need to have any riots about it.
The Mayor has to make the prices go down. He can do it.
Simple. We go to him and tell him, We're not an organization, we're not socialists, we don't want to make any problems. We're just housewives who want the prices should go
down please and thank you very much."

"You are a traitor to your class," called a voice from the
audience.

"Kerosene!" yelled Minnie Fishman.

Jacob Panken stood next to Hannah, clearing his throat like
the voice of doom. He elbowed her in the ribs.

"Kerosene is out of the question," he said firmly. "Burning food is nothing but wanton destruction. The working
class, which creates all value, does not destroy the product of
its own labor. This is senseless. It will only mean less food in

the neighborhood." There were shouts of "Coward!" and "That's right!" but he held up his hand for silence.

"What we need is organization, not sabotage. We must fight, yes, but fight in an orderly manner. I am here to pledge the help of the Hebrew trade unions in getting you women organized, and I personally will head the squad of lawyers to handle your cases if, God forbid, there should be any arrests." Cheers and applause met this offer.

"The capitalists, not the peddlers, are the ones to blame for this food shortage," he continued, "the wholesalers, the beef trust, the railroad magnates, and the profiteers. J.P. Morgan and Company are holding thousands of tons of beef for shipment to Europe—while we go hungry! What we need is a huge, well-organized demonstration of women and children to march on Morgan's office!" The hall went wild. "And on Fifth Avenue too we should march! The Governor will be there on Sunday!" he yelled. "Let the uptowners see how we suffer!"

In no time a committee was set up. Cahan announced that the *Forward* would donate office space on its ninth floor. The Socialist Party had clearly carried the day. As the meeting began to disperse, Hannah stood in the middle of the stage, alone now; the other speakers had left, and she didn't know whether to say anything or not. The boycott was weighing on her mind. Slowly, seeing her there, the crowd grew silent again.

She shifted from one foot to another, red-faced, not knowing how to begin or what to say, before suddenly bursting out in an embarrassed way, "Demonstrations, the Mayor, kerosene, these are all okay by me but will they bring down prices? At my house we have one dollar a day for food, not counting lunches out; the rest goes for rent, gas, coal, clothes, carfare. I can't do it. Prices are too high. I have here a piece of paper with the prices from November and from this week. Before, two pounds of onions were six cents. Now, forty cents."

"A *shandeh!*" called a woman in the audience.

"Cabbage is up from two cents to twenty! Bread, God help us, bread is thirty-seven cents a day!"

"What are we going to do?" wailed a voice in the back. "How will we feed our children?"

"We have to boycott!" said Hannah. "Demonstrate too, but don't forget the boycott! Tell your friends no onions, no potatoes, no chicken on *Shabbos*. Nobody buys till the prices go down! If nobody buys, then who can sell? The peddlers say they're poor like us, they're on our side. Okay, let them prove it; let them join the boycott. One hundred percent boycott and I guarantee you, the prices will go down in a week. The ones who keep the prices up should be driven from the neighborhood! Let them go back to Russia and work for the Czar! You think we can't do it? You think we're not strong enough? You're wrong! Like the saying goes, if God wills it, even a broom can shoot!"

On that note, amid cheers, the meeting came to an end.

By Friday, February 23, 1917, there were no onions or potatoes to be seen on the pushcarts of the East Side, and squads of women roamed the street on the watch for chicken. In front of Garfinkle's Kosher Meat, an army of housewives stood guard with picket signs, while Solly Fein and Rosalie howled abuse from the doorway. A sign in the window said, "Roasting fowl, 32¢ lb.," but to no avail: only two women dared cross the picket line to buy their *Shabbos* hens and as they came out of the store, they had their purchases wrested from their hands and ripped to shreds before their eyes.

"What are you going to make for dinner tonight?" asked Yetta Breynes.

"Noodle pudding and vegetable soup," said Hannah.

"With no onions or potatoes?"

"I've got beets, celery, carrots, garlic," she sighed. "I might try some of those tomatoes they got in Little Italy."

"You ever taste one?"

"No."

"Juicy," said Yetta. "Very juicy. A little messy but okay for soup."

That Sunday the Levys and the Breyneses joined the rest of the neighborhood in the scheduled march on the Waldorf-Astoria to confront the Governor. Hannah carried a sign reading, "Never Mind Riverside Drive, Give Us Food on the East Side." The crowd of five thousand marchers remained orderly except for one incident when a group of housewives pulled a young man out of his automobile and told him sternly, "You have no right to ride in a car when people are starving." The Governor issued a press statement accusing the food rioters of being unpatriotic antiwar agitators inspired by paid agents of the Kaiser.

On Monday the associated poultry peddlers of the East Side decided to join the boycott. They sent pickets to all the butcher shops that remained open, and to the wholesalers as well. That night a brick crashed through Garfinkle's plate-glass window and someone painted a sign on his wall: "Death to Profiteers."

By the next day, Tuesday, February 27, the price of po-tatoes and onions had begun to fall. Chicken soon followed. After the boycott had been in effect for a week, potatoes had gone back to six cents a pound, onions to eleven cents, and chicken to nineteen cents. That night Yakhne Breynes caught sight of Tricker Louis Florsheim unobtrusively leaving the building by a side door, carrying a suitcase. She helped him on his way with a shower of well-placed stones.

All through the next week, Hannah Levy and Yetta Breynes kept up an informal guard before the shop. "Gar-finkle's the one who started the whole thing," they told shop-pers. "He jacked up the meat prices. For him, the boycott is still on." Business picked up in the rest of the street but not at Garfinkle's. Even the credit he offered no longer enticed the housewives of Rivington Street. Three weeks after the meat riot, a sign went up in Garfinkle's still unrepaired store window: "Business Closed for Renovations." A week later, a large horse-drawn van pulled up in front and men began to load furniture into it. Hannah sent Ruby to investigate.

"Moving?" she asked Rosalie Fein.

"You bet," she answered with her nose in the air, "to Central Park West. We're going to open a new butcher shop uptown, where the nice people live."

The sign in the window across the street was replaced by one reading "Store for Rent. Goodwill for Sale. Inquire at Algonquin 2-5900." The store remained empty for some time, however. As Moyshe said, "On Garfinkle's goodwill you could starve to death." But Hannah walked with a new spring in her step. For the first time since 1909, her neighbor-hood was all hers again.

I must make myself worthy, thought Ruby. It was no longer enough to be a designer of beautiful things. Now that there was a man in the picture, she must become a beautiful thing herself. She studied her assets in her hand mirror. She had good hair: golden brown and lots of it. Her eyes were large, blue, candid, and her nose almost perfect, with only the tiniest little bump. But her figure, alas, was like her mother's, too *zaftig* for 1917. Styles had changed and the women's magazines that were her guide had much to say about the new worship of "the little god of Thinness." Despite the new plenty resulting from the food riots, she would have to go on a diet.

"No more potatoes for me, Ma," she instructed Hannah. "No more sour cream and no more bread, either."

"What are you planning to eat?"

"Meat and vegetables."

"Meat?" said Hannah. "Every day? Chicken might have gone down but we're not millionaires."

Ruby shrugged. "Then vegetables."

Vegetables! Hannah wasn't even sure what she meant. Were prunes a vegetable? "Cabbage? Beets?" she asked. "Onions? Pickles?"

"Raw vegetables," said Ruby firmly. "Salads." No one in the history of the Levy family had ever eaten such things and Hannah was sure they would ruin her digestion. But Ruby held firm, so Hannah had to add trips to the Italian market to her schedule. The Jewish peddlers did not stock such exotica as lettuce.

Every morning Ruby studied her face in the mirror with all the concentration of a jeweler looking through his eyeglass. Her skin was not what it should be. Her nose was shiny and her pores were too large and there was a blemish on her chin. This could be fatal. All the magazines were united on one point: "The girl with the best skin wins."

"Many an otherwise attractive girl is a social failure because of a poor complexion," said one advertisement. "If *your* skin is not fresh, smooth, and healthy, or has suffered from an unwise use of cosmetics, see if the daily use of Resinol Soap will not greatly improve it."

Resinol Soap had not solved Ruby's problem. She was considering saving up for a full scientific facial analysis and treatment by a professional beautician. But this was very expensive. Even toiletries were high, and it was hard to tell which were the most essential items.

Was her chin too round, too full? Hannah's chin had become nearly double, at least when she looked down. Ruby didn't want to get like that. Perhaps she should invest three-fifty in a Mary Gray chin strap. But you had to buy Mary Gray Muscle Oil to go with it and that cost another five dollars, or two-fifty for a small one. A wiser investment might be the Mary Gray Reducing Chin Strap. That had an already medicated surface and would remove a double chin permanently. But it cost six-fifty—almost a month's rent. Perhaps she should get skin food instead, or freckle preventative, or eyelash cream to make her lashes grow.

In the end Ruby just took the plunge and decided to start with face powder, still the only generally accepted cosmetic for girls her age, though some fast girls used rouge. She marched down to Toiletries and plunked down her money for Djer-kiss, "that wonderful creation of Mssr. Kherkoff of Paris, the celebrated master of toiletry. It's Frenchy as can be!"

Strolling through the aisles of Berliner's, powdered to a fine matte finish, increasingly spare around the hips and dressed to kill, Ruby felt that epitome of modern sophistication. She caught the eye of more than one of the young male floorwalkers and clerks, but though she smiled graciously at their appreciative murmurs and hellos, she seldom stopped to chat.

Ruby had other fish to fry.

There was one floorwalker she had noticed from the time he came to work, about a year after she did. He was taller than the rest, and funny in his job. He didn't stay on one floor like the other guys but moved from place to place all the time as if he didn't know what he was doing. She found herself hoping he didn't get into trouble, and then wondering why she should care if he did. She didn't even know his name.

She could have found out easily enough by asking one of the other girls, but she didn't want to do that. Show any interest in a guy and it would be all over the store by lunch time; next thing you knew, they'd have you engaged to him. Ruby hated gossip; she knew how it could burn. She never said much when the talk would turn to boys at lunch or in the washroom. Once Milly, who worked near her, poked her in the ribs and said, "Come on, Ruby, give. Tell us the truth, have you got a fellow?"

But Ruby just opened her blue eyes wide and smiled and said no.

Ruby's special relationship to Fritzi Edelin (rumor had it she was being groomed for some high position, no one knew exactly what), and the fact that she spent so much of her own time learning the business rather than socializing, set her apart. It would have been noticeable had she suddenly started asking about any particular floorwalker. She didn't want to risk it.

She did glance at him from time to time, and sometimes she caught him staring back. He seemed to hang around her department quite a lot. He had a different way of carrying himself from most—more classy, and his clothes seemed to fit better. Something about the way he looked at her reminded her of Tricker Louis and she grimaced. She wasn't going to fall into that trap again. She'd never believe another word a man said.

Ruby took her lunch hour late because she had to wait until Fritzi came back from hers in case of any tailoring emergencies. Sometimes, when she was dieting, Ruby skipped lunch altogether and just wandered around the store or went for a walk. But usually she had the hot lunch in the employees' cafeteria on the top floor. By the time she got there, the special entrée of the day was often gone and the room nearly empty. She didn't mind. She'd get soup and a roll, and sit at one of the little tables near the window, where she could look out over the city and daydream.

One day she was awakened from her reverie by the sound of a throat clearing. She looked up, startled. The handsome floorwalker stood beside her.

"May I join you, Miss Levy?"

She gaped. How did he know her name? She looked around; there were lots of empty tables. Why was he coming to her? She almost asked him, flustered as she was; then, realizing this would be terribly rude, gestured at the chair opposite.

"It's a free country," she said with a friendly smile, pleased with her own poise.

She stared at him furtively from under her lashes as she carefully cut a bite of her hard-boiled egg in cheese sauce on toast, the day's special. How clean his hands were. His nails looked manicured.

"What's your name?" she asked him shyly.

"Ben," he said, smiling. "Ben Berliner."

She tilted her head to one side. "Any relation to the boss?"

"Sure," he said. "I'm his son."

Ruby put down her fork and stared at him. Then she realized he was pulling her leg. "Forget it," she said. "I'm not that dumb."

"What do you mean?"

"Mr. Berliner wouldn't put his son to work as a floorwalker. Tell me another."

He laughed. "You don't believe me?"

"Of course not. You men. Always kidding around. You think I was born yesterday? If you were really a Berliner you'd be working in the office."

"But suppose my father wanted me to learn the business from the ground up? What if he started me out in shipping and promoted me to floorwalking?"

"Oh, come on." Ruby was getting tired of the game. "That's ridiculous. A smart man like Mr. Berliner would never treat his own flesh and blood that way."

Nothing she could have said would have won his heart more easily.

At the age of twenty-two, Ben Berliner was his father's son—energetic, businesslike, and family-centered—in all but one respect: He had been infected with a passion for ideas, a recklessness common to many of his generation that gave him a swagger incomprehensible to his parents. Denzell and Tish Sloate had the same strut; Rachel and Sarah had an East Side version of it, and even dreamy Ruby moved with a precipitance unknown to her mother. All of them were buoyed up by the electric air of the times.

Such enthusiasms were considered unacceptable in his social set. Like other recently wealthy German Jews, the Berliners strove to be unremarkable in everything save their money, their culture, and the extent of their charitable contributions. Art, horse racing, and the opera were acceptable diversions for a man, and the conspicuous courtship of chorus girls was a common, if slightly reprehensible, alternative; but an undue interest in politics was so eccentric as to render the bearer suspect. The exotic varieties of what Ira Berliner called "downtown fanaticism"—religious orthodoxy, anarchism, or "this damned nonsense about Palestine"—were reserved for the Lower East Side.

Ben had showed no signs of abnormality as a boy; his scholastic and social career were exemplary, culminating in his being one of the first Jews ever to attend Princeton, class of '12. Ira Berliner was consequently all the more dismayed when he discovered his son had become a Zionist.

Ben had been touched by history years before, in 1905, when the entire Jewish community of New York City had rallied to protest the wave of pogroms in Russia and to find ways to help their victims. Along with the other uptown Jews, Ira Berliner rose to the occasion, sending telegrams to President Roosevelt urging him to sever relations with the Czar, and raising money for relief and guns. He even took his son, then a thin, passionate boy of thirteen, to the protest march that wound the length of the East Side. This demonstration—in which the Levys, along with 150,000 other Jews, also marched—changed Ben's life, open as he was, like so many adolescents, to any seed of idealism flung his way by the winds sweeping through the new century. It was the first mass demonstration he had ever witnessed, the first tme he had even seen so many people in one place for a common purpose; and as the crowd snaked its mournful way through the shabby, narrow streets, he was lifted out of himself. Staring around him at the raggedy families, the bearded old men, the shirtwaist girls, all animated by one need, he felt in the presence of something so grand, so potentially powerful, so rich and varied, so inexhaustible, that he was giddy. His heart moved within him in that heightened sense of solidarity that resembles romantic love, and tears came to his eyes as he thought to himself, We are a people.

The sheltered routines of his own school days and experiences at Princeton—the anti-Semitic jibes of his peers and the social exclusion he suffered as a Jew—confirmed his longing to find that solidarity again. Working in his father's store, he would let his mind wander over the centuries, playing with patterns, looking for redress. Things were not bad for the Jews in America; his own life was extremely comfortable and secure; yet he felt it had no center. Something was missing. The 1914 lynching of Leo Frank, a New York Jew accused of killing a fourteen-year-old factory girl in Atlanta and, after his acquittal, seized and hanged by a lynch mob, moved Ben to action. He sought out Young Judea, a Zionist group on the Lower East Side. His enthusiasm drove his father to distraction. Soon, Ira would have welcomed anything that took his son's mind off Palestine.

"You're an idiot!" he shouted. "What's wrong with New York? We don't need any Zion! America is our Zion!"

But Ben held fast to his beleaguered vision. Incorporated into it was the romantic picture of a girl working beside him on the land, a girl of the people, beautiful, certainly, but practical and robust, a hard worker, no hothouse bloom. Even before he met Ruby Levy, hearing of her from his father, he cast her in this role in his imagination, picturing a dark peasant woman with visible muscles and a strong profile. He was surprised to find her compactly built, with a light and rosy complexion, masses of curly brown hair, and a baby face. She moved through her department with an assurance beyond her years and had the personal authority of one who really knew her business. This was interesting; he didn't know any women like that, at least not young, pretty ones. The girls he met socially presided over charity events and volunteered for good causes but would not have been competent in the business world and would have thought themselves too good for it. He enjoyed the idea of a different sort of woman, a more practical type; and the fact that Ruby was an East Side girl attracted rather than repelled him, for he had reasons of his own to be drawn to that location. Wasn't most of the Zionist movement downtown?

Isabelle Berliner was increasingly concerned about her son's interest in Ruby. He went out with her two or three times a month; it must be serious.

"You'd better get rid of that girl," she told her husband. "You know how willful Ben is. What if he decides he wants to marry her?"

"Stop fussing," said Ira Berliner. "The boy's young. He won't marry for years."

"But, my dear, an Oriental Jew," expostulated his wife. "She has absolutely no background. We must nip this in the bud." Sitting on the edge of their bed, she glowered at him in the mirror as he undid his bow tie. With her jet black hair and elegant bosom showing to advantage in her lace wrapper, she was still a fine figure of a woman and was not above using the fact to press her point. Her husband grinned a little and unfastened his collar stud.

"How much background do we have, my dear?" he inquired mildly. "I seem to remember your father selling sewing machines. And Fritzi says this girl is a genius."

"We have a very successful firm, Ira," his wife said gently. "We don't have to marry geniuses. We can employ them."

"I love you, Belle." He shook his head, laughing at her. "But I'm not going to do what you say. Ben's love life is the least of his problems."

III

Dear Rachel,

We ended the Woman Suffrage Party convention with a huge demonstration, all the delegates, a thousand women, trying to get in to see the President. The weather was ghastly, pouring rain in gales, horrible great winds blowing our banners about. Police were everywhere—they were so scared of us they brought in special troops from Baltimore. But no matter how often we sent little delegations up to the White House doors, there was no sign of life within. The servants kept turning us away and would not take our resolutions. We thought perhaps Mr. Wilson didn't know we were out there. We could not believe he would deliberately ignore such a large number of women from all over the country in that weather. Then, after a couple of hours, a limousine honked its way through our crowd. We saw that it was he and his wife. They looked through us as if we were invisible. That's when I knew we might as well give up on Wilson. He will declare war any day and thinks that nothing else will matter after that and he can do whatever he likes—that is, nothing—about women.

I'm sick with it. It's been such an exhausting winter, standing there day after day with those banners. "Mr. President, how long must women wait for liberty?" Sometimes I think we'll wait forever. I've had one cold after another; my feet are always wet; the relief pickets

never come on time—now I know what you girls felt
like in '09, picketing the Triangle Waist Company in the
middle of February

Our convention was lively. Lots of argument: What
should we do when the U.S. enters the war? There were
plenty who thought we should put away suffrage for the
duration and stick with our country in her hour of need.
Damn fools. Now is our chance to strike and strike hard!
If the Democrats can't stand the thought of a nation divided against itself in wartime, let them make a few concessions to win us around! Imagine him talking of saving
the world for democracy, with half the population disen-
franchised! What sanctimonious cant! The new Russian
government enfranchised its women so they would help
win the war. England will do so as well, mark my
words—let Wilson follow their example if he wants to
talk about democracy!

I don't think he will, though. When he turned his face
away from us in the limousine today, a little chill ran
through me. I think something awful is going to happen
but I don't know what. I fear the worst.

                                        Love, Tish

Rachel saw Roman Zach frequently through the spring and
summer of 1917. His company awakened a restlessness in her
that it could not satisfy, and she began to think of writing.

One day he brought her an engraving of a painting of
Venus standing on a seashell, by an Italian, Botticelli. He
said she looked like the woman in it, and though you really
couldn't tell from a black and white engraving, she was the
most exquisite creature who ever lived. How he wished he
could paint Rachel in such classical drapery, simple and
showing her form.

"I wouldn't like people to know I'd posed like that," said
Rachel, "even if I were wearing three times as much as she
is."

"That's no problem," he said cheerfully. "As you pointed
out, no one can recognize the model in one of my paintings."

She stood in front of the window so the light shone through
her thin muslin draperies, panels that were caught around her
waist with a belt of twisted cord. A fire roared in the grate,
not far away, but the air from the window was wintry; be-

tween them she felt hot on one side, cold on the other, and extremely uncomfortable. Roman carefully arranged the fabric, his hands brushing her skin so lightly that she could hardly feel his touch, placing her hair in locks on her bare shoulders, one spiraling down her breast, another curling back as if windblown. There was in fact a cold breeze blowing in through the cracks around the window, pressing the muslin against her body. Her nipples rose involuntarily, under the pressure of the wind, pointing through the fabric. She caught her breath as he noticed them too, and slowly raised her eyes to his. He smiled a sweet, promising smile that made her breasts tingle and a pang sweep through her legs and up into her stomach. Then he turned and walked to his easel, and began to work.

She stared at him as he laid out the picture, trying to understand the nature of her feeling for him. There was an undercurrent of sensuality in their contacts, never addressed but always there at the back of her mind, disturbing her with its honeyed pain. For she did not love him. She was sure of that.

It was not because she was mourning for her husband. Her love for Denzell had died before he had, starved by neglect. She had fallen in love with an idea of him, a false one, and found the real Denzell almost useless for any human purposes, a handsome empty container once the dream that had animated it was gone. But even in the early days, when she had loved Denzell, there had been none of this aching feeling she had for Roman Zach. Her love for Denzell had been pure, a passionate yearning to merge, to lose herself in the beloved, to be transported to a plane where love alone existed. It had been storybook stuff. This wasn't; she could not identify her feeling for Roman from any of the novels she had read. If she did not love him, what was this weakness that swept her body, this yearning to press herself against him?

They took a break and he made tea, putting out cheese and crackers on a tray. She could not look at his face nor take her eyes from his nervous, brown, paint-stained hands, arranging the crackers so deftly. She imagined them on her body.

Later that afternoon the wind rose, then it began to hail, then sleet. She could not go home in such weather. She grew chilled from posing so close to the window, so he drew the chaise longue up to the fireplace and ordered her to get under the afghan and rest. Staring into the grate, Rachel fell half asleep, drifting in and out of hazy fantasies, imagining him coming quietly over to look upon her while she slept, to confer beauty upon her with his eyes. She felt drugged. Beneath her drowsiness, beneath the heat of the fire upon her cheeks, there was a tension, like one note on a violin played insistently louder and louder. She shifted under the afghan, throwing up one knee protestingly to get some air in all this heat. The sleet pounded on the windows, but near the fire the air was sultry, heavy, still, and she felt a tingling like pain inside her body and then soft fingers stroked the inner curve of her thigh.

She had not heard him come so close. With a sharp breath, she opened her eyes. He was sitting on the floor next to the chaise, fully dressed, with one hand hidden beneath the afghan. She shivered.

"Are you still cold?"

She shook her head, unable to take her eyes from his, a rabbit impaled upon a stare.

"Can I take this off?" he said, touching the afghan. "I want to see you."

She nodded mutely. He folded the afghan carefully and put it aside without removing his eyes from hers. Then gently, slowly, he untied her rope girdle and very tenderly, making each gesture a light caress, removed the muslin draperies from her body, one by one, until she was lying naked on the chaise, the muslin crushed beneath her.

"Odalisque," he said, smiling. She did not know what he meant.

He sat on the floor next to her, still fully dressed, his fingers quietly exploring her limbs, her joints, her skin, each part of her, murmuring descriptions and sounds of praise for the wonder of her coloring, the subtlety of her construction, the delicacy of her parts, until, as his soft fingers returned again and again to touch lightly the curls of hair beneath her belly, touching the rest of her body only to return to the curls and what lay within, she began to be swept by shuddering waves of feeling. She made a little sound of protest, covering her breasts with her hands at such self-exposure, but he just kept on touching her so delicately and gently, giving her to herself, that at last she could no longer lie still as she was supposed to. She began to bite her lip, with the keenness of the fluttering, the combination of her sensations and her worry that he would never lie on top of her and shield her from the light, that he was giving her this but would not take her. She tried to hold herself back in embarrassment, tried not to yield to the flood of emotion that his voice and his fingers created as they touched her with such slow, delicious pressure, but she could not stop herself, she gave in and was carried out of herself, crying out and moving under his hand until his fingers slipped inside her and she gave way in a flood of wetness.

Looking at him with enormous, shining eyes, she reached yearning hands out to him.

"Do you want me?" he whispered, and when she nodded, he stood and began to unbutton his pants. His penis stuck out, erect and large. It looked somehow different from her husband's. She could not think why for a moment, then suddenly she whispered incredulously, "Are you Jewish?"

He laughed and nodded as he lowered himself onto her.

It seemed hours later, lying with her arms around him, that she heard the storm slow and cease outside, and said, "I have to go home."

"I'll walk you," he said. He ran his finger lovingly over her flushed cheek.

She looked at him drowsily. "How come you never told me you were Jewish?" she said. She had never even thought of the possibility.

His body tensed and the lines on his face became hard. It was a long time before he spoke. "I'm the third Jewish artist in my family and the first one not to be destroyed. My uncle and my father were both in love with painting. But they grew up in a small village in Poland, and my grandfather was very pious. Art was forbidden. He tried to whip the dybbuk of painting out of my uncle so many times that he ran away. No one ever heard from him again. My father was delicate. He tried to stop drawing to avoid being beaten and apprenticed himself to a dyer. At least that way he could work with color. And he married to get away from home. But he was only sixteen, and the dyers' vats were too heavy for him. One fell on him while he was lifting it and broke his back. Then my mother brought me here. I grew up in New York."

"Does your mother mind your being a painter?"

"No, she was glad. She wanted me to go to art school. She sent me to the Educational Alliance and then to Cooper

Union. But I didn't know how sick she was. She worked too
hard when I was still young, and got the sweater's disease.
She's dead now." He took a deep breath and shuddered. "Do
you see why I never talk about being a Jew?"

Rachel nodded.

"I am the first generation of Jewish artists," he said a little
unsteadily, "abandoning the old ways, leaving behind superstition with the villages and ghettoes of Europe. There are
many like me: Maurice Sterne, Max Weber, Abraham Walk-
owitz here; Chagall, Modigliani, Chaim Soutine in Paris—we
are painting as no one has ever painted before, least of all
Jews. We will astonish the world!"

Rachel stared at him, wide-eyed. She had never felt such
kinship with a man. She had not known he was like this at
all.

Washington, July 18, 1917

Dear Rachel,

They've started arresting us. I guess with all the diplo-
matic flurry going on with the new Russian government
since the revolution, it was too embarrassing to have us
standing at the White House gates with our signs about
governments deriving their just powers from the consent
of the governed. So they suddenly decided it was against
the law to picket. Only they couldn't find any law it was
against, so they had to arrest us for obstructing traffic.
What a joke—half the time the streets are empty.

We decided to celebrate Bastille Day by picketing
anyway, sixteen of us. We were all arrested. Oh well, as
I said in my speech in court, persecution can only help a
just cause. They gave us sixty days at Occoquan workhouse in Virginia. Actually, they fined us twenty-five
dollars and I think they expected us to pay to get out of
going to jail, but of course we wouldn't pay a fine since
we hadn't done anything wrong.

You should see the workhouse—it looks so pastoral
next to the Tombs. Little white cottages in green fields;
inside, a hellhole. Deliberate humiliation; the Supt., one
Whittaker, a ghastly piglike tyrannical man, grinning
with satisfaction at having so many young white ladies in
his clutches. Most of the prisoners are black. They made
us all strip and walk naked across a big room to a filthy

shower, then gave us horrid scratchy uniforms. They took our own clothes—if Ruby could have seen how I looked!

They wouldn't let us get or send mail; it's all censored. We couldn't see our lawyers or friends. The food was inedible, a zoo of worms and maggots. The smell was so nauseating I began to retch at table—and was told this was strictly forbidden, as the dining room is to be silent, no talking or noise of any kind. We had to share towels, sheets, and soap with the regular prisoners, many of whom appeared to have TB or syphilis. Charming. I didn't wash the whole time. No toilet paper either. We even had to give up our toothbrushes.

After three days the President pardoned us. I gather there were lots of protests outside. As we left, Supt. Whittaker informed us that the next lot of suffrage prisoners wouldn't be treated with so much consideration.

I plan to spend a week in the bathtub, then start picketing again. Hope you are well, give Caro a kiss for me, and tell Sarah she's not the only jailbird now.

Much love, Tish

Deciding at length that since she could not get her husband to deal with Ruby Levy and must do so herself, Isabelle Berliner invited her to dinner. To Ruby, the scented note of invitation was fraught with ominous possibilities. For one thing, it brought the question of her relationship with Ben to the surface of her mind. She liked his company; he was well dressed and good-looking and polite, altogether a credit to her, and he never expected her to pay half when they went somewhere. But marriage?

Although the juices still flowed freely in Ruby's young body, she had been so deeply humiliated by the incident with Tricker Louis Florsheim that the door to her feelings was securely locked. She was not sure how to find the key. While she liked Ben and was obscurely happy with him, he barely figured in her fantasy life, which was almost entirely centered upon her work. She had let Ben kiss her twice in a cab, but gave him no more encouragement than was polite. He didn't seem to object. After all, weren't good girls like that? And if Ruby's mind sometimes wandered to speculations on price, fabric, and fit while he held forth on Theodore Herzl and the

Sultan of Turkey, so sweet was her expression that he had no idea she wasn't listening.

Isabelle Berliner's invitation focused Ruby's attention on the problem and she realized for the first time that if she played her cards right she might be able to marry Benjamin Berliner.

Was this what she wanted?

How could it hurt?

She must be careful to make the right impression on his mother. She wasn't sure she knew how to do this. She consulted Rachel on silverware and table manners.

"But do you love the guy?" said Rachel impatiently, after an hour of beating around the bush. "If you don't, believe me, all the money in the world isn't worth the aggravation."

"I don't know," said Ruby honestly. "I don't *not* love him."

To ensure that she behaved correctly, Ruby borrowed a book from the public library, *Etiquette for Americans,* by a Woman of Fashion. The book gave clear instructions.

"First and foremost, do not feel obliged to talk incessantly. Pauses are excellent things in their way; they accentuate the pleasures of talking, and they give time to eat." Ruby thought she could handle pauses.

"There is one rule about conversation that may be laid down especially for the newcomers in society. Pay outward attention at least to the person with whom you are talking, rather than let your eyes rove in search of somebody else, or perhaps of a mere escape." Ruby decided to pay more attention than usual to what other people said, but to say as little as possible herself.

The Berliners' drawing room was sumptuous though not particularly up-to-date; Ruby judged it hadn't been redecorated in at least ten years. She had heard Mrs. Berliner was very busy with her charities. The room was a magnificent example of the accretive style popular with the older generation rather than the more simplified, linear one that was the growing trend in both fashion and furnishings. There were, for instance, a large number of statues. A bronze shepherdess, naked from the waist up, struck an abandoned pose with two pails of milk; a marble bust of a French lady in a hat shook innumerable carved ruffles gaily at the company. The fireplace, of green faience tile topped with a white marble mantel, held an ornate enameled clock, a battalion of china nymphs and shepherds, and an imposing bronze of a tired horse. The front window was flanked by enormous twin aspidistra plants in Venetian glass urns; it had red velvet drapes with lace undercurtains and gold swags. The wallpaper was red flocked velvet brocade, and an Oriental rug graced the floor.

Before the fireplace stood a large tapestry firescreen, and in front of that was a conversation seat shaped like an S, so that when Ruby and Ben sat on it together, they faced in opposite directions. Mrs. Berliner posed graciously nearby on a blue silk armchair with a heavily carved oak frame; its legs were animals' feet and its arms were grinning lions' heads. There was also a Turkish divan in rose silk with twenty small embroidered cushions on it, and an imposing dark wooden table carved within an inch of possibility. Its legs were in the form of bare-breasted ladies with wings and odd headdresses, its sides depicted hunting scenes, and it was covered with photographs in silver frames, grouped about a Venetian glass lamp whose shade bore three tiers of green silk fringe.

Ruby gathered there would be only the four of them for dinner since one of Ben's sisters was married and had her own house, while the other two were away at school. Presently the company went into the dining room. Rachel had neglected to warn Ruby how much food she would be expected to consume, though she had instructed her to follow her hostess's example on questions of cutlery. It was a good thing she had; there were no less than three forks, four spoons, and two knives. On Rivington Street, they counted one plate per person a considerable achievement; here, there was an incomprehensible array of plates of various sizes. The little plate on the side of the big one seemed to be for bread— hot rolls, rather, Ruby realized as they were passed, soft ones with an indentation like a baby's behind. Another little plate seemed to have no function but to hold up a crystal goblet with half a grapefruit in it. Ruby had no idea what to do with the thing; she was considering picking it up and peeling it when she saw her hostess apply the last spoon in the line, a funny pointy one with a knife edge.

Following the grapefruit in the crystal goblet was clear soup in a low flat plate with little toast cubes floating in it. Then the servants bore in the roast lamb. The meat was served in tiny thin slices with a gob of red currant jelly on the side. There were browned sweet potatoes and roast turnips to go with it, and a side dish that Ruby finally decided was cabbage, baked in a cream sauce. She was thrilled to find a food that was familiar, even though heavily disguised. I guess they are still Jewish in spite of everything, she thought.

The dessert, which came with coffee, was very peculiar. By this time, after two glasses of red wine, Ruby was feeling more at ease and asked, "What is the name of this, please?"

Mrs. Berliner looked astonished. "Why, it's just a plain pudding, my dear. Steamed suet and nut pudding with foamy sauce. Haven't you had it before? What do you have for dessert at home?"

Ruby looked blankly at her, then recollected herself. "We generally skip dessert," she said primly, "for the sake of health and appearance, if you know what I mean."

It was one of the longest remarks she had made yet, thought her hostess. She was demure to a fault, reminiscent of the shy misses of the last century, but "still waters run deep," reflected Isabelle Berliner.

"Tell me about your family, my dear," she said courteously.

Ruby smiled and shrugged. "They're just like anyone else, really," she said. So remote was she from an understanding of the ordinary that she actually thought she was telling the truth.

"Your father," Isabelle pressed on, determined to elicit some damaging admission if possible, "he is religious, I assume, and goes to one of those picturesque little synagogues in a tenement?"

Ruby looked surprised. "Oh, no," she said politely, and took another bite of her suet pudding with foamy sauce.

"He wears earlocks? A long coat? A beard?"

"No," said Ruby, "but he does have a moustache."

Isabelle was puzzled. "I thought everyone on the East Side was Orthodox."

"Mother," said Benjamin in a warning voice.

"Not Papa," said Ruby. "He doesn't approve of that sort of thing."

Isabelle brightened. "Really?" she said. "Is he Reform, like us? Or at least Conservative?"

"Mother," said Ben, "you don't understand the East Side."

"But what else is there besides Reform or Orthodox or Conservative?" asked his mother in honest bewilderment.

"Well, Papa's just an ordinary person," said Ruby. "You know, an atheist. He says religion is like a drug in people's minds."

Isabelle Berliner's eyes opened very wide. She stared at Ruby. "Oh, I see," she said faintly. Clearly the girl's family was particularly outlandish. Ruby herself, while she lacked poise, was not unpresentable. Well, Isabelle did not have to worry about her family yet. The whole thing could still blow over. As she lapsed into uneasy speculation, a lull fell on the table.

"I was looking at the new Paris models today," said Ira Berliner brightly, feeling he should keep the ball rolling. "What did you think of them, Ruby?"

A look of intelligence transfigured Ruby's cheerful features. "Odd," she said oracularly. "If you ask me, it's the war."

"How do you mean, odd?"

"They go in opposite directions. A lot of them are more fluffy and frilly than they've been in ten years, all Marie Antoinette; they even require tight lacing. But a few of them are extraordinary—simple, elegant, rather tubular, hardly any waist, and made of that fabulous new wool jersey. A woman could do anything in them; she could drive a tank and get up without a wrinkle."

"What's wool jersey?" said Isabelle.

"A new fabric they've started making in France," said her husband. "It's wool, but knitted, not woven, so it stretches."

"They haven't really begun to use it yet," said Ruby enthusiastically. "So far they're just cutting it straight, like flannel. But I was playing around with a few yards from the end of a bolt and the stuff is incredible; you can drape it like chiffon, you can cut it like regular wool, and it never gets crumpled. It's ideal for ready-to-wear."

"Ready-to-wear?" said Ira with a laugh. "You mean, for children?"

"For anyone," said Ruby sweetly.

This was going too far. "My dear girl, you know what

Fritzi says," he reproved her. "Our clientele would never stand for ready-to-wear—too many alterations."

"Look," argued Ruby, transformed before their eyes into a career girl, "as long as the styles are fitted and tucked and flounced with hundreds of intricate details, ready-to-wear is out of the question for Berliner's. But—think if the styles change. The models we have from Chanel aren't fitted at all—they're loose, boxy, no waist. It would be easy to mass produce them. The main things you'd have to worry about would be the length and the shoulders, and you could adjust those in only one fitting."

"Do you really think people would buy ready-to-wear Chanels?" said Ben, fascinated by his beloved's transformation from ingenue to hard-nosed designer.

"I would," said his mother abruptly. "I hate those hours after hours I have to spend being fitted, I absolutely hate them. It takes too much time away from my committee work and it's exhausting, and then you don't get the clothes for weeks. If I could get some suits and frocks with no fuss I would be in heaven."

For the first time that evening, she and Ruby exchanged a smile of mutual appreciation, while Ira Berliner stared from one to the other, nonplussed.

"Have the Paris models arrived yet?" asked Ruby one day in March 1917.

Fritzi Edelin groaned. "No, my dear, they haven't, and what's more, we've no word of the ship. We're two weeks behind schedule already; we should be getting ready for the spring show; we've sent out the invitations. I am in despair!"

"Perhaps I should make up a few designs," said Ruby with forced casualness, "just in case."

Fritzi could not believe her ears. "I beg your pardon?"

"I said, I'd like to try a few designs, in case the Paris models don't come in."

Putting her arm around the younger woman, Fritzi walked her through the department. "My dear Ruby, I appreciate your ambition and of course you have talent, but you know Berliner's uses only French designs."

"But what if there are no French designs? Are we going to close down the store?"

Fritzi stared at her in consternation. "But surely they will come!"

"What if they don't?" said Ruby. "At least let me try a few designs. I'll do them on my own time. Then if all else fails, at least we'll have a couple of models."

Fritzi walked in silence for a moment. Finally she said, "I don't see how it would hurt. But remember, you've no guarantee anything will come of it."

"Certainly," said Ruby. "Can I use any of the leftover fall material?"

"What do you have in mind?"

"Jersey," said Ruby. "Black jersey."

Fritzi raised her eyebrows. "For spring? We always show pastels for spring—pink and green and blue and beige."

"I know," said Ruby. "But I've been thinking about black. A straight little suit, loose, with a white blouse. A black chemise with a collar and cuffs, white organdy. You could wear it right from the office or shopping or war work to dinner, even to the theater. Think of the time you'd save. Women are going to be busier now, you know, out of the house more; they won't be able to go home and change for the evening. We'll have to rethink color and style as well. Make everything more informal and adaptable, less fussy."

Fritzi regarded her gravely, then smiled. "This war may be a blessing in disguise."

Ira Berliner and Fritzi Edelin stood against the brocade wall of the dressmaking department two months later, watching Ruby supervise a fitting.

"Ruby's little black dress is selling like hotcakes at a fair," said Fritzi. "That's the sixth one she's sold this week."

"It was a good idea to let her start designing, even if it does set a precedent."

"I never really meant to use her designs," Fritzi confessed. "They were to be a stopgap, just in case. But when the French ones finally came in, they looked so piecey, and hers were so—remarkable. And now they're outselling everything but the Chanels."

"She's very gifted."

"Don't let her hear you say that. I fear her ambitions may

exceed my power to imagine them, and she gets a funny gleam in her eye whenever she mentions ready-to-wear.''

"Well, Bergdorf's is doing it," said Ira Berliner.

Fritzi's face turned to stone. "You're not serious. Why? When? How do you know? Are you sure?''

"I had lunch with Edwin Goodman yesterday. His wife has started working in a canteen for the soldiers, and the store made her a lovely gray uniform for the purpose. Her first day in the canteen she spilled gravy all over it. She, was beside herself—she needed another one the next day and had no time for fittings. So they're going to start a new line of high-priced ready-to-wear for women who can afford the best but don't want to waste time.''

There was a long silence as Fritzi digested this world-shattering information. "It'll never work," she said. "They'll see. Let them fall on their faces. We'll stay as we are.''

He shrugged. "I'm not pushing it.''

Fritzi shook her head. Sometimes she felt the world was changing too fast for her. She looked at him sidelong. "Tell me," she said, "just between the two of us, are you going to let Ben marry Ruby?''

"Let him!" said his father. "I'd be overjoyed. And Isabelle would come around. But he's afraid to ask her. She told him she isn't sure she wants to get married at all, certainly not until she's established in her career.''

"Established!" Fritzi was incredulous. "What does that mean? If she isn't established now, what is it going to take?''

"I don't know," said Ira, taking his leave, "but whatever it is, do me a favor and give it to her. I want to see some grandchildren before I die.''

Fritzi stood some time in deep reflection. Perhaps she had been born too soon. One of the first women to make a career in retailing, she had climbed higher in her chosen field than anyone else before her and had counted herself lucky to be of her own generation rather than her mother's, though it had taken her twenty years to rise to her present eminence and spinsterhood was one of the prices she had paid. She had paid it willingly in exchange for independence and power. Still, the thought that this price might no longer be exacted as a matter of course was intriguing. Ruby's ascent was so much swifter than her own had been; she was still in her early twenties and already her designs were sold in the most prestigious department store in New York. Fritzi wondered if bearing Ira Berliner's grandchildren fitted into Ruby's own vision of her future.

Maybe *she's* the new woman, she thought, and all this time I've been thinking it was Laetitia Sloate.

IV

It was November 1917. Sarah and Avi had been going together for a year and a half and had almost enough money saved up to get an apartment and put money down on furniture. But she still hadn't told him about Joe Klein. She kept remembering her mother's words, flung at her as she berated Ruby on that awful day: "Sarah wouldn't be dumb enough to let a man get her without a ring!" And she remembered the night they'd parted in 1913, when Avi got so furious because she'd danced with Joe and said he'd never marry a girl who cared so little for him.

What would he say when he found out?

The affair seemed so long ago. It had hurt, but time passed and with it went the fears about herself that she had acted out in that miserable relationship, bleeding in the hotel bath and dragging through the months after. In the loneliness that followed her breakup with Joe, she'd forgotten what spring felt like. Now she was green again, the sap running in her veins. Each day the papers were full of the revolution in Russia. Politics had never seemed more promising, the mornings more bright; never had she felt so full of important discoveries, holding them in her fingers like small, bright jewels.

Not all this was because of love. The Equal Voice movement had jarred her from her torpor before she and Avi met again. She was glad she knew that; it made her dependence on him less terrifying. Still, it was Avi she thought of when she eagerly awoke each morning; his name she held in the back of her mind like a magic charm that would somehow keep her safe, just saying it, his name, to herself at odd moments, as a religious woman would breathe a prayer.

Next to this, Joe Klein was ancient history.

But Avi wouldn't see it that way. He was so pure; so uncomplicated in his emotional life. To him, things were simple: You fell in love, you got married, and you loved that one person all your days. Anything else was for other people, not for him and those he cared for. It was funny that he, so sophisticated in his political thinking, was so like a child in this. She remembered something he often said about economics, "Development is uneven," and thought, yes, that's true of people, too.

He would not be able to understand. And he would hate it. But he had to be told nonetheless. To lie to him was unthinkable, no matter what the truth might cost. She made up her mind she would tell him the next Sunday, when they went walking on the waterfront.

Sunday was warm for November. He was happy, but she was preoccupied, rehearsing the words over and over in her mind. "Avi, I've got something to tell you." "Avi, years ago, after we broke up, I did a stupid thing." She didn't know how to begin. The hours passed; their shadows lengthened on the bridge where they'd come on their first walk so long ago. Finally she just blurted it out.

"Avi, I have to tell you something bad. I'm not a virgin."

His face turned white. He stared at her. He shifted a little away from her, down the bridge, and the tiny movement turned like a knife in her heart.

"It was only one man, a long time ago." She spoke in a rush, not wanting him to think it worse than it was. "It was just stupid, Avi. I did it just to prove something to myself. It didn't mean anything."

She could tell he didn't understand a word she was saying. His face was funereal.

"Did you love him?" he said.

"No," she cried, "I hated him!"

He thought it over; then, with a spring of hope in his face, asked, "Did he force you?"

It would have been an easy out, but she would not take it. "No," she said. "I knew what I was doing."

He clasped his hands together and looked out over the railing, staring miserably at the river. "I don't know what to

say," he murmured. "I—" He twisted one hand in an ago-
nized, half-open fist. "It cuts me."

It was even worse than she had feared. It had hit him in
some place she did not know was there, some visceral place
inaccessible to reason. "Do you want to break it off?" she
whispered, terrified. "If you don't want to marry me anymore, I will release you." Her eyes pleaded with him but his
were tormented. He didn't answer.

She took a deep breath and let it out in shuddering gasps.
She knew she was near to disaster. She felt as if two demons
in one of her Bubbe's stories were fighting over her, Pride
and Need. They hovered in the air above the river. Pride, her
terrible demon that had driven him away once before, that
always reared up in the face of any rejection, was so strong
she could hardly keep herself from yelling, "Well, if that's
the way you feel about it, break it off," and running away. (I
have to be careful, she thought, I have to think.) At the same
time Need cried out inside her, "No, no, you can't let him
go, stop him, make him listen, make him see he can't leave
you now. Tell him anything, tell him you'll kill yourself, just
don't let him go away!"

Then suddenly she was clear and cold. Her mind rose like
an angel all white from under the Williamsburg Bridge and
with a wave of its hands banished the demons, as she leaned
there, shaking. This isn't right, what he's saying, she
thought. It's *wrong*. He doesn't want to leave me. He loves
me. This idea that he should leave me is not in his interest
any more than mine. He must be able to see this if I can
explain.

"You are wrong to act this way," she said. Her voice was
low and shaky but gained confidence as she went on. "I will
not let you ruin both our lives because of a wrong idea that is
a relic of the old society we are trying to destroy. I may have
done something foolish years ago, but you are doing it now.
Think, Avi. Look at what you are saying."

He looked at her.

"Do you really think a woman is a man's property, that
she can have only one owner and has to come to him in perfect condition? This idea comes from feudal lords who needed
to make sure the son they left their land to was their own.
You, who have studied so much, surely you know this."

He nodded miserably, but said nothing. Looking at him,

feeling as if she would faint any moment, she resolved to remain calm. It was the hardest thing she had ever done.

"It's not that I believe in the double standard," he said finally in a wretched voice. "I know that's wrong. Women have the right to do anything men do. It's just that—I *feel*—" He couldn't go on. But she wouldn't speak. She waited for him to continue. In a moment he took a deep breath and said rapidly, "You see, I am a virgin and I wanted us to be the same. If one person is not a virgin, it should be the man. That is how the world is. The man should be the experienced one and I am not. I will fail you. You will find me inept."

"Oh, Avi," she cried, reaching for him, beginning to sob. "It's not like that, you won't fail me, you're being silly. You don't know how it was. It was horrible, it was nothing." She wept into his coat front.

"But you don't understand, Sarah," he cried. "I am serious. This is important to me. I want us to be the same. I want us to be equals in our marriage."

"Avi," she said helplessly, "we are not the same. I am a woman and you are a man and we are not equal in the society we live in, in any respect. I can't even vote. You make twice as much money as I ever will. You are bigger than I am and stronger. I am a citizen and you are not. All these things make us different. The fact that I once had a lover and you never did is not the most important difference between us."

He sighed heavily. "I hear what you are saying, and in my mind I understand you. But the way I *feel*—" He hit himself on the breast. "I thought it would be different," he whispered.

"Oh, Avi, I love you. I am so sorry," she said wretchedly, touching his wet cheeks with cold fingers.

She did not see him for a week. She was not completely sure she would ever see him again, though surely he was too principled a man to leave her without a word. He was working things out in his mind and when he had done so to his satisfaction he would come back. In the meantime, she could do nothing. She had never felt so bereft, so powerless, in all her life. She knew how much she needed him, knew what her life would be if he went away. But did he know how much he needed her; did he have as sharp a sense of the aridity of his life alone as she did? She doubted it. He had not given it as much thought as she had. He could make a very bad mistake.

When he came by on Sunday, they walked to Seward Park. He began talking almost as soon as they were outside the door.

"I have thought about it all week. I think it is crucial that we begin our marriage on an equal footing. I cannot get around that. Since you gave yourself to someone else before, I must do the same. I will go to a prostitute."

She stopped in the middle of the street. "Are you crazy?" As he repeated his chain of reasoning, she was astonished by the wave of jealousy that swept through her. "Over my dead body," she said furiously.

"But why? You were with someone else."

"That was after we broke up, years ago. This is now. How can you be so stupid? Think of the dangers, the chance of disease! What if you fell in love with her?"

"Oh, Sarah," he remonstrated, "people do this every day. I'll be careful."

"Careful?" she said. "You won't do it and that is that. I will break off with you if you do. I mean it. You leave me alone for a week, never even stopping by to talk, and then you come up with an idiotic idea like this. I forbid it. If you are so determined to sleep with somebody before we get married, sleep with me."

He stopped walking and stared at her. "How would that help?"

"I don't know, maybe it wouldn't help. You're the one who has such a thing about neither of us being virgins when we marry. This way we wouldn't be."

He looked at her with a funny gleam in his eye, then grabbed her hand and started walking quickly.

"Where are we going?" she said.

"To my house," he said. "Everyone's gone for the afternoon. This may not make us equal but it will get the whole thing over with so I don't have to worry about it anymore. At least it will set my mind at rest." And he pulled her so fast they were almost running by the time they reached Ludlow Street.

Once inside the apartment, she became afraid. She shut the door and stood with her back against it. "I think I've changed my mind," she said. "I don't think this is such a good idea, Avi."

"Yes it is," he said. He began to unlace his boots.

"I don't want to. I'm afraid. It might ruin everything."

"It won't. It's a good idea, the only thing that can get us back to normal and stop us being nervous. Why don't you go into the bedroom and undress? I'll be right in."

She went slowly into his mother's room and sat on the edge of the bed. Outside, she heard one of his boots drop.

It was a cold day and there was very little coal. They lay shivering under the covers, eye to eye, staring at each other as fixedly as two fish cast up on the beach side by side, gasping with nervousness and shock. The sheets were icy.

Finally Avi could stand it no longer and, with a little sneeze, dove under the comforter. It was a big thick heavy one his mother had brought from Russia; she and his aunt had plucked the geese for it themselves. Sarah looked at the place where his head had been. She could see her breath in the air. Her body, naked and still shivering, was beginning to warm up slightly under the comforter. She suddenly felt an added warmth and wetness on her arm, a warm nuzzling pressure. She peeked under the cover and saw the top of Avi's head. He was kissing her arm. His hair was beginning to thin on top, she noted with a pang; in a few years he would be bald. She had never seen the top of his head before. Suddenly it seemed very important to see his face, and she slipped down under the edge of the coverlet and the warm darkness closed over her head like water.

It was an undersea world of shadows and waves and soft lumps and unexpected elbows and muffling billows of blanket. There was very little air. Sarah was reminded of a hayloft she used to hide in as a child in Russia, playing with her sisters. She began to giggle. Reaching out quick fingers, like little nibbling minnows, she tickled Avi in the ribs. He bucked in surprise and said, "Hey," trying vainly to defend himself. In a moment they were wrestling like two little boys, until he had her pinned by the elbows. Her eyes were used to the darkness now and she could see the glint in his as he held her down, looking at her all over for the first time, her small breasts, her ribs sharply outlined under them, her flat stomach and hips, her pubic hair. She began to blush and lay very still. Tentatively he let one elbow go and ran his fingers slowly down her body, exploring its surface as if he were trying to record it with his fingertips. There was a mole on

her left hip where he paused in puzzlement, then put his head
down to see what it was. Overcome by love, she clasped his
head and hugged it to her as she felt him kiss the mole, and
then his kisses traveled delicately up and found her breasts.

She could tell he didn't know exactly what to do next, but
there was no rush. Idly, lightly, she let her own hand travel
slowly down the angles of his body; he sucked in his breath,
and when her hand closed lightly around him, he shuddered
and said, "Sarah." Slowly they moved closer together, pressing against each other, as if for warmth, until they were
touching at every point, and her toes scrabbled round his ankles. Delicately, fearfully, taking it in sips and small motions,
he pushed inside her a little, then more, then more, until
waves of emotion began to shake her body and they held onto
each other for support like trees in a hurricane that left them
gasping, spent, still clinging together under the now damp
and rumpled coverlet.

They lay with their limbs entwined, relaxed and happy.
They had been all right. They had not hurt or disappointed
each other. Neither one was a person who found it easy to let
go. For both, release would always be a struggle, a decision
made moment to moment, point by point. Ecstasy of the kind
known to Rachel, for whom sex was an escape from self
rather than a threat to it, would be something they would
know seldom or might never know. But they were happy.
Sarah stretched lazily, comfortably, next to him and looked
up at his face. He smiled at her, dazzled.

"Oh, Sarah," he said, "I love you so much. I can't wait
till we get married."

"Do you ever wonder why we go through all this?"
moaned Prue Gruening, rubbing her bruised ankle. A slight,
blond girl of twenty from a minister's family in upstate New
York, she had been so impressed by Tish's speeches the year
before that she decided to come to Washington to work for
the Woman's Party. Tish was rather embarrassed by such
hero-worship, but she liked Prue, who had a dry, self-
deprecating wit akin to her own. They palled about together a
good deal, and had just been beaten up by the same gang of
sailors while defending their suffrage banners. They'd stood
valiantly before the White House gates, singing the suffrage
hymn as loud as they could and holding up their signs, but

"Shoulder to shoulder and friend to friend," was soon drowned out by choruses of "Over There."

The Yanks were coming, all right, thought Tish. Things had heated up since the draft began in August; there were so many young men in uniform floating about Washington, looking for a fight. And what better fight could there be than one ✔ith a mob of unpatriotic, unsexed women who were trying to embarrass the government? Especially when the police just stood there and watched. It was all your life was worth to be a suffrage picket these days; and it was hell on banners; they often used up twenty or thirty in one day. There was even a little man who cut the downed banners into squares and sold them for souvenirs. "Captured from a suffragist, 25¢."

The battles with the sailors had a scary, volatile quality and a few of the women had been badly hurt. One had her blouse entirely ripped off along with her suffrage sash; that had certainly amused the troops. Tish herself got a black eye. She had to grin, though, when she thought of her banner; it really got them; it was like waving a red flag at a bull. "KAISER WILSON," it read, "REMEMBER HOW YOU SYMPATHIZED WITH THE POOR GERMANS BECAUSE THEY WEREN'T SELF-GOVERNED? NEITHER ARE 20 MILLION AMERICAN WOMEN. CLEAN YOU OWN HOUSE FIRST!"

"I'm going to take a good long bath," she told Prue. "If we're going to jail tomorrow, we'd better soak while we have a chance."

The sentences kept getting longer. Thirty days. Two months. Three months. The government was thrashing around, desperately trying to make them stop picketing. But the official brutality created its own response as more supporters rallied to the suffragists. The government finally arrested Alice Paul, leader of the Woman's Party, and held her incommunicado, apparently believing that the movement would melt away without her. Tish and her friends protested by holding a mass picket in front of the White House on November 12. They decided to demand treatment as political prisoners, not jaywalkers, if they were arrested, and to go on a hunger strike if this demand was not met.

Forty-one of them were sent to Occoquan workhouse the next day. Superintendent Whittaker's rage at their new tactic was such that many of them were beaten nearly unconscious before being placed in solitary confinement.

Tish had never fasted before. She didn't know what to expect. By the third day of her hunger strike, she had progressed from headache and nausea to running a fever. Her skin was hot and dry, her lips parched and cracking. She felt light-headed and giddy, was a bit weepy, and had trouble remembering names and dates.

That night she had a dream. She was back at Vassar, watching a performance of the *Bacchae;* at the same time she was watching the play, she was also in it and it was real. She was one of the Maenads, maddened with hunger and blood lust, seeing her meat, her man-meat, coming into the clearing, and running after him, baying, panting with mindless hunger, running him down with the other women screaming beside her, tearing him, rending the meat and stuffing great gobs of it into her mouth raw, stuffing in so much she almost 'choked on it, so hungry was she. The bright blood ran down her chin and she looked at the face of dead King Pentheus and saw that he was also her father.

She awoke choking on a scream, her throat dry, terrified. "No," she whispered, stuffing her fists into her mouth and biting them, "no, that's not how it is—oh, how horrible, to have *their* dream!" Even in her sleep, how could she have been so weakened, so hungry, as to see herself as her enemies saw her!

The fourth day, Superintendent Whittaker came to her cell. She could hear him going down the line as one door opened, then another. She did not sit up when he entered. She couldn't.

"I want you to sign a release form. I refuse to force feed you unless you sign a paper saying you yourself are responsible for any injury you may suffer in the process."

Tish gazed up at him unblinking, then shook her head. He glared at her, then left the cell. She heard him make the same request next door.

The next day she was too weak to comb her hair. At midday she heard horrible gagging noises down the corridor. Someone was being forcibly fed. She could not even bring herself to feel much indignation, she was so exhausted. She lay on her cot watching the roaches on the walls. She had lost her horror of them, though she still squirmed when they crawled on her body. The day passed and toward evening she began to feel that she was going to die.

At dawn the prison doctor appeared with Superintendent Whittaker and two guards. They pulled her to her feet and dragged her down the hall to a room with a long table. A matron and four regular prisoners were there. Two held her legs down, two her arms, and the matron held her head and forced open her mouth. With a strength Tish did not know she still possessed, she bit down hard. The matron screamed and slapped her across the face so viciously she blacked out. As she came to, she heard the doctor say, "Watch it, Mrs. Thompkins. We can't have her unconscious. If the food backs up, she'll suffocate."

Tish did her best to resist but she was weakened by days of starvation. As they held her head rigid, the doctor took a length of rubber tubing and inserted it down her right nostril. It scraped like a knife along her throat. Her nose began to leak blood. She couldn't breathe. The whole thing was more ghastly than she had imagined possible.

The food they dumped into her stomach lay there all the rest of the day like a cannonball, indigestible. She kept gagging helplessly, and her nose continued to bleed for hours. Her face ached where she'd been hit, and the muscles of her neck and shoulders were so sore she could hardly move. She had never been in such pain in all her life. She wept through the night, glad that none of the other women could see her.

In the morning they took her back to Washington, to court. The Woman's Party had, with considerable difficulty, obtained a writ of habeas corpus forcing the court to show why it had transferred people arrested in Washington to another jurisdiction in Virginia. The court was swarming with friends and reporters and photographers and lawyers. Mrs. Belmont was there. She screamed when she saw Tish shamble in, supported on each side by policemen, too weak to walk.

Tish's picture appeared in any number of places the next day, including the *New York World,* which ran it next to one from the suffrage parade of the year before, with a caption, "New York Socialite Before and After Her Imprisonment in Occoquan Workhouse." Ruby almost fainted when she saw the second picture. "She looks like death," she whispered.

Tish had indeed been brushed by the wing of the angel of death. Like many who have had such an experience, she began to re-examine her life. Most of the things she had been afraid of paled next to the threat of extinction. Even the pain of love denied burned less intensely than the agony of forced feeding.

How am I to live? she thought. If I live. I can't go on as I have.

The prisoners were transferred from Occoquan to the District of Columbia jailhouse, where they continued their hunger strike. Three days later, the government, unable to countenance either feeding so many of them by force or letting them die of starvation, suddenly released them all. Freedom was ecstasy. They had won, though the fruits of their victory were still uncertain. Tish stayed on in Washington for a week, to regain her strength and be part of the meeting held at the Belasco Theatre to honor the prisoners. Four thousand people fought to get in. Mrs. Belmont spoke: "A flame of rebellion is abroad among women," she said in her strong, plummy voice, "and the stupidity and brutality of the government can only increase the strength of this revolt!"

The day after the meeting, Mrs. Belmont took the train back up to New York and Tish went with her.

Tish came back to New York to see Rachel again, to discharge her responsibilities to herself and know with finality if there was any hope for the two of them. She would either declare her love or fold it away for good; she could not go on caring for someone who gave so little back.

How shocked Rachel was when she saw her. She looked like her own ghost.

Tish smiled. She knew jail had aged her. "Maybe I am my own ghost. I feel as though I've been raised from the dead."

That evening, sitting before the fire, Tish asked, "Have you been getting out more, Rachel, now that the baby's older?"

"I have." She paused. "Actually, I've been going around a bit with a friend of yours, the painter, Roman Zach. He sends his regards."

It was too funny. Tish had never quite believed in her own high hopes, but this was ridiculous, a rapid denouement clearly suited better to a bedroom farce than a tragedy of lost love. "And has he asked you to model for him yet?"

Rachel's blush and the way she looked down at her mending told Tish everything she needed to know. She laughed.

There seemed nothing else to do. Rachel raised her eyes a little fearfully.

"Are you angry with me?" she said. "Was he a beau of yours? I didn't mean to poach but I didn't know; you never said anything. Do you want me to stop seeing him?"

"Of course not," said Tish. "Bless you, lamb, I don't care about Roman Zach. It's you I care about. If he can make you happy even for a little while it's fine with me. It's clear you're fixed on men for good, so you might as well enjoy it."

From the way Rachel's eyes clouded over, Tish could see she neither understood nor cared to do so. Men's women were usually like that; they preferred not to know. It made it easier for them to avoid seeing alternatives and understanding the toll taken by their own choices.

"How long will you stay in New York?" asked Rachel.

"Only a few days," said Tish. "There's a lot to be done in Washington, and as one of the chief martyrs of the Wilson administration, I'll be useful."

"Surely there are others who can do that," Rachel protested warmly, putting down her work. "You're so tired! It isn't fair of them to make you go back so soon. You should stay here for the rest of the winter and let me take care of you."

Tish smiled sardonically at the offer. How delicious it would have seemed only a short time before. She wondered how much care Rachel would really have leisure to give her between Roman Zach and the baby.

"You don't understand," she said, stretching luxuriantly. "I want to go back. I like my work and my friends there are counting on me."

"I thought you'd at least stay through Christmas," said Rachel with a forlorn little pout. "I was going to give a party for you."

Going back on the train a few days later Tish stared out the window, more weary than broken-hearted as the empty fields flew by in the early light. She was thinking of a moment on the picket line in front of the White House, when she and Prue had stood there alone, their backs to the gates, and heard a military parade coming down a nearby street, playing the ubiquitous "Over There."

Prue had given her a long level gaze full of laughter and

said, "Wouldn't mind being over there myself. It's civilized over there." And then she'd winked, and a sudden, completely unnerving thrill of pleasure had run through Tish at the thought. Someday the war would be over and there would be Paris, liberated at last, with its wide boulevards and its quiet cafés, its monuments of culture and its ateliers of advanced art. In Paris a woman could live as she chose. She could run a salon or a gallery or a little magazine; she could be surrounded by women like herself. She could drink small cups of very black coffee; she could admire the gray light that filtered through the medieval courts; she could eat croissants and drink absinthe and dance in the streets. Tish smiled. After the war, she would go to Paris.

One day a little before Christmas Hannah offered to mind Caro while Sarah and Rachel went for a walk through the neighborhood. It was almost like old times, being out together in all the swarms of shoppers, with the cold air crisp in their lungs. They bought some chestnuts in Little Italy and ate them as they walked.

"It's as if you've come back home," said Sarah happily. "I didn't feel like that when you first moved downtown, even though you were right across the Square." She smiled. "This is so nice."

Rachel smiled back and linked arms.

"Tell me about this man, Roman Zach," said Sarah. "What's he like?"

Rachel considered. "He's nice, but he's not steady. He doesn't ever want to get married."

"Maybe that will change when you know each other better."

"We know each other rather well already," said Rachel drily. "No, he doesn't think artists should have families. They should devote themselves to their work. It's all right; I don't need to get married anyway. I have my own money. And nobody minds except my mother."

Rachel's mother had reappeared six months after Denzell's death. One Sunday afternoon she had rung the bell, dressed for company and carrying a sponge cake. She now visited ceremoniously each weekend to see the baby. Rachel had even taken Caro to her brother's flat a few times. They were all rather uncomfortable together, never mentioning the past, but Rachel locked her anger inside when she was with them, for Caro's sake. Now at least Caro would know her roots.

"Do you love him?" said Sarah.

Rachel sighed. "I don't know. It doesn't matter. Men just aren't enough. When we were young, I thought love would change everything. When the right man came along, I would find the meaning of life."

"You can't find the meaning of life in a man."

Rachel laughed. "Same old Sarah, even if you are engaged. Well, where am I supposed to find it, then? I can't find it in politics like you do; I'm just not like that. Sometimes I think the meaning of my life is Caro. But it seems rather a burden to put on her little shoulders."

"There's work," said Sarah.

"You forget, I'm a member of the idle rich," teased Rachel. "I don't work, I just clip coupons. But there is art. As Roman says."

"Art?"

"I'm writing a play," whispered Rachel delightedly.

"You're kidding! For the Yiddish theater? Ruby will be thrilled."

"No, silly," said Rachel. "It's in English. I can't tell you if it's any good. You know that theater that opened last year near my house, the Provincetown Playhouse? Roman knows a man in it who says I should give him the play to read when it's done!"

"That's wonderful," said Sarah. "What's it about?"

"A poor little shirtwaist girl who marries a millionaire," said Rachel demurely. "But in the second act she throws up all her wealth and high position for the love of a poor union organizer, and has an illegitimate child by him. And then in the third act she leaves him too, and goes off with her baby to be a world-famous political agitator for women's rights."

Sarah raised one eyebrow and smiled. "Why, my goodness," she murmured. "Do you think anybody will believe a story like that?"

Rachel's end-of-the-year dividend check was enormous. She blinked. For the first time in her life, she had more money than she knew what to do with. Here was this check and New Year's Eve was coming. Between Sarah's engagement and Ruby's success at work and the Russian revolution, they certainly had things to celebrate. She would make a party and invite all the Levys to be her guests on New Year's Eve at Giovanni's, her favorite Italian restaurant in the Village.

It was a bohemian little place. Lanterns hung on the walls, with dyed fishnet. There were candles stuck in empty Chianti bottles on every table. Hannah was impressed by such details and by the well-dressed customers. Of course, her own companions were not so bad either, she thought. Moyshe looked very distinguished, now that his big moustache and long hair were streaked with white. Ruby was elegant in one of her own designs, a black dress with a white organdy collar and cuffs, and her escort, Ben Berliner, was a very well turned-out young man. Rachel was as lovely as ever, and Roman was certainly interesting, if a bit eccentrically dressed in a red shirt with a polka-dot scarf. The standard fell down when she got to Avi and Sarah, but they seemed so happy Hannah didn't have the heart to carp at their clothes. They were going on, as usual, about the Bolshevik revolution, so young, so full of promise.

"It's the dawn of a new age," glowed Sarah, "not only for Russia—for all the world!"

"I'm waiting to see how it is for the Jews," said Moyshe. Sarah threw him a reproachful glance, but Ben Berliner nodded vigorously.

You'd think Ruby would have had the sense to warn them her boyfriend was a Zionist, thought Hannah; she knows what her father's like. When Ben started in on the Balfour Declaration, and how it meant the Jews could finally settle in Palestine and have a homeland, Moyshe actually got up from the table and started pacing around the restaurant to keep himself from making a scene. Hannah was glad Rachel had ordered so much food. It was harder for people to argue when their mouths were full of noodles.

Roman Zach was the only man there who didn't pick fights. He just smiled and stared around him and drew pictures on the tablecloth, a relatively harmless occupation.

"I like your young fellow," Hannah muttered to Rachel. "Nice and quiet."

Rachel laughed and ordered more wine. As dessert and coffee came, she asked for bottle after bottle until they all were floating, unable even to dispute.

"Hannah, propose a toast," ordered Rachel.

Hannah sighed contentedly. "To happy families," she said. "May we all have one. May we all be as happy always as we are tonight, and also Baby Caro, who I hope is asleep by now."

They smiled at Rachel, and drank.

"I want to make a toast," said Moyshe suddenly, raising his glass. "To my wife, the agitator, who brought chicken down to nineteen cents a pound! Hooray for Hannah!"

They all cheered enthusiastically.

Hannah blushed. She could not adjust to this change in their picture of her. But it was certainly wonderful not to have to see Solly Fein and those Garfinkles around the neighborhood anymore.

"And to think," Avi teased her, "that they told me you weren't interested in politics."

"I'm not," she said loudly. "You think I'm crazy like the rest of you? I didn't do anything at all, only the other ladies were complaining how the prices were so high and I couldn't make my own money reach so naturally—"

They drowned her out. "Pooh, pooh," said Moyshe lovingly. "You can't fool us." And finally she had to join in the joke at her own expense, laughing with them as Moyshe held her knee underneath the table.

"What toast would you like to make, Ruby?" said Ben, gazing at her intently. "What do you wish for in the coming year?" If only she would give him some sign of her feelings, he thought.

She reflected for a moment, then, with a smile so brilliant it made his heart turn over, lifted her glass. "To short skirts in 1918," she said. "Six inches off the ground!"

They clinked glasses and drank. Next Avi refilled them.

"You say it for both of us, Sarahleh," he whispered.

"To revolution," she said so loudly people at the next table turned their heads. "In the United States, in our lifetime! Why should Russia have all the fun?"

"Shh!" said Hannah. "People are looking."

As Rachel gazed around the company, she was filled with so much love it began to overflow and she got a little weepy, being here with these good friends, so steadfast. She filled their glasses once more and raised her own.

"I want to propose a toast," she said in her clear voice. "To us, to 1918, and all its promise! To the bright future!"

"To 1918," they echoed, clinking their glasses and raising them to their lips, smiling at one another.

"To the bright future," they said. But they all meant something different by it.

S0-BQZ-563

"Miss Brandon, the surgeon has declared that no one dies of seasickness. You will not be the first, and certainly not on my watch," Hugh said firmly.

"I. Would. Rather. Die."

At least she was alert. "It's not allowed in the Royal Navy, my dear," he told her kindly. "When Private Leonard returns, I am going to tidy you, find you another nightgown and put you in my sleeping cot."

She started to cry in earnest then, which was a sorry sight, since there were no tears. "Leave me alone," she pleaded.

"I can't leave you alone. I would do anything to spare you embarrassment, Miss Brandon, but you must be tended to."

"The surgeon?"

"Busy. My dear, you'll just have to trust me, because there is no one else."

* * *

Marrying the Royal Marine
Harlequin® Historical #998—June 2010

**Praise for Carla Kelly,
recipient of a Career Achievement Award
from *RT Book Reviews*
and winner of two RITA® Awards**

"A powerful and wonderfully perceptive author."
—*New York Times* bestselling author Mary Jo Putney

"A wonderfully fresh and original voice..."
—*RT Book Reviews*

"Kelly has the rare ability to create realistic yet
sympathetic characters that linger in the mind.
One of the most respected...Regency writers."
—*Library Journal*

"Carla Kelly is always a joy to read."
—*RT Book Reviews*

"Ms. Kelly writes with a rich flavor that adds great
depth of emotion to all her characterizations."
—*RT Book Reviews*

CARLA KELLY
Marrying the Royal Marine

HARLEQUIN®

TORONTO • NEW YORK • LONDON
AMSTERDAM • PARIS • SYDNEY • HAMBURG
STOCKHOLM • ATHENS • TOKYO • MILAN • MADRID
PRAGUE • WARSAW • BUDAPEST • AUCKLAND

If you purchased this book without a cover you should be aware
that this book is stolen property. It was reported as "unsold and
destroyed" to the publisher, and neither the author nor the
publisher has received any payment for this "stripped book."

Recycling programs
for this product may
not exist in your area.

ISBN-13: 978-0-373-29598-2

MARRYING THE ROYAL MARINE

Copyright © 2010 by Carla Kelly

All rights reserved. Except for use in any review, the reproduction or
utilization of this work in whole or in part in any form by any electronic,
mechanical or other means, now known or hereafter invented, including
xerography, photocopying and recording, or in any information storage
or retrieval system, is forbidden without the written permission of the
publisher, Harlequin Enterprises Limited, 225 Duncan Mill Road,
Don Mills, Ontario, Canada M3B 3K9.

This is a work of fiction. Names, characters, places and incidents are
either the product of the author's imagination or are used fictitiously,
and any resemblance to actual persons, living or dead, business
establishments, events or locales is entirely coincidental.

This edition published by arrangement with Harlequin Books S.A.

For questions and comments about the quality of this book
please contact us at Customer_eCare@Harlequin.ca.

® and TM are trademarks of the publisher. Trademarks indicated with
® are registered in the United States Patent and Trademark Office, the
Canadian Trade Marks Office and in other countries.

www.eHarlequin.com

Printed in U.S.A.

To Lynn and Bob Turner, former U.S. Marines.
Semper Fi to you both.

Prologue

Stonehouse Royal Marine Barracks, Third Division, Plymouth—May 1812

Black leather stock in hand, Lieutenant Colonel Hugh Philippe d'Anvers Junot, Royal Marine, stared into his mirror and decided his father was right: he was lonely.

Maybe early symptoms were the little drawings that deckled Hugh's memorandum tablet during endless meetings in the conference room at Marine Barracks. As Colonel Commandant Lord Villiers covered item after item in his stringent style, Hugh had started drawing a little lady peeking around the edge of her bonnet. During one particularly dull budget meeting, he drew a whole file of them down the side of the page.

Hugh gazed more thoughtfully into the mirror, not bothered by his reflection—he knew his height, posture, curly brown hair, and nicely chiselled lips met the demands of any recruiting poster—but by the humbling knowledge that his father still knew him best.

He had written to his father, describing his restlessness and his dissatisfaction with the perils of promotion. While flattering, the promotion had bumped him off a ship of the line and into an office. *I know I should appreciate this promotion*, he had written, *but, Da, I am out of sorts. I'm not sure what I want. I'm sour and discontented. Any advice would be appreciated. Your dutiful, if disgruntled, son.*

A week later, he had read Da's reply over breakfast. He read it once and laughed; he read it again and pushed back his chair, thoughtful. He sat there longer than he should have, touched that his father had probably hit on the matter: he was lonely.

Damn this war, he had thought then. The words were plainspoken as Da was plainspoken: *My dear son, I wrote a similar letter to your grandfather once, before I met your mother, God rest her soul. Son, can ye find a wife?*

'That takes more time than I have, Da,' he had said out loud, but Da was probably right. Lately, when he attended the Presbyterian church in Devonport, he found himself paying less attention to the sermon and more attention to husbands, wives, and children sitting in the pews around him. He found himself envying both the comfortable looks of the couples married longest, and the shy handholdings and smouldering glances of the newly married. He tried to imagine the pleasure of marrying and rearing children, and found that he could not. War had ruined him; perhaps Da wasn't aware of that.

It was food for thought this May morning, and he chewed on it as he took advantage of a welcome hiatus from a meeting—the Colonel Commandant's gout was dictating a start one hour later than usual—and took himself to Stonehouse Naval Hospital. He had heard the jetty bell clanging late last night, and knew there would be wounded Marines to visit.

The air was crisp and cool, but threatening summer when he arrived at Block Four, where his friend Owen Brackett worked his surgeon's magic on the quick and nearly dead. He found Owen on the second floor.

The surgeon turned to Hugh with a tired smile. 'Did the jetty bell wake you?'

Hugh nodded. 'Any Marines?'

'Aye. If you have a mind to visit, come with me.'

Hugh followed Brackett down the stairs into another ward. With an inward sigh, he noted screens around several beds.

'There was a cutter returning from Surgeon Brittle's satellite hospital in Oporto. The cutter was stopped at sea by a frigate with some nasty cases to transfer,' Owen said. 'Seems there was a landing attempted farther north along the Portuguese coast. Sit.'

He sat, never used to ghastly wounds, and put his hands on the man's remaining arm, which caused the Marine's eyes to flicker open.

'Meet Lieutenant Nigel Graves, First Division,' Brackett whispered before leaving.

'From Chatham?' Hugh asked, putting his lips close to the man's ear.

'Aye, sir. Serving on...*Relentless*.' It took ages for him to get out the words.

'A regular mauling?' he asked, his voice soft. 'Take your time, Lieutenant. We have all day.' He didn't; the Lieutenant didn't. It was a serviceable lie; both knew it.

Lieutenant Graves tried to sit up. Hugh slipped his arm under the young man's neck. 'What were you doing?'

'Trying to land at Vigo.'

'A one-ship operation?'

'Four ships, sir.' He sighed, his exasperation obvious. 'We didn't know each other! Who was in charge when the Major died?' He closed his eyes. 'It was a disaster, sir. We should have been better.'

Hugh could tell he wanted to say more, but Lieutenant Graves took that moment to die. Hugh gently lowered him to the cot. He was still sitting there when Owen Brackett returned, enquired about the time of death from him, and wrote it on the chart.

'A botched landing at Vigo,' Hugh said. 'Uncoordinated Marines working against each other, when all they wanted to do was fight! I've heard this before.'

'It makes you angry,' Owen said.

'Aye.' Hugh smoothed down the Lieutenant's hair. 'Each company on each vessel is a well-oiled machine, because we train them that way. Put one hundred of them on a ship of the line, and you have a fighting force. Try to coordinate twenty-five here or fifteen there from three or four frigates operating in tandem, and it can be a disaster.'

The surgeon nodded. 'All they want to do is their best. They're Marines, after all. We expect no less.'

Hugh thought about that as he took the footbridge back over the stream to the administration building of the Third Division. He was never late to anything, but he was late now.

The meeting was in the conference room on the first floor. He stopped outside the door, hand on knob, as a good idea settled around him and blew away the fug.

Why could someone not enquire of the Marines at war how they saw themselves being used in the Peninsula?

'You're late, Colonel Junot,' his Colonel Commandant snapped.

'Aye, my lord. I have no excuse.'

'Are those *stains* on your uniform sleeve?'

Everyone looked. Hugh saw no sympathy. 'Aye, my lord.'

Perhaps it was his gout; Lord Villiers was not in a forgiving mood. 'Well? Well?'

'I was holding a dying man and he had a head wound, my lord.'

His fellow Marine officers snapped to attention where they sat. It might have been a tennis match; they looked at the Commandant, as if on one swivel, then back at Hugh.

'Explain yourself, sir,' Lord Villiers said, his voice calmer.

'I visited Stonehouse, my lord.' He remained at attention. 'Colonel, I know you have an agenda, but I have an idea.'

Chapter One

Lord Villiers liked the idea and moved on it promptly. He unbent enough to tell Hugh, as he handed him his orders, 'This smacks of something I would have done at your age, given your dislike of the conference table.'

'I, sir?'

'Belay it, Colonel Junot! Don't bamboozle someone who, believe it or not, used to chafe to roam the world. Perhaps we owe the late Lieutenant Graves a debt unpayable. Now take the first frigate bound to Portugal before I change my mind.'

Hugh did precisely that. With his dunnage stowed on the *Perseverance* and his berth assigned—an evil-smelling cabin off the wardroom—Hugh had dinner with Surgeon Brackett on his last night in port. Owen gave him a letter for Philemon Brittle, chief surgeon at the Oporto satellite hospital, and passed on a little gossip.

'It's just a rumour, mind, but Phil seems to have engineered a billet for his sister-in-law, a Miss Brandon, at his hospital. He's a clever man, but I'm agog to know how he managed it, if the scuttlebutt is true,' Brackett said. 'Perhaps she is sailing on the *Perseverance*.'

'Actually, she is,' Hugh said, accepting tea from Amanda Brackett. 'I've already seen her.'

'She has two beautiful sisters, one of whom took leave of her senses and married Phil Brittle. Perhaps your voyage will be more interesting than usual,' the surgeon teased.

Hugh sipped his tea. 'Spectacles.'

'You're a shallow man,' Amanda Brackett said, her voice crisp.

Hugh winced elaborately and Owen laughed. 'Skewered! Mandy, I won't have a friend left in the entire fleet if you abuse our guests so. Oh. Wait. He's a Royal Marine. They don't count.'

Hugh joined in their laughter, at ease with their camaraderie enough to unbend. 'I'll have you know I took a good look at her remarkable blue eyes, and, oh, that auburn hair.'

'All the sisters have it,' Amanda said. 'More ragout?'

'No, thank you, although I am fully aware it is the best thing I will taste until I fetch the Portuguese coast in a week or so.' He set down his cup. 'Miss Brandon is too young to tempt me, Amanda. I doubt she is a day over eighteen.'

'And you are antiquated at thirty-seven?'

'I am. Besides that, what female in her right mind, whatever her age, would make a Marine the object of her affection?'

'You have me there, Colonel,' Amanda said promptly, which made Owen laugh.

She did have him, too, Hugh reflected wryly, as he walked from Stonehouse, across the footbridge, and back to the barrack for a final night on shore. *Perhaps I am shallow*, he considered, as he lay in bed later. Amanda

Brackett was right; he was vain and shallow. Maybe daft, too. He lay awake worrying more about his assignment, putting Miss Brandon far from his mind.

Hugh joined the *Perseverance* at first light, the side boys lined up and the bosun's mate piping him aboard. His face set in that no-nonsense look every Marine cultivated, and which he had perfected, he scanned the rank of Marines on board. He noted their awed recognition of his person, but after last night's conversation, he felt embarrassed.

He chatted with Captain Adney for only a brief minute, knowing well that the man was too busy for conversation. Out of the corner of his eye, he noticed Miss Brandon standing quietly by the binnacle, her hands clasped neatly in front of her, the picture of rectitude, or at the very least, someone just removed from the schoolroom herself. Amanda Brackett had said as much last night. She was a green girl.

He had to admit there was something more about Miss Brandon, evidenced by the two Midshipmen and Lieutenant grouped about her, appearing to hang on her every word. She had inclined her head to one side and was paying close attention to the Lieutenant. Hugh smiled. He could practically see the man's blush from here on the quarterdeck.

Miss Brandon, you are obviously a good listener, he thought. *Perhaps that compensates for spectacles.* The moment the thought swirled in his brain, he felt small again. *What a snob I am*, he concluded, turning his attention again to Captain Adney.

'…passage of some five days, Colonel, if we're lucky,' he was saying. 'Is it Oporto or Lisbon for you?'

It scarcely mattered, considering his *carte blanche* to wander the coastline on his fact-finding mission. Perhaps he should start at Lisbon. 'Oporto,' he said. He knew he had a letter for Surgeon Brittle, Miss Brandon's brother-in-law, but he also knew he could just give it to her and make his way to Lisbon, avoiding Oporto altogether. 'Oporto,' he repeated, not sure why.

'Very well, sir,' Captain Adney told him. 'And now, Colonel, I am to take us out of harbour with the tide. Excuse me, please.'

Hugh inclined his head and the Captain moved towards his helmsman, standing ready at the wheel. Hugh watched with amusement as the flock around Miss Brandon moved away quickly, now that their Captain was on the loose and prepared to work them.

Hardly knowing why, Hugh joined her. He congratulated himself on thinking up a reason to introduce himself. He doffed his hat and bowed. 'Miss Brandon? Pray forgive my rag manners in introducing myself. I am Lieutenant Colonel Hugh Junot, and I have some business you might discharge for me.'

She smiled at him, and he understood instantly why the Lieutenant and Midshipmen had been attracted to her like iron filings to a magnet. She had a direct gaze that seemed to block out everything around her and focus solely on the object of her interest. He felt amazingly flattered, even though she was doing nothing more than giving him her attention. There was nothing coy, arch or even flirtatious about her expression. She was so completely *present*. He couldn't describe it any better.

She dropped him a deep curtsy. Considering that it

was high summer and she wore no cloak, this gave him ample opportunity to admire her handsome bosom.

'Yes, Colonel, I am Miss Brandon.'

As he put on his hat again, her eyes followed it up and she did take a little breath, as though she was not used to her present company. He knew she must be familiar enough with the Royal Navy, considering her relationship to a captain and a surgeon, but he did not think his splendid uniform was ringing any bells.

'I am a Marine, Miss Brandon,' he said.

'And I am a hopeless landlubber, Colonel,' she replied with a smile. 'I should have known that. What can I do for you?'

What a polite question, he thought. *It is almost as if I were infirm. She is looking at me as though I have a foot in the grave, no teeth, and more years than her brothers-in-law combined. What an ass I am.*

Feeling his age—at least every scar on his body had not started to ache simultaneously—he nodded to her. 'Miss Brandon, I have been charged by Surgeon Owen Brackett to take a letter to your brother-in-law in Oporto. I suppose that is why I sought to introduce myself, rather than wait for someone else—who, I do not know—to perform that office.'

That is marvellously lame, he thought sourly, thinking of the gawking Midshipmen who had so recently claimed her attention, and mentally adding himself to their number.

The deferential look left her face. 'Taking a letter to my brother-in-law is a pleasant assignment, sir. I am headed to the same place. Do you know Surgeon Brittle?'

'Not yet.'

'If you are too busy to discharge your duty, I can certainly relieve you of the letter, Colonel,' she told him.

'I am going there, too.'

He could think of nothing more to say, but she didn't seem awkwardly waiting for conversation. Instead, she turned her back against the rail to watch the foretopmen in the rigging, preparing to spill down the sails and begin their voyage. It was a sight he always enjoyed, too, so he stood beside her in silence and watched. Although he had scarce acquaintance with the lady beside him, he felt no urge to blather on, in the way that newly introduced people often do.

The *Perseverance* began to move, and he felt his heart lift, so glad he was to be at sea again and not sitting in a conference room. He would range the coast, watch his Marines in action, interview them, and possibly formulate a way to increase their utility. With any luck, he could stretch his assignment through the summer and into autumn.

'I have never sailed before,' Miss Brandon said.

'You'll get your sea legs,' he assured her, his eyes on the men balancing against the yardarms. He hoped it wasn't improper to mention legs to a lady, even the sea kind.

In a few more minutes, she went belowdeck. He watched Marines working the capstan with the sailors, and others already standing sentry by the water butt and the helm. He nodded to the Sergeant of Marines, who snapped to attention, and introduced himself as the senior non-commissioned officer on board. A thirty-six-gun frigate had no commissioned officer. Hugh explained his mission and told the man to carry on.

He stayed on deck until the *Perseverance* tacked out

of Plymouth Sound and into the high rollers of the Channel itself. He observed the greasy swell of the current and knew they were in for some rough water. No matter—he was never seasick.

He went belowdeck and into his cabin, a typical knocked-together affair made of framed canvas, which was taken down when the gundeck cleared for action. His sleeping cot, hung directly over the cannon, was already swaying to the rhythm of the Atlantic Ocean. He timed the swell and rolled into the cot for a nap.

Because Miss Brandon had admitted this was her first sea voyage, Hugh was not surprised when she did not appear for dinner in the wardroom. Captain Adney had the good sense to give her the cabin with actual walls, one that probably should have gone to a Lieutenant Colonel of Marines, had a woman not been voyaging. The Sergeant had posted a sentry outside her door, which was as it should be. There were no flies growing on this little Marine detachment, and so he would note in his journal.

There was no shortage of conversation around the wardroom table. The frigate's officers let him into their conversation and seemed interested in his plan. Used to the sea, they kept protective hands around their plates and expertly trapped dishes sent sliding by the ship's increasingly violent motion. When the table was cleared and the steward brought out a bottle, Hugh frowned to hear the sound of vomiting from Miss Brandon's cabin.

The surgeon sighed and reached for the sherry as it started to slide. 'Too bad there is no remedy for *mal de mer*,' he said. 'She'll be glad to make land in a week.'

They chuckled, offered the usual toasts, hashed over

the war, and departed for their own duties. Hugh sat a while longer at the table, tempted to knock on Miss Brandon's door and at least make sure she had a basin to vomit in.

She didn't come out at all the next day, either. *Poor thing*, Hugh thought, as he made his rounds of the Marine Privates and Corporals, trying to question them about their duties, taking notes, and wondering how to make Marines naturally wary of high command understand that all he wanted was to learn from them. Maybe the notion was too radical.

Later that night he was lying in his violently swinging sleeping cot, stewing over his plans, when someone knocked on the frame of his canvas wall.

'Colonel, Private Leonard, sir.'

Hugh got up in one motion, alert. Leonard was the sentry outside Miss Brandon's door. He had no business even crossing the wardroom, not when he was on duty. *Your Sergeant will hear from me, Private*, he thought, as he yanked open his door.

'How dare you abandon your post!' he snapped.

If he thought to intimidate Private Leonard, he was mistaken. The man seemed intent on a more important matter than the potential threat of the lash.

'Colonel Junot, it's Miss Brandon. I've stood sentinel outside her door for nearly four hours now, and I'm worried.' The Private braced himself against the next roll and wiggle as the *Perseverance* rose, then plunged into the trough of a towering wave. 'She was puking and bawling, and now she's too quiet. I didn't think I should wait to speak until the watch relieved me, sir.'

Here's one Marine who thinks on his feet, Hugh thought, as he reached for his uniform jacket. 'You acted wisely. Return to your post, Private,' he said, his voice normal.

He had his misgivings as he crossed the wardroom and knocked on her door. Too bad there was not another female on board. He knocked again. No answer. He looked at Private Leonard. 'I go in, don't I?' he murmured, feeling suddenly shy and not afraid to admit it. There may have been a great gulf between a Lieutenant Colonel and a Private, but they were both men.

'I think so, sir,' the Private said. 'Do you have a lamp?'

'Go get mine.'

He opened the door and was assailed by the stench of vomit. 'Miss Brandon?' he called.

No answer. Alarmed now, he was by her sleeping cot in two steps. He could barely see her in the gloom. He touched her shoulder and his hand came away damp. He shook her more vigorously and was rewarded with a slight moan.

No one dies of seasickness, he reminded himself. 'Miss Brandon?' he asked again. 'Can you hear me?'

Private Leonard returned with his lantern, holding it above them in the tiny cabin. The light fell on as pitiful a specimen of womanhood as he had ever seen. Gone was the moderately attractive, composed young lady of two days ago. In her place was a creature so exhausted with vomiting that she could barely raise her hands to cover her eyes against the feeble glow of the lantern.

'I should have approached you sooner, sir,' Private Leonard said, his voice full of remorse.

'How were you to know?' he asked. 'We officers

should have wondered what was going on when she didn't come out for meals. Private, go find the surgeon. I am relieving you at post.'

'Aye, aye, Colonel.'

Uncertain what to do, Hugh hung the lantern from the deck beam and gently moved Miss Brandon's matted hair from her face, which was dry and caked. She didn't open her eyes, but ran her tongue over cracked lips. 'You're completely parched,' he said. 'Dryer than a bone. My goodness, Miss Brandon.'

She started to cry then, except she was too dehydrated for tears. Out of his element, he didn't know how to comfort her. Was she in pain? He wished there was a porthole he could open to let in some bracing sea air and banish the odour. Poor Miss Brandon was probably suffering the worst kind of mortification to be so discovered by a man she barely knew. If there was a better example of helplessness, he had never encountered it.

Private Leonard returned. Hugh looked behind him, but there was no surgeon.

'Sir, the surgeon and his mate are both tending to a foretopman who fell from the rigging.' Private Leonard made a face. 'He reminded me that no one dies of seasickness and recommended we get some water and vinegar so she can clean herself up.'

'Private, she can't clean a fingernail in her condition,' he said. He stood there a moment, looking down at Miss Brandon, then at the Private. 'Go get a quart or two of vinegar from Cook and a gallon of fresh water. If anyone gives you any grief, tell them they don't want to know how bad it will be if I have to come up and do it myself!'

The Private stood even straighter. 'Aye, aye, sir. Should I get some cloths, too?'

'As many as you can gather. Good thinking.'

He closed the door behind the Private, who pounded up the companionway, obviously glad to have a purpose. He found a stool and pulled it close to the sleeping cot, which was swaying to the ship's roll. He tried to keep his tone conversational, knowing that nothing he was going to do in the next hour would be pleasing to a modest lady. 'Miss Brandon, the surgeon cannot come, but he has declared that no one dies of seasickness. You will not be the first, and certainly not on my watch.'

'I. Would. Rather. Die.'

At least she was alert. 'It's not allowed in the Royal Navy, my dear,' he told her kindly. 'When Private Leonard returns, I am going to tidy you, find you another nightgown, and put you in my sleeping cot, so I can swab down this one.'

She started to cry in earnest then, which was a sorry sight, since there were no tears. 'Leave me alone,' she pleaded.

'I can't leave you alone. I would do anything to spare you embarrassment, Miss Brandon, but you must be tended to.'

'The surgeon?'

'Busy. My dear, you'll just have to trust me, because there is no one else.'

She hadn't opened her eyes in their whole exchange, and it touched him to think how embarrassed she must be. She was obviously well educated and gently reared, and this was probably the first time in her whole life she had ever been alone with a man who wasn't a relative. He wasn't sure what to do, but he put his hand against her soiled cheek and held it there until she stopped her dry sobbing.

Private Leonard returned with the vinegar and water. He had tucked clean rags under his arm, and removed them when he set down the bucket. 'I'll get some sea water, too, Colonel,' he said. 'That fresh water isn't going to go far, and you can swab her down with salt water.'

'Do it, Private. When you return, close the door and resume your sentry duty. If there are two of us trying to help Miss Brandon, it'll be too much for her.'

He could see that Private Leonard was relieved by that order. He came back soon with two buckets of sea water; God knows there was plenty of it to spare on a frigate in a squall. Private Leonard closed the door quietly.

Miss Brandon tried to sit up and failed. 'If you leave the water, I can do this myself,' she managed to say.

'Begging your pardon, Miss Brandon, but I don't think you even have the strength to scratch your nose right now,' he told her. 'I am so sorry that no one knew the extent of your extremity, or believe me, it would not have come to this.'

She opened her eyes then, and he saw all the shame, embarrassment, and humility in the world reflecting from them. All she could do was shake her head slowly and put up her hands to cover her chest.

It was such a defensive gesture that his heart went out to her. She was soiled and smelly and more wretched that the worst drab in the foulest slum in the rankest seaport he had ever visited. The last thing he wanted to do was violate her dignity, which was all she had remaining. He rested his hands gently on hers. 'Whatever I do for you,

I do out of utter necessity, Miss Brandon. I can do no less because I never back down from a crisis.' He smiled at her. 'My, that sounds top-lofty, but it is true. Take a leap of faith, Miss Brandon; trust me to be kind.'

She was silent a long while, her hands still held stubbornly in front of her. 'I have no choice, have I?' she said finally.

'No, you don't. Take that leap, Miss Brandon. I won't fail you.'

Chapter Two

Miss Brandon didn't say anything, but her hands relaxed. Hugh did nothing for a moment, because he didn't know where to begin. He looked closer in the dim light. She was wearing a nightgown, which chastely covered most of her, so his task was not as uncomfortable yet as it was going to get. He opened the door.

'Private, go in my cabin. Bring my shaving basin, plus the silver cup next to it.'

He was back in a moment with the items. Hugh put his hand behind Miss Brandon's back and carefully raised her upright. He dipped the cup in the fresh water Private Leonard had brought, and put it to her lips.

'It will only make me vomit,' she protested weakly.

'Just swirl it around in your mouth, lean over the edge of the cot and spit it out.'

'On the *floor*?' she asked, aghast.

'Yes, ma'am. The deck—the floor—has suffered some ill usage. I'll never tell.'

She sighed. He held the cup to her parched lips and she

took a small sip, doing what he said and spitting on the deck.

'Try another sip and swallow it this time.'

She started to protest, but gamely squared her shoulders and did as he said. 'My throat is on fire,' she said, her voice a croak.

'I imagine it is raw, indeed, Miss Brandon, considering the ill treatment it has suffered for nearly two days.' It smote him again how careless they had all been not to check on her. 'Try another sip. Just a small one.'

She did, then shook her head at more. They both waited, but she kept it down.

'I'm encouraged. Just sit here,' he told her. 'I'm going to mix some vinegar in this little bit of fresh water and wipe your face and neck. I'll see what can be done with your hair.'

Silent, she let him do what he wanted, turning her head obediently so he could swab around her eyes and nostrils. 'Soon I'll have you smelling like a pickle, Miss Brandon,' he joked, trying to lighten the mood. She did not indicate any amusement, which hardly surprised him. When her face was as clean as he could manage, he added more vinegar to the bucket of sea water and wiped her neck and ears.

Her hair took much longer, as he pulled a few strands at a time through the vinegar-soaked cloth between his fingers, working as quickly and gently as he could. He had to stop for a while when the ship began to labour up and down steeper troughs, as the storm intensified. She moaned with the motion, so he braced the sleeping cot with his body so it would not swing. As he watched her face, it suddenly occurred to him that part of her problem was fear.

'Miss Brandon, I assure you that as bad as this seems, we're not going to sink,' he said. He spoke loud enough to be heard above the creaking and groaning he knew were normal ship noises in a storm. 'Ships are noisy. The sea is rough, I will grant you, but that is life in the Channel.'

She said nothing, but turned her face into his shoulder. Hugh kept his arms tight around her, crooning nothing that made any sense, but which seemed to calm her. He held her close as she clung to him, terrified.

When the waves seemed to subside, he released her and went back to cleaning her long hair. When he felt reasonably satisfied, he knew he could not avoid the next step. 'Miss Brandon, do you have another nightgown in your luggage?'

She nodded, and started to cry again.

'I'd happily turn my back and let you manage this next part by yourself, my dear, but I don't think you're up to it. You can't stay in this nightgown.'

After another long silence during which he made no attempt to rush her, her hands went to the buttons on her gown. She tried to undo them, but finally shook her head. Without a word, he undid her buttons. 'Where's another nightgown?' he asked quietly.

She told him and he found it, fragrant with lavender, in her trunk. Taking a deep breath, Hugh pulled back the sheet. Her hand went to his wrist, so he did nothing more until she relaxed her grip.

'I'm going to roll up your nightgown, so we can best keep the soiled part away from your face and hair when I pull it over your head. Miss Brandon, I regret the mortification I know I am causing you,' he said.

She was sobbing in good earnest now, and the parched sound pained him more than she possibly could have realised. Not only was he trampling on her female delicacy now, but jumping up and down on it.

'No fears, Miss Brandon, no fears,' he said quietly, trying to find a balance between sympathy and command.

Maybe she finally realised he was an ally. He wasn't sure he would have been as brave as she was, considering her total helplessness to take care of herself. Feeling as stupid and callow as the merest youth, he couldn't think of a thing to say except, 'I mean you no harm. Not ever.'

He wondered why he said that, but his words, spoken quietly but firmly, seemed to give Miss Brandon the confirmation she needed of his utter sincerity. She stopped sobbing, but rested her head against him, not so much because she was tired now, but because she needed his reassurance. He could have been wrong, but that was what the moment felt like, and he wasn't one to quibble.

Without any talk, he continued rolling up her nightgown as she raised her arms. His fingers brushed against her bare breast, but they were both beyond embarrassment. Even though the night was warm, she shivered a little. He quickly popped her into the clean nightgown, pulling it down to her ankles, then helped her lie back. She sighed with relief and closed her eyes.

The winds picked up and the ship began another series of torturous swoops through the waves. He braced the cot against his hip and kept his arms tight around Miss Brandon as she clung to him and shivered.

'I don't know how you do this,' she said finally, when the winds subsided.

'It comes with the job,' he replied and chuckled.

'Are you never seasick?'

'No.'

'Are you lying?'

He wasn't, but he wanted her to laugh. 'Yes.' He knew nothing in the rest of his life would ever put him at ease more than the slight sound of her laugh, muffled against his chest.

Since his arms were around her, he picked her up. She stiffened. 'I'm going to carry you across the wardroom to my pathetic cabin, and put you in my cot. You're going to promise me you won't be sick in it, and you're going to go to sleep. I'll come back in here and clean up everything.'

'A Lieutenant Colonel in the Royal Marines,' she murmured, and Hugh could hear the embarrassment in her voice again.

'I can't help that,' he told her, and was rewarded with another chuckle. 'I've swabbed a deck or two in my earlier days.' He wasn't going to tell her how unpleasant that had been, cleaning up a gun deck after a battle. Nothing in her cabin could ever compare with that, but he wasn't going to enlighten her further.

He was prepared to stay with her in his cabin until she felt easy, but she went to sleep almost before he finished tucking his blanket around her. He looked down at her, smelling of vinegar now, but as tidy as he could make her, in his clumsy way. He looked closer. There was something missing. He gave her a slight shake.

'Miss Brandon, where are your spectacles?'

She opened her eyes, and he saw nothing but remorse. 'I…I fear they landed in that basin by the cot, when I vomited.'

She started to laugh then, which must have hurt because her hand went to her throat. 'Don't look so stunned, Colonel,' she told him. 'I am quizzing you. They're in my trunk, next to my hair brush.'

He grinned at her, relieved that she could make a joke. 'I'll get you for that.'

'You and who…?' she began, then drifted to sleep.

He stood there another long moment, watching her sleep, dumbfounded by her resiliency, and not totally sure what had just happened. 'I'd have looked for them in that foul basin, I hope you know,' he whispered, then left his cabin.

He spent the next hour cleaning Miss Brandon's cabin. Before Private Leonard went off duty and was replaced by another sentry, he swore him to utter secrecy on what had passed this evening.

'Sir, I would never say anything,' the Private assured him. 'She's a brave little trooper, isn't she?'

Hugh would have spent the night in her cot, except that it was wet with vinegar and he didn't relish the notion. He could put his greatcoat on the floor in his cabin and not disturb Miss Brandon at all. He put her nightgown to soak in the bucket with sea water, and poured in the remaining vinegar. He found his way to the orlop deck, where the surgeon, eyes bleary, was staring at a forefinger avulsion that gave Hugh the shivers.

'He caught it on a pump, if you can imagine,' the surgeon murmured. He patted the seaman who belonged to the finger. 'Steady, lad, steady. It looks worse than it is, as most things do.'

While the seaman stared at his own finger, Hugh took

the surgeon aside and explained what had happened to Miss Brandon.

'Poor little lady,' the surgeon said. 'I hope you were gentle with her, Colonel.'

'I did my best.'

The surgeon shook his head. 'Only two days out, and already this voyage is more than she bargained for, I'm certain. All's well that ends. Give her some porridge tomorrow morning and a ship's biscuit, along with fortified wine, and all the water she will drink. That should take care of the dehydration.'

Hugh walked thoughtfully back to his deck, after looking in on the unconscious foretopman, with the surgeon's mate sitting beside him. A howl from the orlop told him the surgeon had taken care of the avulsion. *Give me Miss Brandon and her troublesome seasickness any day*, he thought with a shudder.

Counting on his rank to mean something to one of the captain's young gentlemen, he asked for and received a blanket and returned to his cabin. He looked down at her, asleep in his gently swaying cot. *Poor little you. The surgeon was right; you didn't bargain on this*, he thought.

Surprisingly content with his lot, Hugh spread his overcoat and pulled the blanket over him. He woke up once in the night to check on her, but she was breathing deeply, with a small sigh on the exhalation of breath that he found childlike and endearing. Feeling charitable, he smiled down at her, and returned to his rest on the deck.

A fierce and nagging thirst woke Polly at sunrise, rather than the noise of a ship that she had feared last night would sink at any minute. She stared at the deck beams overhead, wondering where she was, then closed her eyes in total mortification when she remembered. *Maybe if I keep my eyes closed, the entire world will move back four days. I will remain in Torquay with my sister Nana and none of what I know happened will have taken place*, she told herself.

No such luck. She smelled of vinegar because she had been doused in it, then pulled from her nightgown and—horror of horrors—been set right by a Royal Marine of mature years who would probably rather have eaten ground glass than done any of the duties her care had required.

If she could not forget what had happened, perhaps Lieutenant Colonel Junot had transferred during the night to another vessel, one sailing to Australia. Failing that, hopefully he had suffered amnesia and remembered nothing past his tenth birthday. No such luck. She could hear someone snoring softly, so she rose up carefully on her elbow and peered over the edge of the sleeping cot.

There lay her saviour, a mature man—not a Midshipman—with curly dark hair going a bit grey at the temples, a straight nose, and chiselled lips that had caught her attention a few days ago, when she was still a reasonable being. He lay on his back and looked surprisingly comfortable, as though he had slept in worse places. He had removed his shoes, unbuttoned his dark trousers, and unhooked his uniform tunic, so a wildly informal checked shirt showed through. The gilt gorget was still clasped around his neck, which made her smile in spite of her mortification, because he looked incongruously authoritative.

He opened his eyes suddenly and he smiled at her,

because she must have looked even funnier, peering at him over the edge of the sleeping cot like a child in a strange house.

'Good morning, Miss Brandon. See? You're alive.'

If he had meant to put her at her ease, he had succeeded, even as he lay there all stretched out. He yawned, then sat up, his blanket around him again.

'Would you like some water?' he asked.

She nodded, then carefully sat up, which only made her lie down again, because the room was revolving.

He was on his feet in an instant, turning his back to her to button his trousers, then stretching his arm up to grasp the deck beam as he assessed her. 'Dizzy?'

She nodded, and wished she hadn't. 'Now the ship is spinning,' she groaned.

'It will stop.' He brought her a drink in a battered silver cup that looked as if it had been through a campaign or two. His free arm went behind her back and gently lifted her up just enough to pour some water down her sorely tried throat. 'Being as dried out as you are plays merry hell with body humours, Miss Brandon. You need to eat something.'

'Never again,' she told him firmly. 'I have sworn off food for ever.'

'Take a chance,' he teased. 'You might be surprised how gratifying it is to swallow food, rather than wear it. Another sip now. That's a good girl. Let me lay you down again.'

After he did so, he tucked the blanket up to her chin again. 'You'll do, Brandon,' he told her in a gruff voice, and she knew that not a kinder man inhabited the entire universe, no matter if he was a Marine and fearsome. 'Go back to sleep.'

She closed her eyes dutifully, certain she wouldn't sleep because she was so embarrassed, except that the Colonel yawned loudly. She opened her eyes at such rag manners, then watched as he stretched and slapped the deck beam overhead, exclaiming, 'I love a sea voyage, Brandon. Don't you?' which made her giggle and decide that perhaps she would live, after all.

When she woke again, it was full light and the Colonel was gone. She sat up more cautiously this time, pleased when the ship did not spin. She wasn't sure what to do, especially without her spectacles, except that there they were in their little case, next to the pillow. *What a nice man*, she thought, as she put them on.

She looked around. He had also brought over her robe, which she had originally hung on a peg in her cabin. *I think he wants me gone from his cabin*, she told herself, and heaven knew, who could blame him?

As for that, he didn't. Colonel Junot had left a folded note next to her robe on the end of the cot, with 'Brandon' scrawled on it. She couldn't help but smile at that, wondering why on earth he had decided to call her Brandon. All she could assume was that after the intimacy they had been through together, he thought Miss Brandon too formal, but Polly too liberal. Whatever the reason, she decided she liked it. She could never call him anything but Colonel, of course.

She read the note to herself: *Brandon, a loblolly boy is scrubbing down your cabin and will light sulphur in it. The stench will be wicked for a while, so I moved your trunk into the wardroom. Captain Adney's steward will bring you porridge and fortified wine, which the surgeon insisted on.*

He signed it 'Junot', which surprised her. When he introduced himself, he had pronounced his name 'Junnit', but this was obviously a French name. That was even stranger, because he had as rich a Lowland Scottish accent as she had ever heard. 'Colonel, Brandon thinks you are a man of vast contradictions,' she murmured.

She climbed carefully from the sleeping cot, grateful the cannon was there to clutch when the ship shivered and yawed. *I will never develop sea legs*, she told herself. *I will have to become a citizen of Portugal and never cross the Channel again.* When she could stand, she pulled on her robe and climbed back into the sleeping cot, surprised at her exhaustion from so little effort. She doubled the pillow so she could at least see over the edge of the sleeping cot, and abandoned herself to the swaying of the cot, which was gentler this morning.

She noticed the Colonel's luggage, a wooden military trunk with his name stenciled on the side: Hugh Philippe d'Anvers Junot. 'And you sound like a Scot,' she murmured. 'I must know more.'

Trouble was, knowing more meant engaging in casual conversation with a dignified officer of the King's Royal Marines, one who had taken care of her so intimately last night. He had shown incredible aplomb in an assignment that would have made even a saint look askance. No. The *Perseverance* might have been a sixth-rate and one of the smaller of its class, but for the remainder of the voyage— and it couldn't end too soon—she would find a way to avoid bothering Colonel Junot with her presence.

In only a matter of days, they would hail Oporto, and the Colonel would discharge his last duty to her family by handing her brother-in-law a letter from his former chief surgeon. Then, if the Lord Almighty was only half so generous as both Old and New Testaments trumpeted, the man would never have to see her again. She decided it wasn't too much to hope for, considering the probabilities.

So much for resolve. Someone knocked on the flimsy-framed door. She held her breath, hoping for the loblolly boy.

'Brandon? Call me a Greek bearing gifts.'

Not by the way you roll your r's, she thought, wondering if Marines were gluttons for punishment. She cleared her throat, wincing. 'Yes, Colonel?'

He opened the door, carrying a tray. 'As principal idler on this voyage, I volunteered to bring you food, which I insist you eat.'

If he was so determined to put a good face on all this, Polly decided she could do no less. 'I told you I have sworn off food for the remainder of my life, sir.'

'And I have chosen to ignore you,' he replied serenely. 'See here. I even brought along a basin, which I will put in my sleeping cot by your feet, should you take exception to porridge and ship's biscuit. Sit up like the good girl I know you are.'

She did as he said. As congenial as he sounded, there was something of an edge in his imperatives. This was something she had already noticed about her brother-in-law Oliver, so she could only assume it had to do with command. 'Aye, sir,' she said, sitting up.

He set the tray on her lap. To her dismay, he pulled up a stool to sit beside the cot.

'I promise to eat,' she told him, picking up the spoon to illustrate her good faith, if not her appetite. 'You needn't watch me.'

He just couldn't take a hint. 'I truly am a supernumerary on this voyage, and have no pressing tasks. The Midshipmen, under the tender care of the sailing master, are trying to plot courses. I already know how to do that. The surgeon is pulling a tooth, and I have no desire to learn. The Captain is strolling his deck with a properly detached air. The foretopmen are high overhead and I wouldn't help them even if I could. Brandon, you are stuck with me.'

It was obviously time to level with the Lieutenant Colonel, if only for his own good. She set down the spoon. 'Colonel Junot, last night you had to take care of me in ways so personal that I must have offended every sensibility you possess.' Her face was flaming, but she progressed doggedly, unable to look at the man whose bed she had usurped, and whose cabin she occupied. 'I have never been in a situation like this, and doubt you have either.'

'True, that,' he agreed. 'Pick up the spoon, Brandon, lively now.'

She did what he commanded. 'Sir, I am trying to spare you any more dealings with me for the duration of this voyage.'

His brown eyes reminded her of a spaniel given a smack by its owner for soiling a carpet. 'Brandon! Have I offended you?'

She didn't expect that. 'Well, n…no, of course not,' she stammered. 'I owe you a debt I can never repay, but—'

'Take a bite.'

She did, and then another. It stayed down, and she realised how ravenous she was. She ate without speaking, daring a glance at the Colonel once to see a pleased expression on his handsome face. When she finished, he moved aside the bowl and pointed to the ship's biscuit, which she picked up.

'Tell me something, Brandon,' he said finally, as she chewed, then reached for the wine he held out to her. 'If I were ever in a desperate situation and needed your help, would you give it to me?'

'Certainly I would,' she said.

'Then why can't you see that last night was no different?'

He had her there. 'I have never met anyone like you, Colonel,' she told him frankly.

He didn't say anything for a long moment. She took another sip of the wine, then dipped the dry biscuit in it, which made him smile.

'Look at it this way, Brandon. You have a friend.'

What could she say to that? If the man was going to refuse all of her attempts to make herself invisible for the remainder of the voyage, she couldn't be little about it.

'So do you, Colonel Junot.'

Chapter Three

'Excellent!' he declared. 'If you're up to it, I recommend you dress and go on deck. The surgeon found quite a comfortable canvas chair—I tried it out—and moved it to the quarterdeck. Believe it or not, it's easier to face an enemy, which, in your case, is the ocean. We can't have that, Brandon. Fearing the ocean is scarcely patriotic, considering that we are an island nation.'

'I believe you are right, Colonel,' she said, amused.

He lifted her out of the sleeping cot, set her on her bare feet, and walked next to her, his hand warm on the small of her back to steady her, across the short space between his door and the door to her cabin. She could smell sulphur fumes behind the door, and was glad he had moved her trunk into the wardroom.

She shook her head when he offered further assistance, even though she did have trouble standing upright.

'You'll learn,' he assured her, then bowed and went up the companionway.

She took what clothing she needed from her trunk, pausing a time or two to steady herself against the ship's movement. She hadn't even crossed the small space back to Colonel Junot's cabin when a Marine sentry came down the companionway, the same Marine who had stood sentinel last night.

'I want to thank you, Private, for alerting the Colonel to my predicament last night,' she told him.

'My job, ma'am,' he replied simply, but she could tell he was pleased.

That was easy, Polly thought, as she went into the cabin and dressed. Her hair was still a hopeless mess, but at least it smelled strongly of nothing worse than vinegar. 'My kingdom for enough fresh water to wash this tangle,' she murmured.

She cautiously made her way up the companionway to the deck, where she stood and watched the activity around her. No part of England is far from the sea, but she had spent most of her eighteen years in Bath, so she felt herself in an alien world. It was not without its fascination, she decided, as she watched the Sergeant drilling his few Marines in a small space. Close to the bow, the sailing master was schooling the Midshipmen, who awkwardly tried to shoot the sun with sextants. Seamen scrubbed the deck with flat stones the size of prayer books, while others sat cross-legged with sails in their laps, mending tears with large needles. It looked endlessly complex and disorganised, but as she watched she began to see the orderly disorder of life at sea.

She looked towards the quarterdeck again and Captain Adney nodded to her and lifted his hat, indicating she should join him.

'Let me apologise for myself and all my fellow officers for neglecting you,' he said. 'Until Colonel Junot told us what was going on, we had no idea.'

Hopefully, he didn't tell you everything, Polly thought, even though she knew her secrets would always be safe with the Colonel. 'I am feeling much better,' she said.

'Excellent!' Captain Adney obviously had no desire to prod about in the workings of females, so there ended his commentary. He indicated the deck chair Colonel Junot had spoken of. Clasping his hands behind his back, he left her to it, resuming his perusal of the ocean.

Polly smiled to herself, amused by the workings of males. She looked at the chair, noting the chocks placed by the legs so the contraption would not suddenly slide across the quarterdeck. She tried not to hurl herself across the deck, wishing she understood how to ambulate on a slanted plane that would right itself and then slant the other way.

'Brandon, let me suggest that, when you stand, you put one foot behind the other and probably a bit farther apart than you are used to.'

She looked over her shoulder to see Colonel Junot on the steps to the quarterdeck. He came closer and demonstrated. She imitated him.

'Much better. When you walk, this is no time for mincing steps.' He smiled at her halting effort. 'It takes practice. Try out the chair.'

She let him hand her into it, and she couldn't help a sigh of pleasure. Amazing that canvas could feel so comfortable. *I could like this*, she thought, and smiled at the Colonel.

He smiled in turn, then went back down the steps to the main deck, where the Sergeant stood at attention now with his complement of Marines. A word from Colonel Junot and they relaxed, but not by much. In another min-

ute the Sergeant had dismissed them and he sat with
Colonel Junot on a hatch.

Polly watched them both, impressed by their immaculate posture, which lent both men an ever-ready aspect,
as though they could spring into action at a moment's
notice. *I suppose you can*, she told herself, thinking
through all of the Lieutenant Colonel's quick decisions
last night. He had not hesitated once in caring for her, no
matter how difficult it must have been. And he seemed to
take it all in stride. 'You were my ever-present help in
trouble,' she murmured.

She gave her attention to the Colonel again, after making
sure the brim of her bonnet was turned down and they
wouldn't know of her observation. While Colonel Junot
was obviously a Scot, he did look French. She realised with
a surprise that she wanted to know more about him.

Why? she asked herself. Knowing more about
Lieutenant Colonel Hugh Junot would serve no useful
purpose, beyond pointing her out as a flirt, something she
knew she was not. 'Bother it,' she muttered softly.

She had convinced herself that the best thing she could
do for the remainder of this voyage was to follow her original
plan and have as little to do with the Marine as possible.
Once he was busy with whatever it was that had taken him
on this voyage, she would be ignored, which suited her
down to the ground. She had never sought the centre of the
stage.

Come to think of it, why was Colonel Junot on this
voyage? *Bother it*, she told herself again. *I would like to
ask him.*

She knew better. Through Nana, she knew these men
sailed with specific orders that were certainly none of her

business, no matter how great her curiosity. 'Bother it,' she muttered again, and closed her eyes.

She slept, thanks to the gentle swaying of the canvas seat, comforting after the peaks and troughs of last night's squall. When she woke, her glasses rested in her lap. Lieutenant Colonel Junot stood next to her chair, his eyes scanning the water. She was struck all over again with his elegance. Compared to naval officers in their plain dark undress coats, the Marines were gaudy tropical birds. He had not an ounce of superfluous flesh, which made him different from the men she noticed in Bath, who were comfortably padded in the custom of the age.

I am among the elite, she told herself, as she put on her spectacles, bending the wires around her ears again.

Her small motions must have caught Colonel Junot's eye because he looked her way and gave her a slight bow, then came closer.

'How are you feeling?' he asked.

'I am better today,' she said simply. 'Perhaps this means I will not have to seek Portuguese citizenship and remain on the Iberian Peninsula for ever.'

He laughed and looked around for something to sit on, which gratified her further. He didn't seem to mind her company. He found a keg and pulled that beside her chair.

He looked at her a moment before he spoke, perhaps wondering if he should. He cleared his throat. 'I suppose you will think me a case-hardened meddler, Brandon, but I have to know—how on earth did you receive permission to travel into a war zone?'

She was surprised that he was curious about her. She leaned towards him. 'Haven't you heard? I am to be a spy.'

'I had no idea, Brandon. I will tell only my dozen closest friends.'

It was her turn to smile and brush aside the crack-brained notion that the Colonel was flirting with her. Now it was his turn for disappointment, because she couldn't think of a witty reply. Better have with the truth.

'I don't know how I got permission, Colonel,' she told him. 'I wrote to my sister, Laura Brittle, whose husband, Philemon, is chief surgeon at a satellite hospital in Oporto.'

'I have heard of him. Who hasn't? That little hospital in Oporto has saved many a seaman and Marine in just the brief time it has been in operation.'

She blushed, this time with pleasure that he should speak so well of her brother-in-law. 'I wrote to Laura and told her I wanted to be of use.'

'I've also heard good things about Mrs Brittle.'

'She's incredible.'

'Aye. And your other sister?'

'Nana loves her husband and sends him back to sea without a tear…at least until he is out of sight,' she said frankly. There wasn't any point in being too coy around a man who, in the short space of twenty-four hours, knew her more intimately than any man alive.

He wasn't embarrassed by her comment. 'Then he is a lucky man.'

'He knows it, too.'

She realised their heads were close together like conspirators, so she drew back slightly. 'Colonel Junot, I thought I could help out in the hospital. Laura said they have many men who would like to have someone write letters for them, or read to them. I could never do what she does, but I could help.' She shook her head, realising how puny her possible contribution must sound. 'It isn't much, but…'

'…a letter means the world to someone wanting to communicate with his loved ones, Brandon. Don't sell yourself short,' he said, finishing her thought and adding his comment. 'Still, I don't understand how a surgeon and his wife could pull such strings. Are you all, by chance, related to King George himself?'

'Oh, no! I have a theory,' she said. 'Tell me what you think. I'll have to show you the letter from the Navy Board, addressed to Brandon Polly, which I received whilst I was visiting Nana. Do you think… Is it possible that Laura or Philemon transposed my name on purpose? Polly Brandon would never do, but Brandon Polly would cause not a stir.'

He thought a minute. 'What is more likely is at one point in the correspondence there may have been a comma between the two names. Orders or requests are often issued that way.'

He looked at her, and seemed to know what she was thinking. 'There now. You've answered *my* question, which surely must entitle you to one of your own. Go ahead and ask what everyone wants to know. How does someone who sounds like a Scot look like a Frenchman, and with a Froggy name, too?'

'I *am* curious,' she admitted.

'Simple. A long-ago Philippe Junot—he had a title, so I'm told—came to Scotland from France as part of the entourage of Mary of Scotland. No one precisely knows how it happened, but he managed to avoid the turmoil surrounding her and blended into the foggy, damp woodwork

of Scotland near Dundrennan. He lost his title, but acquired considerable land near Kirkcudbright.'

'My goodness.'

'My goodness, indeed. The Junots are a prolific breed,
and each generation traditionally rejoices in a Philippe.
My father is still well and hearty, but some day I will head
the family.'

'You chose to serve King and country?' Polly asked,
fascinated.

'I did. Granted, Kirkcudbright is a pretty fishing village, but it is slow and I liked the uniform.' He held up
his hand. 'Don't laugh, Brandon. People have been known
to join for stranger reasons.'

'I cannot believe you!' she protested.

'Then don't,' he replied serenely. 'I love the sea, but I
require land now and then, and an enemy to grapple with
up close. That's my life.'

'What…what does your wife say to all this?' she
asked. *That is hardly subtle*, she berated herself. *He will
think I am an idiot or a flirt, when I am neither.*

'I wouldn't know, since I don't have one of those
luxuries. I ask you, Brandon—why would a sensible
woman—someone like yourself—marry a Marine?'

He had neatly lofted the ball of confusion back in her
court. 'I can't imagine, either,' she said without thinking,
which made him laugh, then calmly bid her good day.

I've offended him, Polly thought with remorse. She
watched him go, then reasonably asked herself why his
good opinion mattered.

Captain Adney's steward kindly brought her bread and
cheese for lunch. She went below later, and found that her

trunk and other baggage had been returned to her cabin. The sentry had moved from the Lieutenant Colonel's door to her own, as though nothing had happened.

When she went topside again, the Captain told her the afternoon would be spent in gunnery practice, and that she might be more comfortable belowdeck in her own cabin, one of the few not dismantled, so the guns could be fired. 'It is your choice, but mind you, it's noisy up here,' he warned, then shrugged. 'Or down there, for that matter.'

She chose to remain on deck. The chair had been moved closer to the wheel—'Out of any stray missile range,' the captain told her.

He didn't exaggerate; the first blast nearly lifted her out of the chair. She covered her ears with her hands, wishing herself anywhere but at sea, until her own curiosity—Miss Pym called it an admirable trait, if not taken to extremes—piqued her interest. Cringing in the chair, trying to make herself small with each cannonade, she watched as each man performed his task.

Someone tapped her shoulder. She looked around to see Colonel Junot holding out some cotton wadding and pointing to his ears. She took the wadding from him and stuffed it in her ears, observing that he seemed as usual, and not in any way offended by her earlier comment. *Perhaps I make mountains out of molehills*, she told herself, as he returned to the main deck, watching the crews there as she watched them from the quarterdeck.

His eyes were on the Marines. Some of them served the guns alongside the naval gunners, and others lined the railing, muskets at the ready, their Sergeant standing behind them, walking up and down. A few Marines had ventured aloft to the crosstrees with their weapons.

Through it all, Colonel Junot observed, and took occasional notes.

It was all a far cry from Bath, and she knew how out of place she was. *I wonder if I really can be useful in Oporto*, she thought. Nana had wanted her to stay in Torquay. What had she done of any value on this voyage yet, except make a cake of herself with seasickness? She wondered why Colonel Junot thought her worth the time of day.

It was still on her mind as she prepared for dinner that evening. Only three more days, she thought, as she reached around to button her last button.

When she ventured into the wardroom, Colonel Junot came up behind her and without a word, buttoned the one in the centre of her back she never could reach. The other men were already busy at dinner; no one had noticed. *I can't even dress myself*, she thought, flogging her already-battered esteem.

Polly had little to say over dinner. For all she paid attention, she could have been shovelling clinkers into her mouth, and washing them down with bathwater. All she could think of was how ill equipped she was to leave England. Probably she should never have even left Bath, uncomfortable as Miss Pym had made her, especially after she had turned down Pym's invitation to stay and teach the youngest class. At least at the Female Academy, she knew precisely where she stood, in the order of things.

Bless his heart, Colonel Junot tried to engage her in conversation, but she murmured only monosyllables. Before the endless meal was over, even he had given up, directing his attention to war talk, and then ship talk. She was as out of place as a Quaker at a gaming table.

Polly had never felt quite this gauche before, almost as though her spectacles were ten times too large for her face, with every freckle—real and imagined—standing out in high relief. And there sat the Lieutenant Colonel next to her, an officer with handsome features, distinguished hair going grey. He was quite the best-looking man she had ever seen, and what had he seen of her except someone who needed to be cleaned up, held over a basin, or buttoned up the back? She burned at her own failings, compared to Colonel Junot's elegant worldliness, and longed to leave the table as soon as she could decently do so.

The dinner ended after a round of toasts to the ship, the men, and the King. She was free to go. She stood, and all the men stood out of deference, even though she knew in her heart of hearts that she was the weakest link at the table.

Polly was only two or three steps from her door, but there was the Colonel, bowing and offering his arm, as he suggested a turn around the deck. She didn't know how to say no, or even why she wanted to, so she took his arm.

The wind blew steadily from the west, making it the fair wind to Spain her brother-in-law Oliver had mentioned during his last visit to Torquay. Polly breathed deep, half-imagining she could smell the orange blossoms in Nana's garden, while she wished herself there.

Colonel Junot walked her around the deck, commenting on the workings of the ship, pointing out the phosphorescence in the water, which he didn't understand, but which intrigued him. She could tell how much he loved the sea, and she felt her shyness begin to recede. He still seemed to be taking care of her, as though someone had given him that role when he first saw her on deck in Plymouth. She knew no one had, which made her feel protected. It was not a feeling she was accustomed to; probably none of Lord Ratliffe's daughters was.

'This voyage has been a real trial for you, Miss Brandon,' he said finally.

She wished he had continued calling her simply Brandon. He steadied her as they went down the more narrow companionway, and into the wardroom again, which this time was full of Marines.

All twenty of the frigate's small complement of Marines had assembled, each carrying a flask. Private Leonard had borrowed a medium-sized pot from the galley, which he set by her door. He saluted the Lieutenant Colonel and stepped forwards, eyes ahead.

'Colonel Junot, if we may take the liberty…'

'By all means, Private.'

The Private looked at her then, flushed, and glanced away, addressing his remarks to someone imaginary over her shoulder. 'Miss Brandon, there's nothing pleasant about vinegar. We decided you should have an opportunity to wash your hair with fresh water. With the Lieutenant Colonel's permission, we decided to give you our daily ration, and we will not take no for an answer.'

He said it practically in one breath, then stepped back. As she watched, tears in her eyes, each Marine poured his drinking water for the day into the pot. When they finished, Colonel Junot went to his cabin and brought out his own flask, adding it to the water in the pot.

'You'll be thirsty,' she protested feebly, when everyone finished and stood at attention.

'Just for a day, ma'am,' the Sergeant of the guard said. 'We've been thirsty before.'

He turned around smartly on his heel, and with a command, the Marines marched back to their posts, or to their quarters between the officers' berths and the crew. Private Leonard remained at his post outside her door, eyes ahead again, every inch the professional.

'Open your door, Brandon, and we'll get the pot inside,' Colonel Junot said.

She did as he directed, standing back as Lieutenant Colonel and Private lifted in the pot, careful not to splash out a drop of the precious fresh water. She had never received a kinder gift from anyone in her life.

The Private went back to his post, but Colonel Junot stood in her room, a smile playing around his expressive lips.

'Colonel, I could have waited until we reached port. They didn't need to do that,' she said.

'It was entirely their idea, Brandon,' he replied, going to her door. 'They only asked that I distract you on deck long enough for them to assemble. Look at it this way: if you ever decide to take over the world, you have a squad of Marines who would follow you anywhere.'

'Why, Colonel?' she asked.

It was his turn to look nonplussed. He was silent a long moment, as if wondering what he should say to such a question. 'Possibly just because you are Brandon Polly, or Polly Brandon. Sometimes there is no reason.'

'No one ever did anything so nice for me before,' she said, wincing inwardly because she didn't want to sound pathetic. It was true, though.

'No? Not even your sisters?'

She could tell he was teasing her now, but there was still that air of protection about him, as though she had become his assignment for the voyage. 'My sisters are different,' she told him, feeling her face grow rosier. 'They are supposed to be kind.'

He laughed at that. 'So is mine,' he confided.

She didn't mean to look sceptical, but the Colonel seemed to be sensitive to her expression. 'Here's how I see it, Brandon—you've made a tedious voyage more than usually interesting.'

She couldn't imagine that tending a female through seasickness qualified as interesting, but she wasn't about to mention it. She knew she should just curtsy and wish him goodnight. She would have, if some imp hadn't leaped on to her shoulder, and prodded her. 'I...I...most particularly like it when you call me Brandon,' she said, her voice low. 'Some of the other students at Miss Pym's had nicknames. I never did.' She stopped in confusion. 'You must think I am an idiot.'

'Never crossed my mind, Brandon.'

She held her breath as he lightly touched her cheek.

'Goodnight, now,' he told her. 'If you need help with your hair tomorrow, I'm just across the wardroom.'

Chapter Four

Hugh couldn't say he had any power to encourage the wind and waves, but he considered it a boon from kind providence that Polly Brandon did need his help in the morning to kneel at the pot and wash her hair, while the deck slanted. They decided that his firm knee in her back would anchor her to the pot, and she had no objection when he lathered her hair, and rinsed it using a small pitcher.

The entire operation involved another pot and pitcher, which led him to comment that between pots and pitchers, women were a great lot of trouble. If she hadn't looked back at him then with such a glower, her hair wet and soapy, he could have withstood nearly anything. He had no idea a woman could look so endearing with soap in her hair. She wasn't wearing her spectacles, of course, which meant she held her eyes open wider than usual, perhaps seeking more depth and more clarity. The effect jolted him a little, because her nearsighted gaze was so intense, her eyes so blue. The shade reminded him of a spot of deep water near Crete where he had gazed long and hard when he was a younger man.

When not coated in vinegar, her auburn hair was glossy. Hugh was half-tempted to volunteer to comb the tangles from her hair, but he had the good sense to strangle that idea at birth. To his surprise, he was finding her uniquely attractive.

Even after two decades of war, he knew enough about women, having bedded them in all seaports when occasion permitted, no different from his navy brethren. By common wardroom consent after one memorable voyage through half the world, he and his fellows agreed that the most beautiful women lived on the Greek isles. He knew at least that *he* had never seen a flat-chested female there. So it went; he was a man of experience.

But here was Brandon—why on earth had he started calling her such a hooligan name?—who, even on her best day, could only stand in the shadow of the earth's loveliest ladies. It was all he could do to keep his hands off her, and he had seen her at her absolute worst. No woman could have been more hopeless than Polly Brandon of two days ago, but here he was, wanting to devise all manner of subterfuges to keep her talking to him. It was a mystery; he had no clue what had happened in so short a time.

He sat down at the wardroom table, hoping to keep her there with him while he thought of something clever to say. To his dismay, she went into her cabin, but came out a moment later with her comb. She was getting more surefooted by the hour, timing her stride to the roll of the ship, but she did plop unceremoniously on to the bench and laughed at herself.

She fixed him with that penetrating gaze he was coming to know. 'You have my permission to laugh when I am no more graceful at sea than a new puppy would be.'

'I daren't,' he said. 'Suppose some day you find me in desperate shape—say, for example, at Almack's? I would hope you would be charitable, so I will be the same.'

'Coward,' she teased. She unwound the towel, shook her head, and began to comb her hair. She seemed to be waiting for him to say something, but when he didn't, she took the initiative. 'Three days at sea and my manners have taken French leave, Colonel. Miss Pym always did say I was too nosy by half, but what are *you* doing here?'

Admiring you, he thought. That would never do; perhaps honesty deserved its moment in the sun. 'I shipped out to the Peninsula because I could not stand one more moment of conference meetings in Plymouth.'

'You're quizzing me,' she said with a laugh.

'Well, no, I am not,' he contradicted. 'I probably should have turned down my promotion from Major to Lieutenant Colonel, but one doesn't do that.'

'No harm in ambition,' she told him, trying to sound sage, and blithely unaware how charming was her naïveté.

'True,' he agreed. 'Trouble is, a step up means different duties at Division Three. Now I am chained to a desk and report for meetings, where I sit and draw little figures and yawn inside my mouth, so my tonsils won't be seen.'

She laughed and touched his sleeve. Just one quick touch, but it made him pleasantly warm. 'Colonel, I used to do the same thing in theology class, where God was so cruel as to make time stand still.'

'Exactly.' *Well, aren't you the charming rogue*, he thought. *No vicar for a husband for you, I should think.* 'As with most things, there is more to it than that. I went to Stonehouse Hospital to visit the newest arrived Marines invalided there. One of them died in my arms, after wishing there was something more he and his fellow Marines could do to end this stalemate with Boney. I chose not to let his sacrifice be for naught.'

Polly nodded, her face serious. He continued, 'I asked permission of the Colonel Commandant to conduct impromptu visits to various ships off the Peninsula, and in Lisbon where a Marine brigade is based. I want to find out how the men feel about what they do, and if, indeed, we Marines could do more. Brandon, these are men with vast experience, who surely have ideas! I have *carte blanche* to stay as long as I wish, and then compile a report. That is why I am here.'

She looked down at her hands, then up at him over her spectacles. 'We are both running away, aren't we, Colonel Junot? I could have stayed in Bath and taught the younger pupils at my school, or at least stayed in Torquay and helped my sister Nana, who is increasing again.'

'But you want to see the wider world, even such a tattered one as this is proving to be, with its everlasting war?'

She frowned, and he could tell she had considered the matter. 'I think we know I don't belong here. Maybe I should have stayed in Torquay.'

Then I never would have met you, he realised. It was such a disquieting thought that he wanted to dismiss it. He chose a light tone, because that was all he could do, and even then, it was wrong to his ears. 'If it's any comfort, I felt the same way at my first deployment in service of King and country.'

'When was that? Where did you go?' she asked, her interest obvious.

What could he say but the truth, even though he knew

it would age him enormously in her eyes. 'It was 1790 and I was bound for India.'

'Heavens. I had not even been born,' she told him, confirming his fear.

Get it over with, Hugh, he told himself sourly. 'I was fifteen and a mere Lieutenant.'

She surprised him then, as she had been surprising him for the three days he had known her. 'Heavens,' she said again, and he cringed inwardly. 'Colonel, I cannot imagine how fascinating India must have been. Did you see elephants? Tigers? Are the women as beautiful as pictures I have seen?'

She didn't say a word about his age, but calmly continued combing her hair, her mind only on India, as far as he could tell. He felt himself relax. 'Do you want to hear about India?'

'Oh, my, yes, I do,' she said, her eyes bright. 'Colonel, I have never been anywhere!'

'Very well,' he began, eager to keep her there. 'We landed in Bombay during the monsoon.'

'You were seasick,' she said.

'I told you I have never been seasick,' he replied, 'and I meant it.'

'Very well. Since I was not there, I shall have to believe you.' She put her comb down and clasped her hands together. 'Tell me everything you can remember.'

If some celestial scamp in the universe—an all-purpose genie would do—had suddenly whisked away all the clocks and banished time to outer darkness, Polly knew she would be content to listen for ever to Colonel Junot. While her hair dried, she and the sentry

who joined them at the Colonel's suggestion heard of
tiger hunts, an amphibious storming of a rajah's palace
in Bombay, and of the rise of Lord Wellington, the
'Sepoy General'. India was followed by Ceylon and
then Canada, as Colonel Junot took them through his
Marine career.

It became quickly obvious to Polly that he loved what
he did, because she heard it in his voice. She saw it in
the way he leaned forwards until she felt like a co-
conspirator in a grand undertaking. His storytelling had
her almost feeling decks awash and seeing rank on rank
of charging elephants and screaming Indians, as he told
them so matter of factly about what he did to support
himself. He was capability itself.

Through years of indoctrination, Miss Pym had
pounded into her head how rude it was to stare at anyone,
especially a man, but the Colonel was hard to resist. A
natural-born storyteller, he became quite animated when
he spoke of his adventures, which only brightened his
brown eyes and gave more colour to his somewhat sallow
cheeks—he had obviously spent too much time the past
winter sitting at conference tables. She was having a hard
time deciding if his finest feature was his magnificent posture and bearing, or his handsome lips, which had to be
a throwback to his French ancestry.

Colonel Junot was different, she knew, if for no other
reason than that he found her interesting. As she listened
to him, injecting questions that he answered with good
humor, Polly discovered she was already steeling herself
against the time he would bow and say goodbye.

'And that is my career, Private Leonard,' Colonel Junot
concluded, looking at them both. 'Private, as you were.

Brandon, excuse me please.' He rose, bowed to her, and went his stately way up the companionway.

'I live such an ordinary life,' Polly murmured, watching him go.

She went on deck at the end of the forenoon watch, pleased to notice the chair she had sat in yesterday had been relocated to its original place, which probably meant there would be no gunnery practice today. She had brought a book topside with her, something improving that Miss Pym had recommended. She decided quickly that a treatise on self-control was a hard slog on a ship's deck where so much of interest was going on. She was happy enough to merely close it, when what she really wanted to do was toss it into the Atlantic. Maybe that wasn't such a shabby idea. Book in hand, she went to the ship's railing.

'Brandon, I hope you are not considering suicide.'

She looked around to see Colonel Junot. 'No, sir. This book is a dead bore and I am about to put it out of its misery.'

He took the book from her hand, opened it, rolled his eyes, then closed it. 'Allow me,' he said, and impulsively flung the thing far into the ocean. 'I hope you were serious.'

'Never more so,' she told him firmly. 'It was a gift from my aunt, who was headmistress at the female academy I attended in Bath, and—'

'I should apologise then for deep-sixing it,' he said, interrupting her.

'Oh, no. Don't you have any relatives who annoy you?'

He thought a moment, then he laughed. 'Who doesn't!'

Walking with more assurance back to her chair, she

seated herself, giving the Colonel every opportunity to nod to her and continue on his way. To her delight, he pulled up yesterday's keg and sat beside her.

'Brandon, give me some advice.'

'Me?' she asked, amazed.

'Yes, you,' he replied patiently. 'Under ordinary circumstances, you appear quite sensible.'

'Thank you, sir,' she teased, and put a hand to her forehead like a seaman.

'I have told you what my aim is on my fact-finding mission.' He must have caught the look in her eye, because he wagged a finger at her. 'Don't you even presume to call it "taking French leave from the conference table".'

'I would never, sir,' she said solemnly, which made him look at her suspiciously.

'Seriously, Brandon, how can I approach Marines?'

She looked at him in surprise. 'Colonel, you would know far better than I!'

'I don't. On this ship, for example—which for our purposes we will call "Any Frigate in the Fleet"—I communicated my wishes to the Sergeant, and he passed them to his men. Everyone is stiff and formal, and I can almost see their brains running, trying to work out what it is I *really* want to know.'

Polly thought about what he had said, but not for long, because it seemed so simple. 'Can you not just sit with them as you are sitting casually with me? Tell them what you told me about the dying Lieutenant, and what it is you wish to do. Look them in the eye, the way you look me in the eye—you know, kindly—and tell them you need their help. Why need you be formal?'

He watched her face closely, and she could only hope he had not noticed her odd little epiphany. 'You *are* kind, you know,' she said softly.

'Thank you, Brandon, but no one can get beyond my rank to just talk to me. There is a larger issue here, one I had not thought of: this may be the first time in the history of the Marines that an officer has actually asked an enlisted man what he *thinks*.'

'That is a sad reflection,' she said, after some consideration. 'Everyone has good ideas now and then.'

'We never ask.'

He was looking far too serious, as though his good idea in Plymouth was already on the rocks. She put her hand on his arm, and he glanced at her in surprise. *Just two days, and then you are gone*, she thought. 'I told you, you are kind. Don't give up yet. You'll find a way to talk to the men.' She took her hand away and looked down, shy again. 'When I was so desperate, you found a way to put me at ease.'

'That was simplicity itself. You needed help.'

'So did the Lieutenant who died in your arms, Colonel,' she told him, finding it strange that she had to explain his own character to him, wondering why people didn't see themselves as they were. 'Just be that kind man and you will find out everything you want to know.'

She stopped, acutely aware she was offering advice to a Lieutenant Colonel of Marines, who, under ordinary circumstances, would never have even looked at her. 'Well, that's what I think,' she concluded, feeling as awkward as a calf on ice.

He nodded and stood up, and Polly knew she had not helped at all. He put his hands behind his back, impeccable. 'I just go and sit on that hatch and call over the Marines and speak to them as I speak to you, Brandon?'

'You could take off that shiny plaque on your neck and unbutton your uniform jacket,' she suggested, then could not resist. 'Let them see you have on a checked shirt underneath.'

His smile was appreciative as he fingered the gorget against his throat. 'I must remain in uniform, Brandon, and the gorget stays. I will try what you say.' He did not disguise the doubt in his voice.

She clasped her hands together, unwilling to let him go, even if it was only to the main deck. 'Colonel, you could practise right here. Ask me questions. I could do the same to you.'

'Why not?' He contemplated her for a moment, and she suddenly wished she was thinner, that her hair was not so wind-blown, and that her glasses would disappear. He was looking her right in the eyes, though, so maybe he didn't notice.

He flexed his fingers and cleared his throat. 'Private Brandon, as you were, please! Let me set you at ease. I'm here to ask questions of you that will never be repeated to your superior. I will not even name you in my report.' He looked at her, his eyes sceptical. 'What do you think so far?'

'You could smile,' she suggested.

'Too artificial,' he replied, shaking his head. 'That would terrify them because officers never smile.'

'I don't understand men,' Polly said suddenly.

'You weren't meant to,' he told her gently, which made her laugh. 'All right. All right. Private Brandon, tell me something about yourself. Why did you join the Royal

Marines? I'm curious.' He peered at her. 'Just tell me something about yourself, Brandon, something that I don't know.'

She thought a moment, and realised with a sudden jolt that she had reached that place where Nana had once told her she would one day arrive. '"Polly, dear, you must never deceive a man about your origins,"' Nana had told her only a week ago.

'My father was William Stokes, Lord Ratliffe of Admiralty House,' she said. 'I am one of his three illegitimate daughters, Colonel.'

To her relief, he did not seem repulsed. 'That accounts for all the years in boarding school in Bath, I suppose. Tell me more, Brandon. What do you like to do?'

'After that, you really want to know *more*?' she asked in surprise.

'Indeed, I do, Private Brandon,' he said simply. 'Remember—I'm supposed to extract answers from you and keep you at your ease. I am interested.'

'Our father tried to sell my older sisters to the highest bidder, to pay off his debts,' she went on.

'What a bad man,' the Colonel said. 'Is he the Admiralty official who died in a Spanish prison and is thought by some to be a hero?'

'He died in Plymouth, and, yes, some think him a hero,' she said, her voice barely audible.

He amazed her by putting his hand under her chin and raising it a little, so he could look her in the eyes. 'You managed to avoid all this? How?'

Don't you have eyes in your head? she wanted to retort. 'Come now, Colonel,' she said. 'I am no beauty. My father chose to ignore me.'

For some reason, her bald statement seemed to embarrass the Colonel, whose face turned red. 'Shallow, shallow man,' he murmured, when he had recovered himself. 'He never really took a good look at you, did he?'

Startled, she shook her head. 'He demanded miniatures of my sisters, but not of me.'

'Thank God, Brandon,' the Colonel whispered, his eyes still not leaving her face. He gazed at her for a long moment, and then seemed to recall what he was doing. He sat back and regarded her speculatively. 'I think I can do those interviews now,' he said. 'If I show a genuine interest in what these enlisted men are telling me, look them in the eyes and wait, I might have success. Is that it?'

'I think it is,' she replied, relieved that he had changed the subject, and a little surprised at how much information she had given him with so little encouragement. 'You're actually rather good at interviewing, I think.' Then she couldn't help herself. 'Only don't chuck them under the chin.'

He laughed and held up his hands in a surrender gesture. 'Too right, Brandon! Wait. You never told me what *you* like to do, only about your dreadful father. There's more to you than him.'

She had never thought of it that way before. 'I like to plant things. Before I left Torquay, I helped my brother-in-law's mother plant a row of Johnny Jump-Ups in pots. We…we were going to do snapdragons next, but the letter came and I went to Plymouth. It's not very interesting,' she said in apology.

'You'd like Kirkcudbright, the village where I grew up,' he said. 'Everyone has flowers in their front yard. It smells like heaven, around July. And it *is* interesting.'

The Colonel put his hand on her cheek then, as he

had the other evening. 'Don't ever sell yourself short, Brandon,' he said quietly. 'Incidentally, I like to carve small boats.'

He bowed and left the quarterdeck for the waist of the frigate, where the guns were tied down fast. She watched as he spoke to the Sergeant of the guard, then sat down on the hatch.

'That's the way,' Polly murmured quietly, her heart still beating too fast. 'Surely they won't remain standing if you are seated.'

Trying not to appear overly interested, she watched as the Marines not on duty approached Colonel Junot. He gestured to them, and in a few minutes, they were seated around him.

'Talk to him,' she whispered. 'Just talk to him. He's nothing but kind. All it takes is one of you to speak.'

One of the Privates squatting on the edge of the gathering raised his hand. Colonel Junot answered him, and everyone laughed, even the man who asked the question. Then others joined in, talking to the Colonel, to each other, and even calling over some sailors.

You just have to be yourself, she thought, imagining Colonel Junot's capable hands carving little boats for children. *Just be the man who was so kind to me.*

Chapter Five

Maybe it was the wistful way Polly Brandon had spoken of snapdragons. As Hugh had tried out his interviewing skills on a squad of obliging Marines, he'd found his mind wandering to the lady in the canvas chair.

He could be thankful he was aboard one of his Majesty's typical warships, which did not believe in mirrors on the bulkheads. He had enough trouble frowning into his shaving mirror the next morning and seeing nothing but grey hair starting to attack his temples. As he stared in total dissatisfaction, a brave better angel of his nature did attempt to remind him of his own words to Brandon a day ago, when he so sagely advised her not to sell herself short. The angel shrugged and gave up when he chose not to admit he was doing exactly the same thing to himself.

'I am too old,' he told his reflection in the shaving mirror as he scraped at his chin, which only made him wince—not because the razor was dull, but because none of those obstacles loomed any higher than the molehills they were to him. All he could think of was his August 9, 1775 birth date in the family Bible back home.

When his face was scraped sufficiently free of whiskers, he sat naked on the cold cannon in his cabin, glumly willing himself to be as practical as he ordinarily was. He reminded himself he was on duty, in the service of his King, headed into the war, and destined to be busy. Another day or two would pass and he would never see Polly Brandon again. For his peace of mind, it couldn't come too soon. Hugh did know one thing—what ailed him had a cure, and it was probably to continually remind himself that he was too old for the bewitching Polly Brandon.

Two days later, he could have made his resolve less problematic if he hadn't been pacing on deck in the early hours, dissatisfied with himself. If he had a brain in his head, he would skulk somewhere on the ship when it docked in Oporto. Brandon would go ashore, and he would never see her again. He could go on to Lisbon.

That was his plan, anyway—a poor one, but serviceable enough. Trouble was, the view of Oporto took his breath away, and he was down the companionway in a matter of minutes, knocking on her door to tell her to step lively and come on deck for a look.

Why did you do that? he scolded himself, as he returned topside. His only hope was that she would look unappetising as she came on deck, maybe rubbing her eyes, or looking cross and out of sorts the way some women did, when yanked from slumber. If that was the case, he might have an easier time dismissing her. He could go about his business and forget this little wrinkle in his life's plan, if he even had a plan.

No luck. She came on deck quickly, a shawl draped

over her arm. He smiled to see that she still couldn't quite reach that centre button in back. *I won't touch it*, he thought. Her face was rosy from slumber, her eyes bright and expectant. She merely glanced at him, then cast her whole attention on the beautiful harbour that was Oporto. She had wound her long hair into a ridiculous topknot and skewered it with what looked like a pencil. She looked entirely makeshift, but instead of disgusting him, he wanted to plant a whacking great kiss on her forehead and see where it led. *Lord, I am hopeless*, he thought in disgust.

She was too excited to even say good morning, but tugged on his arm. 'Where is the hospital?' she demanded.

He pointed to the southern bank. 'Over there, in that area called Vila Nova de Gaia. Turn round.'

She did as he demanded, and he buttoned up the centre button. 'You need longer arms,' he commented, but she was not paying attention to him.

'I have never seen anything so magnificent,' she said in awe. 'Perhaps it was worth all that seasickness. Have you been here before?'

'Years ago, Brandon. I think I was your age.' He chuckled. 'For what it's worth, my reaction was much like yours.' *There, Miss Brandon, that should remind you what a geriatric I am*, he thought grimly.

If she heard him, she didn't seem to mind. Brandon watched as a cutter swooped from the southern shore to the side of the *Perseverance* and backed its sails, then watched as the flag Lieutenant ran up a series of pennants. 'What's he doing?' she asked.

'Giving the cutter a message. Our surgeon told me the hospital sends out this cutter at every approach of the fleet, to enquire of the wounded. Ask the flag Lieutenant what message he is sending.'

Surefooted now, Polly hurried to the Lieutenant. 'He is signalling "Wounded man on board. Prompt attention." He said the cutter will take the message to the hospital wharf and there will be a surgeon's mate with a stretcher there when we dock,' she told him in one breath as she hurried back to his side.

'It appears that your brother-in-law doesn't miss a trick,' Hugh said. 'I'm impressed.'

Polly nodded, her eyes on the shore again. 'I asked the Lieutenant if he could also signal "Brandon on board", and he said he would.' She leaned against him for one brief moment, or maybe she just lost her footing. 'I have not seen Laura in nearly two years.'

The winds were fair into Oporto. As the harbour came nearer, she hurried below to finish dressing. When she came back, she was as neat as a pin. He stood close to her when they approached the mouth of the mighty river, knowing there would be a series of pitches and yaws that might discomfort her, as the Douro met the Atlantic. Besides, it gave him plenty of excuse to grip her around the waist to prevent her losing her footing. He couldn't deny he was touched by how completely she trusted him to hold her.

'I may never get used to the sea,' she confessed, as he braced her.

'It isn't given to everyone to relish going down to the sea in small boats, despite what the psalm says.'

'No argument there,' she agreed cheerfully. 'The less business I have in great waters, the better.'

It wouldn't hurt to ask. 'Of you three sisters, are you

to be the only one who avoids the navy?' *What about Marines?* he wanted to ask.

She wasn't listening to him, but was back at the railing, intent on the shoreline, her mind and heart on her sister, he was certain. He tipped his hat to her and went be-lowdeck to find the letter Surgeon Brackett wanted him to deliver to Philemon Brittle. Better to just hand it to Brandon and let her do the honors. The voyage was over, after all.

He couldn't bring himself to hand it to her, not there at the railing, or after the gangplank came down on the wharf, and certainly not when Polly had thrown herself into the arms of a tall, beautiful woman with auburn hair.

It was a brief embrace. The woman—she must be Laura Brittle—quickly turned her attention to the foretop-man on the stretcher, as her husband planted a quick kiss on Polly's cheek, shook hands with the *Perseverance*'s surgeon, and engaged him in conversation.

'Are you planning to stay in Oporto, Colonel Junot?' Captain Adney asked.

'Perhaps,' he temporised.

'We'll be at the navy wharf today and then sailing the day after, if winds and tide are willing.'

'Very well, sir. I'll sail with you.' He couldn't very well say anything else. He stood at the railing, uncertain, wanting to go down the gangplank and introduce himself, and suddenly shy. He looked at Polly for a clue, and she beckoned him.

That was easy. In another moment he was smiling in-wardly at Polly's shy introduction, and bowing to Mrs Philemon Brittle, who truly was as beautiful as her younger sister had declared. Philemon Brittle held out his hand and he gave it a shake, impressed with the strength of the surgeon's grasp.

'Do join us for luncheon, Colonel, unless you have urgent business that takes you elsewhere,' Mrs Brittle said.

'Since the King of Portugal is probably taking his ease on a beach in Brazil, and Boney is on his way to Russia, if reports are accurate, I am at a momentary loss for luncheon engagements,' he joked, which made her smile and show off the dimple he recognised in Polly's cheek, too.

'Very well, sir. If Marshal Soult should show his brazen face here again, we'll release you before the sorbet. Come, Polly. Colonel?'

He walked up the hill from the wharf with a sister on either side of him. He looked from one to the other, which made Polly stop.

'Laura, this is droll! Colonel Junot is comparing us!'

So much for my peace of mind, Hugh thought, surprisingly unembarrassed, since he had made an obvious discovery that was probably clear to everyone except Polly herself. 'You have me, Brandon. Anyone with two eyes can see that you and Mrs Brittle are sisters.'

'I have told her that many times,' Mrs Brittle said. 'Perhaps she will choose to believe me some day. Thank you, Colonel Junot!' She paused then, and her eyes narrowed slightly. 'Brandon? Apparently you have either chosen a nickname for Polly, or you are on to our own effort to get my sister to Portugal.'

'You *were* right, Colonel!' Polly exclaimed. 'Laura, I don't know why he calls me that, but we did wonder if perhaps some correspondence came from Portugal requesting a Brandon Polly for service.'

'It was the feeblest attempt,' Mrs Brittle said as they resumed walking again. 'Philemon hoped some over-worked clerk at the Navy Board would apparently do what he did. Perhaps I shall call you Brandon, too, my love. Welcome to hard service in the navy.'

If Polly had a rejoinder ready, it went unnoticed when an orderly at the top of the hill called for Mrs Brittle. Alert, Laura put her finger to her lips and listened.

'Ward C, mum! Lively now!'

Without a word of explanation, Mrs Brittle hiked up her skirts to reveal shapely legs and ran up the hill, for-getting her company completely, it seemed. She stopped halfway up and looked back, but Hugh just waved her on. He took Polly's arm, content to walk the rest of the way with her.

'I gather all the rumours are true, Brandon. Wouldn't it be nice some day if your gifted sister could be recog-nised for what she is doing here?'

'I doubt it would concern her,' Polly replied, and he could hear the pride in her voice. 'She would probably just laugh, and say the war is harder on wives like Nana, who wait. It must be so hard to be apart from one's love.'

Maybe I am about to find out, Hugh thought to himself. *Or maybe I am just an idiot.*

They arrived at the convent and were greeted immedi-ately by a nun, who directed them to the dining room. The table was already set; from the looks of things, the Brittles had left their meal when the *Perseverance* docked. Hugh pulled out a chair for Polly, taking a deep breath of her sun-warmed hair as he did so, remembering how he had helped her wash it.

They were just beginning what looked like empanadas

when Mrs Brittle came into the room, hand in hand with a youngster whose hair was the same shade as his mother and aunt's. She knelt gracefully and kissed his cheek. 'Danny, that's your aunt Polly Brandon.' She repeated it in Portuguese. 'His Portuguese is better than mine,' Mrs Brittle explained.

'Laura, he looks like you,' Polly said.

'The hair, anyway,' Laura said as she sat him down on a chair with a medical book as a booster. 'He has his father's eyes and general capable demeanour.'

'Does he run with the herd?' Hugh asked, gesturing towards the courtyard, which he saw through the open door. Other children about Danny's age played there.

'Indeed, he does, which frees me for hospital work,' Laura said.

Polly looked where he looked. 'Goodness, are you running an orphanage, too?'

'No, my love,' Mrs Brittle said. She hesitated, glancing at Hugh, and he understood immediately whose children they were, considering Oporto's sad history with the French invaders.

She reached across her corner of the table and touched Polly's hand. 'When the French came here in '08, they brutalised the young women they did not murder. These children are one result of that misery.'

'Oh,' Polly said, her voice small. 'Where are their mothers?'

Hugh watched Polly's expressive face. *You are so young, so naïve*, he thought. *Let us hope this is the worst face of war you see.*

'Oporto is a sad town, my love,' Mrs Brittle said. She cupped her hand gently against her son's cheek as he ate his empanada. 'We have tried to make life as good as we can for these unfortunates.' She looked at Polly. 'Dearest, this is why we want you here.'

'I don't understand,' Polly said. 'I thought I was to help in the wards.'

'We want you to teach English to the young mothers—some are here—and to the nuns. I haven't time, and they would be so much more useful here. Perhaps, in time, they will find work with the English port merchants, when they return from Lisbon and London.'

'I can teach them,' Polly said. Her eyes on the children, she rose and went to the door, where she could see the children playing. 'Seems a strange way to fight Boney.'

'Not at all,' Mrs Brittle said. She held a cup to Danny's lips and he drank in large gulps. 'Slow down, little one. You'll be back there soon enough.' She looked apologetically at Hugh. 'Colonel, you will find us a strange household. My husband sends his regrets, but ward walking always trumps food. Perhaps he'll wander through tonight for our evening meal, which I trust you will share with us.'

He didn't hesitate. 'With pleasure.'

'In fact, Colonel Junot, you may stay the night here, unless you prefer a smelly frigate.'

'I can do that, too,' he replied, glad for the invitation.

He looked at Polly, but her eyes were on the courtyard. As he watched her, she rose quietly and held out her hand to her nephew, who took it without hesitation and led her from the room in such a forthright manner that he smiled.

'Now there's a lad who has things under control.'

'I told you he was like his father,' Mrs Brittle said, her voice soft with love as she watched her sister and son.

He thought he should make his excuses and leave then. This was a busy woman. He made to rise, but she raised her hand to stop him, then poured him another glass of port. 'As onerous as work is here, we cannot fault the wine, Colonel.'

He drank, pleased to agree with her. His eyes went again to Polly, who was sitting on the grass now, with children around her. He watched as two women about her age came closer, hesitated, and moved closer. 'She's a bit of a magnet,' he murmured, more to himself than Mrs Brittle. 'I noticed that on the ship, too.' He chuckled, then stopped, because Mrs Brittle was giving him that thoughtful stare again.

'I think there were two Lieutenants who would have followed her to the ends of the earth,' he continued, speaking too fast. *Maybe one Lieutenant Colonel*, he thought, glad Mrs Brittle could not read his mind.

'She would only stare at you if you suggested such a thing.'

'I know, Mrs Brittle. She seems to think she is a duckling among swans.'

Mrs Brittle poured herself another glass. 'Thank you for being such a gallant escort, Colonel. I was hoping there would be someone mature like you on board, to shepherd her safely.'

Ouch, he thought, mentally counting every grey hair at his temples. 'You can always count on the Marines, Mrs Brittle.'

Lord, but that sounded feeble, he scolded himself as he said goodbye to Mrs Brittle and walked back to the dock down the well-travelled path, where he planned to retrieve a small duffel of his own and arrange for Polly's luggage to be sent up the hill. The Sergeant of Marines had released his men to shore, where he drilled them. Hugh watched in appreciation and some pride at their neat rank and file. 'We are so few in this war,' he murmured, and thought of Lieutenant Graves breathing his last in his arms. 'I have work to do.'

From the startled look on Laura's face, Polly knew she should have disguised her disappointment that Colonel Junot had left the hospital. 'I…I only wish he had said goodbye, but I suppose duty called,' she said. *And, oh, can I change a subject*, she thought. 'Laura, the young women are so shy. I declare they are like deer.'

Laura removed the medical book from Danny's chair and patted it. Polly sat down. 'You must treat them so gently. They have been through a terrible experience at the hands of the French.' She sighed. 'It is one I can appreciate more than most, perhaps. They were wretchedly ill used, and feel the world's censure.'

'You…you said some of the women returned to their villages and left their babies here?'

'They did, and I call it no foul. Everyone deals differently with violation of such a magnitude. I can assure you the mothers who remained love their little ones, who are surely not to blame for their entry into the world.' She took Polly's hand in hers. 'My dear, you and I know the inside of an orphanage. Only Nana had a home in her early years.' She looked Polly in the eye. 'Is it wrong of me to have thrust you into this?'

Polly shook her head. 'No, a thousand times, Laura. I trust this is one foundling home where the little ones are touched and loved.'

'You know it is,' her sister said firmly, then looked down as her cheeks flamed. 'Other than Nana's embrace when we met in Torquay, my beloved Philemon was the first person who ever hugged me, and I was twenty-seven.'

Polly moved her chair closer and they sat hand in hand until an orderly ran down the hall, calling for Mrs Brittle.

'Duty calls,' Laura said, but Polly heard no regret in her voice.

She stood up, but Polly did not release her hand. 'Tell me you don't mind all this hard work, sister,' she said, tugging on her hand, 'or the fact that you receive no recognition for it.'

Laura let go of Polly's hand gently. 'I only have to look into the eyes of the men I save, or into my husband's eyes, to receive all the reward I need, this side of heaven, my love. You'll understand some day.'

'That's what Nana says, too,' Polly grumbled. 'Some day. Some day.'

Laura laughed. 'Don't be so impatient to grow up! Go back to the courtyard and make some more friends.' She kissed the top of Polly's head. 'And if Danny gets stubborn and won't share, encourage him to do so. Mama says.'

She spent a pleasant afternoon in the courtyard, trying to imagine what Oporto must have been like when the French controlled it and the Portuguese suffered so greatly. She counted ten little ones, all about two years of age, like her nephew. Two of them decided to nap on cots in the shade of a mimosa tree, and three young women watched over them all.

One of the women, Paola, could speak some English, but Polly found herself mostly smiling and wishing she knew more of the language. She did learn a handclapping game in Portuguese, where even Danny corrected her pronunciation. She decided the whole afternoon was a lesson in humility for Miss Pym's star pupil and spent her time more profitably, sitting cross-legged in the grass and folding bits of paper into hopping frogs, a skill she had learned from Nana.

The whole time, Paola sat close to her in the grass, with several children in her lap. 'I am determined to learn Portuguese,' Polly told her, and smiled back when the young girl smiled at her.

The smile left Paola's face when she heard footsteps and looked over her shoulder. Polly watched her freeze and seem to shrink inside her own skin.

She looked around, wondering what could be the trouble. Colonel Junot stood in the open doorway to the courtyard, watching them, a smile on his face. Polly carefully put her arm around Paola, who had moved her legs to the side as though she wanted to leap to her feet. 'No, no,' Polly whispered. 'He is a friend. *Amigo?*'

Paola froze where she was, scarcely breathing. Imagine that much fear, Polly thought. She tightened her grip on the young girl. 'Colonel Junot, if you don't mind, you're frightening this girl,' she said softly.

He stared at her in disbelief at first, and then he sighed and turned away. She heard his footsteps recede down the corridor. *Please don't leave before you say goodbye*, she thought in sudden anguish.

Chapter Six

To Polly's infinite relief, Colonel Junot joined them for dinner. 'I was afraid you had come to the courtyard to say goodbye to me,' she told him.

'Oh, no, Brandon,' he assured her. 'Your sister kindly invited me to eat here and then stay the night. I have been quartered in a chaste cell formerly inhabited by someone—perhaps her name was Sister Quite Prudent—who obviously had God's ear. It can only do me good.'

I'm going to miss your wit, she thought suddenly. *What a short acquaintance this has been.*

Dinner was sheer delight, with young Daniel Brittle sitting on the medical books again, and Philemon actually free to join them. 'What do you think of our society?'

'I like it, Surgeon Brittle,' Hugh said. 'You run a ship-shape operation with good results.' He lowered his voice. 'I'm afraid I frightened one of the young women in the courtyard this afternoon. I suppose one uniform is pretty much the same as another to them.'

'Alas, yes,' Laura chimed in. 'No one wears a uniform here, and our Marine sentries don't go in the courtyard.'

While the Brittles listened, Hugh explained his purpose in coming to Portugal. 'Surgeon Brittle, I would consider it a special favour if you or your excellent wife would show me around the hospital tomorrow. I'd like to reassure myself that your protection is adequate.'

'We can do that.' Philemon leaned back in his chair and glanced at Laura. 'Danny appears to be drooping, Laura. Colonel Junot and I can entertain ourselves with Oporto's major export, if you and Polly want to see him to bed.'

The little boy went with no protest, happy enough for his mother to tuck him in bed, sing a lullaby in Portuguese, and watch until he slept, his arm around a doll made of surgical towels.

'You look a little weary yourself, sister,' Laura said. 'I can't think of a lullaby for your age, but you can tell me about the voyage, and how our sister does.'

Polly decided bliss was a flannel nightgown, two pillows behind her head, and sharing family stories with her sister, a luxury of such magnitude she never could have imagined it only three years ago. She described Rachel at three, and Nana's quiet competence, as counterpoint to the tremendous strain she lived under, and the next expectation, due in September.

Laura listened, adding her own commentary. During a lull, she cleared her throat, then sat up a little higher in the bed. 'Polly, I don't want to pry... Oh, yes, I do! It seems to me that Colonel Junot—heavens, he sounds more Scottish than Macbeth—is your champion.'

Polly stared at her, eyes wide. 'Champion?' she repeated. 'I can't imagine.'

Laura levelled her with a glance, probably one she practised on Danny. 'Confess,' she said.

There obviously wasn't any point in trying to keep the events of the voyage a secret. 'Several centuries back, his ancestors came to Scotland from France with Mary of Scotland. That's why he is "Junnit" now, and—' Polly stopped, and looked at Laura for reassurance. 'As for champion—sister, I don't think I would have survived the voyage without him.'

As Laura listened, only interjecting a faint 'Oh, my', or 'Gracious', as the tale became more fraught, Polly described the whole voyage, leaving nothing out. 'When… when I was feeling better, I honestly tried to avoid him, so he wouldn't have to be reminded of the embarrassing circumstances I had placed him under, but he was just so matter of fact! You would have thought he had done nothing more than…than pull a splinter out of my finger. I tried to be mortified, but he never let me.'

Even Laura, who had probably seen everything by now, stared at her. 'Polly, Colonel Junot may be as rare a man as I have ever heard of! We all owe him a debt.' She thought a moment, choosing her words like ripe strawberries in a summer market. 'That is all you owe him, though.'

Polly watched her sister, unable to overlook the worry in her eyes. She decided to put her at ease. 'Sister, he is much too grand and important to pay me any attention, beyond that which I have described to you.'

She did not expect to feel any pain at that bald announcement, but she did. 'He's a man of some distinction, Laura. Men like that don't…' She couldn't say it. 'Well, they don't.'

'You don't think he's too old for you?'

Surprised, Polly sat up. 'I…I never thought of him that

way.' She swallowed, suddenly wanting this conversation to end, because she felt unwanted tears teasing her eyelids. 'Age never entered in. Heavens, sister, he is a Colonel of Marines! I doubt he will even remember my name next week.'

'Are you so certain?' Laura asked. Suddenly the air hung heavy between them.

It was as if they both decided to change the subject at the same time, and spoke next of inconsequentials. Gradually Laura said less and less. Soon her head drooped on Polly's shoulder and she slept. Polly made herself comfortable, knowing that Philemon would eventually come in search of his wife. Finally, she heard Colonel Junot's firm footsteps receding down the long corridor. Philemon knocked softly on the door, then opened it.

Polly put a finger to her lips, and he smiled to see his wife asleep. Walking quietly to the bed, he picked her up, winked at Polly, and mouthed 'goodnight'. He looked down at his sleeping wife, then at Polly. 'You're just what this doctor ordered,' he whispered, then grinned. 'And you brought along your own Marine for protection.'

'He's not *my* Marine,' she whispered back. Philemon left the room as quietly as he had entered it. Polly frowned at the ceiling. 'What is wrong with my relatives?' she asked out loud.

Hugh's peers back in Plymouth would never believe him if he told them he spent the night in a nun's bed. He woke early, as usual, but felt disinclined to move. Miracle of miracles he hadn't roused earlier, considering the amount of port he had drunk last night, which also accounted for the slight buzz in his brain.

Part of the pleasure Hugh felt was his convivial evening with Philemon Brittle, a remarkable man, if ever there was one. He had handed over the letter from their mutual friend, Owen Brackett, which Brittle read right then, after apologies to his guest.

In the manner of men engaged in years of warfare, they had spent the next half-hour refighting naval battles, discovered they had both served at the Battle of the Nile and Trafalgar, and had decided—Brittle, anyway—each was deserving of confidences.

'Polly's a sight for Laura's sore eyes,' Brittle had said, as they finished one bottle and popped the cork on another. 'She works so hard, and misses her sisters so much.' He poured another measure. 'I hope it is not a felony to bamboozle the Navy Board, but we thought it worth a try to get Brandon Polly here.'

'I've been calling her Brandon,' Hugh confessed. 'I suppose that is rag manners, but it was one way to take her mind off as wicked a case of the pukes as I have ever seen.' He laughed. 'She told me she was determined to take up residence in Portugal and never attempt the ocean again.'

They had sailed into more prosaic conversational waters then, concluding only when the surgeon stoppered the bottle of port, telling Hugh it was time he went in search of his wife.

He had found her in Polly's room. Hugh had continued down the hall, but stood in the shadows and watched as, a few moments later, Brittle came out carrying his sleeping wife. He knew he was a voyeur, but Hugh had not looked away when she woke and her arms went around Brittle's neck and she kissed him.

Well, Surgeon Brittle, I shall have to report to Owen Brackett that you are enjoying a better war than most, Hugh had thought, as he went into his virginal cell and closed the door quietly. His dreams had been livelier than usual that night.

Preparing for the day was no more bare bones than usual. His only misgiving came as he dressed, wearing the black-and-white checked shirt that Polly seemed to have taken a shine to. He tucked the long tails into his navy blue trousers, and stood there a long minute, holding the gorget he had worn around his neck for years. Habit prevailed. He hooked it around his neck, but tucked it inside his shirt because he was out of uniform. Feeling decidedly naked without his uniform coat, he settled for a nondescript waistcoat he usually kept in his duffle as an antidote to cold mornings. *I must look like a brigand*, he thought, then reminded himself that vanity in a Lieutenant Colonel of Marines was out of place.

He retraced his steps to the dining room, hoping to see Polly Brandon. He was disappointed; Laura Brittle sat alone at the table, sipping tea. He hesitated to enter, but she had heard his footsteps.

'Do join me, Colonel Junot,' she called. When he came in the room, she indicated the food on the sideboard. 'Philemon is already ward walking, Danny is in the court-yard, with my sister.'

Porridge, cream, and yesterday's empanadas seemed to be the menu. He filled his plate and joined her as she poured him tea. He wasn't inclined to converse much over meals— maybe this was a consequence of the urgent nature of his wartime life—and she seemed to sense that. When he finished, he sat back. Something slightly militant in her eyes told him she did not suffer fools gladly, or, apparently, Colonels.

'Colonel, as much as you would probably rather not mention it, I must thank you for your unparalleled kindness to my sister on the voyage. She told me how you helped her.'

'It truly was nothing,' he assured her. *That is safe enough*, he thought, daring to relax. 'I only feel sorry it was necessary for a young lady to have to pawn her dignity so completely.' He laughed softly. 'She ain't much of a sailor, but she is a trooper.'

They laughed together. He watched Mrs Brittle's expressive face, seeing so much of Polly in her that it surprised him. Physically they were different—Laura tall and slim, and Polly shorter and probably destined to a life of decisions between one cream bun or two—but he could not overlook the matching dimples and lovely hair.

Then it came; he could see it in her eyes and the way she set her lips in a firm line. He braced himself.

'What do you know of us sisters?' she asked.

He shrugged, not sure of himself, but too stubborn to roll over and play dead. 'I have heard things,' he said simply. 'In fact, she told me about her father.'

He had startled her, but she recovered quickly. 'It's true. We have all decided never to gild a lily, Colonel. Still, I have to wonder why she said so much.'

Hugh said nothing, unwilling to pave her way. He poured himself more tea, then gave Mrs Brittle his full attention. He wondered for only a short moment what her game was, because he realised how transparent he must be to an observant woman who was a great protector of her sisters. 'Say on, madam,' he murmured, bracing himself.

'Nana was able to get away to safety in Plymouth with her grandmother. I had no one's support, so my first marriage lined our father's pockets and fair ruined me. Polly was never a victim because our father never could see past her spectacles. For that, Nana and I are profoundly grateful. Polly sees it differently, I think.'

Chastened, Hugh allowed his gaze to wander. *I was one of those shallow ones, at first, but you'll never hear that from me*, he thought.

What she was telling him became clear. He knew superior intellect had no role in his sudden wisdom because he knew himself well enough. 'Which is worse, Mrs Brittle—to be in peril because of beauty, or ignored because of perceived lack of it?'

'*Touché*, Colonel,' she said, impressed. 'Polly feels like a wren among birds of paradise, although nothing could be further from the truth. But *you* have noticed.'

He looked at her, his heart sinking because he knew she had taken his measure, no matter how well he had thought to hide it. 'You have me, Mrs Brittle. I'll admit that I have become an admirer of your sister. It only took a short voyage.'

'I thought as much,' she replied, her tone in no way calculated to embarrass. 'I have to ask—are you even aware that you have a proprietary air around her?'

It was his turn for surprise. 'No!'

'You do,' she said, giving considerable weight to two words.

He thought a long moment before he spoke, knowing that what he said would end any further connection. 'I'm certain she has no notion of my regard, beyond any consideration of a gentleman towards a female travelling alone. I helped her. That was enough, as far as she is concerned. How could I possibly mean anything to her on such short notice, and in such a circumstance?'

'I trust you are right,' Laura said.

He could hear the finality in her voice. 'I am right, madam. I…I have no plans to pursue the matter, so rest assured.' He made himself smile. 'Nothing like a good war to put the screws on an actual life, eh?'

He should never have said that, because it broke his heart, even as he knew he had ample cause to dislike Laura Brittle.

Not willing just then to stay another moment in Mrs Brittle's company, he stood up. 'Enough said,' he told her, with what he thought was an admirable bit of forbearance. 'I'll only be here the rest of the day, then off to Lisbon on tomorrow's tide.'

It pleased him a little to see her suddenly unsure, as though she regretted her interference in Polly Brandon's life. Maybe she could tolerate his plain speaking, since she was so eager to dish out her own. He took a deep breath. 'You and Mrs Worthy still see Brandon as a child, don't you?'

'She is,' was Laura Brittle's firm reply.

'Take another look,' he said quietly, then bowed and left the room.

Philemon had told Hugh last night where the principal ward was located. He reminded himself that his sole purpose in Oporto was to further his interviews with the Marines serving in small detachments. He would have got off scot-free if he hadn't glanced into the courtyard as he strode so purposefully away, ready to chew nails.

He slowed down; he stopped, making sure he was in the shadow of a colonnade. There she sat on the grass, cross-legged but decorous—Brandon Polly on the Navy Boards rolls, and Brandon for ever in his heart. He knew it now; Laura Brittle had succeeded in convincing him of the matter, even as she pulled the rug out from under him.

Brandon was dressed in something light and her hair was again atop her head in that silly way she had of twisting it there with a pencil or skewer. She had already attracted her nephew to one leg, and a darker-skinned youngster of roughly the same age—some Frenchman's memento— was ready to plop himself down on the other. Her arms were full and her face so pretty in that way of women with children.

How bitter this was. Polly Brandon was precisely the woman he wanted to mother his own children, children destined never to be born because the timing was off, and Napoleon, that bastard, insisted on hogging everyone's attention and effort. *Brandon, you are the wife I will never have*, he thought. *At least there is no crime in remembering you.*

He moved quietly from the shadow and continued his way down the corridor to the convent's chapel, which had been appropriated as the major ward. Philemon had told him that since the French has desecrated it, the Catholic hierarchy in Portugal had been willing enough, and marvellously patriotic, to turn over the use of major portions of the convent to the Royal Navy as a satellite hospital.

He walked into the ward, looking for Philemon Brittle, and found him in a former lady chapel, seated at a desk, poring over a sheaf of papers.

Brittle smiled to see him and indicated a chair. 'Feel

free to talk to my Marine guards,' he said. 'I have them posted in here, as you can see, and by my apothecary, and at each entrance.'

It seemed so few to Hugh. 'Do you feel secure enough which such a small detail?'

The surgeon shrugged. 'I confess I do not think about the matter over much. We're close to the navy wharf for safety—you were there yesterday—and this side of the Douro River is under control. We never cross the river to Oporto proper without an escort, though, mainly because none of your Marines has any faith in the British army's ability to keep the Frogs away.'

They both laughed, as only a navy surgeon and a Marine could who were well acquainted with service jealousies. 'I suppose we're a pack of fools, Colonel,' Philemon admitted. 'There's been no indication of French in the vicinity, but it's lively enough this summer, with Beau Wellesley on the prowl east of us, and Soult and Marmont playing their cat-and-mouse games.'

'And here all is peaceful.'

'For now. My own sources suggest battle soon, although the fleet itself seems quiet.' Philemon leaned back in his chair. 'You'd be amazed how this chapel can fill up with army wounded. They've taken to shipping us their worst cases, even though this was never intended as an army hospital. The advantage is we can get them off the Peninsula sooner, so it works out. I leave it to the Admiralty and Horse Guards to squabble, and let us alone to heal whom we can.'

Philomen peered closer at Hugh. 'But you are not concerned about that, are you?' He paused, but only briefly. 'Did my wife give you what-for over Polly?'

'She said my proprietary air was too obvious, and perhaps I should turn my attention elsewhere, since Polly is so young,' Hugh admitted, miserable and hoping it did not show. 'I assured her I would be gone soon enough and not likely to return. I admit I was not as nice to Mrs Brittle as I should have been. She still sees Brandon as a child.'

Out of the corner of his eye, Hugh could see a nun standing in the doorway. Philemon nodded to the woman, then rose. 'Duty calls. Don't look so glum, Colonel Junot! If it's any consolation, Laura and I don't see eye to eye on some matters. Oliver Worthy and I can both testify to the value of persistence, where the daughters of the late and unlamented Lord Ratliffe are concerned. Good day, now. Feel free to roam the place and question whomsoever you will.'

Hugh did, visiting first two Marines in hospital, and then making his rounds of the building, explaining himself and then questioning. The result was more food for thought, and the satisfaction of knowing he was improving in his offhand interrogations. His pleasure in whatever good he might be doing gave way to a gnawing feeling that he wanted to at least glimpse Polly Brandon again, before he made his way back to the navy wharf and his duty.

He passed through the corridor again, and this time was rewarded. There she was now, her hair more decorous, and her admirers grown to include more children and young mothers, some of whom looked no older than his nieces living so peacefully in Scotland on his land. He had heard stories of the French in Oporto, and the terrible prices exacted so often by conquerors.

He hoped he would not frighten anyone, but he had to

say goodbye to Polly Brandon. There were a few startled glances in his direction as he crossed the courtyard, but no one scarpered away. To his gratification, Polly rose to meet him, a smile on her face.

They met in the centre of the courtyard, and the sun was warm on his back. The scent of orange blossoms was all around, and the peppery odour of roses, fragrances he knew he would always associate with Polly Brandon, even if he never saw her again, which seemed likely, considering her sister's vigilance.

'I approve the shirt,' she told him with no preliminaries.

'I'll pass your encomium on to the Navy Board's chief commissary, who is probably some poor overworked functionary behind a tall desk,' he teased back.

How could he have ever though her plain? Were all men, when faced with spectacles, as stupid as he was? If anything, the spectacles gave her an impish look, especially since they always seemed to be perched a little low on her nose.

He couldn't help himself. He pushed up her glasses. 'You could probably tighten the little screws in the corner.'

Her cheeks grew quite pink then, and he liked the overall effect almost well enough to kiss her, except it had been ages since he had kissed a woman, and he probably wasn't all that good any more, if he ever had been.

Why couldn't he just say goodbye? Just a word and bow and off he would go, back to war. All he could do was stand there, filled with so much regret he wanted to drop to his knees in utter misery.

'You're leaving,' she said quietly.

'Time and tide, Brandon,' he told her. 'I want to talk to the Marines at the wharf, and get on board the *Perseverance*.' Unable to look into her eyes, he looked at the young women watching them. 'You are making friends. Are they to be your pupils?'

'They are,' she said, 'and any of the sisters who care to join us.' She frowned. 'It isn't much of a way to fight Boney, though, is it? Not like my sisters.'

'Be your own person, Brandon,' he said, not meaning to sound like a Colonel of Marines, but unable to help himself. 'I mean… No, that's what I mean.'

'Grow up?' she asked him, her eyes on his. 'And make up my mind about things?'

As he said his goodbye, it occurred to him that maybe, just maybe, he meant something to her. Too bad he had so much to do. Too bad armies were on the march. Too bad Laura Brittle stood in the doorway, watching them.

He wanted to clasp Polly Brandon in his arms. He had watched over her on the *Perseverance* and he was uneasy about leaving her without his protection. *Yes, I am proprietary*, he wanted to shout to Laura Brittle. *Why is it your business?*

He did nothing of the sort. 'Stay off the water, Brandon, and you should be all right,' he said gruffly, then turned on his heel as smartly as any Marine on parade, and left her standing alone in the courtyard.

Chapter Seven

Life at the Convent of the Sacred Name answered every
wish of Polly's heart. She was busy; she was with a
beloved sister; she was doing worthwhile work. In the
month since Colonel Junot left her so alone in the courtyard, she was everything but happy.

A sensible woman, she assured herself that the pain of
his departure would go away. Even her sheltered life in a
female academy had taught her that people come and go,
exerting their influence for a brief time. She remembered
one dance instructor—an Italian *émigré*—whom all the
students had swooned over. He left, after a six-weeks'
course of instruction. By the end of the following week,
all she could remember about him was his last name and
his brown eyes.

Colonel Junot was proving to be more difficult to forget. True, he was handsome by anyone's standards, made
even more beguiling by the unexpected brogue when he
spoke. She, who had endured too many years of constant
reminder about posture—head up and chin back—could
only envy his elegant way of carrying himself. Beyond the

superficial, Colonel Junot was stalwart, capable, and kind, and she had never met anyone like him.

That he orbited far out of her sphere was a given, and should have made it easier to forget him. She couldn't, though. She thought she knew why, but there was no one she could talk to, not even Laura, who had seemed relieved when Colonel Junot was but a distant figure in a scarlet coat, far below at the navy wharf.

I should set Laura's mind at ease, Polly thought, as the days passed. *I'm being foolish to even think Colonel Junot has spared a single thought for me since he said goodbye.* Trouble was, she didn't know what to say, so said nothing, choosing instead to throw herself into the work ordained for her in the convent, trusting to time to smooth away any sharp edges. As the days passed, it did; given another year or two, she knew she could forget Colonel Junot.

The Convent of the Sacred Name had been a large community, before the French desecrated its holiest places, and violated and murdered so many of its gentle inhabitants. Most of the surviving nuns had retreated to the safety of their motherhouse in Lisbon. The few who returned were resolute beings, which made them superbly useful in establishing and maintaining smooth order in Philemon's satellite hospital.

Essentially, these were women not afraid of anything. Philemon explained it to Polly one afternoon when he had a moment to sit in the courtyard with his little son in his arms. 'It's a fine line, my dear. People who endure the worst are either broken by it or strengthened.' He ruffled his son's auburn hair. 'I refer you to your own sisters.'

Polly was not slow to understand. 'These young girls I am to teach—they seem to always move in the shadows.

Where do they fall in the spectrum of what you are saying?'

Philemon passed his hand in front of his eyes, as if trying to brush away terrible visions. 'So many women were treated so cruelly by the French. Many took their own lives. Others were turned off by their families, who could not manage such shame, in the middle of other misery. Mind you, loss of what they call "honour" is a terrible thing to citizens of this peninsula. Bless their hearts, most of these girls still love their little ones, even conceived in such a way. I own that I admire women, and these brave souls in particular.'

Polly leaned against her brother-in-law. 'I should be more than a teacher, Philemon?'

'Aye, much more,' he replied firmly. 'Be a friend.'

That was her mandate, she decided, after another night of tossing and turning in her narrow bed. When she rose with the dawn, she decided that was her last sleepless night; there was work to be done. Everyone around her had been affected by war, which made her concerns puny, indeed. War meant sacrifice; it was no respecter of persons. She could understand that. Obviously Colonel Junot did. When he had left her so alone, he had not looked back.

Before she began, she needed an ally. She found her sister sitting quietly on a bench, obviously enjoying a moment of rare leisure. 'You have a look of enquiry, dearest,' she said to Polly, and patted the bench.

Polly sat down. 'I need an ally—someone who speaks English at least a little, so I can communicate.' She leaned close to Laura. 'What do you call these young girls?'

'I've been calling them "little mothers" in Portuguese—*pouco mães*—because they have been helping me so materially with Danny. I remind them I could never do my work without their help.' She sighed. 'They just don't quite believe they have any value. Learning English would be a start.'

'Who can help me?'

Laura sat back, her eyes thoughtful. 'There is only one woman, Sister Maria Madelena. She is a dragon, but she speaks English and Spanish.'

'A dragon?'

'Indeed. I would say she is more Pym than Pym, without the hypocrisy.'

The sisters looked at each other and burst into laughter. 'Where might I find this paragon?' Polly asked.

'Try the old chapel.'

So Polly made her way to the small chapel, which had existed since the Middle Ages. It was dark and redolent of centuries of incense, but there was a small nun, ferociously clicking the beads on her rosary, impatience evident in every contour of her compact body. She must have heard Polly enter, but Sister Maria Madelena did not turn around.

More interested than frightened now, Polly sat down quietly on one of the few benches near the entrance. She looked around her at the simple stations on the cross and wondered how many prayers had risen through the incense-darkened ceiling, low and decidedly pre-Gothic. *What did they pray about then?* Polly asked herself. *The Black Death? Moors at the gates?*

Finally the click of Sister Maria Madelena's beads ended with a finality that made Polly smile, in spite of her

fears at approaching Laura's dragon. Polly jumped when
the nun slapped the flat of her hand against the stone
floor, as if impatient for God to smile down on the Portuguese, who had been getting the short end of some
cosmic stick for so many years now. She turned around
quickly and Polly swallowed. She opened her mouth to
speak, but Sister Maria Madelena spoke first.

'I need your help, Miss Brandon.'

Surprised, Polly stared at her for a moment. 'Actually,
I…I…was going to say the same thing to you, Sister,' she
managed to blurt out, unnerved by the jagged scar that ran
from under her wimple by her ear, across her face under her
nose, cut through the corner of her mouth, and wound up
on her neck, where it vanished from sight under her habit.

She would have been almost pretty, but for the scar.
Don't stare, Polly tried to tell herself, but it was too late.
All she could do was stare, and wish for the first time that
she could telescope herself back through the weeks and into
Miss Pym's classroom again, where no one saw such
sights.

'I'm sorry,' she said finally. 'I should not stare. Please
forgive me.'

If she expected the dragon to suddenly hiss fire at her,
she was mistaken. The woman smiled, or at least, it would
have been a smile, except that the corner of her mouth
drooped, rendered her more sad than terrifying.

'Considering Our Lord, these are burdens easily borne,'
she said, the voice of practicality. 'We have not met, but I
have heard your name from the *pouco mães*. Sit, sit.'

Her English was excellent, and she wasted not a
moment. 'My dear, what is it you want of me?'

Polly had to laugh then. She needed to make up for her

rudeness, and Sister Maria Madelena did not seem to be one to bamboozle. 'You asked first, Sister,' she said, seeing nothing but kindness in the nun's eyes, belying the fearsome scar.

'I did, but you are the guest here in our convent,' she replied graciously. 'Very well, then. It is not a small thing. Would you be willing to help me at night, when the little mothers cry in their nightmares?'

Polly could not help the shudder that ran through her body. 'What could I possibly do?' she asked, when she could speak.

'Hold their hands. Sit with them until the terror passes. I cannot be everywhere.'

It was simply said, as if she had asked Polly to water the flowers in the courtyard. 'I will help you,' Polly said, thinking how Colonel Junot had helped her without a complaint in her worst moments; surely she could do no less. 'Of course I will help. When do I start?'

'Tonight.' Sister Madelena rose quickly. 'Now I have much to do.' She nodded at Polly and starting walking briskly to the low door, where she ducked and paused. 'What was it you came to see me about, *senhorita*?'

It seemed so unimportant. 'I wanted your help in teaching the little mothers English.' Polly stood up.

'Of course I will help,' Sister Maria Madelena said. 'When you have their hearts, my dear, by watching over them at night, you will easily engage their minds.'

It sounded so true that Polly could only nod. 'Your English is excellent, Sister,' she said. 'Where did you learn it?'

Sister Madelena looked at her, as if wondering how much truth to tell. 'I haven't always been a nun, and I am well named, Senhorita Brandon. I used to be mistress to an Englishman who managed Sandeman's vineyards. He thought if he talked English loud and slow enough, I would learn.'

'How is your hearing?' Polly asked, laughing.

'My English is better. I will come for you tonight after Compline.'

Polly changed her mind several times before Compline, but when there was a soft tap on her door, she rose at once.

'Follow me,' Sister Maria Madelena said, returning with her to the older part of the convent, the section far away from the satellite hospital. 'At first, Surgeon Brittle thought the little mothers would prefer to be together, so we housed them in the old refectory,' the nun said. 'They kept waking each other with tears and shrieks, so we decided on the old cells.'

Polly rubbed her arms, feeling the hairs rise on them. It was the middle of summer, but she shivered. 'Their children?'

'They sleep with their little ones, those who have children.'

Even though every fibre in her body screamed out to stop, Polly let herself be led down the corridor to its intersection, where a padded chair had been placed, looking out of place amid the austerity of a much earlier age.

'Make yourself comfortable here,' Sister Maria Madelena said, as she fluffed up a pillow. 'I will be at the other end of the corridor. If you hear someone cry out, just go to the chamber.'

'And do what?' Polly asked, utterly unprepared.

'What your heart tells you to do.' She left Polly alone.

Polly sat, deeply aware of her utter inadequacy. She leaned back carefully, afraid to make the smallest sound and waken anyone from already uneasy slumber. *You could have stayed with Nana*, she reminded herself. It sounded so cowardly to even think such a thing that she felt ashamed. She thought of Colonel Junot then, and the kindness in his brown eyes when he had told her not to sell herself short. She yearned to see him again so she could tell him she was trying, even as she hoped this would be the night when no one cried out.

She did not get her wish. The smell of incense was cloying but comforting, and there was just the hint of orange blossoms and gardenia from a courtyard they had passed. She drew her legs up under her and rested her cheek on her hand.

Polly sat up, straining her ears. The lowest keening seemed to come up from the very stones on the floor, causing her to clutch at her arms in fear. The sound stopped; she was prepared to swear she had never heard it. When it started again, it was louder, and she knew right where to go, provided she wasn't too afraid to get up from the chair.

Shame on you. Suppose Colonel Junot had chosen to ignore you? Polly told herself. She rose, drew a deep breath, and walked down the corridor, pausing at one door, then moved to the next, until she found the right one. She opened it.

The window was tiny, but the moon shone in bravely, casting its light on an empty bed. Alarmed, Polly closed the door behind her, then let out her own cry of terror as someone grabbed her by the wrist.

The young girl had been hiding behind the door,

pressed against the wall. She barely came up to Polly's shoulder, making her wonder what age the French soldiers considered too young to violate. With a great gulp, she swallowed her fear and put her hand on the girl's hand, not trying to pry off her cold fingers, but just to let her know she had a friend. Whether any of that would be conveyed by her almost-involuntary gesture, Polly had no idea, but it was the only tool in her skimpy arsenal.

Since her Portuguese was non-existent, Polly thought of Sister Maria Madelena's well-meaning British lover and spoke as softly as she could. 'You've had a fright, haven't you? You must be tired. Let me help you back to bed.'

She moved, expecting resistance, but found none. Polly wondered if the girl had been sleepwalking. She led her back to bed, tucked her in, and then looked around for a baby. There was no crib. This must be one of the girls without babies that Sister Maria had mentioned. She found a doll made of surgical towels like the one her nephew adored, and tucked it in the crook of the girl's arm. With a sigh of relief, the girl—scarcely more than a child, herself—rested her cheek against it and closed her eyes as she caressed the towel doll. Polly sat with her until her breathing was slow and steady.

Shaken, Polly returned to her chair in the hall. She sat for only a moment, then hurried to another room, where a shriek was followed by a young child's startled cry. Polly ran to the room to find a young woman huddled on her pillow, her eyes wide and staring. She had wakened her child, who sat up in his smaller bed, crying. Polly went to the child first, soothing the little boy until he returned to sleep.

Polly sat on the bed, her mind a complete blank. In desperation, she started to hum a lullaby she had heard Laura sing to Danny. To her relief, the girl's eyes began to close and her head drooped forwards. She resisted Polly's first effort to induce her to lie down. After two more choruses of the simple tune, she did not object to sliding between her sheets again and closing her eyes. She did not release Polly's hand until she was deep in slumber.

'I understand you,' Polly whispered. 'Colonel Junot held my hand when I could have sworn the ship was sinking. Can I do any less for you?'

So it went all night. She went from room to room down her side of the intersecting corridor while Sister Maria Madelena did the same in the other hall. Some rooms she went to twice to console young girls too soon old. One girl could not be consoled until Polly took her in her arms and held her as a mother holds a child. Her horror at such terrible treatment at the hands of French soldiers turned to rage that anyone would harrow up the innocent. When dawn came, Polly knew she would never be the same again, not if she lived another fifty years.

Exhausted in body, one part of her brain wanted to sleep until the war was over. The other part told her she must return every night, until the last victim in the world had been consoled. She wanted to tell Sister Maria Madelena everything she had learned, but she was too tired to do more than nod, when the nun came to her and said it was time to leave.

They walked in silence. Soon Polly was back in the part of the convent familiar to her. She smiled to hear Philemon and her sister in the dining room, laughing over something, ready to begin their own hard days as she had just ended hers. She turned to the nun.

'How can you do that, night after night?'

'I cannot sleep at night.' The nun looked away, as if wondering what to say. 'I know what it is like.'

Polly didn't even try to hide her shock. 'Oh, Sister,' she said, her voice breaking. 'I…I… Oh, I didn't know.'

'When the French came, Mr Wilson brought me here, thinking it would be safe. We retreated to the kitchen when the…the *crapaud* came. She told me not to, but I tried to defend the Mother Abbess with one of the cook's knives. They took it from me, and then all of them held me down for their own amusement…' She couldn't go on.

'I didn't know,' Polly said again, appalled.

'When I thought they were done, they used my own knife against me. I was determined not to die, though all around me were dead.' She shrugged. 'Who else would bury them?'

Polly gasped. 'Surely you did not…?'

'I had help. Not all of the community were murdered. We made our way down the coast to Lisbon and safety. Mr Wilson was killed here in Porto, defending casks of port—imagine how unimportant that is, Polly. I decided to join the order.'

Polly could not detect an ounce of self-pity in Sister Maria Madelena's voice. 'And you are here again.'

'There is work to be done,' the nun said, her voice brusque again. 'Go to sleep now, if you can. Compline will come too soon, I fear.' She peered at Polly. 'You will join me again tonight?'

'Certainly.'

'Excellent!' Sister Maria Madelena nodded and turned towards the sound of children in the courtyard. 'Your nephew Danny and João have turned into such ringleaders! I had better go administer some discipline, or we will be accused of raising wolves in Porto.'

'João?' she asked, remembering the dark-haired child who played most often with Danny.

'Yes, my dear. He is *my* son.'

Chapter Eight

Polly knew she would not sleep, so she did not try. She sat at the desk in her room, took out a sheet of paper, and began a letter she would never send.

She wrote 'Dear Colonel Junot', then paused, because the word 'dear' loomed up at her like a vulgar word, even though thousands of letters began that way, even those from prosaic counting houses. She drew a line through it anyway, then crumpled the page. She reminded herself that the letter was going nowhere, and wrote 'Dearest Hugh' on another sheet.

Freed of that constraint, she said whatever she wanted. She described the long night of comforting sorrow of such a magnitude she scarcely could grasp it. The words poured on to the page, and another like it and another, as she wrote of the young girl who spent her entire night patting the bedclothes and searching the room for her little one, a half-French infant strangled at birth by a mid-wife in a remote Portuguese hamlet.

She faltered a moment, then wrote of the girls whose troubled minds compelled them to act out their rapes over

and over. Maybe even more frightening were the young
girls who lay perfectly still in as small a space as they
could contort their figures, eyes wide and staring in the
dark.

Exhausted and weary with tears, Polly wrote it all to
Hugh Junot, her friend, so he would know what a pathetically tiny bit of good she was doing at Sacred Name.
'Knowing you'—she put down the pen, unable to continue for a moment. She picked it up, reminding herself
calmly that she did know the man, and knew what he
wanted to hear from her. 'Here is what I have learned: it
is possible to survive, when all hope has perished.'

She didn't need to reread anything, because the experience of that night would never leave her mind, no matter
how many years passed. Polly picked up the pencil again,
rubbing it against the end of the wooden desk to get one
more sentence from the lead, one more line no one would
ever see. 'I wish you were here, Hugh. I would feel more
brave.'

'I miss you,' she said out loud as she folded the letter.
'Your loving Brandon.'

Hugh kept himself supremely busy in Lisbon, which
was not a hard thing to do, considering the confusion,
intrigue, and bustle in the old seaport. Over excellent
port, which only served to remind him of the town he had
just left, Hugh listened as the Major in charge of the
Marine detachment told him of the summer campaigns
underway throughout Spain.

'Where are the armies?' Hugh asked.

'Sir, we believe Wellington is drawing out a fight near
Salamanca. After that, if he wins, the road is open to

Madrid,' the Major said. He tipped the last of the wine into Hugh's glass. 'Could this be our last summer in this wretched country? Shall we drink to that?'

They did. The major invited Hugh to join him at his favourite brothel, but Hugh shook his head, returning some vague regret about reports to write.

Hours later, restless and tangling his sheets into ropes, Hugh wished he had accepted the Major's invitation. He knew how badly he needed the comfort of a woman's body. Trouble was, he only wanted one body, and its owner was far away, unaware of his admiration.

His thoughts were not chaste. He had never wanted a woman more than he wanted Polly Brandon. He got up and went to the window. *How does anyone explain this feeling?* he asked himself as he watched the Marine sentries below, taking their prescribed steps, about faces, and returns. *I never expected this. How is it I have lived on the earth this long, and never felt this way before?* It was just as well he had not accompanied Major Buttram to the brothel; he would only have disappointed whomever he paid to service him.

He was disgusted with himself. In her polite way, Laura Brittle had made it plain he was not to reappear at the convent in Vila Nova de Gaia. She was a sister watching out for her own, and he obviously did not meet her standards. In misery, he knew that if he paraded his rank before Laura Brittle, the family wealth, and a handsome estate in a charmed corner of Scotland, it would make no difference. Laura Brittle thought him too old, and he was not good enough.

He paced the floor, angry at the unfairness of it all. He

tried to remind himself of the misery around him in this tragic country, which had sacrificed so much, but it didn't work this time. He could only think of his sacrifices, and how this war had cost him wife and children. There was no one he could make love with whenever the mood grabbed them; no bright eyes looking into his as they shared the same pillow; no smile to greet him across the breakfast table, telling him prosaically of bills and schooling; no one to sit with in a pew on Sunday morning; no one to tease him when he stepped on her foot during a waltz, as he invariably would have; no one to turn the page for him when he played the piano; no one. It chilled him to the bone and gave him grief beyond parallel.

He sat at his desk. Laura Brittle be damned; he would write to Polly Brandon, even though it was an ill-mannered thing to do. 'My dearest love' came from his pen. He shared his whole heart to her, page after page, leaving nothing unsaid of an intimate nature. He had never been one to gild a lily, either, and he was too mature to begin now. When he finished, he signed it 'Love from all my heart, Hugh', then immediately ripped it into tatters.

'That's out of your system, you randy goat,' he murmured, and took out another sheet. He began this one 'Greetings, Brandon, from someone with rag manners. I suppose I deserve a slap across the face for being so bold as to write to you, but I am wondering how you are.'

This letter was as easy to write as the first one. He described Lisbon, that dirty, charming city so full of intrigue. He wrote of the Marines he had chatted to, his conversations with the great and the lowly. He told her he wasn't satisfied he had learned enough to write a report yet, but that autumn would probably see him back in

Plymouth, doing precisely that, and chained to a conference table again. 'What, no sympathy from you, Brandon? You don't like a whiner? Take care of yourself. Hugh Junot.'

He read it through and found nothing objectionable. Because he had the liveliest confidence the Brittles would make sure Polly never received it, should he be so bold as to send it, he added a postscript on the other side: 'Damn me, if I don't miss you, Brandon.'

He addressed it to 'Brandon Polly, Convent of the Sacred Name, Vila Nova de Gaia', knowing full well he would never send it. Still, it looked good on his desk, almost as though these were normal times and he was writing to a beloved wife far away. There was no reason he couldn't just leave it there and return to bed.

When he woke hours later, he saw that the letter was gone, along with yesterday's towel and last night's slop jar. After his initial jolt, he found himself surprised that Portuguese servants were so efficient. He relied on the Brittles to intercept his bit of nonsense.

Polly knew she would never get accustomed to the misery of her nightly duty at Sacred Name, but as July wore on, she learned to adjust to it. Sister Maria Madelena was right—because of her tender sympathy during nighttime ordeals, the little mothers had no hesitation in sitting with her in the courtyard during the afternoons and learning what little English she had time to teach. It went well; so well, in fact, that she started taking out the letter to Colonel Junot she was never going to post and adding on to it, describing the mothers and children and their efforts to learn English. 'You were right, Colonel,' she wrote. 'I am useful here.'

Her usefulness continued in a way she had not anticipated. She was not even certain she liked the next change—travelling upriver with Sister Maria Madelena to shepherd other young girls to the sanctuary of the Sacred Name.

'How do you learn of them?' Polly asked, as they sat with the children in the afternoon sun.

Sister Maria kissed her son, then sent him back to play. 'There is a network of interested folk who hear things. We take a *barco rabelo* upriver to the village of São Jobim, where we find the young girls waiting for us, some Portuguese, some Spanish.'

'It's not dangerous?'

The nun shrugged. 'Who is safe anywhere in Portugal? There has been no trouble in more than a year, although we always travel with a small detachment of Marines. You will be safe. Ask your sister.'

Polly did. 'I think that is an excellent idea,' Laura told her. 'Sister Maria tells me you already have a wonderful rapport with the young mothers. Perhaps it is because you are so young, yourself.'

'Laura, I am not so young, not compared to some of them. I'll be nineteen this autumn.'

Laura seemed almost surprised. 'Why, yes, I suppose you will,' she murmured. 'I was reminded recently that I am at fault in thinking you younger than you are. You may go upriver.'

Her only regret in the journey was the mode of transportation, one of the flat-bottomed sailing craft used to

transport kegs of port wine downriver from wineries farther up the Douro. The war had disrupted the thriving
business upriver and the *barcos* were used now to transport people across the Douro to Oporto proper, and to
move what wine was available closer to Vila Nova and the
ships anchored at the mouth of the mighty river.

'Ships are the bane of my existence,' Polly muttered the
next morning to the nun as she allowed a Marine to help
her into the craft as it bobbed at the wharf. 'I will claim a
spot near the gunwale and try not to make a total fool of
myself.'

The wind blew inshore, so the *barco* sailed along against
the current, expertly guided by a Portuguese sailor at the
long pole in the stern. She and Sister Maria Madelena
watched the river narrow and its sides steepen as they travelled through the canyon cut by the Douro. Throughout the
morning, Polly watched other *barcos rabelos* coming downstream flying British ensigns. There were wounded men on
the deck, with surgeons bending over them. Last week, news
had reached the convent of a battle in north central Spain in
the Arapiles hills near Salamanca, and Philemon had told
Laura over the breakfast table to prepare for casualties.

'My sister tells me even the army sends the worst of
the worst to Philemon's hospital,' she couldn't help saying
proudly to Sister Maria. 'It was only supposed to be a
satellite naval hospital.' She looked closer. 'Oh, Sister,
excuse me. I didn't realise you were praying.'

It was dusk by the time they reached the village of São
Jobim. 'Ordinarily, we try to leave earlier in the morning,
so we can make the trip in one day,' Sister Maria
Madelena said, as they approached the wharf.

There were few people about. Polly couldn't see any men at all. She looked at Sister Maria Madelena, a question in her eyes.

'The men have gone with the army or the partisans,' the nun explained. 'So it is, in every village in Portugal.'

What happened once the *barco* docked was a marvel of efficiency, testament to how many times Sister Maria Madelena had made this voyage of rescue. From the Marines to the Portuguese mariners, everyone worked quickly. Escorted by the Marines, they were helped ashore and into the church across the square in a matter of minutes.

'I thought you said we were in no danger?' Polly asked.

'That is correct,' the nun replied, as she nodded to the priest approaching them. 'We are merely careful. Good evening, Pai Belo. Do you have someone for me?'

He did, pointing to a young woman huddled on a bench and shivering, despite the warmth of a late July sun only just now setting west across the Douro. Polly glanced at Sister Maria, as her eyes caught the motion of the priest passing a note to her. It was done so quickly she might have mistaken it. Well, never mind, Polly thought, going to the girl and sitting beside her. She knew enough Portuguese to murmur, 'You are safe now', not touching her, but sitting close.

Sister Maria joined her. 'Pai says she is from across the border, where other young girls have come lately.'

'It's so far,' Polly said, resting her hand gently on the girl's shoulder.

'Not so far,' Sister Maria contradicted. 'I come from beyond the border myself. I have a brother—' She stopped, as if to remember him. 'I have a brother there. It is not so far.'

They spent the night in the church, sharing a frugal

meal of bread and cheese, while the Marines ate their own rations and stood sentry duty. Sister Maria and the priest conversed in low tones, with occasional glances at Polly and the young woman—her name was Dolores—who rested, silent and fearful, her eyes wide.

Before the rising sun cleared the canyons of the Douro, they were on the water again, relying this time on the strong current to carry them west to Oporto. After resigning herself to her by now obligatory offering to Neptune or Poseidon, or whatever mischievous god governed the waves that so discomfited her, Polly turned her face to the sun and held Dolores's hand for most of the rapid trip downriver to the sea.

They arrived by noon on the speedier return trip, docking at the navy wharf and sharing a cart to the convent with Laura and other wounded from upriver. Swallowing her fears in the face of her sister's single-minded duty, she let Laura press her into duty, washing dirty limbs and cutting away bloodsoaked clothing. 'If I didn't need you so badly...' Laura began, and then her words trailed off as Philemon—his arm red to the elbow—directed her to another crisis.

After a night of unending work, Polly fell into bed, not bothering to remove her clothes, now as stained and reeking as those of the wounded she had helped. Her head crunched on paper, but she only touched it and closed her eyes.

The warmth of the afternoon sun woke her, coupled with her own hunger and the twine tickling her nose. She brushed at her face and opened her eyes so see a letter bound in heavy paper and tied in a bow. She thought she recognised the casual handwriting, and 'Brandon Polly' confirmed it. Colonel Junot had written to her.

Polly took her time opening the letter, savouring every second. As she opened it, she wondered if Laura knew she had received a letter from Colonel Junot. Maybe in the press of yesterday's activity, someone else had put the message on her bed.

She took a deep breath and began to read. *Greetings, Brandon, from someone with rag manners*, she read. *I suppose I deserve a slap across the face for being so bold as to write to you…* She read the letter, full of news of Lisbon and his work there, ran her finger slowly across his name, caressing it, and read it again. *I have been on your mind*, she thought, so pleased that she hugged herself, then laughed out loud.

It was out of the question that she should be so presumptuous as to answer his letter, and she knew it. She glanced at the letter again, wishing she dared to write back.

If only. The letter contained nothing lover-like or anything that she couldn't show to Laura or Philemon. So she would have thought, if she hadn't turned over the final sheet and seen the postscript. 'Damn me, if I don't miss you, Brandon.'

A pleasant warmth descended on her then. The sole human being on earth who had seen her at her noxious worst missed her. She gently ran her finger across the words. He missed her.

She hid the letter next to the intemperate one she had written to him and never sent. Laura never questioned her about the letter, so Polly knew she had neither seen nor delivered it. Polly gave herself a mental shake and went back to work.

for about ten cups of coffee and no sleep, then bathed her daughter in wildly inadequate . . . a rueful shake and went back to work.

Chapter Nine

Hugh knew Polly Brandon would never answer his letter, if she even received it. He felt a little foolish as he listened every day for the drum rolls in the Marine barracks indicating mail call. He was a Lieutenant Colonel; any correspondence intended for him would have been taken to him. Still, he listened for the drum roll.

He had made the mistake of accepting Major Buttram's invitation to the brothel and spent an hour with a languid lass who otherwise would have pleased him greatly, if he hadn't been thinking of Polly. Too soon he found himself wishing that it was Polly's heels digging into his kidneys as he rode her, and Polly's breath warming his cheek, and Polly's head turning from side to side as he satisfied her, or at least, when she pretended so. Something told him Polly would never pretend, not if he was at the helm.

July turned into August and then early September, as he took one short hop to the Mediterranean on a sloop of war and visited the Marines on Malta, always a charming city to visit. He tried to drink himself silly one night, but that was an even greater failure than the prostitute in Lisbon. He had no real liking for any spirits other than grog, which had always been a source of amusement to his brother officers, who generally assumed he was, at the very least, a Madeira man. All he had to show for an evening in his cups was a head as big as all outdoors and Brandon's inability to maintain stuff in the gut where it belonged.

If women and liquor couldn't assuage him, he had more success writing his report back in Lisbon, busying himself with facts and figures. That lasted about three days, until he found himself staring at the wall and seeing Polly Brandon in the stucco. 'All right, lassie,' he said one afternoon to his wall, 'did ye or did ye not even receive my letter? If ye did, congratulations on having superior manners and not responding. If ye didna, well then, I'm nowhere different than I was when I started speculating. Lord, what a chowderhead. Listen to your sister and stay away from Marines.'

And that was that. Or it would have been, if he hadn't decided to take the next frigate north to Ferrol Station for a look around. His only interesting official correspondence had come encrypted from Plymouth. When the translated message reached his desk, he read of Admiral Sir Home Popham's campaign into the Bay of Biscay, with Santander as the hard-won prize. 'Major Buttram, I want to watch our Johnnies in action,' he said the next morning as he packed. 'Is something heading north at least to Ferrol Station?'

Something was—a sloop of war captained by a young Lieutenant. Considering all of his years rubbing shoulders with the navy, Hugh should have known they could not slide by Oporto without stopping, considering the drinking habits of the Royal Navy's officers. The sloop's skip-per had a heavy purse from thirsty men who wanted to turn gold into port, alchemy common in the navy.

'We'll be here a day at least, I fear, sir,' the Lieutenant said. 'I've promised port to ever so many ships. Um, if you're bored, I hear there are excellent cafés in Oporto, and the women are the…um…easiest in Portugal,' he concluded in a rush, his face red.

The women are not easy in Oporto, Hugh thought sourly. 'I'll remain on board,' he said, and turned on his heel.

By early September, Polly had made four trips upriver with Sister Maria Madelena. Typically, they left before sunrise, to ensure a quick return that day. There were no more lighters descending the Douro, bearing wounded, because the season of campaigning was winding down. Dispatches had reached Oporto that Beau Wellesley and his army had marched in triumph to Madrid, and that several French armies in the region were in motion, as well, some moving towards the capital city and others scattering. No one knew what to believe.

'And still there are those who need our help,' Sister Maria Madelena said, as they came in sight of São Jobim.

Polly knew the routine now. She hurried ashore and followed the sentries into the church, where the heavy door swung shut and was barred. There were two girls this time, one with a baby. Both of them, Spanish sisters, shrank from the sight of the Marines, even though Sister Maria Madelena said '*Ingleses*' over and over.

Polly wished she felt less uneasy about this run. Lately, she had been watching Sister Maria Madelena and the priest more closely. They almost always stepped aside where no one could hear, to talk in low whispers, and sometimes exchange notes. They seemed to be arguing this time. The priest shook his head and there was no note.

'We would be a happier country without *any* soldiers,' Sister Maria said as they prepared to leave.

Polly wondered if she should speak. *What could it hurt?* she thought at last, and cleared her throat.

'Sister, did you feel that someone was watching us this time?' Said out loud, it sounded foolish; she regretted her words at once. Sister Maria Madelena would think her a coward. She never asked about the notes; the one time she had, the nun had ignored her.

'What's this?' the nun asked gently. 'Did you feel a prickling of your neck hairs? Fingers along your spine?'

'I am being foolish, I know,' she apologised.

'No, you're not. I felt it, too. I look around, then I re-mind myself that we are on God's errand.' She shrugged. 'The feeling always passes.'

Maybe for you, Polly thought.

Despite her misgivings, which Polly knew better than to voice again, the trip downriver was as calm as the other ones. She cautiously complimented herself on keeping down that morning's meal, and almost enjoyed the race down to the sea, propelled by a splendid current as the Douro rushed out of the mountains and gradually changed character into a dignified, formidable river that widened with each mile closer to the Atlantic.

They reached Vila Nova as the sun was low in the sky. The slower swells of the turning tide made the bobbing of the small vessel an instrument of torture to her sorely tried equilibrium.

Small, but bristling with guns, a sloop of war was tied to the dock. She glanced at it, then stared, because Colonel Junot stood there, gazing towards the convent. *It cannot be*, she thought first, mainly because she did not want him to see her looking so green under her unlady-like tan, and getting ready to lean over the side of the *barco*. Then, *Perhaps he will not notice me*, she told herself, as she vomited into the river.

If the Spanish girl's baby had not started to cry, maybe he would not have looked around in surprise. When he saw her, he flashed as broad a smile as she had ever seen.

He doffed his hat to her, and bowed.

'I am mortified,' Polly whispered to Sister Maria. 'He probably thinks I get seasick in my bathtub.'

'That is Colonel...how do you say...Junnit? He is the one who...'

Polly nodded. 'I did not really think I would see him again. Perhaps he will not come on shore.'

She couldn't look, but Sister Maria Madelena had no qualms about the matter. 'He appears to be heading to the gangplank, Polly,' she whispered back.

Faster than she would have credited, he was standing beside the *barco*, ready to give her a hand. He helped her over the gunwale and on to the dock, beamed at her, then held out his hand to the young woman with the baby, who hesitated.

'Almira, he is my friend,' Polly murmured in her sketchy Spanish, which changed the girl's worry to relief. Shyly, she handed her baby up to Polly, then took Colonel Junot's hand and let him help her on to the dock.

Suddenly too shy to say anything, Polly stood there with the baby. The Colonel was not smiling now, which caused her to look at him more closely, and then quickly hand the baby over to his mother.

'Colonel?' Something had happened, and she hadn't the slightest idea what it was.

'What were you doing upriver?' he asked, his tone chilly.

She felt like a child under his question. 'We…we retrieve young women from the interior of Portugal who have been…' She hesitated.

'…raped by the French,' he concluded bluntly, as she felt her face flame. He took her arm, a grasp more urgent than angry. 'Brandon, what harsh duty is yours at this convent?'

He took her to a bench and sat her down, then sat down beside her. He seemed to know he was taxing her; she watched him take a deep breath and visibly calm himself. He did not release her arm, but his grip loosened.

She almost wished now she had sent the letter in the bottom of her trunk. It would be easier than explaining to a man what she did. She took a breath of her own. 'Oh, Colonel, it *is* harsh, but not for me. The *pouco mães* wake up at night with terrible dreams. I go from room to room, trying to comfort them.'

His frown only deepened. 'That is not a job for one so young. Is there no one else who can do it?'

She winced, because he had touched a vulnerable place, one that had begun to trouble Laura. 'Colonel, they respond to me, and I certainly have their trust. I sleep in the mornings, and by afternoon, teach a little English here and there, although I must admit I seem to be learning more Portuguese. Some Spanish, too.'

She said that to hopefully make him smile a little, but he did not. What he said surprised her.

He released her arm then and sighed, leaning back

against the railing of the wharf, something she doubted he did very often, considering his military bearing. 'Don't go upriver again, Brandon,' he said finally.

'It's safe, Colonel,' she reminded him. 'Everyone says so.'

'Nothing is safe in the Peninsula,' he replied, and she could not overlook the concern in his voice. 'Armies are marching, and whenever armies march, all kinds of people are put in motion.'

'We don't go so far upriver. Just to São Jobim: six hours up, four hours back, or less.'

'It's too far,' he said flatly. 'Don't do it, Brandon.'

Suddenly, she wanted to agree with him, tell him about her misgivings, and never leave the shelter of the convent again. She might have, if she hadn't looked at Sister Maria Madelena just then, as the nun helped the two sisters with the baby into the back of the ox-led wagon that met every vessel.

She stood up. 'I have to go now,' she told him. 'Sister Maria needs me.'

Hugh had seldom felt helpless in his maritime career. He felt helpless now, because he had no *force majeure* to work on Polly Brandon, nothing a husband would have. He had no tie, no commitment, nothing beyond his feeble effort to get a good woman with charity on her mind to listen to his worries that, for all he knew, were totally unfounded. It was a position he did not like.

Still, he could tell that she left his side reluctantly. For the tiniest moment, he wondered what she would do if he told her he loved her and would she please listen to him? He was being absurd, of course—too bad for her, too bad for him.

Since she seemed disinclined to leave him there, even as the wagon began its slow trip to the top of the bluff, he walked beside her. He noted that her hair was twisted in its funny knot, with a skewer through it. Without thinking, he suddenly pulled out the wooden wand, and smiled when she laughed and hit his arm.

'Laura calls me a ragbag,' she said cheerfully, as she took the skewer from him and wound up her topknot again. 'Nana would scold me and ask how I ever planned to find a husband.'

Just look at me seriously, he thought. *You'd have your answer.* 'It's a good question, Brandon,' he said, thinking how stupid it was the moment he said it.

'Gentlemen never look past my spectacles, Colonel, so it doesn't matter. Philemon tells me to forge my own way, precisely as my sisters have done. Everyone has advice,' she grumbled.

She peered at him then in her kindly way that made him understand, no matter how grudgingly, what Sister Maria and the pitiful female dregs of war already knew: Polly Brandon was good and loyal and not afraid, no matter what she might say about herself to the contrary. They probably did need her. Too bad the thought gave him no comfort.

'Come to dinner this evening,' Polly asked him. 'Colonel? Colonel? When I used to woolgather like you are doing, Miss Pym would rap my knuckles.'

Wordlessly he held out his hand, palm down, and she laughed, even as she blushed. Delightful.

'I must say no,' he replied, as they continued their slow walk to the convent. 'I have already promised myself to the Lieutenant of Marines at the dock.'

She stopped. So did he. A fine frown line appeared between her eyes and she pursed her lips ever so slightly, just enough to make his back break out in sweat. 'Are you avoiding me?' she asked.

'No, ma'am, I am not,' he lied, 'even though dinner with Lieutenant Stephens means the mess hall. It is another opportunity to speak to the men I am interested in hearing from, to complete my report. I have a purpose here, too, you know.'

It came out more sharply than he intended, and Polly had nothing more to say as they walked to the top of the hill. He had shut her down, the last thing he wanted to do, especially when he was so worried.

'Perhaps I could stop by at two bells into the dog watch. That's seven o'clock, Brandon. You need to learn these things,' he added, although why that would be necessary, he couldn't say.

She grinned at him, then hurried ahead to catch up to the cart. He watched her go, admiring her purposeful stride that made her muslin gown sway so nicely, then did an about face and went down the hill.

Hugh hoped he would not see Laura Brittle when he returned to the convent at two bells, full of excellent Portuguese sausage and just enough grog to render him optimistic.

He barely saw Polly. She was lying in the grassy courtyard, dim now with twilight, a child sitting on her stomach and leaning against her upraised knees. The two were silently observing each other, until Polly suddenly darted her fingers into the soft places under his arms and he chortled. Hugh squatted on his heels beside her. The little boy observed him with solemn brown eyes, but did not seem intimidated.

'This is João,' she said. 'João, this is Colonel Junot.'

'You should teach him what my grandmama taught me,' he said. With his forefinger, he began to describe a wide but narrowing circle targeting the child's stomach. '"There was an old bee who lived in a barn, he carried his bagpipe under his arm, and the only tune that he could play was bzzz!"' He aimed his finger at the little boy's navel and zeroed in, to the child's delight.

'Say that again,' Polly demanded, as she raised her hand to do as he had done.

He repeated the little rhyme that every child in Scotland probably knew, as Polly's finger spiralled down, ending in the soft stomach of her totally willing target, who laughed again and made his own buzzing sound, as he tugged at her finger.

'The tough part now is to convince the child he doesn't want to do it any more,' Hugh teased. 'Good luck.'

She smiled at him, which made his heart leap, then continued the finger play. When another child tossed a ball in his direction, João finally moved off. Polly stayed where she was in the grass. 'I didn't think I would see you again,' she said.

'It was a surprise to me, as well,' he told her, as he plucked handfuls of grass and tossed them on her, enjoying her laugh as she let him. 'We are heading to Ferrol Station, where I hope to catch a coastal lighter to Santander. Apparently Admiral Popham has been using his Marines to good effect in taking the town.'

'Is it dangerous?'

He shrugged. 'No more than anything else during a war. When I finish, I will take a frigate to Plymouth.'

She was silent for a long time. He stopped scattering

grass on her and turned his attention to the children at play, obviously getting the last bit of fun out of whatever remained of daylight. He noticed Laura Brittle observing him from the shadows of the colonnade and nodded to her. When he looked back at Polly, she was asleep.

When on earth do you really sleep? he thought, wanting to pick her up and deposit her in a bed of his choosing. *I'm a fool*, he told himself, as he got to his feet, brushed the grass off his hands, and left the courtyard and the sleeping woman who meant more to him than anyone he had ever met.

Philemon sat farther away in the colonnade, holding his son. 'Do that bee thing for me,' he said.

Hugh laughed and did it again. 'It's probably a more popular export than Knox's spare Presbyterianism and oatmeal porridge. Certainly better than haggis, but what isn't?' He sat beside the surgeon.

'You have not been cured of my sister-in-law,' Philemon said, with utterly no preamble.

'No,' Hugh said, amazed at the surgeon's direct approach, but not entirely surprised by it. He had discovered years ago that people with no time to spare seldom wasted words.

'Then you can understand Sister Maria Madelena's need of her. Polly has such a calming effect on those broken reeds she ministers to.' Philemon kissed his son. 'Polly is so self-effacing that she has no idea of her effect on people. Maybe on you, too?'

'You know.'

'Of course I know,' Philemon replied, with all the complacency of a happily married man, damn his eyes. 'I am married to her sister, who has that same effect. I know

Laura Brittle better than any human alive, and I tell you these three daughters of a terrible man are rare and special.'

'Do you want me gone, too?' Hugh said bluntly.

'I don't think so. Don't be discouraged.' Philemon looked at Hugh, as though measuring him. 'I don't know what will happen with you and Polly; wartime is not so amenable to courtship. But things happen.'

'Maybe not right now, though,' Hugh said.

'Maybe not,' Philemon agreed, his voice as kind as one could wish. He nodded to his wife, who was approaching them, her arms held out for her son. 'Laura, take this rascal and put him to bed. I'll see the Colonel to the door.'

He was being dismissed. It was not late, but the Brittles probably wanted Polly to sleep as much as she could, before the midnight hours came when the young women were restless in their dreams.

Philemon was in no hurry to usher him out. They took their time getting to the massive door, with its Marine sentry. Hugh tried one more time.

'I wish Miss Brandon would not go upriver.' He stopped, not mistaking the wary look on the surgeon's face. 'I know, I know! You all think I am being overly proprietary. If the interior of Spain were not in such turmoil this past month, I would say nothing.'

'She's going again tomorrow,' Philemon said.

'No! Don't allow it.'

'We got word at dinner. There was one more girl who made it late to São Jobim. There was some sense of urgency in the communication from the priest.'

'Then insist on more of an escort,' Hugh said.

'Perhaps I can. It's going to be another day trip, that is all.'

'Brandon—Miss Brandon—doesn't have to go, does she?'

'I doubt she sees it your way, Colonel.' The surgeon looked him in the eyes. 'By the way, all mail is delivered to my desk. If Laura had seen the letter you so brazenly sent to her sister, she would have chased you out of the convent with a capital knife.'

'It was cheeky of me,' Hugh admitted. 'Did you deliver it?'

'Guilty as charged, Colonel Junot. You're not such a bad man,' Philemon said generously.

The surgeon's teasing gave him heart. 'Thank you! Now, if you could use your almighty powers of persuasion to convince your sister-in-law to stop those river trips, this Marine could embark for Ferrol Station and then Plymouth with an easier conscience.'

He could tell the surgeon was wavering, but he looked at his timepiece.

'I have to go, Colonel Junot,' he said. 'I'll think about what you suggest.'

Hugh sighed and walked slowly down the hill to the wharf, knowing he would toss and turn all night and probably get even less sleep than Polly Brandon.

Polly had managed to snatch a few moments of sleep in the corridor that night. Before dawn, after a quick kiss on Laura's cheek, she hurried to the wharf. The *barco*, still wreathed in shadows, was the only vessel showing signs of activity. She waited as the three Marines filed on board and sat down near the curved bow. Polly sat near the mast, wrapped her cloak tighter and closed her eyes.

'Goodbye, Brandon. I hope you have a wonderful life, wherever it takes you.'

Startled, she strained her eyes to see Colonel Junot standing on the dock, looking down at her. 'Why, thank you,' she said, wishing she didn't sound so furry with sleep.

He doffed his hat to her and she waved, then closed her eyes again, wishing he had not shown up last night, but determined not to be miserable. As the Portuguese sailor cast off the lines, she felt a sudden thump and a sway. To her utter amazement, she opened her eyes to see Colonel Junot pick his way carefully to the bow. He sat down with the sentries, who looked as startled as she did. He glanced over his shoulder at her.

'I just changed my mind,' he said. His expression suggested to her that he was as surprised as she was to find himself on the *barco*. 'The sloop of war won't get underway until night. You promise me we'll be back here by late afternoon?'

'Certainly. But why…?'

'I have a sudden hankering to see São Jobim, Brandon.'

Chapter Ten

Polly could have told him São Jobim wasn't much of a village. In a peaceful world, one where Englishmen with nothing better to do liked to take the Grand Tour, even the old church was not one of the Seven Wonders.

She couldn't overlook her growing discomfort that he had come along because he was worried about another trip upriver so soon after the last one. She knew he had better things to do, and she doubted he had ever done anything as lowly as escort duty in many years. Still, she had to admit there was some gratification in knowing someone was so concerned about her welfare.

To her relief, she kept down breakfast, which gave her some hope that she could outgrow her tendency to sea-sickness. *Anything is possible, Brandon*, she told herself, as she leaned against one of the wine kegs lashed to the deck. *Perhaps you can outgrow a certain fondness for the man who was so kind to you. Anything is possible, but it might be easier if he had not been so impulsive.*

She watched the Colonel as he sat with the sentries, impressed, as always, by his military bearing. She watched him gesture to the Private beside him, using what she knew were his considerable skills in getting the sentries to talk to him, man to man, and not as Private to Colonel. In his letter to her, he had told her what questions he asked, and how he was becoming more proficient in the art of interview. *At least I think I am,* he had written. *Perhaps I will show you my list of questions and you can tell me if I have forgotten anything.* Polly smiled to herself, wondering if she had memorised his entire letter.

He couldn't have picked a better assignment for himself, she decided, as she watched all three sentries unbend enough to talk and then laugh. The Colonel had a pad of paper resting on his thigh, and he wrote on it with a pencil, not even looking down, doing nothing to call attention to his actions. She knew it was more than mere command that compelled the sentries to relax enough to talk to Colonel Junot. 'If he says he is interested in what you do, he most certainly means it,' she whispered to herself. 'I could tell you that.'

Lulled by the monotony of motion, she closed her eyes again, relieved for no particular reason that Colonel Junot had decided so impulsively to come along. There was no reason she should feel any safer; unlike the sentries, he carried no weapon. In her brief acquaintance with so august a character, Polly knew he was steadfast. That was enough to send her peacefully back to sleep.

When she woke, he was sitting beside her, gazing out at the shoreline. They had entered one of the gorges where the river narrowed and the current grew stronger. The *barco* had begun to pitch and yaw as the two-man crew accommodated themselves to the new forces at play on their flat-bottomed boat. She sat up, well aware that this was the one place in the river's journey where she felt supremely entitled to her queasiness.

'It looks like a rough go here, Brandon,' was all Colonel Junot said.

She nodded, gratified and not a little touched that he had recognised the fact and come back to sit with her through the canyon. 'You're certain you are never seasick?' she asked.

He smiled and shook his head. 'Brandon, I have been bobbing about in small boats since I was not a lot older than your nephew. Do you want me to tell you about it?'

She did, even as she recognised what he was doing to keep her mind off the tumbling water as the *barco* pushed against the current. 'Indeed, I do, Colonel. Talk away, and distract me from all the waves and toothy things probably swimming around right under the water's surface.'

'You are a silly nod,' he told her, matter of fact. 'I am from a stretch of choppy water near Kirkcudbright, in the western part of Scotland. No one in our current genera-tion has much of a clue how our French ancestor managed to end up in such an obscure place, but we're glad he did, cold knees and oatmeal notwithstanding.'

Her mind partly on the rough passage, but increas-ingly more on him, she listened as he told her of a child-hood she could scarcely imagine: the oldest of three children, and the one always inclined to more adventure than his bookish little brother—now a barrister in Edin-burgh—and his sister, who had his same love for tumult but the misfortune of her sex. 'Jeannie should be the Colonel Commandant of the Third Division,' Colonel

Junot told her. 'As it is, she and her husband run the estate west of Kirkie, since our da decided to indulge in a life of leisure in his old age. The estate will be mine some day—hopefully, not too soon.'

'Do you miss it?' she asked, wanting to reach out for him because she knew the upcoming stretch of water was a personal trial.

Maybe she made an involuntary gesture. Maybe he just knew almost as much about water as her brother-in-law Oliver. He took her arm and tucked it next to his side, forcing her to move closer to him, which bothered her not a bit.

'Aye, I miss it,' he told her, his lips close to her ear as the crew manoeuvred the *barco* expertly past the rocks and into a calmer place. 'More lately than usual. Maybe I'd like to drop a line in a trout stream I know about, and sleep in my own bed.'

It was too much. She ducked her head into his shoulder and he pulled her close with his other hand, speaking louder. 'Ah, now, Brandon. Do I have to do the buzzy bee to distract you?'

She tried to laugh, even as she swallowed the gorge rising from her sorely tried stomach. 'No,' she said, wishing she meant it. 'Let go!'

He did instantly, but put his hand inside the collar of her dress, gripping her, as she leaned over the gunwale. 'Brandon, it's a good thing you weren't married to one of Noah's sons. Imagine forty days and nights of this.'

'Don't,' she said as she sat back and he released her. 'I don't even like *reading* that stretch of Genesis.'

He laughed and wiped her mouth with her own skirt. 'I think…this is just my opinion, but perhaps Sister Maria

Madelena will let you stay at Sacred Name in the future, and avoid this watery purgatory.'

'Perhaps. I am inclined to agree.'

After one more visit to the gunwale, Polly sat back for the smooth portion of the ride, where the Douro widened out slightly, and the canyon was breathtaking in its wild beauty. It pleased her that Colonel Junot seemed to enjoy the view, too. When she returned to his side, he took hold of her again. Although she knew they had traversed the last gorge before São Jobim and she did not need his protective hold on her, she remained where she was in the security of his arms.

'Beautiful, isn't it?' she asked.

'Mostly I am noticing what an advantage anyone with a mind for mischief would have, sniping from canyon walls,' he told her. 'Then I notice the beauty of things next, Brandon. It's what I do. How many times have you made this trip?'

Polly decided he could change the subject faster than most people could think. 'This is the fourth or fifth. Why?'

'In that case, then I am impressed with your own toughness, considering how you feel about the water, and knowing these watery traps are here to ensnare you.'

'I like to make myself useful,' she said.

'I understand,' he replied, after some thought. 'Still, this is a war zone—yes, even peaceful São Jobim—and I worry. There's something about this place... Oh, well, I cannot put my finger on it. Brandon, doesn't a quiet life at home sound appealing to you?'

'I've never actually had a home,' she told him, 'but, yes, it sounds agreeable. It sounded agreeable after my first night in the English Channel.'

She wished Colonel Junot would not look at her with such sympathy. Perhaps he was thinking of his own childhood. Since she had never enjoyed a childhood like his, it was hard to miss it, she reasoned. 'I spent my earliest years in an orphanage, and then I went to Miss Pym's Female Academy in Bath.'

That should remind you of everything you need to know about my parentage, in case you have forgotten, she thought grimly. She looked for some disgust, but Colonel Junot seemed unperturbed by her words.

'Take my word for it then, Brandon. Staying at home is a good thing, and I recommend it.'

'You didn't,' she pointed out.

'Of course not. I am a man and I know my duty, even if I do work for the English and my pay chit comes from London.'

Trust you to joke and be serious in the same sentence, she thought. *And to distract me.* He had graciously handed back her serenity, which she accepted without comment. In another minute she disentangled herself from his grip, simply because it was time she remembered.

Polly looked around as the *barco* approached São Jobim. Sister Maria Madelena sat by herself as she always did, her eyes on the rosary in her lap as she fingered it. Their heads together, the sentries were talking as usual, unmindful of the *barco*'s approach to the dock because the duty of snubbing the rope on the cleat belonged to the crew.

What happened next happened fast, so fast she could never have put a sequence to events, even if a jury had demanded it. She looked at the wharf and then the cobbled street where people were usually passing by, especially at noonday. Bells began to sound in her brain, loud and all at once. There were no fishing boats, no vendors, no children at play in doorsteps, no one. São Jobim looked as deserted as villages Laura had described to her in earlier letters, when the French still rampaged in Portugal.

Startled, she turned to Colonel Junot, then tugged his arm. 'Something is…'

'…wrong,' he finished, rising and gesturing to the Marines at the same time, moving fast but not fast enough.

He never got out another word before the shore erupted in flame and smoke. Sister Maria Madelena screamed as the helmsman, a bullet hole drilled through his brain, dropped to the deck. More popping sounds came immediately after each other and two Marines slumped sideways.

Polly took a deep breath, willing herself not to move, even though she wanted to leap up and run somewhere, anywhere. At the same time, Colonel Junot threw her sideways against the gunwale and covered her with his body. She struggled, but he clamped a hand on her head and forced her down into the damp, where river water always puddles. Colonel Junot moulded his body to hers and pulled her in close to him, his hands on her head and belly.

Completely beyond words and thrust into a land of terror she had never known, Polly felt herself start to shake. She stopped when she felt a slight concussion as a rifle ball thudded into Colonel Junot. He let his breath out with a quiet huff that ended in a sigh, but did not loosen his grip on her.

'Colonel?' she managed to ask. She struggled to turn around to look at him, but he was too heavy.

'Hold still, Brandon. My God, don't move.'

Her cheek jammed against the deck, she had no choice but to do what he said. Terrified, she strained to hear his even breathing, knowing he must have been hit, and wondering at his own calmness in the face of calamity.

She thought she heard the remaining Marine returning fire, but then there was silence on the deck. To her frightened reckoning, a century or two must have rolled around before she felt the boat sway as men clambered on to the *barco*, shouting in French. She opened her eyes, which she must have screwed shut, and saw with terror that the damp under her cheek had turned pink.

The soldiers were dressed in green tunics, with reinforced trousers and copper helmets with fur lining that reminded her of pictures of Roman legionnaires. Their boots extended above their knees. 'What? Who?' she managed to gasp.

'Dragoons,' Hugh whispered in her ear. 'How's your French?'

'Adequate,' she told him, amazed that she could even get out another word, much less one that made sense.

'Don't move until I tell you. Oh, God!'

Please, please, don't let them shoot him again, she thought. She listened then, hearing what must have torn the words from him, as Sister Maria began to scream and then plead. More men jumped on the *barco* and then the footsteps came closer. Colonel Junot groaned as someone kicked him, and his hands, so tight around her body, went slack.

Turn and face them, she ordered herself as she struggled loose from the Colonel's limp grasp.

'Don't shoot him,' she said in French in as firm a voice

as she could muster. She twisted around and slowly rose
to her knees for her first look at the deck, which ran with
blood now. So many green-coated soldiers had leaped on
the *barco* that the deck canted away from the dock and
towards the river, causing the blood from the dead
Marines and crew members to pour in her direction as
they came closer. How much of it was Colonel Junot's
blood, she didn't dare speculate. He was unconscious,
with the beginning of an ugly welt on his temple.

Polly knew she would never forget the sight before her.
Her wimple torn away, Sister Maria Madelena knelt
before her captors, who jabbed at her with their muskets,
lifting her black skirt.

'Don't do that,' Polly said, her voice louder.

The soldiers wheeled around in surprise to look at
Polly. Her own knees turned to jelly as their expressions
went from surprise to speculation, much as a cat corner-
ing a mouse. As two of the soldiers swaggered towards
her, one already unbuckling his sword belt, she sat down,
mainly because her knees had stopped holding her up. Her
eyes on the soldiers, she yanked Colonel Junot into her
lap and wrapped her arms around him.

The effort must have roused him. He shook his head
slightly, uttering another quiet sigh. 'Brandon, we're in a
pickle,' he whispered.

She watched the soldiers out of the corner of her eye,
too frightened to look at what was happening to Sister
Maria Madelena, but unable to look away. One of the
Dragoons jerked her to her feet while another slapped her
hard, then slapped her again.

Colonel Junot didn't want her to look, either. 'Keep
your eyes on me,' he ordered. His voice tightened as he

tried to move his arm, the one that must have been hit. 'And if you can think of something… My head…'

Only one feeble idea came to mind, one so puny that on an ordinary day, it would never have seen the light of day. She kissed Colonel Junot on his cheek and then his ear, all the while tightening her grip, looking at the approaching soldiers, who had stopped to watch, wary but interested. 'This is my husband, Lieutenant Colonel Hugh Junot of the Royal Marines. Please do not kill him.'

At nearly the same time she spoke, Colonel Junot did, too, also in French that sounded much better than hers. 'Don't touch my wife,' he said, his voice weak, but with as much determination as she had ever heard from any soul living. 'We are worth more to you alive.'

His eyes so serious, Colonel Junot kissed her cheek. He turned around again and made himself comfortable, his head against her breasts in a gesture both familiar and possessive. The French soldiers squatted on the deck, uncertain and coming no closer.

'Where were you hit?' she asked him softly in English. Then, 'We're married. I couldn't think of anything else.'

'The back of my arm. Nothing much. You can treat it with a strip of petticoat, my love,' he told her. 'As for being married, I couldn't think of anything else, either. I recommend it right now, even though our courtship was amazingly swift.' He took one of her hands that crossed his chest, and slid it inside his uniform jacket in an intimate move.

He sat so calmly that Polly felt herself begin to breathe normally again. 'I don't remember saying yes.' It was the feeblest of jokes in the most dire of situations, but she had to concentrate on him.

'You didn't say yes,' he assured her, settling back more comfortably. 'I told you it was swift. Brandon, we might keep each other alive. I can't think of a better way.' He took her hand out of his uniform front and kissed it. 'Apparently you couldn't, either.'

Sister Maria Madelena shrieked as the soldiers carried her off the *barco*, set her on her feet and stripped off her habit in one wrench, leaving her standing on the dock in her chemise. She dropped to her knees, crouching there with her arms wrapped around her, and looking around wildly.

'We have to do something,' Polly urged, even as the Colonel turned her face gently towards his chest and pressed it there with his hand, shielding her from the terrible sight before them.

'We won't do anything until I see someone above the rating of Private, Brandon. Just hold me. Look at me now. Not at the dock.'

She did as he said, even as she heard Sister Maria Madelena's terrified screams. Her breath must have been coming faster and faster, because the Colonel told her calmly to breathe in and out more slowly.

'We can't help her right now. If we try anything, you will be next,' he said. 'My God, Brandon. What can have happened?'

She shook her head, then looked up when she heard a new voice shouting at the dock. Another soldier ran from the church and was flailing about his own men with his sword, beating them back from Sister Maria Madelena. Polly looked down again, in tears now at the sight of the nun kneeling on the cobblestones, her arms pinned back, her head down.

'It's a Sergeant,' Colonel Junot said, and there was no mistaking the relief in his voice. 'Brandon, help me to my feet.'

Not even sure she could stand on her own, Polly surprised herself by doing exactly what he asked. She hauled him upright, and then braced herself against the gunwale as he sagged against her, then slowly straightened up.

'Don't let go of me,' Colonel Junot ordered. 'Put your hand through my belt. I'll hold you as tight as I can.'

She did as he said, clutching him in a firm grasp. The Colonel leaned against one of the kegs lashed to the deck as ballast. Polly gasped and turned her face into his uniform jacket when one of the soldiers on the dock grabbed Sister Maria Madelena by her arms, slung her over his shoulder and walked towards the church, even as she shrieked and begged for mercy,

'Deep breaths, Brandon,' Colonel Junot said. 'Perhaps I should call you Polly now.'

He stayed where he was, but he stood taller, almost willing himself into his usual impeccable posture and bearing, even though the welt on his face was turning a mottled colour and blood seeped from his sleeve. Polly released him long enough to hand him his hat, then twined her hand through his belt and clutched it.

'Sergeant, I am Lieutenant Colonel Hugh Junot of the Third Royal Marine Division of his Majesty's British maritime forces. I implore your protection for my wife, Polly.'

He spoke calmly, but his voice carried across the bloody deck, where the bodies of the Marines lay sprawled and the *barco* crew was silent in death. Polly held her breath as the French NCO scowled at them.

Decades seemed to pass before he gestured them forwards.

'One foot in front of the other, dear wife,' Colonel Junot said. 'That's how any journey begins.'

Chapter Eleven

Colonel Junot staggered, but Polly held him up, her arm tight around him. She draped his arm over her shoulder and they stumbled across the deck. When they reached the opposite gunwale, the Sergeant nodded to one of his Privates, who held out his hands and helped them to the dock.

'We did not expect to see a Colonel,' the Sergeant said in French. He gestured towards the dead Marines. 'We have been watching, too, for several days. Is the war going so ill for England that Lieutenant Colonels come on patrol? I cannot think you were much help.'

Polly felt Colonel Junot stiffen. 'No, I was not, was I? We are your prisoners, Sergeant.' With some effort, he un-buckled his sword without releasing her and handed it to the NCO, who grinned at the sight. 'I surrender to you and implore your protection for my wife.'

'Not you?' the Sergeant asked, a slight smile on his face, as he accepted the sword, then casually tossed it to a Private, who looked at it and threw it in the river.

'Damn! That was a gift from my father,' Hugh said in English.

The Sergeant laughed at the look on Junot's face. 'Why would anyone want your stupid sword?' he asked in French. 'Why do we even want you, Colonel? Your delicious wife? Now that is another matter.'

'Sergeant, I implore your protection for her,' Hugh said again, his voice softer this time, more pleading. Polly could hardly bear to watch him pawn his dignity, but there was the Sergeant, running the blade of his sword across her breasts now.

The Sergeant apparently had no intention of making anything easy. He walked around them, patting the back of Polly's dress with his sword, then ran the blade slowly down her hips and legs. Hugh set his lips more firmly in a tight line.

The Sergeant continued his leisurely circuit, this time standing too close to Polly and flicking her hair with the point of his sword. 'Here we thought only to bag partisan scum passing information, and what do I find but a Colonel? *Mon dieu*, war is strange.'

She flinched, scarcely breathing. When his words finally settled in on her terrified brain, she wondered if she had heard him correctly. 'Information?' she asked, hoping she sounded much braver than she felt.

Obviously enjoying himself at their expense, the Sergeant smiled broadly as he flicked the blade across the front of her dress, slicing off a cloth rosette. 'And you did not know? Answer this one carefully, *s'il vous plaît*.'

'There was nothing to know,' she replied, trying to slow her breathing so her breasts would not rise and fall so rapidly. 'What can you mean? Sister Maria Madelena and I come to São Jobim to take young women who have been—' She stopped, wondering at the wisdom of saying more about the girls violated by French troops. 'We come here to take young women to a safer place, in time of war.'

The Sergeant was practically standing on her toes now, his eyes on hers. Polly glanced at Hugh, who was breathing shallowly, too. The Sergeant took the pommel of his sword and put it under her chin, raising her face to meet his scrutiny. 'Why is this man along? Your husband, you say?'

'My husband is here because he has been in Lisbon for a month, is headed out on another assignment, and wanted to see me in between. I am certain you understand.'

The Sergeant stared at her. She gazed back, not even blinking. He took the sword from her chin. 'You must be a challenge for him,' he said, stepping back. He looked at Colonel Junot. 'How do you manage her?'

'Very gently,' Colonel Junot said, his voice firm.

'With a whip? How is she to ride?'

Polly felt the blood drain from her face, as Hugh stepped close to the Sergeant this time. 'Sergeant, I resent your foul comments about my lady,' he said, biting off each word, as if he spoke to troublesome Marine Privates, and not the man holding all the cards. 'Do not tell me Napoleon makes war on officers' wives now. I would not have believed him capable of that.'

The men stared at each other. Polly held her breath, waiting for the Sergeant to run the Colonel through with his sabre. At the same time, she felt a spark of pride at Colonel Junot's defence of her, and both of them so powerless.

Hugh spoke first, and his tone was conciliatory now,

although by no means subservient. 'Sergeant, has a mistake been made here? This nun only seeks to rescue those who often get trampled upon in time of war.'

'No mistake,' the Sergeant said crisply. 'None at all.' He shook his sword at Polly. 'We have been watching you.'

'In the greater scheme of things, I can't imagine why,' Polly murmured.

'Oh, you cannot? Let me enlighten you. This way, please, you two. Do you need some help, Colonel?'

'You're so kind to ask,' Junot said. 'My wife will help me.'

Escorted by Dragoons looking hugely interested, they followed the Sergeant across the small square. Polly stopped once when she heard a series of splashes, and looked back to see other Dragoons throwing the dead Marines and crew of the *barco* overboard. 'Sergeant, can they not have decent burials?' she asked, horrified.

'The British? Why, *madame*?' was all he said, sounding supremely bored.

'Don't worry, Polly,' Colonel Junot whispered. 'This is better. The bodies may get snagged on limbs and rocks on the way downriver, but perhaps one of them will reach Vila Nova de Gaia.' He sighed. 'It's puny, but all we have, my dear.'

She was silent then, as the full force of their capture slammed itself home. The village appeared deserted. Who knew what terrors the French had promised to the townspeople if anyone so much as made a peep to the allies downriver? Uneasy, Polly looked up at the Colonel, and was comforted to see him looking at her.

'We haven't had any chance to get our stories straight,'

he whispered in English. 'What say we've been married since June?'

'Where?'

'Vila Nova, where your brother-in-law gave you away.'

Thinking of Laura and Philemon brought tears to her eyes and she looked away. In answer, the Colonel tightened his grip on her shoulder and kissed the top of her head. 'We'll stick together like glue, Brandon,' he assured her. 'I'm not leaving your side.'

They reached the closed door of the church, thick doors that she already knew could muffle any sounds, because she had been inside several times and enjoyed the ecclesiastical quiet within. It was different this time. Shivers travelled up and down her spine as she heard Sister Maria Madelena screaming. Unnerved, Polly stopped, but was prodded from behind. In response, Colonel Junot pulled her in front of him, protecting her with his body.

The Sergeant bowed elaborately and opened the smaller man-gate. 'Do come in, Colonel and *madame*,' he said, gesturing as though he welcomed them to a farmhouse in Gascony. 'Think of this as a wayside shrine on the way to perdition.'

Even at mid-day, the squat building's interior was shrouded in shadow. This was no church of the Renaissance, but a shabby little relic of the Middle Ages, charming in its own way, but not now, and probably never again.

Clad in her chemise, Sister Maria Madelena crouched below the altar, her screams tinged with madness. Before she could react, Colonel Junot turned Polly's face into his tunic. 'Oh, God, don't look!' he said, his voice suddenly filled with horror. She felt his fingers shaking as he forced her against him.

Other hands pulled his fingers away, compelling her to stare at the altar and then up to the large crucifix, where the French soldiers, those students of the Revolution, had crucified São Jobim's parish priest. Naked, pitiful, he hung on the cross, his arms bent at weird angles, his head down as though contemplating the ruin of his pudgy body. In his own death agonies he had moved his bowels.

Polly couldn't help herself. Her knees sagged and it was the Colonel's turn to hold her up. He stepped in front of her, blocking the view, but she knew she would never forget the sight before her. She wanted to close her eyes and keep them shut until the whole nightmare went away and she was back on the *barco*, with nothing more on her mind than negotiating the next stretch of white water. How puny that seasickness had been her biggest fear, how trivial.

Instead, she opened her eyes and looked into the Colonel's concerned face, so close to her own. 'I'll be all right,' she whispered to him. 'The poor man. What did he do to deserve this?'

Colonel Junot shook his head. 'There is a deep game going on here, Polly. I don't think we know even half of it.'

With his help, she stood upright again and turned away resolutely, to find herself looking at Sister Maria Madelena, kneeling and sobbing. Shaken, Polly turned her attention to the Sergeant, who seemed so sure of himself, almost swaggering in his command of this sorry situation. This was probably no more than a typical day for him. 'How can you permit your men to…to…?' She stopped, unable to think of a word to adequately cover what was happening, considering her own genteel Bath French.

The Sergeant mocked her expression, bowed elaborately, and held out a note. 'Perhaps you might consider what she has been doing to *us*!' he declared, triumph in every line of his body.

As she watched, aghast, he stalked over to Sister Maria Madelena and shook her by the hair. Colonel Junot tightened his grip on her when she started towards the nun. 'Don't move,' he whispered. 'These men are wolves.'

'But he's—'

'Stand still.'

She did as the Colonel said, even when the Sergeant tightened his grip on Sister Maria's hair and pulled her head up. 'Tell this Colonel's wife how you have been taking notes from the priest to the Navy docks in Vila Nova,' the Sergeant roared, shaking her head like a terrier with a mouse.

'Sister Maria, you don't have to tell me anything,' Polly said in English, as the Colonel tightened his arms around her.

'Tell her!' the Sergeant demanded of the nun, shaking her again and again until Polly wanted to scream. He looked up at the dead man and let go of Sister Maria Madelena. 'We...persuaded the priest to admit he gave her communiqués to pass on from the interior. Tell her, you whore!'

Polly couldn't stop shaking, not even with Colonel Junot holding her so tight. She leaned back against him, trying to keep the crucified priest and nun out of her sight. 'Sister Maria?' she asked softly, her voice quavering.

The Sergeant released the nun and she struggled into

a sitting position, trying to cover herself with her arms. As Polly watched, horrified, she willed herself into a state of calm and then slowly raised her bruised head and held her hands out, palms up, in supplication.

But it wasn't supplication. Polly jumped when Sister Maria Madelena suddenly clenched her hands into fists. Her tired eyes flashed, and the scar across her face stood out in raw, red relief against her paleness.

'Viva Portugal e viva España!' she declared in a loud voice.

'There's your answer, Polly,' Colonel Junot murmured in her ear. 'She *was* a messenger. Is she even a nun?'

'I…I…I didn't know,' Polly whispered. 'I did wonder once…. I thought I saw a note.' She turned her face into Colonel Junot's tunic. 'I do know she was a victim, too, like the young women we cared for.'

'Madame Junot,' the Sergeant said. He was closer to her now, stepping over the nun, who had slid back on to the stones, exhausted and drained. 'Madame Junot?'

'Polly,' Colonel Junot said in English, 'he is talking to you. Polly, pay attention and remember who you are.'

It was her turn to get a firm grasp on her emotions, to dig down deep inside herself where she had never gone before, and pull out more courage than she knew she possessed. Perhaps the Sergeant would not know how terrified she was. He was addressing her as Madame Junot; she would have to remember that and respond.

'Yes, Sergeant?' she said, as she rubbed her cheek gently against the Colonel's tunic as his hand went up to caress her hair.

'Did you know of this deception? Do answer carefully.'

I am no liar, she thought. She continued to rest her head against Colonel Junot, as she realised it was time to think of him as Hugh, the dearest person in her universe. She chose her French with precision. 'Sergeant, on the last trip, the one yesterday, I thought I saw her take something from Pai Belo. It was the merest glimpse. It could have been anything.'

The Sergeant grunted and took the folded scrap from his tunic again. 'This is what he gave me today, just before we hoisted him on high.'

Polly shuddered as she looked at the bloodstained sheet. To her horror, it was covered with numbers, and she recognised the Portuguese words for 'regiment' and the names of Spanish towns.

'We have other messages,' the Sergeant told her, folding the note. 'How many trips have you made to São Jobim?'

'I hope you are not planning to implicate my wife in any of this,' Hugh said.

She wondered at his ability to sound so protective, when he was as much a prisoner as she. 'Hush, my love,' Polly said. 'This is my fifth trip, Sergeant. That is all. I have only been in Vila Nova for eight or nine weeks, visiting my sister.'

'And not your husband?'

She realised her mistake, and fought down panic. *I am no actress, either*, she thought. 'Sergeant, surely that goes without saying. We were only married in June, and this war keeps getting in our way.'

To her relief, he seemed to find her statement funny and laughed. 'Oh, you British!' he exclaimed, his tone almost fond in a way that Polly found more repulsive than a curse. 'What am I to do with you?'

'What will you do with *her*?' Colonel Junot asked, looked at Sister Maria Madelena.

The Sergeant glanced around almost carelessly, as though she was already someone in his distant past. He shrugged. 'I will turn her over to my soldiers. They will make sure she is dead when they are done. You can watch. In fact, I will insist.'

Unable to help herself, Polly sobbed out loud. 'Shh, shh, my love,' the Colonel crooned, his hand gentle on her hair again. 'I have no say in this, Sergeant, but I wish you would just kill her outright. If she must die—if she is a spy, you have your rights, I acknowledge—then kill her cleanly.'

The Sergeant smiled and squatted on the floor by Sister Maria. He lifted her head by the hair. 'Do you hear that? This Englishman harbours a soft spot for guerillas like you.'

'Viva Portugal,' she murmured.

Her heart in her throat, Polly watched the Frenchman as he squatted there, engaged in thought. He rose then, and inclined his head towards them. 'Very well, Colonel. Since you are so concerned, you kill her.'

Hugh made that same huffing sound that had escaped him on the *barco* when he was shot. He took an involuntary step back and Polly had to steady him as he threatened to topple them both.

'Please, Colonel,' Sister Maria whispered from the floor. 'Please.'

Polly reached both arms around the Colonel and held him as close as she could, her hands splayed across his broad back. He buried his face in her hair, and she just held him.

The Sergeant came closer until Polly smelled all his dirt and perspiration. 'In fact, Colonel, I insist. If you do not kill this spy, I will see that your little wife suffers the fate I originally intended for her, and you can watch that.'

'I will do it,' Hugh said immediately. 'Certainly I will. Hand me a pistol.'

The Sergeant laughed as he gestured to one of his men. 'Don't you wish you had not come upriver today, Colonel?'

While the Sergeant took Hugh aside and handed him the pistol to load, Polly gathered up more courage from a hitherto unknown source. Ignoring the soldiers, she walked to the nun, knelt on the floor and wiped Sister Maria's battered face with the altar cloth. She draped the cloth around the woman's bare shoulders.

'I never meant you to be involved,' the nun whispered.

'I wish you had not invited me upriver,' Polly replied, dabbing carefully around the woman's ears. 'How could you put us in such danger?'

She hadn't meant to be harsh, not with a woman about to die, but she could not help herself. *I can repent later*, Polly told herself resolutely, as she dabbed away. *If there is a later.*

'I love my country more,' Sister Maria said. She grasped Polly's arm with fingers surprisingly strong. 'Watch over João for me.'

Polly nodded, ashamed of herself. 'We will treat him as our own son.' She glanced at Colonel Junot, surprised at herself. *He is not my husband, but that came out so naturally*, she thought.

Sister Maria Madelena nodded, her face calm now. 'Come closer,' she whispered.

Polly crept closer on her knees, as though to arrange the woman's hair.

'I never was a nun. Hear me out! My brother is El Cuchillo, a guerilla of León. He said he would always watch out for me...' Her voice trailed off and she looked up at the dead priest above them. 'Perhaps one of his men is watching now. Be ready for anything.'

'Don't give me false hope,' Polly whispered. 'You have done enough.'

There was more she wanted to say, but she knew it would not make her feel any better. Then the moment was gone, when one of the soldiers grabbed her by both elbows and lifted her off the floor. She shrieked, unable to struggle.

'Polly, my love, steady as you go,' Hugh said, as the soldier pinioned her arms behind her back and led her away from Sister Maria Madelena, who crouched and clutched the altar cover, her face calm.

'Madam Junot, you must not struggle so!' the Sergeant admonished. 'I am handing your husband a pistol now. You are my guarantee that he will not turn it on me.' He shrugged elaborately. 'Call me cautious. I have not lived from Jena and Austerlitz by being overly trusting. You understand?'

'I understand,' Polly replied, her voice soft. 'I'm sorry, Hugh.'

His face pale, his eyes so serious, the Colonel looked at her for a long moment, as though willing her to understand that what was about to happen was not his choice. No matter—she knew that, and tried to communicate her emotions with a return gaze as compassionate as his own.

He squared his shoulders and took a deep breath. 'I will

do this my own way, Sergeant, and in my own time. Don't interfere with me or my wife.'

He stood a moment in silence, head bowed, then walked to the altar, where Sister Maria Madelena knelt. He squatted beside her and carefully draped her hair over her shoulder, away from the back of her neck.

'What is your name, my dear?' he asked, his voice conversational.

'Maria Ponce, from León,' she replied in English, 'although my family is originally from Portugal. Your wife will tell you of my brother.'

He squeezed her shoulder gently, stood up, and cocked the pistol. 'God forgive me,' he said.

'He already has,' Maria Ponce said.

Polly tried to look away, but the Sergeant put the blade of his sword against her neck and gently forced her to watch.

'If there is any foolishness, Colonel,' the Sergeant called, 'I will violate your wife myself.'

'I know that,' Hugh said with a certain weary patience, as though he dealt with a child. 'There will be no foolishness. You have my word as an officer and a gentleman, if that holds any merit with a soldier of La Belle France.'

'It's quaint, but I like it,' the Sergeant said. 'An officer, a gentleman, a murderer. Hurry up.'

Hugh pointed the pistol towards the nape of Maria Ponce's neck, then lowered it. 'No. Not this way,' he said, speaking to the Sergeant. 'I don't want my wife to see this.'

'Poor you,' said the Sergeant, when he finished laughing.

'I mean it,' Hugh said. Polly watched as he seemed to stand taller. 'Sergeant, do you have a wife?'

The Dragoon took the blade of his sword away from Polly's neck. She held her breath. 'I do. She is no concern of yours.'

'What is her name?' Hugh asked calmly, with all the force of his rank and age behind the question, to Polly's ears. *You are so audacious*, she thought. *You are trying to bend this man to your will and you have no power whatsoever.*

'Her name is Lalage,' the Sergeant said, speaking as though addressed by a French officer, and not a British captive. Polly could hardly believe her ears.

'Lalage is a beautiful name,' Hugh said. 'Madame Junot is *my* Lalage. She is my love and my life. Would you want *your* Lalage to witness what I must do here? I cannot imagine a loving husband would do such a thing in France.'

Polly reminded herself to breathe as the two men stared at each other. The Sergeant looked away first. He sheathed his sabre and took Polly by the arm, shoving her towards one of his Dragoons.

'Take her outside. Sit with her on the steps.'

'*Merci*, Sergeant,' Hugh said. 'I would ask all of you to leave. Let this be between me and Sister Maria Madelena.'

'I can't do that!' the Sergeant protested, but his voice had lost its edge.

'You can, Sergeant,' Hugh said. 'If this woman kneeling before you is not dead when I come out of the church, you may shoot me next, after I have killed my own Lalage.'

Again the two men stared at each other. Again the Sergeant yielded. He gestured to his troopers, who followed him into the sun. Polly felt as though she stood on blocks of wood instead of her feet. With a look at Colonel Junot, one that tried to convey every emotion she was feeling, she forced herself into motion and left the chapel of São Jobim.

The sun was hot on her face. She welcomed the warmth, even as she shivered and knew she would never be warm again. The Sergeant sat her down on the top step, then pulled her up gently and took her down several more steps. He sat down beside her, not looking at her.

Polly steeled herself against the sound of the pistol, but when it went off, she still jumped and cried out. The Sergeant gripped her shoulder, but it was not the grip of a captor. He did not release her until she heard Hugh's steps behind them.

He came towards them slowly, going down each step as though he weighed a thousand pounds. Polly knew if she lived to one hundred, she would never be able to entirely erase from her mind his expression. She couldn't interpret it. She had thought to see revulsion at the terrible act he had been forced to perform. There was something thoughtful in his look, instead. If she hadn't known it was impossible, she would have called it relief.

He sat down heavily beside her and gathered her close to him, his grip as tender as the Sergeant's had been.

'Where is the pistol?' the Sergeant demanded.

Hugh shook his head and gestured behind him. 'You can get it. I'm not going back in there.' He looked across Polly at the Sergeant, wonder in his voice now. 'I pointed the barrel right at the nape of her neck. Before I could fire, she grabbed the gun and killed herself.' He began to weep.

It was Polly's turn to gather him close, uttering sounds of comfort that had no language, as he sobbed into his hands. To her surprise, the Sergeant and the Dragoons left them there on the church steps as they went inside again.

'Oh, Colonel,' she whispered into his neck, at a total loss for words.

'From now on, I am "Hugh, love" to you,' he said, after a long moment. 'Never forget it. Our lives depend on it, Polly, dear wife.'

They held hands and sat as close together as they could while the Dragoons finished up whatever business they had in the church. When they came out, the Sergeant gestured for them to stand up.

'What do you intend to do with us, Sergeant, now that Sister Maria has done our dirty work?' Hugh asked.

'Dirty work it is, Colonel,' the Sergeant said. 'Do you know who the whore's brother is?'

'El Cuchillo,' Polly said. 'Sister Maria told me before she died.'

The Sergeant's smile broadened. 'Poor you, indeed, my Colonel! He is a guerilla leader of León, where we are heading.' He sheathed his sword. 'I have always been amazed how word gets around. El Cuchillo will probably assume you killed his sister. You might as well paint a bull's-eye on your back.'

'Perhaps you should just kill me now,' Hugh said, pulling Polly closer.

The Sergeant laughed and shook his head. 'And miss the fun? Never. They say he likes best to kill with a long needle through the eye.'

'Well, into every life some rain must fall, I suppose,' Hugh replied, with just a touch of amusement.

'You're a cool one,' the Sergeant said.

'No, I am not. Actually, let me suggest a very good reason why you should keep me and my wife alive.'

The Sergeant looked down on them from the step

above, perfectly at ease again and in charge, looking for all the world like a cat with cornered mice. 'Colonel, will you never cease to entertain me?'

'Probably not,' Hugh said, his tone equally affable. 'In a word, Sergeant, money. This knowledge is for you alone. You have no idea how rich Madame Junot is.'

Chapter Twelve

'So that is why you married her,' the Sergeant said.

Polly flinched, which made Hugh's heart sink even lower. *Bastard!* he thought. *Damn the man.* But this was no time to argue, so he merely shrugged. 'Think what you will. I am speaking of money. *Dinero, dinheiro, denaro, geld.* Think of all the words for money you have learned as you have tramped through Europe! Imagine that in your pockets.'

He had no idea how this would play. If today was his unlucky day—so far, there was nothing to dispute the notion it could be the unluckiest day of his life—then he had just attempted to bribe one of the few incorruptible men in anyone's army. He stood up, pulled Polly to her feet, and started walking away from the church. One step, two steps, another. The Sergeant did not stop him, but walked at his side. Was it possible even a battle-hardened veteran of Napoleon's campaigns didn't care so much for what had just happened? One could hope; Hugh did. But then,

'A bribe? You want to bribe *me*, Colonel?' the Sergeant asked, putting out his hand to stop them.

I found the only honest man in Napoleon's army, Hugh thought with regret. *Well, then, we have nothing to lose.* 'I suppose I do,' he said frankly. 'One doesn't make Colonel without exercising some initiative. Not in the Royal Marines, at least.'

He knew how that sounded in English. In French, Hugh thought it had a certain Gallic panache. At least the Sergeant hadn't motioned for one of his men to run him through with a sword.

In fact, the Sergeant was smiling—a little smile, to be sure, but a smile. After a long pause, the Sergeant even chuckled. *In for a penny*, Hugh thought. 'It's not for me, especially,' he said. He turned to Polly and gave her a kiss on the temple and a little shake to get her attention. 'And it's not even just for my wife.' He nudged Polly again. 'Shall I tell him, darling?'

He looked her in the eyes and she gazed back through those spectacles that magnified her eyes a little. *Follow me with this*, he thought, trying to communicate through nothing more than a look, something he knew his parents, married years and years, had been quite good at. To his infinite relief, she inclined her head towards him as though the conversation was a delicate one.

'It's this, Sergeant: my wife is in the family way. I especially want her to survive this experience and at least give my estate an heir.'

To her credit, Polly didn't even flinch. He knew she understood his French, because her lips came together in a firm line and she concentrated on her shoes.

'If you can help us, it is worth a great deal to me, Sergeant,' he concluded simply.

They were in the square now. Hugh concentrated all

his attention on the Sergeant, even as his skin crawled at the sound of women and children screaming in some of the buildings. The Sergeant seemed almost reflective, as though he stood in a glade in southern France filled with carnations. *My God, these are hard men*, Hugh thought. He almost hated to interrupt the thought process of a man who obviously had the power to end his life in the next second, but time was passing.

'I know you have a wife, Sergeant,' he said. 'Do you and Lalage have children?' Maybe it wasn't such an unlucky day. While not appearing to stare, Hugh watched the Sergeant's face, and at least thought he saw a slight thawing. He breathed more regularly when the Sergeant gestured with his hand towards a bench and spoke to Polly.

'Madame Junot, let us sit here. You look done for.'

It was probably the understatement of the ages, considering what had just happened in the chapel. Polly nodded, her pale face tinged with pink now, as though she were shy about sharing her *faux* husband's phony admission with a complete stranger, much less the enemy.

Hugh kissed Polly's temple again and whispered in her ear as he sat her carefully down on the bench, 'You're a game goer, Brandon.'

In response, she burrowed in closer to him, shivering in the warmth of the afternoon sun. In a more familiar gesture, Hugh put his hand on her waist and pulled her as near as he could. She responded by resting her hand on his thigh. *Bravo, Brandon*, he thought, enjoying the act.

'Can I get you some wine, *madame*?' the Sergeant asked.

Polly nodded, and the Sergeant gestured to one of his men and made his request. The Corporal shook his head and indicated there was none. The Sergeant merely nodded philosophically. 'We travel light, *madame*. Perhaps he can find something in this pathetic village.'

'Water will do,' she said.

The Sergeant was silent until the Corporal returned with water in an earthen jar. Polly tried to take it from him, but her hand shook so badly that Hugh took it instead and held the jar to her lips until she sipped. A frown on his face, the Sergeant observed her terror.

He spoke at last. 'We have two sons on a farm near Angoulême. It is a small farm.'

Hugh nodded. 'If you will see to my wife's safety, I can promise you your wife will receive whatever sum you consider appropriate.'

The Sergeant nodded, and gazed across the small square of São Jobim, where his men were methodically going through the buildings. He rubbed his unshaven jaw, looking unconcerned as flames suddenly roared skywards from a home. It was just another day in Portugal.

'Of course, I cannot promise anything until we—or she—is restored to Allied lines, but you can trust us to deliver what you wish, and where,' Hugh added, keeping his voice soft, hoping not to distract from whatever the Sergeant might be thinking.

'Because you are an officer and a gentleman?' the Sergeant said suddenly, and his voice was harsh again.

'No. Because I want to be a father,' Hugh said. 'You understand.'

The Sergeant stood up suddenly and slapped his worn gauntlets on his thigh. Hugh had always been a praying man, much to the amusement of his fellow Marines, and he prayed now, as the Frenchman weighed the offer on a scale of delicate balance.

Polly tipped it, to Hugh's everlasting relief. 'Sergeant, what are your son's names? And who are you?'

The Sergeant looked down at her, and Hugh thought he saw pity in the man's eyes, as brown as his own, and something more: a father's love. 'Emile and Antoine,' he said. 'I am Jean Baptiste Cadotte. Colonel, I will help you if I can.'

'I am in your debt,' Hugh replied simply.

'I can promise you nothing.'

'I know that.'

Most of São Jobim was blazing when the Dragoons mounted the horses that had been stabled inside the town hall. Two of the lighter men doubled up and the Sergeant directed Hugh to mount the other horse. He tied Hugh's hands together, then tied Polly's, only not so tight. To Hugh's amusement, Cadotte directed a man to hand her up carefully to sit in front of him. She tried to sit sideways at first, as though she rode a sidesaddle, but gave that up quickly and threw her leg over the saddle, which raised her skirts to her knees. To her credit, Polly scarcely seemed to mind. Directing her to lean forwards, Hugh raised his roped arms and lowered them over her body, resting them against her stomach. The Corporal took the reins and led the horse behind his own.

Polly was still shaking and there was nothing he could do about that. After what seemed like an hour of travel on what was a little-used track, he felt her shoulders lower as her jangled nerves attempted to relax. She said nothing, though, which suited him well enough, since he couldn't think of any words to comfort her. Just as well. Unaccustomed to riding horseback, Hugh felt his inner thighs begin to burn and his buttocks go numb.

* * *

After several hours of steady climbing, Sergeant Cadotte raised his hand and the Dragoons stopped. Everyone knew what to do. In another moment, all the men were urinating into the road.

'My blushes,' Polly said, the first words she had spoken since leaving São Jobim.

Hugh chuckled. 'Boys will be boys,' he told her. 'I hope Cadotte will take a little pity on us, too.'

He did. When the men were standing by their mounts again and eating what looked like hardtack, Sergeant Cadotte sent a trooper to help Polly off the horse. He untied her hands and helped her down, then indicated that Hugh should throw his leg over the saddle and slide off.

'I can't,' Hugh said, looking at Cadotte. 'Sergeant, you'll have to appreciate that I am a Royal Marine and not a horseman of any kind. Undo my hands, please, and I will struggle off and probably fall on my face, to your total amusement.'

Cadotte laughed and told the Private to untie his hands, but was kind enough to steady Hugh as he dismounted. He sank immediately to his knees. All the men in the troop laughed, but Hugh only shrugged and staggered to his feet.

'You meant what you said,' Cadotte murmured. 'Take your wife and go relieve yourselves.'

'*Merci*,' Hugh said with a grimace. 'Just let me stand here a moment and see if there is any blood in my pathetic body willing to circulate to my ass again.'

'But he is never seasick,' Polly said suddenly in French, which made the men laugh again.

In good humour, Cadotte gestured to the stand of trees.

'Have a little privacy, Colonel. That ought to be worth the price of a few cows at my farm by Angoulême.'

'A whole herd,' Hugh said as he took Polly by the hand. 'Come, my love, and let us find a tree.'

To his relief, the Dragoons turned away and squatted on the far side of their horses, some smoking and others conversing. Wincing at every step, Hugh led Polly into the stand of trees. 'Well, my dear, turn your head and give me a moment.'

Her face bright red, she did as he said. When he finished and buttoned his trousers, he pointed towards a fallen log. 'It's the best we can do, Brandon,' he said, and turned around to face the Dragoons on the road while she took care of her own business.

'You needn't stand so close,' she scolded, when she had finished and joined him.

'*Au contraire, ma chérie*, I'm going to stick to you like a medicinal plaster. If you have any inhibitions about that, I suggest you abandon them right here.'

He watched her expressive face, still red, as she considered his words, then nodded. 'Consider them abandoned, Colonel—'

'No. No. "Hugh, my love",' he teased.

'Hugh, my love, you're trying me,' she shot back, which made him smile and took the lump of fear out of his stomach for the first time.

He draped his arm across her shoulder and gave her a squeeze. 'Adventures never are as much fun as bad novels make them out to be, Polly.'

'I can see that,' she said, as she tucked her fingers in his swordless belt. 'Just don't think for a minute you are going to take advantage of me!'

He kissed her temple and whispered in her ear, 'I already did, Polly. You're going to be a mother, remember?'

'How could I forget such an immaculate conception? I defy even the Pope to be more surprised than I.'

They laughed together, which made Sergeant Cadotte turn around in surprise. With a scowl, he motioned them closer to retie their hands and continue the journey.

They travelled off the beaten track until they came to a deserted village just at sunset. The casual way the Dragoons rode into the abandoned town told Hugh volumes. 'I think this must be where they bivouacked on the journey to São Jobim,' he whispered to Polly. 'Look how familiar they are with it. They knew it was deserted.'

He could feel Polly sigh against his chest. 'We might have been travelling on the moon,' she whispered back. 'This poor country. Does no one live in the interior any more?'

'Precious few, I gather. Only think how many armies have picked it clean, like a flock of vultures dining on one thin rabbit.'

Hugh put his head closer to hers to keep his voice low, but also because he could not deny the comfort he derived from her presence. 'I can't help but think this patrol of Dragoons was a forlorn hope.'

'I don't understand.'

He could see Sergeant Cadotte watching them. 'I'll tell you later.'

With help, they dismounted for the first time since the afternoon, with the same results. In agony, he leaned against Polly, who held him up, then kissed his cheek. 'You Marines are pretty worthless on horseback,' she chided.

'Aye, aye, wife. Just wait until you're back on a ship.'

He wanted her to laugh, but tears came to her eyes. 'Hugh, it couldn't be a moment too soon, even if I vomit from Oporto to Plymouth,' she whispered, her face turned into his chest. All he could do was hold her and silently agree, with all the longing of his deepwater heart.

Expertly, the Dragoons took their mounts into the half-burned church while Hugh and Polly stood in the square, then gradually edged over to a bench, where he spent a long moment trying to decide if sitting down again was worse than standing. He sat down gingerly, grateful at least that the bench wasn't going anywhere.

The evening meal—eaten in a barren interior court-yard—continued to confirm his suspicions about the nature of the French army in Portugal. He knew how fond Napoleon was of exhorting his soldiers to live off the land, but the Peninsula was frail and bare. Dinner was a stew of French hardtack soaked in a broth of wild onions and nothing more, washed down, at least, with excellent port someone must have pilfered from farther downriver. The men were already on starvation rations.

They sat close together in the cool evening air that was beginning to feel like autumn. Rains would come soon enough, spreading enough discomfort around to last a lifetime, if they were still prisoners on the trail. *Or we could be dead, my lady and me*, he reminded himself. It was better not to borrow trouble from tomorrow.

His thoughts were unprofitable, so it was with some relief they were interrupted by Sergeant Cadotte, who motioned for them to rise. He felt the hairs prick on the back of his neck. Was this the end, then? Was the Sergeant going to shoot him and turn Polly over to his soldiers? Hugh forced himself to subdue his rising panic.

He could have sobbed with relief when the Sergeant untied their hands, handed him a dusty blanket, and gestured towards a beehive-shaped stone cairn. 'You two will stay in the granary tonight,' Cadotte said.

He had to go on his knees to get into the granary and Polly bent double. The Sergeant put in a bucket. 'For your needs,' he said gruffly, and to Hugh's ears, almost with an undertone of compassion. 'I have no candle or lantern. And do not worry about mice, Madame Junot. It's been picked clean. See you in the morning.' He closed the door behind him and threw the bolt. They were in total darkness.

Hugh stood up, gratified that the ceiling was just tall enough to accommodate him. He put his arm on Polly's shoulder again, and walked with her around the granary, touching the wall, feeling for any weakness. There was none. From what little he knew of Portuguese history, the villagers' ancestors had built the granary to resist Huns and Visigoths and Moors. *They have come and gone and now we are here*, he thought, as the weight of the whole débâcle clamped down on his shoulders like mortar.

With a groan, he sat down and tugged Polly down beside him. Without a word, he sat cross-legged, when he could force his legs to move, and pulled her on to his lap.

It was all the invitation she needed to do what she had been holding back all day. She put her arms around his neck and sobbed into his tunic, as he knew she would. And somehow, he knew she wouldn't be startled if he joined in. They cried together, and soon, to his own sorely tried heart, she was crooning and rubbing her hand on his back.

'I'm sorry you had to be Sister Maria's witness, Hugh.'

Her soft words, whispered through her own tears, comforted him as nothing else could have. He almost believed her.

'I have dealt out my share of death and destruction, thanks to Boney, but I have never been jolted like that before,' he confessed, hardly able to get out the words.

She sat up in his lap and found his face in the dark, pressing her hands against his temples. 'He shouldn't have made you a party to that!'

Her voice was fierce, and he was glad he could not see her face in the darkness. He was a professional Marine engaged in a long war, and that was his life. Either she was the world's greatest actress, surpassed only by Siddons herself, or this young woman sitting on him in the dark didn't want him to suffer for the shocking death he had been forced to deal out. She seemed to care less for her own safety, than that he not suffer. It touched him.

When her tears stopped, she sniffed a few times, then managed a watery chuckle. 'I'm about to commit such a social solecism,' she said. She leaned sideways and he could feel her tugging at her skirt. In another moment she was blowing her nose on the fabric.

'Uh, I do have a handkerchief in my tunic,' he said. 'You should have asked.'

She leaned back against him again, warming his heart. 'Save it. We might really need it later,' she told him. Her voice faltered. 'At least, I hope there is a "later".'

'So do I, Brandon, so do I,' he said.

'That's "Polly, dear",' she reminded him, and he smiled.

'There is something I should do,' she told him. He heard a rip of fabric. 'Hugh, take off your tunic and shirt and let me bandage your arm.'

He had to think a moment like a village idiot, because his wound seemed to have happened years ago. 'It's not bleeding now,' he said.

'Look you here,' she demanded. 'I ripped off this strip and I intend to use it. Do what I said.'

'You're a taskmaster,' he teased, as he unbuttoned his tunic and removed it after she got off his lap. He unbuttoned his shirt and winced when he pulled his arm out of the sleeve. 'Learn that from Laura Brittle?'

'No. From my dear Nana, when she scolds her three-year-old,' Polly retorted.

She felt along his arm, which made him smile in the dark, then rested her finger lightly on the track of the ball that had slammed into him on the *barco rabelo*. 'We will pretend I am spreading on some of the salve that Philemon formulates,' she told him. 'At least it appears to have merely grazed your arm. Are you bulletproof?'

'Nearly so. Ah, that should do it, wife. You're a handy little wench.'

She laughed softly. 'You are a rascal! There is no one you need to impress in this wretched granary. There now. Put on your coat again.'

Polly made no objection when he pulled her on to his lap again. She was silent for a long time, but he knew she wasn't asleep. When she spoke, her voice was timid. 'I should be braver in the dark, but I am not, Colonel.'

'That's Hugh,' he pointed out prosaically. '"Hugh, darling", to be exact. You keep forgetting.'

Her voice turned apologetic. 'I should beg your pardon

for saying we were married, but I couldn't think of anything else on short notice that might help us both.'

'It was the only thing I could think of, too, on short notice.'

'And now you have got me with child, Hugh...'

'...darling,' he finished.

He felt her laugh more than heard it. '"Hugh, darling", then! We will be in trouble if the French keep us for too many months. Even *they* can count!'

He joined in her laughter, but sobered quickly. 'Setting aside our fictitious fertility, we're in murky water, Brandon.'

She nodded and sighed, and he kissed the top of her head before he realised there wasn't any need in the pitch-black granary to fool any Frenchman. 'I fear these French, but we have reason to be wary of how desperate is their own plight.'

'Desperate?' she asked.

'Yes. I learned a great deal in Lisbon about insurgents. They call themselves *guerrilleros*, and they do not play fair. I am reminded of my Commandant's disgust of Americans in that late unpleasantness in the United States. The rebels shot from behind trees, and dropped logs across roads, robbed supply trains, and engaged in vastly ungentlemanlike behaviour.'

'I thought that was the point of war.'

'Well put, Brandon, you practical chit. You don't think armies should just line up carefully and shoot at each other?'

'Seems a little stupid,' she replied, and he was glad to hear her voice getting drowsy. He didn't plan to ever sleep again, but it would be good if she could.

'Apparently those shadowy armies of Spain and Portugal would agree with you. It could very well be that this squad of Dragoons is in considerable danger from guerrillas. Besides that, I think they are a forlorn hope.'

'You did mention that. I don't understand.'

'This may have been almost a suicide mission,' he explained. 'From what I learned in Lisbon, Admiral Popham's landing north of us at Santander is finally threatening French power in León. I think Sergeant Cadotte's commanding officer is desperate to shut off any trafficking in information, because his position is none too secure. Just a suspicion, mind.'

She digested that thought, then stated calmly, 'It's a good thing you have on a red coat, isn't it?'

'And I intend to keep it on, and you close by me at all times.' He kissed her head again and tightened his arms around her. 'It's this way, Brandon—we truly have to think of ourselves as married. We must trust each other completely and look out for each other. I meant what I said about never letting you out of my sight. I intend to watch over you, as I did on the ship.'

'You are the kindest man I have ever met, but you are probably regretting you jumped into the *barco* so impulsively. Was that only this morning?'

He pulled her back against him and rested his chin on her head. '*Au contraire*, wife. That is the one thing about this day that I do *not* regret,' he declared, his voice firm. 'If I had not been along, there is no telling what would have happened to you at São Jobim.'

'Yes, there is,' she replied quietly. 'We know what would have happened to me.'

'Then it was for the best.'

He didn't think his heart could have felt any fuller just then, except that it did when she found his hand, and kissed the back of it like a supplicant. 'I am for ever in your debt,' she told him, then pulled his hand across her body to her shoulder until she was completely entwined in his arms.

There was no reason for him to feel even the slightest optimism, but something about holding Brandon in his arms lightened his mood. 'You know, Sergeant Cadotte was entirely wrong,' he told her.

'Not about Sister Maria Madelena, he wasn't,' Polly said.

'No, he wasn't.' He compromised, found her hand, raised it to his lips, and kissed it. 'I certainly didn't marry you for your money.'

She was silent for a minute, and then started to laugh. There was nothing of hysteria in her laugh, so he found himself smiling in the dark, and then laughing, too.

'You are more of a rogue than I suspected,' she declared, when she could speak.

'But not a mercenary one,' he added, which sent her into another peal of laughter.

It was easier to settle down then, his arms still tight around her. She sighed, laughed low once more, and then slept. He stared ahead into the darkness, knowing that it would be ages before he would not see Sister Maria Madelena pointing the pistol at her own throat.

'God forgive her,' he whispered into the gloom. 'God protect us.'

Chapter Thirteen

Polly panicked when she woke and could not feel her spectacles on her face. Terrified, she patted the ground beside her, trying not to wake up the Colonel as she searched. She stopped only when he gently took her hand and touched it to his uniform front, where she felt the outline of the glass.

'I took them off you at some point last night. What I cannot understand, Polly, dear, is why these pesky things didn't break yesterday. Do you want 'um now?'

She shook her head. 'No. There's nothing to see. Do you think it's morning?'

'It must be,' he told her. He cleared his throat. 'You'll have to excuse my vast indelicacy, but I need to get you off my lap and edge gracefully around this granary for private purposes. You might hum loudly to drown out the symphony, or marvel at the simplicity of male anatomy.'

'That *is* indelicate,' she agreed, then laughed. 'Just do your business! We're not standing much on ceremony, are we?'

'No, indeed. We cannot.'

She helped the Colonel to his feet when he found he could not stand, after all those hours of holding her on his lap. It took him a moment to stand up straight.

'Good God, Brandon. I will announce to you right now that I am feeling every single year this morning! I am also never going to joke again about men on horseback. How do they do it? I am still in pain from gripping that damned beast. My kingdom for an ocean.'

He stood another moment in silence. She was too shy to ask him if he needed assistance in walking across the granary. After copious cursing under his breath that she chose to ignore, he got himself in motion. In another moment, she heard the homely sound of water against the wall.

When he returned to her side, it was her turn, moving slowly in the other direction until she found the bucket. When she finished, she groped along the wall, following the sound of the Colonel's voice until she ran into him again. When she sat by his side this time, his arm seemed to go around her automatically.

He yawned. 'I think I could eat a whole pig, but something tells me we're not going to be well fed on this journey.'

'I must be philosophical,' she told him. 'I told myself when I came to Portugal that this would be a good time to get rid of what Miss Pym called my baby fat.'

'Miss Pym be damned,' he replied mildly, 'and spare me skinny females. I might remind you that you're supposed to be eating for two.'

'Wretch!' she said with feeling. 'Perhaps to while away the hours, we should play a game of "It Could Be Worse".' The words weren't out of her mouth before she saw Sister

Maria Madelena, kneeling in the church. 'No. No. Not that.'

'No,' the Colonel agreed. 'We know it could be worse.' He touched her head with his. 'Tell me something about yourself that I don't know already, Brandon.'

She thought a moment, remembering what he already knew about her that she had divulged on the trip across the Channel. 'You already know I am the illegitimate daughter of a scoundrel whom you have resurrected and made into a wealthy man, for Sergeant Cadotte's benefit, if I am taken care of. That was a nice touch, husband.'

'Why, thank you,' he said modestly. 'If raising the dead to provide money in desperate situations doesn't paint me as a Scot, I don't know what would, considering my own French ancestry.'

She laughed. 'Hugh, darling, I would say your ancestors were quick studies.'

'They were, indeed, Polly, dear,' he teased, unruffled. 'There's nothing like political intrigue, plus menace from Queen Elizabeth and her Privy Council, to sharpen the mind, apparently. The original Philippe d'Anvers Junot obviously knew when to fold his tent and steal away. Evidently he also discovered he preferred oats and Calvinism to truffles and popes. What a resourceful man.'

Her laughter bounced back at her from the opposite wall. 'Your French is so good. Does the ghost of Philippe Junot the First linger in your family's schoolroom?'

The Colonel pulled her on to his lap again, and she couldn't think of a single reason to object. 'Our estate is too new to be haunted, Brandon! Your brain is overactive. We "Junnits" have always learned to speak French. It's a family tradition. I was luckier than most—I have no particular ear for language, but in 1803 before that laughable Peace of Amiens, I spent six months cooling my heels in a French prison. What a tutorial.'

Polly squinted into the darkness, trying to see some evidence of dawn. 'I hope you had more light than in here.'

'Light and then some, Polly, dear. That southern coast of France is devilish hot.'

He didn't say anything else, but she suddenly found herself longing for him to keep talking, to distract her from the granary, her hunger and the itch between her shoulder blades, and the fear that seemed to overlay every rational part of her brain.

'I'm afraid,' she said finally, speaking low, maybe not even wanting him to hear her. 'Please keep talking.'

He did, to her relief, telling her about his childhood in Kirkcudbrightshire, where it rained six days out of seven; the gardens of madly blooming roses in everyone's front garden; the hours he spent in small boats in the Firth of Solway; the year he chafed away at the University of Edinburgh until he convinced his father to see him into the Royal Marines; and his years in deepwater service, doing exactly what he loved.

As she listened to his musical accent and soothing voice, she realised how little her life was, in relation to his, how modest and unexceptional. She knew that most women lived quiet lives at home. Her beloved sister Nana waited, agonised, and bore up magnificently under the strain of loving a man too often gone. Her equally well-loved sister Laura had chosen a different path, but it still revolved around her husband and her son, even as she used her own medical skills quietly in the shadow.

'Women don't amount to much,' she said, when the Colonel finished.

'What brought that on?' he asking, laughing.

'I was just thinking about how little I do, compared to you. We women wait, mostly.' She smiled in the dark, casting away whatever of her reserve that remained of the intimate situation in which she now found herself. 'We have husbands and babies, real *or* imagined, and that is all.'

'"That is all", eh? I doubt even Nana Worthy realizes how much her Captain yearns for her. I suspect she is his centre of calm in a world gone mad. He probably even calls her his True North. I would, and I don't even know your sister.'

Leaning back against the Colonel, Polly digested what he had said. Her first reaction was embarrassment, because this man she admired had no compunction about speaking his mind in such a frank way. She was struck also by her own words. 'We women' had seldom entered her mind before, let alone her vocabulary. Maybe her years as a student, and then the cushion, three years ago, of discovering her own protective sisters, had helped to keep her young. Maybe it was the casual way she now sat on the Colonel's lap and how suddenly she was so aware of his arms around her. Something stirred inside her, and it wasn't hunger or fear.

Maybe it had even stirred yesterday on the *barco*, when she dragged the partially conscious Colonel Junot on to her lap to protect him. Protect him from *what*, when women were so easily thrown aside and trampled on? *I thought I could save him*, she told herself in the gloom of the granary. *I felt stronger than lions, just then.*

'Maybe you'll understand better when you fall in love some day, Polly, dear,' the Colonel said in her ear.

She had to think of something to lighten her mood, which was troubling her almost more than the total darkness and the potential brevity of her life. 'You sound like someone who knows,' she told him.

'Aye, Polly, dear, I know what it is to love someone,' he said after a lengthy pause.

I am put in my place, Polly thought, embarrassed. Of course Colonel Junot had a lover somewhere. Why would he not? Who could there possibly be in the universe who did not think him attractive and worth more than gold?

She couldn't think of another thing to say, but it didn't matter, because the bolt was thrown on the granary's small door, and it swung open to reveal bright morning outside. She squinted in the light, then glanced at the Colonel, who was doing the same thing. She also knew she should get off his lap, but his arms tightened around her.

'I wish I knew what was coming, Polly, dear,' he murmured. He loosened his grip. 'Up you get, but I'm going out first.'

She willingly let him, not eager to have a soldier on the outside grab her hand. With a groan that made the soldiers outside laugh, the Colonel crawled through the entrance. Captured by the irrational terror that someone would slam the door now and leave her there in eternal darkness, Polly wanted to race after him. In another moment, Colonel Junot's hand reached for her. She grasped it for a second, then crouched her way out of the granary.

Polly took his hand again and they stood shoulder to

Polly looked ahead at the mountains and shook her head. 'We're to cross *those*?' she asked.

'It would seem so,' Hugh replied. 'Our Sergeant knows he is in dangerous territory. I'm a little surprised he didn't make me take off my red tunic.' He sighed. 'Of course, any remaining mountain people—*montagnards*—are probably no more fond of the British than they are the French. Portugal is a carcass picked clean.'

'Do you wonder why he didn't just shoot us back there?' Polly asked.

'Polly, dear, I'm actually surprised he let us out of the granary,' the Colonel replied, and tightened his arms around her at her sudden intake of breath. Glancing at the Sergeant, who was watching them, he nuzzled her cheek. 'I don't think he believes I will give him any money for his farm. Men at war tend to be cynical, and who can blame them?'

'Then why are we alive?'

'Polly, dear, I wish I knew his game.'

It was no game, she decided, after three days of weary riding through narrow mountain passes that made her close her eyes and turn her face into Hugh's tunic. Her jaws ached from gritting her teeth as the horses—the big-boned animals that French cavalry used—sidled along nearly imaginary trails far above boiling mountain streams.

She knew the heights bothered Hugh, although he did not admit as much. Once when their horse stumbled, sending rocks plunging down into the gorge, he came close to admitting his own fear. 'Polly, dear, I would trade about five and a half years off my life this moment if we were suddenly transported to the deck of a frigate.'

You must be sorely tried, to admit as much, Polly thought, as she screwed her eyes shut against that awful moment when they would plunge off the mountain face. 'Hugh, darling, you must have mice in your pockets,' she managed to squeak out, when she could talk. 'You know how *I* feel about life on the rolling wave.'

He was silent for a long moment, then all he said was, 'Bless your heart, Brandon, you're a rare one.'

She didn't feel like a rare one. She was grimy, smelly, and hungry, with filmy teeth and a constantly growling stomach. The blood from the noisome floor of the church at São Jobim had stained her light blue muslin dress, which was also torn now, and muddy from a night spent shivering in the Colonel's arms as they were tied to a tree. Still, she decided the tree was better than the claustrophobia of the granary, if only she weren't so cold.

Somewhere, far below in the lovely coastal valleys of the Rio Douro, it was late summer. Here in the *tras o montes* region, autumn had begun, and with it a light mist that fogged the upper valleys and brought relief only to the Dragoons. Now the troopers travelled with caution, but visible relief, because the mist obscured their presence from watchful partisans. They stopped for nothing after the second day, when even the hardtack gave out.

'Tell me, Hugh, darling, are the French so poor they cannot even feed their soldiers?' she asked the Colonel after one noon stop when the only refreshment was cold water from a stream.

'It's not that they cannot, but that they choose not,' Hugh said, as they walked shoulder to shoulder along the bank. 'Napoleon believes that his *Grand Armée* should feed itself in the field.'

'I don't think much of that,' she retorted.

Hugh laughed softly. 'You should demand that Sergeant Cadotte take you to Napoleon so you can give him a piece of your mind.'

Polly glared at him. 'I know you're hungry. Don't try to tell me you're not.'

'I'm hungry,' he agreed, 'but I've been hungrier. Brandon, as long as we get drinking water, we'll be all right. You'll be amazed how long we can last without food.'

'Mostly I'm tired,' she admitted, and stopped walking. 'What can I do about that?'

'Get something to eat,' he said wearily. 'Bit of a vicious circle, ain't it?'

She couldn't help the tears that spilled on to her cheeks then, even though she tried to brush at them. It would have been easy to do that if her hands hadn't been tied. As it was, she couldn't hide them.

To comfort her, Hugh raised his tied hands and dropped them around her, pulling her close to him. With a shudder, she rested her cheek against his chest as his chin came down on the top of her head.

'*Why* did Sister Maria Madelena do what she did?' Polly asked.

'For love of her country, I expect, and fierce anger at the French and the way they treated her,' the Colonel replied. He peered at her face. 'Have you never loved something enough to risk everything, even your life, for it?'

'I suppose I have not,' she said, after some thought. 'Have you?'

'Oh, yes,' he said, more promptly than she. 'Perhaps that is why I am a Royal Marine until I die.'

She thought that over, then dismissed the idea. *Maybe I will understand when I am older*, she told herself. 'But why did she involve me?'

'That we will never know, Polly, my love,' he said.

'It's "Polly, dear",' she reminded him.

'I thought I would change the dialogue a little, Polly, dear,' he replied. 'Variety is, after all, the spice of life, or so I am told. I doubt you want a boring, predictable husband.'

She had to smile then. 'When I get home to England, I am going to vie for the attention of an apothecary or perhaps a comptroller.'

'Too boring by half,' he said, his voice light. 'You'll rue it the moment you get in bed with him.'

Startled, she looked up at him, and saw the laughter in his eyes. He glanced over at the bank. 'Uh oh, the Sergeant is watching.'

He kissed her then, pressing his bound hands against the small of her back and then raising them to her neck. She had never been kissed on the lips by a man before, but she knew better than to draw back or act surprised, not with the Sergeant watching. She returned his kiss, surprised a little at the softness of his lips, since he did not look like a soft man. Their lips parted, and he kissed her again and again, little kisses that made her lean into his hips, to her surprise and embarrassment.

When they finished, he asked in a low voice, 'Is he still watching?'

Suddenly shy, she turned her head to look. Sergeant Cadotte was looking at the water, then tapping his boot with his riding whip.

'You're a scoundrel, Hugh, darling,' she whispered into his neck. 'I'm not so certain he was ever looking.'

She laughed then, and stirred in his arms, which was the Colonel's cue to raise his arms and release her.

'Perhaps he wasn't,' he said with remarkable aplomb, 'but at least you are not so unhappy now.'

She certainly wasn't, she reflected, as they travelled into the afternoon of another dreary day. Only the warmth in her middle, which began and spread downwards when she leaned so close to the Colonel, gave her any satisfaction. That she was out of her element, she knew beyond a doubt. So was the Colonel, and for all she knew, despite their hardness, the Dragoons, too. They were captives riding with hunted men trying to get back to their own lines. Sergeant Cadotte must have been a farmer before Napoleon came calling, yet here he was.

'I can't forgive them for what they did to the priest and to Sister Maria Madelena,' she murmured, half to herself, later that day.

'Nor should you, or trust them for even a second,' Hugh said. 'Still, if we had met these men while strolling in Vauxhall Gardens, we would probably just have nodded and smiled. War changes everyone.' His hands tied, he nuzzled aside her hair with his lips and kissed her ear, biting gently on her earlobe. 'Maybe even you, Brandon.'

She looked around, but the Sergeant was not watching them. 'Hugh, darling, you are taking advantage of me,' she said, feeling that warmth again.

'And who would not, in my boots?' he said complacently. 'Polly, dear.'

There wasn't even a deserted village for shelter that night. They dismounted into mud and gravel. When the rains came, Sergeant Cadotte rummaged in his pack for an oiled slicker, which he draped over Hugh's shoulders. Polly shivered in his arms, unable to keep her teeth from chattering with the cold.

She had not complained when the cold rain started to fall. Come to think of it, she never complained, Hugh realised as he held her close. She said nothing about her empty belly, even though he heard her stomach growl and she winced from the pain of it. She had grown quieter and quieter as the hours passed, and Hugh wished with all his heart that he could make her comfortable, even if for only a moment.

They were not in as bad shape as one of the Sergeant's men, a Private gone unconscious with the cold and deprivation. There was no shelter beyond the dripping trees for a bivouac that night, but two Dragoons had put their slickers together and with some sticks, created a rude shelter for their companion.

'Poor man,' Polly said, as she stood in the shelter of Hugh's arms. 'He's going to die, isn't he?'

'Probably. You'll have to ask your brother-in-law why some men are impervious to a little cold, and others succumb. He's the enemy, Brandon,' Hugh reminded her.

'I know. I know. Still…' She let the sentence trail away.

She surprised him by turning around to face him, burrowing her head into his chest as they stood together, hands tied in front of them. She took his hand and raised it to her breast. 'I don't want to die before I have even lived,' she whispered. 'Don't let that happen to me, Hugh, if you are my friend.'

'I'm your husband, Polly,' he whispered, feeling exactly that. 'I'm proud of you, the way you have borne up under this misery. You're brave and kind.' Unsure of himself, he knew he should make light of what he was saying. 'And an excellent mother to our child.'

She glanced up at him then, her pretty blue eyes so tired and filled suddenly with tears. 'Don't tease me about that, Hugh,' she whispered back. 'I…I don't want to die before I have a child! Don't ever tease me any more about that.'

Words failed him. He raised his bound hands, wanting to pull them free so he could caress away her tears; scrabble in the sparse vegetation to find something—anything—to feed her. In the horror that was São Jobim, he had sworn to protect her with all the fervour with which he had sworn, as a lad of fifteen, to defend King and country. In fact, the two were inextricably bound together in his mind. He wanted to touch her gently until they were content enough in this miserable wilderness where the heavens had opened up. He wanted to assure her that she would not die until she had lived, but he could promise her nothing of the kind.

'No more teasing, Brandon,' he said. 'Don't let me shock you, but I feel exactly the same way about the very same thing.' It struck him then that he understood her completely. 'I…I don't think I have even started to live yet, either, and we know how old I am.'

She hesitated and he leaned closer to her. He thought he knew what she was too shy to ask, this young woman who had been raised properly and carefully, but who must have been aroused as he was aroused when he kissed her ear and then her neck, earlier that afternoon. This was all so strange—no one could seriously fall in love under such conditions.

Or could one? He didn't dare think it was possible. Lord knew he had tried to think of the Brittles' objections to him. But as the rain thundered down, he kissed her with all the fervour of his heart. Because the others were gathered around the dying trooper, this was the most privacy they had enjoyed since the granary. To his joy, she kissed him back, little inarticulate murmurs coming from her throat that made his body yearn for her as he had never yearned for any female in his life. He knew without a qualm that for the rest of his life, he would cherish and protect this woman to the end of his strength. He had sworn to do it, on his honour as a Marine. Was there more? Time might tell, if there was time, and he had his doubts.

He kissed her nose next, then stepped back, shrugged out of the slicker and left it wrapped around his love. Without a word to her, he strode to the circle of Dragoons, calling for the Sergeant. When he had the harried man's attention, Hugh just held out his hands wordlessly. *'S'il vouz plaît,'* he said simply.

Brandon was beside him then, doing the same thing. 'Please, Sergeant,' she said. 'Perhaps we can help your man.'

'And do what?' Cadotte snapped.

Hugh knew that whether seconds or decades would be allowed to pass in the life of his loved one, he would never be more proud of Polly Brandon than he was then. 'I can hold him in my arms,' she said. 'Men are well enough, Sergeant, but women are better. You know they are.'

Cadotte looked at the two of them. Without a word he untied their hands. Polly bobbed a small curtsy that made her look suddenly young. She gave Hugh such a look that he felt his insides begin to smoulder, then shouldered her way through the troop of Dragoons, those men who only a week ago would have raped and killed her, and sat down beside the unconscious Dragoon.

Humming softly, she let one of the men help her lift the dying man into her lap. After only the slightest hesitation, she began to smooth his dirty hair from his forehead. Someone handed her a dry stocking, and she wiped the grime from his face, bending lower over him until her breasts touched his chest. She did it deliberately, wanting the dying man to know he was with a woman.

Hugh watched in humble amazement as his green girl sent her enemy to his death peacefully. She unbuttoned the Dragoon's ragged green tunic and pressed her hand against his chest, stroking him until his eyes flickered open. He tried to speak and she leaned closer.

'Emilie?' he asked, with the smallest bit of hope in his voice.

'*Oui,*' she replied. '*Dormes-toi, mon chéri.*'

With a look of surprising contentment, he died. Polly Brandon closed his eyes and began to cry. As Hugh listened, she seemed to cry every tear that had ever been shed over every soldier in every war since the Lord God Almighty cast Satan from heaven and the trouble really started.

Still enveloped in the too-large slicker, Polly Brandon stood as chief mourner as the troopers buried their comrade. Hugh helped dig the grave, needing the release of hard work to calm the fires in his body. He could have cried at his own weakness, when he had to stop because he was exhausted. No one noticed because all the men, equally starved, were taking turns.

No one said anything over the grave. Polly cried. Hugh

held her close, then turned around, walked to the Sergeant and held out his hands, to be bound again. Cadotte shook his head. He pointed to the foot of a large tree. 'Sleep there,' was all he said. 'We ride at dawn. I'll bind you then.'

Without a word, Hugh wrapped the slicker around both of them and sat Brandon down under the tree. His hands free, he pulled the slicker over them, protecting their heads from the rain, and pulled Brandon close. With a sigh, she rested her head on his chest, her arm possessively around his body. In a matter of seconds, she was breathing evenly.

'Please, Polly, I need your comfort,' he whispered, wishing she could hear him.

She did, which humbled him beyond anything. Without a word spoken between them, without even opening her eyes, she unbuttoned her dress. She untied the cord holding her chemise together, took his hand, and placed it on her bare breast with a sigh. It was warm and softer than he could have imagined. He cupped her breast carefully in his hand as his eyes closed, too. He tried to open his eyes when she put her hand inside his tunic and shirt and stroked him as she had caressed the French Dragoon. All he could do was succumb to his best night's sleep in recent memory, as the rain poured down.

Chapter Fourteen

If the burial didn't change everything, crossing an un-named mountain stream did. What surprised Hugh about saving Sergeant Cadotte's life was the ferocious way Polly Brandon did all he demanded without question. She had the heart of a Marine, and this unexpected discovery bound him to her tighter than the cords shackling them. Not only did he love her; he respected her as a brother in arms.

They had come to the river at dusk one week later. They had been slowly winding their way down to it for most of the day on the precipitous switchbacks that Portuguese mountain passes were notorious for. He knew how terrified Polly was, shrinking back against him as they travelled the dangerous trail, their hands bound and at the mercy of the Corporal, who had roped their horse to his.

One of the Dragoons on the narrow file in front of them had lost his life around a sharp turn when his horse made a misstep and trod upon thin air. The man shrieked all the way to his death. Polly's sharp intake of breath and the shaking of her shoulders told him volumes about her own state of mind.

She had borne up well against the journey. Even the Sergeant had remarked on that to him the night before, when he had tied them to a picket stake and laid down next to them, spreading his blanket over them all, which had touched Hugh.

'I wish matters were different for your lady,' was all the Sergeant said, and it was quietly spoken, as Cadotte turned on his side to sleep, his back to them.

My lady, Hugh thought, as he cuddled Polly close. He knew her body well by now. His acquaintance with it had begun on the voyage from Plymouth, but he had taken pains not to embarrass her, even as they had to manage private functions in sight and sound of each other. She had accepted their constant closeness for her protection. There was nothing missish about Polly Brandon, which eased his plight. When she had so generously comforted him two nights ago, he knew he was in her debt for ever.

He wished she did not continue to chafe about the impulsive gesture that had caused him to jump into the *barco* in Oporto. He knew it still bothered her that he could be safe downriver, and by now, at Ferrol Station, or even in Plymouth. Not even the reality of her probable fate at the hands of Cadotte's troopers seemed to assuage the guilt she felt at endangering his life, because she had insisted upon accompanying Sister Maria Madelena on the ill-fated journey.

'It's my fault you are here,' she told him after the Dragoon fell to his death.

'Polly, dear, life is strange,' he had said, and it sounded so facile to his own ears, something uttered vapidly in a drawing room to impress fops.

Obviously unimpressed with his philosophising, she had said nothing more to him. It chafed him that she felt so alone in her misery. He knew she liked him, but he also suspected she had not invested her heart in him, as she would have if they were actually married, instead of submitting to a great fiction to stay alive. Something told him she needed to discover how much she loved him, if she even did.

They came to the ford of the stream before dusk. The Sergeant sat in his saddle, his leg across the pommel, in that casual way of his that Hugh could only envy. Cadotte watched the stream for some moments, as if weighing the value of crossing now or waiting until morning. The mist that had been falling on them for days must have fallen as rain higher in the mountains, because the stream boiled along like a river. To cross now or not? Hugh almost smiled to himself; he knew what command decisions felt like.

'We will cross now,' the Sergeant said finally, and gestured his men forwards.

'How?' Polly murmured, into Hugh's tunic.

It was a good question. There was little remaining of the stone bridge that had once spanned the stream, more properly a river now. One army or another had blown it into gravel years ago, leaving behind only stone pillars at either bank. Some enterprising soul had rigged a rope across the expanse. Hugh pointed this out to Polly.

'I suppose we are to grip the rope as the horse does his best,' he told her, trying not to sound as dubious as he felt.

'Then the Sergeant had better free our hands,' was all she said.

The Sergeant seemed disinclined to agree, which

hardly surprised him. What did surprise him was the way Polly argued with the Frenchman, holding her bound hands in front of her and then waving them about, which made the Sergeant's face twitch in what Hugh had decided was as near as the man ever got to smiling.

'You insist?' the Sergeant said finally.

Polly stared him directly in the eyes and nodded vigorously. 'I insist.'

'You have no power to make me do anything, Madame Junnit,' he said.

'I know that, but I still insist,' she replied.

Sergeant Cadotte turned to him and threw up his hands in a Gallic gesture. 'Is she always so much trouble?'

'This and more,' Hugh answered. 'Humour her.'

The Sergeant did, gesturing for his Corporal to untie them. The Sergeant had the sapper find him a longer rope and told his Corporal to tie it around their waists, binding them together.

'We would be safer if you didn't fetter us,' Hugh said.

'I don't care about your safety,' Cadotte snapped, obviously weary of decisions and complainers. 'I want you across the river together, or not at all.'

Cadotte sent half his troopers across the stream. Hugh watched as they guided their mounts into the swift-moving water, grasping the rope as the water tugged at them.

'I do not think it is more than four feet deep. I fear the current. Can you swim?'

Polly nodded, her eyes on the water. 'Miss Pym is a modern educationist. She took us river bathing in the Avon.' She glanced back at him, and he saw the worry in her face take on a calmness that impressed him.

'However, the Avon never looked like this. It's rushing so *fast*.'

He kissed her cheek impulsively. 'D'ye know, Brandon, one of the many things that impresses me about you is that you're not afraid to admit you're afraid, but you plug along anyhow.'

His reward was a faint smile and a shake of her head, as if she thought him two-thirds barmy. Perhaps she did; maybe he was. Who understood women?

The Corporal crossed next, holding tight to the rope and calling for them to do the same, as he kept a firm grip on the rope around their waists. The stream caught them, and Hugh felt the mighty pull of the water. Polly whimpered, then was silent as she glided her hand along the rope. He could feel how tightly she gripped the horse's flanks with her legs.

'You'll do, Polly, dear,' he said loud in her ear, to be heard above the sound of the water.

When they reached the opposite shore, he had to coax Polly to let go, finally just twisting her fingers from their death grip on the rope that spanned the stream. Her face was pale and her eyes huge in her head, as the Corporal tugged their mount on to the bank. Only then did her shoulders slump. 'Thank God,' she said simply.

Hand possessively on her shoulder, he turned in the saddle to watch Cadotte cross. No sooner than it took him to blink, Hugh watched as the Sergeant plunged headfirst into the river as his horse stumbled over rocks slippery with moss. He came up sputtering and grasping frantically for his mount, but he was already downstream of any aid.

'Stand up, man,' Hugh muttered to himself as he quickly undid the knot tying him to Polly. 'It's not that deep.'

As he had remarked to Polly before their crossing, it wasn't the depth, but the current that was playing merry hell with Sergeant Cadotte. He retied the rope around Polly and dismounted, his eyes on the Sergeant, who was watching his startled troopers with desperate eyes. He tried to speak as he was swept downstream.

'Polly, I'm going in,' Hugh said as he took off his tunic and gorget and handed them to her. 'Convince the Corporal to let loose of our horse and follow me along the bank with that rope. Get ahead of me and think of something!'

As he unbuckled his shoes he looked back to see some of the men unlimbering their weapons. *Fools*, he thought. *And the French think they will win this war?* He dived into the water.

There was no thought in Polly's mind except to do exactly as the Colonel said. Scarcely breathing, she watched him make powerful strokes to the middle of the stream, then let the current carry him towards the floundering Sergeant as he tried to swim. Polly pulled at the rope connecting her horse to the Corporal's to get his attention. 'Let me go,' she shouted. 'Then follow me. And for God's sake, stop them from firing. Hugh is trying to *help*!'

The Corporal must have thought she could do some good. After a spare second to stare at her and mull her demand, he did as she said, untying the rope from his pommel and tossing it to her. Grasping the reins for the first time, she dug her heels into the horse and was rewarded with an unexpected burst of speed from an animal probably as tired and hungry as she was. She could hear the Corporal shouting something to her in French, but she ignored him, putting all thoughts aside of what would happen to her if both men died in the river and she was left to face the troopers alone.

To her relief, she heard the Corporal pounding his horse along behind her. She watched the river, which had narrowed and deepened, and the Colonel, who swam with one arm clasped around the Sergeant now. She urged the horse on until they were nearly parallel to the men in the river. In another hundred yards of pounding along the bank, she was ahead of them.

Once through the narrow gorge, the river widened again and the current slowed. She glanced over her shoulder to see Hugh gradually angling towards the shore, fighting the lessening current. He tried to stand up once, but the river yanked them down again.

Polly glanced back to see the rest of the troopers following the Corporal. Her horse was flecked with foam by the time she came to another ford where the bank gradually inclined to a sandy beach. Throwing herself off her horse, she gestured to the Corporal, who dismounted, too.

'Can you swim?' she shouted.

He returned a blank stare, and she realised she was speaking in English. She repeated her question in French, and he shook his head.

It's up to me, then, she thought. *Oh, I don't like adventures.* She handed him the end of the rope tied around her waist, and told him to hang on tight as she went into the stream, recoiling in shock from the cold, and then struggling to stand upright.

The water came up to her chest and the current knocked her over. She struggled to her feet again, then looked at the bank, where the troopers had dismounted and were helping the Corporal with the rope.

Falling and rising several times, and encouraged by the troopers on shore, Polly fought her way to the middle of the stream where the water boiled around a significant boulder. She heaved herself against the protecting rock, letting it anchor her, gratified to see the rope stretching almost taut as the troopers pulled just enough to keep it level, but not to yank her into the stream.

Eyes anxious, she watched for the men. *Please, Hugh,* she thought, *please, Hugh.* It was not coherent or profound, but as she said his name over and over, she realised there was nothing she would not do for this man. He was no longer a Colonel, a Marine, a man she had only met a few months ago. Proper or not, their trials had bound them together tighter than a trussed Christmas goose. He owed her no more than she owed him.

She waited there, her teeth chattering, as the Colonel and the Sergeant swung around the bend of the river. Hugh quickly saw what she had done, and struck out for the space between her and the bank. He grasped the rope with a waterlogged yell of triumph and clung to it as the troopers on shore dug in against the impact.

The force of two men hitting the rope yanked her into the channel again, as she had known it would. She took a deep breath and clung to the rope as the current pulled her under and then downstream. His face a study in concern, Hugh tried to reach for her. She shook her head, and held up the end of the rope that bound them to shore, so he would not worry.

She had no reason to fear. Gradually, the troopers pulled the three of them towards the shallow bank. It was just a matter of hanging on now, and she had the rope tied around her waist. She watched in relief as the two men crawled ashore and slumped on the sand, then let the troopers pull her ashore. She sank face down beside the Colonel, pillowing her cheek against the sand. The water lapped at her legs still, until one of the troopers gently grasped her under her arms and pulled her higher up on the bank. She put her hand on Colonel Junot's back, content just to touch him.

When he was breathing evenly again, he heaved himself on to his back and slowly turned his head towards her. 'Words fail me, Brandon,' was all he said, as he closed his eyes.

Suddenly terrified, she crawled closer, then straddled him, shaking his shoulders and crying. 'Don't you dare die right now!' she sobbed. 'We have miles to go!'

She stopped when he grasped her wrists. 'Polly, dear, I am quite alive.'

She collapsed on top of him then, crying, and not moving until he muttered something about swallowing half of the river, and would she please get off his stomach?

She did as he said, helping him into a sitting position, while he coughed until water dribbled down the front of his checked shirt, torn from his rough passage over rocks and past snags of timber.

She thought of the Sergeant then, but the Corporal was already beside him, turning his leader on to his side as water drained from his mouth. Cadotte opened his eyes and he stared at Colonel Junot in amazement.

'*Mon Dieu*, you saved my life,' he said, when he could talk.

To Polly's amusement, the matter seemed to embarrass the Colonel. 'Yes. Well. Of course I did! Do you take me for someone raised by crofters?'

'But you saved my life,' the Sergeant repeated. He lay back, exhausted, his head against his Corporal's leg.

'Let me assure you, Sergeant Cadotte, I have no love for you at all,' Hugh said. 'Not one scrap of affection. But somewhere near Angoulême there are a woman and two children who think you are worth saving. I did it for them.'

With some effort, the Sergeant managed that twitch that passed for a smile. 'You could have saved yourself some money,' he countered, still stubborn.

'I told you I am an officer and a gentleman. Why won't you believe it?' Hugh said patiently, as though he spoke to a child. 'Polly, dear, are you and our little one all right?'

Drat the man. Why did he have to embarrass her? 'Yes,' she replied, her voice steely.

He patted her leg, then rested his hand on her thigh, giving her a roguish grin and daring her to take exception to his fond, husbandly gesture. He glanced at Cadotte. 'I dare you to submit her name for one of Napoleon's new Legions d'Honneur.'

The Sergeant's lips twitched again and he let out a bark of laughter this time that quickly turned into a coughing fit.

'Lord, you are droll, Colonel,' he said, after his Corporal raised him into a sitting position. 'I will give her something better. You two can ride without your hands tied now.'

The Sergeant surprised her again. He reached across the short space that separated them, took Hugh's hand in his and kissed it, then reached for Polly's and did the same.

* * *

There was daylight left, but no one questioned the Sergeant's decision to backtrack to the bridge and move east just far enough to be among the trees and out of sight. There was even shelter of sorts—a gutted stone farmhouse with interior walls remaining, but no roof. Rendered stupid by exhaustion, Hugh allowed Polly to help him from the horse. Her efforts embarrassed him, but all he wanted to do was lie down and never cross a river again.

'If I see so much as a tin bathtub in the next four or five years, I swear it will unman me,' he told her as she helped him into the wholly inadequate shelter of the tumbled stones.

'You're the one who told me adventures really weren't much fun,' she reminded him.

She was as wet as he was, but he let her help him from his shirt and trousers and wrap him in a blanket smelling strongly of horse. Not until he was lying beside a bonfire, built by one of the troopers, did she think of herself. His men were taking care of Cadotte in much the same fashion on the other side of the interior wall, in what must have been the hut's great room in better days. She cajoled another blanket, looked around to make sure none of the troopers were in sight, and took off her dress.

His eyes could barely stay open, but he watched her stand there in her chemise for a long moment, then sigh and lift it over her head, until she was naked.

'Not a word out of you, Colonel,' she murmured, as she sidled in next to his bare body and pulled both blankets over them. With a sigh, she pillowed her head on his arm, closed her eyes, and slept.

He couldn't help himself. He reached across her body and gently touched her breast. Knowing he deserved a slap to his face, he smoothed his thumb across her nipple, which only elicited a small sigh from her as she burrowed into his warmth. He reminded himself he was an officer and a gentleman as he ran his hand along her rounded hip and stopped there—the spirit as unwilling now as the flesh was weak. He just wanted to sleep until the war ended and he was home again in Kirkcudbright, with his father and sister there to fuss over him.

When he woke several hours later it was dark and Polly was whimpering. Careful to keep the blankets around them both, he propped himself up on his elbow, the better to see her. He watched her expressive face a moment in the faint glow of the bonfire, which had worked its way down to glowing coals, and carefully removed her spectacles. One of the lenses was cracked in the corner now. He set the spectacles on a niche in the wall behind them, a place where a *paisano*'s wife had probably kept her favourite saint.

Polly stirred and cried out, but she still slept. He lay back again, enjoying the feel of her body against his, warm for the first time since he had dived into the river after the Sergeant. As his eyes closed in weariness, he was sure of nothing, except that he relished this woman. How odd it was that in all of his thirty-seven years, he had finally found the woman he wanted like no other, and they were smack in the middle of a war, prisoners, even.

Hugh woke later when Polly stirred in his arms, weeping this time, but still asleep. In his years in both barracks and the fleet, he had heard many a young Marine, newly scoured by battle, do precisely that. His reaction had always been to pat them on the shoulder, so he did that now.

'I'm sorry,' she whispered, as she woke. 'What must you think of me?'

'I think you're magnificent and braver than lions,' he whispered back.

Wordlessly, she turned over to face him and put her arms tight around him, drawing him close as she muffled her sobs against his chest. 'It's too much,' she managed to gasp out, when she could speak. 'Just too much. Is this ever going to end?'

He held her close, cherishing the feel of her breasts against his chest, her hips so close to his. His lust turned to tenderness; all he wanted to do now was touch her shoulder again, as he did his young Marines, and send her back to sleep as he watched over her. It wasn't too much to ask, and God was kind for a moment. She sighed, relaxed, and slept.

He thought she would sleep for the night, but she woke a few minutes later, patting his cheek to rouse him. He looked around in alarm, then settled down when she put her hands on both sides of his face and her forehead against his.

'Hugh, you need to know something,' she told him, her eyes earnest, but with another emotion visible. 'I don't know how you feel about this, but I have to be honest, don't I?'

Mystified, he nodded.

'You may not like it, but I suppose that doesn't matter,' she said. 'How do I say this? Don't let me die without making me a woman.' She put her hands over her face. 'I am so ashamed to say that.'

He took her hands away. 'Don't be. There aren't enough honest people in the world.'

Her words came out in a rush then. 'I know I am probably asking too much. I swear it won't go any further. I mean, here you are, a Lieutenant Colonel, someone of importance, and we know who I am.' She faltered. 'I just wanted you to know.'

She looked ready to apologise further, but he put his fingers on her lips. 'Stop right there, Brandon,' he whispered.

Her face clouded over, but only until he grasped her shoulders and pulled her close for a kiss. She clung to him, her face against his chest, so he kissed her hair this time.

'Brandon, you're not asking too much. Not at all.'

She raised her head to look at him, and he saw her shyness. 'Hugh, I'm just not sure what to do.'

'Nor am I,' he replied, 'except that everyone thinks we're already married.'

'We look like we are right now,' she pointed out, ever the practical one, which he had decided weeks ago was only one of her many charms. 'My goodness.'

'You're not afraid to give up your virginity to me?'

She shook her head, and her humour came back like a brief candle. 'This sort of thing wasn't covered at Miss Pym's, but I have no intention of going to my death without even a memory of a man's love. I refuse to just take the words of poets and sonnets, even Shakespeare's.'

He doubted he had ever heard a more honest admission in his entire life, even as Polly Brandon's eyes closed. She struggled to open them. 'Drat,' she muttered softly. 'Heroines in novels don't fall asleep at times like this.'

Laughing softly, Hugh cradled her in his arms and watched in amusement and love as she sighed and slept. Exhausted, he did the same.

Chapter Fifteen

At peace with himself after Brandon's declaration, Hugh waited until she slept, then left the warmth of her body, careful to tuck the blankets around her. He found his clothes—still damp—and put them on. At least his thorough dousing in one of Portugal's nameless rivers had cleansed his skin and made his smallclothes less objectionable. He smiled in the dark to think of what his Colonel Commandant in Plymouth would think of his filthy state.

I used to be a bit of a military fop, Hugh thought as he buttoned his trousers, which hung loose on him now. Amazing what three weeks on short rations and then no rations could do. He glanced at Polly. He decided that, as much as he admired her, he preferred the Brandon with more meat clinging to her.

He put his gorget around his neck again, always feeling a relief at having it hanging there, as it had for twenty years now. He knew he should wear it outside his uniform tunic, but there was some comfort from feeling the cold metal gradually warm against his skin, as it reminded him who he was. He glanced at Polly again, as unexpected emotion welled up in him. *I wish I had a ring for your finger right now*, he told himself. *Maybe you are not my actual wife; maybe there never will be one, but you should have a ring. Something eye-popping to impress our lovable Sergeant Cadotte.*

He stood a moment looking down at her, suddenly indecisive. If she should wake up while he was gone, what would she do? He chanced it, because he smelled something cooking in the next ruined stone room. Something told him he and Brandon had nothing to fear now from the Frenchmen. Their Sergeant was alive because he and Polly had acted.

Squatting by the fire, Sergeant Cadotte looked up when he came around the corner. 'You see before you a miracle, Colonel Junnit. I do not refer to myself, although I remain in your debt,' he said.

Food. Hugh felt his stomach contract and then release its grip on his spine, where he was certain it had cowered and clung for the last week. 'May I have some?' he asked, squatting beside his enemy.

After a glance at his Sergeant, the Corporal ladled what looked like porridge into a tin cup. Hugh took it from him with no preliminaries, scooping up a spoonful and blowing on it.

'One of my troopers went to take a piss by the sheepfold and noticed the stones,' Cadotte said.

'I don't understand,' Hugh said, after he swallowed a glorious mouthful of the bland mixture. It was wheat, probably cracked with the butt of someone's musket and boiled in river water. He knew he would never eat anything so delicious ever again, not if he lived to be a dribbling old man in a kilt in Kirkcudbright.

Cadotte raised his eyebrows. 'I know Portugal better than you. When they do not feel confident enough to build granaries such as you are already familiar with, the farmers dig grain pits and mark them with a cross of stones.' He finished his cupful. 'I cannot imagine how this was overlooked.' He nodded to his Corporal, who ladled out another cupful of wheat porridge. 'This is for your wife.'

Hugh finished his cup. He wanted to ask for more; for a second, he even wanted to eat the small share meant for Polly. 'Delicious,' he said, taking a swipe inside the cup with his finger and then handing it back to the Corporal.

Before he could take the cup for Polly, he heard an unearthly wail from the other side of the wall and leaped to his feet. He ran around the tumbling wall, the Sergeant just behind him, to see Polly sitting up, keening like an old woman from his home parish who had lost her whole family.

She burst into tears when she saw him. Hugh slid on his knees by her, careful to cover her again, and then hold her close. 'Polly, I was just around the corner! Oh, damn my eyes, Sergeant!'

She held herself off from him for a small second, then burrowed into his embrace with more tears. 'You were gone!' she managed to gasp. Hugh doubted any accusation at the eternal bar of God on judgement day would have even one-tenth the terror for him as her plaintive sentence.

He feared he couldn't hold her any tighter without cutting off her breathing, but she kept pressing closer, her tears spilling down her face until he could not help but cry, too, trying to shield himself from the Sergeant so his enemy would not have cause to gloat over his anguish at leaving Polly alone for even a moment.

He did manage a look at Cadotte, when Polly's tears turned into hiccups. What he saw brought tears to his own eyes again. The Sergeant sat cross-legged, elbows on his knees, his hands covering his face. Hugh kissed Polly's head, looked up at the dark sky. The matter had borne itself home to him more forcefully than any emotion of his life that no matter what happened, Polly was his wife. He had vowed at São Jobim to protect her, and he had just failed her miserably.

Finally she lay silent in his arms, worn out and staring at nothing. His face a study in calm, Sergeant Cadotte leaned across the small space separating them and touched her shoulder. 'Madame Junnit, let your husband help you with your clothes and come to our fire. We have food. He had only left you to get you some, too.'

She nodded, but said nothing. The Sergeant got up and returned to the other side of the wall.

'Can you forgive me for leaving you?' Hugh asked, feeling more wretched than the rawest recruit caught sleeping on duty.

'It's…it's the dream I wake up with every night. I was afraid you had left me to the troopers,' she whispered. 'You would never do that. I *know* you would never do that, but I was still afraid. I'm sorry.'

If she had ripped open his back with pincers and poured lime juice inside, he could not have felt worse, but there was only remorse in her voice, and no accusation. He didn't deserve such kindness.

'I'm the one to apologise, Polly,' he whispered back. 'I will never do that again.'

'Brandon, please,' she told him, with a trace of her former sass.

'Brandon only and always, except in company,' he said. 'Polly, dear.'

She tried to chuckle, but it came out in a sob instead. All he could do was hold her until she pulled away from him and let loose of the blanket. Without a word, she raised her arms so he could pull on her chemise, then let him help her to her feet so he could drop her dress over her head in the same way. He hadn't even needed to unbutton it in the first place, because it hung on her. With her hand on his shoulder, she let him help her into her stockings and shoes again. She stood still, a dutiful woman, as he carefully hooked the curved bows of her spectacles around her ears again.

They stood so close together that when her stomach growled, he wasn't sure if it was her or him. 'That is so unladylike,' she said. 'What a relief that I am not a lady.'

Hugh thought to himself that he would some day like to throttle this Miss Pym, who had been so careful to instruct this dear person in the reality of her illegitimate life, and what little she could possibly hope for. Suddenly, he wanted to consult Philemon Brittle, and meet Captain Worthy, and ask them how they managed their wives, these sisters who were unique in all the world.

'You're lady enough for me, Brandon,' he said gruffly, and kissed her.

Her arms were soft around his neck, then her fingers were in his hair, pulling at it, which he savoured more than he would have thought possible, considering his typical fastidiousness. Neatness be damned, he thought, knowing he reeked and his hair was greasy and he hadn't shaved in weeks. All he wanted to do was kiss Polly Brandon, like a brainless schoolboy.

'And for all intents and purposes, we are married,' he whispered to her, his lips still practically on hers.

She didn't hesitate, but what she said had the power to turn him to jelly. Amazing creatures, women. 'Don't you forget that and leave me alone again, Hugh Junot.'

As she sat close to her beloved, warm by the fire and honestly full of wheat porridge that had nothing whatever to recommend it except that it was hot and filled her stomach, Polly felt something incredibly close to happiness. There was no reason she should feel that way, not with the rain starting again, and sitting across from Sergeant Cadotte, the Corporal, and nine troopers—no, eight now, after the fall this morning. Hugh's arm was around her, and she felt safer than she knew she had any right to.

She looked down at her hands in her lap, wondering if the Frenchmen were sound sleepers, because she intended to give herself to Colonel Junot, that orderly, dignified, maybe a little vain, Marine who had become the man she needed now. For nearly two weeks now, they had lived every day as though it was their last on earth. Something burning deep in her body told her she would not willingly surrender her life in the middle of a war without knowing his love. If they only had one night together, it wouldn't be enough, but it might have to do.

Jesting aside, they weren't married and there was no way they could be right now. Maybe she was her mother's daughter, after all, because she didn't care about the niceties, the banns, the seals, the signatures. She wanted the man beside her. What made the matter so sweet was that she thought he wanted her, too. Outwardly, nothing had changed. He held her as close as he ever did, keeping up their subterfuge with the enemy. He called her 'Polly, *chère,*' as he always did around the Sergeant. Maybe it was the way he looked at her now.

She looked at Hugh and smiled, happy to see the relief in his eyes, and a little embarrassed she had frightened him so badly when she had called out and he had come running. So be it. She had been terrified to wake and find him gone. She would make it up to him. She could do no more right then except turn her face into his shoulder and kiss it, which made him swallow a few times and raise his face to the dark sky.

Maybe he knew what she was thinking. Hugh kissed the palm of her hand and tucked her fingers inside his tunic, which almost gave her the giggles, because it re-minded her of a portrait of Napoleon she had seen once. When she patted his chest and withdrew her fingers, he got to his feet with a wince and a groan and tugged her up after him.

He released her and held out his hands, wrists together, to the Sergeant. 'No more, Colonel,' Cadotte said in a quiet voice, one that would not carry to his men, who were starting to bed down on the other side of the fire. 'If I cannot trust you after what happened at the river crossing, then I know nothing about character.'

'*Merci,*' Hugh said, inclining his head in what Polly thought could pass for deference—they were, after all, prisoners. Not even a river rescue had changed that. He turned to her then, and put his hand against her back. 'Come, my dear, let us go to bed.'

Sergeant Cadotte wasn't quite through. He held another blanket. 'The nights are getting colder,' was all he said, as if daring them to thank him.

She knew what she was going to do that night, but was too inexperienced to even frame a declaration. Tomorrow they would probably be joining the main body of the French regiment, and all chance at either privacy or life would be over. When the Colonel handed her the extra blanket, then walked away—keeping himself in her sight—to finish his private preparations for sleep, she spread out the blanket close to the wall. There was little privacy there, but she felt a certain security in the embrace of old stones and rubble.

Hugh stood on the perimeter of their ruined chamber, his back still to her, just looking into the darkness. He must know what she was going to do; it wouldn't have surprised her. By the time he turned around, she had removed her dress and was kneeling on the blanket, lifting off her chemise.

He watched her, a slight smile on his face. After a quick look around, he was kneeling on the blanket, too, removing his clothing. She could have sighed with relief. She was grateful he did not tell her what a supremely stupid idea this was, because giving away her virginity was a serious matter. She was only going to do it once, and thank God it was going to the man she trusted, to initiate her into an experience that might be brief.

When she was naked and unspeakably vulnerable, he helped her tuck the other blanket over her, his face more serious than she could remember, even after these weeks when little had been remotely amusing. Looking into that middle distance again, he removed his trousers and smallclothes and then lay down with her under the flimsy protection of the blanket.

Wordlessly, Polly moved into his embrace. For a long moment, he just held her close to him, running his hand along her arm, which was prickled with gooseflesh from the cool of early autumn in the mountains. With his other hand, he gently touched her body, seeming to find the most enjoyment in tracing the womanly swoop from her hip to her waist, and then to her breast, as she lay sideways, facing him.

The rhythmic motion of his hand relaxed her, then began to frustrate her as she began to grow almost too warm for the thin blanket. Working up her courage, she took his hand and placed it on her breast.

'Touch me wherever you want,' she told him. 'May I do the same?'

When he removed her hand, and raised up on one elbow, she was struck dumb with mortification until he took the moment to remove her spectacles, reach over her body, and place them in the little niche. He put her hand around his still-peaceful member. 'Share and share alike, sweetheart. It's not that I don't want you to see everything clearly, Brandon—oh, you know what a peacock I am! You wouldn't be disappointed,' he whispered. 'I would hate for your spectacles to fall victim to passion, when they have survived everything else.'

She chuckled, disarmed and relaxed. Tentatively, she began to stroke him, enjoying the feeling, but equally amazed by what was happening to her own body, as she touched his. All the blood in her core seemed to be rushing towards her loins as she stroked Hugh Junot—not a Colonel, not a Marine, not a fellow prisoner, but a man with her best interest at heart—and felt him begin to grow under her delicate touch. It was a power she could never have imagined. For a tiny, delicious moment, as though the thought came from another galaxy, she remembered telling him how much she enjoyed making plants grow.

She realised her eyes were squeezed shut, so she opened them to see what he was doing. To her increasing warmth and utter gratification, his eyes were closed and he had a slack look on his face, in vast contradiction to his usual military demeanour. She was a total amateur, and this man of experience was putty in her hands.

She kept her touch gentle, exploring him, running her hand next across the junction where his hip and thigh met. Miss Pym had taken them once to a gallery, where she had admired the cool marble men with sculpted bones and muscle. There was something elegant about the way Hugh Junot worked. Why quibble? All bodies had the same hip-and-thigh junction, but to feel another's skin and bone under her probing fingers was a glory she had not anticipated, in her rush to lose her own virginity. Perhaps this was less about her, and more about them, an epiphany that took away her breath for a moment.

She began to breathe deeper then, because he was touching her now. His fingers were soft as he probed into her body, taking his time as though they had hours and privacy and endless freedom to examine the nature of men and women. She had thought his probing, which grew more insistent, might be painful, until she realised that she was turning into liquid.

'Is this going right?' she asked, wondering for a moment why her mouth didn't work as well as usual.

'Superbly well, Brandon,' he said. She was glad to note she wasn't the only one having a tussle with speech. He sounded less than sober, slurring his words in a way that smacked of brandy.

She had been lying on her side, with his leg thrown over hers. Suddenly it wasn't comfortable; she turned on to her back and put her arms around him. His swollen member grazed her leg now as he gathered her closer, kissing her breasts, and then carefully taking her nipple into her mouth, which made her sigh.

He kissed her lips next, and then her neck. *'Madame Junot, je t'aime,'* he whispered. 'You're the bonniest lass in the universe and I am happy to be your man.'

She pulled him closer, not sure what to do with her body. It seemed almost to be thinking independently, as she felt more heat gather around her loins. *I wish you would enter me*, she thought, then realised he was probably not telepathic. 'I wish you would enter me,' she whispered.

'In a minute, Brandon. Let's have all the fun we can for as long as we can,' he told her.

In small circles, he began to massage her mound of Venus, sitting up so she saw his erect organ and she could watch what he did to her. She could not help thrusting up towards him then, which embarrassed her at first, but not for long. She decided enough was enough, and reached up to pull him down to her again. She clung to him, her fingers splayed out on his spine. She found herself pushing on his buttocks and starting to pant in his ear. She wasn't sure about the protocol, but it seemed a good thing to run her tongue inside his ear and breathe a little harder.

The result amazed her. Who knew that ears were so useful to lovemaking? Not her. Now it was his turn to mutter something indistinct and raise himself directly over her, one hand under her back and the other on his member as he coaxed her legs a little wider apart and slid himself inside.

It wasn't a totally uncontested passage. He positioned her more firmly under him and advised her to breathe deep breaths. It was good advice, because she relaxed after a momentary twinge, then decided on her own to wrap her legs around him, as he went deeper at a sedate pace: no hurry. He must have approved, because it was her turn to discover the delights of a tongue in the ear and reflect—as well as possible, anyway—on what that did to her mind.

And then it was all rhythm, which pleased her enormously. She had always been musical. The rhythm climaxed into a greater stiffening inside her, then a huge relaxation that filled her with peace, even as Hugh bowed over her body and try to stifle his groans into the hollow of her shoulder. She kissed his hair, sweaty now, and felt them turn into one being.

She would have liked the moment to have lasted longer, but as they lay together, she could almost feel the waves of exhaustion pouring off both of them. She opened her eyes to see his closed, his face a testament to fatigue. 'Oh, my dear,' she whispered, her hands on his hair. Eyes still closed, he smiled and kissed her forehead. Still inside her, he turned carefully on to his back, pulling her on top of him. In another moment he slept, and so did she.

He woke her before daylight, and made love to her again, moving slowly because he had little energy. As dawn came, they went through the entire ritual again, this time with more confidence. Their slow, deliberate pace this time aroused her beyond her ability to refrain from crying out in pleasure, as waves of rhythm seemed to spill from her body into his. He quickly put his hand over her mouth, and kept it there as he bowed his head over her, then put his face into her shoulder to silence himself, as he followed her in pleasure.

When they were more entirely satisfied than she ever would have thought humanly possible, he cuddled her close to his side. 'Brandon, I think Cadotte's Corporal will have to sling us over the horse today like meal sacks,' he whispered, and covered her mouth again when she giggled. 'Can you fathom our potential, if we ever get anything to eat?'

'I wish you would not talk of meal sacks! Lord, I am hungry. Let me remind you we have been married since São Jobim.'

'I feel that way, too,' he agreed, feeling reflective. 'Seriously, you know we have to have someone exhort us and counsel us and remind us that marriage is a remedy against fornication, and we have to sign papers and cry banns, and Lord, I have that all out of order. Maybe I should ask someone for your hand in marriage, but who that would be escapes me. Cadotte?'

She smothered her laugh in his bare chest, then grew serious. 'Nothing's happened in the right order. And please don't think I am angling for a proposal. You have not compromised me because I asked for what you gave.' *There*, she thought. *I am honest.*

Hugh reached over and handed her her spectacles, contemplating her. 'Hold that thought, Brandon.'

He kissed her forehead. It was so chaste, so disarming,

that she felt her heart turn over. Polly sat up and put on her spectacles. 'I mean it, Hugh,' she told him quietly.

Again he looked at her in that thoughtful way that she suddenly knew, with a real pang, that she could never tire of. 'Perhaps I should get dressed now,' she said, a little unnerved by his level gaze.

She dressed quietly, and then it was her turn to admire him in the low light. He had not an ounce of extra flesh anywhere, especially now that they were starving, courtesy of the enemy. She wanted to ask him how he managed to maintain such posture; maybe he would tell her that was a requirement of the service. When times were better, she would ask. She decided she had no commentary to make about his manly parts. Maybe Marines were just supposed to be impressive everywhere.

He laced up his smallclothes and put on his black-and-white checked shirt again, tucking the gorget inside, and then doing up the few buttons that remained. The shirt was ripped and well ventilated, and she smiled to herself when he frowned. *You are a vain man, Colonel Junot*, she thought. *Let us hope your hair never dares to fall out.*

She felt no need to look away when he strode to the edge of the ruin laughingly called a room and relieved himself. She felt a sudden breath of fear when he finished and stepped back in surprise. When he did not return to her immediately, she thought he must have trod upon something in his bare feet. He stood there a long while, then backed up a few paces before he turned around.

She wanted to ask him about that, but her eyes were closing again. When he knelt beside her and whispered for her to go back to sleep, she was happy to oblige. He put his lips close to her ear then.

'If I am not here when you wake up, don't worry, my love. I'll just be around the corner, talking to our favourite jailer.'

She nodded, pleasantly aroused again when he ran his tongue around the inside of her ear and took a tentative nibble on her ear lobe.

'Well, well, Brandon, you're a tasty morsel. Let's hope we find some more wheat today, or your succulent accessories might be in danger.'

'You're such a smooth talker,' she said, as the little flame in her body tamped itself down and let her slumber again.

'I am, indeed,' he told her as he lay down beside her once more. 'I'll just rest here a moment.'

He returned to sleep even before she did, to her amusement. Her spectacles were off, so she got as close to him as she could, admiring his face in repose, hoping their children would look like him. She lay back herself then, nearly overcome with the tantalising thought that they might have a future.

And if we don't, at least I have been loved, she told herself, upon reflection. Maybe it took the clear light of dawn to remind her of her place in life. She got up on one elbow to watch him again, knowing she would never tire of her private view, even as she weighed the probability of a real marriage, and not one engineered to fool the enemy into keeping them alive. The realist in her told her such a thing would never happen, no matter what he said when in the grasp of passion. The dreamer in her admonished her to be peaceful and contemplate what she had given away, and received in return.

It was the fairest trade of her life; of that, she had no doubt.

Chapter Sixteen

Hugh hadn't meant to sleep again, not with the Dragoons moving about in the other room. Careful not to disturb Brandon, he raised up on one elbow to watch her lovely face. He lay back for another moment, thinking of his father's letter last spring, admonishing him that it was high time to set up his own nursery.

He yearned to be a father. He had to give Da credit for starting him thinking along concrete lines. His thoughts had begun to solidify at Sacred Name, when he had watched Brandon playing with the little ones in the court-yard. He thought of Sister Maria Madelena and Brandon's promise in the death house of São Jobim to raise João as her own. So be it. They would, and gladly. *There was an old bee who lived in a barn*, he thought, eager for his own father to teach that silly rhyme to a grandson or daughter. Or João. As Scots went, his father was a tolerant man. As Hugh considered it, his father also was dead right about what had ailed him. *I hope I live to tell you, Da*, he thought.

Still, marriage was a serious venture. There was not

one thing Brandon had to offer that he could not get from a lady of higher degree, except her own dear self. Lying there next to her, he contemplated his career in ruins, his peers mocking him in barracks and wardrooms around the globe, his sister shocked and his father dismayed. Or not. *We live in uncertain times, Brandon, dear*, he thought, *and I do not mean the war.*

He rose quietly and dressed, gratified that Brandon did not wake up, and joined his enemies. The Dragoons were tending to their mounts, but Sergeant Cadotte stood by the glow of last night's fire, contemplating the coals as he sipped from his tin cup. He poured Hugh a tin cupful of liquid from the pot and held it out.

Ever hopeful, Hugh looked into the cup. It contained nothing more than boiled water, with what appeared to be a thin smear of wheat from last night's poor banquet. He took a taste. Obviously the French had better imaginations than he did. No stretch of his imagination was going to turn it into coffee or tea. Still, the cup was warm in his hands, and the air had a decided chill.

'Colonel, I am sorry we cannot give you and your wife more privacy.'

Oh, Lord. You must have heard us last night, Hugh thought, and felt his face grow warm. At a loss, he took a sip. 'We tried to be quiet,' he said finally.

'Ah, but I am in command here,' Cadotte replied, with that hint of a twitch around his lips. 'As you well know, Colonel, that means I sleep lighter than any trooper.'

'I understand, Sergeant,' Hugh said, and smiled. The Sergeant was the enemy, but he was also a man.

It was time for a massive change of subject, and Hugh had less trouble with that. The Sergeant was younger than he by many years, but every bit as experienced in the ways of war. Hugh knew he could not offer advice, but he also knew how heavy command could feel, especially when there was no one to talk to.

'Sergeant, we are being followed.'

'I know.' Cadotte gave one of those Gallic shrugs that Hugh knew he could never manage, not after all the family's years in Scotland. 'I think we have been followed since São Jobim.'

'I would agree.' Here was the dilemma. Should he say more? Hugh took another sip, deciding that he liked hot water well enough. 'Sergeant, how close are we to the Spanish border?'

He could tell his question had surprised the Sergeant of Dragoons, perhaps even knocked him off balance a little, never a bad thing with the enemy. *You are wondering why I am not asking you to just let Brandon and me go?* Hugh asked himself.

Hugh had to give the Sergeant points for shrewdness, though.

'Colonel, we are close to the border, which will work in my favour, not yours,' Cadotte replied, regaining his poise. 'When I join up with my Lieutenant and our larger force—hopefully today, if not tomorrow—the *guerilleros* who seem to be content to track us will fade into the background. I think they are not now strong enough to attack us.'

Hugh could think of another reason, and wondered why the Sergeant had not. There was no sense in alerting the man. He went back to the original point. 'Sergeant, why does moving into Spain work in your favour?'

Cadotte almost smiled then. 'Colonel, Colonel! You

know as well as I do that northern Spain is still well pop-
ulated with French troops. Any hope you have of liberation by your allied troops are getting smaller the farther
north we ride.' He replaced the threatening smile with
something perilously close to scorn. 'We may have experienced a setback at Salamanca, but—excuse my plain
speaking—Wellington is an idiot to besiege Burgos.'

Is that so? Hugh thought. Good thing Cadotte had not
been sitting at the conference table in Lisbon last month,
hearing of Admiral Sir Home Popham's successful raid
on Santander, on the Bay of Biscay. It could be that even
as they stood sparring with each other before a fire in a
battered Portuguese farmyard, the balance had changed.
Or not, he had to admit to himself again. There wasn't
much about war that was predictable. He thought briefly
of the happy times when he knew exactly where he was
going in life, and tucked them away as the idiocy they represented.

'I, for one, would not mind if you just left me and Polly
here to fend for ourselves.' Surely it didn't hurt to ask.

The Sergeant was silent, so Hugh finished his hot
water and handed back the cup. Cadotte shook his head
slowly, and Hugh sensed his regret. 'Colonel, I would do
as you ask, except for one reason.' The Sergeant looked
at his men, who by now had bridled and saddled their
mounts. 'Them.'

Hugh understood perfectly, even as his heart sank.
'Ah, yes,' he said, keeping his tone light. 'How would it
look if the leader released his prisoners?'

'What would you do in my position?'

You have me, Hugh thought. 'Precisely the same thing,
Sergeant. Excuse me now. I will wake up my wife.'

* * *

Still, Hugh had to reflect over the next two days that Sergeant Cadotte was not as confident as he seemed. The Sergeant did not go back on his word to keep them unfettered, which was a relief. They were travelling out of the mountains now, skirting along the foothills, heading for northern Spain. The Sergeant seemed to know precisely where he was going, but he seemed in no hurry to get there, despite the hunger that rode along with them.

'It's odd, my love, but I think our Sergeant is almost daring our invisible *guerrilleros* to attack us,' he whispered in Brandon's ear as they followed the Corporal through the protecting underbrush.

He had told her yesterday of his suspicion they were being tracked, and she had surprised him. 'I thought so,' she had said, in that practical way of hers.

'Brandon, sometimes you amaze me,' he had told her.

'That's good,' she said complacently.

He had let out a crack of laughter at that, which caused the Corporal to turn around in the saddle and glare at them. Sergeant Cadotte even stepped his horse out of line and watched them for a moment, frowning.

'Perhaps he doesn't want us to have too much fun,' Brandon said. After the Sergeant resumed his place in line again, she turned her face into his tunic, lowering her voice. 'What I don't understand is why they have not attacked us.'

'Sergeant Cadotte seemed to think they are a much smaller party than we are,' Hugh whispered back. 'I don't think that's the reason.'

'You think they are larger?' she asked, after a long consideration.

'Much, much larger, my dear,' he had replied. 'I think they are waiting to attack until Cadotte takes them to his Lieutenant and his force.'

'Goodness,' Brandon had said, and nothing more.

Her pointed reminder to him not to underestimate her led him to the only reason for her silence—she knew, or at least suspected, how much more dangerous their situation had become. He could only hug her tighter, aware that she really couldn't know how terrifying a pitched battle would be, when the *guerrilleros* finally decided to attack with overwhelming numbers. Their own chances of surviving such a mêlée were not much better than a snowflake in a furnace, but she didn't need to know that.

The wheat lasted to noon on the second day. By night-fall, Sergeant Cadotte had led his little troop back to his regiment as accurately as a homing pigeon. Before he took them in, he bound their hands again, but not as tight as before.

'The devil we know, dearest,' Hugh whispered in her ear as he settled his bound hands around her again. 'What this will amount to, I have no idea, but we have a new set of captors.'

What it amounted to was a look of amazement on the face of Sergeant Cadotte's Lieutenant, a young man probably in his first command who stared at them, then turned on Cadotte, who had dismounted, along with his troop. After another furious look in their direction, the Lieutenant of Dragoons kneed his horse directly into the Sergeant, practically bowling him over.

'He's an ugly one,' Hugh said into her ear. 'He's never

learned what I learned in my first year as a Lieutenant: it's your NCOs who keep you alive.'

Rubbing his arm, Cadotte kept his face impassive as he took the brunt of the Lieutenant's sharp tongue. 'I can't follow what he is saying,' Polly told Hugh. 'It's too fast for me.'

She felt Hugh's sigh. 'It's what you probably think it is, dearest. He's asking our Sergeant why in God's name he did not kill us at São Jobim.'

Here it is, she thought, surprisingly calm. *After weeks it has come to this. Hugh and I will not live to see the sun go down. I only hope to heaven they are quick.*

'Will we die now?' she whispered.

He kissed the top of her head. 'We might. Polly Junot, you've been the best wife a man could hope for.'

His eyes still on the Sergeant, the Lieutenant shouted an order to Cadotte's Corporal, who walked towards them and held out his arms for her. They had done this for weeks now. Hugh lifted his arms up and Polly swung her leg across the pommel and allowed herself to drop into the Corporal's arms.

The Dragoon settled her on her feet, bending close to her this time to whisper, 'Speak only English, Madame Junnit.'

She knew better than to look at him, especially since the Lieutenant was staring at her, his eyes angry, his hand patting his sabre. She stood still, eyes down, as the Corporal helped Hugh from the saddle. When he stood beside her, she whispered. 'The Corporal told me to speak only English.'

'Then trust him,' Hugh replied. 'I have only one feeble card to play. Tally-ho, Brandon.'

Putting himself between them, the Corporal took them by the arms and walked them towards the Lieutenant. He stopped, but the Lieutenant beckoned them closer. When they were standing close to his horse, he suddenly took his foot from the stirrup and shoved Hugh to the ground.

Polly wrenched herself from the Corporal's grasp and threw herself down beside Hugh, who was shaking his head, as if to clear it. Grasping his arm with her bound hands, she tugged Hugh into a sitting position, as the Lieutenant danced his horse around them, almost stepping on her. She glanced at Sergeant Cadotte, noting the dismay on his face, and the two red spots that bloomed on his cheeks.

'I don't think that was called for, Lieutenant,' Polly said, after taking a deep breath. She put her bound arms around Hugh and hugged him to her.

'*Parlez-vous francais?*' the officer asked, putting his foot back in the stirrup.

She shook her head. 'Through an unfortunate confluence of events, we found ourselves prisoners.'

'I speak French, Lieutenant,' Hugh said. 'My name is Lieutenant Colonel Hugh Philippe d'Anvers Junnit, of the Second Division, Royal Marines. This is my wife, Polly Junnit.' He hesitated. 'Perhaps you are more familiar with the French pronunciation—Junot.'

Whatever his failings as a Lieutenant, the young officer seemed to have heard of the name, Polly realised, as she watched the man's face. In fact, he grabbed at his reins and stared at Hugh on the ground before him, then dismounted.

'What did you say?'

Hugh repeated himself.

The Lieutenant shook his head in disbelief. 'Junot?'

Hugh nodded. Polly held her breath as the Lieutenant, hands on his hips, glared at Hugh, who smiled back. 'Where *is* my dear uncle Jean-Andoche?'

'Sergeant Cadotte!' the Lieutenant yelled. 'Front and centre!'

Looking almost as amazed as the Lieutenant, Cadotte came quickly to attention, the red spots in his cheeks even more pronounced now. 'Sir!'

The Lieutenant tapped Cadotte's shoulder with the crop. 'Why did you not tell me his name was Junot?'

'Sir, I…' Cadotte began, his voice mystified.

'Help me up,' Hugh told Polly. She did as he asked. He staggered and shook his head again. 'Lieutenant…'

'Soileau.'

'Lieutenant Soileau, it is not your Sergeant's fault. I introduced myself to him as Lieutenant Colonel Hugh Junnit, which is how we pronounce the name in Scotland.'

'Scotland?' Soileau repeated. 'Junnit? Good God. Are you a *spy*?'

'Sir, I am a Royal Marine in his Majesty's service,' Hugh said, drawing himself up and managing to look so masterfully offended that Polly stared, too. 'It happens there is a branch of the family in Scotland, and it is a long story. But tell me, how is my dear uncle? Is he with Clausel or Massena? Does he have his marshal's baton yet?'

Good God, he is amazing, Polly thought. She looked at the Lieutenant, who had the stunned look of an ox banged on the head and ready for slaughter. She watched as he took a moment to collect himself.

'How can I be sure you are who you say you are?'

'Ask my wife.'

The Lieutenant barely glanced at her. 'Bah! She speaks no French, and from the way she is looking at you, she would probably tell me you were the second cousin of Our Lord Himself, if you wanted her to.'

'She is a dear thing, isn't she?' Hugh said agreeably in English. 'Polly, dear, perhaps the kind Lieutenant will untie your hands so you can reach up and unsnap my gorget.' He continued in French, 'My name is engraved on the other side. It's also tattooed on the inside of my left leg.'

The Lieutenant's mouth dropped open. 'The Royal Marines require *that*?'

'Lieutenant, were you never drunk, nineteen, and in a foreign port?'

Lieutenant Soileau shook his head, then gestured to Cadotte to untie Polly's hands. He seemed unaware that the Sergeant's troopers had gathered around, their tired faces lively with interest.

'Thank you, Sergeant,' she said in English, then unbuttoned the top two buttons of Hugh's tunic. He bent down obligingly as she pulled out the gorget he had tucked inside his shirt and unsnapped it from the chain. She held it out to the Lieutenant, who did not take it from her, but read the inscription.

He read it again, aloud this time, and stood another moment in thought. 'As we speak, your uncle is with our glorious Emperor and the *Grand Armée* in Russia,' he said finally, his voice subdued, as though he did not believe his own ears.

'What a shame for me!' Hugh exclaimed. 'I would like to have seen him and exchanged pleasantries. Since the war, family reunions have been impossible.'

Don't press your luck, you scoundrel, Polly thought, as she put the gorget back around his neck and tucked it inside his shirt.

Hugh's lips were close to her ear. 'I'm out of ideas,' he whispered. 'Brandon, this would be a good time to faint.'

With a sigh, she did exactly what he asked. A man couldn't hope for a better wife.

Chapter Seventeen

She must have been convincing. After a suitable amount of time, she moaned and opened her eyes to find herself lying on a camp cot in a tent blessedly warm.

She had known Hugh would catch her on the way down, especially since he had engineered the faint, so never having lost consciousness, it was no surprise to see him kneeling beside the cot, his eyes full of concern, and something else that made her heart leap a little. She touched his face.

She hadn't meant to unman him, but her touch filled his eyes with tears. 'Lieutenant, can you send someone for a little water? Just a sip would be so kind,' Hugh said. He took her hand in his, kissed her palm, and tucked it close to his chest. 'You're better than Siddons,' he said in English. 'Although I suppose after weeks in captivity, it ain't hard to look wan.'

'It's easier than I would have thought,' she murmured to him, putting her hand over his. 'What is this supposed to get us?'

'Some sympathy?' he whispered back. 'Heaven knows, *I* feel sorry for us.'

Lieutenant Soileau snapped out an order and in a moment Hugh was helping her into a sitting position for that sip of water. She took one sip, and with what she hoped was a die-away look on her face, begged her husband to let her rest again.

He did, with a perfectly straight face, and Lieutenant Soileau himself tucked a light blanket about her. He motioned to Hugh and the men withdrew for a brief conference. With a sigh, she resolved to let her husband worry about the pickle they were in, and resigned herself to sleep. At least they were still alive.

When she woke later, Hugh sat in a folding camp chair by her cot, head back, eyes closed. She knew he needed sleep, but she wanted information more, so she put her hand on his thigh and squeezed it. His eyes opened in an instant. He looked wildly around the tent first, as though wondering where he was, then smiled down at her.

'Do we live to fight another day?'

'We do, Polly, dear,' he told her. 'I fear, though, that our good Sergeant Cadotte had to endure a blistering scold for not killing us at São Jobim. I couldn't hear the whole thing, but Cadotte may have even been busted down to Corporal.'

'I *am* sorry for that,' Polly said. 'I should sit up, but for the life of me, I don't want to.'

'Then don't. Lieutenant Soileau graciously consented to your remaining in his tent tonight. He even promised some food, but don't expect much.' He grew serious immediately. 'I think Lieutenant Soileau is taking us along with his force to General Clausel, who had withdrawn to Burgos, where our own dear Wellington is laying him siege. Who knows what will happen then, except that I am so glad Cousin—or Uncle—Junot is somewhere in Russia.'

'You don't even know if he is a relative, do you?' she asked.

'Haven't the slightest,' Hugh replied cheerfully.

'What will Clausel do with us?'

'Probably pass us off to someone else, as Lieutenant Soileau is eager to do.' He hesitated then. Polly knew him well enough to know something else was percolating in his fertile brain. 'I can't gild this, my darling, but I rather think the *guerilleros* who have been dogging our steps will make their move tomorrow. Clausel might be the least of our worries.'

She mulled over that bad news during dinner, which was tough beef in a wine sauce, bread pudding made of hardtack, but soaked in rum sauce with raisins, and excellent port. By the time the meal was over—Lieutenant Soileau had shared it with them—all she wanted to do was sleep.

Lieutenant Soileau had no intention of allowing Hugh to run tame in his tent for the night. So he told Hugh, who translated for her. 'You already know. He is taking me to the detention tent for another of our typical nights in the hands of our enemies, Brandon. I'm sorry.'

She was powerless against the dread of having Hugh Junot gone from her sight. 'Tell Lieutenant Soileau I will go with you.'

The detention tent was no worse than other nights on the trail from São Jobim to this nameless spot in the foothills, and far better than the granary. While Lieutenant Soileau looked askance, Hugh made himself comfortable against a meal sack, obligingly held out his hands to be bound, then patted his thigh. Ignoring the Lieutenant, who refused to bind her hands, Polly sat down beside Hugh and rested her head on his leg, tugging the extra blanket around her. She was asleep in minutes, happy to be where she was.

They were up before daylight, prodded by the sentry, who grudgingly loosened Hugh's bonds so he could attend to his private business and shooed Polly from the tent while he did so. Lieutenant Soileau's blanket around her, she waited serenely in the mist, watching the Dragoons at their breakfast fires. Sergeant Cadotte and his men squatted by their own fires, and she noted with some relief, at least, that the Sergeant seemed to have retained all his rank.

As she stood there, Cadotte brought her a tin cup of what turned out to be chicken broth. She drank it gratefully, surprised there had been a chicken still on the loose in this picked-over terrain. The fowl must have been as determined to live as the Junnits.

'I am sorry we got you in trouble, Sergeant,' she said in French, after looking around to make sure Lieutenant Soileau was not in sight.

He shook his head. 'Junot. Junnit. Good Christ, woman!' Cadotte looked around, too. 'I could not have killed you. It never was the bribe your husband so generously offered, and you may tell him that.'

'Why, then?' she asked, curious.

'That nun was a spy and I did my duty,' he told her. 'You, however, were in the wrong place at the wrong time. God help me, but I don't customarily make war on women.' He looked away, as if contemplating his own family. 'Heartless as I was at Sâo Jobim, God forgive me.'

She handed back the cup. He took hold of it, but did not take it from her. His fingers touched hers. 'Be careful today. I'll watch you two if I can.'

You're my enemy, she thought, grateful for Cadotte. *We owe you so much. 'Merci,'* was all she said.

Cadotte was obviously one of the smaller cogs in the battalion, but he still managed to secure the same horse for them. She noticed he did everything quickly, before Lieutenant Soileau had the opportunity to impose his own regulations. Polly held her hands out to be bound, but Cadotte shook his head. 'Not this time, Madame Junot. Keep your hands low in your lap, and I do not think the Lieutenant will notice. Be watchful and think quickly.'

When he touched his finger to his helmet and turned away, Polly twisted around to look at Hugh, who was watching the Sergeant with his own troubled expression. 'I'm afraid,' she whispered.

'I am, too,' Hugh murmured back. 'Keep your eyes on Cadotte. He'll help us, if he can.'

The column rode into a misty morning, the forest abnormally quiet of birdsong. Although admonished to silence by Lieutenant Soileau, there was no way to totally quieten the creak of harness, clink of mess kit, or the sharp strike of horseshoe against stone. Polly strained for the sound of other horses and men riding on their periphery, but she heard nothing.

The mist gave way to a morning as beautiful as any she had ever seen, the air crisp and the landscape scrubbed clean by the rain that had fallen in the night. They continued their downward path until Polly saw open ground in the distance.

'The plains of León,' Hugh said, and there was no mistaking the relief in his voice. 'I believe we are less than eighty miles from the Bay of Biscay.'

It might as well be a million miles, she thought. Hugh seemed to read her mind. 'Now we will turn east towards Burgos, I suppose,' he said. 'Ah, well.'

Lieutenant Soileau called a rest. When they were in the saddle again, Sergeant Cadotte stepped his horse out of the line and waited a moment until they were beside him.

'This is the last pass to the plains, Colonel,' he said, keeping his voice soft and looking straight ahead, ignoring them. She barely saw his hands move as he placed a knife in her lap. 'Watch for an opportunity and take it. *Bon chance.*' He touched spurs to his mount and moved up into the line, in front of his Corporal.

Polly could not stop the fear that seemed to ripple down her spine. She took the knife, and cut through Hugh's bonds, as he continued to envelop her in his grasp, his hands in front of her. 'Don't drop the knife,' he told her. 'Do what I tell you when the moment comes.'

It was then that she heard other horses and riders, but they were above them in the pass. Some of the Dragoons were looking up, too, and gesturing. It was just a man here and a man there, standing, observing, dressed in brown to blend in with the dry plains of León. When the column turned, she saw Lieutenant Soileau in the vanguard, his head inclined towards one of his Sergeants, who pointed with some emphasis.

'Lieutenant Soileau is too green for this assignment,' Hugh whispered. 'He is in over his head. He's ignoring his Sergeants. Brandon, it's going to be bad!'

He grasped her around the waist then, his hand tight.

At a word from Cadotte, who rode ahead, the Corporal loosed the rope that bound his horse to theirs. Polly snatched the rope, leaning forwards across the horse's neck.

When she tried to rise, Hugh pushed her down again into the animal's mane, and leaned over her. He edged off the path just as the noonday calm erupted in screams and gunfire. 'Get off and slide down the embankment,' Hugh ordered, loosing his grip on her and lifting her leg over the pommel. 'Don't look back!'

She did as he said, as the *guerilleros* seemed to rise like rapid-growing plants from the hillside, and rain down fire. She stood at the side of the road, rooted there in her fear, as the Corporal suddenly slapped his ear, slumped across his horse's neck, then plopped in a heap at her feet, a bullet drilled through his brain.

Polly needed no other encouragement. She slid down the slope, rolling and scrambling up and falling again as the column dissolved in gunfire. Horses screamed and pushed against each other as everyone tried to take cover. Other Dragoons had dismounted, true to their training, and were firing now from positions along the embankment she had slid down.

Scarcely breathing, she watched for Hugh through the growing smoke of the muskets, realising with an ache that he had not been so far from her side in weeks. She began to cautiously climb up the embankment, looking for him. Relief coursed through every fibre of her body as she saw a scarlet tunic and then Hugh as he slid off his horse and tried to follow her down the slope. As she watched in horror, one of the Dragoons pulled out his sidearm and aimed it right at Hugh.

'Hugh!' she shrieked. He had no weapon. She raced up the slope, blotting everything from her mind except Hugh. It wasn't so far, and she suddenly felt strong, despite days of starvation, cold rain, and despair. Suddenly, she knew what it felt like to risk everything for what she loved the most. She understood what Sister Maria Madelena had tried to tell her at São Jobim.

As puny as it was, the Dragoon hadn't expected an attack from the rear. Polly scrambled to her feet and lunged for the horsehair tassel hanging from the man's helmet, jerking it with all her might. It earned her a clout on the shoulder, but he fell backwards, tried to struggle to his feet, then was stopped for ever by a bullet from a musket—friend or foe she had no idea.

Polly sobbed out loud, then shrieked as Hugh grabbed her around the waist and ran down the slope. Not until he found a fallen tree and pulled her behind it did he release his grip.

They lay in a jumble, arms around each other, until the firing stopped. She wanted to say something, but she knew it would only come out as babble, so she was silent, feeling her heartbeat gradually slow, and the tingling feeling leave her arms and legs until she felt as heavy as the log they crouched behind.

'I told you to go down that slope and not look back,' Hugh said finally.

'He came between me and you,' she said, touching his face as though she had never thought to do that again.

He didn't say anything more, but gathered her closer. They lay there, listening, until the voices above them were Spanish instead of French.

'Do you know any Spanish?' Hugh asked.

'Not much. Do you?'

'Precious little.' He sat up cautiously. 'It galls this Scot, but all I can remember is *Ingleses*. I have to tell them I am English.'

'I'm coming with you.'

'You are not!' He took her chin in his hand and gave it a little shake. 'And don't give me that mulish look, Madame Junot! Stay here. I won't ask you twice.'

He sat on the fallen log, brushing futilely at his scarlet tunic, which was torn, stained, and bloody. Most of the gilt buttons hung by threads. He pulled his gorget out of the front of his tunic and settled it where it belonged. He glanced at Polly.

'You're probably going to tell me I'm a dandy and I don't smell very good, either,' he muttered.

'You certainly don't,' she teased, then reached for him. 'Please be careful, my love. My love,' she repeated, enjoying the way it rolled over her tongue.

'Your love,' he mused. 'Brandon, I think—no, I know—your sister wanted you to wait a few years and then fall in love with a solicitor, or maybe a ship builder.'

'Probably,' she replied agreeably, since he was going to be a dunce. 'I will be a sad disappointment to them, but not to me. I never wanted to harm anyone, but Boney gave me no choice. It's my fight, too.'

He looked at her in admiration, then gently pushed her spectacles higher up on her nose. 'I still can't believe they are not broken.' He started up the hill, moving deliberately, his hands up, calling *Ingleses* every few feet until he was on the road again. Polly held her breath, fearing a volley of rifle fire, but the only sounds she heard were weapons being thrown on to a pile and the groans of the wounded, followed by shrieks. *Dear God, they are killing the wounded*, she thought. *What kind of men are these?*

When she did not think she could stand it another minute, Hugh came halfway down the slope and gestured to her. She wavered, not wanting to see the carnage on the road, but uneasy to be so far away from her love. Hugh won out, as she knew he always would, and she climbed the slope.

He grasped her arm to pull her on to the road, then held her tight, face against his chest. 'We won't be here long, Brandon. They have no plans to bury the dead or aid the wounded.'

'Are we…?' She couldn't even think of the word. It had been too long.

'Free? Indeed, we are. We are in the hands of General Francisco Espoz y Mina, himself.' He pointed to a tall man, hatless, bending over what remained of Lieutenant Soileau. 'He speaks only Basque, but his Lieutenant, Feliz Sarasa there, speaks Spanish and English.'

She only nodded, her eyes huge in her face, as she watched the killing ground. 'Are they all dead?'

'If they aren't, they soon will be. The *guerilleros* aren't inclined to give quarter. Seems a pity, almost, doesn't it?'

She nodded, unable to take her eyes from the dead, who systematically were being stripped of what clothing might be useful in the guerilla cause, and then rolled unceremoniously down the slope she had just climbed.

Hugh's grip tightened involuntarily. 'Look you there. Sergeant Cadotte.'

She followed where he led, picking her way through

the French until the hem of her skirt was crimson. She knelt when Hugh knelt by the side of the Sergeant, who lay with one leg bent in an odd direction, his hands bloody from clutching his stomach.

'He's barely alive,' Hugh whispered. 'What I would give to have your brother-in-law here, except I fear it would do no good.' He put his hands on both sides of the Sergeant and leaned close until his lips were practically on Cadotte's ear. 'Sergeant, can you hear me?'

The dying man's eyes opened finally. Polly could hardly bear to look at him, but when she did, she saw no fear, only weariness.

One of the *guerilleros* knelt beside Cadotte, too, his knife out. Hugh shot out his hand to stop the man. 'No, *por favor*, no,' Hugh said. '*Este…este hombre…*' He stopped, his Spanish exhausted.

'*Su amigo?*' the *guerillero* asked, a look of incredulity on his face.

'He saved our lives,' Hugh said, leaning over Cadotte, shielding him with his own body. 'Please leave him to me.'

The *guerillero* obviously didn't understand, but shrugged and moved away, looking for enemies without friends. Hugh turned back to the Sergeant of Dragoons and carefully put his arm under Cadotte's shoulders, raising him up slightly.

'*L'eau,*' he gasped.

Polly looked around. The Corporal lying nearby still had his canteen attached to his belt. Trying not to look at his ruined face, she cut the canteen with his knife and brought it back to Hugh. He tipped a little of its contents into Cadotte's mouth. The water only dribbled out the corners and from the wound in his neck, but the Sergeant said '*Merci,*' anyway.

She decided she could not be afraid of this dying man and tried to think what Laura would do. She took him by the hand and was rewarded with the slightest of pressure against her fingers. It could have been her imagination.

'Sergeant, we owe you our lives, twice and three times over,' Hugh said, his mouth close to Cadotte's ear again. 'I remember your wife's name, but is there a direction besides just Angoulême where I can send her funds for your farm? Is there a parish?'

The Sergeant was silent. 'I asked him too much,' Hugh said in frustration and near tears himself.

'Lalage.' In spite of his vast pain, Cadotte seemed to caress the name. A long moment passed, then, 'Sainte Agilbert.' He smiled at Polly. 'If...girl, name...Lalage.'

Polly raised his bloody hand to her cheek. 'I promise.'

Cadotte nodded slightly and turned his head a fraction of an inch towards Hugh again. 'Cows. A new fence.' He sighed, as though thinking of the farm he would never see again, and a woman named Lalage. The sigh went on and on, and he died.

His face a mask of pain, Hugh gently released the Sergeant and pulled Polly close to him. 'I wish I had not deceived him.'

'Lalage is a beautiful name,' Polly said through her tears. 'We will use it some day, husband.'

He managed the ghost of a smile. 'No one will understand.'

'Do you care?'

He shook his head and kissed her temple. 'When the war is over, we will mend a fence near Angoulême. There will be a lot of cattle for it to contain.'

Chapter Eighteen

They were in the saddle again in less than an hour, riding at the front of the column now, next to a Lieutenant of Pakenham's division, and dressed like one of Espoz y Mina's ragtag army.

'Wellington has sent a few of us into the hills to ride with the *guerilleros*, Colonel Junot, although I cannot for the life of me understand why,' he said cheerfully as they rode along. 'Good show this morning, eh?'

I wonder what this irritating Lieutenant would do if I suddenly knocked him out of his saddle? Hugh asked himself, his mood sour and his mind dark.

He knew how Brandon felt. As they rode away from the bloody ground, she turned her face into his chest and sobbed, which only made the British Lieutenant look at her in amazement.

'I say, Colonel,' he whispered. 'Doesn't she understand that we have freed you from the French?'

Hugh returned some non-committal answer, knowing it was fruitless to explain to this ninny that in any war, especially one fought as long as this conflict, there comes a time where reasonable men and women have had enough. His own heart was heavy enough, thinking of Lalage Cadotte and her two sons whom she would continue to raise alone. He didn't want to think how many sad little families there were in France, in Spain, in England.

That's it, he told himself, discarding every reason why the world would think theirs a foolish match. *Polly is my love.* He decided then that his home with Brandon would not be a sad one. He longed to take her to Kirkcudbright. He wanted to walk along the shoreline, watch the fishing boats, breathe deep of the fragrance of his late mother's rose garden, and imagine the delight of a young child skipping along beside him. He knew he was duty-bound to the Marines until the war ended, at least, but there wasn't any reason Brandon herself could not be his proxy, and settle into that lovely life he suddenly wanted for himself.

He looked down at her, wondering if she even knew how much she probably loved him, she who would have killed that Dragoon on the slope. If she did, something told him she would never allow herself to be settled so far away from him. He swallowed as his own heart raced uncomfortably at the idea of such a separation. Scotland could wait, as long as she was safely tucked into his quarters in Plymouth. Even then, he thought it would be hard to kiss her goodbye every morning and attend to his deskbound duties a building away. He wondered if a time would ever come when he would feel easy again without her in his line of sight.

They rode as hard as the French soldiers now lying slaughtered had ridden, in that last pass before the moun-

tains gave way to the vast plain of León. At first, he listened with half an ear to the voluble Lieutenant who rode
beside him, learning of Wellington's triumphal entry into
Madrid, then the need to move north and invest the strong-
hold of Burgos. There was hopeful talk of wintering in
the Pyrenees and moving on France in the spring, rather
than enduring another dreary retreat to Portugal and the
safety offered by the lines of Torres Vedras and the Royal
Navy close offshore.

In late afternoon, the *guerillero* leader the Lieutenant called Espoz y Mina stopped the column and
rode with his English-speaking Subaltern along the
column, falling in beside the Lieutenant. Through in-
terpreters, he told them his army was taking the road
east to Burgos.

'*El jefe* wants you and your wife to continue with a
smaller column to the Bay of Biscay,' the interpreter said.

'I won't argue,' Hugh told him. 'After a month in the
saddle, this Marine would like to clap his eyes on a fleet.'

'You will, then,' the interpreter said. '*Vayan con Dios.*
I will leave you with another interpreter.' He nodded to
the Lieutenant on foot, who gave them a cheery wave and
peeled off with the long column. The smaller unit watched
until Espoz y Mina's army turned on to what looked like
no more than a cow trail, but pointed east to Burgos. The
new interpreter, a long-faced Basque named Raul Etchemindy, rode beside them.

The smaller column continued north and turned
slightly west, as it sought the relative safety of another
mountain pass. 'This area is still patrolled by the
crapaud,' Etchemindy said. 'That will change, God

willing, if your Wellington invests Burgos.' He shrugged philosophically. 'If not, then we fight another year.'

The rains came again as the tired horses plodded into a village Hugh never would have seen from the plains below. Small and self-contained, he wondered if it had been guarding the pass since the earliest days of Roman conquest.

Brandon had said next to nothing through the long afternoon, and he was relieved to hand her off carefully when he halted his horse in the village square. His buttocks on fire, he dismounted with a groan and barely had time to blink before the horse was whisked away down a side street. He looked around. All the horses were gone now, hidden from French eyes.

He put his arm around Brandon, who leaned against him. 'I'm so tired,' she said.

Then it was their turn to be taken in hand by Etchemindy and whisked away into a small, fortress-like house. Chattering in an uninflected language he did not understand, two women pried Brandon from his side and led her away. He stood there a moment, indecisive and uneasy to have her gone, then turned to Etchemindy.

'You are safe here,' his Basque said in good, workaday English. 'In the past four years, we have had English visitors. Sometimes they even bring us weapons, but never enough.'

'Perhaps we can change that,' Hugh said, interested.

'Possibly. We are riding to Santander as soon as your wife is able, *señor*. The fleet has brought more weapons for the Spanish army, but we in the hills need an advocate.'

'We can leave tomorrow, and I can help you,' Hugh told him. 'Admiral Sir Home Popham is my friend.'

Etchemindy clapped Hugh's arm as his solemn expression gave way to a smile. 'It is a doubly good thing, then, that we did not shoot you on sight, and wonder later who the man in the scarlet coat was!'

Etchemindy led him into a heavy-beamed room dark with the wood smoke of centuries, sat him down, and offered him a bowl of soup. Hugh felt his hunger pangs increase at the sight of meat floating in the thick broth. His host handed him a hunk of dark bread, which made a heavenly sop.

He ate too fast, knowing he would suffer for it by morning. He was reaching for more bread when he noticed one of the women hovering in the doorway, beckoning to him. *Brandon*, he thought, alarmed, and rose at once.

The woman whispered to Etchemindy, who turned to him. '*Señor*, follow my wife.'

Outside a closed door, the woman spoke at length to her husband, who gestured Hugh closer. 'Your little lady is just sitting in the tub and keeps asking for you.'

Hugh let out the breath he had been holding, relieved. 'It is this way, Señor Etchemindy. We have not been separated for some weeks now, and I confess I am feeling lost without her, too. With all due respect and thanks to your wife, may I go in and take care of things?'

Etchemindy nodded. 'Goodnight. If we are not being presumptuous, we can find some fresh clothing in the village.'

'Not presumptuous at all,' Hugh said. 'It's been a long time.'

The wife whispered again to her husband, who laughed. 'She says she is going to burn your clothing, no matter what you decide.'

'Wise of her!'

When the Etchemindys had returned to their great room, Hugh knocked softly and lifted the latch. What he saw touched his heart. Just as Señora Etchemindy had said, Brandon sat in a tin tub, head down to one side, shoulders slumped. Her hair was tumbled around her shoulders, but it was dry. She just sat there, as though too stunned by the day's events to move.

He just looked at her, seeing again how young she was, how utterly spent. She was a woman with the courage of a lion, who would have killed for him, but there she sat. *Do I sympathise?* he asked himself. *Do I tease her? Do I just tell her I love her?*

'Brandon.'

She gasped and looked around, and the relief in her eyes scored him right to the bone. He felt his own heart lift, and he knew he had been hungrier for the sight of her than that whole bowl of stew, as good as it had tasted. A room without Polly Brandon in it was a room not worth inhabiting. It was a simple truth, but deeper than a well.

He was at her side then, squatting by the tub, his arms around her awkwardly. She didn't try to kiss him or say anything, but clung to him, her arms strong around his neck. She was a woman who would never fail him or tease him or play a missish card. She had a heart of oak, first requirement of a Royal Marine.

He kissed her cheek. 'Brandon, I suppose you will have a thousand objections and try to stop me from sac-

rificing myself, but here it is. Brace yourself. I love you.'
It sounded so good to his ears he said it again. 'I love you.'

Her voice was small. 'Enough to marry me?'

'More than enough. Laura Brittle knew. I knew it, even
though I didn't dare say anything. And then I tried to
change my mind.' He rested his cheek against hers. 'Are
you certain you want to splice yourself to a chowderhead?'

'When I saw that Dragoon point his sidearm at you…'
she began. She sobbed and tightened her grip.

'Is that a yes?' he asked, cradling her in his arms and
soaking his sleeves.

She nodded.

I daren't be a watering pot, too, he thought, *else she
will change her mind.* He tickled her knee instead, content
to be easy with the lovely body he already knew. 'You
know, Brandon, we will return to Plymouth and I will dutifully take my place at the conference table, probably
never to roam the world again,' he said into her ear. 'No
more adventuring in foreign waters. I shall leave that to
the Lieutenants and Captains in my division. You'll be
stuck looking at my sorry visage over breakfast and
dinner tables. I can't live without the sight of you.'

'I feel the same way,' she whispered. 'As for roaming
the world again, you will, but you will be duty-bound to
write me long letters!'

She was patient with him as he poured water over her
head and worked soap through her tangled hair, digging
with his fingernails until she sighed with pleasure. He
washed her hair twice more, then devoted his attention to
the rest of her.

It was easy to linger over her breasts, which had lost
some of their heft, but none of their attraction. He shook

his head at the sight of her ribs. Where had his plump Brandon gone? A few good meals would change that. He had no doubt that his cook in Plymouth would not rest until the Colonel's lady was better fleshed.

She stood when he asked, and let him leisurely lather her hips and thighs and the space between. In fact, she began to breathe hard and clutch at his hair, as he bent to the task. She gasped, pressing his hand into her soft folds, making sure he didn't miss a thing. His thoroughness was gentle. She clutched him convulsively, then kissed the top of his head after she found release.

He rinsed her off as she laughed softly, then wrapped a towel around her and moved her closer to the fireplace. As he dried her, he couldn't help but think how it had all started on board the *Perseverance*, and her so seasick. He had cared for her then and he cared for her now.

'Thank you for saving my life,' he said into her bare shoulder, as she finished drying herself. 'What an inadequate statement, Polly!'

'I would do it again,' she said, turning around.

He picked her up and deposited her in the bed. 'You're my hero, Brandon.'

She blushed becomingly, and held out her hand to him. 'I'd rather just be your wife, and sing lullabies to our children. You can have the adventuring, Hugh. I don't mind.'

'That's fair enough.' He sat beside her on the bed. 'I don't mean to be squeamish, but your bathwater is daunting. Perhaps Señora Etchemindy can get her little Etchemindys—I saw them peeking around the stairwell—to empty this, move it into the kitchen, and fetch some clean water.'

He looked at her. She was asleep, her hand limp on her bare breast. He laughed softly to himself and covered her with the blanket.

Hugh took his time bathing in the kitchen, once the tub had been emptied and moved from the bedroom. Señora Etchemindy had retired for the night, so Hugh entertained his host with the whole story, from his impulsive leap into the *barco* at Vila Gaia to the ambush on the mountain pass. Etchemindy nodded and smoked his pipe.

'That nun at São Jobim was no nun,' Etchemindy said.

'I didn't think so,' Hugh said, soaping up, 'but she had been violated like so many of Portugal's fair women.' He looked at Etchemindy, soap in hand. 'Some women withdrew, some descended into madness, some coped, and some, like Sister Maria, turned it into a great thirst for revenge.'

'No different than men,' Etchemindy commented. 'Sister Maria Madelena passed on valuable information to your navy. She paid a high price.'

Hugh had nothing more than a towel to wrap around his middle when he padded back down the hall, because Señora Etchemindy had taken out everything except his gorget to the burn pit. Her husband assured him that the village wasn't so destitute that it couldn't come up with adequate fabric to hang on his frame, come morning.

The fire had worked its way down to hot coals and a red glow. He breathed in the fragrance of pine oil and pronounced it better than anything he had smelled in weeks. Autumn was well advanced now and the tang of wood smoke reminded him pleasantly of home.

Brandon was sitting up in bed.

'You were supposed to be asleep,' he told her as he discarded his towel and climbed in beside her.

Polly said nothing, but wrapped her arms and legs around him, working her way into his core. She kissed him with a ferocity that stunned him at first, then built a bonfire in his own body. All he could do was show her how much he loved her by easing himself as deep inside her as he could, all the while kissing her open mouth. They were bound up tight in each other arms.

When she cried out, he felt no need to cover her mouth. The walls were thick, and he knew the Etchemindys were understanding. He could have been quieter, too, or maybe not. They had survived; this coupling was a triumphant victory over death, as they told each other of their love and celebrated their survival with their bodies.

Their next coupling at dawn gave them both a chance to watch each other make love. He had never really noticed before that she had a light sprinkling of freckles on her breasts. Maybe, after peace came and he had some free time, he would count each one. He liked the comfortable way she rested her legs on his legs, and massaged his buttocks with her strong fingers.

Drowsy and satisfied, they lay close together later, listening to the Etchemindys moving about in the great room. 'We're going to the coast,' he told her. 'Admiral Popham is there, and we will join the fleet. Brandon, the fleet is big enough to have a chaplain, and when I am on sea duty, my ship is also my parish. Will you marry me there without any further delay?'

She nodded. 'I will probably have to explain a lot to my sisters.'

'I doubt it.' He raised up on his elbow for a good look at her. 'Brandon, do you realize that at every stage of this journey, no one ever doubted we were married?'

She considered it. 'Did we just always seem married?' she asked, caressing him.

'I've felt that way since the *Perseverance*,' he confessed. 'Don't laugh!'

Her hands were soft on his face. He kissed her palm. 'Colonel, you're a looby. You know that's impossible.' She rubbed her nose against his cheek. 'Well, maybe not impossible. I wanted to think along those lines, except that Laura talked me out of it. But I'm young and foolish. How can you explain *your* behaviour?'

He couldn't think of a thing to say. He just cuddled her closer, until Señor Etchemindy knocked on the door, reminded them there was a war on, and invited them to breakfast.

'There is a pile of clothing outside the door,' Etchemindy said. 'I think you will be suitably disguised, Colonel Junot.'

Hugh decided he liked Polly Brandon very well in the ankle-length skirt, white blouse, and shawl of the local woman. He laced up her leather shoes and earned a flick to his head with her finger when his hands wandered farther up her legs than the stockings.

She laughed out loud when he dressed—courtesy of the village priest—in black soutane, cape, and broad-brimmed hat. The priest had thoughtfully furnished a crucifix for his neck and a prayer book. 'Now you must behave, Père Hugh Philippe d'Anvers Junot,' she teased.

'Let us pray no one needs Last Rites,' he retorted, and frowned at his patched sleeve. 'I look better in scarlet.'

'You are a man milliner,' his love accused.

'Guilty,' Hugh agreed affably. 'It used to be my little secret, but I suppose marriage lays one open to all sorts of charges. Dash it all—everyone in the Third Division knows I am a peacock!'

Polly was generous. She kissed him and murmured something about how grateful she was that he wasn't perpetually clad in a bloody apron like Philemon, or smelling of brine and tar like Oliver, her brothers-in-law. 'I could probably even take you to Bath and show you off,' she told him, tucking her arm in his as they went to the great room, 'providing I felt like parading you about in front of Miss Pym, which I do not. I intend to admire your remarkable posture and creaseless tunic without an audience!'

'I'll even take it off for you,' he whispered, the soul of generosity.

He hoped she would laugh and blush, but she surprised him. Unable to keep the tears from her eyes, Polly leaned her forehead against his arm. 'My love, I never thought we would have a chance to laugh about a future, did you?'

'No, I didn't, Brandon,' he replied, as honest as she was. 'We owe Sergeant Cadotte a debt we can never repay.'

'We can repay some of it,' she said. 'Some day.'

Breakfast was bread and blood sausage, washed down with milk. Hugh just sat and enjoyed the pleasure of watching Brandon eat until she finally had to hold up her hands in protest against one more bite.

Not one to be sceptical of any man's opinion, Hugh

still had to ask Raul Etchemindy how an odd couple such
as they were now—maiden and priest—could possibly
travel north through territory still patrolled by the French.

Raul seemed not at all perturbed. He broke off a piece
of bread and dipped it in his jug of milk. 'You're not the
only visitors to our village, Colonel. I think I can guarantee you as safe a ride to Santander as you can imagine.'

As it turned out, he did. Hugh decided never again to
doubt Providence.

'Wait here,' Raul said. He hesitated at the door, listening intently, which made Brandon tuck her hand in
Hugh's and look at him with concern in her eyes. She was
even tensed for flight, which told him volumes about her
trust for anyone except him.

'Let's see what this new development is, my love,' he
told her calmly. 'Raul, don't think I have rag manners, but
how *are* we getting to Santander?'

'Would you like a carriage ride with a Frenchwoman?'

Polly shook her head. 'We would not,' she declared
firmly. 'No French ever again. I would rather walk to Santander.'

'Polly, let us reconsider your firm stance against anyone of French origin,' he told her, putting his arm around
her. He looked at their host, saw the smile in his eyes, and
remembered Lisbon. 'Señor Etchemindy, might this lady
be of middling height, trim, and with red, curly hair?
Young, too? Not much older than my wife?'

Enjoying himself hugely, Raul nodded.

Polly looked at Hugh suspiciously, but he only kissed
her hand, so tight in his. 'If this is who I think, I heard of
this paragon in Lisbon,' he told her. 'Her name is Madame
Felice Sevigny, and she is the answer to more than one of
our prayers, actually.'

'The very woman, *señor*. I believe I hear her carriage now.'

Hugh didn't precisely drag his love to the front door of the Etchemindy dwelling, but she did remind him of his favorite hunting dog—when a pup—who had to be coaxed towards open water. 'Trust me, Brandon,' he whispered. 'Our fortunes have turned.'

They were standing in the doorway as a mud-stained carriage came to a halt in front of the house and the door opened. Raul helped down a kindly looking female, not much taller than Polly and barely any older, whom he engaged in conversation. The result was several glances towards them standing in the doorway, then a bow, rather than a curtsey.

'That's odd,' Polly said.

'Not so odd,' Hugh contradicted. 'Ah, here she comes.'

The female in question patted her handsome black hair where a portion of it peeped out from a bonnet that must have come direct from the Rue de Rivoli or a Parisian boulevard close by. She strode across the muddy space to the Etchemindy's front door, and into the house in a businesslike manner, forcing Polly, her eyes wide now, to back up into Hugh's arms.

When she and Raul were inside and the door shut, she nodded to Hugh, and turned her attention to Polly. With a flourish, she lifted off her bonnet, which carried away her hair, too, and bowed again.

'Madam, James Rothschild at your service.'

Chapter Nineteen

Polly stared in astonishment at the young man before her, then clapped her hand over her mouth and laughed out loud. 'Oh, I do beg your pardon!' she said a second later, then turned to Hugh, who seemed to be enjoying her discomfort hugely. 'Husband, you owe me more than an explanation. I think you owe me a lengthy visit to a modiste when we return to England.'

James Rothschild's eyes were merry. 'My dear Madam Junot, I could not resist, so blame me!' He nodded next to Hugh. 'You, sir, seem to know my secret. One for the confessional, eh? Does chastity wear a little thin on a Royal Marine, Père Junot?'

Hugh laughed and turned over his crucifix. 'I attended a secret conference in Lisbon this summer, but never thought to actually meet you. Polly, dear, James Rothschild and his esteemed father in Frankfurt are bankrolling this war through their London office and James's brother.'

'We are, indeed,' Rothschild said. 'Do your fellows know I have set up a house of business in Paris, right under

Napoleon's nose? No? I hide in plain sight, Madame Junot.'

'How on earth…?' Polly began.

'Trade secrets,' he replied, shaking his head. 'Let me only tell you I travel back and forth between France and Spain, a little bullion going to the Corsican's generals, but much more to Wellington and his allies.' His smile was almost cherubic. 'We have an excellent record of backing winners.'

And that was all he would say about that, turning his attention and all of his charm upon Polly then. 'My dear madam, although you are charming in that rustic garb, let me give you another dress, so you can travel as my French companion.' He glanced at the Colonel. 'Your husband can continue in his role as father confessor.'

A nod and a word to Etchemindy sent one of the smaller Etchemindys dodging puddles out to the carriage, where he retrieved a travelling case and hat box. Rothschild indicated Hugh was to take it.

'Colonel, assist your wife in changing into something more suitable for this next leg of our journey.' He peered into Polly's face with enough intensity to make her blush. 'Something warm in burgundy, if I have it on this trip. She has such lovely eyes.'

'I tell her that often, so you needn't,' Hugh assured Rothschild, which made Polly accuse him of jealousy a few minutes later, when he was unbuttoning her.

'You have me there,' he said. 'Who could blame me?' He kissed her neck. 'He is right; you do have lovely eyes.'

'Even with spectacles, the bane of my existence?' she asked, then felt immediately embarrassed because she had no experience in fishing for compliments.

'Even with spectacles,' he assured her. 'I like them, actually.' He struck a pose, which made her smile, since he was still dressed as a priest. 'Polly, you know me well enough to know I am not precisely a deep thinker, given to introspection.'

'I could disagree,' she interjected.

He bowed. 'Thank you. With or without spectacles, you're obviously an intelligent female. Think how brilliant and wise you will make me look!'

She gasped and thumped his chest, then laughed when he caught her up in his arms again. 'That was the most shallow thing anyone has ever said to me!' she declared.

'But it made you laugh and forget our circumstances for a moment, didn't it?' he teased, then turned immediately serious, or possibly half-serious; she knew she couldn't be sure. 'Brandon, the only problem you might have with spectacles is that all of our babies will want to snatch them off your face. Resign yourself to that.'

'Hugh,' she said softly, and it said the world.

There was no burgundy dress among James Rothschild's catalogue of disguises, so she settled for a dark blue wool travelling dress that screamed Paris-made from every discreet, impeccable seam. It was too big, built for a man's shape, but Hugh looped a sash twice around her waist and called it good. A pelisse of similar hue and a straw bonnet completed the outfit and turned her from a Basque *paisana* into a travelling companion for a distinctly average-looking Frenchwoman with impeccable taste.

After hugs for her hosts, Polly let Hugh hand her into the closed carriage and seat her beside Rothschild, who had replaced his wig and bonnet covering his own red hair. He brought out his tatting. 'My mother taught me,' he said, expertly throwing the little shuttle. 'I have made enough lace to trim petticoats for every sister and cousin I have, and I have a lot of them.' He glanced at Hugh. 'You'd be amazed how something as domestic as this deflects any number of questions from guards and sentries.'

James Rothschild played a deep game, and he distracted her with it through miles of uncomfortable travel, telling them of smuggling goods in all sorts of ways. 'My dears, this coach has a false floor,' he told them. 'And my petticoats—trimmed with tatting or otherwise—have deep pockets.'

He was only one in a far-reaching network of couriers and spies that spanned continental Europe and spilled into England, where his older brother Nathan had established a branch. 'Our business is money, so we appreciate the value of enterprise and commerce in a free environment. This war will end eventually, and the Houses of Rothschild will reign supreme in Europe,' he said, then made a face when the carriage hit a larger-than-usual pothole. '*Oi vey!* Meanwhile, our backsides suffer. My Hebrew ancestors would tell you it is hard to start dynasties.'

They travelled through two French sentry posts, both well guarded with troops, which told her volumes about the ever-present threat of *guerilleros*. Rothschild, or rather, Madame Felice Sevigny, barely looked up from her tatting, and even handed it to one guard while she searched in her reticule for the safe-conduct pass. His audacity took away Polly's breath.

Nightfall found them in León, also patrolled by the French. With remarkable aplomb, Madame Sevigny asked for her usual room and added one for the priest. They ate in a private parlor, but not until the last dish was removed and hot water brought up did Rothschild remove his wig and hike up his skirts, to rest his white-stockinged legs and chic half-boots on a settle. Hugh tugged at his priestly skirts and did the same thing, which made Polly roll her eyes and throw up her hands.

She started the night on a pallet in the same room with Rothschild, clad in a nightshirt, who had taken a yarmulke, phylacteries, and blue-fringed shawl from some recess in his portmanteau and was rocking back and forth, deep in prayer. She watched him, touched at his devotion and wondering how much courage it took for him to practise this huge deception on Napoleon. Madam Sevigny, née Rothschild, may have tried to let them think it was all for business, but Polly knew enough of men now to reckon that even vain ones like Hugh were fuelled by higher motives. *So am I*, she told herself.

When he put away his religious artifacts, Rothschild climbed into bed and told her goodnight. 'I'm certain if you tap on the next door, there is a priest who would probably do you a bout of no good,' he teased. She blushed in the gloom, blew him a kiss, and left the room.

Rothschild was right. Their bout of no good calmed her nerves and soothed that part of her, somewhere under her skin, that seemed to hum with tension. 'This is disconcerting to the hilt, Hugh, darling, but I only feel safe when you are covering me,' she whispered, blushing as she said it.

'Happy to oblige, even though it's *my* sorry ass

winking at the ceiling,' he said cheerfully, his breathing still ragged. 'At least I weigh less than when our journey began.'

'It seems so long ago now,' she murmured, drowsy. When he left her body, but continued to hold her close, she kissed his arm and pillowed her head on it. 'How soon will we be at the coast?'

No answer. Her hero slept. He even snored a little.

In two days they arrived at Gijón, where Hugh sighed with relief to see the Bay of Biscay, sparkling in the sun. 'God, I love the ocean,' he said.

'We are less than fifty miles to Santander,' Rothschild said, putting down his tatting. 'Here is where I trade *haute couture* for rough trousers and a sweater, and take a fishing smack to La Rochelle.'

'You amaze me,' Polly said.

He shrugged, then tied off the length of tatting, which he handed to Polly. 'Sew this on a petticoat and think of me.' Rothschild took out a handkerchief. With a glance at Hugh, he dabbed at her eyes. 'No tears, Polly! You and your excellent husband will come and see me in Paris when this is over. I never knew a woman to tear up over tatting before.'

The plans changed as soon as Rothschild went on board the fishing boat and spoke to the Captain. After that brief conversation, they were all on board to hear the good news that the British fleet was in no apparent hurry to leave Santander. 'The Captain says he will take us to the fleet, Colonel,' Rothschild said. 'You'll be in Santander by morning.'

Bundled against wind and rain, they spent the night on the deck of the fishing smack. Polly visited the rail several times to retch her stomach out, while Hugh came to the rail to look for the first sign of the fleet. 'I'll feel so much easier when we are on board Popham's flagship,' he told her once, when their trips to the railing intersected.

Morning brought more mist, but not enough to disguise the breathtaking sight of Admiral Sir Home Popham's 100-gun ship of the line, and the frigates and smaller ships, a bomb kedge among them, hovering close by like chicks around a hen.

'Thank God,' Hugh said fervently. 'Polly, we made it.'

They said goodbye to James Rothschild after breakfast, which Polly was wise enough to forgo. After a glance at Hugh, he hugged her and kissed both cheeks, French fashion. 'Be careful, James,' she told him.

Rothschild looked over her head to Hugh in his priest's garments and kissed Polly again. '*Au revoir*, fair lady. We'll meet again in Paris. *Shalom.*' With a wave of his hand, Rothschild returned to his fishing net.

The fishing smack's jollyboat skimmed across the bay to the largest ship in the fleet. Because they approached the flagship as an unknown quantity, they were met on deck by a whole contingent of Marines, bayonets at the ready and commanded by a Captain of mature years who took one look at Hugh the priest and saluted, to the amusement of nearby seamen.

'Colonel Junot! We thought you were dead!'

'A vast understatement, Captain Marten. I do hope my Colonel Commandant in Plymouth has not replaced me yet.' He glanced at Polly, amused. 'My love, I am about to revert to my frivolous ways and ask Theodore Marten, whom I have known for years, if he has some more suitable clothing.'

'I knew you were a man milliner,' Polly said.

Hugh took her arm and led her closer. 'Captain Marten, this is my wife, Polly Junot, and she is abusing me because I am a peacock.'

Captain Marten snapped to attention again for her benefit. 'Sir, I knew right away after that exchange that she was your wife. Who else would treat you that way, sir? Welcome to Admiral Sir Popham's flagship, ma'am. Colonel, allow me to escort you and your lady to the old man himself.'

To Polly's amusement, the old man was as astounded as his Captain of Marines to see Lieutenant Colonel Hugh Junot—thinner, looking more righteous than usual, but obviously no worse for wear.

''Pon my word, Colonel, we have been scouring the coast for news of you,' he said, pouring them each a glass of Madeira. 'And is this Polly Brandon, risen from the dead as well? There is an anxious surgeon's wife on Oporto who has been pelting me with letters, and an equally anxious frigate captain who should be at Ferrol Station but who is patrolling this coast, looking for his sister-in-law.'

'It is Oliver,' Polly said with relief. 'I have so much to tell him.'

'And we have much to tell you, Admiral,' Hugh said. 'But first, there is a delicate matter that demands your assistance and your discretion. May we speak privately?'

They could, after the Admiral shooed away his secretary and other crew members. Hugh quickly explained their situation and requested a wedding in the Admiral's great room at the earliest possible convenience. There were no flies on the Admiral; he summoned his chaplain immediately while Hugh procured himself some clothing

from slops—nothing fancier than dark trousers and another black-and-white checked shirt. 'I have my limits,
Polly,' he told her, as he patted his gorget, which now lay
on the outside of his shirt. 'I won't be married in priest's
clothing.'

'I still look better than you do,' she teased.

'You always will, my love,' he told her.

I believe him, she thought, a little surprised at herself,
considering what a splendid man Hugh Junot was. *I am the
most beautiful woman who ever lived*, she thought, watching
her husband—in fact, if not by law yet. 'We have been
through more than most, my love,' she said, her voice low,
but not low enough that Admiral Popham did not hear, and
then turn away, muttering about something in his eye, and
complaining that his steward hadn't a clue about dusting his
quarters.

They waited while Popham demanded one of his
Midshipmen to run up the numbered flags that would
summon the Captain of the *Tangier* to the flagship immediately. Then they waited a little longer for Captain
Oliver Worthy—anxious at the summons and frowning—
to gasp and throw open his arms to embrace his sister-in-
law, as soon as he came into the great cabin.

'We needed another witness, Worthy. I thought this
was one way to get a lick of work out of you and then send
the *Tangier* back to Ferrol Station,' Popham said gruffly.
He nodded to his chaplain, who stood ready. 'C'mon,
man. This won't wait. Splice 'um! There's a war on!'

Admiral Popham dropped his anchor on her when the
ink wasn't yet dry on the marriage lines. 'Mrs Junot, take
a long look at your husband and give him a kiss. I'm

sending him with Captain Marten and his Marines to Burgos with siege guns for Wellington.'

'Then I am coming, too,' she said, as the blood rushed from her face at the Admiral's news, so drily delivered. 'I…I really don't know what I will do if he is not in my sight.'

'That is not possible, Mrs Junot,' the Admiral said, and she felt her heart slide into James Rothschild's shoes, because she knew he meant it.

'I'll take you to Oporto, Polly,' Oliver said. 'Duty is duty and no one knows that better than your husband.'

She looked at Hugh, pleaded with him with her eyes without saying a word, and saw in his glance that he felt precisely the same way, even as he agreed with her brother-in-law.

'I must obey, Brandon,' he told her.

They all looked at her, each man with some anxiety, and she knew why. She was a woman, weak, missish, and prone to tears. This was their world and she had intruded in it from São Jobim on. No matter how much Hugh Junot loved her, and she knew he did, he was a Marine and the world was at war.

I could cry, she thought, *or I could be the woman my sisters have become; the woman I want to be.*

'I know you must obey, Hugh,' she told him. She turned to Oliver. 'I would love to sail to Oporto with you, or even go back to Torquay and Nana, but I would like to remain here with the fleet, at least until I know what happens at Burgos.' She looked at Admiral Popham. 'I did learn some skills at the satellite hospital, if your surgeon might have need of them. If not, I can stay out of everyone's way.'

'It could be that I must remain in Burgos, or follow the

guns, if we are successful, and winter in the Pyrenees,' Hugh said tentatively.

'Or retreat with Wellington to the lines of Torres Vedras,' she said. 'So be it. Just let me know, one way or the other, and I can return to Oporto on a coasting vessel.'

The men looked at each other, and then at the Admiral, whose decision it was. He removed his wig, scratched his scalp, and replaced his wig. 'Done, madam,' he said. 'You may remain with the fleet here in Santander, until we know where this Marine of yours is headed.' The Admiral chucked her under the chin. 'I suppose I am a fool for love,' he told her. 'Let's send Oliver packing, and find you a berth somewhere on this big ship, shall we?'

'Furnish it with a bucket,' her lover and newly licensed husband said. 'She's my darling, but she is no seaman.'

They laughed. Hugh took her hand and kissed it. 'I'm going now to speak with Captain Marten and find out what the duty entails.'

After he left, and before she had a moment to pine, Oliver tucked her arm in his. 'Polly, if you won't come aboard the *Tangier* and let me take you to Oporto, please write a letter to Laura. I will deliver it inside of a week.'

She took a deep breath. 'I have a lot to say to her.'

It was only a brief letter, because the *Tangier* had to sail. It came from Polly's heart, begging Laura's pardon for doing precisely what she had counselled against, but assuring her sister that she knew her heart, even as she did and as Nana did. '"I trust you will come to love my husband as your brother,"' she wrote, choosing each word with care. '"We will be in Plymouth at the Marine barracks, and you are always welcome in our home."'

She showed it to Oliver, who had been given leave to

relax in the Admiral's quarters and drink the man's Madeira. He nodded, and patted the banquette beside him.

'I wish I could take you back to Torquay, but I understand, truly I do,' he said, then tightened his grip on her shoulder, at the mention of his and Nana's home. 'I didn't tell you the best news. Nana was confined with our son only three weeks ago. Polly, I was there. I was *there!*'

It was too much. He couldn't say anything else. They were still sitting close together when Hugh returned to Popham's great cabin. He sat beside her, his hand on her knee, and looked at them both. 'Should I be suddenly afraid that my new relatives are emotional southerners?' he asked, his Scots accent never more pronounced. 'Oliver, does it take official wedding vows to bring out the fearful truth?'

'Sister Polly, you have married a Marine, a Scot, and a Lieutenant Colonel,' Oliver said solemnly. 'I am not certain which will give you the most trouble.'

'None of them,' she replied. 'I know this man's heart.'

Chapter Twenty

She slept with her husband that night in quarters off the Admiral's cabin, accustoming herself to the motion of a sleeping cot again. They lay tight as sardines, swinging gently as the ship of the line moved on its anchors. He told her of the letter he had sent with James Rothschild, requesting him to forward it through his secret channels to his brother Nathan in London. It was a request for a tidy sum from his banker to be sent through James in Paris to Lalage Cadotte in the parish of Sainte Agilbert.

'Providence sent us the only man in Europe who could actually get that money to our Sergeant's widow before this war ends,' he told her. 'We will still go and see her later, but at least we know she will soon have what we promised her husband.'

'Bless you,' Polly said. 'And João at Sacred Name?'

'He'll come to Plymouth with us, just as we promised his mother in São Jobim, my love.' He turned towards her, his hand inside her nightgown now. 'Give a Marine some comfort,' he whispered, his lips on her breast. 'You're my only girl in a port, and I can't waste a moment. Time management, wife.'

Admiral Sir Home Popham and his Captain commanding kindly allowed her access to the quarterdeck, where she stood at the rail for long hours, looking south towards Burgos. She had said an appropriate farewell to her husband belowdeck as the circumspect wife of a Lieutenant Colonel should, but came above deck to watch the Marines and seamen, aided by brown-suited *guerilleros*, move three eighteen-pounders from the fleet to be used as siege cannon at Burgos. After they were out of sight, she longed to tug at the lace on Sir Home's sleeve and demand to know how long the men would be gone. Instead, she chose discretion and kept her own counsel, as Hugh would want. She passed her nineteenth birthday alone, her mind and heart on her husband, adding his own mantle of duty to her shoulders. She was strong enough to bear the weight of it, and had not a doubt of her own courage.

To her relief, the Admiral had no intention of pulling up anchor until he knew what had happened at Burgos. The rains gave way to unexpected sleet in mid-October and a choppy anchorage, which sent her belowdeck, white-faced and trembling, to kneel over the bucket in her quarters.

Less than a week later, the detail returned, but without the cannon. Even Admiral Popham stared in surprise to see them. ''Pon my word, Mrs Junot,' he said, handing her the glass and pointing. 'There had better be an adequate explanation!'

There was, and it was delivered by one of Wellington's aides-de-camp, looking decidedly out of place among his naval brethren. 'The General sends his compliments, Admiral Popham. I am to tell you that he has lifted his siege and is returning to Portugal. Your guns are no longer required.'

'Admiral, General Wellington sent his ADC to us when we were still fifty miles from Burgos,' Hugh added. 'He couldn't sustain a siege and he decided it was time to retreat to Portugal.'

Popham frowned and deliberately looked all around the deck. 'Then where, Colonel, are my flaming guns?' He stared down his long nose at Captain Marten, his chief Marine officer on the flagship, who had accompanied the guns, too. 'Sir? Did they take wing?'

Captain Marten blushed. 'No, sir, not at all. Colonel Junot suggested we give them to General Espoz y Mina and his *guerilleros*, who so ably assisted us in the transport.'

'Hmm,' the Admiral said, returning his gaze to Hugh. 'I trust you have an excellent reason why this was a good idea?'

'I do, sir,' Hugh replied, not ruffled at all by the stare from an Admiral of the fleet. 'The rain was bogging down our own retreat, and Espoz y Mina can find good use for the guns in his operations here in León.' He glanced at Polly and smiled. 'Polly and I have seen him and his troops in action, sir. I think his army is worth three of any bona fide Spanish army. I take full responsibility.'

'Good of you,' Popham murmured, but with no malice.

'Sir, if I may, any muskets, rifles, and materiel you have not handed over to the regular Spanish army should be given to the *guerilleros*,' Hugh said, pressing home the point. 'Do this, and León will be pacified before winter ends.'

Admiral Popham nodded. 'You guarantee these ragged men can do what a Spanish army cannot?'

'Admiral Popham, no man can guarantee that. My advice is to trust him. Espoz y Mina's brand of hit-and-run war may become a standard of warfare, in future.'

'I doubt that very much, Colonel,' Popham said, after a long pause and much scrutiny of Colonel Junot, who did not squirm. 'Care to make a wager?'

The tension on the quarterdeck vanished when Hugh gasped theatrically. 'Not with my wife standing here, Admiral! She will give me a regular bear-garden jaw, if I gamble away my pay chit.'

'I wouldn't, you know,' she told him later, when they stood on the deck of the frigate *Aurora*, which had peeled off from the fleet towards Oporto with them aboard. 'The Admiral will think I am a shrew.'

Hugh kissed her cheek, and wrapped his borrowed boat cloak tighter around both of them. 'No, no. He's a married man, too.' He sighed then, and gently rubbed his thumb under her breast, more for comfort, to her way of thinking, than any greater design. 'I don't know what I accomplished during this sojourn in the Peninsula, as far as military matters go. I have a wife—the best one imaginable—but the notes I took from all those interviews must be scattered from here to breakfast. My conclusions about the *guerilleros* will be met with scepticism—you heard the Admiral—because no one understands this kind of warfare yet.'

'You can still write a report about that,' she pointed out.

'I can. I can also urge my Commandant Colonel that our Marines be used here and there among the *guerilleros* as liaison. They'll be better than that ninny from Wellington's army. Certainly more flexible.' He pulled her closer. 'Is it enough?'

'Probably not for you,' she said. 'Will you be content to sit at a desk in Plymouth now and make policy?'

'And not go gallivanting off to the Peninsula?' He kissed her fingers. 'Aye, Polly, dear, because I know that when I come home each night, you will be on the other side of the door.'

She had no resistance to that. After a quick scanning of the deck, she turned around in his arms and kissed him, pressing against his body so brazenly that she was glad his cloak enveloped them both. *Better get the man belowdeck and roger him royally*, she told herself. She knew that as soon as the frigate began its dance on the Atlantic rollers, she would be kneeling by that bucket again, with love a long way from her mind.

He kissed her back with some fervour, but then he sighed, and rested his chin on her head. 'Brandon, I have to tell you something.'

'That you love me?'

Hugh held her off a little, his face serious. 'When we were fifty miles from Burgos, where the ADC joined us, so did El Cuchillo.'

She thought a moment, then tensed. 'Dear God. Sister Maria Madelena's brother?'

'The very same. He came right up to me out of the shadows and stood practically on my shoes. What could I do? I didn't know whether to fight or run, but then he clapped his arms on my shoulders and kissed me on each cheek.'

Hugh couldn't help himself then. He sobbed out loud, trying to smother the sound in her hair. Polly held him closer. 'She spared you!' she said fiercely. 'I'll remind you of that whenever you need to hear it!'

She wiped his eyes, kissing his lips and neck until he could speak again.

'That was what he told me, too, my love. We didn't know it, but the deacon at São Jobim witnessed the whole wicked turn of events from the choir loft. He carried the tale to El Cuchillo, and it was El Cuchillo who took word to Oporto that you and I were still alive. He…he just wanted to assure me he knows the truth.'

'Poor man,' she murmured. 'Did…you tell him of our plans for João?'

'Aye, and he gave me his blessing again. Polly, I want to be a good father.'

'You will be,' she said, running her hand along his face, caressing him. 'And to all our other children,' she whispered.

'Is that an announcement, Polly, dear?' he asked, and he sounded so eager.

'No. It's just a fact,' she said. 'I even predict that when we get to Oporto, my sister will give you a hug and a kiss.'

'I doubt that,' he said. 'She doesn't like me.'

'She will! Philemon will be our advocate, Hugh. Did you know it was Philemon who delivered that letter you so incautiously wrote to me?'

The frigate began its Atlantic roll. He walked her carefully to a nearby hatch and sat down, his cloak still tight around her. 'He did tell me that, and gave me some reason to hope.' He glanced at her. 'Polly, do you think you and I will disagree on things, as the Brittles do?'

'I think you can count on it,' she told him. 'I have a brain; so do you. How could we possibly see eye to eye on everything?' She moved herself into his embrace, wrapping her arms around him. 'I never told you this, but I wrote you a letter, too, only I never sent it. You can read it, when we get to Oporto.' She sighed. 'It's not cheerful reading.'

'It's not a cheerful war. You know that better than any female, Brandon. We're returning to Stonehouse Barracks and I am going back to boring desk duty, where I will write that report—as much as I can from memory—and strenuously argue for the Marines to be used as liaison with *guerrilleros* like Espoz y Mina.' He twined his fingers through hers. 'Maybe there will be time for you and me and João to visit Scotland, but I doubt it.'

'What will I do?'

He kissed her hand. 'You can begin by decorating my quarters. I'm embarrassed for you to see them now, but that can't be helped. And just think—you can spend leisure time playing "There was an old bee" with João.'

'I can,' she agreed, feeling impish. Either the waves weren't rolling too high yet, or she was finally developing those mythical sea legs her Marine spoke of. More immediately, she saw a future belowdeck in a sleeping cot with her husband. *I used to be a lot more circumspect*, she thought, as she leaned closer to him. *Thank goodness that passed.* 'I have a version of my own for you. "There was an old bee…"'

'Brandon, you scamp,' he exclaimed, even as he made no effort to stop her pointing finger, which was more of a caress than a circle, and targeted south of his stomach. 'No one's ever done the bee like that before. No, don't stop.'

'"…who lived in a barn,"' she continued, not even bothering with the circle any more, but touching him where she knew it would do the most good, considering her designs on her husband. She began to undo the buttons on his trousers. '"He carried a bagpipe…"' she began, but he stood up then.

'"…under his arm,"' he continued, as he kept the cloak around both of them and started with her for the gangway. 'So glad you remember that little ditty, except that I may never be able to look at it in the same way again. I believe you are a rascal, Brandon.'

Thirty minutes later, he was deep asleep, cradling her in his arms, as he had protected her from Plymouth to Santander, and apparently back again. She thought about looking for her nightgown, but that was more effort than she deemed strictly necessary. Besides, she might just have to take it off again, and she knew how Hugh, darling, felt about effective time management.

As Colonel Junot slept the good sleep of the thor-

oughly rogered, she pillowed her head against his chest.
So much had happened since early summer, when she had
left Plymouth as a green girl. Autumn was almost winter.
Wellington and his troops were slogging back to Portugal.
The war was her companion, but no war lasted for ever.
Duty called her Colonel, and always would, but she expected no less. In the grand scheme of things—where
armies marched and tyrants decreed—perhaps nothing
had changed. In her heart, everything had. She listened
to the ship's bells, content to watch over him.

* * * * *

COMING NEXT MONTH FROM

HARLEQUIN®
HISTORICAL

Available June 29, 2010

ALASKA BRIDE ON THE RUN
by **Kate Bridges**
(Western)

PAYING THE VIRGIN'S PRICE
by **Christine Merrill**
(Regency)
Book 2 in the *Silk & Scandal* miniseries

UNTAMED ROGUE, SCANDALOUS MISTRESS
by **Bronwyn Scott**
(1830s)

THE MERCENARY'S BRIDE
by **Terri Brisbin**
(Medieval)
Book 2 in the *Knights of Brittany* trilogy

REQUEST YOUR FREE BOOKS!

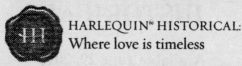

HARLEQUIN® HISTORICAL:
Where love is timeless

2 FREE NOVELS PLUS 2 **FREE GIFTS!**

YES! Please send me 2 FREE Harlequin® Historical novels and my 2 FREE gifts (gifts are worth about $10). After receiving them, if I don't wish to receive any more books, I can return the shipping statement marked "cancel." If I don't cancel, I will receive 6 brand-new novels every month and be billed just $4.94 per book in the U.S. or $5.49 per book in Canada. That's a saving of 20% off the cover price! It's quite a bargain! Shipping and handling is just 50¢ per book.* I understand that accepting the 2 free books and gifts places me under no obligation to buy anything. I can always return a shipment and cancel at any time. Even if I never buy another book from Harlequin, the two free books and gifts are mine to keep forever.

246/349 HDN E5L4

Name _____ (PLEASE PRINT) _____

Address _____ Apt. #

City _____ State/Prov. _____ Zip/Postal Code

Signature (if under 18, a parent or guardian must sign)

Mail to the Harlequin Reader Service:
IN U.S.A.: P.O. Box 1867, Buffalo, NY 14240-1867
IN CANADA: P.O. Box 609, Fort Erie, Ontario L2A 5X3
Not valid for current subscribers to Harlequin Historical books.

Want to try two free books from another line?
Call 1-800-873-8635 or visit www.morefreebooks.com.

* Terms and prices subject to change without notice. Prices do not include applicable taxes. N.Y. residents add applicable sales tax. Canadian residents will be charged applicable provincial taxes and GST. Offer not valid in Quebec. This offer is limited to one order per household. All orders subject to approval. Credit or debit balances in a customer's account(s) may be offset by any other outstanding balance owed by or to the customer. Please allow 4 to 6 weeks for delivery. Offer available while quantities last.

Your Privacy: Harlequin Books is committed to protecting your privacy. Our Privacy Policy is available online at www.eHarlequin.com or upon request from the Reader Service. From time to time we make our lists of customers available to reputable third parties who may have a product or service of interest to you. If you would prefer we not share your name and address, please check here. ☐

Help us get it right—We strive for accurate, respectful and relevant communications. To clarify or modify your communication preferences, visit us at www.ReaderService.com/consumerchoice.

HHIO

HARLEQUIN®

A Romance

FOR EVERY MOOD™

Spotlight on

— Heart & Home —

Heartwarming romances
where love can happen
right when you least expect it.

See the next page to enjoy a sneak peek
from Silhouette Special Edition®,
a Heart and Home series.

Introducing MCFARLANE'S PERFECT BRIDE
by USA TODAY *bestselling author Christine Rimmer,*
from Silhouette Special Edition®.

Entranced. Captivated. Enchanted.

Connor sat across the table from Tori Jones and couldn't help thinking that those words exactly described what effect the small-town schoolteacher had on him. He might as well stop trying to tell himself he wasn't interested. He was powerfully drawn to her.

Clearly, he should have dated more when he was younger.

There had been a couple of other women since Jennifer had walked out on him. But he had never been entranced. Or captivated. Or enchanted.

Until now.

He wanted her—*her,* Tori Jones, in particular. Not just someone suitably attractive and well-bred, as Jennifer had been. Not just someone sophisticated, sexually exciting and discreet, which pretty much described the two women he'd dated after his marriage crashed and burned.

It came to him that he...he *liked* this woman. And that was new to him. He liked her quick wit, her wisdom and her big heart. He liked the passion in her voice when she talked about things she believed in.

He liked *her.* And suddenly it mattered all out of proportion that she might like him, too.

Was he losing it? He couldn't help but wonder. Was he cracking under the strain—of the soured economy, the McFarlane House setbacks, his divorce, the scary changes in his son? Of the changes he'd decided he needed to make in his life and himself?

Strangely, right then, on his first date with Tori Jones, he didn't care if he just might be going over the edge. He was having a great time—having *fun,* of all things—and he didn't want it to end.

Is Connor finally able to admit his feelings to Tori, and are they reciprocated?
Find out in McFARLANE'S PERFECT BRIDE
by USA TODAY bestselling author Christine Rimmer.
Available July 2010,
only from Silhouette Special Edition®.

Copyright © 2010 by Christine Reynolds

SSEEXP0710

INTRIGUE

BESTSELLING
HARLEQUIN INTRIGUE AUTHOR

DEBRA WEBB

INTRODUCES THE LATEST
COLBY AGENCY SPIN-OFF

MERGER

No one or nothing would stand in the way
of an Equalizer agent…but every Colby agent
is a force to be reckoned with.

Look for

COLBY CONTROL—*July*
COLBY VELOCITY—*August*

www.eHarlequin.com

HI69483

HARLEQUIN Presents

Bestselling Harlequin Presents® author

Penny Jordan

brings you an exciting new trilogy…

Needed:
THE WORLD'S MOST
ELIGIBLE
BILLIONAIRES

Three penniless sisters:
how far will they go to save the ones they love?

Lizzie, Charley and Ruby refuse to drown in their debts.
And three of the richest, most ruthless men in the world
are about to enter their lives. Pure, proud but penniless,
how far will these sisters go to save the ones they love?

Look out for

Lizzie's story—**THE WEALTHY GREEK'S**
CONTRACT WIFE, July

Charley's story—**THE ITALIAN DUKE'S**
VIRGIN MISTRESS, August

Ruby's story—**MARRIAGE: TO CLAIM HIS TWINS,**
September

www.eHarlequin.com

HP12927

Silhouette

Desire

USA TODAY bestselling author

MAUREEN CHILD

**brings you the first
of a six-book miniseries—**

Dynasties: The Jarrods

Book one:

CLAIMING HER BILLION-DOLLAR BIRTHRIGHT

Erica Prentice has set out to claim
her billion-dollar inheritance
and the man she loves.

*Available in July
wherever you buy books.*

Always Powerful, Passionate and Provocative.

Visit Silhouette Books at www.eHarlequin.com

SD73037